PORTRAITS

a novel by
Cynthia Freeman

BANTAM BOOKS
NEW YORK · TORONTO · LONDON · SYDNEY · AUCKLAND

This edition contains the complete text
of the original hardcover edition.
NOT ONE WORD HAS BEEN OMITTED.

PORTRAITS
A Bantam Book / published by arrangement with
Arbor House

PRINTING HISTORY
Arbor House edition published November 1979
Literary Guild edition January 1981
A Selection of Doubleday Book Club
Bantam edition / October 1980

The author gratefully acknowledges permission to include excerpted lyr-
ics from the song "Some of these Days." Copyright 1910 by Wm. Foster
Music Co. Copyright MCMXXVII by Shelton Brooks. Copyright assigned
to Jerry Vogel Music Co., Inc., 58 West 45th Street, New York, New York
10036. Used by permission of copyright owner. Reproduction prohibited.

ISBN 0-553-24790-5

Published simultaneously in the United States and Canada

Bantam Books are published by Bantam Books, a division of Bantam
Doubleday Dell Publishing Group, Inc. Its trademark, consisting of the
words "Bantam Books" and the portrayal of a rooster, is Registered in
U.S. Patent and Trademark Office and in other countries. Marca Regis-
trada. Bantam Books, 666 Fifth Avenue, New York, New York 10103.

PRINTED IN THE UNITED STATES OF AMERICA

KR   28 27 26 25 24 23 22 21

I dedicate this to my daughter, Nini,
and my son, Shelly,
from whom I drew the inspiration.

ACKNOWLEDGMENT

There are not enough words to express my deepest gratitude and profound thanks to my publisher, Don Fine. No author has been more privileged than I to have worked with an editor such as he. The arduous task of having written *Portraits* could not have been accomplished without the understanding that I received.

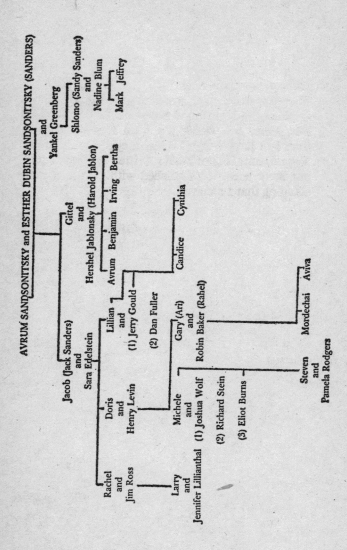

AVRUM SANDSONITSKY and ESTHER DUBIN SANDSONITSKY (SANDERS)

Jacob (Jack Sanders) and Sara Edelstein

Gittel and Hershel Jablonsky (Harold Jablon)

Yankel Greenberg and Shlomo (Sandy Sanders) and Nadine Blum

Rachel and Jim Ross

Doris and Henry Levin

Lillian and (1) Jerry Gould (2) Dan Fuller

Avrum Benjamin Irving Bertha

Mark Jeffrey

Larry and Jennifer Lillianthal

Michele and (1) Joshua Wolf (2) Richard Stein (3) Eliot Burns

Gary (Art) and Robin Baker (Rahel)

Candice Cynthia

Steven and Pamela Rodgers

Mordechai Aviva

CHAPTER ONE

JACOB WAS born in a village which is no longer on the map. History and war have changed that. But at the time, it was on the border between Poland and Germany. His father died when Jacob was three, leaving his mother, Esther, with two small children—a five-year-old daughter, Gittel, and little Jacob. But Esther was a woman of enormous strength and little time for sentimentality. After she buried the dead, dried the tears, she knew there was only one thing for a widow to do, and that was to get married. After a year of mourning, Esther Dubin Sandsonitsky met Yankel Greenberg at the house of Tante Chava. There they were married. What did love have to do with it? He provided a roof over her head and she provided him with a wife who cooked, cleaned and worked from morning to night.

She soon found that her marriage was not a happy solution, nor even an acceptable one to a woman of her pride and independence. Soon after the nuptials, Esther found herself not only pregnant, but a slave to Yankel and his three sons, who were uncouth, lazy and demanding. As Esther scrubbed away, she planned that as soon as the child she carried inside her was born, she would pick up and leave. A roof and a bed hardly warranted the kind of abuse she and her children took from Yankel and his sons. True, she didn't have a profession, but one thing she could do was cook. She'd make a living and survive without the benevolence of Mr. Greenberg.

After the nine months passed, a son lay in her arms. When the circumcision was healed, she packed whatever belongings she had, stole the money Yankel hoarded under his mattress, took her three children and without a word she left. Logic made the decisions for Esther.

She deposited four-year-old Jacob with the family of a distant relative who lived in a small village in Poland. They were hardly overjoyed at having another mouth to feed, but as Esther handed them a few of Yankel's zlotys their resis-

1

tance seemed to soften. She assured them they need not worry, that Jacob's board would be taken care of.

That night a bewildered Jacob cried as he lay on the thin blanket covering the floor in the corner, which was to be his for the next few years.

With Gittel and baby Shlomo, Esther boarded the train for Germany. Logic, however, did not replace her longings and regrets, and she sat up for two nights and days thinking about Jacob. But what could she do? What? It wasn't easy being a woman in the first place. How could she take care of three children and work? She shoved aside the guilt, realizing there were no alternatives.

When they arrived in Frankfurt, they went directly to the small hut, on the edge of the city, where Esther's parents lived. Fatigued and weary, she knocked at the door. The house seemed even smaller than she had remembered when she married Avrum Sandsonitsky and had gone to live in Poland.

After a few days of rest and reunion, Esther left Gittel with her family, knowing the little girl would be loved. It was different for a girl. Somehow Jacob would adjust. He was a boy and boys didn't require the same attention or affection. Besides, her mother was too old and sick to take care of two small children. Amid a tearful good-by, once again Esther boarded the train, this time to Berlin.

For the first time in a long time, Esther began to think maybe God loved her a little, that He'd not forgotten she existed, for soon after her arrival she found a clean room with a kitchenette and, added to this windfall, the landlady fell in love with the baby. How lucky could Esther get? The landlady said she'd be overjoyed to care for the little one while Esther worked. In return for any *kinder gelt*, Esther could clean on her day off. She assured Esther the work wouldn't be too difficult—the basement, windows, woodwork, kindling the furnace, a few more chores as they arose. The deal consummated, Esther immediately weaned baby Shlomo away from her breast. Heaven looked down on her once more, for within a week she found a job cooking in a kosher restaurant not too far from where she lived. Again, Esther had a plan.

The next year was dedicated to one thing—saving enough money so that she could go to America. She would go first with Shlomo, open a small restaurant, establish a home and send for her other children. Her frugality with her hard-earned wages and the money she had stolen from Yankel

2

finally brought about the moment of departure, and without a moment of indecision she quit her job, left Berlin, and returned to Frankfurt to see her family before setting off for America.

As Esther stood before her parents' house, she felt a nervous quiver at the pit of her stomach. This would be the last time she would see her parents, of that she was more than sure, but this final, painful severing would mean a new and, Esther hoped, a better life for herself and her children. There were beginnings and endings. That's what life was made up of.

CHAPTER TWO

ESTHER BECAME a part of the multitude of rejected humanity that waited in droves at Ellis Island. If the great American watchword was "Give me your poor," then her dream had been realized. The disenfranchised of the old world stood on the threshold of the new, waiting to be embraced. They were weary, dirty, tired, bewildered people who had traveled a long distance from the lands of their birth. This promised land seemed as unprepared for them as they for it. They were herded from one place to another and separated into different ethnic groups—Poles, Irish, Russians, Jews. It was little different from the cattle boat from which they had just disembarked.

The immigrations officer looked at Esther's name tag pinned to her coat. Boy, this was a tough one. Sands-o-nit-sky? To hell with it. The name was stamped Esther Sanders.

What Esther found in America the Beautiful was a dark, rat-infested room on the fifth floor of a five-story building on Rivington Street. Poverty anywhere was ugly, but here it seemed unrelievedly so. At least in the village she'd left in Poland there was a tree, a little garden, a little space, a patch of blue sky, a *shul*. And Berlin had been heaven compared to this promised land. And for this she had dreamed, yearned, never spending a cent that wasn't a matter of life or death. The heat, the stench, the crush of humanity seemed worse than in the ghettos of Europe. Here, everyone screamed at the fruit vendor for a penny, at the fish peddler for a pound, and the butcher would steal you blind if you didn't watch the scales every moment.

3

So this was the *goldeneh medina*. This was the place where the streets were lined in gold?

With Shlomo in her arms, she started to look for a store she could turn into a restaurant, but it seemed that half of the East Side was made up of restaurants. What they didn't need was another one. Besides, when she found out what it cost to buy a stove and equipment, she knew it was out of the question. She couldn't put her money into something so uncertain; if things didn't work out she'd be penniless. No, she'd have to do something else to live on in the meantime. And so Esther went to work for Kreach's Restaurant, where she all but collapsed during the summer standing over the steaming pots and worrying about her future. Things were not working out as she'd dreamed, and for once Esther's hopes and plans were faltering. But at least Shlomo, thank God, was taken care of. In the same building where she lived, Esther became acquainted with a Mrs. Rubinstein, who had seven children. For five dollars a month, taking care of another one was no problem.

Esther had been working at Kreach's for some months when she came through the back door at six o'clock one morning and heard wails of sorrow from Mrs. Kreach. Alarmed, Esther ran to Mrs. Kreach and looked down at the floor where Herman Kreach's lifeless body lay. His eyes, still open, had a look of surprise. Esther unthinkingly took charge that day, helping Malka Kreach with the most immediate arrangements until the widow's family finally came and took over.

When an exhausted Esther left at the end of the day, she knew it was only a matter of time before Mrs. Kreach closed the restaurant and Esther would have to search for another job. Or was it? Another plan began to take form in her mind, and with it, new hope that she might yet reunite her family.

After the mourning period was over, Esther approached Mrs. Kreach.

"Now that Herman's gone, how are you going to run the restaurant alone?"

Malka winced at the mention of Herman's name, then sighed deeply.

With tears she answered, "To tell the truth, I don't know. In the meantime, maybe you should look for another job. I don't feel well myself. To tell the truth, I'm lost without Herman."

4

"You want to sell the restaurant?" Esther asked without preamble.

Bewildered by the suggestion, Malka simply stared. Sell, sell Herman's sweat? Sell what Herman worked so hard for? Never took a day off except *Shabbes*? But she was too sick now to manage the restaurant, and besides, she knew little about handling money. Herman had taken care of everything, from the moment they had married, when she was fifteen and he seventeen. When they had set out to make their fortune in the land of opportunity, the opportunities they found had amounted to ten years of drudgery. With the untimely death of Herman, she was left without a penny in the bank, for they had only managed to live from day to day on the restaurant's earnings. The future looked bleak. They had not been blessed with children who could have taken care of her in her old age. Malka sighed. Maybe a dollar in the hand was better than . . .

Malka was suddenly brought back from her reverie. Vaguely she asked, "What did you say, Esther?"

"That no one knows more than me what it means to be a widow, but in time you'll get over it. You're a young woman."

Malka blew her nose on her apron, wiped the tears and shook her head. "Sure, a young woman. I'm twenty-six."

"You're still not exactly an old *yenta,* and in time you'll get married."

Malka looked at her in horror. "Never, after Herman."

"That's what I said when my first husband died. I was younger than you and I was left with two small children. It could be worse, Malka. I didn't have a business I could sell."

"You were luckier than me. At least you had the children." Malka started to cry again.

Esther took her hand and said, "Very lucky, sure, *mazel tov.* I had to be both mother and father and make a living so my children should have to eat. Malka, the restaurant is the answer for you. You can't run it and I'm willing to buy it."

Malka knew she was right, but she also knew the restaurant was the answer for Esther. Poor Esther, Malka thought, it's not easy being a woman alone, with two children in Europe to bring over. How painful it must be parted from your flesh and blood.

Malka sighed deeply and shook her head. "All right, I'll sell."

Esther stopped shaking inside. Evenly, she asked, "How much do you want?"

Want? Why were the decisions of life so difficult. How much was it worth? "How much do you want to pay?"

"Five hundred dollars," Esther answered quickly and with a tone of finality.

Ten years of Herman's life was worth only five hundred dollars? Malka sighed, remembering the day she and Herman had first stood outside and seen the sign, KREACH'S KOSHER RESTAURANT. They had thought they owned the world then.

"All right, I'll sell," she said again. "I hope you make a living for your children."

Esther was beside herself, but she managed to contain her excitement and replied calmly, "I'll give you two hundred and fifty dollars today, and the rest I'll pay out in six months."

Malka wanted to protest that she wanted it all now, but something about Esther's manner stopped her, so she merely nodded her head.

The place was filthy. Esther bought a gallon of yellow paint and a large brush, and for three nights in a row she painted. Then she changed the oilcloth on the tables, varnished the chairs, took down the Kreaches' sign and put up her own. Finally, Esther was in business.

Three months after Esther had become an entrepreneur, she sent for Gittel. When she saw her child come through the gates of Ellis Island, her heart began to pound. Gittel wasn't a little girl anymore; she was ten years old. Unbelievable—she had grown so that Esther could scarcely believe her eyes. Why were memories so unrealistic? Somehow, she could only remember a small child of eight, waving good-by, and here was a self-possessed little girl coming toward her.

Soon they were holding each other, their tears and words overlapping, and suddenly the worry and the loneliness of the past few years was dispelled. They were together now. Esther composed herself, wiped the tears and held the little girl at arm's length, observing the whole of her. Swallowing the lump in her throat, she said, "Come, Gittel, we'll go home."

CHAPTER THREE

JACOB WASN'T sure if he was seven or eight years old, but one thing he was certain of: no one loved him. In all the years he'd lived with his relatives, there had never been a word of endearment, never a kiss or a hug. No one wiped away the tears or consoled him or held him through the nights of despair. The money his mother sent for his keep and the brief letters did nothing to alleviate the pain of feeling he was neither needed nor wanted. Why had she sent for Gittel but not for him? Was he that unimportant to her? Well, as far as he was concerned, he was motherless, fatherless and penniless. So he was going to have to be a man and stand on his own.

Whatever Jacob's age, he was bigger and stronger than any of the other little boys in his village, and the thick curly head of blond hair and the deep blue eyes certainly made him the most handsome. If anyone had bothered to observe the boy in the last few weeks, they would have seen a change in him. There was still the haunting look in his eyes that made him seem older than any child had a right to, but his manner had taken on a calm resolve. For some time now, he had thought carefully about his life, and if there were many uncertainties that remained, one thing he was not uncertain about and that was what he now had to do.

One night, after everyone was asleep, he quietly got up, went to the meager larder, broke off a large piece of black bread and stuffed it into a small sack. He climbed through the rear window and, once outside, he put on his shoes and ran across the field until he reached the huge tree where he'd hidden the sharp knife in a hollow. Quickly opening the sack, he stuck the knife into the bread. His journey had just begun, but he never once looked back.

He walked for three days, resting only when he was too exhausted to go on. But the urgency to escape compelled him to continue almost beyond his endurance. He slept for only a few hours each night, in a hayloft, a meadow, a forest, wherever he happened to be. He kept alive by stealing a few eggs, which he cracked and swallowed whole. At first he almost gagged, but he forced himself to hold it down, and the rumbling in his stomach subsided. When he came to a stream, he would bend down, cup his hands in the cold water and drink until his belly bulged. Once he was even lucky enough to spear a trout with his knife, though he had to eat the fish raw.

Finally, he felt a little less apprehensive, having put many miles between himself and his captors. But Jacob needn't have been so concerned. It was several days before anyone even realized he was missing and the worry he caused was not

7

because anyone fretted that perhaps he had met with danger, but because he had the *chutzpah* to steal the bread from his benefactors, who chose to forget that he had not lived on their charity but on Esther's hard-earned money. However, their anger was assuaged when a ticket and a little money arrived, shortly after Jacob's departure, to take him to America. Unfortunately, Jacob would not be the recipient. How could he be? So they chose their Mottel, to carry the torch of freedom to the golden shores of America.

If Mottel and his family were jubilant about his imminent departure, it was no more than Jacob felt at this moment. He had finally arrived at the train station. It really didn't matter how long it had taken or what he had gone through; he was here and the last leg of his journey to freedom was at hand.

He waited in the shadows until the train was about to move out, then he jumped aboard and darted, unseen, to the first row of unoccupied seats. He crouched beneath it in the corner, praying he would not be detected. From that position all he saw were feet and all he heard was the sound of the giant wheels grinding along the railroad tracks.

For hours he remained immobile, then something terrible happened. He had to urinate. Unable to hold back, he wet his pants. He spent the night feeling cold and uncomfortable, but he consoled himself with the thought that as the night wore on it brought him closer to his destination.

The next morning, when he awoke from the screech of brakes, he was in Frankfurt. He had scarcely changed his position all night and he felt too stiff to move. But with sheer animal determination, he willed himself to stretch his legs, and with the same instinct, he sensed when it was safe to crawl out. When the last of the feet were seen, walking slowly down the aisle, he peered out cautiously, got up and walked rather closely next to a young couple, as if they were his parents. At last he stood on the platform, watching people coming and going, embracing and kissing, and he felt a surge of happiness, as if he belonged among them. He knew he was free at last.

After many inquiries, Jacob found himself in front of his grandparents' house. His pulse racing, his breathing staccato, he knocked on the door and waited expectantly. At last he had come home to love and be loved. He had dreamed of this moment for so long. Grandparents were ... so special. He had never met them, only seen them in the faded photograph he carried, but still the feeling within him was overwhelming.

He waited, knocked again, still no answer. This time he pounded.

He looked at the door for a long moment. For some reason he could not fathom, his hand shook as he turned the knob and opened the door.

All the furnishings had been removed. Frantically, he walked from room to room, opening closets, praying there would be some clue as to what had happened to his grandparents. But the house offered no answers. Slowly, he walked back to the front room and stood in the middle, trembling. Then he noticed that there were some old papers and letters in the fireplace. Quickly, he retrieved them. Sitting down on the bare floor, his pulse raced as he picked out the first one. It was a letter written by his mother, but since he could scarcely read, he was only able to make out a few of the words and the date, January 7, 1899.

Suddenly he became aware that he was not alone. He looked up and saw an old man framed in the doorway. Frightened, Jacob got up, putting his hand on the hidden knife, and asked, "Who are you?"

"I live in the house next door and saw the door open. What are you doing here, young man?"

Jacob looked at the old man, whose face wore a thousand folds and creases.

"I'm looking for my grandparents," he replied, his voice quavering.

The old eyes softened. Quietly he answered. "From the looks of you, you must have come a long way."

Jacob nodded. "Yes, a very long way."

The old man shook his head sadly. He took so long in answering that Jacob finally whispered, "Where are they?"

Without looking at the boy, he said, "Dead . . . I'm sorry." He could not stand the agony in Jacob's eyes. He was too old, too old, and he had no more grief to share. Feebly, he turned and left, shutting the door behind him.

"They're dead?" Jacob mumbled uncomprehendingly to himself. Then he looked down at the letter in his hand. Quickly he ran to the door and called after the old man. "Wait . . . please, please would you read this for me?"

The old man looked down at the small boy, took the letter and read it in a low voice.

My dearest mama and papa,
    My heart broke when I left, knowing I would never be able to see your sweet faces again, for I will never be able to

9

save enough to send for you. New York is a jungle, and I doubt I will ever be able to get used to it, but at least I know Gittel is taken care of and loved. I find great comfort in that, and in knowing I have been blessed with good parents. I was fortunate in one thing—I found a job working in a restaurant. And Shlomo is well. I receive little word from Poland about Jacob, but all must be well since I have had no complaints.

May God be good and keep you for many years to come. Please write often. Your letters are my greatest joy. The address is ...

Jacob wasn't listening anymore. All he could hear, reverberating in his ears, was her love and concern for Gittel and Shlomo. But for him? Nothing.

He thanked the old man for his kindness, took the letter, put it in his pocket and walked back to his *bubbe*'s house. Knowing where his mother was brought him small comfort; she neither loved him, nor wanted him.

In frustration and anger, Jacob took the knife and stabbed it into the wall, then sat on the floor and cried himself into exhaustion.

For the next two weeks, Jacob spent his days roaming the Jewish district of Frankfurt like an alley cat, staying alive with whatever food he could steal.

At night he would return to sleep on the floor of his grandparents' house. His dreams were nightmares, and he awoke from them shaking, drenching in perspiration.

Death was something Jacob had become acquainted with very early. His father had died when Jacob was only three, but the terror of it had remained with him, and was now intensified in his dreams. He remembered the still body of his father, stretched out on a wooden slab. There were coins covering the closed eyes. His face had been the color of yellow wax and his lips purple. Jacob had witnessed the ancient Jewish burial rite. His father had been put into the ground, covered with only a shroud. Then handfuls of earth were thrown into the pit until it was covered over. Jacob's dreams revived the memory of the traditional *minyon* of ten men assembled in a very small room, sitting on the floor. Their lapels were cut in the traditional gesture of mourning, and they wore no shoes. He heard the mournful chanting of the *Kaddish*, glorifying God's name. The sound had been so eerie he had hidden in a closet, but there was no escape from the distorted, dizzying chanting of his dreams. Those were Jacob's most vivid childhood memories, and the images were indelibly imprinted. And now, with the death of his beloved

10

grandparents, he relived the haunting knowledge that no matter how much he longed for them, they would never return to give him what he so badly yearned for . . . to be loved. He was still a little boy, and yet already too old for his age.

The days stretched into weeks, and one day a man and woman entered the house unexpectedly. Jacob's heart pounded as he stood rigid against the wall, his hand poised on the ever present knife in his pocket. "What do you want? What are you doing?" he demanded.

The man looked at the piercing, defiant blue eyes. "Me, you're asking? What are *you* doing here?"

"This is my house. Get out."

A tough little *dybbuk*. This one will wind up in jail. "Your house? Why, you bought it?" He laughed coldly.

"No, but it's mine."

"Oh, I see." He looked at Jacob, who stood like a trapped little animal. "You ran away from home, yes?"

Jacob stared back without answering.

"God will punish you for bringing so much worry to your parents."

Jacob answered, "I have no parents. They're dead."

There was no compassion in the voice that replied, "So, you're an orphan. You found this house vacant and you moved in. You could go to jail for that."

Jacob swallowed his fear. "This is my house. It belonged to my grandparents."

The man narrowed his eyes. "To your grandparents? You have papers to show they gave it to you? You little liar, I just bought it. I'm going to take you to the—"

Before the man could say more, Jacob ran from the house down the streets, into the alleys, as fast as his sturdy legs could take him.

For the rest of the day he hid in a deserted basement. They had taken his house away from him. It was his legacy. He loved that house because it held the memories of his *bubeleh* and *zayde*. One day, he promised himself, if he did nothing else, he would come back and redeem what belonged to him. His house. Yes, at least that . . .

CHAPTER FOUR

THE NEXT few years found Jacob sleeping in alleys and doorways and supporting himself at odd jobs. He delivered meat for a butcher and always managed to cut a chunk of salami and hide it in his shirt. For the tailor, he delivered a suit minus the vest—and by the time the customer had a chance to complain, Jacob was miles away, working in a fish store.

His first real job came to him miraculously when he was thirteen. If there were anything to be grateful for in this world, it was the day he saw a sign in Mendlebaum's window, advertising for an apprentice.

Mr. Mendlebaum was a small man with a sparse head of gray hair upon which he wore a skull cap. On his wire-rimmed eyeglasses were specks of ivory from the umbrella handles he carved. The decorations of Mr. Mendlebaum's masterpieces fascinated Jacob.

At first Jacob worked in wood. Carefully and slowly, Jacob began to copy Mr. Mendlebaum's designs. He worked far into the night, trying to master the technique of his mentor, whom Jacob thought was the only kind human being in the world. Jacob was afraid to like him too much, because liking and loving always seemed to end in disappointment, disillusion and pain. But in spite of himself, he found he was unable to hold back the flood of affection for both Mr. Mendlebaum and his wife. In turn, they soon came to regard him as a favored grandchild. He was frequently invited to dinner.

The best days was *Shabbes*. His mouth watered on Fridays as he whittled away contentedly. The aroma of *gefilte fish*, chicken soup and fresh baked *challah* found its way from the back of the store where the Mendlebaums had their rooms.

At three o'clock, the blinds were drawn and Mr. Mendlebaum would rest and prepare for the Sabbath. Jacob would go to the boarding house where he lived in an attic room, take his weekly bath, and change into the one decent suit he owned. At sundown, he and Mr. Mendlebaum would go to *shul*. How proud he was to stand beside Mr. Mendlebaum, who had bought him a *tallis* and *yarmulkah*. As Jacob touched the fringes of the *tallis* with reverence, he would glance from time to time at the man beside him. He was the

12

zayde returned to him. Jacob willed himself to believe that Mr. Mendlebaum was in fact his grandfather.

When the service was over, Jacob's new *zayde* would put his arm around the boy and wish him *Shabbat shalom*. It was difficult for Jacob to hold back the tears. Then the two would return to *Shabbes* dinner. Life had become good for Jacob.

One morning, Jacob arrived to find Mr. Mendlebaum was not at his worktable. For a moment he was filled with apprehension, but his fears were quickly dispelled when he heard Mrs. Mendlebaum calling from the back of the store.

"Jacob, I want you to meet someone."

Quickly, he went to the sittingroom.

"Jacob, I want you should meet Lotte." With pride she continued, looking at the young girl, "This is our granddaughter. She came last night from Berlin."

Jacob stood mute, looking at the beautiful creature. He was wise in the way of many worldly things, but thus far he had never thought of passion. All his sexual drives were funneled into the business of survival, leaving him little time to dwell upon his physical fulfillment. This was the first time Jacob felt the stirring of desire. The sensation both disturbed and embarrassed him.

Lotte was fifteen and yet she looked younger than Jacob, who, though a few months her junior, stood a head taller and looked years older. She was round and soft. Her burnished brown hair fell demurely below her shoulders. When their eyes met, he felt dizzy from the stirring in his loins. When she smiled and acknowledged the introduction he mumbled something under his breath, quickly looking down at the floral carpet.

All morning he worked furiously at the ivory carvings. Today he did not join the Mendlebaums at the noonday meal. Against Mrs. Mendlebaum's gentle urgings, he refused the meal, saying he wasn't hungry while feeling guilty that perhaps he'd hurt her.

That afternoon was the first time the sharp instruments slipped, cutting his thumb deeply. He was angry at himself because his mind had been in the back of the store rather than on his work. He took out the white rag he used as a handkerchief and bound the wound tightly.

By four o'clock the pain was almost excruciating. Jacob had never been talkative, but today his silence had been so complete Mr. Mendlebaum was more than concerned.

"The finger bothers you? Here, let me see it."

"It's nothing."

"Jacob, don't be so stubborn, so brave. Go back and soak it in hot water."

"It isn't that painful." Jacob shrugged.

"The look on your face tells me different. You can hardly hold the tool."

"I'm sorry. I . . . I got clumsy."

"Oh, Jacob, Jacob, what am I going to do with you? It's no sin to be human. If it hurts, it hurts."

When Jacob continued to work, Mr. Mendlebaum sighed and said, "All right, that's enough for today. The ivory will be here tomorrow. Now, go inside and eat something."

"Thank you very much, but I'm not hungry."

"Then go home."

Jacob looked at Mr. Mendlebaum. Was he angry? No. The eyes were kind.

"Are you sure it's all right?" Jacob asked.

"It's all right." Mr. Mendlebaum shook his head and smiled. "If I get a rush order, I'll send for you." On the way out he called to Jacob, "And don't forget to soak the thumb. A nine-fingered carver I don't need."

The night passed miserably for Jacob. He got out of bed a dozen times, and paced back and forth. His feelings were terribly confused and the heat of the attic so oppressive there was little to relieve his depression. He put on his shoes, fumbling painfully with the button hook. It had to be his right thumb, couldn't have been the left. To hell with it. He slammed the door as he left, then bounded down the four flights of stairs, two at a time.

Once in the street, he ran for blocks. Finally winded, he sat on a bench under a gas lamp until the panting stopped.

For how long he sat staring out into space, he did not know. When he was more composed he got up and walked with his hands in his pockets. As he passed the stores he saw his image reflected in the windows. Stopping in front of Frankel's Bakery, he took a closer look at his silhouette. It was as though he were seeing himself for the first time. He was a man! Much too large and much too tall for his age.

What had happened to him today was frightening because he'd come face to face with his manhood. He had known the awakening of suppressed desire the very first moment he had seen Lotte. The sensation of wanting a woman had jolted him. He now knew a different kind of love; not just the love and longing of the heart alone, but the love of someone with whom he desperately needed to share his physical self. But

14

with his revelation came the self-discipline. He would never touch Lotte, never. She was the grandchild of his beloved benefactor.

The change in Jacob greatly disturbed Mr. and Mrs. Mendlebaum. Politely but firmly, he refused their invitations to dinner. He no longer attended *shul* on the Sabbath. Of all his avowed disciplines, this was one of the most painful.

When Lotte wandered into the store, he was polite but reserved. The conversation she tried to engage him in brought no response and left her in utter frustration. She was terribly smitten with him and unable to understand his dislike of her. At night she cried bitterly, because of his rejection.

For days she avoided coming through the front of the store. But the more he ostracized her, the more she wanted to see him.

Finally, one day, she sat across from him and watched as he worked.

It was almost impossible to keep working with her so close, but Jacob did not look up.

Trying to keep her voice even, she asked, "Jacob, I want to be your friend. Why do you hate me?"

His eyes on the carving tool, "How can I hate you? I don't even know you."

"You act like you do, like you resent me."

"That's your imagination. I'm only an employee. How should I act?"

"Like a person, a pleasant person. Besides, you're not just an employee. My grandparents love you."

Jacob swallowed as though something were caught in his throat. If only she would go away and leave him in peace. God, he wanted her so.

"Well, they do," she continued.

"I don't know why they should."

"Neither do I. I think you're the most miserable person I ever met." With that she got up and ran from the store, leaving Jacob in a pool of perspiration. After this encounter, Lotte resolutely stayed away, though the separation was an agony to her. Jacob, for his part, continued to keep his distance from the Mendlebaums and their granddaughter, though he felt extremely guilty about his seeming ingratitude to the Mendlebaums.

One day, two weeks later, Mr. Mendlebaum cleared his throat as he whittled away at the lion's head. "Jacob."

"Yes?"

"Jacob, why have you been avoiding us lately?"

How could he lie to this man? This was one of the most difficult things he'd been called upon to do. "I'm sorry if it seems like that, but I've made friends with a few boys and I'm seeing a girl."

"Oh? You're seeing a girl?"

"Yes."

"What kind of a girl?"

"A nice girl, a very nice girl."

"Do I know the family?"

"I don't think so. She lives on the other side of town."

"You like her?"

"She's a nice girl."

"I know, you said that a number of times. But do you like her?"

There was a long pause. "I . . . I . . . guess so."

"You guess so?"

"Yes."

"Well, then, since you're not in love with her, I wouldn't ask you to bring her to the picnic."

"What picnic?"

"My lodge is having a picnic this Sunday and I think you would enjoy it. There will be other boys and girls. You'll see, you'll enjoy it."

I'll die, Jacob thought.

CHAPTER FIVE

NO MATTER how hard Jacob tried to make time stand still, Sunday came. He had been up since dawn, watching the sun rise. It held the promise of a glorious summer day. He washed his hair and shaved. The blond stubble had become more abundant in the last few weeks. After combing his hair, he held the comb up to his lip and looked at himself in a piece of broken mirror he had found in the rubble out in the backyard. With a mustache he could pass for eighteen, even nineteen. Maybe he should grow one. It would give him an air of distinction. Should he wear his suit? Was it right? He'd never been to a picnic. He decided to take the chance. If he was careful, nothing would happen to it.

At nine o'clock sharp, he knocked on the Mendlebaums' back door.

It was opened by Lotte. Without a word, she turned and walked away.

Awkwardly, Jacob went into the sittingroom and stood with his cap in his hand.

"Good morning, Jacob, you look so handsome! Sit, sit. I have a few last-minute things to put in the basket," Mrs. Mendlebaum said as she made her way to the kitchen.

Soon there was another greeting.

"Good morning, Jacob, it's a lovely day for a picnic," Mr. Mendlebaum said cheerfully. "You wouldn't be too warm in that jacket?"

"I don't know. Shouldn't I wear it?"

"A sweater would be better. Wait, I'll go get mine."

Mr. Mendlebaum was at least three sizes smaller than Jacob was, but he'd wear it if it killed him. Soon Mr. Mendlebaum handed the sweater to Jacob, and he struggled into it.

Mr. Mendlebaum smiled. "Take it off, I thought it would fit. It happens to be a sweater my son sent to me for Chanukah, and it's too big. I seem to shrink."

"You didn't shrink, only Aaron seemed to think you are the same size you were when he had to look up to you. You must have looked very tall," Mrs. Mendlebaum laughed. "Here, take one of the baskets and Jacob can take the other."

"No, Mrs. Mendlebaum, I can take both."

"Then you, Max, take the blankets and the pillows."

"Pillows we don't need."

"Pillows we need. What if someone wants to take a nap?"

"Pillows we need." He nodded.

"They're here," Lotte called out excitedly from the back porch.

Within seconds they were climbing aboard the large horse-drawn wagon. The greetings were profuse. When Jacob was introduced he was embarrassed by the knowing smiles. Ah, Max Mendlebaum had made a *shiddach,* a match. This handsome young *boychik* had been embraced for his carving ability alone? Nonsense. Then the ladies' heads turned to Lotte, who sat to the right of her grandmother as Jacob sat at the other end next to Mr. Mendlebaum.

Soon the notions of romance were forgotten, and more pressing conversations of news and gossip began as the wagon bounded along the country road.

Jacob sat rigidly, all too aware of Lotte, but the constant conversation distracted him and made time rush by so rapidly that before he knew it they had arrived at the campsite. The wagon came to a halt and everyone disembarked.

Jacob had never seen anything quite so magnificent as the wooded area. He looked up and saw the trees silhouetted against the sheer blue sky. White clouds floated by. He accompanied the others to the clearing surrounded by a meadow and, putting down the baskets, he walked to the edge to look out into the distance. With a feeling of reverence he stood in the peace and tranquillity. Never had he known such a moment, but it ended all too quickly when he heard Lotte saying suddenly, *"Bubeleh* wants you to come and eat." Without another word, she turned and walked away. He followed her.

The excitement was thick in the air as everyone sat down at the long wooden benches. The tables were laden with food of all kinds. It was evident the women had been preparing for days, and each was more proud of her contribution than the next. There was an endless exchange of platters: chicken, corned beef, thin-sliced brisket, hard-boiled eggs, salads, bread, pickled beets, cucumbers, tomatoes, kosher dills, fresh fruit, a compote of dried apricots and pears, raisins, beer. Then the array of cakes: sponge cake, cookies, strudel, honey cakes, *mandelbrot.* The joy of eating, the sheer sensuous joy.

Jacob had never seen such happiness and affection. It was as though they were all one big family. He could no longer resist acknowledging that there were mothers who loved their children, fathers who provided for their families, children who weren't abandoned and left to survive on their own almost from the cradle. Suddenly, Jacob was seized with a feeling of loneliness and pain. Had he been so unworthy? His own mother had never loved him. If only his father had lived, maybe his life would have been . . . God, why was he thinking about that now? This was a picnic where everyone was so happy. But he wasn't like the others. They belonged to someone, and he didn't belong to anyone or anything. He was a stranger in their world.

"So why aren't you eating?" Mr. Mendlebaum asked.

Jacob looked into the old man's eyes, so kind, so trusting. Why couldn't you have been mine, Jacob wanted to say to him.

"What, you don't like the food? Why aren't you eating?" Mr. Mendlebaum repeated.

"I'm full."

"From what are you full? You hardly ate anything. Here, drink some beer. *L'chayim*," Mr. Mendlebaum said, lifting the glass.

"*L'chayim*," Jacob answered.

"You're having a good time?"

"Oh, yes, a very good time."

"You see? I told you there's nothing like a picnic. *L'chayim*, drink, it's good beer. My friend Mr. Finkel makes it."

Jacob took a large swallow and soon he felt lightheaded, giddy.

"To you, Mr. Mendlebaum. *L'chayim*," he said, lifting the glass.

"Thank you very much, *mazel tov*, but don't drink too much. You won't be able to play ball."

As the women were clearing the tables and putting the leftover food away, some of the men began to play pinochle. The little children played hide-and-seek. Couples strolled arm in arm into the woods. The big boys chosé up sides for soccer. Jacob was asked to be goalie because he was the biggest. But being the biggest wasn't the best. He had never played soccer, much less seen it played. At first he refused, then he was prodded by Mr. Mendlebaum.

"You'll play, you'll learn. There's nothing to it. Irving, explain to Jacob how simple it is."

After the rudiments and rules were explained, Jacob tried keeping up with the others. He got kicked in the shins. The ball landed on his head, staggering him for a long moment. But he would stay if it killed him; he wouldn't let Mr. Mendlebaum down.

After a half hour of grueling defeats, he began to get the hang of it. And suddenly he felt a rush of power. God, he loved it! He slam-banged the ball around, never letting anyone get the edge on him. He'd had no idea how marvelous the feeling of competition and winning was; he felt like a giant. When the game was finished he wanted to go on. The boys congratulated him. Would he join their team? Sure, why not? This was turning out to be a good day after all. He was making friends and, besides, when he played soccer he hadn't thought of Lotte once. He loved the camaraderie of the boys as they all walked down to the lake to take a swim and wash off the perspiration. They jumped in with their underwear on. After the swim, they lay basking in the sun to dry off. Jacob lay looking up at the sky. From that position, the world looked quite beautiful.

Now the dwindling afternoon was beginning to leave its rendezvous in this meadow and move on to another place. Soon everyone was seated once again at the long wooden tables, and the platters of cheese, assorted smoked fish, herring and sour cream, the rolls and breads were being passed around. Mrs. Findelstein, with the pink cheeks and the perpetual smile, was pouring apple cider into the large mugs.

This time, Jacob needed no prodding. He ate with relish and drank his cider. *"L'chayim,"* he said to Mr. Mendlebaum.

Mr. Mendlebaum shook his head and winked. *"L'chayim."*

Now the festivities began in earnest. There were songs everyone knew except Jacob, but he clapped along. Then the boys and girls formed a circle and the folk dancing began to the accompaniment of a concertina. Jacob had never danced, but then he'd never played soccer before and he had never known what true laughter was, so he did what the others did. He bowed, the girl curtseyed. There were no partners and Jacob was very happy until he had to circle around Lotte. When she extended her hand, he refused to touch it. Angrily, she thought, this is really too much. It was rude, arrogant, infuriating. Why her grandparents liked him, she'd never know. She wanted to cry. Throwing back her hair, she moved on, glaring back at him.

He wanted to die. He could no longer be this close to her, this aware of her. All day he'd tried not thinking about her, but now it was impossible. He left the dancing and walked to the lake. As Lotte saw him leave, her anger increased.

She excused herself and went after him. Catching up, she called out, "I want to talk to you." He stopped walking, but he couldn't turn to face her. Angrily, she continued, "You're the rudest, the most arrogant, ungrateful boy I have ever met. I want to know why you hate me so much. I never hurt you. In the beginning I tried being your friend. You humiliated me in front of the others by refusing my hand in a simple dance. Am I that dreadful?" He did not answer. Lotte insisted, "Well, am I? Say it."

He swung around and faced her. In the lengthening shadows she looked so beautiful and small and vulnerable. It took every bit of discipline not to grab her and hold her close, to make her almost a part of his own body. He swallowed hard and the muscles in his jaw tightened. His eyes became cold and his breathing labored. "Leave me alone. Do you hear what I say? I don't want to have anything to do with you."

20

Shocked, she lifted her arm in a reflexive motion and started to slap Jacob in the face, but he caught her wrist and held it, glaring at her.

"You're hurting me," she said finally, with tears in her eyes. "You're a brute and a bully and I hate you. I *hate* you."

"I love you, you stupid girl, I love you." He hadn't meant to say it, but it had been said and now there was nothing that would change it. He released her wrist as she stood looking at him in utter disbelief and confusion. At last, she whispered, "You what?"

"I love you. I didn't want to, but I do."

"Then why have you been so mean to me?"

"Because it was the only way I could stay away from you."

"I don't understand you, Jacob. If you love me, why do you want to stay away from me?"

"Because I thought wicked things."

"What wicked things? It's not wicked to love someone, to want to kiss someone."

"It's more than that. I want more than to kiss you. That's how it is with men when they love."

Lotte had only a vague idea of what men and women actually did. But what she was feeling for Jacob was something she'd never felt before, so strong she wanted to be held tightly, to feel his arms encircle her, to have their mouths touch. Standing on her toes, she reached up and kissed Jacob. There was a moment of innocent embrace as Lotte's lips met Jacob's. Overpowering desire washed away his reluctance, and suddenly his responses were hungry and eager. He put his hand inside her blouse and felt the soft round breast, the small distended nipple. In spite of his building passion something down deep jolted him back from the brink from which there would be no return. My God, he had touched her, known her softness. He had violated a trust. This was Mr. Mendlebaum's grandchild. With great difficulty, Jacob released Lotte. Looking into her eyes he said, "Come, Lotte, it's wrong for us to be here together."

"You do love me, Jacob?"

"Yes, but I'm ashamed of what I did. I hope you forgive me. I had promised myself I would never——"

She put her finger up to his lips. "I'm not ashamed. I love you, Jacob." . . .

That night brought Jacob a great many decisions to be made. He wanted to marry Lotte but how could he? How

21

could he provide a living, a home? He scarcely earned enough to provide for his own needs. If only his legacy hadn't been taken away from him, his property, then he could have carried Lotte over the threshold of his *zayde*'s house, rightfully *his* house. But redeeming his property was as far beyond his reach as marrying Lotte was at this moment.

By dawn, all the debates had come to an end. Now, he was compelled to deal with the realities of life. If he stayed and continued to see Lotte, he would not indefinitely be able to steel himself as he had done today. Tomorrow, the next day, the next week, eventually it would happen. He was only human, made of flesh and blood, and there was a limit. He knew the answer . . . there was only one alternative. He had to leave and go to America. It was the only place on earth that held the promise of his future hopes. Only in America.

Quickly, he packed his meager belongings in a sack and left the attic. It had been his home, a place of contentment, but he was compelled to move on. It was the only way he could eventually give Lotte what he felt she was worthy of.

Softly, he knocked at her window. She got up from her bed and quickly slipped into her robe. Quietly, she walked past the closed door of her sleeping grandparents and met Jacob on the back porch. He did not attempt to kiss her. She started to reach up to him, but he held her hand gently. "What is it, Jacob?"

"Lotte, I've been awake all night."

"Why, Jacob? You seem so upset. You do love me, don't you?"

"Oh, yes, Lotte——"

"Well, then?"

"I want to marry you, Lotte, but I have to go away and I want to know if you love me enough to wait."

"Wait, Jacob?" she said, confused. "You mean because of our ages? When my parents meet you and see what a wonderful young man you are, they'll consent."

"It has nothing to do with my age, but with your future. I can't make a living here, I have nothing to give you. So I must go to America, I can make money there——"

"Oh, no, please don't go, Jacob. Please come to Berlin. You'll find a job, I know you will."

"No, Lotte. Listen to me carefully. There is no future here in Europe for a person who has no trade. I'll be a poor man all my life. It's only in America that I can succeed——"

"Jacob, don't go, *please* don't go." And she began to cry.

22

"How much do you love me?" he asked, taking her face in his hands.

"With all my heart, Jacob."

"Do you love me enough to wait? It may take some time."

"Yes ... but I beg you, don't go, Jacob."

"I must, Lotte, it's our only chance. The time will go fast, and before you know it I'll send for you."

"Oh, Jacob, I will miss you so."

"And I'll count the days, but there's no other way." He took out a letter and handed it to her. "Will you give this to your grandparents? I love them more than my words can say. I will write you every day." They clung to each other fiercely, then Jacob gently put her from him and turned to go. Lotte watched as he flung the sack over his shoulder and walked down the street until he was lost from sight.

CHAPTER SIX

IT WAS December of 1907, and the old vessel turned and twisted like a toy in the midst of the mighty Atlantic. The ocean seemed angry and hostile today, as the giant waves shot up like white fangs, then cascaded down in an icy torrent across the bow.

Below the decks, hoards of immigrants were being tossed about in the stormy seas. Some writhed in pain from hunger, holding their swollen bellies. Others, too weak to cry out, lay oblivious to the misery around them. Some wished that death would overtake them, and others prayed to survive.

Deep in the bowels of the ship, Jacob shoveled the coal into the furnace. Its appetite seemed insatiable. As soon as the monster was fed, he slammed the iron door shut. Breathlessly, he wiped the perspiration from his forehead with his blackened arm. When the shift was over he would hold onto the rail with his raw hands and ascend the catwalk and then, unsteadily, inch his way along the narrow corridor until he reached his quarters. Too exhausted to wash, he would all but collapse in his hammock and fall into a deep sleep.

During the two weeks since he had signed on at Hamburg, Jacob had not seen daylight. When the storm lessened he would go up and breathe in the crisp night air. Standing at the rail, he dreamed of Lotte. She was what sustained him during this ordeal; the very thought of her fortified him. Yes, he would conquer the world for her, no matter how difficult the times that lay ahead of him.

The long journey had at last come to an end as the old vessel weighed anchor in New York harbor. It began to move in slowly while the torrential rain pounded against the portholes. The wind howled mournfully.

Weak and bedraggled women, men and children, families who until now had been faceless, formless creatures, began to emerge from below. Many cried with relief from the agonies they had endured. Some, too bewildered by the reality, that they had survived, stood mute on the deck almost unaware of the downpour and the cold. Others, too weak to stand alone, clung to one another for support.

For a brief time Jacob observed the human fodder, of which he was a part, and in that moment he was filled with a special feeling for them. But he also admonished himself. Life hadn't treated him with any special privileges. He'd known deprivation, hunger and the fight for survival, and he had endured them all alone. Remember that, he told himself . . .

Quickly, he picked up his duffel bag, swung it over his shoulder and walked down the gangplank. He went to the shipping office and waited in line to receive his wages. He looked at the money being placed in his callused hand. A dollar a day, the stingy bastards. He stuffed the twenty-one dollars into his pocket.

He found a room in a flophouse on the Bowery for twenty-five cents a night. Shedding his wet clothes, he collapsed on the iron cot.

In the morning, when he opened his eyes to the bleak winter day, his mouth was dry and his stomach empty, but he could not find the energy to get up. He looked around at the human debris that lay as listlessly as he. For some, he suspected, this was their natural habitat. Suddenly, the oppressive sight gave him the energy to get up, to get on with his new life.

Getting out of bed, he began to dress. As he put on his trousers he instinctively felt for the small wad of money, but it was no longer in his pocket. Frantically, he looked under the iron cot and found that his duffel bag had been stolen. In a rage he screamed out, "You goddamn bastards, who stole my money!" The men barely lifted their heads. "I'll kill you if you don't give me back my money." No one responded. He looked at the man next to him, then grabbed him by the throat. "I'll kill you! You stole my money." The frightened man mumbled something in intoxicated incoherence. For the first time, Jacob realized he spoke in a language no one seemed to understand. Breathing hard in fury, he let the man drop. Thank God they hadn't stolen his coat. Putting it on, he bolted from the room.

The streets were covered with a white blanket of snow and ice so slick it was almost impossible for him to walk. Shivering, he huddled in a doorway, not knowing what to do. Everything was gone. The money, his immigration papers . . . All he had was the tattered, faded, old letter Esther had written to her parents so long ago and a picture of Lotte in his innerpocket. He took it out and looked at it. It's all right, Lotte, they won't beat me. I've come this far . . . It's a hard lesson, *no one* will ever do it to me again. Putting the picture back into his pocket, he sat rubbing his hands together for warmth. Spending his energy in anger would not return his loss, so he turned his thoughts to more immediate things. How was he going to eat today, and where would he sleep tonight? He was so deep in his thoughts he did not notice that he was under the scrutiny of a burly uniformed figure.

"What are you doing here, me boy?" asked the suspicious Irish cop.

Jacob looked up into the cold red face, shook his head and gestured that he could not understand.

"Ah, so you're one of those ignorant Poles or Kikes? Naw, can't be a Sheenie. Too blond and blue-eyed for that . . . don't have a hooked nose."

Jacob was at the point of utter frustration; he didn't understand a word the man was saying, nor could he make himself understood. He tried to gesture that his money had been stolen. Abruptly, Jacob was pulled up under the armpits and shoved against the wall. The man in the heavy navy-blue overcoat with the shiny brass buttons moved his hands up and down Jacob's body. He went through Jacob's pockets but all he found was the picture of Lotte and the letter from Esther. Looking at the picture for a moment, he put it back. In bewilderment, Jacob watched the lips move. "So you've no papers. I've seen the likes of you, thinkin' it's so easy jumping ship. Well, boyo, you're gonna be learnin' different." He took out a set of handcuffs and clasped them on Jacob's wrists.

Jacob realized now that the officer thought he was a criminal, but his protests fell on uncomprehending ears as the officer led him to the police station.

He waited on a hard bench for a very long time. Finally he

found himself standing before another man who was sitting at a desk. "What's your name?" he asked, staring at Jacob.

Jacob shook his head mutely.

"I asked, what's your name?"

Jacob held out his hands and shrugged in utter helplessness.

"So you don't understand a word, is it now. There ought to be a law makin' you foreigners speak English. O'Toole," the man called out.

"Ya, chief."

"Take this one, hold him and call the immigration department. He ain't got no papers."

Jacob was taken away and put in a cold damp detention hall. He sat frightened, wondering what his crime was and what the penalty would be. He wasn't alone. The room was full of men who had jumped ship. Italians, Poles, Russians . . .

At four o'clock in the afternoon, Jacob was led once again down a long hall and shoved into a room. His heart quickened when he heard the door behind him shut. He stood at attention and watched two men—one an immigration officer, the other an interpreter—sitting at a desk thumbing through a sheaf of papers.

Jacob looked from one to the other, increasingly alarmed as he waited for them to break the silence. My God, what was going to happen to him? When he was finally summoned to the desk, it seemed he'd been standing for hours. He came forward without hesitation.

The interpreter handed Jacob a large chart, on which was written boldly: "I am Polish, I am Russian, I am Greek, I am . . . When Jacob's eyes lit on the sentence he almost went limp with relief. Shaking his head in disbelief, his blue eyes soberly fixed on the interpreter, he said, *"Ya, ich bin Deutsch."* The interrogation began in German.

"Where did you come from?"

"Frankfurt."

"What is your name?"

"Jacob Sandsonitsky."

"But that isn't a German name."

"No, I am a Jew."

"Tell me how you got here."

Jacob began the story of his departure from Hamburg, how he had paid for his passage by working, ending finally with the theft of his money and his stolen papers. Jacob trembled as the questioning continued.

When had he left Frankfurt and arrived in Hamburg? He had very little difficulty remembering that month; it had been after the picnic on that beautiful late summer afternoon in August. But the thought was cut short by the urgent need to respond. His answer was August 18, 1907. Why had he remained that long in Hamburg and how had he sustained himself? The answer was that the ship was being repaired and outfitted for the voyage, so he had worked as a deckhand and stevedore. The questioning continued. What, then, was the departure date of the ship from Hamburg? November 22. And its arrival? December 10. Did he have any family here?

This was the only time Jacob hesitated, but the answer could be crucial. He did not know what his crime was, but now he understood they suspected he was here illegally. Quickly, he dismissed the pledge he had made not to seek out his mother. He answered, "Yes, I have a mother, a sister and a little brother here."

"Where are they living and what is the address?"

This time Jacob faltered. As he took out the old letter from his pocket and handed it to the interpreter, he prayed his mother would be living in the same place. He swallowed hard as the pain in his chest stabbed like a knife. At this moment, his trust in God was all he had left. He prayed the truth would redeem him, as he began to recount the events that had brought him to this moment. His mother was poor and had been widowed when he was a young boy. She had come to America without him, leaving him with his grandparents in Frankfurt. Only in this one instance had he lied. Quickly, he continued. After their death, he had moved from place to place, and somehow if and his mother had lost touch.

Did he know if she was still alive?

Was she alive? Jacob wondered. The question evoked a torrent of guilt. Although he was certain she had never loved him, the idea she could be dead was something he found impossible to face. In that brief moment, his mind darted back to a yellow, waxen face, a still body, closed eyes, coins, *Yis-gad-dal v'yis-kad-dash* . . . He wanted to put his hands over his ears to stop the sound of the mournful chant. "No," he said shakily, "she's alive, I know she's alive. I'll find her."

The interrogation was concluded. He was told that he would be detained until all the facts were checked out and that he would be notified. He was then taken from the room and led to a darkened cell.

27

As the days passed, he seesawed between feeling completely and helplessly abandoned and feeling a hard, angry core of bitterness. A lot had happened in his young life, but at least he had always been free. The confinement, the stench and the overcrowding were torturing him. For two weeks, the old nightmares of death returned to plague him, and one afternoon he was just falling into yet another troubled sleep when he was jolted awake. "Jacob S-a-n-d-s-o ..." Jacob did not understand English, but he knew his name.

Quickly, he got up off the cold cement floor and answered, *"Ja, das ist mein Name, Jacob."*

The guard motioned for him to follow. He was ushered into the office he'd left fifteen days ago, with the same men present. Jacob, however, scarcely looked like the same boy. His hair was dirty and unkempt, his stubble was now a beard, and his trousers hung loosely from his body ... he had lost at least ten pounds. He looked ten years older. It took all the strength he had to stand as the men continued with their paperwork. At long last, the interpreter handed him a paper to sign. He explained that everything had checked out and that Jacob could remain in the country temporarily. He was given a list of instructions; he had to find immediate employment, locate his mother, and report to immigrations in two weeks, at which time determination would be made as to whether he could stay in the country permanently. Were there any questions? Since he had no money, Jacob asked where he could sleep tonight.

For the first time, almost unwillingly, the interpreter really looked at Jacob. The man hated his job, despised the world for what it did to a handsome young boy like this one. Hell, he was no boy. Two weeks ago, maybe. But there was no illusion left in those clear blue eyes.

In German, the man answered, "Go to the Salvation Army. They'll give you something to eat and a place to sleep."

"The army?" Jacob asked, confused.

"It's not a regular army; it's a Christian charity that helps people."

"But I'm a Jew."

"They don't care what you are." He wanted to add, because they're Christians. So was the country, born and created out of the Christian ethic. Oh, what the hell. Perfunctorily, he handed a card to Jacob. "Here's the address, in English. Show the paper to anyone. They'll know where it is."

Jacob looked at it curiously and put it into his pocket. On his way out he said in German, "Thank you." The man shook his head sadly. Yeah, thanks a lot. You got a lot to be thankful for.

The snows had come and gone. Now the streets were slick and the air raw and cold, but Jacob didn't care. He was free. God had given him his freedom. He wanted to go to *shul*. A haunting memory came back. Mr. Mendlebaum, his *zayde* and he used to go to . . . The son of a bitch who had stolen his things should only rot in hell. More than the money, it was the duffel bag that was the greatest loss. The only thing that meant anything to him was in it. His *tallis* and *yarmulkah*, his legacy from his beloved Mr. Mendlebaum.

The next morning, Jacob was told where the Jewish section of the East Side was. The streets were crammed with dirty tenements, but at least here he was among his own people, and to speak his own language was like honey in his mouth. He went to the house where he thought Esther lived and knocked on a door. Apprehensively, an old woman peered out. "Please, lady, I want to ask you a question."

She squinted at him suspiciously. "So what's the question?"

"My name is Jacob Sandsonitsky. My mother is Esther."

"Your mother is Esther?"

"Yes, do you know where she lives?"

Reassured, the woman's expression softened. "Tell you I can't, but help you I can. I haven't seen her in years. She's a funny lady, you should forgive me, but she never comes to see her old friends. When she lived here, everyone was so good to her."

Jacob's mind wandered back in time, to when he had been a bewildered little boy. He couldn't even remember his mother kissing him when she said good-by. But this was not the time for recriminations. If he was going to remain in America, he had to find her; life had made the decision. "You were saying you could help me find her?" Jacob asked anxiously.

"Yes. Although this is a big place, still people talk. I hear that she owns a restaurant."

"Where?"

"That I don't know, but if you'll go to the wholesale fish market on Fulton Street, I know they'll be able to tell you."

Jacob nodded, then asked for the directions. She said if it

29

wasn't so bitterly cold, she would show him herself. After she wrote out the streets in Yiddish, the old lady felt a sadness as she saw Jacob leave. Such a nice boy. Would he like to come back and visit again? Yes, he would like that very much. When he closed the door behind him, however, both knew he never would.

CHAPTER SEVEN

As THE old lady had predicted, yes, the fish market sold to Esther. Where was the restaurant located? On Canal Street. "Could you write out the directions?" Jacob asked.

"Look, I'm busy. You'll ask, you'll find." The man picked up a crate of fish.

Angrily, Jacob followed him. "Can't you at least tell me how to get there?"

Putting down the crate, he looked irritably at Jacob. What was he in—the direction business? This was Thursday, the busiest day in the week, and this *momzer* was taking up his time. Reluctantly, the man motioned Jacob toward the entrance, where he would be pointed in the right direction. Then, quickly, the man disappeared into his office, slamming the door shut before Jacob could ask the name of the restaurant.

From time to time, he stopped a passerby. It was always go right, go left—nobody had any time. Jacob plodded along the street, unable to read the signs. It seemed he had walked for miles. Well, if he could find America, he'd find Canal Street.

He walked on and on, stopping at every restaurant he came to. Suddenly his heart pounded in excitement. There it was! Esther Sandsonitsky's Kosher Restaurant. A trembling fear grew in him as he crossed the street. A bell rang as he opened the door and rang again as he closed it. He stood alone among the vacant tables and chairs. There were no customers today.

Soon a woman emerged from the back. Wiping her hands on her white apron, she told him to take any table. Then their eyes met. She was not his mother. His mother was much taller than this woman. His mother was blonde, this woman had gone totally white. And yet . . .

"Jacob . . . ?"

My God, it *was* his mother. He shook his head in disbelief. "Yes, my name is Jacob."

30

She stood in front of him, trembling. Suddenly, she slapped him across the face.

He was so shocked he could not speak. Then an overwhelming anger took hold of him... honor thy mother and father, indeed. Quickly, he turned and walked toward the front door, but she ran after him.

"Wait, Jacob," she said, putting her arms around him, sobbing now.

In a state of total confusion, he merely stood.

Wiping her eyes on her apron, she said, "Come, Jacob, come and sit down."

That was it? Not "I'm happy you're here, happy to see you"? But then, what could he have expected. She didn't love him, he'd known that ...

"No, I can't stay," he answered bitterly.

"I'm ... I'm sorry I hit you." She bit her lip. He turned to leave, but she grasped his arm and went on. "It was because of all the years of worry, because you ran away and I never heard from you."

"And that worried you a lot, you cared so much for me?" He almost spat out the words. "Why did you leave me, and take Gittel and Shlomo?"

"Because Gittel was a girl and Shlomo was a baby."

"And I was nothing? A dog treats its own better than you treated me. Why didn't you send for me?"

"I did."

"You sent for me?" Jacob said after a long, stunned silence.

"Yes, I sent a ticket and money to bring you over."

"How long ago was that?" he asked in disbelief.

"About six, seven years ago. I no longer remember."

About seven years ago? That was just about the time he'd run away. He couldn't believe it ... she *had* sent for him? Then, suspiciously, "You got the ticket back, and the money?"

"Of course not. Who sends back money and tickets? Come, Jacob, sit down. You look like you could stand a good meal. We have plenty of time to talk and plenty to talk about."

When he thought of the immigration officer, he reluctantly obeyed.

Esther sat across the table, watching her son eat. The deep resentment and hostility were written in his eyes, and both knew it would be difficult for him to forgive her. But then, the years had taken their toll on both of them. Who asked you, when you were born, what you wanted? You took what you were given. She knew how deep the hurt went, and this first meeting wouldn't bind the wounds, but what could she have done? Nothing, and she wasn't going to allow Jacob to make her feel guilty. If life had been kinder to her, she would have been a different woman, a different mother.

Jacob's feelings had calmed. As he watched her over the rim of the coffee cup, he observed again how much she had changed. It was the white hair that startled him so. What did he feel for her? He couldn't say. But this woman was his mother and maybe, given time, he might overcome the long years of loneliness and bitterness. For the moment, the feelings lay quietly submerged.

When he finished eating, they sat awkwardly, not knowing how to begin or where.

"Well, Jacob, you enjoyed the dinner?" Esther asked, clearing her throat.

"It was very good," he answered the stranger across from him.

After a pause, Esther asked, "Tell me, Jacob, how long have you been here?"

"A little over two weeks," he answered tonelessly.

"Oh? That long? What did you do?"

"Nothing."

"You couldn't find a job. I know it's very hard."

"I suppose, but I didn't need a job. I was taken care of by the government of the United States."

Esther inclined her head and looked sideways at Jacob. She wasn't sure if he was joking but the thought immediately vanished as she noted the set of his jaw and the hardness around his mouth. "What happened?"

When Jacob recounted the ordeal, Esther was almost speechless, but her concern, perversely, touched off a raw nerve in Jacob. "Why are you so shocked? I lived in places almost as bad most of my life. The only difference was at least they didn't put me behind bars." The muscles in Jacob's jaw knotted. "Prison is where I got my first look at this promised land."

Another long silence between them, like a barrier.

"Would you like a cup of tea?"

"Sure, that's always good. Helps to wash down the anger, am I right, mama?"

"Jacob, you're very bitter and I can't say I blame you, but it doesn't help."

"No, it doesn't help. What does, mama?"

"Come right out and say it, Jacob. You hate me."

His eyes suddenly glistened as he stared at her for a long moment. He said nothing.

Silence. Their eyes met briefly, then Esther looked down and brushed away the crumbs on the oilcloth.

"But still, you came here . . . and found me . . ."

"The truth is, I made up my mind a long time ago I never would, but the immigration people said I had to have a family in America. Otherwise, they'd have sent me back."

Esther bit her lower lip. "Well, at least you're truthful. But you listen to me, Jacob. You want to punish me for something I couldn't help. That's all right, but no matter what you feel, I did the best I could."

"I don't think so," he shot back. "You sent Gittel to *bubeleh* and *zayde* but left me with strangers. I didn't mean anything to you—"

"That's not true. They were old people. My mother was sick, and two children would have been too much for her."

"Sure, my needs were so great."

"All right, that's enough. Think what you want. Nothing I can say will do any good."

He watched as she got up and poured some brandy into a small glass. Her hand shook slightly as she raised the glass to her lips and quickly drank it down. His emotions became confused. She looked so fragile, so vulnerable, that he hated himself for having been so cruel. She too had suffered, and she was his mother. He sighed deeply. Maybe having vented his anger would make the past easier to accept, take away the sharp edge. When Esther came back and sat down, he wanted to say he was sorry, but somehow the words just wouldn't come.

Trying to push aside the angry words, Esther asked with great difficulty, "What did make you decide to come to America?"

"I'm in love with a girl. We wanted to get married, but I couldn't make a living. What chance does a Jew have in Europe? *Bubeleh* and *zayde* lived and died in that little hovel, and I wonder if they ever had enough to eat."

Until now, Esther had tried to avoid asking too many questions, but now it didn't matter. Nothing, it seemed, would change Jacob's condemnation of her. She asked why he had run away, how he had survived on his own, and he told her the entire story. It felt good to let it out. Once he started, he couldn't stop. He ended with, "The only kindness I ever had in my life was from the Mendlebaums. I thought the whole world was a sewer until I met them. Thank God, I did."

When he finished his story, Esther sighed, got up and poured tea into a glass and handed it to him. He took a sip, then asked, "Now tell me about you."

"What's to tell?" She shrugged. "I came here, lived in a place with Shlomo where I needed a club to beat off the rats. I'm not feeling sorry for myself, that's just the way it was. Then I went to work for the people who owned this restaurant, he died, and I bought it."

"You make a good living?"

She blinked her tired eyes. I made enough for your keep and to feed my children, she thought, but said, "It was a living. At least I have a better place to live in. I haven't shown you, but there's an apartment in the back."

"Where's Gittel?" Jacob asked, stirring the tea.

"Where's Gittel?" she sighed. "She got married."

"You don't sound very happy about it."

"What's to be happy? She couldn't wait. At sixteen, she was afraid the great bargain she got, she wouldn't be able to get later. I wanted her to finish school at least."

"What does he do?"

"What does he do?" She laughed coldly. "As little as possible."

"How do they live?"

"In a beautiful place on Delancey Street, two rooms. I help pay the rent and they eat here. Except right now, it's a little hard for Gittel. In about two weeks, she's going to have a baby, so I take the food over there every night."

"And Shlomo?"

"He's a good boy, goes to school and to *cheder*. He's ten now."

"Ten?" Jacob said in disbelief. My God, where had the years gone? Jacob couldn't remember him at all. Yes, he could, vaguely. A tiny thing wrapped in a bundle of blankets, who seemed always to cry until he was taken to Esther's breast. Jacob recalled his resentment of the new one being held so tenderly. Had she held him that way once . . . ?

He got up and walked to the window. It had begun to snow gently. For some reason he could not articulate, he felt a strange sense of longing. He had wanted to hate his mother, he had tried to hate her. It was the only defense he had, the only tool to fight with, and it had given him strength. But now that he'd seen her, some of the armor had been chipped away—but just some. One didn't live with the feelings Jacob had harbored for so long and then all at once feel reborn.

Still, his hostility seemed more subdued, and he felt a sense of peace he'd never known before.

Jacob was so deep in thought that the sound of the bell ringing as the front door opened startled him. A little boy ran past him, went to his mother and kissed her lightly on the cheek. Shlomo was always in a hurry. Before Esther could get his attention, he was already in his room, taking the straps off his books and removing his wet coat and cap.

Esther went after him. "Shlomo, come, I have a surprise for you."

Shlomo followed her into the room.

"This is your brother Jacob."

Jacob watched as the little boy's eyes widened, then glistened with tears. Shlomo had dreamed about his big brother. He needed a man he could look up to. He loved his mother and Gittel, but a boy should have a man to talk to, to guide him.

Jacob looked down at the boy with the large, brown, soulful eyes. They did not resemble each other at all. Shlomo was smaller than Jacob had been at the same age. The fact that they were of different fathers did not occur to Jacob. All that he cared about in this moment was that the little boy was his brother. Esther stood by, watching with tears in her eyes. Shlomo clung to Jacob, and Jacob held his brother close. This was a different love from any Jacob had known.

Shlomo looked up into Jacob's face. "I knew you'd come some day. Mama always said you'd come."

Jacob picked Shlomo up in his strong arms. "I guess mama was right."

In the shadows, Esther whispered to herself, Thank you, God, for your goodness. At last I have my family together. She went to the front door and locked it, then turned around the sign. Closed. Today, she didn't need any customers. Esther hastened to the back of the store and began to get things ready for Gittel. When the basket was filled, she put on her coat and hat, then went to join her sons. "Come," she said, "get ready now. We'll go to Gittel's." Looking at Jacob's thin coat, Esther added, "Shlomo, bring your brother the woolen muffler and the leather gloves. Oh, and in my drawer you'll find my knitted hat." Esther was once again in command, the strong Esther of old, the undaunted, indestructible Esther.

When Shlomo came back and handed Jacob the long plaid scarf, he put it on, letting it hang. Esther stood in front of him. He was a head taller than she, and she had to reach up as she adjusted the scarf into a cravat. She smiled, which was something Esther hadn't indulged in for a very long time, but he was really so handsome and her pride was enormous. "There, at least it will keep your neck warm. See if the gloves fit."

Jacob felt a sudden desire to take her in his arms and kiss her, but he couldn't. Instead, he smiled and picked up the basket, and the three of them set off in the cold winter evening to his sister's house.

Winded by the four-flight climb, Esther stood in front of Gittel's flat. "You wait here," she said. "I want to go in and tell Gittel first. You understand?" Jacob nodded. He waited nervously as Shlomo stood looking up adoringly at him.

After what seemed an interminable length of time, the door opened and Gittel stood framed in the doorway. For a moment she could not move; it was all too unbelievable. Then she was in his arms, holding him close as the tears tumbled from her eyes. Looking up at him, she explored his face with her hands, touching his cheek. "Oh, Jacob, our dearest Jacob, you've come back to us. Mama always knew you would. There was never a day we didn't speak of you."

And there was never a day I hadn't hoped it would be this way, he thought, too choked with emotion to speak. He wiped the tears from his eyes with the back of his hand.

"Come, my wonderful brother, come," she said, leading him into the sparsely furnished kitchen.

Gittel's husband was seated at the table. He rose for the introduction. "Jacob," Gittel said, "this is my husband, Hershel."

Remembering what his mother had told him about Hershel, Jacob felt a stab of resentment. What had Gittel seen in him? He was a small, thin, joyless man of about twenty-five who looked as if he'd never seen the sun. Why hadn't Gittel waited? She was so lovely, with honey-blonde hair and eyes as blue as cornflowers. There was a slim delicacy about her, even now with her swollen stomach. As he looked from one to the other, he thought scornfully that Gittel's husband had never made a living for her, protected her as he would Lotte. And the *shnorrer* had even allowed his mother, who worked so hard, to pay his rent. Jacob was brought back from his thoughts when his mother said, "Now, sit down, we'll eat. Jacob, you'll make the blessing."

Gittel and Shlomo could not take their eyes from Jacob.

There was very little conversation during the meal, but as they drank their tea and ate the sponge cake, there was an avalanche of questions.

Jacob tried to avoid the bad times, which only left him the time with the Mendlebaums, and Lotte.

Gittel smiled. "So you're going to get married. I can't believe it."

"And you, Gittel. It's hard to believe you're going to have a baby." And as though speaking to him, he added, "It seems we were kids ourselves only yesterday."

"Yes, Jacob, but we're together now, thank God. Life is good——"

"Yes, I guess maybe there's a reason for everything."

As Esther opened the door to the restaurant and took him to the back apartment, he knew the past had to be put to rest and that all that mattered was now. He was home at last.

Quickly, Esther put clean sheets on the narrow iron cot in Shlomo's room as Jacob watched. The first bed that belonged to him, the first real home he had ever had.

As Esther climbed into bed that night, she lay gazing up at the dark ceiling with a grateful heart. God had returned her son.

It was a night of peaceful, contented sleep for Jacob and for Esther.

CHAPTER EIGHT

FRIDAY, BEING the start of *Shabbes*, was a bad day to look for work, so Jacob cleaned the apartment and scrubbed the accumulated grease from the kitchen walls.

That night they went to Gittel's for *Shabbes*.

Jacob felt a deep joy as he watched his mother light the candles and say the prayer. Even his dislike of Hershel was overlooked in this moment of rejoicing. Nobody cooked like his mother—the *gefilte fish*, chicken soup with *kreplach*, *kugel, challah,* chopped liver, chicken—it was like a banquet.

The next morning, as Jacob sat having rolls and coffee with Shlomo, his mother handed him a red velvet sack embroidered with the golden *Torah*. He did not have to wonder what was inside—he knew. Taking the *tallis* in his hands, he touched the fringes reverently. The silk was yellowed with age. When he looked up there were tears in Esther's eyes. "This was your father's. Wear it, Jacob, as proudly as he did."

Not holding back the tears, he embraced his mother. She felt so comforting in his arms. And she, in turn, felt the strength inside him.

As they prayed that Saturday in the little *shul* on Hester Street, his memories came flooding back to him. He looked up to the women's section and saw his mother's smile, then went back to his *dovening*, raising his voice to equal the elders' as they chanted the hauntingly beautiful liturgy that had been heard for two thousand years. Shlomo stood proudly, swaying with the same rhythm as his brother.

At three o'clock in the morning there was a frantic banging on Esther's door. Jacob almost collided with Esther as they both hurried to the front of the store. Opening the door, they found a frightened and near frozen Hershel. He blinked the snow from his eyelashes as he entered. Trying to catch his breath, he said almost incoherently, "Gittel . . . Gittel needs you." Without questions, Esther hurried into her clothes, as did Jacob.

"What's wrong?" Shlomo asked as he watched Jacob put on his trousers.

"It's Gittel. It's all right, go back to sleep. I'm going with mama."

"Me too," he announced, jumping out of bed.

"No, Shlomo. It's not necessary, you go back to sleep."

"But I want to go."

"If I need you for something I'll come back, all right?"

Reluctantly, Shlomo got back into bed as Jacob pulled the covers up under his chin and ran his hand affectionately across the boy's face.

Gittel's contractions were coming so quickly that Esther knew she had to act fast. The midwife who was supposed to deliver the baby had come down with pleurisy. There being no time to find another midwife, Esther took charge. She called from the kitchen to Jacob, who paced the narrow hall outside Gittel's room. "Yes, mama," he answered nervously.

"Go with Hershel to Mrs. Goldstein's house. She's the midwife. Tell her about Gittel and ask her to give you the instruments."

Within less than fifteen minutes they were back with a paper bag. Jacob felt a wave of nausea as he watched Esther drop the scalpel and scissors into the boiling water. Hershel went out into the hall, shutting the door behind him, and leaned against the wall, dripping with perspiration. He put his hands to his ears to shut out the cries of pain.

Quickly, Jacob went to Gittel's room, pulled up a chair and held her hand. He wiped the perspiration from her face with a damp cloth as she writhed in agony.

"Squeeze my hand . . . hard . . . harder . . ."

"Jacob?" she cried out.

"Yes, I'm here, I'm here. Squeeze hard."

Esther bustled into the room with the midwife's instruments and looked under the sheet to examine her daughter. My God, her grandchild was about to be born. "Jacob, help me move Gittel around closer to the edge of the bed."

As Esther adjusted the pillow under the girl's head, the last scream was felt almost as much by Jacob, who watched Gittel's child being pushed into life. At last, it was done, it was over. Jacob stood back and watched his mother. Soon the child was taken out of its veil of placenta, held up and slapped on the tiny buttocks.

Jacob smiled almost sadly when he heard the baby's first cry. If he had feelings other than love for his mother, at this moment he realized she too had suffered bringing him into life. Today especially he saw her through different eyes.

After she had cleaned the child, sponged Gittel, changed the sheets and tidied up the room, Esther stood with the basin in her hand. "Well, Gittela, you're a mother . . . now sleep, *mein kind.*"

When she turned and started to leave, Jacob took the basin from her hands, placed it on the floor and put his arms around her.

She looked up. "You're a fine man, Jacob—like your father, may he rest in peace." Then she went out.

"Jacob?" Gittel said weakly, holding out her hand.

He went to her and sat on the edge of the bed. "Yes, Gittela?"

"Thank you for being strong. Poor Hershel was so frightened."

It wasn't fear, but weakness, Jacob thought. He kissed her lightly and left.

Opening the front door, he saw Hershel sitting on the stairs, looking up at him expectantly. It took all Jacob's strength to control his anger.

Hershel's mouth was slack. "Well?"

A silent pause, and then Jacob said, "You have a son.

When you die you'll have someone to say *Kaddish*." Jacob ran down the stairs, two at a time.

This day found Jacob a very happy young man. He had gotten a job. The work was hard but out in the open air instead of in some unventilated loft. And the money was good—nine dollars a week.

When he went to Gittel's for dinner that evening, he walked in to find Esther taking off her coat.

From the look on Jacob's face, she asked, *"Nu?"*

"I got a *job*."

"Mazel tov, where?"

"On the docks."

"On the docks, working in this kind of weather?" she asked, putting on the white apron. "Jacob, those men are bums. With bums you don't have to—"

"That's right," he said, interrupting her. "I don't have to associate with them."

She struck a match to light the stove and he watched the tip smolder when she blew it out. "Listen, Jacob, I don't want you—"

"I took it, mama. No use talking. You know how much it pays?"

"I don't care how much. I still don't—"

"Nine dollars a week. More than I could make in a factory."

"Nine dollars a week?" Shlomo put in. He'd never heard of so much.

"That's right, Shlomo, and I'm going to make more too. You, I'm going to send to college and you, mama, I'm going to give half every week."

"Me, you'll give half? I don't take money from my children and Shlomo can marry a rich girl. She'll send him to college and you'll save the money so you can get married." They all laughed.

"What's so funny?" Gittel asked, coming into the kitchen with her six-day-old son.

"Shlomo's going to get married," Jacob told her.

"I am not," he said, turning red. Then, excitedly added, "Jacob got a good job, nine dollars a week!"

"Oh, *mazel tov*," Gittel said.

"Sure, some *mazel tov*. He's going to be working like a *goy* on the docks with bums. Bums, that's what they are," Esther said half angrily.

Jacob paid no attention as he peered down at the baby. So beautiful. Imagine, a little human being, and this had come from the ordeal of last week. He couldn't get over it.

When Hershel walked in from the bedroom, Jacob looked at the slippers on his feet.

"You have a good rest, Hershel?"

Hershel looked at him sourly. He hadn't forgotten the congratulations he'd received the night the baby was born. "Yeah, I was a little tired when I came home."

"I can imagine. It's hard working in a pool hall. Racking up the balls is enough to make any person——"

"All right, everyone sit down and eat," Esther said, when she saw Gittel swallow hard. Then she shook her head at Jacob to keep him quiet.

When they were all seated at the table, Shlomo said to Hershel, "Jacob got a good job."

"Just eat before it gets cold," Esther snapped, wishing the meal were over already. She would warn Jacob later not to antagonize Hershel. It only hurt Gittel, and she knew Jacob would never want to do that. And of course, whatever Jacob did, Shlomo thought he could get away with too.

That night, after promising his mother he would be more polite to Hershel, Jacob sat down and wrote a long letter to Lotte.

February 11, 1907

Dear Lotte,

Not a day has passed that you have not been in my thoughts. During that long voyage, I would lie awake in the dark and feel as though you were there with me. It made it easier to endure our separation. I keep your picture close to my heart and I look at it every day.

So much has happened since I arrived I don't know where to begin. I suppose I'll tell you first about my family. It is like we have been together all our lives, I just can't get over it. You'll love my mother, and I know she will treat you as she does my sister Gittel. My little brother Shlomo, who is ten, speaks of you as though he knew you. My sister had a baby boy last week. He is so beautiful.

America is a good country, and I can hardly wait for you to come and share it with me. I know that will not be too far away because I got a good job. I am going to save most of my money because I am living with my mother, who owns a restaurant. Everyone is so happy about us. I am the happiest person on earth to have found so many that love me, *especially* you. Please write as soon as you get this letter. Oh, I almost forgot to tell you, my nephew's name is Avrum, after my father. On Sunday he's going to have his *bris,* and the party will be at my mother's. My only regret is you will not be here.

Please give my deep affection to your grandparents. I miss them very much and will never forget how good they were to me. My regards to your mother and father and I hope they know how much I care for you. Please assure them they do not have to worry about your future.

Well, Lotte dear, I will close now, but before I do, again I want you to know how much I care for you.

With deep respect,
Jacob

Before putting it into the envelope, he reread the letter. It didn't really say what he felt. But those were feelings no decent man expressed to the woman he was going to marry. And besides, he could never put them into words. For some feelings, there were no words.

Quickly, Jacob folded the letter and sealed it.

The snows of winter had come and gone, and the heat of summer settled on them with a fury.

Jacob had become accustomed to the scenes of the East Side, the familiar daily sights of humanity locked together in a common fight for survival. It was not the poverty that bothered him so much, since he'd known nothing else. But his burning desire to bring Lotte over became more difficult to bear with the passing days.

He had been painstakingly frugal with his money, but at the end of six months he had saved very little. It was quite simple; he had to earn more money. But how?

At noon, when the whistle blew, Jacob walked to the shaded side of the warehouse, wiped the sweat from his forehead, then sat on the concrete and braced himself against the wall. It was so hot that he didn't feel like eating. Instead, he took the small English primer from his back pocket and began to study.

The burly Irishman sitting beside him asked, "So, you're going to be a professor, arrre ya?"

Jacob smiled, "I wouldn't mind." Jacob had been going to night school three times a week to study English. Between the lessons and his eagerness to learn he now had little difficulty in speaking or understanding the language.

"Well, professors ain't no better than the likes of you and me. We work hard for what we get, and that ain't nothin' to be ashamed of."

42

"Ashamed, I'm not, but a little more money I wouldn't mind making," Jacob said, shrugging.

"I ain't gonna be faultin' you for that. It's a struggle, and hard raising a family. But I'll take this to the potato famine we had when I was a young one back in the old sod."

Jacob nodded. He understood about famines and hunger, but still, in this land of opportunity he wasn't making much progress, and his need for Lotte was becoming more and more acute. At the rate he was going, it would take a long time and that he couldn't accept.

"Still," the Irishman said, looking at Jacob's strong shoulders and arms, "it shouldn't be so hard for a big buck the likes of you to be earnin' a little extra."

"What does my size have to do with it? I don't get paid more because of that."

"Take a look at those fists. You got a *forrtune* in them, me boyo." The older man laughed.

"In my fists?"

"And that ain't no lie."

Jacob was beginning to get interested. "Explain it to me."

"You been to a prize fight, ain't ya?"

"No." Jacob shook his head.

"You was never at a fight?"

"Never."

"Well, now me boy, how would you like to be going with me? I go ever' Tuesday and Thursday nights."

"How would going to a fight make me money?"

"Let me tell you what I have in mind. I think you ought to be thinking about gettin' into the game. There's a lot in it."

Jacob took a look at his hands. He could make money with them? The man said they were worth a fortune. If he was telling the truth then that would mean he could bring Lotte over sooner. And what was going to school compared with that?

"Where is this place?" Jacob asked eagerly.

"On Chrystie Street there's a big gym. It ain't Madison Square Garden, but that's where some of the big ones got started."

Thoughtfully, Jacob took out the corned beef sandwich and offered half to the Irishman. As the two men ate, Jacob thought, this really is a wonderful country. Where else could a Jew and an Irishman become friends? Although Jacob was not yet aware of it, Patrick Michael O'Leary and Jacob Sandsonitsky had just become partners in a new venture.

43

When Tuesday finally arrived Jacob was filled with an assortment of guilts. He knew his mother would object to his going to a prize fight ... she didn't believe in fights of any kind. She would object to his getting involved with what she thought were bums and lowlifes, and she would certainly forbid him to mingle socially with *goyim*. They drank whiskey, smoked cigarettes, slept with bad women; in short, they were without morals. For two thousand years, the Jews had lived with a rigid code of morality, but the *goyim* were so mixed up they didn't even know who God was. They worshipped idols, pagans, like in Egypt.

Jacob left his mother to meet Patrick with many misgivings.

He sat on the wooden bench next to Patrick, listening to the sounds and repulsed by the sights. The crowds roared as an upper right landed, hitting the opponent so hard he hung like a doll on the ropes, then dropped to the canvas. Two new contenders replaced the last. Again the bell rang and the fighters came together. There was a brutal foray.

It seemed to Jacob the referee took his time in separating the fighters. One to the right, then the left, short jabs to the kidneys, then biff, bang, one to the jaw, and it was over as the winner held up his arms clasping his hands together over his head. Shifting gracefully from one foot to the other, he laughed triumphantly. The crowd went wild.

Jacob despised it. This was not a contest; it was a savage, pagan rite, it was the Roman arena, the pogroms. He looked around at the evil delight on the faces of the spectators. They wanted blood. And this is what men did for money?

On the way out Patrick said, "Well, boyo, now you saw your first prize fight. That's what you call sportin' fun." When Jacob didn't answer, Patrick smiled and said, "You thought it was a little too much, did ya? Well, let me tell you, me bucko, life ain't exactly a circus." Laughing, he cuffed Jacob on the arm and added, "The first time it might seem a little rough, but the next time it won't seem so—"

"There won't be a next time," Jacob answered quietly.

"Ho, now, me boy. Weren't you the one sayin' just the other day how much you wanted to make more money?"

"Yes, but I didn't think that a prize fight was—"

"Let me stop you right now. What you saw tonight was the manly art of self-defense. Now you just think about it, me boy. I've been around fighting all me life, and let me tell you, if I had your body and those hands instead of being the leprechaun I am, I'd have been in that ring tonight. Now I'm strong enough, mind you, to work the way I do. Make no mistake about that. But you got something I ain't; you got the makin's of being a champ. I can spot 'em a mile away."

"I don't want to be——"

"Wait now, just wait till I've had my say. With the proper training, the right manager, why you'll never hit that canvas. The ones you saw tonight are sluggers, flat on their feet. Maybe you don't know it, but I've watched you work, and you ain't no ordinary buck."

"I'm not going to fight."

"Well, that's fine with me, but you're missing a golden opportunity. You know how much those bums got tonight?"

"I don't give a damn."

"Okay, but I'll tell you all the same." Patrick came closer to Jacob and almost whispered, "Ten dollars. That's a hell of a lot of money, wouldn't you be thinkin'? Ten dollars for a night's work."

"What does the loser get?"

"What he deserved, about three. As I said, there are winners and losers. You're a winner. Go home and sleep on it. You could be a rich man in no time at all."

Jacob went home, but he didn't sleep. Instead, he lay awake in the dark, unaware of Shlomo's soft breathing. The thought of Lotte kept nudging his conscience. If he wanted Lotte as much as he said he did, wasn't she worth fighting for? But what would his mother say? He wouldn't be able to tell her. He could hear her arguments; Jews don't fight, it's against our religion and a sin against God. But ten dollars a fight, two nights a week, was twenty dollars, multiplied by six months—more money than he needed to send for Lotte. If he continued as he was going, it could take years. That thought frightened him. Patrick said he was a winner. If he could make enough money in a short time, he could not only marry Lotte but save enough to get started in a business. Fighting was considered the manly art of self-defense. If he'd known *that* he wouldn't have lost his legacy, *zayde* and *bubeleh*'s house. . . .

The next morning, he sought Patrick out. "I did what you said, I thought about it. How do I become a fighter?"

Patrick smiled, thinking, money is the greatest little whore in the world, that and jealousy and lust.

"Meet me at the gym tonight and we'll start trainin'. I don't want you to do nothin' until you're ready."

"How long will that be?"

"In a few months."

45

"Months?"

"Maybe sooner. Leave it in my hands, trust me. I have an instinct about these things." . . .

Every night after supper Jacob met Patrick at the gym. At first, Jacob spent hours jumping rope, then graduated to the punching bag. On Sunday mornings after Patrick's early Mass, the two met in Central Park and Patrick clocked the miles Jacob ran. Jacob's stamina was more than Patrick could have hoped for. He was going to make this Jew into a champ.

The time had come for Jacob's first bout. Jacob waited his turn, nervously pacing back and forth. The heavyweights were always the last. That's really what the crowd wanted to see, the heavyweights.

As he climbed into the ring, Jacob's fears were more real than his opponent—he was frightened because his mother and family didn't know what he was doing, frightened because he might hurt his opponent, frightened because he might lose. Winning was so important. It meant his life, his life with Lotte.

Then the first round began with the ring of the bell, and unsure of himself, he sparred with his opponent, played with him.

Patrick stood at ringside, gesturing as he instructed Jacob . . . a jab to the rib, another, dance away and never let the bastard get in too close. Hit the kidneys, dance away. Come in close and keep the right up, the head covered. Wear him down, keep jabbing. Don't be in a hurry, easy, easy. A jab and dance away.

When the bell rang, Jacob sat down in his corner, perspiring and winded, as Patrick handed him a glass of water. Jacob swished it around in his mouth, spat it into the bucket, and put the mouthpiece back in.

Round two began, and Patrick kept up his ringside patter. Keep him away, he's getting tired. Now, knock the stuffing out of him, a right, a left, another right, another left. Think about Lotte, me boy, you're doin' this for Lotte. Keep punching, gettin' closer, one to the jaw. It's time for the kill.

Suddenly, the crowd went wild. Jacob looked at the unconscious man on the canvas. Blood was coming from his mouth, and his eyes were swollen shut and black and blue from the pounding he'd received. Jacob didn't have a scratch.

He ran down the short dark corridor, slammed the door

and vomited. He could still hear the roaring of the crowd, stamping for him to come back, but all he wanted was to get his money and get away from this place as fast as he could.

When O'Leary entered, Jacob was getting into his coat.

"By Jesus, you were a tiger in there, did everything like I said. You're a killer, me boy," he said, shaking his head in admiration.

"Just give me my money," Jacob said woodenly.

Patrick took a good look at Jacob. He decided he would only take a fourth of the earnings for tonight. Patrick had never had the likes of this one before, and he could wait until the boy was hooked before he collected his fifty percent. Slowly and deliberately, Patrick peeled off the money, knowing how impatient Jacob was, then counted off seven dollars and placed it in Jacob's sweating palm.

Jacob was sick. It was blood money. A man could have been killed for seven dollars. But he had more coming to him than seven dollars. "Where's the ten dollars you promised?"

"Hold on there, me boy. You don't get the whole thing. I got something coming; I'm your manager. In fact, I should be gettin' half. The gym gets a bit too, you know. You'd better wake up, Jackie Sanders, *champ*. You got to pay money to make money."

Jacob closed his fist hard around the money and ran out, leaving Patrick standing in the middle of the room. Patrick smiled, not at all worried. He would think it over. He'd be back.

Patrick was a very good judge of human nature. Jacob would never have believed himself capable of sinking as low as he had tonight. It was vile, reprehensible. No, there were some things a man would not do for money. But that still left him exactly where he was a few days ago. Where and how would he be able to earn sufficient money to bring Lotte over? Even if he got an additional part-time job, he would earn only a few extra dollars at the most, and time was so important. His want, his need for Lotte was an all-consuming thing now.

So Jacob lay awake, finding that the struggle to totally dismiss the money was a battle much greater than the one he'd fought tonight. Maybe, if he could keep thinking that the end justified the means, then maybe he could consider the fighting as just another job, another challenge to deal with. If he could only remember, when he was in the ring, that he was fighting for his future security, forget he was dealing with a man, block it out of his mind... Suddenly there was a new thought. Would the man he was fighting have any qualms about beating the hell out of him? Why should Jacob worry about him when no one had ever worried about Jacob. His past bitterness suddenly welled up in him. Who gave a damn what *his* life had been like? He had been kicked out of his grandparents' house, his property and then his money had been stolen, he had been thrown in jail for no reason. Why shouldn't he at long last have some happiness, the happiness of having Lotte at his side? Why shouldn't he grasp this opportunity. Why... ?

The next morning, Jacob was in such a hurry to see Patrick that he didn't notice the women haggling with the pushcart vendors, nor the people taking their thin mattresses off the fire escapes, where they had slept the night before to avoid the unbearable heat inside. He stopped just briefly to watch a group of boys beating one another up. That was stupid, unproductive, he thought. If you're going to fight, at least get paid for it. Fight for a purpose, fight for someone you love.

Jacob put on his mental blinders, refused to consider the man he'd fought as anything more than a punching bag. He pushed aside any previous revulsion he'd felt. He would not condemn what he was doing, not when he counted out the money. In the last few weeks, he had stashed away thirty dollars, which he'd earned from "the art of self-defense," plus twenty-one he'd earned from the sweat pouring out of his body as he unloaded freight in the scorching sun. His assets were now fifty-one dollars, and *no one* would steal this from him. But there was just one little matter he was going to take care of, and that was his dear friend, Mr. Patrick O'Leary.

After the fight on Tuesday night, Jacob stood wiping his face on a towel. His body ached from the blows he'd received. Tonight he'd come up against a big bruiser, not as fast as Jacob, but when he connected a body blow, Jacob had been staggered. Jacob had almost met his match in this one.

With a broad grin, Patrick hoisted himself onto the table. "Well, me boy, you showed that crowd what real pugilistic ability looked like. Your footwork was beautiful, and the way you kept your distance, waitin' for the openin'—why, when you landed that blow, I swear by the saints it could have been heard in Brooklyn. You're gonna be—"

"I want more money," Jacob said as he buttoned his pants.

48

The smile froze on O'Leary's face. Why the dirty, money-hungry Kike. No wonder Jesus chased them out of the temple. Taking out his handkerchief, Patrick wiped the sweat from his brow. Slow down, O'Leary, don't want to lose the big bucko Jew pigeon. The smile returned. "So, it's more money you're wanting, is it?"

"Yes." Jacob nodded as he slipped into his jacket.

"And how much more would you be wantin'?"

"Ten dollars."

Patrick slapped the side of his thigh and let out a booming laugh. "Well, now, it's one thing to be wantin', but where in the saints are you goin' to be gettin' it from?"

"From you."

"From me, is it now?"

"That's what I said, from you."

Jacob's American schooling on the docks had been illuminating. He had learned to recognize the guises of prejudice, which existed even in this so-called land of opportunity, and he had consequently become wary of anyone who offered something as an "opportunity." These bitter lessons had been completed with the discovery that O'Leary was cheating him, that O'Leary was getting twelve dollars, not ten. Jacob spilled his guts and got only five, and that Irish Jew-hater wound up with seven.

Jacob came closer and looked down at Patrick. Patrick knew this was one Jew he would never have any sport with. He remembered the time he and his cohorts had cornered a young Jewish dockworker and ripped off his pants so they could see his smooth shiny penis, minus the foreskin the Lord had provided. The young boy had never returned. But Jacob would, and with a vengeance.

Patrick got off the table. "Now, Jackie, me boy, you've got to be sensible. How in the name of heaven can I give you ten dollars?"

"You'll have to ask heaven. That's what I want or I don't fight."

"You're going daft, me boy. Now, Jackie, I'm your manager and I'm entitled to—"

"Not when I get five and you take seven. Not for the kind of punishment I take."

Patrick knew he had been found out, and became conciliatory. "All right, Jackie, tell ya what I'm going to pro—"

"My name is Jacob, and I want ten or I don't fight."

"Eight."

Jacob still needed the Irish bastard, he still had plenty to learn. "For the next two fights only. I'm beginning to fill up the house. You say you're my manager? Okay, then get fifteen dollars a fight."

"You're a plucky lad." Patrick shook his head and laughed. "That I'll be giving you. I'm not quite sure how Hallihan's gonna go for it—"

"With your Irish mouth, you'll talk him into it." Jacob turned and slammed the door behind him.

Patrick smiled, scratched his head. Damned if he didn't admire the cocky bastard. Pity he wasn't an Irishman.

CHAPTER NINE

JACOB, HOT and sweaty after a hard day's work, came through the front of the store and walked past the customers. Going to the back, he saw his mother ladling out four plates of cold borscht. "It looks like business is good today, mama," he said, kissing her on the cheek.

"Very good. You smell terrible. Go get washed and come eat. Oh, Jacob, you got a letter from Lotte."

Quickly he went to his room, where Shlomo was studying.

"Well, Shlomo, how's the schoolwork going?" Jacob asked, taking the bailing hook out of his back pocket.

"Fine, I got a good report," he said, handing it to Jacob.

Jacob smiled and said, "I'll bet you're the smartest boy in the class."

"Well, not the *smartest*."

"Who's smarter?"

"Oh, they got a lot of smart guys in class."

"Who? Name me seven." They laughed.

"You got a letter from Lotte. Bet you're happy."

Jacob nodded as he sat on the edge of the bed and tore open the envelope. His expression changed as he took out the letter. It was so short.

Dear Jacob,

I received your letter. I hope you will forgive me for not answering sooner, but I have been very busy. I got a job working for a dressmaker, and I enjoy the work so much.

Bubeleh has not been well and my mother has gone to see her. I wish I could have gone too, but I can't leave my job and I have to take care of my father. My sister helps, but she goes to school. Besides, I'm the oldest so it's only right. I should take the responsibility when my mother is gone.

I hope you are well and your family is fine. I guess your nephew is getting to be a big boy. I hope your job is good and that you are happy. Everyone sends their love. There really isn't anything else to say.

Love,
Lotte

Jacob sat on the edge of the bed, staring down at the letter. In his mind, he reviewed the previous letters. Dearest, dearest Jacob, they began. Or, My dearest Jacob. I dream about you all the time. Darling Jacob, I cry myself to sleep. You are always in my thoughts and I count the months, the days, till we will be together . . .

Those had been the early letters, and they had brought Jacob so much joy. But the more recent letters had seemed less amorous, and increasingly formal, and today's letter left him altogether bewildered, let down. It seemed so impersonal.

Shlomo looked at Jacob's face. He got up and sat alongside his brother.

"Jacob," he said softly, "are you sad?"

The little boy's voice startled him. His eyes left the letter and looked at the boy's sensitive face. As though trying to sort out the pieces, he answered, "Yes, Shlomo. I think that's what I feel."

"Why?"

"I'm not sure."

"Is it something Lotte said?"

"It's more what she didn't say."

Shlomo took the letter and read it. Handing it back to Jacob, he said, "It's because she didn't say she missed you. Maybe that's why."

Jacob shook his head slowly. "Yes. I have a funny feeling, that maybe she doesn't . . ."

"Jacob, she *loves* you, but she's very busy and working so hard. Maybe she doesn't have the time to . . ."

Jacob was only half-listening to Shlomo. They'd been separated now for nearly a year, and in that time Lotte had poured out her love over and over again. Being separated, how much could one continue to say? She had a great many responsibilities, and working as hard as she was left her with little time to write love letters. Besides, he thought guiltily, he had never really told her the truth. He had told her that life in America was wonderful, that his family was wonderful

But he had never told her of the ordeals he had suffered when he first arrived, or that he resorted to brutality in order to save enough money. He never told her how worried he was about his future, about being able to provide a good living, a nice home.

Jacob reread the letter. Suddenly the letter seemed quite sensible, mature. There was no reason to repeat the sentiments that had been expressed over and over again for the last year. Perhaps he was only telling himself the things he wanted to believe, Jacob thought, but suddenly he felt better, much better. He smiled at Shlomo, put his arm around him. "You *are* the smartest boy in the class. Not only that, but you're a lot smarter than I am. Now, let's wash up and have supper." ...

After serving her sons, Esther sat across from them, watching Jacob as he ate. He was going to be sixteen years old next week, but he looked twenty. He also looked very tired. He worked all day, unloading those heavy crates, and every night he went to school. But what worried Esther most was why he stayed out so late. He rarely came home before eleven.

"Jacob, I want you to stop going to school every night. A doctor you're not going to be. You already speak very good English."

He continued to eat, without looking up at her, but suddenly the food would hardly go down.

"Jacob, I'm talking to you."

"I heard," he mumbled.

"Listen, Jacob, you can't do so much. A person also needs to rest."

"I rest, I rest."

"Don't be stubborn with me, Jacob. This may be America, but I'm still your mother."

"I'm sorry, and I'm *not* being stubborn. I just want to learn." He listened to the lie and despised himself for it.

"I admire you for that, but it's too hard to work all day and then go to school every night. It's too hard." Esther took a sip of her tea and peered over the rim at him before she continued. "And as long as I'm talking already, why do you come home so late? School is over at nine o'clock."

"I go with some boys I met," he answered quickly, swallowing hard.

"Till eleven o'clock every night?"

"I need a little change. I can't just work and go to school, mama. A person has to have a little fun."

She didn't like the way he said fun. Was he going to bad houses? No, not Jacob, he would never do anything like that. He would be pure when he went to his marriage bed. She was certain. Dismissing the thought completely, she said, "All right, but you shouldn't come home so late."

"Listen, mama, I don't want to be disrespectful, but I am not a child."

"You're my child no matter how old you are. Besides, what do you do till eleven o'clock?"

Jacob was getting nervous. The conversation becoming more complicated, the deception damned difficult. "I go to school, and then I go out with a few fellows I met to see a picture, have a cup of coffee, play cards, whatever. I don't want to talk about it anymore." Jacob got up quickly, kissed his mother on the cheek and said good-by to Shlomo.

As he opened the door, Esther called out to him, "I want you home early."

He looked back at her. "I'll be home when I'll be home. Don't worry, I'll get enough rest."

Esther sat shaking her head. Was it good, this new country? It wasn't really good for Jews anywhere, but at least in Europe there was a quality of family life and respect that was soon lost in America. . . .

When Jacob looked back, he could scarcely believe that it was a year ago, almost to the day, that he had arrived in America. He dismissed the welcome he had had on his arrival as his mind moved quickly to how much he had accomplished. True, he had done things he was not proud of, but pride would not have given him what he needed so desperately. With the money he had saved, he could now bring Lotte over, and at long last he no longer need live with the guilt and stress of his deception. Thank God, for being so good to him. He had five hundred dollars now, and at last he could stop fighting. Last night was indeed the last time he was going to take the body blows, which had been more painful than he had let on. The greatest pleasure was yet to come. In the morning, he would tell O'Leary.

At supper that night he said, smiling, to his mother, "You'll be happy to know I quit school, mama."

"You did?" She smiled back weakly. Poor Jacob, he wanted the education so badly.

"Yes, and I won't be out late anymore. Also I want to tell you I lied. I don't have any friends. I got a job at night, working overtime, to save enough money to send for Lotte."

Beaming, he continued, "I never thought the day would come. She means so much to me. I know you'll love her, she'll be like a daughter."

"If you love her, then so will I. If anyone deserves some happiness, it's you, my dear Jacob."

"Deserve, I don't know about, but I was blessed the day I met her."

"You deserve," Esther assured him.

When he went to his room, he found Shlomo doing his homework as usual.

Jacob looked over at Shlomo and smiled as he sat down to write to Lotte, scarcely able to contain his deep joy at the thought that soon she would be with him. The loneliness of the past would soon be over.

The next morning found the streets blanketed with snow. Jacob put on his heavy new coat—his one extravagance—and hurried out to buy the greatest luxury he could imagine he would ever possess. A ticket for Lotte. His heart pounded when he looked at the ticket. She would travel in style. She was going second class, not steerage like cattle, not Lotte. The thirty dollars extra was worth it. He put the ticket into the addressed envelope, sealed and posted it. . . .

Breathlessly, he walked into the warehouse and signed in. He was a little late this morning, but it was the first time. Besides, this was a very special day.

He had just started to work when Patrick O'Leary saw him. "Well, now, don't we look handsome this morning, all bundled up like a teddy bear in that lovely new coat. By the saints, if you don't look like a captain in the merchant marine. Couldn't have bought that on the pittance you earn here, now could you, Jackie?"

Jacob knew the Irishman was seething under the friendly facade. He was more than seething, and had been since the night Jacob had demanded the ten dollars a fight. He'd seen the venom in the Irish eyes but he didn't give a damn. Besides, the bastard had made his demands to Hallihan. Seventeen dollars, he said, or we go. Plenty of places for Jackie Sanders to fight. Seventeen dollars. He got it.

Jacob took the bailing hook and brutally stabbed into a bail of cotton. When he looked up, it was into the face of O'Leary.

"You're making quite a name for yourself, *champ*, and lifting those bails helped to build the muscles."

Jacob ignored him. As he climbed up to attack another bail, he said, "I'm not going to fight anymore."

O'Leary froze, narrowed his eyes. So it was a little more extortion was it? But he'd play along with the Christ-killer. As O'Leary shifted a huge crate into place he said, "Now, what's this I'm hearing. Not going to fight anymore? Why Jack . . . Jacob . . . you got a big future ahead of you. You're not going to be a dockworker all your life? That's not for the likes of you, me boy. Why, I got plans for us. Fact is, tonight there's going to be a big promoter watching you. Convinced him to take a look. That's the kind of talent I think you've got. Like I said from the very beginning, you're gonna be a champ—"

"I'm not going to be there tonight, or any other night."

"Now, Jacob, that's what I call a little deceitful. Especially for an upstanding young Jewish lad with integrity. Why, your Bible teaches you about loving your neighbors and righteousness. That's what you've been taught, to respect your elders and not betray a friend."

Jacob turned away.

"Now, Jacob, I would suggest you be fightin' tonight. I went to a lot of trouble to get this."

"I told you, I'm through fighting," he said, looking Patrick in the eye now.

"Why didn't you tell me Tuesday?" Patrick asked, his fists in his pockets and his jaw clenched.

"Because I made up my mind last night."

"I see, just like that."

"Just like that."

O'Leary ran his tongue around his dry lips, then smiled. "Well, me boy, I think you're going to live to regret this. There are damn few people get the kind of golden opportunity I'm handing you. You could be as big as the likes of Sullivan. Don't be throwin' it away so lightly. Think on it. I'm a patient man. You give me the answer by quittin' time."

"I don't need any time, the answer is no." Jacob turned and hoisted himself up to the last row of cotton and began to maneuver it down.

When the noon bell rang Jacob sat on a crate inside the warehouse. Although the day was bitterly cold, he unbuttoned his heavy jacket, took off the leather gloves and put them into his slashed pockets. He had worked up a good sweat this morning from the freight he had loaded, but he had never felt happier. O'Leary was out of his life and Lotte was coming back into it. With the thoughts of what the future held he unscrewed the top of the thermos and began pouring out the yellow chicken soup, thick with noodles, large chunks of chicken, carrots and celery. He smiled, hearing the echo of his mother's voice ringing in his ears. "I want you should eat a hot meal, and I want you should eat it all. Not a drop you should leave." It was a quart. Contentedly, he started to eat when he saw O'Leary and three of the biggest men on the dock come toward him. Well, it seemed he wasn't through with O'Leary just yet . . . quickly he jumped off the crate, grabbed the bailing hook from his back pocket and waited.

"So, you're goin' to quit the ring, are you now? Well, the boys and me want to give you a little farewell party." With that, he nodded at the three men and they lunged at Jacob. One grabbed and twisted his wrist until the hook dropped to the ground.

O'Leary said, "Okay, drag him to the corner. We wouldn't be wantin' anyone else to enjoy this."

Jacob heard the Irishman saying above his screams, "Here, let me stick a rag in his mouth, the lousy bastard. No one's goin' to outsmart O'Leary."

Jacob was beaten until the blood came from his mouth. His cries of pain were muffled as they savagely pounded away at his body, his head, his face. His left eye was completely swollen shut and he could hardly see out of the right one. The last thing he remembered was the voice of O'Leary . . . "All right, boys, take the bastard's pants off. I want to see the size of the Jew. Saints above! If it don't look like a stud." O'Leary bent over Jacob. "Well, now this time, Jackie, how would you like to feel the crunch of them big balls? I've almost have a mind to do it." Jacob could scarcely hear; everything was slipping away. . . .

Jacob lay unconscious. O'Leary was kicking him in the ribs. "Okay, boys, let's get the hell away from here."

Jacob lay unable to move. For a moment he wondered if he were dead. But if you're dead, you don't feel any pain. His lips were as swollen as his eyes. His ribs must have been broken, his chest felt as though it had caved in. The throbbing in his head was torture. He tried calling out, but his voice would not obey. Vaguely, he heard someone speaking. It was coming from very far away, from an echo chamber. Now it was coming closer.

The voice was saying, "Can you manage to sip this?"

He felt a glass tube being forced between his lips. He tried to swallow, but couldn't. Then he felt a gentle hand on his wrist. It lingered on the pulse, then was gone.

"Can you hear me?" the voice said, very close to his ear.

Jacob tried to respond, nothing came out.

The voice repeated, "Can you hear me?"

Jacob mumbled, but the voice didn't seem to understand.

The tube was being forced between his lips once again. "Sip slowly."

Painful as it was, this time the water traveled from the glass tube to his stomach. Weakly, he groped for the hand.

"Yes, what do you want to say?"

"Where am I?" he whispered, forcing himself to be heard.

"At Bellevue Hospital. You've been here for three days."

Three days! His mother must be frantic. Things were beginning to get clear. "How did I get here?" he asked haltingly.

"By ambulance. Don't talk, I'll tell you all I know. You were unconscious when you arrived, badly beaten." More like half dead, she wanted to say. It had been nip and tuck until the internal bleeding had been stopped. "My name is Miss Hanson. I'm one of the emergency nurses and I've been looking after you. Now you mustn't be frightened. I know you can't see, but that's only because your eyes are so swollen. There was no real damage to your eyes. You have three broken ribs, which have been taped; that's why your breathing is so painful. Now, you rest, and the doctor will be in to see you soon."

Jacob reached out to her.

"Yes?" she asked, holding his hand.

"I have to go home. Please . . ."

"I don't think that will be possible, not for at least a few days."

"I must go home. Please, my mother will be—"

"I see. We didn't know anything about you. There was no family reference in your belongings. The only thing we found was a gym membership card, with Jackie Sanders written on it."

"My name is Jacob Sandsonitsky."

"Does your mother have a phone?"

"No."

"Well, then we'll have one of the social workers notify her. Can you give me her address?"

Painfully, he whispered it to her. . . .

Jacob was quite right; Esther had been frantic when he had not come home that first night after work. She waited through a sleepless night, and when the morning came she took the subway to the docks. She went immediately to the office and inquired about her son. They looked up his work

57

record and found he had not signed in for work. That was all the information they had. She went out among the men, making inquiries, but no one seemed to know what had happened to Jacob.

The only course left was to ask the police for their help. They took down all the information Esther could give them, but they were so perfunctory, so unsympathetic, that Esther left the station house in tears.

Not knowing what else to do, she went to Gittel's house. When she got there, Hershel was home. Helplessly, she asked him, "What shall we do?"

"I don't know where to start. He didn't have any friends, no one," Hershel said, scratching his head.

"Oh God, I'm beside myself. Jacob would never do this, unless . . ." She bit her lip.

"Listen. I'll go down and use Mrs. Greenblatt's phone."

"Who will you call?" Esther was almost afraid to ask, but not knowing was worse.

"The hospitals."

Hospitals? My dear God, if I have sinned, don't punish me like this, I beg you.

When Hershel returned, Esther searched his face. She knew before he said a word.

"I called Mount Sinai and Bellevue. They don't have him."

Esther knew Jacob was dead. Getting up, she said, "Well, I'll go home. Shlomo will wonder where I am." . . .

Esther closed the restaurant and sat in her room. She waited in torment. Jacob, Jacob, where are you?

Shlomo did not go to school. Hard as he tried to reassure her that Jacob was all right, his words went unheard.

At five o'clock that night, Esther opened the door to a stranger.

Her heart pounded as the man asked, "Are you Jacob Sandsonitsky's mother?"

She nodded.

"Well, Mrs. Sandsonitsky, your son is in Bellevue Hospital, recovering from an accident."

Esther could not answer.

It was Shlomo who asked, "What kind of an accident?"

"Well, son, he was beaten up pretty badly, but he's much better now."

Before he could say another word, Esther ran to her room, put on her hat and coat and went immediately to the front of the store. Her son was alive, and that's all she would concern

58

herself with at the moment. "Where do I go to find out what room he's in?"

"He's in a ward. Go to the admitting office and they'll—"

"Thank you, very much. Shlomo, go get ready." . . .

Esther and Shlomo walked down the long aisle between the iron beds until they came to Jacob's. The only thing she recognized was his blond hair. She gasped and steadied herself, holding on to the iron footrail. His face was smashed in, his eyes so swollen she wondered if they could ever heal, and his hands were bandaged. But this was not the time for tears. Composing herself, she spoke in a soft but even voice. "Jacob?"

"Mama . . ." He put out his hand to her, and she held it tightly.

"Yes, Jacob."

"Shlomo, where's Shlomo?"

"Here, Jacob, on the left side." Shlomo held Jacob's groping hand.

"I want to go home, mama."

"Yes. Yes, Jacob, I'll take you home."

"They said I can't go."

"They said, they said? Who are they? You're my son, and what I can do for you they can't. I'll be right back. Shlomo, don't talk too much to Jacob, let him rest."

Esther went down the hall hurriedly. She stopped at the nurses' station. "I would like to get my son's clothes. He's going home."

"What is your son's name?"

"Jacob Sandsonitsky."

"I have no authority to dismiss him," the nurse said after looking at Jacob's chart.

"You have no what?"

"Authority. Only the doctor can let him go home. Do you understand?"

"Sure, I understand, but I don't need a doctor to tell me I can take my son home."

"I'm afraid you'll have to . . ."

"I'm afraid you don't know Esther Sandsonitsky. Bring my son's clothes. I'll get him dressed."

"Now you listen to me," the nurse answered, measuring out the words. "Your son has been seriously hurt. Not until the doctor says he can be—"

Esther had had enough. "Now you listen to me, young lady, a greenhorn, I'm not. You go tell the doctor I am taking my son. But first, bring me his clothes."

The nurse turned and walked down the hall. When she returned it was with a young intern.

"I'm Dr. Lee. I understand you want to take your son home?"

"You understand right."

"I would be against that."

"Maybe you would, but I wouldn't."

It was moments like this he wished he had gone into his father's hardware business. Jewish mothers were damned formidable, obstinate. "If you take your son out of here, the hospital will not be responsible. Do you understand what I mean?"

"Of course I understand. What am I, a dummy? I'm an American," she answered indignantly.

"He requires care. I mean, he needs nursing care—"

"So what he can get here he can get at home. Better. A mother is not a nurse and a nurse is not a mother?"

"All right. Miss Williams, get a release form." This one was hopeless; no use arguing. Turning back to Esther, he said, "You'll have to pay for an ambulance. The hospital will not provide that."

"So who's asking for charity?"

Jacob was grateful to be home, where all the familiar sights and sounds had such meaning for him. The room he shared with Shlomo, his bed with the marvelously clean sheets, the sounds of pots being put on the stove and dishes taken out of a cupboard . . . But best of all was the feeling of love.

Esther fed him, bathed him, nourished him with her devotion. Shlomo hurried home each day to help, and at night he read beautiful Jewish poetry to Jacob, and books about the founding fathers, the building of America, the Civil War, the freeing of the slaves. What a country! Imagine, no more slaves. They were all free men, not like in Poland and Russia, where Jews lived beyond the pale or in ghettos. Except it was also a country where a Jew could be beaten up because he was a Jew. . . .

The days went by peacefully as Jacob's health and strength were restored. His eyes were almost healed, and although his ribs were still painful, now he could get out of bed and walk around. Gittel came every day with the baby, who was now crawling and getting into everything. Little Avrum, Avrumchik. Oh, if papa, his namesake, had only lived to see. If only he'd lived . . .

CHAPTER TEN

Now THAT Jacob's health was returning so quickly, he began to think what he would do about a job. He was strong as a bull, but to go back to work on the docks was out of the question. That brave, he wasn't. His mother had been right; *goyim* were bastards. He would never trust them as long as he lived. But he shoved the thought aside as he realized that Lotte's letter would be arriving in the next few weeks. When he received it, he would have to look for a flat.

So Jacob's immediate concern was a job. There were few choices and fewer jobs. Reluctantly, he went to work in a sweatshop off Second Avenue. The conditions were foul, unfit for human beings to work in. He despised what was called the needle trade, but he learned to work away at the machines, making suits for other men to wear. Still, at least he was among his own people. In fact, he almost convinced himself it was the best thing that had happened to him. He was out of the freezing cold and he was earning six dollars a week. Later, when he and Lotte got settled, he would get into a small business, a fruit stand maybe. . . .

As the month dragged on, his anxiety grew to what bordered on obsession. He'd had no word from Lotte, he couldn't think straight or do anything right. He began to wonder if she'd received the letter at all. The thought made his stomach do somersaults. In the morning he would set off for work exhausted from not having slept the night before. He cursed the mails. Well, there was only one thing to do—write another letter to Lotte. It wouldn't speed up anything, but no matter how long it took, at least eventually he would know whether she had received the ticket.

One night when he returned home, Shlomo was waiting and excitedly called out, "The letter from Lotte came today."

Thank God. Jacob hurried to his room, sat on the edge of the bed and tore open the envelope. His hands began to tremble as he sat staring at it. First he looked at the ticket, then at the unread letter. Taking a deep swallow he began to read.

Dear Jacob,
    Please try to understand and forgive me for what I am

61

going to say. I was in love with you, you must believe that, but it was the first love of two young people experiencing life for the first time. Unfortunately, time makes many changes. Perhaps if you had remained, I would never have thought of anyone else. I know you will be hurt about this. The truth is always painful, but I should have told you sooner. There is no way to say how sorry I am, but I have met a man who is a little older. He has a very good business and can take good care of me and also help my parents. By the time you get this, I will already be married. Truly, to think I would be the one to hurt you . . .

Jacob could not finish it. He felt as racked with pain as when he had been beaten, but this time he had no physical adversary. He got up and smashed his fist against the wall, then he ran out into the cold night, blinded with tears. He slipped and fell on the icy sidewalk, got up and went on. He wanted to die, kill himself. What was there about him? How could Lotte have destroyed him so when she knew how much he loved her? He thought again of all he had done for Lotte, of all that he had suffered for her, and suddenly he prayed that she would be punished for what she'd done to him. And he swore to himself that no one would ever make him feel like this again, *no one*. He hoped she would never have a moment's peace in her life.

Jacob did not know what street he was on, nor what saloon he was in, it didn't matter. He only knew hatred and anger and, worst of all, the frustration of not being able to strike back at Lotte any more than he could have struck back at O'Leary.

All that was left was the world.

The next morning he woke up in the somber gray dawn and let his gaze wander about the dirty room. The mattress springs stuck into his aching ribs. His head pounded. When he rallied himself out of his drunken stupor he realized a nude body lay close to him. Unsteadily he got out of bed, throwing back the covers. He looked at the girl. Her arms were black and blue. There was a gash on her lips and a large reddish area on her swollen cheek. Her eyes were frightened as they met his. Heavily, he sat down on the edge of the mattress. She flinched as Jacob moved his hand to cover her body with the sheet.

"You're afraid of me? Why?"

Swallowing hard, she said, "Because of what you did to me last night."

Jacob narrowed his eyes. "What did I do?"

She hesitated, pulling the sheet up under her chin without answering.

"Nothing will happen to you, tell me."

"Well," she started slowly, "I met you coming out of the saloon and asked if you'd like to come home with me." She hesitated.

"Go on."

Taking a deep breath, she said, "You were pretty drunk. Then, when we got here, you asked if I had some whiskey. You won't get upset?"

He shook his head. "Just tell me what happened."

"You drank the whole bottle and then . . . you went kind of crazy."

"Crazy?"

"Yeah. I mean for no reason, you began to beat me up. I never had a guy do that—a lot of other things but never that. I thought you were going to kill me. You kept hollerin' out 'Lotte.' I really think you thought I was this Lotte."

Jacob was stunned. He couldn't remember any of it. He shut his eyes and held his head with his hands. My God, he could have killed this girl. Of course, he wanted to punish Lotte. Yes, it was Lotte he had been beating.

The long silence was so great the girl was beginning to wonder what he was planning. Running her tongue around her dry lips, she asked quietly, afraid to antagonize him, "Are you all right?"

Jacob was brought up sharply. "Yes, I'm all right." Looking at the girl he asked, "Why didn't you try to get away?"

"Listen, you're very strong. Besides, you locked the door and threw the key away."

Jacob sighed and rubbed his throbbing forehead. "What else did I do?"

"Well, you knocked me down on the bed. I got to be honest, I never had a guy do it so hard. I thought my insides was going to bust."

He couldn't listen to any more. Quickly, he got up and started to dress. Still frightened, she asked, "How you gonna get out, mister?"

Jacob took the jacknife out of his back pocket and stuck it into the lock. One turn and the door opened. He reached inside his coat pocket, took out whatever money he had and, without counting it, put it on the dresser. He looked at the girl once more, shook his head. "I'm sorry. I really mean that." And as he turned and hurried from the room he was even sorrier that it had not been Lotte. . . .

He didn't go to work that day. What difference did it make? What difference did anything make?

After wandering aimlessly for hours, he went home. He passed Esther in the kitchen without a word. She followed him into his room and watched as he took off his shoes and lay down. Putting his hands behind his head, he stared up at the ceiling. What he saw were the bruises he had inflicted on the young prostitute's body. The first woman he'd ever taken, a whore, and he couldn't even remember what it felt like. And it was his beloved Lotte who had driven him to such ugly violence.

This time, Esther did not question why he had not come home. Quietly she said, "Jacob, I know how sad you are. And why."

He wanted to put his hands over his ears and shut out her voice. He couldn't stand the sound of it; it was false. All the anger and suspicions of her came back . . . she'd only taken him in because of her own guilt . . .

Esther tried to comfort him. "You've been hurt terribly, Jacob, but believe me . . ."

He refused to listen to her, refused to believe her. Where was she when he was a little boy, on his own, by himself? It was damned easy for her now to be the good kind mother, now that he was a grown man. Well, no matter how hard he'd tried, the hurts and memories wouldn't die. And why should they . . . ?

He got off the bed, went to the kitchen cupboard, took out the brandy and started to drink.

Esther stood watching. "Jacob, this is not the answer." Gently, she tried to take the bottle from him.

Breathing heavily, he looked at her.

"Please Jacob, let me try to help you."

"You helped me enough. Do me a favor, leave me alone." He returned to his room and lay down, turning his face to the wall.

For the next few days Jacob neither ate nor left his bed. Whenever Esther tried to bring him food, he ignored her. Not even Shlomo could divert him. He would speak to no one.

Esther never left the restaurant. In fact, she scarcely slept at night, lying half awake and listening in fear of what Jacob might do. Her worst, most secret fear was that he might do away with himself . . . She had said nothing to Gittel, knowing it would only add to her problems. Hershel had lost his job and they were barely surviving. But now the burden of silence was becoming too great; she simply had to share it. Leaving Shlomo with Jacob, she went to her daughter's flat and implored her to come talk to Jacob.

When the two women returned, Gittel went to Jacob's room. Closing the door behind her, Gittel sat on the edge of the bed and looked at him. He almost frightened her. He hadn't shaved or washed. His hair was unkempt, his eyes were flat, haunting. She took his hand gently and, trying to keep her voice even, said, "Jacob, I wish I had known. I would have been here sooner. You know that, don't you, Jacob?"

No answer.

"Jacob, mama told me everything. You must listen to me. I know how terribly hurt you are. To love someone as you did and not have it returned is very painful. But when you met Lotte you were so young. It was the first time a girl came into your life. Please try to understand, you knew each other a very short time. In fact, you didn't know each other at all. Maybe if you'd been able to stay and allow your friendship to grow this wouldn't have happened. But you left, and even one year makes a very big difference, especially in a girl's life. Lotte grew into a woman. I think what she did was very cruel, but you mustn't let this ruin your life. She really wasn't for you. If it had been meant to be, this wouldn't have happened. Please, please, don't let this make you so bitter. You're very young and I know you will meet someone worthwhile . . ."

For the first time in five days, Jacob spoke. The anger in his eyes was not for Gittel. "I will never love or trust any woman again. I will never get married . . . never." His voice was a monotone but his intensity was beyond doubt.

Kissing his hand, then holding it to her cheek, Gittel said, "What you feel now is very deep hurt, but time will heal it. You mustn't think every woman is like Lotte."

He flinched at the sound of her name. "I'm not going to find out. You're the only good woman I know."

"Thank you, but mama's a good woman too."

She saw the muscles in his jaw tighten.

"She did the best she could for us, Jacob. You mustn't blame her for what you feel she did when you were a little boy. You must forget, Jacob. If you try to punish her you only hurt yourself. Let the past go, Jacob. Forget *that*, and forget Lotte. For your own sake."

Nothing had changed in his expression, but she prayed

something of what she'd said would get through. She waited as the long silence hung between them. All that could be said had been said. It would take time for Jacob. Still, in her heart, she knew nothing lasted forever. The threats he made today would change when he met the right girl. She tried very hard to convince herself of that.

Finally Gittel said, "Jacob, would you do me a favor?" She waited. When he did not answer she continued. "Please get out of bed, take a bath and eat something. You'll feel better. Will you do it for me, Jacob? Please." Slowly she pulled back the covers and waited.

He looked at her. She was right, he decided. I'm damn well not going to let any of them beat me down—no more. Getting out of bed, he looked at his reflection in the mirror. Like a bum on the docks, he looked.

Gittel shut her eyes and, in her innocence, thanked God as Jacob opened the door.

As the months passed, his acute bitterness took another form. Jacob retreated into himself. He stopped going to *shul* and spoke as little as possible to his mother. He had, in fact, become like a boarder. Each week he paid for his room and board. When Esther tried to refuse it, Jacob told her in no uncertain terms that he would not live on her charity and that if she didn't stop objecting he would take a room somewhere else.

Even with Shlomo there was not the closeness they'd once had. And although his love and admiration for Gittel remained, even with her he was remote and withdrawn.

He had no desire for women, sex was something he now totally rejected.

The only salvation in his life was his new job. He found employment in a glass factory in New Jersey.

In spite of the distance, he was the first to arrive and the last to leave. The work was hard, but that was what he needed—to work hard for *himself*. He was going to go into business, be somebody, his own boss. Not dependent on anybody, on any of *them* . . .

In the next year, Jacob's salary was raised from nine dollars a week to sixteen. His loyalty as a worker had not gone unnoticed. He had never been late, never grumbled about working overtime, never complained about conditions, did his work, kept to himself and refused to join the men who wanted to organize . . . Although he was only seventeen he was promoted to foreman.

When he returned from work at night Jacob used the back door, avoiding Esther and her customers. This evening as he was taking off his coat, he looked across the inner hall to the kitchen and saw a young girl standing at the sink washing dishes. For a moment he was surprised. Was business so good that his mother needed help? He shrugged his shoulders and went to his room where he found Shlomo studying.

The boy looked up from his book. "You're home early tonight. How come?"

"Things were a little slow. Where's mama?"

"Why do you ask? She's waiting on customers, didn't you see her?"

"No, I came through the back," he answered, taking off his shirt.

"Why didn't you say hello? It wouldn't hurt, you know."

"I was all sweaty. I want to get washed up."

"Oh . . . well . . . Mama got a girl to help."

"I saw," he answered. Sarcastically he added, "Now, she won't have to work so hard."

"She didn't do it for that reason," Shlomo snapped back.

"No? Then why?"

"Because the girl had no place to live. And she's not just a girl, her name is Sara Edelstein."

"What does that have to do with her working here?"

"I just told you, she has no place to live."

"Where's she gonna sleep, in the kitchen?"

"No, in mama's room, until she can get a job. In the meantime she'll help."

"So she's going to live here?"

"Yes, mama got a cot for her."

"In that case, I'm leaving."

"Wait a minute, Jacob." Shlomo jumped up from his chair. "You should be happy mama's got someone to help her. Besides, what do you care if she stays here?"

"But I do care. I don't want a girl . . . a stranger living —"

"She's not a stranger. She's a distant relative of Hershel's and her father just died."

"But we're not her relatives . . ."

"She doesn't have anyone else and Gittel likes her, feels sorry for her—which is something that it wouldn't hurt you to do."

Jacob narrowed his eyes on Shlomo. He was about to answer when Shlomo went quickly on. "You know what your problem is? You think no one in the world has suffered quite as much as you. You're the only one who had a terrible childhood, who ever had a girl turn him down. Everyone else had a great life—"

"Well, your life was just a little bit easier than mine—"

"Yes, a whole lot. And mama's too and Gittel's—we had all the luxuries."

"What's that got to do with this girl living here? Why doesn't she live with Gittel?"

"Because Gittel's living in two rooms and she's going to have another baby."

Jacob was stunned. "Another baby? When did you find out?"

"Couple of days ago."

"Why didn't anyone tell me?"

"Because you've been feeling so sorry for yourself, you've kept as far away from all of us as possible."

"Okay, all right, I think you told me enough. So I'm a louse, right?"

"Wrong. Underneath that suit of armor is a very nice person with a good heart. You're a *mensch,* Jacob, and being a *mensch* is the most important thing a person can be."

Jacob stood studying Shlomo. The truth hurt, but it was indeed the truth. He *had* acted like a louse—to his mother, to Gittel, to his own brother.

Jacob shook his head in wonderment and smiled for the first time in months. Putting his arm around Shlomo's shoulder, he said, "Remember I once said you're the smartest one in your class? I also said you were smarter than me. You are, Shlomo . . . you are."

"I'm not. You're still the smartest *and* the best."

As Jacob left to clean up, Shlomo said, "And Jacob, it wouldn't hurt if you went to *shul* with me."

"On Saturday." Jacob nodded.

Not that Jacob gave a damn about Sara or any other girl, but he couldn't help noticing that she was different from anyone he'd ever met—so educated, so . . . He couldn't quite fathom how or why she had come to be living in a place like the lower East Side of New York. Of course, Shlomo had told him the reasons, about her father dying and all, but in spite of himself she was a source of curiosity. At night he lay awake in the dark, wondering about the life that had given Sara her elegance and her aura of breeding and culture, but the life he envisioned was quite far from the truth. Jacob would have been shocked had he known that Sara Edelstein's beginnings were in many ways quite similar to his own. They were just variations on the same theme.

CHAPTER ELEVEN

As HAPPENS with a great many people, she knew only the apparent facts of her mother's and father's life. And what she knew, she had pieced together. Her mother, then Molly Pollack, was a young girl from Warsaw who worked in a millinery shop. Molly's family were all dead, except for one brother who had migrated to the United States, to Oakland, California. Sara knew her father had come from a distinguished family that lived in Zurich, but that her parents had married against the vehement protests of his family and were disinherited. It seemed Harry Edelstein was married when he met Molly Pollack. Divorce was unheard of in those times, but nonetheless his wife divorced him. Now he found himself not only disgraced but without any money.

During his first marriage he had been taken into his father-in-law's established jewelry business—not as a salesman, but as an elegant manager. Harry knew nothing whatsoever about gems or jewels, but in his case, it wasn't necessary. His charm and polish, his ability to greet and handle the elite trade on an equal footing was his prime function. He had been raised in an affluent family who felt that a young man had to have a knowledge of art, be well-traveled and accomplished in literature to be suited to take his place in society. If Harry hadn't been such an impulsive young man, these accomplishments might have secured his life's future. As it was, after leaving his father-in-law's business he was completely unprepared to make a living.

Harry and Molly went to Brussels, where Sara was born a little less than nine months later. Her father had relatives in Brussels who were in the business of manufacturing fine linens, and Harry prevailed on them to give him a job. While they didn't condone what he had done they were people of compassion and they gave him a job. However, Harry was unaccustomed to menial labor and he lasted in the position for only a very short time. Then he went from one thing to another, barely making ends meet. As the larder grew bare, love and passion began to diminish, and both Molly and Harry found themselves greatly disappointed. Molly had only been a milliner and was surely not his equal intellectually, but she was more than equal when it came to the things she wanted out of life—and what she wanted was not to be poor. Harry, in his turn, had been captivated by Molly's great beauty and thought she would give him the love and passion he'd never had in his previous marriage. Both were mistaken. Sara could still remember the violent argument that had ended with Molly shouting that she was through, that he'd ruined her life and her chances of meeting and marrying a rich man. She wanted a Jewish *get;* a divorce.

Since they had been married by an Orthodox rabbi, they did not have to concern themselves with the civil courts; rabbinical laws considered and ruled on divorce. After careful examination of every possible course, Molly and Harry's marriage was terminated and they went their separate ways, Molly taking her belongings and her child and moving to a small hotel.

In the months that followed, Molly met a dapper, handsome man who wined and dined her, gave her extravagant gifts and was enormously fond of little Sara. Louie Carr was everything Molly wanted in a man, and especially in a husband. The only thing she found herself debating was Louie's profession. He was a gambler. Very high-class, to be sure, but still it could be the Savoy today and the next day . . . Well, why worry about that? Louie was a master, a genius at his craft.

Soon they were married and lived luxuriously in the finest hotels, dined at the finest restaurants, bought the most expensive clothes and enjoyed the finest in theater. Louie indulged Molly and Sara shamefully and adored doing so. To Louie, money was good only for one thing—to spend. . . .

After three months of wedded bliss, quite early one morning Louie entered their suite, put his pearl-gray felt fedora in the hall closet, walked into the small salon and poured a large brandy into the snifter. As he settled himself into the satin brocade chair, the mantel clock chimed. It was three in the morning.

A yawning Molly slipped out of bed and walked into the sittingroom. Louie looked up and smiled that roguish smile

70

she found so irresistible. He got up and put his arms around her slim waist as she reached up to kiss him. He nibbled on her ear and whispered, "Did you miss me?"

"Of course. How did it go tonight, Louie?"

"Well, to be honest . . . I took a heavy loss at *chemin de fer*. But there are winning streaks and losing streaks."

"I know tomorrow will be better."

Taking her hand he led her to the settee. "Would you like a brandy?"

She tilted her head to one side and asked, "Why . . . do you think I need it?"

"I'm not sure," he said, but he filled a glass for her, refilled his own and sat down next to her. Lifting his glass he said, *"L'chayim."*

"What are we drinking to?"

"To taking a trip."

"Where and why?"

"The where is South Africa—Johannesburg to be exact—and the why is there's a casino I can buy into. It also has an added bit of revenue . . . girls."

"You mean a whorehouse?"

"Oh, Molly, that's shameful," Louie answered, shaking his head.

"So what would you call it?"

"A whorehouse with a gambling casino," he answered with a laugh. "But very elegant, very exclusive."

"Absolutely not."

"You surprise me, Molly. I thought you were more worldly than that."

"Worldly I am, but I'm not taking my child to a whorehouse."

"I've thought about that too."

"Really? You seem to have thought about a great many things."

"Believe me, Molly, I have. Gambling isn't a very secure way of living and there's no real future in it. You see, it's our future I'm concerned about. Here we have the opportunity to get into something—"

"What about Sara?"

"As I said before, I thought about it—a great deal, I might add."

"And?"

"I think she should have the best. You know how much I love her . . . as though she were my own child."

"Come to the point."

"The point is, I think she should be put into the best boarding school money can buy."

"I'm not putting my child into a boarding school. The answer is no."

Her anger didn't bother him a bit. Taking the glass from her hand, he took her in his arms, kissed her and held her close, as he explained his reasoning to her.

Molly thought seriously about it and somehow what he said did make sense. It wasn't forever, Louie said. Girls from the best homes—rich homes—went to fine boarding schools, and she'd become a lady. If you loved your child, you made sacrifices. Besides, there was one other rather disturbing thing to consider; Louie told her he'd go without her, and then where would she and Sara be? He was trying the only way he knew to secure their future. With great reluctance she finally answered, "All right, Louie." . . .

Sara was enrolled in one of the best schools, but for all the "advantages" she was terribly lonely and missed her mother and Louie. She often cried herself to sleep at night and her frequent letters to Molly always asked when they were coming to visit. It had already been two years since they'd promised, but unfortunately Louie's plans had not matched his prophecies.

When Louie and Molly arrived in Johannesburg they had found that the casino was shabby and rundown, and it had taken a large chunk of Louie's limited capital to refurbish the casino. By the time Louie was making a profit, the local constabulary had put a padlock on the door; gambling was one thing, but prostitution was another. Now without the added revenue of his voluptuous hostesses, Louie could barely survive—which left Molly sitting on the edge of the bed asking, "What are we going to do *now?*"

He sat in the chair opposite her with his hand cupped under his chin. When the answer was not forthcoming, Molly continued. "There's nothing here for us, Louie. And besides, I haven't seen Sara for two years. I can't stand the pathetic letters, they tear me apart. Soon we won't be able to keep sending money for the school anyway, so while we can still salvage something—sell. I want to go back."

"I'll raise the money to pay off the police . . . everyone can be bought off."

"Don't be foolish, Louie. Even if you could, they'd milk you for all you've got. Listen to me, sell the casino for whatever you can get."

What the hell, Louie thought, she was right. Besides, owning a casino was not all it was cracked up to be. He still had his skill; that was something no one would take away from him. They could always go to Monte Carlo and he'd have no problem getting a job as a croupier. Dealers made money if they knew how—and Louie knew how. "All right, Molly, start packing."

A smile broke across her face. It was the first time she had smiled with honesty in a long time. "When will we leave? I want to write Sara."

"As soon as the casino is sold. As a matter of fact, I have someone who wants to buy. We won't get what we put into it, but what the hell. I'll make it up in no time at all."

By now, Molly had heard that so often she paid little attention to his optimism. Besides, she was too happy at this moment to challenge him—she was going to see Sara . . . .

When their steamer arrived in Brussels, Sara was waiting. Molly ran down the gangplank and grabbed her in her arms. Sara was now seven and she was beautiful. Louie's prediction about Sara, at least, had been accurate. She was a poised, lady-like and mature child. In fact, it was difficult for Molly to believe Sara was so young; she spoke and acted like a grown-up.

If Molly was happy, Sara's joy at seeing her mother and Louie was overwhelming. What excited her most of all was that she no longer had to go to that dreadful girls' school; she was to live with mama and Louie in a grand hotel and she would attend a daily academy. She adored Louie. He was so gay, cheerful, devil-may-care, and always so elegant and impeccably groomed that Sara almost forgot he wasn't royalty.

For the next few months Sara's life was filled with every luxury, but best of all was that she was no longer lonely.

And then one day she returned to find Molly packing. "What are you doing?"

Molly looked at her for a moment, saw the frightened eyes and quickly pushed aside her own misgivings as she casually answered, "We're moving."

"We? Where are we going?" Sara asked haltingly.

"To an apartment," Molly said, continuing to take things out of the closet.

"Why don't we stay here?" Sara was close to tears.

"I don't—hotels are not a place to make a home." She wasn't going to tell Sara that Louie was on a losing streak and that they were going to be evicted.

"But we're going to live together? I mean, you're not going to send me back—"

"Of course not, what a silly question."

The adjustment was very difficult for Sara. She'd made friends at the girls' academy, but now she would no longer be able to go to the birthday parties, and suddenly there were no more pretty party dresses. As glad as she was to be with Molly and Louie, they didn't seem very happy. Molly couldn't help but notice Sara's troubled face, but she refused to dwell on whether Sara was disappointed with the shabby little bedroom she slept in or whether Louie thought the dingy apartment beneath his dignity. She had enough on her mind. Louie had become so compulsive in trying to recoup his gambling losses that they were now down to their last few dollars.

No question, Louie was definitely on his downers. The once charming devil-may-care Louie had become sullen. He complained constantly that Lady Luck was conspiring against him. He swore that never in his life had he encountered such a losing streak; it went beyond his comprehension. In the next few years they moved from one place to another, each cheaper than the last. Sara changed schools three times and became a very withdrawn, self-contained child. . . .

At three o'clock in the morning, Louie climbed into bed, took the sleeping Molly in his arms and kissed her gently. She opened her eyes. At Louie's amorous touch, she knew instantly his luck had turned.

After the passion had spent itself she said, still lying in his arms, "Well, one thing you didn't lose is knowing how to make love."

He laughed. "That I'll never lose and another thing I won't lose is my confidence."

"Really? It seems to me that lately you haven't been the Louie of old."

He smiled in the dark. "So sue me. I've got a right to complain once in a while, but I'm not complaining anymore."

"How much did you win?"

"A fortune."

"How much?"

"Enough to buy you a beautiful new wardrobe and tickets to Monte Carlo."

The announcement had far from the desired effect. Molly jumped out of bed and switched on the lamp. "When in hell is this moving around going to stop? I'm sick and tired of it and

74

I can't keep dragging Sara from one place to another, one school to—"

"Keep your voice down. Now, once and for all time, Molly, I make my living gambling. You knew it when we got married so don't try to remake me. I am what I am . . . Do I make myself clear?"

There was a long silence as Molly stood there, staring at him. She was, in a way, frightened of him . . . he was a man she could not manipulate . . . he wasn't Harry. Gradually the look on her face softened. "What about Sara, and what about Monte Carlo?"

"I'll answer the last first. I've been offered the opportunity to manage one of the most exclusive casinos on the French Riviera, which is quite an honor—and you'll be able to strut about like a queen. Now, I love you and I love Sara, but in my business a child is in the way. I feel very bad about that, as bad as you do . . . but facts are facts."

She swallowed hard. "You mean we'll have to send her to a boarding school?"

"No, not this time. At the moment all I have is enough to get us settled and buy you some new clothes."

"And if I didn't get the clothes would there—"

"No. I don't have a year's tuition—but later, absolutely."

She sighed, knowing she had a real choice to make this time. Did she lose Louie for her child? She loved them both, but what would her life be without him? The sad truth was that children grew up and eventually one was left alone. Sara was already nine years old and before you could turn around she would be a young woman, ready to marry. Where would that leave Molly? She wasn't getting younger and who would she ever find who compared with Louie? There were no alternatives, no more decisions, only capitulation and compromise. "All right, Louie . . . what do you suggest we do with Sara?"

He smiled at her, knowing how difficult the choices had been, and took her in his arms and kissed her. "You're a sensible woman, Molly, and you won't regret this. Now about Sara . . . What I think she needs is to live with a nice family."

Molly thought for a long moment. The idea seemed reasonable. Sara would be in a wholesome atmosphere, would have the stability of familial surroundings—something she'd never really had. In fact, the idea even began to appeal to Molly . . . except where would they find such a place?

Reading her thoughts Louie said, "I've already contacted a

family where I think Sara will be very happy. They're lovely people and they have three children—boys, nice little boys."

"How old are these boys?"

Sensing Molly's disapproval he answered offhandedly, "I'm not sure. The oldest I think is about thirteen and the others are probably eleven and nine."

"I don't like it, Louie, not one damn little bit—"

"Come now, Molly, what do you think's going to happen? This is a fine, lovely, Jewish family."

"In lovely Jewish families the boys are saints? Boys are boys, Jewish or *goyim*. At that age they know all about little girls."

"I take it back, Molly, you're not such a sensible woman. In fact, I think you have a very suspicious mind."

"You bet . . . when it comes to my child, I certainly do."

"And I don't? She's as important to me as she is to you. Would I even suggest this lovely home if I thought for one moment she wouldn't be safe? I'm really very upset and insulted."

"Why should you be insulted?"

"Because I'm the one that found the place and you don't seem to think I take my fatherly responsibilities very seriously."

Molly looked at Louie. He always knew the right thing to say at the right time, always pushed the right buttons—leave it to Louie. "So tell me about this lovely home and these nice boys and this wonderful family, and where do they live?"

"You have a funny little habit, Molly. You ask so many questions in one sentence, I don't know which one to answer."

"You'll find a way. Soo?"

Louie laughed. "Their name is Bromberg. They live in a modest two-story house in the Jewish section. Victor Bromberg has a wonderful bakery—small, but makes good money. Mrs. Bromberg—her name is Clara—is a real Jewish mother-type. The house and the children are immaculate, and the Brombergs are very religious. I think the situation is ideal for Sara, and when you see it so will—"

"All right, enough talk. I'll get my coat and hat and we'll go to see this marvelous home." . . .

Molly's worries were laid to rest when she sat in Mrs. Bromberg's parlor. The smells that emerged from her kitchen were intoxicating and the smell of roasting brisket reminded her of home.

After drinking a glass of tea and eating homemade strudel

and sponge cake, Molly left with a slightly lighter heart—but she would only be totally content when she'd seen Sara's reaction.

That night Molly sat with her child and explained the situation—or as much as Molly felt Sara needed to understand. She asked Sara to be brave, but above all to remember that she and Louie loved and adored her. There were things in life that required great sacrifices, and since they were a family they had to make the best of the situation. It would only be a short time until Louie got settled in his new position and they would be together again . . . that was a sacred promise.

But for all Molly's reassurances, Sara cried long and hard. "Why can't I go with you, mama? I won't be in the way."

Molly wiped the perspiration from her forehead and tried once again. "It's not a question of your being in the way. I just explained why. As soon as we can manage it you're going to be with us . . . Now please, Sara, you're a big girl. This is as hard for me as it is for you, so don't make it harder." She took her child in her arms and kissed her. "Trust your mother, please . . ."

Sara wiped away her tears. "All right, mama . . . but you will come for me soon?"

"Of course. Louie and I want you as much as you want to be with us . . . more. You're my child."

"And you're my mother," the girl said simply.

Putting the little girl's head on her shoulder she whispered, "I know, darling . . . how well I know."

CHAPTER TWELVE

HAD THE lovely Jewish family lived up to Louie's expectations. Sara might have adjusted easily. At first she was eager to please the Brombergs, but she soon discovered that the family that had appeared so proper and hardworking had a meanness of spirit she had never suspected or even encountered elsewhere.

What Mrs. Bromberg had acquired was not a boarder but a kind of Cinderella servant; before school and late into the night Sara did all the scrubbing, washing and polishing that gave the house the cleanliness Molly had so admired. Her only reward was a small portion of food that she ate alone in the kitchen.

It still might have been bearable if she'd been left to herself, but with her arrival those three nice Bromberg boys swore a truce among themselves and now directed their abusiveness toward her. Their games ranged from practical jokes to slapping and pinching and using foul language—but like the good little boys they were, they were careful to hide these small pleasures from their adoring mother.

The event that brought things to a head was one that Sara would long remember . . . One night when she was asleep, the oldest boy, Carl, crept into her room. She woke up with a start when he crawled into her bed, but before she could cry out he was on top of her, with one hand over her mouth and the other struggling to pull up her nightgown. As his hand closed over her breast she gave a wrench, freed herself and screamed out. Before he could put his hand over her mouth again to quiet the outburst, Clara came rushing down the hall. Now she flung open the door and stood trembling with anger. "What is this!"

Carl jumped out of bed and pointed in righteous indignation to a very frightened Sara. "It's her fault, mama. She asked me to do it to her. I didn't want to but she got me all excited . . . It's hard to stop when a girl throws herself at you—"

Clara looked menacingly at Sara. Of course Carl would never do such a thing if he hadn't been tempted. He was a fine Jewish boy with morals. But he was a young man already, with a young man's desires, and when he was tempted . . . Well, she would not allow this little tramp to remain in her home and corrupt her boys. She had probably made advances to all of them, even her little Morris . . .

"I didn't do anything, Mrs. Bromberg . . . honest. Carl—"

"I don't want to hear your lies. You're going to get out of my house, you hear? Out!"

"I have no place to go." Sara was crying now.

"You should have thought of that before you corrupted my son."

"I didn't . . . He came—"

"I've heard enough. You'll write to your mother today, you hear? And I'll have plenty to tell her when I see her . . . You'll come to a bad end, but you're not my concern, thank God. In the meantime I don't want to see you. Stay in your room and stay *away* from my sons." And with that she turned and left, with Carl following her.

When Sara finally stopped sobbing, she sat down to write to her mother. She swallowed hard, praying her mother

78

would believe her. She felt terribly confused—and without knowing why, very guilty. . . .

It was late of an evening when Louie returned from the casino to find a very distraught Molly smoking one cigarette after another. She thrust a letter into his hand, then stood glaring at him as he read.

His outrage matched hers. "That miserable little son of a bitch, I should beat the hell out of him. Sara's not going to live in a place where there are boys and that's definite. This time will be—"

"Listen, Louie, and listen carefully. *This* time I'm going to bring Sara back—and that's final."

He tried to take her in his arms to soothe her, but she backed away. "Not this time . . . I know all your little tricks, but no matter what you say it's not going to work. Sara's coming here, you understand me, Louie?"

"Now, Molly, you're very upset—"

"Damn it, shouldn't I be?"

"Of course, and I'm just as upset as you are—"

"I doubt it."

"That's like a slap in the face."

"Maybe that's what you need to wake you up . . . I want my child and I'm going to get her."

Louie poured two brandies, handed one to her. "Sit down, Molly, there's no need to fight me. I want Sara as much as you do."

She looked at him. Had she really won this round? The acute anger began to subside and she sat down and sipped at her drink. The look on Louie's face as he took her glass to replenish it told her, yes, she had won—and victory tasted very good. Although still resolute, she began to relax.

Louie took her hand and kissed it, then her lips. "Molly, darling, don't you know how much I want Sara, how much she means to me? Of course you do. I know you want to bring Sara now, but let me ask you something . . . Sensibly and logically, where is she going to live? In a hotel . . . in one room, if that's—"

She jumped up. "Damn it, Louie, this time you're not going to outtalk me. If you didn't gamble so much, if you got rid of that horse—who's more expensive to support than a child—if you were content only managing the casino, you *could* make a good living. We could have an apartment and live like human beings. But you make it sound like someone's putting a gun to your head and forcing you to—"

"What kind of a living?"

"Better than you're making now, when everything you earn you use to gamble or support that—"

"I do it because that horse is a winner."

"You're an idiot, an absolute idiot. When did that horse win? Not once . . . Now, I'm going to give you exactly one minute for an answer. Get rid of that horse, stop gambling, operate the casino or I'm leaving you—once and for all. I'm not going to spend the rest of my life this way, Louie."

"You mean to say you'd walk out on me?"

"You can make a safe bet on *that*."

"Damn it, Molly, give me a chance to get myself settled—"

"You just ran out of time. Keep your horse and to hell with you . . . I'm leaving. That's it, I've had enough of this."

"Fine, but you'll regret this, Molly, leaving a husband who loves you, supported your child and clothed her. It's not my fault if things don't always go . . ."

Molly wasn't listening.

Louie kept up the tirade as he watched her pack. She put on her coat and hat, picked up the house phone and asked to have the bellboy come for her bags.

"What are you going to use for money?" he asked. "You don't have any money. How are you going to live?"

"Don't worry about me . . . I have a few dollars I saved for just such an emergency."

"How much?"

"Enough to take me to Brussels, and a little extra. It'll do until I get a job. I'm not afraid . . . I was a milliner once and I can do it again."

"Molly, you're the most stubborn woman I ever met."

"So the next one you get won't be so—"

"Okay, Molly, *okay* . . . I'm not going to beg. You go ahead and do what you want. At this point I just don't give a damn any more." Digging into his pocket, he pulled out a small roll of bills and threw them on the bed.

His gesture was very grand. A real sport to the end.

CHAPTER THIRTEEN

THIS TIME the smells coming from Clara Bromberg's kitchen were not so intoxicating. Molly stood in the parlor with Sara at her side and listened to Clara's tirade about Sara's conduct—the hardship Clara had endured, the responsibilities of raising a girl ... especially this one. Why, Sara had eaten them out of house and home and the money Molly and Louie sent had barely covered the board.

As she listened to Clara's baseless charges, Molly's anger grew until she could stand it no longer. Her anger erupted in a torrent of abuse that left Clara white with shock. Molly ended breathlessly, "You know what I should really do? Put that louse in jail for trying to rape my child—and you for being a white slaver." With that said, she took Sara by the hand and walked out, slamming the front door so hard the oval glass broke and shattered into little pieces. . . .

That night Molly and Sara slept together in the best room in the best hotel in Brussels. Sara's joy in cuddling next to her mother was immense. She was almost afraid to fall asleep for fear that when she woke up her mother would not be there ... that all this had been a dream.

When morning came and Sara saw Molly sleeping alongside her, she felt more secure. She was so proud of the way Molly had lashed out at Mrs. Bromberg. Her mother was her protector. No one would ever abuse or hurt her again ...

When Molly woke up she kissed Sara and held her close. "Well, what would you like to do today?"

"I'd like for us to be together, but I have to go to school."

"Not today. Besides, you're changing schools ... you're not going to be living in that neighborhood again."

"Oh, mama, I love you so much—"

"And I love you ... Now, what shall we do?"

"Anything." Sara smiled with overwhelming joy.

"All right, first we'll have breakfast sent to the room, then we'll go shopping. I want to buy some new clothes for you."

"Mama?"

"Yes, angel?"

"Do you have enough money for all this?"

"A child shouldn't have to worry about money. That's for a mother to do."

"But you said that things were very bad for Louie ..."

"I know, but it got better. Louie gave me plenty of money when I left him." If it were only true ... But Sara was going to have new clothes; she'd outgrown the ones Molly had sent from Monte Carlo. Of course they couldn't stay here, but Sara needed a treat. And if she lived frugally, the *francs*

Louie had given her would tide her over until she got a job—which she knew she would have no trouble getting. Forget it. Today she and Sara were going to enjoy.

That evening as they sat having a fine dinner, Molly noticed Sara's eyes were not happy, in spite of the fixed smile on her lips. "You're happy, darling, huh?"

"Oh, yes, mama," Sara responded quickly.

"Then why do you look so sad?"

"I'm not, mama, I'm so happy."

"I mean, inside . . . down deep. You can tell me."

Sara took a sip of water. She knew something was out of focus. She had paid no attention when Molly had said, "when I left him," but suddenly the words came back to her. "Mama . . ."

"Yes."

"Do you and Louie still love each other?"

Molly suddenly felt shaky but she pursed her lips and answered, "What a question! Of course we do. Why should you ask something so foolish?"

"I don't know . . . I guess it's because I thought we were finally going to be a family."

"We are."

"Not without Louie."

Molly swallowed hard. "Listen, Sara, you're a big girl . . . so now I'll tell you. Louie's trying to get into a new business and we agreed that maybe it would be best if you and I stayed here until he got things settled. Also, I want to help him, so I thought it would be good if I took a job. I used to be a good hat designer, you remember?" Molly hurried on. "You see, a wife should help her husband."

"But couldn't you design hats in Monte Carlo?"

"Would Louie let me do that! No, not there. It would embarrass Louie, hurt his pride because his wife had to work. Men have a lot of pride, darling. I had to plead with him to do my part."

Sara didn't believe a word of it . . . Her mother was going to get another divorce, and all because of her. She was in the way. It was her fault that her mother was giving up the man she loved . . . sacrificing her life. Poor Louie had been so good to her, sent her all those beautiful presents from Johannesburg when she was in that expensive boarding school. Louie had given her all that and now mama had left him. She just knew it. If only she hadn't written that letter about Mrs. Bromberg. But what else could she have done?

She would have been thrown out into the street. Still, Sara felt a huge guilt . . .

"Are you listening to me, Sara? Everything will be all right. Now eat, it's getting cold and we don't want to come in the middle of the first act. *Swan Lake* is your favorite ballet."

She really didn't want to go, not with all she had on her mind. . . .

The next few weeks found Molly and Sara living in a moderately priced *pension* in a moderately exclusive district. Sara was enrolled in school and Molly went in search of a position—but it seemed there was no need for her services. She even considered working in a clothes shop as a salesgirl, but after an exhaustive search, that too proved fruitless.

Now the enormous determination she'd had when leaving Louie was beginning to crumble and she began to regret her decision. She'd had no idea how important Louie was in her life, how much a part of her he had become. She was beginning to discover that life without Louie was lonely, terribly lonely. As much as she adored Sara, the girl did not fill up the void. For all his instability, Louie was gay, exciting, gregarious, caring—and above all, he loved her the way a man should love a woman. She missed sharing life with him and she missed their intimacy and the loving touch of his hands, the feel of his body . . .

That night she decided to write, but she would take it very slowly. She knew Louie would be thrilled to hear from her, but let him worry a little. She would tell him what a marvelous job she had, how busy her social life had become. . . .

When Molly received Louie's letter she cried. It was hardly the response she had expected; she's been so sure Louie would beg her to come back. But as she blew her nose and wiped her eyes, she suddenly knew that Louie was on to her game and the realization was galling. All right, Louie . . . we'll play this out to the end.

Louie was walking across the lobby toward the restaurant when the clerk called out to him.

"A letter arrived this morning, *monsieur*."

Louie recognized the handwriting immediately. It was from Molly. If he needed anyone in the world, it was Molly. The months she had been away seemed like forever. But when Louie read this letter, he was shocked. She really meant to leave him, permanently . . . Maybe she had met someone. Molly was quite a beautiful and sensual woman. Damn it, he was going to get her *back*, no matter what. He no longer cared about winning the game they were playing. He only wanted to win Molly.

Dear Molly,

We've been apart now for too long and I'm not going on with this nonsense. I love you more than ever before . . . I reach over in the middle of the night hoping you are there, then I awake to the realization you have left me.

I wasn't the worst husband in the world. And if I haven't been the best father, you know it wasn't because I didn't want to be. We've been through all the whys and wherefores, so I'm not going to go into them. I did the best I could, and in your heart you know it.

I'm not going to beg, but if you are the woman I know you are, you will come back to me, where I know you belong. I never make idle promises and I will not do that now. I have done a great deal of soul-searching. I'm going to sell the horse and I promise never to gamble again. My position at the casino will be more than enough to afford us a gracious living.

I ask only one thing from you, and I know you will see the wisdom of this. For the time being, put Sara in a very good school, then come back and look for a lovely small house. Furnish it any way you like, then we will send for our lovely daughter. Once and for all, we will be a family. That is my vow. But Molly, I need your strength to inspire me, to keep me from slipping back. Remember one thing—I love you more, both of you, than words can say. I will write to Sara to assure her that it will not be too long before she joins us. This I pledge.

With all my devotion,
Louie

Amid tears and promises, Sara was once again installed in a boarding school. It wasn't the most expensive or exclusive, but it had a lovely homelike atmosphere—which helped keep down Molly's guilt. At least Sara would be well cared for and, above all, not abused.

Molly's reunion with Louie set aside any trepidations she had felt about their future. This was where she belonged. Louie was her home.

For several months they were very happy together and spent much of their time planning for the day when Sara would be able to join them. But Louie, inevitably, was growing restless; abstaining from gambling was almost more than he could bear. The expenses of decorating the house they had bought were growing, and still he bought more, wanted more . . . always more.

Eventually, in spite of himself, he went back to gambling. . . .

Sara, of course, never knew about the unending cycle of arguments, tears and reconciliations between Molly and Louie. Over the next four years she received letters from Monte Carlo, Paris, New York, and finally she heard that Louie had bought a small but exclusive hotel in Seattle, Washington. It was only much later that she learned that her mother's love for Louie had finally run its course. Molly had lived through too many failures and broken promises with Louie; with no change in sight, his charm had finally worn very thin.

When she left him this time to set out for Oakland, California, they both knew it was truly over. Her brother Morris and his wife lived in Oakland, and she would find a job. In the meantime she had just enough money for Sara's passage to America and her own fare to Oakland.

At first Sara had dreamed about all the places Molly and Louie visited, about how happy she would be when she was reunited with them and about all the luxuries they had promised her. But her fantasies and her faith in Molly's promises gradually faded. With all of their traveling and expenses, somehow there was never enough money to send for her.

Sara had never expected to stay at the school for very long and so she had kept aloof from the other girls. By the time she realized that she might be there for a long time, it seemed too late to make friends with them. Besides, the visits from their parents and the tales of their holidays with their families only seemed to reinforce her feeling of isolation, of not being wanted.

When she received her mother's letter, postmarked Oakland, California, U.S.A., she was no more curious about where Oakland was than about the contents of the envelope. For ten years now she had read variations on the same letter, and the old phrases meant nothing compared with the hope life had suddenly presented her. Sara had finally reached out for the one person who might still want her, and for once she had received a promise that was not empty. She tossed the unopened envelope aside as she sat down to write to her mother about it.

Dear mama,

I can't go on living the way I have, without any hope. My father's relatives here in Brussels have given me his address and I have been corresponding with him. He not only wants me, but has sent money for me to come to America. I feel at long last I will have a home where I am loved.

My childhood has been spent in the most dreadful anticipation. However, now that I am a woman of fifteen, I have accepted the fact that you never meant me to live with you. I always knew down deep in my heart that you and Louie thought I would be in the way. Now I must try and make something of my life, and papa will see to that. I only wish it could have been sooner.

I want you to know I still love you and always will. But now you and Louie won't have to sacrifice for me anymore. I hope you are well and doing fine. I will write to you when I arrive in New York, which is where papa lives. Incidentally, he has remarried and is very happy, as I am sure you are.

> With deepest affection and love,
> Sara

When Molly received the letter, first shock, then tears came. And came and came, until she thought she would die.

Her daughter, it seemed, had become a stranger.

CHAPTER FOURTEEN

SARA WAS met by her father in New York. Between her memories and her fantasies she had pictured him as a handsome dark-haired gentleman, with lovely, smiling eyes. Although the change in his appearance was more than surprising, the realization was forgotten as they embraced, unaware of the milling crowds at the pier.

Soon Sara saw the sights of New York for the first time as she and her father walked to the subway that would take them to the East Side. Down there it was like a carnival: pushcarts on all the sidewalks, half-naked or raggedly clothed children running in the streets, men dressed in long coats and black large-brimmed hats that topped the curls in front of their ears. Mothers sat on the doorstoops in front of decaying buildings. There were mattresses on the fire escapes and clotheslines festooned from one building to the next. The air was filled with smells of fermenting garbage, dill pickles, herring, and the large twisted pretzels made of soft dough and sprinkled with salt crystals. The vendors' cries echoed in the streets and Sara heard odd chants from open windows. How extraordinary, how truly extraordinary . . .

"Sara, before I take you home, I would like us to have a few moments together."

Oh, how she adored Harry's smile, his pink cheeks, his almost silver hair, his cuddly round tummy . . . He reminded her of *Père Nöel* at Christmas time in Brussels. "Oh, yes, papa, I would love that."

They went to Esther Sandsonitsky's restaurant. When Esther brought their ice cream soda and apple strudel, Harry said. "This is my daughter, Esther, can you believe it?"

Esther smiled. "It's always nice when children come home to their parents."

As Esther walked back to the kitchen, Harry said, "I . . . I can't get over the miracle of this. I know I sound like a phonograph record going round and round . . . but how did this happen to me?"

"It's a miracle, papa. More for me than for you—" She could scarcely take her eyes from him. It was as though they had never been apart . . . "Miracles do happen, papa."

"Darling, I want to say a few things to you before I take you home to meet my wife."

"Yes, papa?"

"Well, my wife—her name is Lisa—is really a very nice lady. But she's just a bit aloof when you first meet her. She's German and doesn't show her feelings too much . . . It doesn't mean she's not loving, but she has a . . . a dignity about her that you might take the wrong way if you don't understand her."

Sara thought fleetingly of Mrs. Bromberg, then said, "Papa, will you be honest with me? She didn't want me to come, did she?"

"That's not true . . . She was very happy when I told her—"

"Then why should you feel you have to explain her to me?"

"Well, the truth is . . . your mother is a very warm, outgoing person and I don't want you to . . . to . . ."

"Compare them?"

"That's *exactly* what I mean."

"Well, you're right about my mother. But as you know, I've never been with her long enough to feel her great warmth. I

87

don't want to say anything unkind, papa, but the truth is, she was no more a mother to me than I imagine she was a wife to you—"

Harry tried not to show the bitter memories. "Well, honey, be that as it may, I suppose we can't help being what we are. I just want to say that my wife will be delighted to have you . . ."

Poor papa really couldn't tell her she wasn't wanted. "I understand, papa. Be assured I will be most courteous and obedient. I intend to do my part and make life as pleasant as possible."

Her father looked at her. At fifteen Sara was indeed a woman . . . she understood things, apparently had guessed that he'd had to cajole Lisa to allow Sara to come. "You're a very understanding young person, Sara."

"Well, papa, I've had the advantage of knowing all different kinds of people. Don't worry, papa, I'll get along with your wife . . . just trust me."

He smiled. "I do, darling . . . I think I told you she had a delicatessen on Rivington Street, and after school maybe you could relieve her."

Sara smiled back. Mrs. Bromberg was apparently alive and living on Rivington Street . . . "Of course, papa, I will be more than happy to relieve her." . . .

Harry's description of his wife was fairly accurate. If she was much prettier and perhaps less formidable than Sara imagined, the new Mrs. Harry Edelstein was still a woman who tolerated no challenges to her supremacy. Yes, this was Mrs. Bromberg—a little slimmer, but . . .

The familiarity hardly made the adjustment easier. Sara could not get used to the noise, the smells . . . once more she was obliged to be patient. In a few years, she told herself, she would be able to get a job and live uptown. The lower East Side was not for her. She was going to be somebody. She started to study typing . . . but that dream lay far in the future. Papa had wanted her, and for now that knowledge would have to be enough. . . .

On the first Saturday when she went to *shul* and sat next to Lisa she felt peculiarly out of place. It was not like the synagogues she knew; it was more like a store with a loft where ladies sat upstairs and the men downstairs. Everything was strange, everything . . . except uptown. For a long time she couldn't fathom why people living so close to great art and the best in theater never made an attempt to go. True, it cost money, but the people she lived among now never even did the things that were free, like walking in Central Park. She was a newcomer and she had already seen more of New York than anyone she had come in contact with. Of course, papa was different. He had seen more in his time, and now his days were spent slicing Lisa's pastrami and corn beef just to make ends meet. Poor man ... What was he really suited for? Oh, papa, Sara thought, if only you hadn't been so impetuous when you were young. I might very well be an heiress instead of a maid. But she at least knew there was a world out there, and that one day she was going to have it. . . .

It was Sara's sixteenth birthday, almost a year later, but it was not a happy day. She opened the package from her mother and looked at the hat and the letter inside. The words in the letter were the same and so was mama. That would never change. But other things had changed. Dear God, how they had changed.

The day before, her adored father had been trampled by a peddler's horse. The animal had reared as Harry was crossing the street. The only blessing was that Harry had died instantly. With his passing, all her dreams seemed buried inside his pine box, laid in the cold ground.

After the days of mourning were over, Lisa said, "Now that your father is gone, Sara, I need the room. I'm taking a boarder in."

Sara looked at her. "What would you suggest I do ... I mean, where can I live?"

"Gittel likes you. Maybe she'll make room for you."

Sara shifted uncomfortably before she asked, "Ah, did my father leave anything to me? I mean—"

"I know what you mean. But let me tell you, my dear, your father was not my partner. This business was mine when I married him and everything he had was what he got from me—the shoes on his feet, the food—"

Hershel was a distant relative of Lisa's, and when Sara told Hershel and Gittel of her problem they were outraged and persuaded Esther to take the girl in.

Which was how she happened to be standing at Esther's kitchen sink when Jacob first saw her.

CHAPTER FIFTEEN

DESPITE JACOB'S curiosity about Sara, he had not responded to Shlomo's suggestions of charity and understanding about her dilemma.

Every morning they passed each other in the narrow hall, almost colliding, and the contact only heightened his antagonism. As he sat across from her at supper he wondered who she was that his mother should embrace her as though she were part of the family... What was she doing that she should be fed and housed from mama's sweat? She did the dishes, helped wait on tables? Big deal. She not only got room and board, but five dollars a month. A sixteen-year-old girl couldn't get a job? She and Hershel were two of a kind, living off of anyone's muscle. He made it a point to ignore her, but he was disturbed to find himself dwelling on his dislike of her almost constantly.

He found himself thinking about her even at work. Why didn't she put her long black hair up into a bun instead of letting it hang, practically getting it into the food? Why did she have to stare back at him when he looked up from eating? Those brown eyes, so big, so innocent... He'd seen a girl with innocent eyes once before in his life... And how come she had so many nice things—the beautiful hat and especially the pretty nightgowns and robes? She even had the luxury of using their bath. Most women went to the *mikva*, the public baths. Even Gittel did, and she had to bathe Avrum and the new baby Benjamin in the sink, and either run down the hall to the toilet or use the chamber pot under the bed. Added to her sins was that while she was living in his house and was only a servant she completely ignored him. Some *chutzpah*. She didn't even go to *shul* to say *Kaddish* for her father. He would speak to Gittel about her.

On Sunday as Jacob sat in Gittel's kitchen sipping a celery tonic, Gittel answered the knock at the door. Of all people in the world... There she was, dressed like she was going to a ball—wearing a straw hat trimmed with violet velvet ribbons and field flowers, a white organdy and lace blouse, a navy-blue skirt and elegant beige suede shoes that were laced with silk strings. If Gittel were dressed like that she'd look like a princess too, but then Gittel had class even when she wore her faded blue cotton dress.

Jacob got up, leaving the unfinished celery tonic, and kissed his sister and the babies good-by. He said he would try to see her *alone* next Sunday and left without a word to Sara.

The two young women sat facing each other.

"You look beautiful, Sara."

"So do you, Gittel . . . you look happy. Does having a new baby do that to a woman?"

"Yes, a family and a good sweet husband are the most important things, in a woman's life . . . Sara, if I ask you something you wouldn't be hurt?"

"No. What did you want to ask?"

"I've noticed you and Jacob seem so—I don't know how to put it . . ."

"Distant?"

"Yes. Yes, why is that?"

"To be honest, Jacob has been making a point of ignoring me. I don't understand it and it makes me angry. Who does he think he is?"

Gittel looked at Sara over the rim of the glass. She knew why Jacob was rejecting Sara; he saw Lotte in every girl. But she also knew Sara was too proud and independent to make any overtures. Sara was not like her. When Hershel had come into Gittel's life she was the one who had broken down his defenses, shy as she was, but Sara was different. Still, she would have liked for Jacob to become interested in a girl . . . it would be so good for him. Finally Gittel said, "He doesn't hate you, Sara. In fact I think Jacob likes you."

Sara laughed and shook her head. "Oh, Gittel. If a young man likes a girl he doesn't make a deliberate effort to offend her. People don't have to love each other to be civil."

"Sara, Jacob had a very bad thing happen to him. He was very much in love with a girl and they were going to be married. He worked day and night to save enough money to bring her over from the old country but she found someone else. Now he doesn't trust any girl. It's an old story. I know he's wrong, but he's still hurt and he's afraid of being hurt again. If only someone understood him . . . I mean a girl." Gittel bit her lip, remembering the aftermath of his severing with Lotte.

Sara looked almost interested. "I'm sorry to hear that. I suppose it explains a great many things about Jacob's attitude toward me, but I still don't think he should take out his feelings on me. Why should he punish me for what this girl did? Do you think that's right?"

"Of course not, but Jacob just can't seem to get over it. Well, at least you know now it isn't because he doesn't like you."

Sara shrugged. "I know what it's like to love someone and not have it returned. You never get used to it, but you have to go on living—"

"Have you ever been in love?"

"Not with a man, but there are all kinds of love and when it's not returned it hurts—"

"Then you understand?"

"More than I did before. About Jacob, I mean . . ."

"Then I'm happy I told you . . . it makes things easier when we understand why people act the way they do."

"In some cases," she replied, thinking of Molly. . . .

That night Sara lay awake in the dark listening to Esther's even breathing and thought about Jacob. Although she couldn't yet acknowledge it, Jacob was the first boy who had ever attracted her. However, Sara had as many misgivings about the opposite sex as Jacob had, but for far different reasons. She had never forgotten that dreadful night when Carl Bromberg had tried to rape her and for that reason she had been more than grateful that Jacob paid no attention to her when she first came to live with Esther. Her fears were soon laid to rest when she realized Shlomo was the sweetest, dearest person, and Jacob the rudest and most arrogant. And now that she understood Jacob's coldness she wasn't against being friends. She had no reason to be afraid that he might— No. In fact, now she felt just the opposite . . .

As they walked home from *shul* on Saturday Sara decided that today was the day to begin their friendship. He was merely being a petulant little boy and if she waited for him to make the first move she could be old and very gray.

At lunch Sara said to Shlomo, "How would you like to go to the nickelodeon tonight?"

Shlomo had spoken to Gittel about Sara and Jacob and approved of her plans for them. Gittel was playing the part of the *shadchen,* the matchmaker, and the role became her. He answered, "I have a date. If I'd known sooner I would have made it another time."

Sara smiled. "I'm glad you have a date—it's nice to go out with someone. Do you like her?"

"Oh, well, I wouldn't say I'm really crazy about her. To tell the truth, I'd rather be with you."

Jacob kept eating. How could a woman like Sara go out with a boy like Shlomo? She was sixteen . . .

That afternoon Sara asked Esther if she would like to go to the picture show, but Esther excused herself. She really didn't like Charlie Chaplin, even though she understood he was Jewish. What Yiddish actor played parts like that? Boris Thomashefsky—now there was an actor. If Sara would excuse her tonight she promised they would go to the Yiddish theater next week.

Jacob chomped down hard on the chicken leg. Sure, mama would take her, and the Jewish princess would let mama pay for the tickets. But somehow Jacob heard the echo of Shlomo's words: "You're a *mensch* and that's the best thing a person can be . . ." He supposed it wouldn't hurt him. As an older man he supposed he should take it upon himself to at least see that she got there safe and sound. When all was said and done, Sara was a baby when it came to this tough neighborhood. She really shouldn't be allowed to go to the pictures alone. Not that she was his responsibility, but he'd do it for Shlomo . . . In a voice far from warm, Jacob announced, "All right, come on, I'll take you."

Jacob looked sideways at Sara in the darkened theater. She was obviously enjoying the comedy but he was angry at himself for playing nursemaid. He wasn't even watching the screen. Well, the evening would pass, and he wasn't going to go on being her great protector. Not even for Shlomo.

When the lights came up, for a moment Jacob was startled. Had she noticed that he had been looking at her? Well, so what if she had.

As they walked out into the warm evening Jacob asked tonelessly, "Would you like a soda?"

"Yes, but I'll pay."

That did it. He stopped and stood towering above her. "Let me give you a little good advice. When a fellow takes you out, don't ever ask to pay for him or he'll never take you out again."

"Thanks for the advice, but when I go out with a fellow I wouldn't think of it."

He swallowed hard. None too gently, he took her by the elbow and led her down the crowded streets until they reached Esther's restaurant. Then he hurried to his room and slammed the door.

"Did you have a good time, Jacob?" Shlomo smiled.

"I'm warning you, Shlomo, tonight I don't want to hear any of your great philosophy." . . .

The next few weeks found Jacob's anger a bit more subdued. He was not especially friendly when he passed her in the kitchen on the way to his room to clean up after work, but Sara was satisfied with his grunt. One night at supper she decided to try for more. "It must be fun to take the train every day to New Jersey."

He didn't look up from his soup. "Yeah, I like it."

"I'm going to Coney Island this Sunday."

This time he looked up from his soup. "Coney Island? By yourself?"

"No, with Gittel, Hershel and the children."

Why hadn't they asked him? "How can Gittel take a little baby to the beach?"

"Very simple . . . on the streetcar."

"I don't mean that."

"Well, what do you mean?"

"She . . . well, you know how she feeds the baby—"

"Nursing mothers don't have to stay home for years, you know. Do they, Mrs. Sandsonitsky?"

"Absolutely not. Why don't you go, Jacob?"

They hadn't asked him, so why should he *shlep* along? "I don't like crowded beaches."

"Why don't you come, Jacob? You might like it," Sara said.

"No."

"Well, it's up to you."

"Why don't you go, mama?" Jacob asked.

"Because Mrs. Lipsky is sitting *shivah* for her mother. Otherwise I would."

"Oh . . . And you, Shlomo, as long as the family—"

"I have to study for a final exam."

On Sunday morning Jacob decided to go. Why should they have all the fun? Hershel especially—the hard worker, the big breadwinner. If anyone needed a little relaxation it was he, Jacob. You bet he was going—and he'd enjoy it if it killed him.

Hershel and Jacob got into the striped bath suits they had rented and waited on the beach for the girls. They were taking so long Hershel went into the water, holding Avrum as he kicked and splashed around.

Along with the two baskets of food, Esther had included a

94

jar of chicken fat to fend off the scorching sun. Jacob was unscrewing the top when he saw Gittel and Sara approaching from a distance. But it was Sara who caught his eye.

Her black bathing suit was so form-fitting, so revealing . . . Yet at the same time her pleated skirt and oval neckline trimmed with white made her look very much the regal young lady. His gaze wandered down her full figure to the black bathing shoes laced to the calves of her slender legs, then back up again. Curly wisps of her long black hair poked out from under her bouffant cap and she was twirling a French parasol over her shoulder. My God, she was the . . . most disturbing person he had ever met. Suddenly, memories of Lotte were gone.

"Would you like to join me in a dip?" Sara asked.

He composed himself and hoped God would protect him from any signs of the throbbing between his thighs. As he stood up and brushed off the sand she reached out her hand to him and the two ran toward the water.

Gittel smiled. They hadn't asked her to join them. . . .

After lunch the children were put down for naps and Gittel and Sara adjusted the umbrellas to shade them. Hershel was fast asleep—which was not surprising, Jacob thought. He asked Gittel why she didn't take a dip, assuring her he'd keep an eye on the children. She hesitated and then ran to the blue surf, glad of a few moments of freedom.

Sara looked at Jacob. "Your back is getting red . . . let me put some Vaseline on it before you burn to a crisp."

"Mama says chicken *schmaltz* is better."

"You'll forgive me, but Vaseline is better," she said.

Jacob closed his eyes as she put her greased palm on his shoulders and massaged them.

"Thank you . . . that's fine."

"You're sure you don't—"

"I'm sure." Jacob lay down and covered himself with a blanket of sand up to his neck.

Sara lay almost within touching distance. From under his half-closed lids, he watched as she put the French parasol in the sand to shade their faces and then covered her legs, her abdomen, then her bust in sand.

Jacob was less than tranquil. He was full of conflicting thoughts. He really wanted to dislike her, really . . . but—

"Aren't you glad you came, Jacob?"

"What?"

"I said aren't you glad you came?"

95

"Yeah."

"Well, you could show a little more enthusiasm than that. You know you're having fun, why do you hold back?"

"Who's holding back?"

"You are. You're afraid you might enjoy yourself—"

It was becoming too much. The sound of her voice, lying in the sand so close to her . . . It was sheer— "Sara."

"Yes, Jacob?"

"I think maybe we should get married."

"You think so?"

"Yes."

"Well, when did you decide that?"

"A minute ago." He waited. "So?"

"I think that might be very sensible."

"That's what I thought."

Jacob jumped up from his mound of sand and suddenly Sara found her hand in his as he lifted her to her feet. With the sand still clinging to their bodies he took her in his arms and kissed her with a force that surprised them both.

It was difficult, very, but he managed to say, "I . . . I love you, Sara."

"And I love you, Jacob. I think I have for a little while now."

He kissed her once again as Gittel approached. She took in the scene at a glance and was smiling knowingly.

Jacob picked up his oldest nephew and said, "Avrumchik, say hello to Tante Sara."

She kissed the chubby cheek and then turned to Gittel. The two embraced as Gittel said, "You see? I told you."

"You did . . . Gittel, I'm so happy." . . .

Sara and Jacob waited for the streetcar that was taking Gittel and her family home. The lovers were going to complete the evening by going on all the rides at Coney Island.

Jacob held her hand on the carousel and held her close as they came down the winding chute-the-chute. Her lips tasted better than the pink cotton candy and he kissed her in between bites of ice cream.

What a wonderful day, Sara thought. There'd been few precious moments in her life, and suddenly she wanted to share this one with her mother. Late that night she sat down to write to her.

Dear mama,

Life works in mysterious ways. It seems we are deprived of one thing, then blessed with another. I thought it was the end

96

of all my dreams when papa died. While he was alive, I could indulge my fantasies. As you know, I hoped to become a secretary. I'm afraid I inherited something of you—my ambitions—and like you I cannot stand mediocrity or poverty. But there is no need to repeat the past years' events.

I hope you are sitting while reading this. I am going to be married. Jacob is the son of Mrs. Sandsonitsky. Should you wonder if I am in love—well, yes, I am. Jacob is not the kind of young man I thought I would be attracted to. He is rather a complex person, very difficult to know in the beginning, less educated than I, but I think we will be very happy together.

There is something strange that draws me to him. Perhaps it is because I know he too has great dreams, and with his ambition I have no doubt they will come true. He is the most handsome young man I have ever seen. I know we are right for each other and that together we will achieve a future life we both deserve. I need a home and someone to love and protect me.

I was sorry to hear about your separation from Louie and about your financial difficulties, and I regret that you will not be with me on my wedding day. But please do keep writing. Your letters mean so much to me.

Love,
Sara

Molly was desolate when she received Sara's letter. She would not know the joy of seeing her child married. Her emotions that day brought back many painful memories. She knew that Harry had given up a great deal for her and she shook her head sadly when she thought that if she had been the kind of wife to him she had to Louie, Harry might have been changed, things might have worked out. If she had stayed, who knew what direction Sara's life would have taken. Harry's family was affluent and perhaps they would have embraced a grandchild . . .

But how foolish it was to dwell on what might have been. When she married Harry her thoughts had been unrealistic, clouded as usual with her visions of grandeur, and she hadn't changed from that day to this. When she left Louie and moved to Oakland, California, to be with her brother and his wife . . . that too was the result of illusions. Not having seen each other since they had been children, Molly and Morris were unknown quantities to each other. Molly was not accustomed to living in someone else's home, and Rose's large brood of noisy children grated on her nerves.

So Molly had moved out and taken a dingy room in a boarding house, but the job she found in the hat factory paid less than enough to maintain even that meager style of living. With all things considered, she began to have second thoughts about having left Louie. It had become a litany: Louie was kind, comfortable, her loneliness was unbearable, her misery intolerable . . . The tears flowed as she wrote to him, but this time Molly was too late. He had died of a coronary. Whatever was left from the sale of the hotel would be hers, but at this moment her only worldly possession was a pair of small diamond earrings.

The next morning she pawned them and sent an eiderdown quilt to her daughter Sara as a wedding gift.

It made her feel at least a little more like a mother.

CHAPTER SIXTEEN

THE WEDDING was none too soon for Jacob. How much could he take with Sara sleeping in the next room, just the other side of the wall.

Esther made the wedding arrangements and the *shul* was scheduled for the next Saturday night, right after sundown.

It seemed an eternity, but Saturday finally came. They stood under the blue velvet canopy and pledged their everlasting love. He lifted her veil . . . what a face, such a face. She drank from his cup of wine. He took a sip, then stomped on the glass.

"*Mazel tov . . . mazel tov . . .*" Esther's restaurant was packed with people from the neighborhood. Such a gorgeous wedding, such a beautiful bride, such a handsome groom, such lucky people. . . .

They honeymooned at Coney Island on Sunday and Monday—Jacob was given the day off with his boss's blessing and a wedding gift of ten dollars—and after their honeymoon Sara and Jacob stayed with Esther until they could find a flat.

The newlyweds took Esther's double bed while she shared a room with Shlomo. The arrangement, although temporary, didn't please her. It didn't seem quite right for a mother to be sleeping in the same room with a growing son. As she blushed in the dark at the sound of heavy breathing and squeaky bed springs on the other side of the thin wall, she thought how happy she would be when they found a place of their own. That's where lovers should be. Alone . . . .

Esther said a silent prayer of thanks, when Sara told her,

"Mama, we found a place uptown, in Washington Heights. Only two flights up and right near the bathroom. It will be so lovely when we fix it up, and Jacob loves it. Don't you, Jacob?"

He returned the smile. "It's real pretty."

"Where's Washington Heights?" Esther asked.

"A very nice neighborhood," Shlomo told her.

"Wait till you see it, Shlomo," Jacob said. "Sara's got so many good ideas. I never saw anything so beautiful."

At first Jacob had been uneasy about the rent. But after all, he wasn't exactly a poor man, not with six hundred dollars in the bank, in cash . . . in the vault. He had a good job, his salary was seventeen dollars a week and just recently his boss had said he would get a raise. With all that, why shouldn't he move up in the world, why not? He had Sara to thank for all this. She had shown him a different world and he could well afford it. If not for her, chances were he eventually would have married some girl whose world was limited to Rivington, Ludlow and Delancey Streets. The right wife showed a man how to live. No question about it.

When young Mr. and Mrs. Jacob Sandsonitsky spent the first night in their home, the smell of fresh paint still remained. Sara was truly amazing, Jacob thought as he surveyed the apartment. The kitchen was lime green with white woodwork and crisscross organdy curtains hung above the sink. On the window ledge were four pots of pink geraniums, and on top of the shiny yellow linoleum stood a round golden-oak pedestal table with heavy claw-and-ball feet. Surrounding the table were five tall chairs with spindle dowels held together by a wide carved panel. Jacob was fascinated with the carving. For a fleeting moment he was taken back to Frankfurt, to the umbrella handles, the ivory and wood chips on the worktable, Lotte . . .

Quickly, he walked into the bedroom, and the sight erased his memories as his gaze wandered from the imitation lace curtains to the flowered wallpaper they had had so much fun in choosing and hanging, from the dresser to the oval mirror attached by two crescent-shaped arms, to the comb, brush and mirror that lay on the white dresser scarf. Jacob's heart skipped a beat when he looked at the tall brass bed. He touched the pink satin comforter—so inviting and soft, like Sara's body, like Sara.

Tonight he would lay his head against the down pillows inside the white eyelet pillow slips. It had been expensive, but what was two hundred dollars compared to what he had received. In Jacob's wildest dreams, he'd never imagined living in such style. Sara had not only lifted him to unbelievable heights of passion, but had provided a world he had never before known existed.

Jacob's delight was only exceeded by Sara's. Her chief thought when he had asked her to marry him was that she needed to have a home and to be loved. But she had thought Jacob was a poor young man, and now that she had acquired what she had so longed for all these years, her devotion to him was even greater. If only mama could see the way she was living. . . .

The first Friday night they were settled in their new home the family came to dinner.

Sara brought the boiled carp to the table on a large blue willow-patterned platter. It looked delicious, with sliced carrots layered on top and parsley surrounding the edge. But when Sara started to serve them their portions no one could look at her. She had forgotten to gut the fish. Mortified, she quickly removed the platter and brought out the chicken soup. But it was watery and the *matzo* balls were hard as rocks. Then the chicken, but it was underdone. The *kugel* was like glue, and the *tsimmes* . . . Oh God, the whole thing was a complete disaster. She had worked from early in the morning, thinking how proud Jacob would be. The only salvation was the sponge cake and that must have been an accident.

Frustrated and embarrassed, she barely heard the conversation around her as the family sat drinking tea.

"I knew you were beautiful, Sara, but I didn't know you had such talent. The flat is so pretty, like you," Gittel said.

Sara smiled thinly.

"Well, Jacob, how does it feel to live in such a mansion?" Shlomo asked.

He beamed. "How does it feel? Wonderful."

"Sara, you're such a good housekeeper, everything is neat as a pin. That I should live to see my son so well off and happy, makes my heart really overflow," Esther said. Somehow, the past was very close tonight. She well remembered Jacob's troubles and she was deeply, sincerely happy for him.

Hershel said nothing. He wished them what they wished him. Jacob was a smug upstart and he, Hershel, was green with envy. Imagine how Gittel must feel, he thought, living in two rooms with two babies . . . .

100

Sara cried as she lay in Jacob's arms that night. "I'm so embarrassed. The dinner was terrible and I wanted it to be so wonderful."

He wiped away her tears. "It wasn't that bad . . ."

"It was terrible."

"And if it was? So, it's only a meal. You did the best you could and—"

"I'll bet your mother thinks I starve you."

"My mother doesn't think anything like that . . . you know her better."

"All the same, our first dinner—"

"From where should you know how to cook?"

"Well, I'm going to learn. And I'll be as good as your mother, you wait and see."

"And if you don't, I'll still feel the same about you."

"Just the same, I will learn. You're never ever going to say your mother's cooking is better than mine."

"Would I ever compare—"

"Yes, husbands have a habit of—"

"That's enough already, Sara . . ."

Soon the tears were gone . . . All was forgotten as the satin comforter slid to the floor unheeded . . .

CHAPTER SEVENTEEN

SARA NOT only learned to cook, but to grasp the edge of the bed when she tried to turn over. In her sixth month her belly was larger than Gittel's had been at her ninth. Her legs were swollen and she had gained thirty pounds. She was so ill from the pregnancy and the oppressive September heat that she had to stay in bed most of the time.

All in all, impending motherhood left Sara so disenchanted that she wrote and asked her mother to come. Jacob was alarmed by her condition and helped all he could, and yes, she loved Jacob's family. But no matter what, a mother was still a mother.

The answer Sara received did nothing to lift her depression.

My darling Sara,
    Nothing would keep me away if I could come, believe me.
But I opened a secondhand store with the money I finally

received from the sale of the hotel and have no one to take over. Darling, if I don't work, I don't eat. Please God, if things begin to get better and I make a little money, the first thing I'll do is come to see you and my new grandchild.

I pray you are feeling better by the time you get this letter. Give my love to your wonderful husband. I keep looking at the wedding pictures. They are my greatest happiness. May God continue to be good to you. I always miss you and love you. You are all I have now.

Your mother

You are all I have now . . . When did she, Sara, ever have Molly? Sara cried now for the same reasons she had cried in her childhood. Mama was never there . . . never. Still, poor mama—living alone must be hard, especially since Louie had really been her whole life. Sara had confused feelings of wanting and guilt. Mama's life, she reminded herself, was sadder than hers. She at least had a home. She had Jacob.

November came and with it a bitter cold that even penetrated their warm little apartment. Sara was bundled in Jacob's heavy flannel robe when she heard the door open. Awkwardly, she managed to get out of bed and trudge into the kitchen to greet him. He took off his coat and hung it in the tiny closet. She reached up and kissed him, then saw the expression on his face.

"Jacob?" Sara asked.

He didn't answer.

"Jacob, you're tired. Come, sit down, I'll get supper."

He stood holding onto the edge of the sink.

"Did you have a hard day?"

"Hard? They let me go. I'm out of work—"

She sat down heavily before she asked, "Why?"

"Why? Because my boss has a nephew who came from some damn place and he was given my job."

"But you've been working there so long."

"So what does that mean? Blood is thicker than water. He didn't even give me a day's notice."

"Couldn't you have taken a job for a little less pay in the meanwhile?"

"Don't you think I asked? My boss said very apologetically that, no, business wasn't good enough to put on an extra man. You know what he had the *chutzpah* to do? Give me a written recommendation. I told him he could wipe his rear with it. In a sweatshop I don't need a recommendation."

Oh God, their beautiful home. "You'll find another job . . ."

"For what kind of money?"

"So it will be a little less."

"Much less . . . we can't live here, Sara."

She wasn't listening. This apartment was their first home, *her* first home. Jacob felt much the same, but there was more bitterness as he recalled how he had lost his grandparents' home, how he had struggled for so long when nobody gave a damn. His experience of injustice had not hardened him to it. On the contrary . . .

"Jacob, please don't be hasty. Let's stay here and see if—"

The answer was a flat no. . . .

He found a two-room flat on Rivington Street for nine dollars a month. Sure, the flat on the Heights was beautiful, and he could afford it when he was earning a large salary. But now it was a luxury and he could no longer indulge Sara. He only had three hundred dollars between his family and starvation. No one knew the misery he felt when he helped Sara up the three flights of stairs. His pride had been so shredded he could hardly meet her eyes.

The kitchen was gray, food stains and grease clung to the walls. The bedroom was small and faced an alley. Their furnishings looked ludicrous in these surroundings, especially the satin comforter and the lace-trimmed pillow slips. The toilet was at the far end of a narrow hall. A building like this should only burn to the ground, Jacob thought. The millionaires uptown were getting rich on the misery of people like him.

On November 30, 1910, Sara gave birth to a blonde blue-eyed baby girl after eighteen hours of excruciating pain that made her swear she'd never have another.

Jacob had never doubted that a man of his virility could have anything but a boy. Even Hershel could make sons. But when he held the little girl in his arms, any such feelings vanished—she was *his*, and his love was greater than anything he'd known. Much to Sara's irritation, the baby was named Rachel after Jacob's grandmother. She argued with Jacob that the child should be called Denise, but his objections had overruled hers. When she looked at the child at her breast, she felt almost envious of the affection that Jacob showed the child. Even at the height of his passion he never gave her the tenderness he gave to his child. Sara felt left out, rejected.

She had endured the long pregnancy and the labor pains because of Jacob, but now he seemed lost to her in the pleasure of fatherhood. . . .

In the weeks to come, Jacob spent every weekday looking for a job. One late afternoon he came home to find Sara, in the usual heavy sweater, standing at the sink as she prepared their dinner. She glanced up. "So how did it go . . . you found a job?"

"I found a job."

"*Mazel tov*. Where?"

"At a factory, making umbrella handles." Mr. Mendlebaum's presence was vivid in Jacob's memory.

"I guess you're pleased . . . since it used to be your trade. How much does it pay?"

"Nine dollars a week."

"You like the job?"

"Like it? It's a job . . . what do we have for supper?"

"Meatballs. Where is the job . . . I mean is it—"

"Uptown."

Where they once lived.

They went their separate ways, she to the stove, Jacob to see the baby. . . .

The next two years passed slowly for Sara and Jacob, but if they hardly noticed the passage of time it was not because life had improved. Sara's unhappiness resulted in arguments, then utter silence. Jacob became sullen and withdrawn. His hopes, dreams diminished, as did Sara's. Both felt their situations would never improve, and somehow they blamed each other.

Sara even began to punish Jacob—she would not have recognized it as that—by depriving him of herself. At night, she turned her back to him and stared at the wall. And he reached out more, and more, to his child for solace.

CHAPTER EIGHTEEN

HERSHEL AND Gittel's life had, surprisingly, prospered. Hershel now had a fine job working for a pawnshop on Ludlow Street. Each day he set off with a small case filled with diamond-studded earrings, wedding rings and gold watches, and he proved to be quite effective at selling.

Gittel gave birth to another son and they moved to a three-room flat. Gittel was more than content. Hershel was making a steady living. In fact, they had even saved a little money. These were the best years Gittel had ever known.

Esther was both happy and unhappy. She was pleased for Gittel, but she wept for Jacob and Sara. She well knew her son's fierce pride and Sara's needs. If business were better she would have given them some money. Added to her concern, Shlomo quit school in his junior year and went to work at the Fulton Fish Market. Esther tried to convince him to finish school, but he said he felt obliged to help support the family.

Jacob was furious that Shlomo would insult him by offering his help. But when he bought things for Rachel, whom they both adored, Jacob looked the other way.

It was an unexpected opportunity that fell into Hershel's lap. And once again coincident with someone else's disaster.

One morning he walked into Abrams' Pawnshop to replenish his case, and found his boss slumped over the counter. The man's eyes were open, but Hershel knew from the way his head lay that Mr. Abrams was dead. He felt the pulse to be sure . . . but no beat. As Hershel stood looking at the dead man his thoughts were all on the living . . . Mr. Abrams had no family, no one at all. So who would fall heir to the fruits of his labor? The government, but Uncle Sam could hardly be called a relative.

Hershel went to the front of the store, locked the door and pulled down the shade. Then he began stuffing his pockets and his case with rings, earrings, watches, brooches— whatever he could put his hands on. He opened the metal strongbox, took whatever cash was there and laid it on top of the jewelry in his case. Nervously, he locked the case and hurried home.

In spite of the cold day, he was drenched in perspiration when he reached his flat.

Gittel was so busy with the children that she didn't hear him walk in. He hurried into the bedroom, where he could be alone. He had too many pressing questions to answer. What should he do with the loot? Where could he hide it? Would the police suspect him? Question him? Hershel admonished himself . . . why was he so upset about all this? Who knew how much merchandise Abrams had? He didn't even know, and he'd worked for Abrams. Abrams didn't keep any inventories and Hershel was positive that he had taken only jewelry that was years overdue. Maybe he shouldn't have been so hasty, but done was done. Now, where should he hide it? In the closet, under the pile of dirty clothes? It wasn't safe, but for the time being it would have to do. Hershel went into the kitchen and sat down at the kitchen table. Benjamin climbed onto his father's lap and put his head against Hershel's chest.

"When are you going to wash the clothes in the closet, Gittel?" he asked.

"When I have the time. To tell the truth, I've been so busy I almost forgot but I'll do it tomorrow. You have enough —"

"No problem . . . Listen, Gittel, I have something to tell you. Sit down."

"What's the matter, Hershel? Here, let me get you a cup of tea."

"No. Listen, Gittel, I have something very sad to tell you."

Her heart pounded. Was it mama? "Sad, Hershel? What . . ."

"Mr. Abrams died. When I went to pick up the jewelry this morning, I found the poor man gone."

"Oh, my God, he was such a nice person. Poor man, there's no one to even say *Kaddish* for him. Too bad when you have no sons. How lucky we are—"

Her words reminded him of the night Avrum was born, when Jacob had loomed over him on the steps and said, "You have a son. When you die there'll be someone to say *Kaddish* for you." But he looked at Gittel and quickly continued, "It's sad, but he lived a good life. If he didn't make arrangements, I'll take care of it. Now, of course, Gittel, I have to get a new job."

She hadn't thought of that and suddenly she panicked. "What are you going to do?"

"Don't worry, Gittel, I'll make a living. Trust me, we won't starve."

"Whatever happens, Hershel, it doesn't matter so long as we're all together."

He nodded. "I have to go and take care of Mr. Abrams. God should only rest his soul in peace, such a nice man." . . .

After Hershel let himself into the store, he ran out and frantically summoned a policeman.

"My God," he said, "I can hardly believe it. Yesterday he was fine . . ."

"Well, that's life," said the policeman, "that's what people die from . . . living."

106

"What's going to happen now, what should I do?"

"Don't do nothing ... don't touch anything. You know his family?"

"He has none. I was like a son, though, I loved him."

"Yeah, that's kind of tough, but we all got to go."

"What's going to happen to the store?"

"I suppose the sheriff will padlock it, but first I have to notify the chief to call the coroner."

"Mr. Abrams and I never talked about it, but I don't even know if he took care of—"

"Funeral arrangements, yeah. I been around you people enough to know you have to make certain arrangements. Now give me your address in case we have to get in touch with you." ...

Hershel saw Mr. Abrams buried, then waited out the next few days in fear and anxiety.

The amount of jewelry Mr. Abrams had stashed away boggled the minds of the police who inventoried it. The gold pieces alone were worth a fortune, they told Hershel. He could have killed himself for being so honest, but his reprieve had finally come. He was not interrogated nor under any suspicion. Why should he be? There was certainly no foul play. It was a heart attack.

When Mr. Abrams' case was closed, Hershel felt it was safe to take his merchandise to a fence and convert it into cash. He was shocked at the amount—fifty-seven hundred dollars, not including the cash he'd taken. He felt like a millionaire.

That evening at dinner he said, "Gittel, I've saved a little money. I was always worried about losing my job and the only time you don't have to worry is when you're your own boss."

She sighed. "How true that is."

"Well, I'm going to be my own boss."

"You are? Oh, Hershel, I'm so happy, tell me—"

"Calm down, I'll tell you. I'm going to start a small business and we're going to move."

"You mean to a cheaper place until—"

"No, I mean away from New York."

"Away from New York? Why, Hershel?"

"What kind of business could I start here, another delicatessen? I haven't got a trade and I can't—"

"But my family ... your family, Hershel. How can we pick up and leave them?"

"I thought about it, of course I did. But our future's not here."

Silence. She was afraid to ask, afraid to hear the answer . . . "Where, then?"

"To Cleveland."

While she recovered from the shock, Hershel thought about the decision he had made. If he went into business here, people would wonder how he had acquired so much money, and that he couldn't risk. He still woke up in the night, drenched with perspiration, thinking the police would discover the missing loot . . . "Listen, Gittel, I'm thinking of the children. This is no place to raise them. They'll grow up without ever seeing a tree. What chance do we have here? None. I thought of Cleveland because it isn't too far for your mother to take a train. At least we can live like human beings there."

Biting her lip, she asked, "What made you think of Cleveland?"

"I know a man who moved there. I happened to meet him the other day when he came to visit his parents, and he said Cleveland was the best decision of his life. It's a wonderful city and his wife loves it there too."

Oh God, Gittel thought. She would be having to leave mama, her brothers, Sara and little Rachel . . . Why was life so complicated? "When will we be going?"

"I'm going first. I can't have you come till I find a place and a business."

"When are you going?"

"Tomorrow."

Gittel sat with Esther in the restaurant as the children played at a nearby table. "I'm not complaining, mama, but I can't get over Hershel moving us to Cleveland. Don't you think there's something he could have done to get into a little business here, mama?"

"He could have, yes, but in my heart I know Hershel is right. I don't think there's a worse place than this. When I came from the old country I hated it. For the bums, the East Side is good . . . but I hated having to bring up Shlomo here. That he turned out so good is only by the grace of God—"

"There are good children and families here, too, mama."

"True, but they'd be better off somewhere else. Listen to me, Gittel, this one time I give Hershel a lot of credit. His concern about his wife and family is wonderful. He's turned

108

out to be a good husband, Gittel—a very good man. Go with an easy heart, Hershel is right."

"I know, but I still love you, my family, and to think you won't see the children breaks my heart."

Esther had thought about this too and had come to a decision. "You know what? When you get settled, I'm going to sell the restaurant. The great riches I have here I can have in Cleveland. I saved a few dollars through the years. And when we get settled then Jacob can move—why not? The whole family will be together. You know something, Gittel?"

"What, mama?"

"I suddenly got a lot of hope." And to think Hershel should be the one to make such a great change in all our lives, she thought. . . .

Three weeks later, Hershel sent for Gittel and the children.

When they arrived they stood on the sidewalk in front of the new store as Hershel pointed up to the sign above the door—HAROLD'S DRY GOODS.

Gittel wept happily and asked, "Why Harold's?"

"Why not? A new life, a new name . . . this is America."

Harold Jablon had emerged and Hershel Jablonsky had vanished.

Gittel hugged her husband as he put the key in the latch and marched ahead of his family toward the back of the store to the five-room apartment.

Two years later Esther sold the restaurant. From the moment the sale was finalized until the time of her departure she continued to tell Shlomo that his opportunities were in Cleveland. Look what a good living Hershel was making. The children were living in fresh air and they and the new baby girl, Bertha, were going to grow up among civilized people. Wasn't Shlomo eager to see Gittel's children?

Yes, but if Jacob couldn't go then neither would he.

"Jacob's going to come eventually. Why are you being so stubborn, Shlomo?"

"Because Jacob needs some family too. With everyone leaving he'll feel very alone."

Esther nodded her head slowly. As usual, Shlomo was right. Poor Jacob would be alone. At this moment it seemed to her that the children were smarter than she'd ever been. . . .

Before getting on the train at Pennsylvania Station, Esther

looked from one face to the other. She felt torn apart and suddenly remembered the first time she'd left her children. Had Jacob really forgiven her? Sometimes she wondered. But she couldn't be in two places at the same time. Once again life had taken her by the hand. . .

In spite of himself, Jacob too remembered that first parting. Gittel always came first.

Sara's thoughts were with Hershel, the one they'd always criticized. Hershel was making a home and a good living for his family, but Jacob, strong as an ox, was still carving umbrella handles and earning nine dollars a week. There was no justice in the world. For all her cultured background Sara lived in poverty, and Gittel, who had never gone to school, had it very good indeed. Sara and her mother had something in common—they seemed to know how to pick the wrong men.

Three weeks later they received a letter from Esther in which she enclosed a snapshot of a storefront and the sign above the door. ESTHER SANDERS DRY GOODS.

Where else but in America?

CHAPTER NINETEEN

THE DAY Sara discovered she was pregnant was the same day Jacob told her Germany was at war with France and England. When she cried it was not because of the war but because she didn't want this child. She'd been so careful not to conceive and had in fact discouraged Jacob's advances. But something was wrong. Well, the whole thing had been wrong from the day she was born, so why should anything be so different now . . . When she wrote to her mother about her situation and Molly wrote back that children brought luck, Sara wanted to scream out. If they brought so much luck why had Molly resisted being so blessed? Then she admonished herself. Molly had sent her some money although she was barely making a living out of the junk store she ran, and it hurt Sara to think of her mama living in the back of a store.

Sara gave birth to a second girl on January 10, 1915. No matter how she tried, she simply could not accept the fact that she was only twenty-two years old and burdened with two children and a husband with no future. She had become so fat after bearing the children that she swore she'd *never* have another. She had nothing in common with the mothers who sat on the stoops and discussed everybody's business but their own. She had to get away. So from time to time, out of desperation, she took the subway with Rachel and the baby and went uptown although she had barely enough for the fare.

As she walked along Fifth Avenue she wondered how God could single out certain people to have the riches and good things in this life and others to be deprived and unloved. Her excursions only increased her longings, making it almost impossible for her to return home. The contrast between her dingy flat and her memories of Central Park, the governesses tending children who wore organdy dresses with wide pink satin sashes, the smartly dressed women who lived in mansions—it all brought back the promises Louie and Molly had made and the hopes she had felt in the early days of her marriage. But her marriage was just another broken promise.

Jacob couldn't help but be aware of her resentment, but it made him feel betrayed. She should have been his comfort and helped him to shut out the mean world. Instead she made him feel less than a man, made him feel impotent. Was it his fault things had turned against them? Had he denied her anything he was able to give her? No, but all she had done was make life harder for him.

One night their resentment exploded into an argument. Sara had brought up Hershel's success just once too often.

"I'm sick and tired of hearing the same thing over and over again." He shoved his plate away and got up from the table. Standing over her, he said, "You should have married a millionaire. A lot you have to complain about. When I married you, what was the dowry you brought me? I even bought you the dress. What did your mother ever do for you—"

"Don't talk about my mother."

"Why, does the truth hurt?"

"You know as well as I do that she doesn't have anything."

"She had enough to support a pimp—"

Sara slapped Jacob in the face.

He took hold of her wrist as he tried to calm himself. After a long tense moment he said, "You listen to me and listen carefully. Don't *ever* do that again. I warn you, Sara, and don't push me too hard . . . As for your mother, it's funny how you tell me how bad your life was, that you didn't have a mother when you were a little girl, and then you defend her to me—"

"She's my mother no matter what she did. You don't have a right to talk against her . . ."

"But I'm your husband. What about your loyalties to me?"

"I'm as loyal as any wife. I live with you and make a home and—"

"And also make my life hell."

"Then why don't you leave me."

"Don't think I haven't thought of it."

"What's keeping you?"

"My children . . ." He ran from the room, down the stairs and into the street. When he got to the river he sat on a bench and thought about his so-called marriage . . .

Meanwhile Sara started to pack. Enough was enough, and if this was what she could look forward to the rest of her life . . . she'd go to California to her mother.

Suddenly she sat heavily on the bed and began to cry. She must have gone mad. Where would she get the money to go to California and how would she support herself and two children? And then a further sobering thought came . . . She'd been selfish. Jacob was, after all, suffering as much as she was; his life had been nothing but hardship from the day he was born, and he was doing the best he could. If she could think a little less about herself and a little bit more about him maybe life would be a little more endurable. But she'd spent so much of her life vacillating between love and resentment. She prayed that if God could help her with anything, it would be to change her nature . . .

When Jacob came back she was sitting at the kitchen table, waiting for him. He walked toward the bedroom without a word.

She called after him but he slammed the door.

She went to him and watched as he let his shoe drop to the floor. "Jacob, I'm sorry . . . really I am."

No reply. The trousers were tossed onto the chair.

"I've been wrong, taking my feelings out on you."

He laid his shirt on top of the trousers. In his union suit he got into bed.

Sara went to the bed. "I know I've been wrong." It wasn't easy for her to say that, but Jacob didn't make up easily. "I apologize, Jacob . . ."

112

No answer.

"Jacob, for God's sake, what can I say except that I'm very sorry I—"

"You can leave me alone," he answered, turning toward the wall.

She hadn't felt so abandoned or alone since she had been a little girl, begging her mother to let her come with her, and she cried now, softly, through the night as she lay alongside Jacob.

The greatest joy in Rachel's life was meeting papa at the subway every summer evening. How proud she was now that she was six and could go alone. Everyone said she looked like papa, same blonde hair and blue eyes . . . and papa was so wonderful. He took her to a place in a basement that sold charlotte russe. Papa always smiled and watched as she ate hers, but he never had one. Hand in hand, they walked home through the crowded streets. Rachel was very happy that Doris was still a baby and that she didn't have to share these precious times with papa, and sometimes it was even good to get away from mama. She didn't know why mama often made her feel so bad, like she'd done something wrong. "The reason you don't eat your supper," mama would say, "is because you always eat sweets before." But Rachel didn't care, she liked charlotte russe more than supper. More important was meeting papa; that was the nicest thing in her life and she wouldn't stop even if mama got mad. And mama could get mad. The things she said to papa . . . although things had been better since Doris came into the family. She really didn't like Doris at all. The only people she really loved were papa and her Uncle Shlomo. . . .

Fortunately, Rachel couldn't see what was happening between Jacob and Shlomo. For the first time in their lives there was a breach between them, and Jacob suffered badly for it.

The day America declared war on Germany, Shlomo went to Jacob to tell him he was joining the marines.

After the first shock Jacob said, "Oh, no, you're not going to join anything. You're only nineteen."

"Jacob, I didn't come to ask you but to tell you."

"And I'm telling you *no*."

"Jacob, there's a war going on—"

"Don't tell me about the war. I read the papers."

"Then if you read the papers you know I'll be drafted anyway. I don't want to go into the army."

"Damn it, I say *no*. You hear?"

"How could I help, you're yelling so loud. But it doesn't change a thing."

Jacob went wild. Grabbing Shlomo, he punched him in the stomach, then slapped him in the face. Shlomo staggered and fell to the floor.

When Jacob saw the blood dripping from Shlomo's split lip he was on his knees in a second, holding Shlomo to him like a child and wiping away the blood. "My God, Shlomo, I don't want anything to happen to you. It would kill mama . . . me too if anything—don't do it."

Shlomo rallied himself and stood up unsteadily. He looked at Jacob, then put his arms around his brother. "Nothing's going to happen to me." . . .

The day Shlomo left, Jacob was as bereft as the day his father had died. When Jacob cried for Shlomo, and prayed he would come back safely, he was also, of course, crying for his father . . . for his father who had never come back.

CHAPTER TWENTY

FOR THE first time in Molly's life she happened to be in the right place at the right time. With the outbreak of the war, defense plants in Oakland were booming and the influx of people needed what Molly sold—secondhand furniture.

Six months after the declaration of war she had enough money to buy two flats in East Oakland. She no sooner had the deeds in hand than she sent off a letter to Sara and enclosed tickets and money. . . .

The day Sara received the letter she threw her arms around Jacob's neck when he came home and kissed him over and over again. When she showed him the letter, though, he hardly shared her excitement.

"Jacob, what's the matter? I thought you would be so happy."

He was thinking of Hershel, who had allowed Esther to pay the rent and give them food. And now Jacob was about to do the same thing he had so despised in Hershel.

"Jacob, look at the tickets and the money. Don't you realize what a wonderful chance this is?"

His eyes focused on Sara's face. The baby came and sat on his lap and when he felt the soft black curly hair and the little head against his chest he wondered what choice he really had.

"I don't understand you, Jacob—"

He put the baby down and took Sara in his arms. "Don't try to understand me. No one can look inside someone else's head. I'm happy but I just wish I could have done it—"

"Oh, Jacob, that's just foolish pride. Wouldn't you help your children if they needed it? Wouldn't you?"

But that was different; he was a man, a father. Still, Sara was right—he was being selfish. So he swallowed his pride, accepted the hundred dollars and looked at a smiling, jubilant Sara.

The only moment Sara felt sad was when she saw all her beautiful furniture being taken out of the dirty flat and loaded into the peddler's wagon. But why should she dwell on the past now? The old dreams had been replaced by new ones. And at long last, mama was actually waiting for her.

Sara and the children were excited by the long train ride and spent much of the trip exclaiming over the countryside they watched from the windows. Jacob, however, was not quite so excited. He was unhappy with the food, which wasn't kosher, and he despised the confinement. The trip was becoming boring and his restlessness made him irritable.

When the train finally came to a halt at the Oakland station, Sara ran to her mother's waiting arms. Mama had changed so. Her hair was streaked with silver, lines were etched in her face . . . She remembered the day when she had stood on a pier in Brussels and watched a regal Molly walk down the gangplank, dressed in a dove-gray velvet suit and a feathered toque. But all the childhood dreams and disappointments—the overlapping love and hate—all were forgotten as Sara clung to Molly. They were together at last.

With happy tears Sara said, "Mama, this is Jacob and your grandchildren."

Molly embraced Jacob warmly but he felt awkward. It wasn't just the shame of accepting charity. He resented what this woman had done to Sara, leaving her so alone in the world. His mother had done things he could never completely forgive her for, but at least she hadn't abandoned him for a lover. She had struggled to try to bring them together . . . Jacob picked up Doris in his arms and mumbled an introduction.

Molly noticed his stiffness and remembered the letter Sara

115

had written to tell her she was getting married. She had described Jacob as "rather a complex person," but to Molly he seemed cold and unfeeling. Well, he was Sara's husband and this was no time to dwell on his dark nature.

Molly took Doris from Jacob's arms and devoured the child with hugs and kisses, then took Rachel's hand in hers and excitedly led the way out of the station to the jitney.

When they were seated on the bus, Rachel looked at her father and couldn't understand why he wasn't enjoying himself. Even mama was happy. She was laughing and crying and grandma was saying how happy she was that they were going to be living with her after all this time. She just wished that papa would smile. Rachel felt uncomfortable, as if this was something she was responsible for.

They got out of the jitney at Seventh Street and Rachel forgot the upsetting thoughts as they started to walk up strange new streets. They passed a church that didn't look like anything she'd ever seen—not a *shul*. It had a big cross on top of a peaked roof, and there was a statue of some kind. The wooden houses, each with a flight of wooden stairs that led to the front door, looked just as odd to her. But the flowers were pretty and she knew the green patches in front of the houses were grass because she had played on grass in Central Park. Suddenly it all felt very strange to her. It was all so quiet and there was hardly anyone on the streets. . . . But the queerest sight of all was grandma's house. It wasn't like the others at all. It was two stories and had two doors sort of next to each other. Mama said a family lived in the bottom part and grandma lived upstairs. But how come the two doors were on the same level?

Rachel's confusion was cleared up after grandma unlocked the door. The stairs inside went up and up and up. Then they were in the hall with a wooden banister. It was so *big* and so was the parlor, as mama called it. Rachel especially loved the cupids that were painted on the round table and lamp. But best of all was the diningroom. In the center of the table was a cut-glass bowl with wax fruit. They didn't look like wax . . . They looked real. She wanted to pick up the banana and bite into it. Then her eyes wandered to the china cabinet. Gosh, grandma must be rich, she hadn't ever seen anything like it . . . it was filled with dishes standing up against the back with lots and lots of cups and saucers. Also little dolls, not the kind you could play with, mama said they were porcelain . . . She couldn't believe her ears when she heard grandma say to mama she had practically stolen the diningroom set

116

from an old widow. Her grandma stole! Well, grandma had said practically, but stealing was stealing. That's what mama had said when she'd just taken Izzy Greenblatt's ball. She could still feel the sting of mama's hand on her bottom, even though it happened way back when she was four . . .

As mama set the table and grandma heated the food in the kitchen, Rachel noticed the hole in the linoleum, but she didn't want anyone to feel bad so she didn't say anything. Now she was watching grandma taking things out of the big brown wooden icebox. Grandma handed her a plate of chopped liver and another of kosher dills, and she took them into the diningroom and put the plates on the table.

Pretty soon everyone was eating and talking . . . everyone except papa . . . he was just eating.

That night, after she and Doris were in bed, Rachel said, "It's kind of scary. It's so quiet . . ."

There were no sounds from the El, no sirens, no pushcarts being rolled over the cobblestones . . . nothing.

Rachel asked again, "Don't you feel funny, Doris?"

No answer. Doris was sound asleep.

The next week Jacob found a job working in the Chevrolet plant, but the great American dream had been slightly exaggerated by his mother-in-law. A job was easy to get, but the salary wasn't that much more than he'd made in New York. Sara was so happy that the children were thriving, but he hated California. It wasn't going to be easy being a Jew in Oakland, California. In New York he'd spent so much time surrounded by his own people and by reminders of his heritage that he'd *almost* taken it for granted. Here he was surrounded by *goyim*. He almost felt like a *goy* himself. . . .

Rachel loved California at first. The only drawback was school. She was put in the second grade when she should have been in the third, and it embarrassed her because she was taller than the other children and a little older. Another thing that annoyed her was that mama made her come home for lunch when she wanted to eat at school like the other kids. She envied them their metal lunch boxes and peanut butter sandwiches, small bottles of milk and the graham crackers. But no, she had to bring Doris home . . . Take care of your sister, Rachel, you're the oldest . . . Was it her fault she was the oldest? Why didn't mama pick Doris up?

When she found out the reason—that mama was going to have a baby—Rachel was excited but she also felt vaguely uneasy. Somehow it embarrassed her and she warned Doris

117

not to tell anyone in the neighborhood about mama. But Doris was so thrilled that she couldn't keep such a secret. She was going to have a baby brother or sister—although she really hoped it would be a brother.

When Rachel found out Doris had broken her word she was furious. She stayed after school that day and played on the swings for a while, then she merely sat looking at the kids in the sandboxes or swinging on the metal rings. When the playground finally closed she wandered around the streets aimlessly, then stood in front of a church.

The doors were open and she could see colored people inside. She walked up to the door and listened to their rich voices as they sang. She was surprised by the handclapping and swaying—almost dancing—that accompanied their songs and by the occasional voice that rose above the others singing "Hallelujah."

When Jacob came home, Sara was distraught about Rachel's disappearance.

"What time does she usually get home?" Jacob asked.

"Just after two-thirty."

"Don't worry, I'll find her."

He ran down Molly's stairs, then up one street after another. Finally he saw Rachel framed in the doorway of the church.

"Rachel—"

When she turned and faced her father, her heart pounded. She really shouldn't be here; these people were *goyim*. "Yes, papa . . ."

"Come, your mother is very upset."

He wasn't mad. "I'm sorry, papa . . ."

"All right, but from now on go straight home after school."

She loved papa. Taking his hand she felt just the way she used to when she met him at the subway and they went to get the charlotte russe.

When Sara heard the front door open, her anxiety ended and her anger began. Rachel was genuinely sorry for having worried mama in her condition, but Sara took hold of her, pulled down her pants and spanked her hard. It didn't stop until Jacob called out above Rachel's cries, "Leave her alone . . . Do you hear me? Leave her alone, and don't ever lay a hand on her again—"

Molly rushed out of the kitchen. "And don't you ever shout at my child. Who do you think you are?"

118

Since they'd been living with Sara's mother, it seemed they never had a word that Molly didn't interfere with. She made insinuating remarks, reminding him of his responsibilities and saying how difficult it was to raise a family without any money. And Sara never contradicted her, never came to his defense against a mother who had all but abandoned her when she needed her most . . . .

Jacob grabbed some clothes and stuffed them into a suitcase. He'd had enough.

Sara called out after him, but the front door slammed. She stood motionless and frightened in the hall.

"Don't cry, Sara. I know men, he'll come back . . ."

Sara turned on her mother. "You know men! But what do you know about me? You think I don't know how much you regret sending for us? The strain is too much for you, the children are in your way—just as I would have been. All you ever needed was Louie, Louie—"

"How dare you speak to me after all I've done . . . What do you want from me?"

"What I've always gotten from you. Nothing. You should have kept out of things. It was between Jacob and me."

"I couldn't see him talking to you that way and do nothing."

"Your concern is very touching . . ."

Sara went to her room, lay down heavily on the bed and cried until her lids closed in unhappy sleep.

Rachel didn't sleep at all. Her guilt was too strong. It was all her fault . . .

Nor did Jacob, as he lay in the sleazy hotel room. He shouldn't have lost his temper that way, not with Sara in that condition. But he'd had enough of Sara's mother and he knew there was only one way out. He had to earn more money so he could be rid of Molly, once and for all.

The next day he found out that the shipyards were in need of expert riveters. He went to the Pacific Iron Works, filled out an application and waited to be interviewed. Jacob, of course, didn't know a rivet from a monkey wrench, but he got the job.

The first day he watched while he worked. Whatever the man beside him did, he did. After a week he became so good that he went to the office and quite confidently asked for a raise. If he didn't get it he would quit, he said. A man of his experience didn't have to work for peanuts and he could get a job anywhere. With the war going on, experienced men were needed.

Jacob not only got the raise but was elevated to foreman. Thirty dollars a week was more money than he ever thought he'd make.

On Friday afternoon he left work early, went to the hotel to change his clothes, then went to Rachel's school and waited for her to come out. When he saw her he thought his heart would break. Two weeks. She looked so *tiny* . . .

"Papa!" she screamed, running toward him. "Oh, papa, I'm so happy to see you. I thought you were never coming back and I cried."

He swallowed. "Come . . . I'll buy you an ice cream."

It was like New York, waiting for papa and going to buy the charlotte russe . . .

They sat at the round table in the ice cream parlor. "Rachel, how is mama?"

"Fine."

Jacob noticed Rachel's eyes lower. "Is she really?"

"I suppose . . ."

"What do you mean?"

"Well . . . she cries and cries. She and grandma fight all the time. They say terrible things to each other."

"They do?"

"Yes, mama says she had no right to come between a husband and wife."

Jacob's face softened. "She . . . I mean, mama said that—"

"Yes."

Rachel felt the warmth go through her when her father smiled.

"Now listen to me, Rachel. I want you to go home and tell mama that I have a very good job and I'm making a lot of money. You tell her as soon as I find a nice place, I'll let her know."

"Oh, *papa*, you really mean it?"

"Of course. I want you to be very careful not to lose this," he said, handing Rachel some money in an envelope. "Now you'd better go home before mama begins to worry."

"Why don't you come too?"

"No, Rachel. I'm not going back to your grandmother's. But inside the envelope is the name and address of the hotel I'm staying at. Tell mama if she wants to see me, I'm there every night after work."

Forgetting the melted cone on the table, she got up and put her arms around his neck. "I love you, papa . . ."

He only nodded. He couldn't say, "I love you too, Rachel," but she knew he did.

120

On Sunday, Sara and the children went to see Jacob. There was no bitterness now. Who had been right and who had been wrong didn't matter. All that mattered was that they knew they needed each other.

Jacob showed Sara the new house that he'd rented. The livingroom was badly in need of paint but it was better than Rivington Street. And Sara liked the large kitchen and the glassed-in back porch.

There was a little garden in the backyard and a tall hollyhock grew in front of the worn wooden fence.

They climbed the stairs to the two bedrooms. Sara liked it. She wished she had the furniture from Washington Heights, but . . .

Reading her mind, Jacob said, "If you feel well enough, there's a furniture store on Fourteenth Street. We can pick out what you need."

"How will we pay for it?"

"They have time payments. You like the house?"

"Yes, Jacob. *Yes* . . ."

CHAPTER TWENTY-ONE

ONCE AGAIN their lives were beginning to come together, and Sara seemed quite content. The only sore point was that Jacob refused to allow Molly in his house. Sara and her mother had their differences but both were able to forget and forgive easily. Not so with Jacob. He held his grudges.

Sara tried to explain how mama was, but Jacob didn't want to hear about it. So Sara kept peace by not bringing it up. She went to see her mother as often as she could and just prayed that eventually Jacob would forgive.

As Sara's time approached she wrote out long lists for Rachel.

1) Change Doris' bloomers every day or she'll forget.
2) Don't bother making Doris' curls.
3) Don't use too many towels so there won't be so much to wash. The bath towels can be used a few times.
4) Be sure to have the soup hot when papa comes from work. Be sure and put the meat in the same pot.
5) Doris can help with making the beds. Let her hang out the clothes, she's old enough.
6) Rachel, you wash the dishes and let Doris stand on a box so she can wipe them.

121

7) Keep the kitchen clean and the living room dusted. Use the carpet sweeper twice a week.
8) Wipe out the tub after the bath.

Sara thought she'd covered just about everything. Everything except the pregnancy.

On December 25, 1917, Lillian Sanders was born at the Peralta Hospital in Oakland, California. Eight pounds, two and one-half ounces with a head of black fuzz and dark eyes to match. She would look just like Sara.

Jacob now was sure he would never have a son because he knew Sara would refuse to have another child, accident or no. But still, this was his baby and he was pleased by what a pretty little thing it was.

"She's a darling little girl, don't you think, Jacob?" Sara knew how hard it was for Jacob, but it wasn't her fault if they couldn't make boys.

"Oh, yes. She's darling." Jacob nodded.

"How are things at home?"

"Just fine . . . everything's running like clockwork, but I'll be happy when you can come home."

And he would. He wouldn't tell her about last night, about how delirious Doris had been. Her fever was so high that she rambled on and on, scaring him half to death. He stayed up half the night sponging her with towels. Thank God, today she was better.

"Well, I'd better go now and let you get some rest."

"Stay a few minutes longer."

"I would, but I don't think I should leave the children too long."

"You're right. Give them my love."

"I will." He kissed her and left. . . .

The day before Sara was due to come home, Molly came with a heavy basket of food, changed the linen, put out fresh towels, scrubbed the kitchen floor, cleaned the bathroom—and cried. Why was Jacob so angry? She shouldn't have interfered but she really meant well. Molly wouldn't tell Sara that she had gone to the house one evening to try to make amends and Jacob had all but thrown her out. She hadn't been the best mother in the world, but now that she was trying to make up for lost time it seemed Jacob wouldn't let her. Why should Jacob protect Sara from her own mother? She just couldn't understand it.

122

Rachel and Doris stood breathlessly on the front porch and watched as papa helped mama and the new baby up the wooden steps.

Doris had picked a bunch of marigolds in the backyard and handed the bouquet to her mother. Sara accepted them although she held in her breath. How could anything so pretty smell so terrible. Still, she was so excited to be home that she hugged Doris and thanked her.

The door closed as the family followed Sara and the baby up to the bedroom.

Rachel looked at the infant with disdain. God, she was ugly. Even the blue blanket she was wrapped in didn't make her look pretty. Doris, however, was captivated . . . madly in love with her baby sister. Doris felt very grownup today; after all, she had become an older sister.

As the weeks went by, Sara worked, took care of her children, kept house. Thick barley soup and noodle *kugel* were staples.

Wheeling the baby in the buggy, she would walk up Seventh Street and buy brisket at the kosher butcher. It was almost as good as New York. The fish, however, was not. In New York there was white fish, good carp, but here she bought whatever she could for *gelfilte fish*. As she had promised Jacob after that disastrous first dinner as a bride, she would excel in cooking, and she had . . . her *challah* was every bit as good as Jacob's mother's, in fact better . . .

Shabbes nights were observed with mixed feelings. Lighting the *Shabbes* candles Sara was sad that not more than a few miles away was her mother . . . Still, when she looked around her table and observed her children, especially Doris' round eyes focused on papa saying the *baruch* and the *motzim*, she counted her blessings . . . .

Jacob felt guilty because he had to work on Saturdays, the one day of the week when he should be with his family. How could you be Jewish here? This was a new land, different from the East Side where they could be open about being Jewish. How they observed Friday nights was a miracle. Jacob Sandsonitsky was living like a *goy*. He had even taken a *goy* name—Jack Sanders—and like a *goy* he rode on Saturdays and carried money in his pocket. What kind of a religious Jew did that? God would simply have to forgive him because his family needed to be fed and clothed. If it were known he was a Jew he might be out of a job. The men he

123

worked with made jokes about Kikes but Jacob turned a deaf ear to them. Jacob Sandsonitsky would have knocked the hell out of them, but Jack Sanders compromised.

Jacob had to admit that although he had compromised his religious convictions at least he had bought his family some security. His mother had always observed the Sabbath, but how had that helped her children? His children would never have to struggle as he had. Financially, things had worked out beyond his wildest dreams. He had saved seven hundred dollars and bought a Dodge for fifty dollars from a man who was going into the navy. They had a little furniture, a nice home to live in. So all in all, things were going well. Maybe he never set foot in a *shul,* but life was better than he'd ever known it to be. And Sara had changed in many ways. She seemed more contented, and she watched the children like a hawk and fed them three large meals a day. Children needed food, Sara said, and if anyone agreed it was Doris. She could hardly wait to come to the table. She was a nice fat little girl with dark curly hair.

Rachel was the only one who was slender and that seemed to worry Sara a great deal. She was terribly finicky and—just different.

Rachel, Sara was sorry to admit, was not sweet-natured like Doris or Lillian. She was overly sensitive, sullen at times, and she kept to herself and showed no affection toward the baby or Doris. Yes, there was something strange about Rachel. Everything was a matter of life and death. She had to study, she had to get the best grade, she couldn't stand to wear the same underpants more than once . . . Who did she take after? It had to be Jacob's family. Well, maybe she was just going through a phase. Doris was more like herself . . . pliable, happy and lovable . . . Look how she rushed home from school every day to take the baby Lillian for a ride in the buggy. One would think nobody else had a sister. As for Lillian, all you had to do was feed her.

Even Jacob had changed. His life was dedicated to keeping a roof over his children's heads and shoes on their feet. He was proud that they were never going to know what he'd gone through, and Sara was happy to see him so content.

Still, Sara would have liked him to have been more demonstrative. But she had no doubt that he loved her and his family. It was merely his way.

124

JACOB WAS as excited as anyone at the announcement that the war had ended, but peacetime had its price for Jacob. He was called into the office and told the shipyard was laying off men. Jacob was the first to go. His services as a foreman were no longer needed and he was to remain only for the rest of the week.

He didn't tell Sara at first. He didn't have the heart to, and he was preoccupied with the injustice of it—just when life had been going so well. . . .

And then a few months later the influenza epidemic struck, and Sara made gauze masks that, Doris noticed with alarm, covered the nose and mouth. Mama told Doris and Rachel to run right home after school and never, never remove the mask. Doris couldn't take Lillian for a walk because there was this terrible disease from a place called Europe and people were, mama said, dropping dead like flies. How could people drop dead like flies? But if mama said so, it must be so . . . mama knew everything. . . .

Sara began to notice the changes in Jacob. He was silent at dinner and he scarcely ate. He got up during the night to go down to the front room and sit in the dark. It bothered her, but she had assumed he was probably overworked and tired.

However, this evening she could no longer assume.

Jacob lay in bed with his hands behind his head and stared up at the ceiling.

"Jacob . . . I'm not complaining, but you've been so quiet lately. I would think with the war over and Shlomo coming back you'd be . . ."

"Happy?"

"Yes."

"I'm happy for Shlomo and that the war is over—but I'm also out of a job."

"Why?"

"Because the country doesn't need any more ships. They've got enough ships but not enough jobs."

Finally Sara said, "There has to be something else you can do—"

"You think so? Well, I've been looking but there are no

125

jobs. It seems the world needs wars so a man can provide for his family . . ."

"Jacob, what's going to happen to us?"

"I wrote to my mother and—"

"You told your mother, but you didn't tell me?"

"Now don't start with your temper, please. I hoped I'd have an answer about how things are in Cleveland before telling you."

"What can your mother do?"

"Since I haven't gotten the letter, I don't know . . ."

She bit her lip to stop the tears, then said softly, "Jacob, I know how you feel about my mother, but she is my mother and really she's a very good woman. Please let me ask her if—"

"Sara, I don't want to make you feel bad, but I won't take *anything* from your mother."

"Why do you dislike her so much? After all, Jacob, she didn't do anything so terrible to you."

Some people you just don't like, Jacob thought, and he was repulsed by the notion of her help. Besides, she was barely making a living.

"Jacob, if we stayed, maybe between what you and mama have saved we could open a furniture store."

Jacob looked closely at her. Of course she wanted her mother; it was the first time she'd had a chance to be close to her. Molly, he supposed, wasn't *really* such a bad person, and sometimes he wondered if he wasn't taking it all out on Molly for what he'd gone through as a kid, on account of his mother . . . Think about this, he instructed himself . . . Sara and the children loved California. He badly missed his own family, but maybe it was important for a woman to have her mother. Sara had missed so much . . . Maybe if God was good to him and they pooled what they had, got into business and made a little success, he and Sara would be able to go east from time to time on a little visit . . . "Sara, do you think your mother has any money?"

She smiled. "She has the flats and if she sold the store . . . I think she would be thrilled, Jacob."

Jacob wasn't thrilled. Molly would be putting up most of the money and it made him feel damned uncomfortable. But on the other hand . . . "Okay, Sara, talk to your mother and see how she—"

"Oh, Jacob, I love you, thank you so much. But come with me, please. Let bygones be bygones."

126

Pride was not easy to swallow. Not for this man who had had it taken from him so early, and so often . . . Still, for Sara and the children . . .

Molly got nine hundred dollars for the flats and three hundred for the junk, but she was so happy her children were staying and that Jacob was speaking to her that the money was the least important concern.

The only thing that mattered at this moment was the large painted sign going up over the door—SANDERS AND CARR FINE FURNITURE.

Jacob thought about his father as he watched it go up. It should have been Sandsonitsky . . .

The day of the grand opening came, but not one customer.

"It's the first day," Sara said. "Wait till the store becomes better known."

Jacob waited through the next three months of the worst weather in years. It rained most of February and March, but worse than that was that there was no business. He thought he'd go out of his mind walking up and down the store with only the occasional customer to divert him. For lack of things to do, he began to play solitaire. Molly and he began to grate on each other's nerves. She suggested that rather than do nothing maybe he should vacuum the store, polish the furniture, do the repairs. And while he was doing all that, he asked, what was she going to do?

Unimportant things began to build into arguments. If things kept up this way, Jacob thought, two things would happen; they would all starve and he would wind up choking Sara's mother. Better to leave now. . . .

"Sara, I really tried, but I can't go on this way. She's impossible to get along with."

"Please, Jacob, give it another chance—"

"No. No more chances. It's not good to be partners with relatives. Tell her to give me my six hundred dollars. I want to get out of the store—she can have it."

"Jacob, she sold her house and her store so you would be able to make a living for us . . ."

"You're saying I didn't support you?"

"You're twisting my words."

"Sure, and your mother's an angel to get along with. Listen, you tell her I want my six hundred dollars back." . . .

The next day a miserable Sara went to see her mother.

"I don't have it, Sara," Molly told her. "Everything is in the store and the furniture. Let me tell you about your husband—"

"I don't want you to say a word against him, do you hear me?"

"But you listen to him complain about your mother?"

"He never says anything against you."

"Sure, he loves me. I sacrificed my own old age so that you and the children could have enough to eat and this is my thanks."

"That's why Jacob's so upset. You kept throwing it in his face."

"Oh, so he does talk about me?"

"For God's sake, mama, keep quiet. I'm sick and tired of being in the middle. You weren't such a perfect mother..." The minute she said it she was sorry. Her mother was right—she had sold everything for them. And Jacob was right too—Molly was impossible to get along with. She blew hot, she blew cold.

"Mama, please sell the store... or I know Jacob will leave me—"

Molly sighed. "All right, all right, go home and tell your wonderful husband I'll sell..."

Sara found Jacob waiting in the front room of their house. "Jacob, mama said she'd sell."

"That's very kind of her, but if she can sell that store you can use my head for a chopping block."

"What do you want from her, Jacob? She's a poor woman trying to do the best she can."

"I want her to liquidate."

"Liquidate?"

"That's right."...

The original investment had been Molly's twelve hundred dollars and Jacob's six. After the liquidation they came out with seven hundred dollars.

All Jacob wanted was enough to go to Cleveland; three hundred dollars would be enough. In spite of it all, Molly was heartbroken. She'd wanted them to take the whole thing. Somehow she'd get by... go back to the hat factory. But Jacob said she'd sacrificed enough for her children. From now on, he'd carry the burden.

That night Jacob reread a letter his mother had written several months ago. His eyes skimmed down to... "Please come, Jacob. I don't have much, but you can live with me until you have a place of your own. Remember, I'm your mother . . ." Jacob sat deep in thought remembering the day he'd received that letter. If he had listened to his heart then, he'd have been three hundred dollars richer and a million times less upset.

The departure was very painful, and Jacob was not unaware of Sara's distress as he watched mother and daughter cling to each other with tears in their eyes.

At last Molly came over to him. "I know I'm not the easiest person in the world to get along with, Jacob, but I hope you won't hold it against me. I really meant well."

Jacob nodded. Everybody *meant* well.

CHAPTER TWENTY-THREE

SARA FELT that this journey was taking her backward. At this moment all the arguments with Molly seemed so unimportant. Once again she was going into an alien world . . .

As they stepped off the train, all of Jacob's family were there to meet them. Today the signs on the doors of Harold's Dry Goods and Esther Sanders Dry Goods read "Closed."

As the family sat having dinner at Esther's Jacob looked around the table. How much they'd all changed. Mama looked older, her hair whiter, and Gittel's eyes seemed very tired. Hershel, on the other hand, seemed rested. He was just as joyless as ever, but now there was an arrogance about him.

Jacob looked at Hershel's sons. Strange, he thought, Hershel's boys were going to be tall—like Jacob. For a moment the thought made him sad, but when he looked at his daughters he couldn't help but smile.

Sara's thoughts were not as happy. She was—admit it—envious of Gittel and her well-dressed children. Hershel wasn't as tall and handsome as Jacob, but at least he provided well for his family.

Gittel thought Sara had changed a great deal. She supposed she would always remember Sara as that charming girl she'd first met, old for her age . . . Sara at Coney Island . . . delightful in that black bathing suit. Now there seemed to be a kind of bitterness about her. Nothing that Gittel could exactly put her finger on . . . maybe it was all her imagination, the long trip with three children on a train, Jacob without a job. Of course Sara would be worried. And leaving her mother must have been very difficult. How well she remembered leaving Esther to come to Cleveland . . . .

Doris was mostly overwhelmed with Uncle Shlomo. She'd never seen anything so gorgeous as this man with his shiny brass buttons on the dark blue uniform, the silver metal, the red stripe down the sides of his light blue trousers, the black polished shoes and the white hard hat with the black visor, which he'd now taken off. She'd only seen men like Uncle Shlomo in the newsreels the few times she and Rachel went to the movies on Saturdays.

Looking around the table, Rachel felt nearly as uncomfortable as her mother with all the relatives, especially with her boy cousins. Then she looked at Bertha. She really would have loved a big hair ribbon and barrettes like her cousin had. Her line of thought was lost as she heard the conversation going on between papa and Uncle Shlomo. Papa looked plenty upset; she could always tell.

"Why didn't you write and tell me you were joining up with the marines again?"

"Because I thought it would be better to tell you when we were all together," Shlomo answered.

"But why did you join up for four more years?"

"Jacob, I joined again because it was impossible to get a job."

"But what are you going to do when the four years are up and you still can't find a job? You can't make a career out of it. *Goyisher* bums stay in the army, lazy bums . . ."

"Have some more tea and some strudel," Esther said quickly.

Both brothers ignored their mother's attempt to change the subject.

"There are no bums in the marine corps, Jacob. It happens to be the most respected branch of the service. Besides, since I didn't go to college, I don't exactly have a profession. The marines' benefits are good."

"*Mazel tov*. Where are you going to be stationed, in Washington with the President?"

"No, the Philippines."

"Couldn't you have at least stayed in the United States?"

"You go where they send you. And besides, I'm very happy about it. How else would I get to see the world?"

"Why, it's such a beautiful world?"

"I don't know yet, I haven't seen it all. When I come back I'll let you know. Now, welcome home to Jacob, Sara and the children."

"Thank you, Shlomo Sandsonitsky. I mean Sandy Sanders—that's some name. Only in America—from Shlomo of Poland to Sandy of the United States Marines."

"You're welcome, *Jack Sanders*—"

"Enough," Esther said. "Shlomo's only home on leave so let's have a little peace. Gittel, it's getting late and the children are getting tired."

Gittel got up and went to Sara. "Darling, we're all so happy you're here."

Sara sighed. "Me too," she lied.

"Tomorrow night, you'll come to my house for supper. Now let me kiss my beautiful nieces." She bent down, then looked up at Sara and Jacob. "You're still very rich." . . .

Esther was awake until very late that night. She shuddered to think how angry Jacob would be when he found out it was not Hershel who was the breadwinner but Gittel. She worked in the store and took care of the house and the children while Hershel did as little as possible. There would be many arguments that would come . . . And she worried about Jacob's future. She would gladly have given him her store, but the few bolts of cloth on her shelves barely made enough to feed and clothe her, and she had no money to offer him. Then her thoughts went to Shlomo . . . She too had been very upset when he'd come home after the war and told her he had reenlisted. However, the more she thought about it the more she realized that Shlomo was more realistic in accepting situations than Jacob. When Shlomo decided there was no future for him in the civilian world he pulled himself up by the bootstraps and did the next best thing. Well, maybe in the morning things would look a little brighter.

Three weeks later Jacob found a store.

It was way out on the fringes of Cleveland in a place called Collingwood, but the rent was cheap.

With the few dollars he had he stocked the store with the minimum amount of yardage, mostly gingham, cotton, braids, thread, pins and an assortment of ribbons. Hershel offered his opinion that Jacob would never be able to make a living with such a small inventory.

Jacob listened as Hershel went on, "If you don't have it on the shelves, you can't sell it. What if a customer walks in and asks for blue serge?"

Jacob held down his temper. He knew Hershel's apparent concern was meant to make him feel more insecure than he already did. "When I've been in business as long as you, I'll have blue serge in stock."

Hershel was enjoying himself. He knew Jacob was jealous as hell. He could tell the night they'd come to dinner at his home.

Puffing on his cigar, Hershel said, "I told you there's no reason to turn down the offer I made you, Jacob. You'll pay me back when you can. I wasn't going to charge more interest than the bank gets." He felt safe making the offer, knowing Jacob would never accept it.

Jacob made up his mind that his day would come. He wouldn't live in the back of a store forever. If he had Hershel's money, his wife and children would at least live in a house. . . .

It wasn't too long after the JACK SANDERS NOTIONS AND DRY GOODS sign went up that Jacob and Sara became aware they were living in a very anti-Semitic neighborhood.

Sara was quite nervous when a customer noticed her slight accent and asked what nationality she was. When Sara answered that she was from Belgium, the lady said that it must have been a lovely country before the war. Lovely, replied Sara. The dear lady had really only asked because she wasn't quite sure, and, she wanted Sara to understand, Collingwood prided itself on not renting or selling to Jews. Thank the Lord there weren't any in this part of town . . .

Jacob was very disturbed by this incident. Of all places they could have lived, it had to be with a bunch of Jew-haters. They were afraid it might be discovered they were Jews, and they lived too far from the kosher butchers on Euclid Street to keep a kosher house. Like it or not they were compelled to live like *goyim*. It only seemed possible to be Jacob Sandsonitsky on the lower East Side of New York. His children would grow up half-Jews and half-*goyim*. . . .

She adored the black galoshes that snapped up the calves of her pudgy legs. She loved the plaid muffler around her neck and the stocking cap she pulled over her ugly black hair. But best of all was trudging through the snow to school. At lunchtime the children sat around the big pot-bellied stove and took out their peanut butter and jelly sandwiches on white bread. Doris felt badly because mama didn't make the thick meat sandwiches on black bread anymore or give her a little cup of fruit and a thermos of hot chicken soup. When she asked why, mama said, "Eat what the other children do and don't talk about it . . . Just keep quiet, Doris."

Doris enjoyed the games the children played until the bell rang and she returned to class only reluctantly.

132

Of all the things Doris enjoyed, class was not one of them. She really hated her teacher. She asked the dumbest questions. If you cut an apple in half and gave your friend half of your apple then obviously you'd have the other half to eat for yourself. Furthermore, she didn't care at all how Jack and Jill got up the hill, nor was she interested that they were going to fetch a pail of water. Doris also knew that Cinderella wasn't Jewish. No Jewish girl would have lost her glass slipper. Her mother would have killed her. And if Old Mother Hubbard was Jewish, she wouldn't have let her children go hungry. Papa always said that children had to have a roof over their heads and food in their stomachs but Old Mother Hubbard's cupboard was always bare. . . .

Doris's teacher always seemed vaguely affronted by her questions and said the class would get to it later. So Doris was bored and spent a lot of her time making up answers to her own questions. But there was one question that bothered her, and one night she brought it up at supper.

"What's a Kike?"

Sara and Jacob stopped eating and looked at each other.

"Where did you hear that word?" Jacob asked.

"At school. The kids said that they don't like Kikes or Catholics. Is a Catholic the same as a Kike?"

"No, just eat and don't say another word," Jacob told her.

Doris was mystified by their attitude and frustrated that no one ever answered her questions. She still didn't know what a Kike or a Catholic was, but it had to be something bad, like saying "okay" instead of "yes." At age seven, it was all very confusing.

When spring came, the five of them would take the streetcar every Sunday to spend the day at Esther's, where the whole family congregated.

Jacob noticed that Hershel had put on weight and was looking very prosperous. A diamond ring flashed on his pinky finger and he smoked his long black cigar. "Twenty-five cents," he said, blowing the smoke toward Jacob. Always the same questions. How were things in Collingwood? Very good, great. Really? Nevertheless, if Jacob needed any stock, Hershel would be more than happy to sell some to him, since he knew Jacob had no credit. Then Hershel would go on to boast that he now had three machines—an automobile, a washing machine and a vacuum. "Jacob, you really should get a washing machine for Sara."

Yes, sure. Next week ... God in his wisdom should only make Hershel's tongue fall out of his mouth.

Summer descended upon them like a blast furnace.

On Saturdays Doris went with Rachel to take a piano lesson for twenty-five cents, and in order to save the carfare they walked.

After the lesson was over they bought ice cream cones and sat in an old, old cemetery on a tombstone, licking them. Delicious, Doris said. Next week she was going to get chocolate. Rachel paid no attention to her. As Doris contentedly licked her cone, her eyes wandered to the dusty moss-covered hundred-year-old tombstone and read the name and date. She asked, "I wonder who Fanny Pride was?"

Stupid Doris, always asking such crazy questions. "How would I know," Rachel answered.

"I didn't say you knew, I said I wonder."

Oh God, what a pest. "I guess she was a woman."

"Well, I know that ... Fanny's a girl's name ... I wonder if she was a mother."

"Stop wondering and eat your ice cream, it's melting."

"I think it's really nice here, it's so quiet."

"Can't you ever keep quiet? That's all you ever do is talk."

"Well, what else is a person supposed to do with their mouth?"

"Eat. Which is something you don't have a problem doing."

That was really very mean, Doris thought, and wondered when Rachel would realize that she was at least a *person* ... After all, she was almost eight years old.

Jacob sat on the short flight of steps leading to the back rooms. The heat was impossible and the flies even worse. If he bought nothing else, Jacob was going to buy a screen door. Sara was handing him a cold drink when a customer walked in.

"Good afternoon, Mr. Sanders. Did you ever see anything like it? I swear this is the hottest July I can remember."

Jacob nodded. "What can I get for you?"

"I'd like a yard of red satin ribbon."

Jacob took the ruler, measured out one yard of ribbon, put it in a small paper bag and handed it to the customer.

"How much is that?"

"Ten cents."

The lady paid and blew a wisp of hair off her wet forehead.

Jacob stood in the middle of the store, watching the woman leave. Ten cents . . . that made about a dollar for the day's earnings, and it was four in the afternoon. He looked at his hands, those enormous hands . . .

He went to the front door, slammed it closed, locked it and called out to Sara.

In a moment she stood framed in the doorway with Lillian in her arms. "Yes, Jacob, what's wrong?"

"Nothing's wrong. Everything's suddenly right . . . we're getting out of here and moving back to California."

"Oh, my God. Jacob, you really mean it?"

"Do I look like Hershel? I don't sell ribbons for ten cents a yard."

"How will you get the money?"

"I'll beg, borrow or steal, but I'm getting out of this damn store." . . .

From the goodness of his heart, Hershel bought Jacob's stock for twenty-five cents on the dollar.

Jacob had eighty dollars. He moved Sara and the children to live with his mother until he could find a job and an apartment in Oakland. He would send for them soon. . . .

CHAPTER TWENTY-FOUR

THIS TIME the train ride had been slightly different than the first. It was still long and exhausting, but it was terribly lonely without Sara and the children.

When he reached Oakland he stood on the platform watching other passengers going their separate ways with the families and friends who had come to greet them.

Jacob stood alone and felt the past come back to haunt him. Once before in his life he had waited on a platform with no one to greet him. How old was he? Seven? It was Frankfurt, but this was Oakland, California, U.S.A.

He picked up his paper suitcase and walked out of the station. He found a rooming house on Jackson Street near Seventh, where the dregs lived, he knew. But after he'd bought the train ticket for thirty dollars he had only fifty left . . . he couldn't be too choosey.

The next morning he went to the Chevrolet plant where

he'd once worked. They weren't hiring. This wasn't war-time.

For one whole week he wandered around, but it seemed there was simply no work.

His loneliness was so unbearable that at the end of the week he even went to see Molly. She had opened another junk store with the money she'd salvaged from the furniture liquidation, and for her life had once again fallen into a familiar pattern.

Jacob sat with her now at the round table in the back of the store and drank a cup of tea.

"For some people life just doesn't work out," she said, thinking of Louie. "My God, the mistakes we make and the regret we have."

"That's true," he answered. "But people make their own breaks—and I'm going to make mine, believe me."

Molly shook her head. If Jacob had read the letter she'd received only yesterday from Sara, he wouldn't be so full of himself. It began . . .

Dear mama,
  I'm so miserable, sometimes I want to die . . . What kind of a life is this? My mother-in-law isn't the angel Jacob thinks she is, and I know she isn't happy with us here. Gittel's children are more important to her than mine, and of course it hurts my feelings. Hershel says terrible things about Jacob. I know he does it deliberately to try to antagonize me against my husband. He says Jacob will never amount to anything, that he has no ambition, that I should never expect anything to change, that Jacob is hopeless. Although I try not to listen, it leaves doubts in my mind. I'm simply desperate, mama. How long can I go on like this? If you can help, I beg you, mama, try . . .

"Jacob, have you heard from Sara?"

"Sure."

"What does she say?"

"That she misses me and hopes we can be together soon."

"And?"

"And what?"

"Nothing . . . Do you think it'll be long before you find a job?"

"Listen, I'm doing the best I can."

"How long can Sara go on like this? It's hard for her, Jacob."

"And what about me? You don't think I miss my wife and

136

children? I'm alone, but at least she has the family in Cleveland. Who do I have?"

"Jacob, if I ask you something, you won't get mad?"

He shrugged.

"I have a few dollars. Please let me give it to you to bring Sara—"

"Thank you very much, but I have to do this on my own. No more loans, thank you."

"This is not a loan . . ."

"That's very kind, but I know your life too. Save it for your old age. Besides . . . somehow, I know I'm going to make it—"

"Well, *mazel tov,* no one would be happier than me." . . .

On the way back to his room, he stopped in front of the pool hall and watched the men queuing up. Out of sheer loneliness he walked in, sat down and watched. He turned to the man sitting next to him. "You play?"

"Yeah, do you?"

"I have, once or twice."

"Would you like a go at it?"

"No thanks, I'm afraid I'd be a pigeon. But I like to watch."

"And I like to play. Takes my mind off a hard day's work."

"Yeah, what do you do? What kind of job have you got?"

"I work for a meat packing plant."

"Do they need any extra help? I need a job."

"I don't know, why don't you try?"

"I will. It's something I never even thought of. By the way, my name is Jack Sanders," Jacob said, holding out his hand.

"Smitty. Nice to know you. I'm going to get a beer, feel like one?"

"Sure." Jacob took out a dime and handed it to his new friend, who soon returned with two foaming mugs.

As they sat and drank, Jacob began to feel a little better. He questioned Smitty about his job and the name of the place where he worked.

"The Hayward Meat Packing Company."

"How long have you been there?"

"Since I was a kid."

"I think I'll go tomorrow morning. By the way, is it important to have experience?"

Smitty laughed. "When they bring those cows up on the chute, all you got to know is how to hit 'em over the head."

That notion didn't exactly appeal to him, but still... "Thanks a lot, Smitty. I really appreciate this... maybe I'll see you tomorrow."

"Sure, Sanders, I have lunch out in the back lot. Let me know how it turns out."

Jacob left the beer, said goodnight and went back to his room. He could hardly wait for morning to come. . . .

God was good to him. He got a job with the Hayward Meat Packing Company, starting salary twenty-five dollars a week.

He lived frugally but it seemed impossible to bring Sara and the kids out. How could he rent a house and furnish it? As little as it took to keep him, he still had to pay rent, eat three meals a day and pay for a streetcar. He sent a little money to Sara every week, but at the end of the month he was lucky if he had fifteen dollars left.

After three months, he could no longer stand the separation and the letters from Sara had been more and more openly unhappy.

Finally he forced himself to go to Molly. "If you still want to, I'll take you up on your offer, but under one condition. The money is only a loan. I have to bring Sara and the kids out, I have to—"

Quickly, Molly got up, went to the secret drawer and took out two hundred dollars and handed it to Jacob.

"God bless you, Jacob," she said.

Jacob nodded uneasily as he looked at the money in his hand.

He wanted to give it back and run away. But the loneliness overpowered his reluctance to accept her charity.

He put the money in his pocket and forced himself to thank her.

CHAPTER TWENTY-FIVE

THE LONELINESS of his childhood had never really left him. When he saw Sara and the children getting off the train, he realized more than at any other time of his exile how desperately he had missed them.

He had taken two rooms and there Sara and the children had finally come home to him. . . .

When Sara registered Rachel and Doris in school she was shocked. If they were afraid to admit they were Jews in Collingwood, here she knew that was one fear she could eliminate. The neighborhood was more than half black, with a few Chinese and only a token number of whites. Boarding schools and Brussels seemed very far away. How strange, Sara thought, as she walked back to her rooms with Lillian holding her hand. After seeing this school she wondered if she had been so terribly abused after all. But as she recalled the longing she had felt and her frustration at not having anyone to guide her she decided that children were better off with their mother, no matter how modest the family circumstances, than being alone in a fancy school. Her children would grow up better adjusted, with fewer fears than she'd had. . . .

Jimmy Smith's one claim to fame was the announcement of his birth in the Chicago *Tribune*. He grew up in a house with too many siblings, too little money and a mother whose affections were devoted to the wares of the local bootlegger. His father worked at the stockyards and at age ten, when Jimmy decided it was time to get out and make it on his own, he followed in his father's footsteps.

By the time Jimmy was nineteen there was very little about the cattle business he didn't know. Jimmy had never planned to leave Chicago, but then he had never planned to get married and start a family either. He confided to his father, "I knocked up a girl and I've got to get the hell out of Chicago." With his father's blessings he hopped a freight train and wound up in Oakland, California.

He looked for the only kind of employment he knew, and went to work for the Hayward Meat Packing Company.

The most important day in the life of one Jacob Sandsonitsky, better known as Jack Sanders, was the night he walked into a pool room and met Jimmy Smith, better known as Smitty. . . .

After working at the Hayward Meat Packing Company for three months, Jacob decided he wasn't going to spend the rest of his life hitting cows over the head. At lunch one day he said to Smitty, "How'd you like to be my partner? I'm going into business for myself."

Smitty looked at him and laughed. "You got to be out of

your mind. You know what it takes to get into the cattle business? What the hell have I got?"

"It's not money I need but someone who knows the business inside out."

"You're nuts. How would we make it without dough?"

"I've got some, enough to start."

"Start what?"

"I've been looking and I've been listening. Buying calves is the cheapest and that's where we begin."

Smitty wasn't laughing now. After a long moment he said, "It's a hell of a long shot, but what do I have to lose? It's your dough and a job like this I can get anywhere. Okay, Jack, you've got yourself a partner."

Tomorrow was Thanksgiving. Tears stung Sara's eyes as she looked at the two-burner hot plate and the crayon drawing of a big turkey that Doris had made for her and Jacob. She put aside the drawing as well as her painful feelings when the door opened.

"You're home early, Jacob?"

He kissed her on the cheek, took off his jacket, went to the small corner sink and began to wash his face.

"Jacob, why are you home so early?"

Wiping his hands on the towel, he looked at her and smiled. "I just quit my job."

For a moment all she could do was look at him. "You . . . what? Jacob, what's *wrong* with you? You must be crazy—"

He sat down alongside her and took her hand. "No, I'm not crazy. This is the first time in my life I'm absolutely completely sane."

"I don't know what you're talking about. How are you going to make a living?"

"I'm going into business for myself."

"With what, what kind of a business?"

"I told you I work with a guy by the name of Smitty. You know the story of how I got the job. Smitty and I are going into business for ourselves."

"You can't be serious, Jacob. It takes money to get into business."

"I have to start somewhere. We're going to buy calves in the country, slaughter them ourselves and sell to the Chinese butchers. They're not too particular what they buy."

"I think it's crazy, absolutely crazy. How are we going to live in the meantime?"

"With your mother."

140

That meant still another school for her children . . . and another move to the back of a store. For a moment she looked at Jacob and saw Louie's face. Gamblers . . . "You're sure you know what you're doing, Jacob?"

"You bet. Sara, do you believe in fate?"

"At this point I don't believe in anything."

"Well, maybe you don't, but I do. The luckiest thing that ever happened to me was the night I met Smitty. Sara, as there's a God above us, I'm not just going to make a living, I'm going to be rich—"

Yes, it was Louie speaking, from Johannesburg, Brussels, Monte Carlo. . . .

This time he felt no guilt or shame when he asked Molly to loan him an additional three hundred dollars. She'd get all her money back, plus interest.

He bought a secondhand Dodge truck and moved Sara and the children to Molly's place.

Doris and Lillian loved the excitement of living in the back of grandma's store—especially Doris. She loved to wander through the maze of junk and make up stories about the people in the old tintypes in the gold oval frames. She loved to take Lillian to Fremont Park to show her off, and then go to the United Biscuit Company, where huge bags of broken cookies were sold for a nickel. Broken or not, they were delicious.

But best of all were Saturdays, when she *shlepped* Lillian to the movies, where the serials started at ten in the morning. Doris was always the first in line, grasping the brown paper bag filled with sandwiches, sponge cake and fruit to be eaten at noon while William S. Hart and his horse were falling off a cliff. She was madly in love with William S. Hart because he was so brave. Somehow he always seemed to defy the Indians —at least twenty at a time—while jumping from one side of the horse to the other. She wondered if William S. Hart was Jewish. If only she could look like Mary Pickford. Doris wondered if Mary Pickford was Jewish . . . .

The one cloud in Doris's life was school. She still found the classwork boring. Even worse was that the teacher's response to her questions had passed from annoyance to studied avoidance. Well, maybe next year would be better.

Doris was not alone with her crosses to bear. Sara could not understand how Rachel could be so different from the other children, so difficult to handle and so moody. Rachel was even less happy with their move than Sara was. She hated sleeping with Doris and despised living in the back of grandma's store. There was absolutely no dignity in living with all that junk in the store. She remembered the beautiful furniture her mother had sold before they first came to California and how her mother had missed it. But everything had changed so much, especially mama. If Rachel said the least little thing mama didn't like she was slapped, but what made mama the angriest was that Rachel wouldn't give her the satisfaction of crying, no matter how much it hurt. When she cried, it was alone. How could her mother discuss her so openly with grandma? If your own mother didn't think you were anything, then how much of a person could you be? Mama criticized everything she did. She was never paid a compliment, and everything she did was taken for granted. Nobody knew how lonely she was . . . There didn't seem to be anyone who understood. And since she'd grown up, even papa and she had grown apart . . . .

At thirteen, the only comfort in her otherwise joyless and friendless life was the Fulton Theater, where she went alone on Saturdays. The make-believe world seemed more real than her own. She felt a strange closeness to the actors on the stage, as if she were more related to them than to her own family, and she found herself becoming immersed in their make-believe lives.

When the matinee was over she would leave with a strange sadness. Going back to grandma's junk store depressed her after the magical places she had just seen, so she usually delayed the return home as long as possible. She would walk down the street to the corner of Fourteenth and Harrison, turn into the Clinton Cafeteria and wait in line with a tray. Walking close to the counter she would look at the different colors of shimmering Jell-O topped with snowy white whipped cream and the crisp salads garnished with small plump tomatoes and black olives. There were enchiladas in large oblong steel pans, creamed chicken and garden peas on the steam tables. It was all so serene, so tranquil, so *different* from home . . .

This time she had the creamed chicken and a square of corn bread. It was worth the long walk to and from school every day to save up the nickels for this treat. When at last she returned to the junk store she walked to her room without a word of greeting to anyone and shut the door. She wanted to preserve the calm, dreamy feeling, but peace was not to be hers for long.

Sara stood framed in the doorway. "How dare you not let

142

me know when you come home. Do you care at *all* how hard I work? Now get up and come and have supper—"

"I'm not hungry."

"You're not hungry? Fine. You think you're punishing me? Well, we'll see . . . just wait till your father comes home—"

Sara slammed the door and went into the kitchen where she found Molly. "She's impossible, completely impossible. Mama, how did I ever have such a child?"

"She's only thirteen . . ."

When I was thirteen, Sara thought, I would have given the world to have a mother who cared where I was and how I spent my time. Sara felt as if her life was choking her. She was still going to be a better mother than Molly had been, but she wasn't about to get any further into the trap than she already was. She was pregnant, but this was one child she wasn't going to have.

That night Jacob was met at the door by a very upset Molly. "Jacob, I don't know what to do, Sara's locked herself in the bedroom and refuses to speak to me or come out—"

"Why? What happened?"

"I don't know, she takes everything so to heart—"

"Did you have another one of your fights?"

"No. Rachel upset her but I really don't know what the child did that was so serious. In fact, Jacob, Sara's been so nervous lately. I know it's not easy all of us living here in such conditions . . ."

He hurried back to their room and knocked on the door. "Sara, let me in."

No answer.

He was about to insist when he heard the key turn. Opening the door, he looked at Sara's red-stained eyes and watched as she crossed the room to sit on their bed. It wasn't Rachel that had upset her, not really. She couldn't understand how hard he was working to make life better for them, that this bad time wasn't going to last forever. Something down deep in him knew what she was feeling . . . after all, he'd felt it himself many times . . .

"Sara, I'm trying, and things will get better—"

"It has nothing to do with your trying or not trying."

"Then what was it Rachel did that upset you?"

"She upsets me most of the time, but she's not my most important problem."

"What then?"

Her eyes seared through him. "I'm pregnant."

For one brief moment Jacob wanted to hold Sara very

143

close and tell her how happy he was, but that moment was lost in Sara's next words.

"Tomorrow I'm having an abortion."

Jacob stood rooted to the floor, speechless. She was destroying . . . no, killing, something that was a part of him too. The decision, by God, was not only hers. "Oh no you're not. I swear, Sara, if you do this I'll never forgive you . . . I mean it . . ."

"Then I'll have to live without your forgiveness. I will not have this child or any other. Three is enough, I've suffered enough for them. I won't sacrifice myself any more. *No more* . . ."

Jacob paced the floor, then turned, looked at Sara and said quietly, "Please, Sara, don't do this . . . it might even be a boy . . ."

Was that the only consideration? Did he expect her to keep having babies until they hit the jackpot? "No, Jacob, I will *not* have this child."

He sat down on the straight-backed wooden chair and put his hands over his eyes so Sara would not see the tears.

"I need fifty dollars, Jacob."

He sat for a moment longer remembering the night Gittel's first child was born and his words to Hershel. "You have a son. When you die there will be someone to say *Kaddish* for you." He got up, counted out the money and placed it on the dresser, and left the room without a word.

For three weeks Jacob stayed away and roamed the countryside, trying to come to terms with his bitterness over Sara's decision, and for three weeks Sara did almost nothing but cry.

The abortion had been done in the back of a dirty barbershop and for several days the bleeding was so profuse that Molly thought Sara might die. She too had pleaded with Sara not to go through with it, but no amount of reason or logic did any good.

As for Jacob, to all outward appearances he was a man of great physical and emotional strength; no one would have guessed his deep, intense fear and loneliness. When he finally did come back Sara was hugely relieved. She'd felt as lost and helpless without him as he had felt without her. Although she would never admit it, she had felt misgivings about taking a life Jacob had so wanted and she now lived with an unexpected burden of guilt. The child had been a boy—would have been—but of course she could never let Jacob know.

144

They would never be able to reveal their feelings to each other, and it was more than a week after Jacob's return before they could even face or speak to each other. Eventually conversations around the table with the children began to draw them into meaningless talk. If their lives did not always run smoothly and if there were times when they grew apart, nothing would change the great need they still had for each other.

CHAPTER TWENTY-SIX

SMITTY TAUGHT Jacob every trick, every piece of territory, which ranchers to buy from, what to look for when evaluating a calf.

Calves were three dollars a head, so Jack's two hundred dollars bought a truckload. There was just one hitch. Smitty told Jacob that they had to do something a little irregular— their own slaughtering. The cost of sending the calves to be slaughtered would eat into the profits and they could wind up with practically nothing. Smitty suggested they rent a barn or a garage in a remote place, so they wouldn't have the law on their tails.

They found the perfect place in Emeryville, way back in the hills. Smitty and Jacob slaughtered the calves, hung them just long enough to drain the blood and get rid of the body heat, and the next day sold whole carcasses to the Chinese butchers, who were no more impressed with government regulations than were Smitty and Jacob.

The hides were sold for four dollars a skin to a tannery, the innards for fifty cents a pound to a feed mill, and the hearts, livers, kidneys, heads and hooves brought an additional seventy-five cents a pound. That was the beautiful part about the cattle business; nothing was wasted. From an initial cost of three dollars per head, the total yield realized a profit of twenty-eight dollars.

At the end of three months Jacob put seven hundred and fifty dollars into Smitty's sweating palm and told him that the partnership was terminated.

At first Smitty was furious, but he couldn't really say that Jacob was being unfair. Smitty had made a lot of money, although he hadn't invested a dime. Besides, Smitty wasn't one to be tied down to such a large responsibility, and the work and the living conditions were grueling. Jack was a tough guy to work for. Everything had to be his way, and he was like a mechanical man who never knew when to stop. Smitty missed the pool hall and the occasional glass of beer. So, with all things considered, he didn't feel he'd been given such a raw deal. The partnership was terminated, but not the friendship.

Jacob decided he'd learned all Smitty could teach him, the rest would come from his own acquired experience. Smitty went back to work at the Hayward Meat Packing Company and now Jacob did the work of two. He slaughtered and skinned his own calves, delivered to the trade, traveled through the countryside to Salinas, Modesto, Watsonville... he stopped at every farm along the way.

In the next few months, he learned everything that remained to be learned about the business. At long last Jacob had come out of the dark tunnel, into the warm California sun.

If Jacob felt guilty about ending the partnership with Smitty he still knew it was a wise decision. Now all the profits were his. He had earned them and now he would use them. Finally he would have a house of his own.

Jacob's supreme moment came when he announced, "Sara, I found a house in West Oakland."

Sara's heart pounded. Was it possible that she would stop living in back of stores? She was too stunned to respond, but her thoughts were clearly written on her face.

Jacob smiled. "It's true. Come, Sara, get the kids and tell your mother to close the store. I want you to see it."

There was such excitement as the family piled into the truck that Jacob laughed out loud. As they drove along Fruitvale Boulevard Sara asked him, "How did you find this house?"

"Funny how things fall in my lap, like with Smitty. I stopped for coffee and met a butcher I know. He happened to tell me his mother died and left him a house. I asked him if he wanted to sell and he said yes—as soon as possible, because he doesn't want to pay the county taxes. I went to see it and all I can say is it's the most beautiful house I ever saw in my life."

Her heart pounded even harder. "If it's so gorgeous, why is he selling it?"

"Because he's an old bachelor and doesn't need all that space."

Sara relaxed. "How much did you pay for it?"

"Twenty-five hundred dollars."

"Jacob, we don't have that kind of money—"

Jacob had it, but he was careful not to divulge too much to Sara. Washington Heights was still very fresh in his memory. "That's true, but I'm giving him a down payment and a note for the balance . . ."

At this point Sara was no longer listening. The only thing she could think of was being her own mistress and of the hell she'd gone through living in such close quarters with mama and the children with never a moment of privacy, nowhere to hide—the same as it had been with Esther. It was about time she took charge of her own life.

Deep in thought, she was startled when Jacob came to a halt in front of the house. Everyone got out of the truck. Sara couldn't believe her eyes. The small dingy houses in the neighborhood only emphasized the charm of the lovely old two-story wooden house. Leading to the front porch were four wide stairs and a banister on each side. The peaked roof was trimmed with filigree moldings.

Jacob took the key from his pocket and opened the door wide.

The moment Sara entered she wanted to get down on her hands and knees and kiss the floor. Breathlessly, she looked around.

The square hall was paneled in gray gumwood. Her gaze wandered to the heavy newel post and banister leading up to the second floor.

Jacob beamed as he showed his wife and her mother through the house.

The livingroom was spacious, with a tall wood mantel flanked on either side by round columns. Between the columns a mirror reflected Sara's image. She could visualize it in winter, could almost smell the scent of burning logs. She followed Jacob into the adjoining diningroom where the wood panels towered to within two feet of the twelve-foot ceiling, ending with a cornice that ran around the entire room. How beautiful, Sara thought. She could already visualize decorative plates along the wall. The built-in buffet with the leaded glass doors must have held the previous owner's best china.

Jacob hurried Sara and Molly into the enormous kitchen. The brown linoleum would have to be replaced, Sara thought, but she smiled as she recalled their first flat with the lime green kitchen and yellow linoleum. This was a far cry from Washington Heights.

Jacob led her to the glassed-in back porch, where an old Maytag washer still remained.

Molly summoned her back to the kitchen. "Look, Sara," she said, sliding back the narrow wall panel. Sara looked from the kitchen side into the diningroom. The opening was between the upper cabinet and the counter of the buffet.

Sara smiled at her mother. "Jacob was right, it is beautiful."

Molly shook her head as she remembered the house in Monte Carlo. When had she ever really forgotten? Sara thinks she's the only one that's ever been deprived, she thought, and I also remember having to sell my flats so Sara could have this. She tried to dismiss the jealousy. She wanted Sara to have this. Still, Jacob had never mentioned giving her back the money he owed her . . .

They could hear Doris and Lillian running from room to room upstairs. When Doris saw her mother come to the second floor she said breathlessly, "Five bedrooms! Which one can I have, mama?"

"We'll see . . ." Sara said walking past her, scarcely hearing, thinking of the past, the future . . .

Of course, that's so like mama, Rachel thought. How nice if mama had said, "What room would you like, Doris, which one would please you?" But mama was too concerned with mama. Poor papa . . . well, at least she wouldn't have to sleep in the same room with Doris anymore. Whichever room she got would be hers and no one would invade her privacy.

Rachel grimaced when she heard Sara's voice rising at Lillian, who had climbed into the bathtub and was splashing in the running water. "What are you *doing?* Oh, God, that's all I need now is for you to come down with a cold, I don't have enough to do—"

"Everyone come up quick," Doris called from the attic. "Look," Doris said, holding up the lid of the large cretonne-covered chest.

The family looked inside. There were satin dresses, wide-brimmed plumed hats, veils, beads and fans. It was Doris's treasure chest . . . hers.

"Jacob, we'll have to clean this junk out."

"No," Doris cried out, "it's mine. I want it . . . please."

Sara looked at her. "It's a bunch of old rags. God knows how long they've been here . . ."

"I don't care."

Hesitating for a moment, Sara finally said, "All right, but

148

don't touch them until I take a look. They might have moths or lice or God knows what . . ."

Sara didn't hear Doris' thank-you. She was looking about from one object to another. Four white wicker chairs, an old rocker, three oval tables with white marble tops, a red velvet sofa with a broken leg, a dresser, gold-leaf frames and family portraits . . . Is that what our lives become at the end, she wondered, a bunch of discarded portraits? Quickly she dismissed the thought; she was being altogether too philosophical today.

"Jacob, is the man going to take all these things?"

"No, whatever's here goes with the house."

"I see . . . well, what do you think we should do with it all?"

"Keep it, what else?"

"But only until we can buy new, you mean . . ."

"Of course. You like the house, Sara?" He knew she did but he wanted to hear her say it.

"Yes, Jacob, yes. The furniture's not quite what I want, but it will be all right when I'm finished——"

"I know you always had good taste, Sara. Now, you haven't seen everything yet," he said as he started downstairs with the family following. He took them down the driveway and showed them the garage and adjoining building which had once been a small barn. To the side was a small garden. Although it was now overgrown with weeds, Sara could see the roses and the daffodils.

"It's beautiful, Jacob. Well, you finally got a little *mazel*," Molly said.

"You make your own luck," Jacob answered.

"Luck helps a little on its own," Sara said, defending her mother.

"You think what you want, but all the luck Jacob Sandsonitsky got, he made." . . .

The rest of the week Sara and the girls scrubbed and cleaned every nook and cranny. The old pots and pans were sterilized, then placed in the cupboard.

Dishes and silver were no problem. Molly had more than she'd ever sell. Nothing matched, but Sara was more than content to wait.

The windows were washed with vinegar-water and dried with newspaper. As Sara washed the stained-glass window on the front door she remembered how Molly had shattered Mrs. Bromberg's glass door. How she hated Mrs. Bromberg and her hypocrisy. Hershel was just as hypocritical, but if he could see where they were living he'd eat his heart out. For all his showing off, Gittel was still living in the back of the store. Sara smiled. She had married the right man. For now . . .

CHAPTER TWENTY-SEVEN

SARA BEGAN preparing for Passover. Although it had been a long time since she had kept kosher, Passover still had special meaning.

Jacob brought home a crate of fresh farm eggs, a sack of onions and potatoes. He drove Sara to Klein's on Seventh Street, where she bought *matzo . . . matzo* meal and wine. Then they went to Rothstein's for the chicken and the fish.

That afternoon, as the huge pot of carrots, onions and fishheads were bubbling, she took a moment to sit down for a cup of tea and a piece of strudel. After today all the bread and cake would have to be finished or thrown out; for the next week only *matzo* and *matzo* meal could be used.

After tea, she began making the fish paste into perfect oval shapes. With that complete, she carefully dropped each one into the boiling stock, covered the pot and lowered the flame. The aroma was sheer heaven. Next she set herself to the task of cakemaking. With a hand beater, she beat the frothy whites until they stood in stiff peaks, then folded them into the egg yolks and added the sugar and *matzo* meal. While the sponge cakes were baking, she cleaned the chickens that she would cook the next morning.

Today Sara was happy. Life was good and it promised to be better. Sara had a home.

When the doorbell rang, Sara wiped her hands on her apron and went to the front door. When she opened it she could hardly believe what she saw. "*Shlomo*, my God . . . when did you get here?"

"This morning." He laughed and took her more than ample body in his arms.

"I'm so excited, oh, Shlomo . . ."

"Well, are you just going to let me stand here?"

"*No.* Come in, come in." She took his hand and led him to the kitchen. "Sit down, Shlomo, I'll get you something to eat—"

"Thank you, Sara, but I had lunch."

"A cup of tea?"

"That would be nice. It's been a long time since I sat in someone's kitchen and had a cup of tea . . . You look wonderful, Sara."

"And you too." Putting on the water, she went on, "Tell me about yourself, everything . . ."

"Everything? You sure you want to know?" They laughed.

Sara smiled wickedly. "You know what I mean. Why didn't you let us know you were coming?"

"By the time you would have received a letter I would already be here."

"Are you here to stay?"

"Yes."

"You mean you're discharged from the marines?"

"No, I was just transferred back to the States. I'm stationed at Mare Island."

"How long will you be there?"

Shlomo laughed. "The marines don't take you into their confidence—you go where they send you. But I have a feeling I'll be here for a while."

"But you don't have to go back today?"

"No, I'm on leave for three days."

"Oh, thank God. Then you'll stay here with us, Shlomo."

"I'd love that . . ."

Sara poured the tea and put a plate of cakes on the table. "Please eat the strudel, I really hate throwing it out. Tomorrow's Passover, you know . . ."

"I know." Taking a sip of tea, Shlomo looked across the table. "I can see you're happy, Sara."

"Yes." She sighed. "This is the first time I've really ever had a home."

"It's lovely and you deserve it."

"Well, thank you, life hasn't been so easy for any of us."

"And Jacob?"

"I think he's the happiest and busiest man in the world."

"I'm glad. I always knew Jacob would make it."

"He's making a good living. Of course, nothing is perfect, Shlomo. Jacob's inclined to be rather difficult when it comes to money . . ."

"I suppose when you've been poor all your life, Sara, it can get very frightening to part with money."

"For some people—"

"Well, I don't know, Sara, I always saw something very special in Jacob."

"Special I don't know about, but I guarantee you no one

151

works harder. I really didn't think he was so smart. I suppose you're right, Shlomo. In his way he *is* special. But then, so are you. If things had been different for you, you'd have made a lot out of yourself. I know you always wanted to go to college—"

"Tell me about the children."

"Well, they're very nice little girls . . . although Rachel is a little difficult . . . It's hard to believe that a mother shouldn't be able to understand her own child but she's . . . well, defiant and quite stubborn, keeps to herself . . . I don't know who she takes after, but in some ways she is quite a lot like her father . . . I don't know, Shlomo, they all have a lot more than we ever had. A mother and father to provide for them—"

"And the other two?"

"Doris is . . . what can I say? She hates school, she's no student . . . Doris has two loves—talking and going to the movies . . ."

"And the little one?"

"Not so little anymore. She goes to kindergarten . . . Listen, what can I say? They're children. Now, tell me, Shlomo, have you met anyone?"

"I've met a lot."

"But no one special?"

"In the marines you don't meet the kind of girls you'd want to bring home to mama. Besides, I'm not looking to settle down. Now, tell me about your mother. You must be thrilled to be together finally . . ."

As Sara went on, Shlomo thought how much she had changed from that sad, beautiful young girl who had first come to live with them. Although he still loved her deeply, there was an underlying discontent in her that disturbed him. She loved her children and yet she spoke of them as if they were a burden—unlike Gittel, who thought the sun and moon set on her children. Sara didn't have it any harder than Gittel, but she seemed to dwell on her own hardships and sacrifices. He hoped it was just his imagination, but he suspected it wasn't . . .

Sara heard the sound of the truck turning into the driveway. "It's Jacob. Wait till he sees you—"

When Jacob walked into the kitchen and saw Shlomo he was speechless. He put down the boxes he was carrying and took Shlomo around the shoulders and they embraced. For a moment they were back in Esther's restaurant . . . I knew some day you'd come back. Mama always said you'd come home . . . Jacob released his brother and looked at his new uniform. All thoughts of his aversion for it were forgotten in his joy at seeing his brother.

"When did you get here?"

"This morning."

"I can't get over it. You're home to stay?"

"Well, not exactly, but I'll be stationed Stateside for a while."

Jacob's disappointment showed. "Well, one of these days when you get the craziness out of your system, you'll come into my business."

It wasn't all that crazy, Shlomo thought, better than he would have done in the civilian world. If he stayed in the marines he'd have a pension for the rest of his life and the experience he'd had was something money couldn't buy. The world was a big place and he'd seen a great deal of it . . . these last few years the Philippines, Singapore, Siam and the Far East. His life had widened, but Jacob wouldn't be too interested . . . "Sara was telling me how much you love your business and that you're making a good living."

"Better than I ever thought. I paid off the house as well as the loan from Sara's mother. The important thing is to stay *out* of debt. You got to have money to make money and if we're careful, as there's a God in heaven, I'm going to make a barrel."

"There's that much money in meat?"

"You bet, but the real money's not in calves, it's in cattle. Next week I'm going to buy my first cows."

"You sound really excited, Jacob."

"Why not? Look at the partner I'm going to have." Jacob beamed at his younger brother.

"Some partner, with my great capital, you'll become a millionaire overnight."

"I'll become a millionaire anyway. It's you I need, not the money."

The conversation was interrupted as Doris came bounding into the kitchen with Lillian not far behind.

It all smelled so delicious, but when she saw her uncle she forgot even the delights of Passover.

"Uncle Shlomo!" she screamed, and flew into his open arms.

He kissed her and held her chubby body. "You're such a big girl now and so beautiful. I would never have recognized you."

She was beautiful? Nobody had told her that before. "Thank you, I'm so happy to see you."

"Me too. And this is the baby?"

Doris watched as Shlomo picked up Lillian. For a moment she was jealous. When she grew up, she would marry him. She loved him even more than she loved William S. Hart. And besides, he was her relative . . . .

When Rachel opened the front door and started for her room Sara called out, "Rachel, I have a surprise."

"What?"

"If I tell, it wouldn't be a surprise."

"Let me put my books away first."

Sara grimaced. Why couldn't she ever do what she was asked? "Leave your books on the stairs and come down."

Reluctantly, Rachel did as mama requested. When she saw her uncle, there was genuine surprise on her face. He was the handsomest man she'd ever seen—except for papa. Her heart beat peculiarly and her knees nearly buckled as he took her into his arms. Slightly frightened of her feelings, she shyly returned the embrace, then awkwardly stood looking at him without knowing what to say.

He held her at arm's length. She was exquisite, so tall and slim. She had Jacob's blond hair and startlingly blue eyes, and her skin was as translucent as fine porcelain. "I can't get over you, Rachel. You're not only beautiful but you're already a young lady. I almost forgot that you were thirteen."

"Fourteen, this year," Rachel answered, lowering her eyes in embarrassment.

"All right, Rachel. Go change your clothes and come right down. I want you to help," Sara said.

Looking up into Shlomo's eyes, for once she was grateful for mama's command. She ran up the stairs.

The next day Jacob showed Shlomo the stores he sold to and began to explain his business. He told him about how he and Smitty had started, the problems he'd had, the hardships and how he had conquered them. He confided that although it was illegal, they slaughtered their own calves.

"Not that anything was ever easy, but this time, Shlomo, I really worked. In the beginning I didn't have the price for a room, so even in the dead of winter I slept in the back of the truck and froze my ass off. But it was worth it. You know how much money I have in the bank?"

"No, Jacob, how much?"

"Five thousand dollars."

154

"That's a lot of money."

"At one time I would have thought it was a fortune, but money's strange. The more you make the more you need if you're going to get ahead, keep going . . . It's not really very much, Shlomo. I'd hardly call myself a rich man."

"Sure sounds like a lot of money to me."

"It is, but not compared to what I'm going to make. And this I promise you, Shlomo, no matter what I have to do, one day I'm going to own a plant of my own. My only problem is with Sara."

"In what way?"

"She refuses to understand that the money I have now is the capital I need to build on. She wants to furnish the house but that's a luxury I can't afford to give her now. To be honest, Shlomo, I don't have the easiest life with her. She doesn't understand that the business has to grow, has to provide us with some security before she can start spending every cent I make. So I have to be careful what I tell her about the business."

"You've changed, Jacob."

"Sure I have. You know something, Shlomo? I never told her this, but when I slaughtered my first calf I threw up . . . I was sick for a week. But I had to forget, not think about it." For a moment the echoes of the past came back . . . forget it's a man you're fighting, fight for love, fight for Lotte . . . "I had to keep remembering the kids and Sara and our future."

"And now?"

"It's easier now. You have to get pretty hard if you want to survive. Say . . . who knows that better than you? What about the war? I bet it's tough to kill a man, even if he *is* the enemy—"

Shlomo didn't answer. He wouldn't tell Jacob now, but he was not going into business with him. He was going to reenlist.

CHAPTER TWENTY-EIGHT

LIFE, IN its inexorable fashion, went on.

Molly's death affected Jacob more than he would have imagined. It wasn't, truth to tell, that he missed her so much as that his own childhood fear of death came back to haunt him, and he began to reflect on his own mortality. Remembering his childhood nightmares, he refused to allow the girls

155

to attend the funeral. Sara was so devastated that her protests were subdued, and her bereavement lasted for a longer time than was customary. She was inconsolable, and now remembered Molly only as the mother she would have liked her to have been.

With Molly's death, Sara had only her children to cling to. Jacob was consumed with his work and the closer he came to achieving his goals the further apart he and Sara seemed to grow. He was away much of the time now in Oregon, Nevada, Wyoming and Montana, where he bought cattle on speculation and then sold them to the stockyards in South San Francisco.

Jacob was, in fact, so preoccupied that he had little time to notice that his children were growing up in rather odd directions. Nor did he seem to feel the same devotion toward Gittel and his mother. He responded less frequently to their letters, although he always remembered to enclose a small check. . . .

Thursdays were especially difficult for Sara. As soon as the children were off to school, she started with the heavy cleaning and then would bathe, dress and go to Seventh Street to shop for *Shabbes,* usually returning with a heavy bundle late in the afternoon.

But this particular day she was so tired and the day so hot that she decided to do the shopping the next morning. So she wouldn't bake *challah.* They could live without it for one week. Sometimes she wondered why she even bothered to work this hard for one meal. Rachel seemed to be the only one of her children to whom it mattered, and that was probably just her perverseness. So far as Sara was concerned it was another day in the week, but Jacob insisted that at least this little bit of tradition be carried on, even though he was away so much of the time. It was his mother's cooking that was the real tradition for him, Sara thought, more than the observance of the Sabbath . . .

When she finally finished scrubbing the kitchen floor she took a large glass of orange juice and a book and went out to the backyard to relax, looking up at the branches of the linden tree, thinking about the passing years. Her mother's death had left a void in her life, in spite of all their disputes. Now she was no one's child and she had lost her one confidante. The children were growing up and she was, face it, growing weary. For all her fine education she was scrubbing floors and living in a house that was still unfurnished. Jacob's traveling and business expenses never seemed to leave

156

enough money to spend on her or the house. It was like Louie and Molly, always traveling, always spending . . . stop thinking about the past, Sara warned herself, it only makes you more unhappy. It was good advice, but Sara had never been an expert in taking advice . . . even from herself. No wonder she failed to recognize the same trait in her daughter Rachel as her own . . .

She got up and went into the house, had just begun to shell the peas when she heard the front door open. It was only three, a little early for the children to be home from school.

She started to open the door leading from the kitchen to the front hall when she heard Rachel's voice. Rachel was not alone. Slowly and carefully, Sara opened the door a crack and froze when she saw Rachel being kissed by the Cantino boy, the son of the neighborhood grocers.

Rachel stood with her eyes closed as Joe kissed her again. Then she said, "I think you'd better leave. My mother might come home—"

"Just one more kiss, Rachel."

"No, *please,* you have to go—"

"You like my kisses, don't you?"

"*Yes,* but no more. I'll see you tomorrow."

After Joe had left, Rachel leaned against the door, remembering the taste of his lips on hers. I love your sweet delicious kisses, she whispered to herself. She had never been kissed before and had just discovered how incredibly wonderful it could be.

She had no sooner walked into her room to change her clothes when Sara flung open the door and stood there, looking at her.

Rachel was surprised to see her. On Thursdays mama never came home much before five—

"How long has this been going on?" Sara asked, almost too softly.

"What?" God . . . mama must have seen her.

"Don't pretend with me, miss . . . and wipe that innocent look off your face, if you please. Now just when did you become involved with that little tramp?"

"Joe's not a tramp," Rachel snapped back. "And I resent the way you said *involved*. It sounded so nasty—"

"Nasty? Don't you think I know what goes on with—"

"Mama, nothing's going on, as you put it. He's merely been walking me home after school . . ."

Sara came close to Rachel. "Why were you home so early today?"

"We had an assembly and got out early."

"What did you do earlier?"

"Why don't you say what's on your mind and get it over with."

"I'll tell you what's on my mind. You're a little too pretty and a little too bold, but you're not going to wind up like Ruby Fox. Oh, no. Not one of my children. I've worked too hard to bring you up as a decent girl, poured my life into all of you—"

"You have a strange mind, mama. What kind of a mother *are* you to trust your children so little? Damn you, I hate you, I *hate* you . . ." She was crying openly now.

Sara grabbed her and pushed her against the wall. "So you hate me, do you? I'm sorry your father's not home to hear this. I want you to stay in your room." Sara turned and left, slamming the door.

Rachel stumbled to the bed, sobbing, and lay down. Her mother was crazy . . . it had all been so innocent. Oh, God, if she could only run away. Please God, let me die. Anything would be better than this. And so, indeed, it seemed . . .

Sara went to her room. From where she sat on the bed she could see her image in the mirror on the dressing table. What she saw was a little girl in a bedroom, screaming for help. But her mother wasn't there to help her. No one was there except Carl Bromberg, trying to rape her. She shivered at the memory. But Rachel wasn't a ten-year-old and she wasn't being raped. Sara couldn't understand it. Sex was something a woman submitted to, but from her own experience it was not something that a decent woman either talked about or ever enjoyed. Rachel was too beautiful and too impetuous for her own good. Sara would have to do something about that. She couldn't afford to send Rachel to a boarding school. So what was the next best thing . . . ?

The next morning Rachel sat nervously on a bench outside the mother superior's office at St. Frances parochial school while Sara went in alone.

"I'm very happy to meet you, Mrs. Sanders. Won't you sit down."

Sara sat in a straight-backed chair on the other side of the nun's desk. "First, I want to explain that I have a problem. As you'll see, my daughter is quite . . . shall we say, attractive? That can be a problem at her age, as I'm sure you can understand. And she's become a little too conscious of boys. I want her to go to a girls' school. She's a rather headstrong and difficult girl, she needs discipline and guidance . . ." Sara

158

saw only genuine concern in Mother Teresa's eyes. She went on. "Now before we go any further, I must tell you, we are Jewish. Is that a problem?"

"Not at all. As I told you over the telephone yesterday, Mrs. Sanders, we welcome children of all faiths. There is, of course, a question of your daughter's scholastic records. Our requirements are quite high—"

"You'll have no problem. She's a very good student—excellent, in fact. But there is one other thing, Mother Teresa, which I'm sure you'll also understand. Although we're not terribly strict about our religion we are true to our beliefs . . . I don't want Rachel to attend anything religious."

"Let me assure you there's no need to be concerned about that. We have many girls of different faiths."

"Well, thank you for your understanding. I know Rachel will prove to be a real asset."

"I'm sure. Now, I'd like to see Rachel alone." . . .

Sara had no problem with Rachel, who seemed completely indifferent to the change. At first all that concerned her was getting through the next few years until she could leave home, but as time went on she found herself loving the serenity of the convent.

The one Sara had a problem with was Jacob.

"What goes on when I'm away? I come home to find you've put Rachel in a *Catholic* school? I want her out of there and I mean this minute. Are you crazy, sending her to a convent?"

"Sit down, Jacob, and don't scream. Unfortunately, I have to make the decisions when you're not here. Now wait, let me finish. Do you know why I had to do this?"

"No, you tell me."

"Rachel has been carrying on with a boy. By accident, I found her and this boy, making love—"

"Making love? Where?"

"Here in the house. Rachel has become boy-crazy."

"Who's this boy?"

"What difference would it make if I told you?"

"I'd knock the hell out of him, that's what—"

"And if you did, there'd be another boy. Don't you see? Rachel is a girl who attracts boys. She's a beautiful girl . . ."

"What actually happened, Sara? Did he . . . ?"

"No, thank God. It didn't get to that. But he and Rachel weren't kissing like innocent children. I'm not a fool, Jacob. She's been going behind our backs and seeing this boy."

"But why did you have to send her to a convent?"

"Because she needs to go to a girls' school and because of the same old problem with money. Sending her to a convent was the cheapest. And let me tell you, Jacob, it's the best thing that could have ever happened. They know how to discipline—"

"I don't like it, Sara. I'm going to have a talk with Rachel. I'll lay down the law—"

"You think that'll do any good? Don't be silly. If she wants to do something, she'll find a way. But at least now she won't be so tempted. I make sure she comes home right after school. And I've left instructions that if she's ever absent I'm to be notified immediately."

Jacob put his elbows on the table and held his head in his hands. "My God, what's happening to our family . . ."

Sara couldn't contend with that . . . "Nothing's happening to our family. Rachel just needs watching and that's what I'm doing. If she doesn't grow up to be a decent girl, at least I'll have nothing to reproach myself for. I did what I had to do, Jacob."

"But a convent?" He shook his head.

June came and none too soon for Doris. School let out for the summer on the fifteenth. It was a time for helping mama with the jams and the jellies and for producing the little plays that Doris wrote. The chest in the attic provided most of Doris' costumes but Sara was never quite sure whether she would find her imitation lace curtains at the window or on Doris. Among all the parts that Doris played her favorite role was that of the bride. Only if it was impossible to get a kid on the block to be the groom would Doris relinquish her favorite role to play the man's. On the days of performance Doris arranged the orange-crate seats in front of the improvised stage and then took on her role as ticket-taker to collect the safety pins and marbles that were the price of admission.

Best of all, summer was a time when she could go to the little creek she had discovered and spend some time alone. It wasn't really a creek at all, but a ditch where the spring rains left an inch or two of stagnant water. The earth on either side had eroded so that the tree roots were exposed like giant gnarled spider legs. But to Doris it was the most perfect spot on earth.

She loved to lie against the earth and peer up at the lacy patterns of the tree branches against the sky. Here she could dream and think and try to sort out the puzzle of her feelings and thoughts, wondering why mama and Rachel seemed so

160

unhappy so much of the time, thinking how lovely and funny most things seemed to her. Was it wrong to feel like she did when the others seemed so unhappy...? Oh, she had her problems too, it was just that nobody seemed to notice, which in a way bothered her and in another way made her glad. It made what she felt more private, all her own. She liked that. School was her special problem, for lots of reasons. Mama thought she was stupid because of her bad grades, but the truth was that she was so much brighter than the other kids that she had no patience with her homework. Another problem was that she'd become an object of curiosity, and rejection, because she was the only Jew in the school. She was never invited to her classmates' parties, although at lunch period the girls openly discussed whose party they were going to after school. As if that weren't bad enough, her weight and her dark curly hair brought on calls of "Hey, fatso" or "hey, nigger-wool..." Between being fat, curly-haired and Jewish, she began to think of herself as a real oddity.

Things were no better at home. She had seen the anger unleashed on Rachel for fighting back and she was terribly afraid of displeasing mama, of not being loved. But unlike Rachel, who refused to be beaten down, Doris never fought back. Rebellion only increased the tensions that already existed.

Her mother loomed large in Doris's bundle of confusions. Sara swung from one extreme to the other. She either criticized and shouted or was terribly protective, fighting with papa whenever he scolded the children. It was in those moments she thought mama loved them more than papa did.

If papa complained that she should lose weight and get better grades, mama told him to mind his own damn business. He was away so often, mama said, that she was left with the responsibility of raising the family, and he had no right to interfere. Doris' emotions swayed back and forth. Papa loved her, papa loved her not; mama loved her, mama loved her not...

Papa seemed like a vague figure who came and went in the background of their lives. She felt ill at ease with him, but secretly she would have loved him to take her in his arms once in a while, the way other children's fathers did. There were things papa did that made her feel bad inside whenever she secretly felt angry at him. He never broke a promise. When she asked for a pet, papa remembered to bring home a puppy. Which was more than mama did; she never seemed to

161

keep her word. "What do you want me to bring you from downtown?" she would ask Doris and Lillian. The two girls would wait patiently after school, and when they heard the key turning in the latch they would run to greet mama and help her with the packages. They waited until mama put the things away, but there were no books for Doris, no doll for Lillian ... Mama had forgotten, as she forgot so often ... Who could believe her?

Doris could remember vividly how mama had often complained to grandma about how difficult it was raising children, about the sacrifice and the money it cost. Mama used to say that if her life had been different she would never have married so young. That always made grandma angry. She would say that she was sick and tired of being told how badly Sara had been treated as a child. Then she would go out of the house, leaving mama in tears. No sooner had grandma left than mama would cry about how alone she was ... how she had no one in the world except her mother and now to be treated this way ...

That was something Doris would never quite understand. Didn't mama have papa? And her children? It all seemed so strange. Mama would run to the telephone after her fights with grandma and plead with her not to be angry. "I'm sorry, mama, who else do I have to talk to but you?"

But it was Rachel who got the worst of mama's anger. Why? Rachel was really so nice. Doris would never forget a few months back when she'd gone to the lavatory at school and found her underpants spotted with blood. She was so frightened that she left school without asking permission and ran all the way home ....

Sara heard the front door slam and came into the front hall as Doris was running up the stairs to her room. "What's the matter? Why are you home this time of day?"

Doris was already in her room, lying on her bed sobbing.

Sara came in and looked at her. Suddenly Doris was in her arms. "What's the matter?"

She was too ashamed to tell; it had to do with a place nice girls didn't talk about. She just knew it was wicked and mama would hate her.

Sara spoke quietly. "Doris, tell me."

"I want to see Rachel, even though she's in bed with a cold."

"Why Rachel?"

"I can't tell you, mama."

"But you can tell Rachel?"

162

"Yes . . ."

Soon Rachel was standing near the bed. "What's wrong, Doris?"

"You won't tell mama?"

"No. What is it?"

"I'm bleeding . . ."

"Where?"

"Down in my drawers. I'm going to die, Rachel, I just know it."

"Doris, you're not going to die. It happens to all girls. You're just a little young. It doesn't happen at ten too often, but it's normal, Doris. You're getting a menstrual period, that's all."

"A *what?*"

"A menstrual period. It happens to all girls."

"Not to boys?"

"No, just girls."

"Why?"

"Because that's how God made it, Doris. It has something to do with children, after you're married."

"Do you have . . . menstrual periods?"

"Yes, mine started at thirteen."

"Why didn't you ever tell me?"

"Because it's something . . . you just don't discuss."

"Was mama mad?"

"No, for once."

"I'm so embarrassed, Rachel."

"You don't have to be. I should tell you, you're going to have a period every month. Now come to my room and I'll tell you how to take care of yourself."

Rachel had even gone to mama and told her that she should have explained to her daughters about becoming a woman, and mama in no uncertain terms had told her that no one had ever told her anything and she'd survived and, what's more, she didn't appreciate her own daughter lecturing her, thank you very much. Doris might have been upset by the argument, but she was so excited about finding out that she'd become a woman that she could hardly wait for her next period. . . .

She would never forget how wonderful Rachel had been to her that day, Doris thought as she lay now in her private place looking up at the trees that clouded her summer hideaway. Life had its ups and downs, but there were wonderful times—like this very moment—when she could be alone and dream that one day she'd be a great movie star like

Gloria Swanson. She had made up her mind she was going to be an actress, and nothing in the world would stop her. She'd go to Hollywood or maybe she'd go on the stage. Uncle Shlomo would help her; he always said she was a born actress. Uncle Shlomo . . . she really loved him and she wondered if anyone in the whole world ever loved her as much as he did. When he was home on leave he gave her money to go to the Orpheum Theater, where she would stay all day and watch the acts over and over again. She saw the greatest: Fanny Brice, Al Jolson, Belle Baker, Ted Lewis and Sophie Tucker. When she went home she would go up to the attic and put on the wide-brimmed satin hat with the plumes and the beaded satin dress and then perform almost word for word the routines she had seen.

She was aroused from her daydreaming when she noticed how late it was. She stood up and stretched, then sighed. She really didn't want to go home. . . .

Sara came into the room and gently shook Doris and Lillian. "You'd better get up. We have a long day ahead of us."

The two girls scampered out of bed and headed for the bathroom, but it was locked. Rachel was in there and this would take all day. Impatiently, Doris looked out the back window and saw Shlomo and papa cleaning the truck. Papa was really so handsome and tall, she thought. Mr. Hanson down the street looked a lot like papa. Well, not a lot, but they both had dark blond hair and blue eyes. Papa was as tall and strong as Mr. Hanson and she'd bet papa could have knocked Mr. Hanson out for making her feel so uncomfortable the day she went over to try and play with Gerta.

"You don't belong here, go home. Gerta can't play with you."

But Gerta liked Doris, so the next day on the way to school she caught up with her. "I'm sorry my daddy said that to you, Doris. I like you even if you are a Jew."

Even if you are a *Jew?* What made the Sanderses so different from the Hansons, and what did being a Jew have to do with it? Was it bad to be a Jew? Papa didn't look so bad. . . .

"I got to go to the bathroom, Rachel. I can't hold it in much longer," Lillian called out, keeping her legs crossed tightly.

There was no response.

Lillian knocked hard on the door. "Let me *in*, Rachel."

Rachel opened the door, and Lillian quickly ran past her.

"For heaven sakes, can't a person even go to the bathroom in *peace*," Rachel said.

"Peace? My gosh, you've been in there an hour," Doris said.

"I have not. Why do you always exaggerate?"

"Well, darn close to it. There are other people who have to pee too, you know."

"You're positively obscene, the language you use is disgusting."

"I don't know what obscene is, but you're inconsiderate."

"You've been reading the dictionary again. Inconsiderate is a pretty fancy word for someone so illiterate."

Doris's face flamed. There was a limit to the insults she was going to take. Even though Rachel had been nice enough to tell her she could have children when she got married.

Sara had just reached the top of the stairs. "I see the fights are already starting. I want this to stop, do you hear me?"

"Rachel started it."

"I did not."

"You did—"

"That's enough. Rachel, go get dressed and come downstairs and help."

Some Fourth of July, Sara thought. Couldn't there ever be one day without them fighting? She wished they didn't have to take the kids to the country. Just once. She hurried to the linen closet to get the white cloth and blankets. On the way downstairs she called, "Hurry up. I need you, Rachel."

I need you, Rachel. Mama didn't need Rachel—she needed a slave. Why did she have to be the oldest, Rachel thought as she was carrying out the food. Sara had prepared enough meat, salad, bread, cakes and pies to last a year. It made Rachel ill.

Doris and Lillian sat together in the back of the truck and Rachel sat across from them. "What have you got? A can of worms?" she asked Doris.

"No. Firecrackers . . ."

"Firecrackers? You've got enough to blow up the world."

"She's been saving them up for a long time now," Lillian said.

"It looks like she's been saving them for years."

"I have not. I started last month—"

Putting up the tailgate, Jacob looked sternly from one to the other. "Now, before we leave, I'm going to warn you. I don't want *any* fighting today."

"Rachel starts it."

"I know, Doris, you're an angel."

He always seemed to defend Rachel, Doris thought ... why did she always have to be in the middle ... ?

Sir Lancelot, the puppy Jacob had given Doris, barked and whimpered and ran around the yard. Doris' heart broke whenever they left him alone.

"Papa, can we take Lancelot along, please?"

Jacob looked at the mongrel with the elegant name.

Lillian put in, "Please, papa ..."

"Absolutely not," Sara decreed.

Jacob started up the motor and let it idle for a moment.

"Could we, papa?" Doris asked, ignoring mama.

"It's better if we don't. He could wander off and get lost in the woods."

Well, at least papa was nicer about it, even though it broke her heart. And in a way she guessed it did make sense. She would die if anything happened to Sir Lancelot ....

As they drove along Fruitvale Boulevard past the beautiful orchards of apricots, pears and apples Doris wondered how any day could be so wonderful. "This is God's earth and all the things that dwell herein ..." That was what the pastor said when Doris went to Bible class one day after school with Jennie Harrison. Doris thought the hymn they sang was so pretty that she had sung along. "Yes, Jesus loves us ... Yes, Jesus loves us ... and Jesus is the Lord." Doris was humming the tune inside her head.

What was the difference between the Lord and God? At Passover papa had read from the *Haggadah* that the Lord was one and that next year they would be in Jerusalem. She wanted to go to Jerusalem because that's where all her people had come from five thousand years ago, but maybe it wasn't such a nice place after all. That's where Jesus had chased the Jews out of the temple, which seemed kind of funny considering Jesus and his family had been Jewish, the same as the Sanderses. The Hansons loved Jesus even though he was Jewish, but they didn't want Gerta to play with her because she was Jewish. It was all very confusing.

Jennie Harrison had asked her to go to the Baptist church last Easter and Doris was so thrilled to be invited that she wore the white dress with the eyelet embroidery mama had

166

made from one of the petticoats she'd saved from when she was a girl and lived in a place called Brussels. Doris thought she looked quite elegant as she bounded down the stairs to the kitchen. Sara turned around and asked where she was going. Doris' heart beat a little too fast when she lied, "To see the parade on Broadway..." "Take Lillian," was the reply. She really didn't want to because sometimes Lillian let things slip, and she knew mama wouldn't want them to go to the Baptist church—even if Jesus was Jewish. But she wanted to hear the songs.... Besides, Jesus loved them. Reluctantly, she took Lillian.

It was during that Easter service that Doris learned the Jews had killed the Son of God and that they were consequently scattered to the four corners of the earth to burn in hell for all eternity. Although the Sanderses had never killed anyone she felt terribly guilty, and the prospect of burning in hell was a frightening one. She couldn't understand why it was that although the Sanderses believed in God they did not believe in his Jewish son. There was certainly a lot to learn.

On the way home Jennie said it was nice that Doris and Lillian had attended because even though they were heathens Jesus would save them if they believed in him. They would be forgiven if they converted and were baptized. She pleaded for Doris to do it before it was too late to save her soul. Doris didn't want to lose Jennie's friendship and so she said she'd give it serious thought although she knew she'd never do it. Jennie was so happy that she put her arms around Doris' plump body and said the Lord would reward her in heaven because she had saved a soul. She was so happy that she paid Doris a real compliment and told her that she liked Jews better than niggers. But the baked ham that was served at the Harrisons' Easter dinner was the deciding factor for Doris. She almost gagged at the sight of it. Not being kosher was one thing, as mama pointed out, but eating ham was strictly forbidden. You could get a terrible disease....

The aroma of the delicious food in the agateware roaster brought Doris out of her reverie, along with the sound of Lillian calling out to papa to please stop the truck because she had to go. Jacob parked on the side of the road, while Lillian pulled down her pants behind a bush. Sara handed her a roll of toilet paper, which she always carried on excursions into the country, and a damp cloth to wipe your hands. When Lillian and mama came back to the truck papa said, "If anyone else has to go, they'd better go now because I'm not going to stop till we get to Elum Rock." Rachel would rather die than do anything so undignified and Doris was glad she didn't feel the need.

Once again on the road, the orchards were now left behind. Here the hills had turned golden brown and looked as though they were dying of thirst. But they hadn't gone too far when once again papa pulled over and stopped the truck, got out and bought a basket of plums and another of green figs from the roadside stall.

Four eyes peered out beyond the steel-mesh panels and watched papa paying the farmer. When he came back and placed the baskets of fruit on the floor near Lillian, Sara said, "No one eat the fruit until it's washed."

Doris groaned. She would have loved to bite into a juicy plum. She was hungry, a chronic condition for her . . .

At long last the journey ended, as Jacob drove the truck off the road and parked under a clump of eucalyptus trees. Everyone got out and stretched and Shlomo picked up the baskets and carried them down the slight embankment to the edge of the rippling spring.

Within minutes, Sara and the girls had the cloth and the blanket spread out. Everyone was hungry and they piled their plates with food before they settled back to eat and laugh.

- After the girls had rested, Sara said it was all right to change into bathing suits and wade in the stream. She put the food away and then lay down to read while Shlomo and Jacob played pinochle.

The picnic and the surroundings had evoked the memory of a different picnic in a different world for Jacob. He wondered how Lotte was and if the Mendlebaums were still alive. When he looked around at his children he realized that even if they weren't boys he was still happy they were his. Actually, he had Lotte to thank for all his blessings. Sara was far from the perfect wife, but she was certainly superior to Lotte. Sara was no *yenta*. He would never let her know it but he envied her education and there were times when he felt inferior to her . . . She was a good mother to the kids and if she wanted them to grow up to be good and decent women, no one could condemn her for that. He was pleased with his family and very proud of what he had accomplished in so short a time. He'd provided a good life for his children. For sure they would never go hungry or be frightened and alone the way he'd been, he thought as he heard the happy voices and the sounds of splashing water and watched Doris float on her back and Rachel swim breaststroke with a bathing cap

168

down to her eyebrows, and Lillian sit on a rock watching the fish scamper away.

Early that evening they set off their own fireworks display. Shlomo lit the punk and everyone listened excitedly to the sound of the firecrackers going off and watched the sparklers and the rockets flash in the darkness.

When they all got back into the truck and started on their way home everyone was tired but very content, especially Sara. There had been no fights. Jacob hadn't had to scream, "That's enough, that's enough fighting." On the drive back he even started singing "Juanita," and Doris and Rachel joined in, harmonizing with his voice.

The day was coming to a close. Its memories would be stored away, to be taken out at another time—like the portraits in the attic.

CHAPTER TWENTY-NINE

THE FIRST day of school seemed like torture to Doris after the last three months of pleasure. But for Rachel it was heaven to get away from the conflicts of home. She loved the convent. At St. Frances she was not subjected to the discrimination that Doris faced at her school. The nuns were kind and gentle and Father McDougall was just about the handsomest man she'd ever seen, including even Uncle Shlomo . . . Except it did seem strange he could never marry.

The only time she felt different was when the other girls went to prayers. She would stand to one side of the open chapel doors and hear the sounds of "Hail Mary, full of grace." It was so beautiful that she longed to be a part of it . . .

One day she managed to get up enough courage to step inside. When she saw the students kneeling in prayer, she was awed by the great hush in the room and she felt very much alone. She would have stayed but someone tapped her gently on the shoulder. She turned to see Reverend Mother Teresa summoning her. Rachel followed her down the hall and into her office.

"Sit down, Rachel. You know your mother would object to that, don't you?"

Rachel nodded.

"Well, then, we have to do as your mother wishes."

A tear fell on Rachel's cheek.

"Why are you crying?"

At first she couldn't articulate her confused feelings.

"Are you unhappy, Rachel?"

"Yes." Her head was bowed as she looked down at the terracotta tiles beneath her feet.

"Would you like to talk about it?"

Rachel took out the handkerchief and wiped her eyes. "Is it a sin to hate your mother?"

"Yes, it is, Rachel. Your own teachings are the same as ours. You must honor your father and your mother."

A long silence lay between them before the nun went on. "It is wrong to hate, Rachel. The person it does the most harm to is the person who hates. And you, dear child, are too lovely a person to harbor such feelings."

"But how do you love someone who treats you without any kindness, or respect?"

"Is it possible, Rachel, that you're being overly sensitive?"

"I don't think so. My own mother talks about me. She's told me over and over again that she's too young to have a daughter my age, that she can't cope with me. Nothing I do seems to please her. She's angry all the time ... And my father's away so much that he's like a stranger in the house. I don't know if he really loves us. He almost cringes when we try to kiss him—" Rachel was crying again ...

"Rachel, I would like to have your mother come and see me."

"Oh, please, no ... If she even suspected I talked about her with you, she'd be very angry. She wouldn't understand at all. She thinks she's the perfect mother who's done nothing but sacrifice for us ..."

"And you don't think she has?"

"No. She thinks she's the only one who ever suffered. But if her childhood was so bad, wouldn't you think she'd want ours to be better?"

Mother Teresa swallowed hard. "Well, what do you feel should be done to let her know how very unhappy you are?"

"Nothing. She'll never change ..." Rachel sat trembling inside. Taking a deep breath, she said, "Reverend Mother, I want to become a nun."

Mother Teresa paused before she asked, "When did you think of that?"

"For some time now—"

170

"What are your reasons, Rachel?"

"I don't like being Jewish."

"Why do you suppose you'd like being Catholic any better?"

"Because it's so beautiful. And besides, people hate us because we're Jews. Everyone in our neighborhood hates us . . ."

"And do your sisters suffer from this the way you do?"

"No. Doris doesn't let anything bother her, and Lillian is too young to understand."

"Rachel, let me tell you something. I come from a country that very much dislikes Catholics. To be a Catholic there is to suffer too, and very often to die. It means to be without a job, with hardly enough food to survive on—and only because we're Catholic."

"What country is that?"

"Northern Ireland. And the pity is, it's the Irish who fight the Irish. It's been going on for hundreds of years, and I pray I am wrong but I see very little hope that things will change . . . Rachel, I'm afraid your reasons are not quite the right ones to become a nun."

"If I said it was more than that would you believe me?"

"I would believe anything you tell me."

"I've had the calling."

Mother Teresa took off her wire-rimmed glasses and wiped them before she asked, "And when did this calling come to you?"

"I've felt it for a long time now, but this morning I felt something so spiritual I just knew down deep in my heart . . . you must believe me . . . I felt the presence of God."

"Rachel, my dear child, I know you believe what you have told me, but you must listen. The reason you feel as you do is because of a spiritual need and a need to find what you lack at home. Catholicism is a very difficult religion to take up. It is demanding to the point that Catholics born into the faith cannot always live up to what the Church demands. What is your rabbi's name?"

"We don't have a rabbi. We don't even go to a synagogue. The only thing Jewish in our home is food, and only for very special days. That's my mother and father's way of being Jewish."

"Your holy days are not observed?"

"No, Easter is the only one. We have a ceremony, I suppose you could call it . . ."

"Your Passover."

Rachel was shocked that a nun should know about Passover. "You've heard of it?"

"Yes, indeed. You've seen the picture hanging in the chapel hall? That, Rachel, is the Last Supper, but it's more than that. It was in Jerusalem and the Passover was being observed by Christ."

"It was?"

"Yes. Would you do something for me?"

Rachel looked at the nun's kindly face. "I'd do anything for you, Reverend Mother."

"Then, on your own, I want you to find a synagogue and attend Friday night services. I also want you to go to Sunday school. Will you do that?"

Rachel sat silent for a long, long moment. "Yes, Mother Teresa. And thank you ... If it's not irreverent, is it all right if I say I love you?"

The sister held back the tears. "To be loved by you is a very great gift. That I will always keep in a very special place in my heart." As Rachel started to leave, Mother Teresa added, "And, Rachel, try to remember that if God can forgive us, then we must learn to forgive one another."

"I'll try ... but I don't know very much about God," she said quietly, closing the door behind her.

Mother Teresa could not dismiss Rachel from her mind. The inner beauty she had was being crushed, it was understandable how such a girl could be drawn to the Church ... Catholicism was a compelling religion and it had all the ingredients that would draw a young girl who felt unloved and had virtually no faith to sustain her. It was difficult to resist the compassionate eyes of Jesus as He looked down from the cross, difficult not to be touched by the sight of the son who lay in his mother's arms both as man and child ... from the manger to the cross. Of course Rachel had been affected by it and had interpreted it as her way out, but that was not the reason to become a nun. Mother Teresa felt she had done the right thing, but she prayed that God would ease the path for Rachel . . . .

Rachel willed herself to forget the moment of what she considered her deliverance when she felt that she had been called, and turned to try and find solace among her own. She did not find companionship but she did find a great beauty in the history of the Jews and their struggle for survival through five thousand years. She also found a great many new confusions about her family. Her father often said how difficult it was for American Jews to hold on to their beliefs and perpetuate their faith while living in a gentile world. How wrong he was. He seemed totally oblivious to the fact that every Friday night Jews worshipped with their families at temple services—in Oakland, California, of all places. To her knowledge, he had never made the effort to cling to the faith he so often said he had been deprived of. Through the months of study she began to realize that it wasn't that papa couldn't have held on to his religion. She knew in her heart it wasn't just America that had changed him, but that he had fallen away from the tradition because of other needs that she didn't fully understand.

She began to feel that one must have faith and an understanding of one's religion if one was to understand who and what one was. She knew she would always remain a Jew, in spite of the fact there was nothing at home to sustain her faith, and no matter where she might go, or who she might be with. . . .

CHAPTER THIRTY

IN DECEMBER the houses on the Sanders' street were transformed with holly draped around window frames and fragrant wreaths with red satin ribbons that hung on the doors. Through the windows could be seen the trees that glittered with lights and strands of silver tinsel. It was a time for presents and Santa Claus, a time of brotherhood and good will, midnight Mass and Christmas pudding.

Doris and Lillian went up and down the block, captivated by a world of make-believe and enchantment. Doris loved beauty so, and she longed to reach out and embrace what in her heart she felt she was being deprived of . . . .

When she took Lillian downtown and saw the rush of holiday shoppers, a loneliness came down on her.

The stores were all shimmering with silver icicles.

On the corner a man dressed in red flannel with a long white beard tinkled a silver bell and called out "Merry Christmas" to the passers-by.

Parents and children pressed down the store aisles, their arms laden with packages in green-and-red ribbons and holiday wrappings.

The two girls took the elevator to the toy department, where Lillian played with the beautiful dolls, then wound up a toy and watched it in wonder as it walked away, turned around, then fell on its side. The most fun of all was the red-and-yellow automobile, just large enough for one. Lillian pedaled up and down until she was pulled up by the shoulders and told in no uncertain terms that she was to leave the department.

"You take your hands off my sister," Doris said, looking up what seemed like ten feet into the eyes of the lady manager. The woman's lips were pursed, her eyes narrowed. "Then you tell your sister to join you, young lady, and leave immediately."

Doris stood her ground. "We will if we want. This is a free country—"

"But the things in this department aren't."

Doris gave her a dirty look. "All right, Lillian, we're not going to buy the skates and the car in this lousy store." She took Lillian's hand, and with all the dignity she possessed she kicked the manager in the shins.

They ran through the crowds, ducking and weaving, until they found themselves on the street in front of Capwell's Department Store.

Catching her breath, Lillian looked up at Doris and asked, "Were you really going to buy the skates and car for me?"

"Well . . . not really. I just wanted to show that terrible person she couldn't treat you that way."

Disappointment written on her face, Lillian said, "I wish you were . . . but anyway you were nice to say so."

"Maybe next year . . ." Her face brightening, she said, "You know what, Lillian?"

"What?"

"I've got money. Let's go to the Pig and Whistle for ice cream." . . .

They sat in a booth, looking at a menu. The prices were a little higher than Doris had expected: hot fudge sundaes were twenty-five cents, marshmallow and chocolate was twenty-five cents, maple and—

"What are you girls going to have?" the waitress asked.

Without hesitation Lillian replied, "I'm going to have a banana split."

Thirty-five cents . . . Doris almost fainted; they wouldn't have enough for carfare. "Lillian, I don't think you should have that. You won't be able to eat dinner . . ."

"Oh, it won't spoil my appetite."

"What are you going to have?" the lady asked as she took in Doris' pudgy form.

"A glass of water, please . . ."

Doris watched as Lillian devoured the sundae. First the maraschino cherry found its way to Lillian's mouth, then a spoonful of vanilla ice cream, next chocolate, then strawberry and a dab of whipped cream.

"Is it good?" Doris asked, her mouth watering.

"It's okay. You want a bite?"

"Well, maybe a little one." She reached across with a teaspoon and helped herself to the three flavors.

"Why don't you take some more?"

Doris was about to accept but just then she looked up and saw the waitress passing by. "No, it'll spoil my appetite." She drank the water.

After Lillian had scraped the bottom of the dish she wiped her mouth and asked, "What are we going to do now?"

"Walk home."

"Walk!"

"Sure, it's not far."

"Doris, we can't walk home. We'll never make it . . ."

"Of course we will."

Lillian sighed. After all, Doris was older and if she said so . . .

After they had walked seventeen blocks, though, Lillian sat on the curb and panted. "I can't go any further."

Doris sat down next to her. She had raised a blister on her heel. "Just rest. Tell you what, let's pretend we're explorers or Indian scouts."

"I don't want to be an Indian scout . . . let's take the streetcar."

"It's so close to home. You can make it, Lillian."

Lillian grimaced. "Okay, I'll try, but if I can't make it can we take the streetcar?"

"Absolutely."

The last twelve blocks proved almost beyond their endurance and Lillian began to cry. "I think you're mean, Doris."

Doris took out her handkerchief and wiped Lillian's nose. "I'm sorry, let's sit on the curb."

"Why didn't we take the streetcar?"

"Because I lost the carfare."

"You did? Where?"

"When we left the Pig and Whistle."

"Oh, gosh, I'm really sorry."

"Don't be, but don't say anything or they'll think I'm not a responsible person."

"I won't, Doris."

"Well, sometimes you forget."

"But I won't this time, promise."

"Okay, let's start for home. Pretend you're an Indian going through the woods."

"I'd rather be Becky Thatcher."

"Okay, be Becky Thatcher." . . .

Doris walked the last few blocks home without shoes. The throbbing blister was running and red . . . It was killing her.

When they got home they were hardly able to make it up the stairs. They flopped onto the bed in Doris' room. Bed had never felt so good, Doris thought, and she was never more grateful than at this moment that mama was out grocery shopping.

"See," she said to Lillian, "it helped being Becky Thatcher."

But Lillian was already fast asleep.

On Sunday night the family was sitting down to dinner when Doris asked, "Mama, could we have a Christmas tree?"

Jacob put down his fork and looked at Doris. "No, and don't ever mention it again." Unaccountably, the memory of Patrick O'Leary sprang to his mind. "Not *ever*."

"Why not, Jacob? They see it all around them. Where are we living, in Palestine?"

"Damn it, Sara, when I say no, I mean no!"

"That frightens me a lot. We live among *goyim*, so they—"

"I said I don't want them to have it. It's up to you to see that they get a little religious training."

"Really? With Father Gallagher and Pat Heanny and the rest of our *goy* neighbors?"

"Why don't you join a synagogue and become active, meet some other Jews?"

"Wearing what? The beautiful clothes you buy me? Besides, when do I have time with this big house? My religion is cook-and-clean. We don't even go to a movie or take a vacation—"

Rachel had had enough. "You should hear yourselves. Doris asked for a Christmas tree and instead of answering her you're having your own personal fight. Why didn't either

176

one of you explain to her why? I think you're both *awful*—"

Sara got up and slapped her. "Don't you ever dare talk like that again—"

It stung but Rachel didn't flinch. Instead she ran out of the room, up the stairs, slammed and locked the door, then lay down on the bed and cried as though she could never stop.

Jacob was stunned by Rachel's behavior but also deeply upset that Sara had slapped her.

Doris wished she could die. It was all her fault. If only God would strike her deaf and dumb . . . Why couldn't she learn to keep her mouth shut? "I don't want a Christmas tree."

"If you want it, you can have it," Sara said adamantly. "It's only a tree. Christmas has nothing to do with it."

Jacob got up and ran up the stairs, with Doris going after him. When she walked into her parents' bedroom she saw that he was flinging clothes into a suitcase.

"What are you doing, papa?"

"Leaving—"

"I don't want a tree. Please, papa, I don't . . ."

But Jacob didn't hear her.

Doris heard the back door slam, then the sound of screeching tires and a sharp turn out of the driveway. Then . . . nothing. Nothing but the sound of her own fear . . . . She knocked on Rachel's door. Crying, she called out, "It's me, Rachel. Can I come in?"

She heard the sound of the key.

When the door opened she saw her sister's tear-stained face.

"Rachel, papa left and it's all my fault—"

"No, it's not, Doris. If they had any understanding none of this would have happened—"

"But, I shouldn't have mentioned the tree."

"The tree had nothing to do with it . . . don't cry. They'll make up. They need each other. Believe me . . ."

"They won't, Rachel. Papa was awfully mad and if they get a divorce it will be my—"

"Listen, Doris. If they do it will be *their* fault. They're taking their troubles out on us."

"I don't understand any of it, Rachel."

"How could you? They don't even understand themselves."

"But I'm eleven years old."

"And I'm sixteen . . . so what. Come and sit down . . ."

Doris settled herself on the edge of the bed.

"Now listen to me, Doris. The reason we shouldn't have a Christmas tree is because we're Jewish and Jews should be faithful to their religion. Christmas is for Christians, and to have a tree would be like stealing something that doesn't belong to us. Do you understand?"

"No exactly . . . Yes, I kinda do. But it's all so beautiful, Rachel, and we don't have anything . . . Nothing beautiful, I mean."

"Yes, we do, Doris, only mama and papa don't try to show us."

"Show us what?"

"Chanukah. It's not all tinsel and trees, Doris. But I've been going to Temple Sinai and I know there's a lot to our religion that is beautiful."

"What's Chanukah?"

"It's sort of like Christmas. We have a *menorah*—that's a candelabrum—and one more candle is lit each night for eight nights."

"Yeah, but that's not really like Christmas, Rachel. Gee, downtown everyone is buying presents . . ."

"Well, at Chanukah we're supposed to give presents. In fact, the girls that go to confirmation class have been bringing in their presents to show them off."

"They get presents?"

"Yes, one every day for eight days."

"Gee. How come we don't?"

"Because we're Jews in name only, and our parents don't seem to realize what we're missing."

"Golly, it really is all mixed-up. How come you know so much?"

"Well, thanks to mama I learned it at St. Frances, through Mother Teresa. I have *her* to thank. You know, Doris, I even wanted to be a nun . . ."

"Oh, my God. Papa would have really been mad. If he didn't even want a tree in the house—my gosh, Rachel!"

"Well, don't worry. I'm all over that."

"How come you never told me about going to confirmation class? And what's that, anyway?"

"It's sort of like when Gina Soracchi had her first communion, remember? You said she looked like a little bride." Rachel smiled. "You love brides . . . Well, anyway, our confirmation isn't quite like that, but it's lovely and all the girls wear white dresses."

"And veils?"

178

"No, but it's beautiful."

"You still didn't say how come you never told mama and papa."

"Because I didn't think anyone would care . . ."

"Where did you get the money?"

"From my summer job. I saved most of it."

"Gosh, you're terrific. I'd sure like to be confirmed . . ."

"Well, you're a little too young. The truth is, I'm a little older than I should be, but the rabbi is a wonderful man and he helped me a lot."

"And you never said a word about it . . ."

"Who cares?"

"I do."

"Well, then, why don't you tell mama you want to go to Sunday school and that Lillian should go too?"

"You think I should?"

"Yes, it's about time we all found out why people don't like us. One of the reasons we don't like being Jewish is because other people make us feel inferior, but the rabbi says we're the ones the whole world copied and we should be proud of our heritage. We gave our Ten Commandments to everyone, and the Bible too."

"Gosh . . . you're so smart, Rachel. I love you—even though I haven't always felt that way. Besides, you're a swell person."

"Thanks, Doris, so are you. It's a shame we weren't taught to love each other more—"

"I thought you just loved someone. No one taught me to love Lillian."

"Well, you have to have some examples . . . most people don't treat their children the way our parents do. Who talks against their children the way mama does? You'd think she had the rottenest kids in the world. If we grow up with an inferiority complex it won't be just the Christians who did it to us." Rachel looked at Doris for a moment. "I'm going to the high holy days . . . to temple."

"Can I go?"

"If you want to."

"I'd *love* to."

"Then we'll go together."

"Do you think mama and papa would be upset?"

"If they are, that's their problem."

"Can we take Lillian?"

"Sure."

"Where will we get the money?"

"We'll just walk in. We're really supposed to be members to get regular seats, but we'll find a place."

"You think I should talk to mama about Sunday school and all . . . I mean tonight?"

"I'd wait until tomorrow, Doris."

"You know, Rachel, sometimes I feel sort of . . . sorry for her."

"I do too—because she's so mixed up—but I don't love her, Doris. I'm sorry, but I don't."

"Don't you love papa either?"

"I used to . . . a lot. When I was a little girl, I thought he loved me too. That was before you were born, but he's changed—or maybe mama changed him, I don't know. Anyway, I'm going to be of age in another year . . ."

"What are you going to do then?"

"I'm going to college."

"College?"

"Yes, I want to make something of myself. I don't want to be like mama."

"I'm going on the stage."

"If that's what you want, I hope you make it."

"That's what I want." . . .

Doris lay awake for a long time that night, thinking about her parents and about the things Rachel had told her. She still found it all very confusing but when she finally fell asleep it was with the happy thought of going to Sunday school . . .

Down the hall Sara lay alone in the dark with many confused thoughts too. She missed Jacob terribly and berated herself for not being able to bend to his will, but she couldn't give in the way Gittel gave in to Hershel. Sometimes she felt that she had to fight to prevent her family from consuming her identity, but at the same time she really loved them and wanted to protect them, make a good home for them. She was always there when they came home from school, but they seemed to appreciate so little of what she tried to do for them . . . especially Rachel. She didn't want to hurt Rachel, but Rachel should be old enough to try to understand her for a change.

Why didn't Jacob see how much she needed him to support her, to stand with her when it came to the children? His ideas were so old-fashioned. Imagine leaving the house because Doris had asked for a tree. They lived in a gentile world and having a Christmas tree wouldn't have done any harm. As far as she was concerned, it was just a thing of beauty which had

180

nothing to do with religion. My God, she knew more about Christmas than Jacob knew about Chanukah, but her days in a gentile boarding school had never corrupted her. She was as good a Jew in her heart as anyone. What did all the running to a synagogue mean? One was either good or bad. That's all the religion a person needed. Her children knew they were Jews. She did everything to make them aware of their *Yiddishkeit.* When Passover came, look at the table she'd set ... and at how hard she'd tried to make the high holy days special. God, oh God, why didn't they understand? Oh mama, mama ... I love you, but I have tried to be everything you weren't ... All I wanted to do was make a good and comfortable home for my family ...

She cried into her pillow. Oh, Jacob, I'm so miserable. I'm only trying to be a good wife and mother and struggle with you, but you don't understand that there's more to living ... There's a world I can't enter because you say we have no money for it ... How can I go to temple when I don't even have a dress? Don't you understand, Jacob? I can't compete so I have to stay in my kitchen and cook. Don't you think I know there's more than that? Please ...

After a sleepless night Sara found it difficult to get out of bed. She was very subdued as she sat in the kitchen, drinking a cup of coffee.

Doris wasn't interested in her scrambled eggs, not today. She knew her mother had cried last night and in spite of Rachel's reassurances she still felt that she was responsible. If only there was something she could do to make it up to mama and papa ... "Can I get you another cup of coffee, mama?"

"No, Doris, thanks. Just eat."

Lillian said nothing. Nor did Rachel, but for different reasons. Rachel missed papa but she almost hoped he'd stay away long enough for mama to be really frightened that he might never come back. Of course he would never do that, but still ... he had been right about the tree, which showed he had *some* feelings about being a Jew.

"You feeling all right, mama?" Doris asked.

"Yes, fine, Doris."

There was an awkward silence.

"Mama, if you don't mind, I'd like to go to Sunday school," Doris said softly.

Sara looked at her wearily. First a tree and now Sunday school ... "All right."

"Why didn't we ever go before?"

"Because, Doris, it didn't seem necessary. We know we're Jews ... I don't really feel like going into it this morning. But you'll go. It will make your father happy."

"And what about Lillian?"

"Naturally. And you too, Rachel."

"I already do."

Sara bit her lip. "You do?"

"Yes."

"I see. And you didn't think you should tell me?"

"Would you have cared, mama?"

"Would I have cared? What's wrong with you, Rachel? Why do you always fight with me? What have I ever done to deserve this from you?"

Maybe I should ask what did I ever do to deserve a mother like you? Rachel thought.

Sara went on, "What are you trying to do—punish me, Rachel? Haven't I given you the best of it all? Sent you to private school so you'll grow up to be a fine woman? I have to sacrifice to pay tuition and buy uniforms, and this is my thanks?"

Couldn't mama have said, I'm so proud of you, Rachel? No, she had missed the whole point and turned everything around to martyr herself.

"Please answer me when I'm talking to you, Rachel."

"There's nothing to say." Rachel got up and left Sara crying as she sat with her head on the table between her hands.

Both Doris and Lillian sat there, feeling upset for mama. She was good in her way. She did sacrifice to send Rachel to private school. Maybe Rachel should have been a little more understanding herself ...

Jacob looked out at the bleak December morning. He disliked this time of year. It meant not working and that made him restless and irritable. His joy was what hard work brought him. ... At this moment, though, his thoughts were in the kitchen, where Sara and the children sat. After two days of being alone he missed his family so much that he ached with loneliness. Strange, he thought, when he was away on business he was never lonely. Home was always there to go back to. But this was different.

Sara wasn't really so wrong. Living among *goyim*, what kind of Jews could they be? He suddenly felt like a hypocrite. He hadn't been in a *shul* for how long now? Even in Cleveland they had lived like *goyim*. What did the tree really

182

mean? It was an ornament, that's all it meant to them. It wasn't worth breaking up a family over. It was even more strange when he thought about Lillian's birthday being on Christmas . . . the twenty-fifth of December, when another Jew was supposed to have been born.

He packed his things and paid the hotel bill. It was enough already. On the way home he bought a four-foot fir tree. . . .

Doris thought she was dreaming when she heard the truck come to a halt in the garage. She jumped out of bed and ran to the hall and looked out through the back window. "Papa's home," she screamed out and then bolted down the stairs.

Sara was standing at the sink when he came in carrying the tree. She closed her eyes. Thank God . . .

Then she turned around and they stood looking at each other, not knowing what to say. I would have died if you hadn't come home, Sara thought.

If she had only said that one simple phrase out loud, how much it would have meant to him, to them both. Her words at that moment, when he was caught in embarrassment and pride, might have brought them closer. But they had never said such things to each other . . . never knew how . . .

"Where's Doris?"

"I'm here, papa." She hugged him and said breathlessly, "Oh, papa, I'm so glad you're home."

He felt uncomfortable even with Doris' show of affection. Still, he wanted to hold her to him. But, of course, he didn't. "Thanks, Doris. Now, here's your tree."

"It's . . . pretty, papa. Thank you." She was as embarrassed by it now as he.

He nodded, then went into the livingroom and placed the tree in front of the window. He could barely stand the sight of it. *Goyim*, America, *Sanders*. . . .

When Rachel returned from her late afternoon Christmas job at Woolworth's she was disappointed when she saw the tree in the livingroom. Papa had no more conviction than mama had. She had admired his forbidding a tree in the house, but now . . .

When Jacob met her in the upstairs hall he suddenly realized how much she'd grown. Gone was the little child he'd adored so. She was still exquisitely blonde and blue-eyed, but she was no longer a little girl. She was a young woman . . . Why hadn't he noticed? He could no longer hold her close, much as he wanted to. It was only when his children had been babies that he could openly express his affection. They had seemed so helpless, so dependent . . .

"How are you, Rachel?"

"How am I? I'm disappointed, papa. The other day I admired you a great deal, but I'm sorry to say I don't quite feel that way now. We're Jews, papa. You should know that better than any of us. Do you realize how confusing it is for children who don't know what they are? Trees are for *goyim*, not Jews."

And, of course, damn it, she was right. He had wanted to make Doris happy and show Sara that he was open-minded, but he should have held to his convictions. At this moment he despised the tree almost as much as he despised himself.

December 25 was, ironically, also Lillian's birthday, and the first treat of her day was to lick the chocolate icing that remained in the bowl after Sara had frosted the cake for her birthday.

After dinner she opened the presents. Rachel had bought her a doll, and Doris had bought a pair of skates from the money she had been saving by not buying ice cream and candy bars or taking the streetcar if she could avoid it. Best of all was the pair of patent leather Mary Janes with the black grosgrain bows from mama and papa. She had wanted them for so long now, but mama had always said, "We don't have money to spend on foolishness. You need school shoes."

Her pleasure in putting them on almost overcame the guilt she felt over her parents' sacrifice. "Oh, mama, papa, thank you so much. They're beautiful."

"Take good care of them," Sara answered, and she meant it. Her children were going to grow up realizing they couldn't have everything they wanted. They had to learn to appreciate that parents had to deny themselves for their children. Too much was taken for granted. She remembered the beautiful dresses Louie had sent from Brussels and the gorgeous hats and outfits mama sent from Monte Carlo, but that had hardly been a sacrifice—not one that meant anything. She would gladly have traded all the fancy clothes for the love and devotion she'd given her children . . . Yes, her children were going to realize that being protected and cared for by your parents was more important than being indulged. . . .

The next morning, Lillian could hardly wait to show off her new shoes. Taking her doll, she walked over to Haley Welch's and rang the bell.

Haley had always been nice to her, although they were not really best friends. Lillian had become intrigued with her from the moment she learned that Haley was born with some kind of "deformity" and had a silver pin in her left leg, which made her walk sort of strangely. The two girls stood on Haley's front porch now.

"Look what I got," Lillian said, pointing down at her feet and feeling like Cinderella.

"They're pretty. What else did you get for Christmas?"

Still looking down at the shiny leather, Lillian answered, "Skates and a doll."

"I got nineteen presents."

"I got twenty." Lillian knew she shouldn't have lied, but she was embarrassed. It seemed so strange to have been born the same day everybody was celebrating Jesus' birthday too. Still, it did make her feel rather special . . .

"Well, I got to go home now," Lillian said haltingly, hoping Haley would invite her in. She smiled eagerly when Haley asked, "Would you like to see my presents?"

"Sure."

She followed Haley up the stairs and came face to face with the magnificently adorned tree, so different from the untrimmed and unloved tree in her own livingroom. She couldn't take her eyes from the cotton snow around the base, the jewellike ornaments, the gingerbread Santa Claus and striped candy canes . . . And the little Lord Jesus that stood looking down from the very top. The remnants of yesterday's festivities were very much in evidence—boxes contained gifts which had not been put away, crumpled ribbons and wrappings in the fireplace.

Haley's older sister came into the livingroom wearing soft fleecy slippers. She looked so pretty, almost as beautiful as Rachel . . . She was going with a boy and Haley had told Lillian they were going to get married.

"Hi, Lillian. Your doll's very pretty."

"Thank you, Alice. These are my new shoes . . ."

Haley was about to show Lillian all the presents she'd gotten when Mrs. Welch came into the livingroom. "Well, now if it isn't Lillian. Looks like Santa was surely good to you."

Haley's mama had a strange kind of sound to her words. It was an Irish brogue, someone had said.

"Oh, yes, Mrs. Welch."

"Haley . . . you'd better send your little friend home now and come have your breakfast."

"All right . . . I'll come over later and see your presents."

Lillian nodded mutely. Why had she said she'd received twenty presents . . . What was she going to do?

It started to rain, which only added to her dilemma. She stood on Haley's porch for a few moments, thinking about her new doll and her new shoes. She'd promised mama she'd take good care of them 'cause they'd cost a lot of money... She took off her sweater and bundled the doll and shoes inside.

By the time she reached home her clothes clung to her like a second skin and her hair was dripping. She ran up the stairs, her stocking feet leaving wet footprints on the floral carpets. Her nose was running and she was shivering, but she hardly noticed. At least her precious gifts hadn't suffered.

She hung the wet clothing in the bathroom and changed into dry clothes, then apprehensively stared out the window, watching the rain pound against the pane. She prayed it would continue all day so Haley couldn't come over and catch her in her whopper of a lie.

"Where did you go?"

Lillian turned from the window, startled to hear mama's voice.

"To Haley's. I wanted her to see my things. Then it started to rain—but I didn't get my shoes wet."

Sara looked at her as she sniffled. "Here, let me feel your forehead. You seem warm to me. Do you feel all right?"

"Yes, mama..."

"Did you wear your sweater?"

"Yes, mama, but... I had to take it off, to wrap up my doll and shoes."

"That's why you've come down with a cold. What makes you *do* things like that, Lillian?"

"Mama, you told me to take care of them... the shoes, I mean—"

"Use your head, Lillian, you're a big girl, for heaven's sake. I didn't want you to go running down the street practically barefoot in the pouring rain. That's just plain silly."

Lillian bit her lip.

"Now, you get into bed and I'll have Doris come in and play with you."

"Thank you, mama."

Sara shook her head and smiled... a thin smile, but a smile all the same.

As Sara was on her way out Lillian called, "Mama, if Haley comes, tell her I'm sick in bed?"

"Fine. I'll bring you some hot soup."

Lillian was happier at this moment than she'd been on her

birthday. Mama was kind, she felt secure because Haley couldn't see her, because Doris was going to come in and play with her . . . Life wasn't so terrible after all.

CHAPTER THIRTY-ONE

IT WAS going to be a glorious spring. Doris noticed that the daffodils and irises had begun to bloom along the edge of Mrs. Cleary's lawn, and the few maples on the street had begun to sprout new green leaves. She loved it when they turned brownish-red and gold in autumn, loved to hear the crunch as she stepped on them. Both seasons were nice, but March was a time of anticipation.

She had just turned twelve in January, and now maybe she could find a summer job, make a little money to buy birthday gifts for the family and anniversary presents for mama and papa. Of course she was too young to be an usherette at the Tivoli like Rachel, or to work in the five-and-dime, but there had to be something she could do. Being seventeen sure had its advantages. Rachel could work and buy things for herself that mama and papa wouldn't give her—like the blue crêpe de Chine slip trimmed with écru lace. Still, no matter how old Doris got, she'd never have the nerve to talk back to mama the way Rachel had. That slip had started some fight . . .

"You spend your money on nothing but luxuries. How about buying school shoes?" Sara had said.

"Parents are supposed to buy the necessities for their children."

"You're telling me what my responsibilities are?"

"Maybe someone should."

The slap Rachel had received still reverberated in Doris' ears. Suddenly she couldn't wait to get to school.

When she crossed the vacant lot across from the school she saw a crowd gathered out in front of the building. That was odd. Usually all the kids were in the playground before the bell rang. Curiosity made her hurry her steps.

She looked at the faces of the students. "What's wrong?" Doris asked Irene Fratis.

"Isabelle Larson was killed by a hit-and-run driver."

She'd seen Isabelle only yesterday . . . Isabelle was a nice girl, she always spoke to Doris . . . In fact, everyone liked Isabelle . . . "When did it happen?"

"After school, yesterday."

She never knew anyone young died. Grandma had been so old when she died. Papa hadn't allowed them to go to her funeral, but Doris had gone down the street to the wake for Mrs. Shields' old mother and seen her laid out on a slanted board surrounded by lots of beautiful flowers and tall candles. Everyone had been happy and they were serving refreshments in the livingroom. "It was a blessing to have died so peacefully," everyone said. "She had a long and rewarding life and gave the Church ten children, two nuns and three priests." "Oh yes, Maureen McDermot deserved her reward in heaven . . ." Well, so dying had its rewards . . .

Isabelle was going to be buried at Holy Cross Cemetery on Thursday and the whole school was going . . . .

That day, after school, she asked Rachel what to wear to the funeral.

"Who died?" Rachel asked.

"A girl at school . . . Isabelle Larson. Her father's Danish and her mother's Spanish. What do you wear to a funeral?"

"You're not going to be the belle of the ball, so I wouldn't worry too much."

She didn't much care for Rachel's answer, but she wanted to look nice so she ignored it. "Is it okay if I wear my pink pleated dress?"

"I suppose."

"You ever been to a funeral?"

"No . . ."

"Didn't you ever know anybody who died?"

"Oh, stop being so ghoulish, Doris."

"There's nothing ghoulish about it. Mrs. Shields' mother died and I went to the wake."

"You would."

"What do you mean, I would? Almost everybody in the neighborhood went."

"What did you wear then?"

Rachel was being really snippy . . . she could sure be insulting when she wanted. "My everyday dress," Doris answered, "but it wasn't a funeral. It was like a party. Everyone was drinking and eating sandwiches."

"Really? I bet Mrs. Shields' mother wasn't having much fun."

"Sometimes I actually hate you, Rachel."

"So? You have enough company in this house."

"Oh . . . go sit on a tack." . . .

188

On Thursday, Doris was up at the crack of dawn. She wanted to take a bath and get dressed before mama got up . . . she knew there'd be objections to her wearing her best dress to school. But this was something special.

According to the kids, Isabelle looked absolutely beautiful. Some of them had been to see her.

Carrying her white cloche hat in one hand and her shoes in the other, she crept down the stairs and went into the kitchen. She took out the cornflakes, sugar and milk and ate quickly, then fixed three pieces of toast, buttered them, heaped on apricot jam and made a triple-decker sandwich that she wrapped in wax paper. She put on her shoes and hat, feeling quite elegant. She didn't care who wore what, she'd never have to apologize. . . .

There was no one standing in front of the school when Doris arrived. She wished she had a wristwatch. Well, when she went to work, she'd buy herself one. But by then maybe papa would be able to.

He said he had just made some money out of something very bad . . . All the cows in California had a terrible sickness called hoof-and-mouth disease and papa went all the way up to Nevada and sent cattle to the stockyards in South San Francisco. It had really been fun waiting for the train papa was coming home on. She just loved the way he looked as he got off the train, wearing his cowboy boots and the Stetson hat. He and mama had had a terrible fight. Mama asked why he couldn't give her some of the money to furnish the house decently—and, boy, did he get mad.

"Sara, I shouldn't tell you anything. The minute I make a little money, you want to spend it on furniture. I can't do it now, can't you understand? My business requires capital, not furniture."

"It's a funny thing, though. Money for a new car you've got."

"What do you want me to do, take a bus? I need a car for business and the old one was ready to fall apart."

"Listen, Jacob, how long do you think I'm going to go on living like this?"

"As long as it takes me to accumulate enough to open a small plant. You're not the only one who has it hard. You think it's easy for me, running around the country in all kinds of weather? If I listened to you, I'd go broke—"

"You know what you are, Jacob? The tightest, most penny-pinching man in the world. If your children meant anything to you . . ." But papa ran out of the house and into his car . . .

No, Doris decided, she'd better not ask. . . .

Soon the students and faculty were all assembled and the special buses were waiting. By nine o'clock, everyone was in their seats and the excursion began. There was a wonderful kind of excitement with everyone on the bus. Not that anyone seemed especially glad or anything; it was just that everyone was being so nice today. There were none of the cracks that were usually directed at Doris. Of course, except for the kids on the block, no one had ever seen her dressed up. And the hat hid her hair, which helped. It made her feel like a . . . well, a lady. . . .

When the bus drove into the cemetery grounds Doris found the silence eerie, and the large marble gravestones were both beautiful and frightening. This was nothing like the dirty, deserted, hundred-year-old cemetery where she and Rachel used to eat ice cream cones in Cleveland. Here was a deep green carpet of lawn that seemed to go on and on for miles. The gray stonework lambs and angels made her flesh crawl.

She was hurried along to the chapel with her class and they were seated in long narrow pews. The organ music was sad, and Isabelle's family was weeping softly. Doris was shaken by the wails of the lady with a black veil covering her face.

Then the priest came in, dressed in a long black skirt and a white lace tunic, with a narrow *tallis* around his neck. He delivered the homily in a heavy monotone, something about how this blessed child had been taken because God wanted to keep her from harm. Now she was in the arms of Jesus. Her soul lived in heaven with the Lord, who had died on the cross to make the world . . .

Doris tried to shut out the sounds of his voice. Maybe she should have listened to Jennie Harrison. Her soul would probably burn in hell for all eternity.

For a moment she could not get up as the teacher directed the children to pass in single file to view their friend Isabelle for the last time.

When Doris looked down into the coffin and saw Isabelle lying so still and waxen, well, she couldn't help it . . . she felt sick to her stomach. Her legs trembled so that she wanted to hold onto something for support but she was afraid to touch the box Isabelle lay in. The cloying smells of carnations, roses and gardenias made her weak. When she doubled over, the

190

teacher quickly took her out of the line to one side. She had to get out of there. All she could feel was coldness, fear . . . someday she would be dead, and so would mama, papa, her sisters and Uncle Shlomo . . . Tears ran down her face. She was too upset to go to the gravesite. Barely above a whisper she asked, "Miss Thomas, may I please be excused?"

"All right, wait in the bus." . . .

For weeks afterward she would wake up screaming, in a cold sweat. Drenched, she would change into a fresh nightgown but it was usually some time before she could stop crying. The dark terrified her so much that she was afraid to turn off the light. God also terrified her, but she spoke to no one about her fears.

Compared to Doris' usual appetite she ate very little. Usually, she was the first to sit down to a meal and the last to leave. In the past, food had filled the emptiness left by too little show of affection, but now . . . Besides, what good did it do to love anyone when they were going to die? . . .

Sara was disturbed by Doris' remoteness. Was it that she was going through some phase of adolescence? Was she beginning to notice boys? The idea took hold and began to grow beyond all proportion. She remembered the problem she'd had with Rachel and that Cantino boy, and her own painful recollection of Carl Bromberg climbing into her bed was still with her . . . the feeling of his body hovering on top and savagely trying to find his way between her thighs made her shudder even now. Was that why she'd reacted to Jacob the way she had . . . ?

In the beginning of their marriage she'd rejected him as carefully as she could without letting him know why . . . that sex was something that made her flesh crawl . . . Of course she would have three children, but that would have nothing to do with the joys of love—not on her part, anyway. Like any healthy man, Jacob had stong physical needs, and he'd also wanted a family . . . a son. Sara repressed the guilt she still felt over the abortion . . .

So much time invested, so many tears shed and so many disappointments. Still, she loved them, and they *were* her responsibility. When Doris started to menstruate, Rachel had told her and taken her to task for not preparing them for the natural events of womanhood. Now she just assumed there was no other reason for Doris' becoming so withdrawn; it must surely have to do with the discovery of her own body.

191

Inwardly she felt a resentment that bordered on anger, but she must try and handle this. . . .

"Doris, I'm afraid I don't like the way you've been behaving lately. You've changed . . . why?"

Doris sat silently for a moment. Why? Because we're all going to die, she wanted to say. Looking at her mother now, the notion was far too painful to accept. She remembered her mother's long mourning and her father's reluctance to have her go to her grandmother's funeral. She understood death a lot better now than she had then. But her hesitation was taken by her mother as an indication that perhaps she was right in her analysis . . .

"Have you done anything to be ashamed of?" her mother asked.

Doris felt as if her mother's penetrating eyes could almost look inside her. But what did mama mean . . . ashamed? She wasn't ashamed, only very, very sad.

"Well, Doris?"

"No, mama. What do I have to be ashamed of?"

"What do the boys and girls do after school?"

"They play basketball, football or go home, I guess . . ."

"And you?"

"I come home."

"But sometimes you're late . . . Why?"

"I go to the library."

"That's all?"

"Yes, I love the library."

"You like boys?"

Doris really hadn't thought about it. Yes, the girls talked about a lot of things, things that happened in dark movies, in the back of cars, in the bushes . . . But Doris had shut out even her own curiosity, knowing that no one would want to neck with fat Doris. No one even asked her to dance on assembly days. She always served the punch or was on the hospitality committee. She felt left out and of course she dreamed, but—

"Do you, Doris?"

"Do I what, mama?"

"I asked, do you like boys? If you do, say so."

"I suppose so . . . but—"

"Doris, I'm not going to prolong this. I'm your mother and it's my duty to tell you that boys can get a girl into a lot of trouble."

She knew what mama meant. Ruby Fox had had an

192

illegitimate baby and now everyone ignored her. Poor Ruby had been expelled from school. They all knew that Mike Dugan, the school football hero, was the father, but he was still the captain of the team and the kids still carried him on their shoulders when each game was over ... "I know, mama ..."

"Tell me honestly, have you ever had anything to do with a boy?"

Doris could feel an indignant blush come across her face. "No, never—"

"Don't use that tone of voice to me, young lady."

"I wasn't using any—"

"You were. Do you know about boys and girls?"

Doris wanted to cry. She had never even discussed this with Rachel. "Yes ..."

"You do? Well, then I want to warn you, Doris. Don't ever let a boy touch you. I mean even kiss you. Kissing can pass on terrible diseases that some boys get."

Doris hadn't the slightest idea what sort of diseases boys got and she didn't care. She'd never been asked to kiss anyone, so that was one worry her mother could forget. Why did her mother feel she had to bring up something that made her feel embarrassed and unclean?

"And don't dance too close to boys," Sara went on.

Who wants to dance with a blimp? Doris thought angrily. She got up from the table. "I'm awfully tired ... I have a terrible headache. If you don't need me for anything, I'd like to lie down—"

"Why should you be so tired?"

"I just am ..."

"I think you're getting very lazy, Doris."

"I'm sorry you feel that way, mama."

"One thing I'll say about Rachel, she at least doesn't mind work. That's why she gets good grades and you don't."

Why couldn't her mother shut up and leave her alone? She hadn't slept in a week, not since Isabelle ... She wanted to hit her mother, but the anger was immediately turned inward. If her mother died, she'd never forgive herself for having such thoughts. "All right, what do you want me to do, mama?"

"The wash. I can't take care of everything. Go take an aspirin. And remember what I told you before." ...

The Sanderses always seemed to go their separate ways. When Jacob was home, he went to bed at eight and Sara either read or sewed. Rachel and Lillian studied, while Doris found herself writing plays. As a result, she had to cram for examinations, but her mind was so keen and her memory so photographic that she could remember practically verbatim an entire page . . . The only time the whole family was together was at the dinner table.

Just before the Jewish holidays Rachel looked around the silent table and watched as everyone ate. She debated for a moment, then summoned up the courage. "I'm going to temple on Rosh Hashanah and Yom Kippur."

Jacob remembered Rachel's speech to him after the incident with the Christmas tree. He had felt like a hypocrite but had continued to make excuses for himself, saying that he was too occupied with the business of making a living, providing security for his family. Suddenly his childhood memories were very clear, and it brought a lump to his throat when he recalled standing in the little *shul* alongside of Mr. Mendlebaum. When his mother had handed him the *tallis* in the red velvet case with the gold-embroidered *Torah*, she had said, "Wear it with the dignity your father wore it." It had taken Rachel to remind him how far he had fallen away from his heritage. When had he lost that spiritual need? Well, there were no Jews in his world, and since his social contacts were nonexistent he doubted if many Jews living in America, especially in West Oakland, were able to keep to the old ways. It seemed that only in the ghetto of New York could one really be a Jew; in the larger world, being a Jew meant bartering one's very existence. How could he have continued to be Jacob Sandsonitsky? He hadn't changed the name out of shame; the new name had simply made it easier to become part of the melting pot. America was a great country, but it demanded compromises . . .

Sara had never felt the same loss Jacob had. She had come out of a totally different set of circumstances. Her link with Judaism had only come when she lived with Esther, and even then it was more gastronomical than spiritual.

Jacob could understand her feelings, since she hadn't really been exposed to religion as a child. But his own childhood had exposed him to Judaism but deprived him of a father to learn from. Perhaps if he'd had sons Jacob would have been more aware of the need to pass on Jewish ideals. Still, he felt ashamed of having neglected his children's spiritual needs . . .

". . . and I'd like a new dress, papa," Rachel was saying.

"How much will it cost?"

"I don't know."

194

"How much? A thousand dollars? With the clothes you buy, you mean you don't know?" Sara said.

"About fifteen dollars, papa."

"So you'll go buy a dress. Tell me, Rachel, what *shul* are you going to?"

"It's not a *shul*, it's a temple."

"What's the name of the temple?"

"Temple Sinai."

"Sara, we'll all go."

"You have to be a member, papa, and you have to pay."

"So . . . Sara, find out how much it costs."

"Why do you want to become a member, Jacob? When will you go?"

"When I'm home. If not, you'll go with the girls."

"They already go, Jacob."

"To Sunday school only, papa."

"Keep still, Rachel, this is between papa and me. I'll call tomorrow. And incidentally, Jacob, since you're in such a generous mood, we all need clothes—including you."

Rachel was very pleased with herself . . . she'd beaten mama with papa . . .

As for Doris and Lillian, they couldn't quite believe it. They were going to have their first store-bought dresses. But their hopes were short-lived. Sara took the wooden dome off the Singer sewing machine and within four days the dresses were done.

They were even more disappointed when Rachel came home with a blue jumper and a polka-dot blouse with a large bow that tied at the neck. She looked like an angel, and her slim body made Doris envious. Funny, she ate the same things. How come Rachel was so thin and she was so fat? Doris was even more upset when mama bought a beautiful brown silk dress and a pink feathered hat from the Gray Shop, and the most gorgeous brown suede shoes and bag to match. It must have cost a fortune. For once, papa didn't say a word when she gave him the bill for forty-nine fifty for the dress and fifty dollars for the shoes and the bag. When papa tried on his suit and gray fedora from Hart, Schaffner and Marx, he and mama and Rachel looked so elegant that Doris felt she and Lillian were being treated like stepchildren. She was embarrassed by her plaid dress with the sweet little white collar and cuffs. She not only looked like a blimp, but like a juvenile of ten.

Lillian seemed satisfied with the yellow silk. But, after all, she was only a little kid. What did she know . . . ?

On Rosh Hashanah eve, dinner was served early. The dishes were scraped and left in the sink to soak in the Fels Naphtha soap because mama wanted to get dressed.

The girls were waiting in the livingroom when mama and papa came down the stairs.

Rachel stared when she saw papa holding the red velvet sack with the gold-embroidered *Torah*. Well, no use procrastinating. "Papa, you don't need that. No one wears a *tallis* and *yarmulkah*."

Jacob was astonished. "What kind of a place is this?"

"It's reformed."

"Reformed from what, Judaism? If you'd told me, I wouldn't have gone."

"I love your sudden interest, Jacob. It's all or nothing with you," Sara said.

"I never worship without a *tallis*."

"God will forgive you. You haven't worshiped for so long that a *tallis* more or less—"

"I asked you to join a synagogue, didn't I?"

"Please, for once let's not fight. It's Rosh Hashanah," Rachel said, almost in tears.

Jacob put down the velvet case and walked quickly from the room, with his family following. . . .

They sat in hushed reverence, listening to the organ playing as the choir sang. Two huge floral arrangements of gladiolas and mums stood on the pulpit, and beyond were enormous golden candelabra. Exquisite walnut carved panels covered the eastern wall. Suspended from the ceiling hung the ruby-red glass eternal light in front of the doors which would later reveal the *Torahs* with their silver crowns.

Jacob's gaze wandered to the balcony, to the golden pipes of the organ and the choir dressed in black robes, then to the stained-glass windows. His attention was diverted by the rabbi, who stood before the congregation looking like a Harvard professor or even a judge, but for the neatly folded *tallis* over his long black robe. Jacob not only felt uncomfortable, but totally uninspired as the rabbi began.

He read in English from the prayer book as the congregation sat silently. Then the cantor replaced the rabbi and sang to the accompaniment of the organ, the pauses in his singing punctuated by the choir's "amen."

So this was a temple? If anything needed reforming, it was Temple Sinai. This was not Jewish, these were not Jews. Hatless! What was there to indicate this was a Jewish house

196

of worship? Jacob felt alien, out of place. It was about as Jewish as the church he had called Rachel out of so long ago. The only difference here, it was so quiet, if a pin dropped the organ would stop playing. They didn't even call the man up there rabbi; he was addressed as doctor . . . Doctor of what? No wonder Rachel loved it—it must be just like the Catholic church. He hated being here and once again he was angry with Sara for sending Rachel to a convent.

His anger was no greater than Doris' fears. The flowers, the organ and the flickering candles made her feel faint. She prayed she wouldn't throw up as she almost had at Isabelle's funeral. Please, let it be over. She didn't want to be here, it wasn't at all like Sunday school.

Rachel sat watching her mother and smiling to herself. If the lights went out, mama would fall asleep. The only thing that was important to mama about this occasion was the new clothes. My, how regally she had descended the stairs, as if she were a queen.

Lillian squirmed in her seat. She opened and closed her purse, tugged at her white cotton gloves and looked around the sanctuary at the solemn faces. Her lovely brown eyes looked up to the vaulted ceiling, then across to the balcony. She counted the ladies dressed in red, then in green, orchid and blue. The red were more predominant. Suddenly she felt mama's arm on hers. "Stand up when everyone else does."

Lillian bolted up and then watched mama carefully for her next cue. Suddenly the congregation was seated once again.

The president of the temple rose to make a few announcements about upcoming events. Then the rabbi wished him a happy Rosh Hashanah and shook his hand and the president took his place next to the cantor. After the rabbi intoned the benediction, the cantor came forward and the entire congregation—except the Sanderses—sang the closing hymn.

> The Lord of all, who reigned supreme,
> Ere first creation's form was framed;
> When all was finished by His will,
> His name Almighty was proclaimed . . .

It went on for four more stanzas. And for this Jacob had paid one hundred and twenty-five dollars for seats? What kind of a temple asked money for tickets? It was like going to the Orpheum.

Toward the end of the service the mourners' *Kaddish* was said.

As Lillian started to stand, she was held down by Sara. It was certainly very confusing. First she was told to get up when everyone else did, and here mama and papa were standing and a lot of other people were saying something in a foreign language: *"Yis-ga-dal, v'yis-ka-dash."*

She whispered to Rachel, "First mama wants me to stand, then she doesn't. How come we're not and mama and papa are?"

"Because you're not supposed to if your parents are alive. It's a prayer for the dead."

Doris overheard and started to tremble inside. She felt ill throughout the *Kaddish* and the concluding hymn. She was never more relieved than when the rabbi pronounced the benediction and she saw the congregation leaving their pews and walking up the aisle. Once outside, she took a breath and exhaled deeply. People stood on the broad stone steps between the beautiful marble columns, exchanging holiday greetings with family and friends. For once she didn't envy the conversations in which she had no part.

Making their way through the crowd, the Sanderses walked up the street to the parking lot and got into their Dodge sedan.

Jacob started the engine and drove out. Silence prevailed. No wishes for a happy Rosh Hashanah, no embraces or kisses, nothing . . .

Rachel pursed her lips in the dark. What could she have expected? Her parents just didn't have any feeling for their religion. Money was papa's god and martyrdom was mama's. Or so it seemed to her seventeen-year-old mind.

Halfway home the silence was broken when Jacob announced: "I'm not going back to Temple Sinai." He almost spat out the words. "If that's reform, it's no better than being with a bunch of *goyim.* What kind of a religion is that?"

"I thought it was very impressive," Sara said.

Rachel laughed to herself. The beautiful temple and the ladies' elegant dresses were what impressed mama. She didn't understand the significance of tonight's service. She heard papa saying, "It was as religious as the Baptist church and just as Jewish."

"That's because you have a closed mind. If it's not like the little *shul* on Hester Street with all the *Yiddles* in their *tallises* and *yarmulkahs,* wailing and pounding their breasts, it's not Jewish. There's so much noise and confusion going on you can't even hear. How stupid, women sitting upstairs separated from their husbands. I think it's archaic. If a husband and

198

wife can sleep in the same bed, then I think they can sit together in temple too."

"Church, you mean. Listen, Sara, I want to join a *shul* . . ."

"Absolutely not. I'm not going to bring my children up with all those *meshuggeneh* rituals. This is America."

"You went when we lived in New York."

"Of course. What should I have done—stayed home with all the family going? But I didn't like it. I wasn't raised that way."

"I know, you were raised like a princess."

"Yes, I was, and I think my spiritual values are as great as yours. You didn't have a *bar mitzvah,* you never went to *cheder,* you don't even understand Hebrew. So what are you making such a fuss over? You're still living in the old country, except you aren't—"

"And you're living like a queen. When did you ever have so much? From your mother?"

"Don't talk about my mother. At least I developed an open mind from her."

"I'm not going back again, you hear? I don't have to spend my hard-earned money to sit with a bunch of *goyim* who don't even cover their heads. And I don't want any of the children to go again. Some religion . . ."

Rachel bit her lip. She would go whether papa liked it or not.

The argument went on until they reached home. Happy Rosh Hashanah. . . .

It was three in the morning when Sara got out of bed, walked down the darkened hall to the bathroom and saw a beam of light coming from under Doris' door.

Doris slept so lightly that she bolted up in bed as she heard the knob being turned. Maybe the angel of death had come to claim her—

"Doris, what are you doing with the light on?"

"I don't like to sleep in the dark."

"You don't like to sleep in the dark? What are you, a baby? Turn the light out, the electric bills are high enough," and Sara switched the light off as she closed the door behind her.

Doris cowered under the sheets. Covering her head, she pleaded, "If you're there, God, please listen. I don't want to die, I don't want to die . . ." She cried until she fell into exhausted sleep. . . .

On Yom Kippur Rachel came to the table dressed in her blue jumper.

"What have you got that on for?" Sara asked as she served the chicken and the noddle *kugel.*

"Because I'm going to hear *Kol Nidre.*"

Sara waited for Jacob to answer, but he said nothing. Having warned them on Rosh Hashanah that none of them were permitted to go to the reformed synagogue again, she thought he would forbid Rachel to go this evening. To her amazement, he said nothing and simply continued to eat.

When the meal was finished he announced, "Everyone get dressed, we're going."

Doris ran to the sink and this time threw up.

"I don't know what's wrong with her lately," Sara said, as she took a damp cloth and wiped Doris' flaming face. "You feel better?" Sara asked with genuine concern.

"No, I don't, mama."

Sara looked at her. She'd lost weight, her eyes were hollow and almost glazed. "Next week we'll go to the doctor."

Doris had never been to a doctor before. Mama must have guessed she was going to die. "No, I don't want to go to a doctor, I'm not that sick—"

"We'll see . . ."

"I can't go tonight, mama. My stomach hurts."

"What do you mean . . . where?" Jacob asked.

"Just all over. May I please be excused? I want to go to bed."

Jacob recalled how ill Doris had been when Sara had given birth to Lillian. Then he could hover over her, kiss her and hold her. Now he couldn't do it, much as he wanted to. All he could say was, "Go to bed, Doris. You'll feel better."

"Thank you. Have a happy Yom Kippur, papa, mama. You too, Rachel and Lillian." . . .

Doris heard the front door close and listened to the silence. She had never been alone in the big house before and suddenly it became more forebidding than even Temple Sinai. She was going to keep the light on till mama came home. . . .

This evening, when Jacob heard the sound of the *shofar* blown, somehow all his disenchantment vanished and was replaced with a deep sadness. Good God, didn't the loneliness ever leave the heart? This evening he missed his mother terribly, and thoughts of Shlomo and Gittel only deepened his feeling of need. Sara . . . more and more there seemed so little understanding, compassion . . . he couldn't even confide in her . . . but tonight was the Eve of Atonement and such thoughts should be far from his mind.

He forced himself into forgetfulness by immersing himself in the service, and suddenly he found that he *was* touched by the violin playing the hauntingly beautiful strains of the *Kol Nidre*. It had never sounded so poignant to him, and in his heart he blessed Rachel for awakening this feeling in him. Tonight the resentments were gone, the old days of *shul* blown into the past. He joined in the responsive reading.

As though the congregation and the rabbi were of one voice, they intoned: "Thou are my hope, my immovable rock, my stronghold. O God, strengthen and sustain me, for without Thee I am all too weak. Hear me on this solemn day, on which Thou hast promised to purify the sinner and efface his guilt."

The congregation was then seated and listened to the organ play softly as the choir sang.

Followed by the meditation:

O God and Father, I come into Thy benign presence to lift my voice in penitent prayer. This Day of Atonement is a messenger from on high, calling me in love to return to Thee. May it be Thy will, O Master of the universe, that I may hear and heed Thy voice. Thou hast given me the understanding to distinguish between good and evil and hast bestowed upon me freedom of will to choose between them. Often have I disregarded Thy words and strayed from Thy paths. But in Thy mercy dost Thou give me the means of turning from my evil ways and of coming back unto the path on which Thou desirest me to go. . . .

This evening Jacob listened to the rabbi and felt almost as if he were speaking directly to him.

"We have turned aside from Thy commandments and from Thy beneficent ordinances, and it hath not availed us. Thou art righteous in all that has befallen us, for Thou doest justice, but we have wrought evil.

"What shall we say before Thee, who art on high, and what shall we recount unto Thee, who dwellest in the heavens? Dost Thou not know all things, both the hidden and the revealed? Thou knowest the secrets of eternity and the hidden thoughts of every living being." . . .

At ten the next morning Jacob sat with Rachel in the synagogue. He would have liked to have shared this moment with Sara, but she said she would stay home with Doris and meet him for the memorial service.

He stayed all day. Not a drop of water had touched his lips . . . his mouth was dry. Somewhere deep within him he felt the need to remember his past hunger and how good life had since been to him. Today he did not feel omnipotent. Today he felt cleansed. . . .

At three o'clock, Rachel left the sanctuary and Sara now sat beside her husband. The doors were closed and the mourners remained. The solemn service of the *Yizkor* began.

After the choir's song, the rabbi came forward, stood before the congregation for a moment, then began, "O, what is man, the child of dust? What is man, O Lord? The eye is never satisfied with seeing; endless are the desires of the heart. No mortal has ever had enough of riches, honor and wisdom when death ended his career. Man devises new schemes on the grave of a thousand disappointed hopes. Discontent abides in the palace and in the hut, rankling alike in the breast of prince and pauper. Death finally terminates the combat, and grief and joy, success and failure, all are ended. Like a child falling asleep over his toys, man loosens his grasp on earthly possessions only when death overtakes him. The master and the servant, the rich and the poor, the strong and the feeble, the wise and the simple, all are equal in death; the grave levels all distinctions and makes the whole world kin."

The service continued with the silent devotion as each mourner recalled the memory of his departed loved ones.

Jacob wept at the memory of his father as he recited from the *Union Prayerbook* . . . "Thy memory, my dear father, fills my soul at this solemn hour. It revives in me thoughts of love and friendliness which thou didst bestow upon me. The thought of thee inspires me to a life of virtue and when my pilgrimage on earth is ended and I shall arrive at the throne of mercy, may I be worthy of thee in the sight of God and man . . . May our merciful Father reward thee for the kindness thou hast ever shown me; may He grant thee eternal peace. Amen."

And Sara whispered in longing, "I remember thee in this solemn hour, my dear mother. I remember the days when thou didst dwell on earth and thy tender love watched over me like a guardian angel . . ."

Soft weeping seemed to echo through the quiet synagogue.

Once again, the congregation joined the cantor and the choir as they all raised their voices . . . "Open unto us, O God, the gates of mercy, before the closing of the gates, ere the day is done. The day vanishes, the sun is setting; let us enter Thy gates."

202

Now the rabbi intoned: "The day is fading, the sun is setting; silence and peace of night descend upon the earth. Vouchsafe rest, O God, unto our disquieted hearts; lift up the soul that is cast down. Turn, in Thine all-forgiving love, to Thy children who yearn for Thy mercy; turn, O Father, to all the fainting hearts, to all heavy-laden souls. Let this hour bring us the assurance that Thou hast forgiven, that we have found favor in Thy sight. Consecrate our hearts unto Thee, and make them Thy living altars, whereon shall return the holy flame of devotion to Thee."

Jacob and Sara then stood with the others and listened to the benediction. "Let the year on which we have entered be for us a year of blessing and of prosperity." . . .

Jacob looked at Sara. Both with the same wish—that they should be more understanding, more loving and forbearing. In that special moment, all hostilities were gone. Jacob took her to him, kissed her and said, "Have a good year, Sara."

"And you, Jacob. A good year . . ."

Together they went home to their children and at least for this special evening they all sat together, in love and in peace.

CHAPTER THIRTY-TWO

RACHEL THOUGHT she'd performed a miracle. Hardly able to contain herself, she went to Mother Teresa and told her what had happened.

If anyone shared her joy, it was Mother Teresa. "You see, Rachel? Faith *can* move mountains."

Rachel truly believed that—for a while. But then, gradually, mama seemed to lose the peace she had found and once again became as irritable as before . . . the same old complaints were revived. And papa also lapsed into the same old pattern. He worked harder than ever and was away for even longer periods of time.

How naïve she had been, Rachel thought. Going to temple for one service didn't change a person. Only constant devotion and dedication would do that. The rabbi had said Judaism was a tree of life, a living thing that had to be embraced daily as a way of life, a guideline of morality. People's natures didn't change because of one glance at what heaven might be. Mama couldn't help being what she was.

Rachel had seen how touched papa had been on the Day of Atonement, but in spite of that and in spite of his complaints about living among *goyim,* he was a man who lacked faith— or who had traded it? That night had stirred their faith, but only their lives could sustain it . . .

Now all Rachel could think about was getting away, going to college. Thank God, only three more months and she'd be graduating. . . .

But the old feeling for papa was still there. He'd been away on a trip for so long now and when she heard the sound of wheels in the driveway she hurried down the stairs and ran to meet him, throwing her arms around his neck and kissing him.

He was embarrassed by her unusual display of affection, but managed to greet her with a small peck on the cheek.

"I'm so happy you're home, papa, I just couldn't wait."

"Me too, Rachel."

When they went into the house Sara turned from the sink to give him her standard greeting. "How was it you didn't call? You were gone ten days."

"I was up in hell and gone, without a phone."

She shook her head. "Go wash up. Dinner's ready . . ."

As they ate, Rachel said, "You know I'm graduating this June."

Jacob couldn't believe it. She was eighteen years old now. Imagine, that little girl who used to wait for him at the subway . . .

His fond memory was cut short when Rachel continued, "I want to go to college."

"College? You don't have to go to college—"

"I don't have to, but I want to."

"College isn't necessary for a girl."

"Why, papa?"

"Because—"

"Because why, papa?" Rachel was not only nervous but angry.

"Because a girl doesn't need that kind of an education. You're already educated enough."

"Nobody's ever educated enough."

"I'm still not sending you to college."

"You haven't answered me yet, papa."

"So, I'll answer you. Why should I spend all that money? You'll just get married and it'll all be wasted."

"Oh, my God, I simply can't believe this. How do you know I'm going to get married?"

"Why, what are you going to do? Become an old maid?"

Sara sat listening and watching as Rachel's anger brimmed over.

"But if I were your *son*, you'd send me, wouldn't you?"

"Yes, if you were a boy, it would be different."

In spite of herself, Rachel began to cry, which, of course, was the last thing she wanted to do ... show him what he'd consider her feminine weaknesses ... "I think you're the most unbelievably selfish man in the world. It's only the *money* that bothers you, that's what it is. You never had an education and of all people you should know how important it is. You've talked about it often enough. About your poor unfortunate childhood and how—"

"That's *enough*." For the first time in his life, he started to raise his hand against one of his children, but he caught himself and continued, "I'm not your mother, you can't talk to me that way and don't *ever* raise your voice to me, young lady ... Yes, you bet it's the money, at least partly. I don't apologize ... I worked damned hard to give you what I didn't have, and if it's not enough ..."

But Rachel no longer heard as she ran out of the house and down the street. God, if only she could run away, but where and with what ... ?

Jacob, God help him, was honestly surprised by her outburst. *His* childhood came rushing at him now ... Damn it, he'd starved, slept on bare floors and in alleys, been so hungry his stomach had shrunk. It had been no damned picnic clawing his way up to where he was. And now he discovered that his children took him for granted, just the way Sara did. It was as though they all felt it was coming to them. He was someone who made their life comfortable, but beyond that he was no one to them. And God help him if he ever denied them anything their hearts desired ...

He looked at Sara. "I don't understand ... If I'd had a father like I at least try to be to my children, I would have kissed the ground he walked on."

"Now you know what I mean, Jacob. Whenever I tried to tell you how difficult Rachel was, you fought me—"

More to himself, he said, "I can't get over her talking to me like that ... no respect. I never noticed before—"

"Of course you didn't. You're not home long enough to notice much of anything about the children."

Doris and Lillian sat listening to themselves all being lumped together as the "children" ... Were they *really* such bad and difficult children ... ?

Unaware of their presence, Jacob went on, "I'm knocking myself out so they can have. What am I doing it all for if not to secure their future? Never mind what I said, even if I didn't have the money I'd send her to college if I thought she should go. But she needs a college degree to wash diapers? Am I wrong, Sara?"

"No." She shook her head in agreement. "Look what my fine education did for me—I can quote Shakespeare while I'm doing the dishes. What Rachel needs is to go to work and find how hard it is to earn a dollar. I'll tell you something, Jacob. Rachel's inclined to be very extravagant. She spends her money on nothing but luxuries, and that's something I'm not going to give her."

Doris sat biting her lip. Quietly, she said, "Why do you want me to get such good grades, papa? I mean, if you don't think an education is necessary ..."

Jacob looked at her with mingled confusion and anger. "From you, I don't need any philosophy, young lady. If you graduate high school, we'll be lucky."

She held back the tears, then silently got up and left the room, with Lillian following. ...

June came and Rachel graduated. The occasion was far from happy. Most of the older girls were going to college and some were engaged, but she had neither to look forward to.

Rachel was understandably subdued in spite of the excitement of kisses, congratulations, picture-taking and happy families that closed the graduation ceremony.

Jacob refused to come because he still disapproved of her having gone to a convent. But Sara was there, feeling as she had from the start that she'd saved Rachel from temptation by sending her to St. Frances.

Doris and Lillian were proud as could be that their big sister had graduated with highest honors and hugged her as they told her so ...

"Oh, Rachel, you were so beautiful," Doris said.

"Thank you ..."

"You were," Sara said. "I was right, wasn't I? Someday, Rachel, you'll learn to be grateful that I insisted. A mother has to direct her children. Papa and I are very happy for you." She kissed her oldest daughter. "Very happy."

206

"Yes, I know, mama ... I really do," Rachel answered.

If Sara noticed that Rachel was barely able to meet her glance, today it was disregarded. "Now, we'll all go out to lunch and celebrate. This, my children, is a wonderful occasion."

And not one sigh escaped her lips.

After graduation Rachel avoided the family as much as possible. When her father was home she rarely spoke to him. She all but ignored her mother and told her nothing about her plans. She knew she had to go to work, but she wasn't going to sell dresses for other women to wear. Not her. So temporarily she worked at Withorn and Swan department store during the day and enrolled in a class at night school to become a comptometer operator.

While looking through the want ads she had discovered there was not only a demand for this skill but that the pay was excellent with the promise of raises. At least there was some future in it. . . .

After the six-week course was over, Rachel applied at the telephone company in San Francisco and was hired. For once she felt free. Commuting on the ferry boat gave her a feeling of exhilaration. Still, her emancipation went only so far. Secretly she wanted to move out of the house and live by herself, but she knew what *that* would create. And in spite of all her bravado she was fearful about cutting the umbilical cord so completely. Her feelings mystified her, but they could not be denied either . . .

Every week she bought new clothes for herself . . . she loved fine things and having had so few of them she now indulged herself.

One day, while cleaning Rachel's room, Sara found a receipt for twenty-five dollars for a *pair of shoes*. Was Rachel earning *that* kind of money? Sara looked inside the dresser drawers and found the neatly placed silk, crêpe de Chine and satin nightgowns and slips. Sara looked at the labels—Leibes, Ranschoff, I. Magnin ... well, she and Rachel would have a long talk.

That night, Sara didn't wait to be invited in. She opened the door as Rachel was unbuttoning the front of her blouse. Seeing her mother's reflection in the mirror, she turned around, lifted her chin and waited. Mama clearly had something on her mind.

"You have some lovely things, Rachel."

"Thank you. I get my good taste from you, mama."

Sara narrowed her eyes. She wasn't going to fence tonight. Without hesitation she asked, "How much do you earn?"

"What difference does it make?"

"Let me warn you, Rachel, don't provoke me. I asked you a question."

"I make enough to take care of myself . . ."

"Really? It must be a good deal to buy such expensive things."

"I earn it, so I have the right—"

"You have a right? Do you? Well, from now on, young lady, you also have the right to pay for your room and board."

"Why, mama, are you *jealous?*"

Sara lost control, slapped her across the mouth. "Don't you ever talk to me like that again, do you hear?"

Rachel almost cried out, but she dug her nails into the palm of her hand, pulled a cardboard dress box from under the bed, and without another word began to pack.

"And where do you think you're going?"

Rachel took out the clothes from the closet and folded them neatly into the box.

"I asked—"

"To the YWCA, not that it's any of your business."

"If you leave this house, you'll never step foot into it again. And that I promise."

In spite of her show of bravado, Rachel was frightened, but she forced herself to go on with her packing. When she'd finished she put the top on the box, took twenty dollars from her purse and threw it on the dresser. Then, without another word, she walked out of the room and down the stairs.

Sara heard the front door slam. God, what had she done to be so punished? How could she cope with someone as difficult as this? How could a girl—a *decent* girl—leave her home?

When Jacob came home he found Sara weeping. "Rachel left the house . . ."

He was still terribly hurt at Rachel's outburst the night she had asked to go to college. But no matter, she was his child, and he was her father whether she loved him or not. He would not leave her out there alone, abandon her the way his mother had done . . .

"Left the house? How could you have allowed that—?"

"Don't you start at me, Jacob. I've been through enough. For one solid week it's been hell—"

"Why did she leave?"

"You don't know Rachel yet? I asked how much she earned. After all, was that so unreasonable? Don't I have a right to know? I was trying to make her understand she shouldn't spend everything, that a person should save a little."

Jacob sighed. "Where is she?"

"At the YWCA."

"Did you call?"

"I'm her mother—she should have called me."

"Still, she's just a child."

"A child? Eighteen is a child? I was a mother at her age, and making a home. Not if hell freezes will I give in to her this time. Besides, if I did there'd be no living with her—"

"Don't be foolish, Sara. You're hurt, I understand that, but we have to go and get her—"

"Not me, you go. She loves *you* a lot too . . ."

"Well, she thinks I did something terrible and she's angry. She'll get over it."

"A lot you know. She's as stubborn as a mule and just as selfish. She never offered to contribute a dime."

"She doesn't have to, this is her home."

"All right, Jacob. As usual, stick up for her—"

"Oh, for God's sake, Sara. Whatever I say is wrong. It always ends up this way—with us fighting. I'm going to bring her back."

"You do that. And tell her next time she can step on me," Sara called out as Jacob slammed the back door. . . .

Jacob found his daughter sitting on the edge of the iron cot against the wall, in a room just large enough for a dresser and a chair.

"Mama tells me you left the house. What kind of a decent girl does that? A girl from a good Jewish home? Now, get your things together and I'll wait for you downstairs in the lobby."

"I'm not going back . . ."

He was running out of patience. "Now listen to me, Rachel. You're not the easiest person in the world to get along with, and neither is your mother. But you belong home and that's where you're going. So get dressed."

Rachel wanted to resist, but this past week had been unbearably lonely. Bad as it was at home, there were things she missed. Perhaps the mere familiarity of it? Here she felt an isolation and aimlessness that had badly frightened her. For all the problems, home was home. What else was there for her? She had no friends to turn to. Imagine, eighteen and

209

she'd never even really kissed a boy. Mama took care of that a long time ago. It would be awful to face mama, but . . .

If Sara was relieved she didn't show it, and Rachel didn't expect it. Rachel, though, told herself that striking back wouldn't solve anything. She wasn't capitulating, not for a moment. It was just a question of self-preservation.

She ended up paying twenty-five dollars a month. Papa objected loudly but she didn't back down. She had her self-respect, and it did make her feel a little more independent. God, couldn't they see that . . . ?

Not until the day Rachel came home from work to find that Shlomo was there on leave did she feel any real lift to her spirits. How handsome he was in the magnificent uniform . . . she almost trembled as he looked at her, holding her at arm's length. "Rachel, you're a woman, a beautiful woman. How did you grow up so fast?"

"It wasn't so fast, you just weren't around often enough."

"Obviously a great mistake on my part . . ." He kissed her on the forehead and held her against him. When he let her go he shook his head. She was truly exquisite, so poised, her blonde hair still like strands of silk, and those blue eyes . . .

"How long will you be here?" Rachel asked.

"A week."

"I'm very pleased you've come." Oh God, if only she could tell him what she really felt . . .

"I am too, Rachel. You'll have to tell me about yourself and what you've been doing."

She smiled. "I'm sure that would be boring. It's you we all want to know about."

"After dinner," Sara said. "Papa's getting washed up."

At dinner Shlomo couldn't take his eyes off Rachel. Sara had done a good job, no question. But Sara wouldn't be able to keep her much longer. Of that he was certain.

Later the family all sat in the livingroom and listened to Shlomo tell them about the exotic places he had been, the different cultures he had seen. The children were fascinated by him. He could speak Chinese, Japanese, Filipino . . . They wanted him to go on and on, but it was well past Jacob's bedtime, and reluctantly Doris and Lillian said goodnight and went up to do their homework. Rachel would have liked to stay but she felt awkward. In fact, there hadn't been a moment since he arrived that she hadn't been aware of his presence . . .

210

Doris had always dreamed of being a bride. She bought magazines and was an authority on the subject. In her fantasy she was always tall and thin, floating down the aisle in a cloud of white veils and lace. Then she and her groom went off to a romantic island, floating in the blue Pacific. She had planned the whole marvelous event. The reception would be here at home, and mama would make all kinds of marvelous sandwiches and salads. But the cake was to come from a bakery. It would be three layers, with a bride and a groom standing on top . . . Tonight as she and Lillian lay in bed, she asked, "Lillian, can you keep a secret?"

"Of course I can. That's almost insulting."

"Well, sometimes as I've told you, you do forget. But you won't tell? Promise?"

"Promise."

"All right, I'm going to marry Uncle Shlomo." Mrs. Sandy Sanders . . .

Lillian sat up in bed and switched on the bedside lamp. "That's crazy. You can't marry a relative."

"Oh, yes, you can. Didn't our cousin Bertha from Cleveland marry her cousin, on Uncle Harold's side?"

"Well, maybe that's different, but your uncle? Besides, he's an old man . . ."

"Oh, he is not, Lillian. A lot you know about romance."

"Well, I know a little bit about it. Billy Hines walks me home every day," she answered indignantly.

"That's different. Incidently, did he ever kiss you?"

"Oh, Doris! Of course not. I don't go around kissing boys. Remember what mama said about getting diseases . . ."

"How do you know about that?"

"Because I overheard her telling you. I'm not so dumb."

"I didn't say you were dumb. I meant . . . oh, I don't know what I meant. I only know I'm going to marry Sandy."

"Sandy? You mean Uncle Shlomo?"

"Well, only until we're married."

"How do you know he wants to marry you?"

"Because of the way he kisses me. A person can just tell, that's how."

"Well, I saw him looking at Rachel tonight."

Doris had too. "So what if he did. I didn't see him kiss her like he kissed me when we left the room . . . Anyway, I don't want to talk about it any more." And with that she turned off the light, shut her eyes and lay awake in the dark for a very long time.

Rachel stared up at the ceiling. She could simply find nowhere to hide from herself tonight. He had aroused feelings in her she had never felt before, feelings that were disturbing, exciting, confusing ... She dreamed what it would be like to lay in his arms, to be fondled, caressed and told how beautiful and desirable she was. She was so madly in love with him that she was convinced there could never be another man in her life. Somehow it seemed she had known for a long time, but had only now realized it. He had, after all, sent her special presents and letters from all those places ...

Turning on the bedside lamp, she went to her special hiding place and took out the packet of letters he'd sent through the years. She read the last one now, the one he'd sent before leaving Singapore.

My dearest Rachel,
You have no idea how delighted I was to receive the invitation announcing your graduation. I was bursting with pride that my little Rachel had become the most beautiful woman. The pictures you sent me made me realize how much I had missed, not seeing you grow up. The loss is mine.

However, I must say that when I showed your picture to my buddies they thought you were my sweetheart. I told them you were my very own sweet Rachel, with the halo of blonde hair and the eyes like blue sapphires.

Don't let anyone run off with you, Rachel, not without my consent. I'm concerned who you marry. Don't be in a hurry—there's a world to see and explore. I love all my nephews and nieces but there is something special in you. Congratulations, dear sweet Rachel, and may God love you, as I do.

Sandy

She held his letter close to her as she would have loved to hold him. He was sleeping in Lillian's room, just down the hall. What were his thoughts? Did he feel the way she did? She was sure of it as she slipped the letter back into the envelope. . . .

After an almost sleepless night Rachel was awakened by the alarm clock. She clicked the button off and lay in dreamy thoughts before she suddenly got out of bed ... It was six-fifteen and she had to catch the seven o'clock commuter train to connect with the ferry.

She hurried through her morning shower. When she

212

walked out of the bathroom, her heart began to pound as she almost collided with him. "Good morning—"

Sandy smiled. "You're in such a hurry?"

"I know. I overslept—something I never do."

"You sound like you're in the marines." He laughed.

She could only smile, mumble something insane and run to her room, where she now leaned against the wall and wondered if he could tell . . . did he suspect? She prayed he couldn't—then prayed he could. . . .

That night she hurried home, only to find the most painful disappointment. Jacob had taken Sandy to the country for a few days. She could hardly eat, sleep was nearly impossible. She withdrew into almost total silence. Immediately after dinner she went to her room and paced the floor. Why did he go away with papa? Didn't he know how she felt? Or had he left because he too felt the nearness of the hall, which was all that separated them?

The next evening Rachel decided she simply couldn't go home to dinner. The last few days had been unbearable, so instead she decided to have dinner at a small tea room that catered to ladies only. As she waited for her salad her thoughts were full of Sandy . . . She looked about the room . . . When they—Lord, she meant "she," of course—when she had a home of her own it would be like this, with a Windsor table and chairs, country floral wallpaper and matching draperies. Beyond the windows were flower boxes of spring blooms. Yes, her house would look more like this . . . She was depressed by the way her family lived, with the awful old furniture. Why didn't papa spend some of his money and fix up the place? At least she wouldn't be embarrassed to bring someone home then. Then again, she didn't have friends to entertain, so what difference did it make? If they wanted to live like that, let them—it was their business. But it was hers to see that her life took a different direction. . . .

It was eight o'clock when she put the key in the door and was halfway up the stairs when Sara slid open the livingroom doors to the hall and without preamble asked, "Why didn't you come home for dinner?"

Rachel looked at her mother in amazement. To mama, she was still a little girl going to the convent who had to be carefully watched. "Because I didn't feel like it."

"I must say, you're getting to be quite an independent woman."

"You might say that," Rachel said.

Sara's anger began to build. "What did you do after work?"

Rachel felt like saying, I lost my virginity tonight. Instead . . . "I decided to have dinner out."

"Where?"

"At a *restaurant*."

"Really . . . Who did you go with?"

"Someone from work . . ."

"Oh, you made friends at work?"

"Of course, mama, people like me. I'm very popular."

"Especially with the men, I imagine—"

"Especially." She wouldn't give mama the satisfaction of knowing there were no men in her office. Just sad girls, all cogs in a giant wheel pumping out figures for American Telephone and Telegraph, but not on her life would she let mama know that. She would very much have liked to tell mama that she was jealous of her job, that mama couldn't quite keep her under her iron thumb anymore.

Sara ran her tongue around her dry lips. "I'm going to warn you, Rachel, I won't have you talk to me in that tone of voice. From now on, I want to know where you go and I want you to call. Do you hear?"

"It would be difficult not to—"

Sara ran up the stairs and was about to slap Rachel when the front door opened.

Jacob and Shlomo stood below.

Rachel was so mortified she ran to her room, slammed the door, then pounded on the wall until her knuckles bled.

Sara walked down the stairs, seething. "I only wish you'd been here a little earlier."

Jacob's face was pale. He had forbidden Sara to hit the children. After all, he'd left her once because of that. "What happened?" he asked with unmistakable anger.

"You should have heard the way she talked to me—"

"How?"

"Like I was an interfering stranger, and all because I had the temerity to ask why her royal highness hadn't come home to dinner. She didn't even consider I might be worried that something had happened to her. It's simply too inconsiderate, I can't take this, Jacob. I want you to talk to her—"

"But you were about to hit her. You weren't hit enough in your own childhood? You forgot?"

"Why are you bringing that up? I didn't deserve it, I wasn't like Rachel . . . I tell you, Jacob, there's a limit to my endurance. I'm not a saint." She went off to the kitchen, lay her head on the table and wept until her whole body shook.

Jacob looked at Shlomo and shook his head. "I don't know, I can't understand. What's wrong with kids today?"

"Go up and talk to her, Jacob."

"No, I can't. Not now . . . I'm too upset."

"Jacob, she needs you . . ."

"Rachel doesn't need anyone. Sara's not altogether wrong, believe me . . . You should have heard the mouth she opened to me one day."

"Jacob, Sara's too emotional—and Rachel's a very sensitive young woman."

"How do you know so much? Correct me, but as I recall you just got here a few days ago. Besides, what do you know about raising children?" and he went into the livingroom and sat down heavily in his chair. . . .

Shlomo shook his head, went upstairs and knocked at Rachel's door. "It's me, Rachel."

She held her breath. "Please, go away. *Please.*"

"I just want to speak to you."

"Not now, I can't—"

But it was what she wanted more than anything in the world . . .

The house was very still. Rachel put on her flowered robe, went to the bathroom and washed her face and combed her hair, then stared at her reflection. All the red was gone from her eyes. She tinted her cheeks and lips lightly, then walked quietly across the dark hall to Shlomo's room. She knocked softly. The door opened.

"May I come in?" she asked, trembling.

"Of course."

When Shlomo shut the door, Rachel went into his arms. Clinging to him, she kissed him with such passion he felt himself grow hard. Gently he took her arm from around his neck and held her at a distance.

"Rachel, I think we'd better talk tomorrow—"

"No . . . now."

"Not tonight, Rachel, not here—"

"Why not? You love me. We love each other and I want you to make love to—"

"No—no, don't say it."

Desperate, she let her robe drop from her shoulders. Her slim body was like delicate ivory. Her breasts were soft, firm.

He picked up the robe and handed it to her, saying gently, "Put it on, Rachel."

She looked stricken. "Don't you want me? Don't you find me desirable at all? I thought—"

"Rachel, I'm your father's brother—"

"Half-brother. Besides, what does that have to do with this? I love you, Sandy. Please take me with you . . ."

"Rachel, you don't know what you're asking."

"Yes, I do. I've thought of absolutely nothing but us, you and me."

"You're not looking for me, Rachel, you're looking for an escape. Believe me, that's what this really is—"

"How can you say that to me after the letters you sent and the presents?"

"What letters?"

"The love letters . . ."

Oh, my God, she had read into them what she needed to hear. "Rachel, those weren't *love letters*. They were letters written to someone I love very dearly, as I do all of you . . ."

Slowly Rachel stepped into the robe and tied the sash around her waist. "So all these years I waited for nothing. I thought if there was one person in the world I could count on, it would be you. My mother's right. I *am* nothing, I *am* stupid—"

"You mustn't say that. You're a beautiful young woman and you're going to find a very lucky young man who loves you as you should be loved."

She stood silent for a long moment. "Well, dear uncle, you taught me a very valuable lesson tonight . . . I'm never going to love *anyone* again."

"You're hurt and . . ."

But she had already turned and walked out of the room before he had a chance to finish.

He sat now on the edge of the bed. Face it, he *had* wanted to hold her tight and not only to comfort her . . . But such feelings aroused in him not only were dangerous but also of no importance. What was of real concern was that she clearly meant what she'd said, that she'd never allow herself to be vulnerable to anyone, and it was partly his fault. But what could he do about it except pray that he hadn't, even if unwittingly, helped to destroy the last small vestige of love that she had left . . .

He dressed quickly, packed and wrote a note that he propped against the pillow. He looked at the room, knowing he would never be able to come back. . . .

Jacob was not only bewildered but also angry at Shlomo's abrupt departure. He had dreamed that the two of them were at last going to be partners but now Shlomo was going back to the marines. Jacob needed someone of his own to depend on in his business. If only he'd had a son ... What perplexed him most was that in the last few days, as they had traveled together through the countryside, he thought that Shlomo had finally shown some enthusiasm for his work. Now, suddenly, he was reenlisting for another two years. Shlomo was a mystery. What in the world was the great hold the marines had on his brother?

Fortunately, if Shlomo had his way, Jacob would never find out.

CHAPTER THIRTY-THREE

IT WAS 1928, and America was riding high. The nation was rich and powerful, the economy solid. Businesses were thriving and everyone was buying stock—even Jacob's barber.

Jacob was draped now in a white cloth and sitting in a revolving chair as Guido Ranzinni clipped away at his thick blond hair. He observed Guido's smiling face in the mirror.

"I got a house paid for. A brand new Chevrolet—green, the color of money. I'm a happy man, Jack. My sons are goin' to have what I never had. Joey's going to the college ... he's gonna be a doctor. Pretty good for a barber who couldn't read or write, huh? From me and Maria, two dumb kids from Naples. With these scissors and a little luck I've done okay. But I really made a killing the other day."

"Yeah? How?"

"I bought a stock called Goldman Saks. I never heard of it, don't even know now what it's all about, but my broker says buy, so Guido buys. Smart man, my broker."

"Who is he?"

"Wonderful man, his name is Joseph Calla. You should go see him, Jack."

"I don't like stocks."

"You're crazy, everyone's making a fortune. I made three hundred dollars in one day. Did you ever hear of anything like it? I could have stood on my feet for the rest of my life and never make what I did last year. I learned how from Calla. I buy and sell, keep most of the money, put it in the bank and buy on margin."

217

"I still don't like stocks . . ."

"A smart Jew like you don't want to make a killing?"

The comment didn't anger Jacob because he knew there was no malice in it. In fact, Guido put them in the same bag. Wops and Kikes had to stick together, he had often said.

"Of course I do," answered Jacob. "Who doesn't? But I only know how to buy cattle. I don't like to invest in anything I can't control."

"That's foolish. The richest men in the world are in the market and they can't control it any more than you can."

Jacob knew how much money everyone was making, but he was afraid to invest. His own business was almost as much a gamble as the stock market was, in some ways even more so. The truth of the matter was that although he knew it was important to buy in volume he didn't always have the cash to buy the amount of livestock he needed. Most of the time he traded on a bank draft, when in fact the money wasn't in his account. But thank God he'd become good friends with the local bank manager. The man covered for him because he knew that not once had Jacob defaulted. Still, he frequently spent a sleepless night praying that by the time he sold the cattle he'd be able to cover the draft and come out with a profit.

These were different times than when Jacob started. Prices fluctuated so fast from the time of purchase to the time of sale that if it hadn't been for his uncanny skill in buying right he could easily be operating in the red. Yes indeed, these were different times. Today farmers had radios and listened to stock prices. But Jacob pitted his brain against the ranchers and there were few who did better than he. He played the percentages. Many of the heifers were underweight but he bought them deliberately. He made sure that his cattle would gain weight in transit, because every pound gained was a dollar earned. Which was why he traveled with them, even slept in a caboose . . .

As Guido removed the white apron from Jacob's neck, sprinkled talcum powder on a round brush and began to dust away the tiny stray hairs, he said, "You go see Calla. I'm telling you, Jack, climb on the gravy train."

After he left the shop Jacob sat in his car for a long time debating with himself. Guido's words had had more of an impact than he wanted to admit. "I could work a lifetime . . . I'm a happy man . . . two dumb kids from Naples . . ." Well, Jacob wasn't such a happy man, but in its fashion life had been good to him too. He wasn't *rich*, of course, but he had more than most, and more than anyone knew, including Sara and the kids, and for good reason. He'd become so secretive, thanks to their pressures, that he didn't even tell Shlomo, though he wondered now if that hadn't been a mistake . . . maybe if he'd told him more he'd have stayed, not reenlisted . . . Still, what he'd seen and learned was that you couldn't trust anybody . . . hadn't his whole life been proof of that? Sometimes he did feel bad . . . though he could never bring himself to tell her so . . . that he held back from Sara, but then he reminded himself that if he let her have her way she'd have them bankrupt with her craziness about furniture, her refusal to understand that the money he needed to buy his cattle didn't grow on trees . . . All right, maybe he did overdo it, maybe he could loosen up a little more, except once you started with that . . . The overwhelming fact for him was that from his sweat and hands and brains he had created security for his family, and he was determined that the source of it . . . his business . . . should grow. One day he would own his own plant . . . Still, "go see Calla, climb on the gravy train" kept reverberating in his head. Sometimes maybe you did have to risk a little to get ahead. . . .

Jacob sat now in Calla's office in the Bank of America Building as the broker explained, "In order to make money, Mr. Sanders, you know as well as I do that you've got to invest a sizable sum."

"What's a sizable sum?"

"Well, all things are relative, but let's say if you could spare five thousand dollars, that could start you out with a fair portfolio."

Jacob groaned inwardly. Sure, he had the money, but to *gamble* five thousand dollars?

Calla continued, "I'd suggest putting three thousand in Goldman Saks—that's the best buy on the market at twelve dollars a share. Then there's a new issue out on an airline that's going commercial—"

"Airline stock? I wouldn't invest a quarter."

"All right, here's a gilt-edge stock. AT&T. There . . ."

Jacob wasn't listening. Goldman Saks was the buy. Twelve dollars into five thousand meant owning four hundred and sixteen shares. Jacob's hand shook as he wrote out the check. . . .

He read the financial page every night. It was going up and up and up.

After eight months Jacob became nervous. The stock had jumped to sixty-five dollars a share. Of the twenty-seven

219

thousand dollars, he took twenty-two of it and put it in the safe-deposit box and reinvested the original five thousand, plus what he bought on margin. He now owned railroad, oil and AT&T stocks. Not so bad. Jack Sandsonitsky had a real stake in the *goyim*'s America . . .

To own a meat packing plant, that still was the ultimate, and now it was almost in the palm of his hand. Mr. Fratis, who had owned and ran the Hayward Meat Packing Company, had died, leaving no sons to carry on the business. It was an established and well-respected business, and it was up for grabs.

When Jacob had worked for the Hayward Meat Packing Company, he had been concerned with keeping his family's security uppermost in his mind and suppressing his revulsion over slaughtering the cows. The idea that one day he might own it would have seemed as ridiculous as going to the moon. And now? He hungered for it. The plant and the five acres of pens and feed mills were his ladder to success—no more speculating at the stockyards. But buying it would mean selling the stocks, which had now earned him two hundred and twenty-five thousand dollars. The choice lay between the riches promised by the market and the attainment of a longtime dream. He would have liked both, but Mrs. Fratis wanted cash. She was a tough old lady who could not be bargained with. So Jacob sold to buy a dream.

On January 5, 1929, Jacob disposed of his stock and bought the Hayward Meat Packing Company. He paid seventy thousand dollars in cash to Mrs. Fratis and used the rest of his stock earnings to establish a line of credit. With a bank loan he modernized the plant and hired a small office staff. Smitty, who still worked at the plant, became a truck driver. Jacob hired two additional drivers and bought three new trucks.

This would have been, should have been, Jacob's happiest moment, except for two things. Shlomo was still in the marines and he needed someone to keep an eye on his interests. He couldn't be everywhere . . . And Sara still badgered him . . . wanting to furnish the house and all the rest of it. The arguments were becoming more frequent, more extreme. But he would not, could not, budge from his position . . . She was not going to dominate his life no matter how much she tried. She'd deprived him of enough, deprived him of *herself*. Now she would wait until *he* was ready. She had hurt him more than even he knew. She had turned against him during the times when it seemed that everything in life was conspiring against him. Now, the money at least helped. His new company would help more. . . .

Shortly after Jacob was firmly established in the plant he became consumed with another vision—to own a large ranch up in Klamath that consisted of four hundred and fifty acres of perfect grazing land and two hundred acres of planted alfalfa. But its greatest asset was what every cattleman most valued—water. The irrigation ditches were already there and an added attraction was that a Santa Fe spur track ran through the property. This not only meant less expense in transporting his cattle, but the railroad had to rent the land in order to have access to the track. No longer would he be obliged to buy the cattle in Montana, Wyoming, Oregon and Nevada, and once he acquired his own breeding stock the profits could be enormous. The cattle could be shipped to the Hayward Meat Packing Company, fed and fattened in his pens and feed mill—and all the profits would be his.

He would miss the camaraderie of sitting around a poker table with the ranchers he once bought from, and drinking a little straight whiskey. They never discussed business when playing five-card stud, but when all the fun and games were over the serious trading began. "Okay," the discussion began, "what do you want a head?" The answer was always the same. "Make me an offer." And no matter what the offer was, it was never enough. But Jacob loved this sparring.

He also loved riding herd and seeing his own brand sear the butt of a bull. He loved the glow of coals as the branding irons heated, and the sizzling of burning hair and the pungent odor of the smoke. Yes, the best time was roundup . . . "Don't hurry the cattle when you make a drive," he'd call out to the men. The fat on the cow was worth more than the wages of the few cowpokes who were driving them. "Go slow," he admonished them, "don't let them get nervous or tired out. Don't tackle them too hard." Yes, that was the adventure that Jacob loved. He'd never been more happy than when he was riding behind a bunch of fat cattle. This was a side of him that Sara had never known. It was a private side and it had given him many good memories. But like all good things, it had had its run, and now needed to be put aside for a larger and better future . . .

He bought the ranch for five hundred an acre and put down a minimum payment. The bank carried the balance, but this time he wasn't frightened. It would pay off. . . .

When he told Sara what he had done, to her it meant that

221

their lives would grow even further apart. But wasn't that to be expected? she thought. Her mother, her father, and now Jacob—sooner or later they had all left her to herself.

And now Jacob did spend more time away from home than ever before. Sure, he had asked her to come up to see the ranch, told her she might enjoy it, that the house was beautiful, that from time to time she should leave the kids and come up to stay. But what would she do up there alone in that kind of wilderness? Jacob would be working all day . . . Sara refused even to see it.

As Jacob's world widened, Sara's narrowed to an intense focus on her only remaining outlets. Jacob, she felt, was closing her out. What more natural than that she should become increasingly possessive of her children, more assaulted by anxieties and grievances, more difficult to live with. . . .

Jacob had been so busy that he had little time to concern himself with what the stock market was doing. So in September of 1929 he was stunned by the events that had brought him to his current prosperity—the crash, which came like a thunderbolt, with panic its aftermath . . .

Guido Ranzinni sat in his barber shop in a state of shock. Yesterday he was a rich man, today he was a pauper . . .

People were jumping out of buildings. Committing suicide was a daily occurrence, and those who had criticized Jacob for not staying in the market began to think of him as a financial genius.

Jacob was well aware that for once his life had brought him a little luck. He could have been in Guido's position if Fratis hadn't died at the right time. Moreover, in spite of the Depression, his plant survived. He owned the property free and clear and had sufficient cash stashed away in a vault box. He began to wonder if perhaps luck had less to do with it than he'd thought when he first heard about the crash. After all, the best school in the world was life, it had taught him not only to learn from his errors but how to survive. If he hadn't been robbed in that flophouse in the Bowery he might not, for instance, have realized the importance of a vault box. He made sure that he always had a certain amount of cash he could put his hands on. Banks were necessary institutions—for loans only.

Harvard Business School he didn't need to teach him that.

CHAPTER THIRTY-FOUR

RACHEL STOOD on the corner of Montgomery and Market Streets, waiting for a streetcar to take her to the ferry building where she would make the crossing from San Francisco to Oakland. It had started to rain, and here she was without an umbrella. She waited in a doorway, tired and disgusted.

Where *was* her life going? Nowhere. She had saved a little, hoping that maybe this summer she'd be able to go to Vancouver, but the Crash had taken care of that. Still, she was one of the lucky ones. There had been a drastic cut in her salary, but many of the girls in her office had been given notice. In the last year she had dated a few men, but no one who really interested her. Most recently she had dated Maury Cohen, who was madly in love with her and had begged her to marry him, but she had turned him down flat. He had been merely an excuse to get out of the house, but she didn't really like him. He was poor *and* obnoxious—a combination she could do without . . .

Seeing the streetcar approach, she ran toward the curb. She didn't see the car that turned the corner just at that moment, and she was so surprised by the torrent of water that splashed up at her from the gutter that she lost her footing at the curb. She lay sprawled on the pavement, drenched and stunned. Her purse was open and all the contents scattered. Her lovely hat was askew and her best coat ruined. She was so angry she wanted to cry.

The driver of the car parked to one side, got out and began to help her up.

"Are you hurt?"

Rachel blinked the rain from her eyes without answering him.

With the rain dripping from the rim of his hat he went on, "I'm so sorry, are you hurt?"

Looking at her coat, she answered, "With no thanks to you—no."

"Look, please. I'm sorry. I insist on paying for it."

Rachel wasn't listening. She had just realized that the streetcar had gone past her stop, and she shook her head angrily.

"I don't know what to say, really. I know this sounds forward, but may I please drive you to where you're going?"

Shivering, she looked at the man in the handsome suit, then at the Cadillac convertible. He was about forty, she guessed, and his voice seemed decently kind, sincere. She hesitated, then, "All right."

He helped her into the car, then retrieved her purse and its contents. By the time she removed her hat to shake off the rain he was behind the steering wheel. "Now, where can I take you?"

"To the ferry building."

As he drove down Market Street he said, "I'd like to introduce myself. I'm Jim Ross."

"My name is Rachel Sanders," she said, looking in her purse to see if anything was missing.

"May I call you Rachel?"

"I can't see that it matters . . ."

"But it does, since I intend to replace your coat."

"Don't be ridiculous, I wouldn't accept that—"

"I insist. I was the one who ruined it."

"I still couldn't let you do that."

Silence. Then awkwardly Jim said, "I want to apologize again. You're absolutely drenched, and that fall you took must have shaken you."

"I can't say it was exactly fun." He glanced at her beautiful face as she continued, "If we don't hurry I'll miss the ferry."

"Where do you live?"

"In Oakland."

"I see. Well, again, may I say how sorry I—"

"That's very nice of you. If you don't mind, will you let me off under the canopy?"

Jim Ross was so taken with the exquisite Rachel that he hadn't realized they were in front of the building.

Helping her out he asked, "Where can I reach you?"

"Why?"

"Because I insist on replacing—"

"Please forget it, Mr. Ross. You've been very kind." She got out of the car and ran inside the building.

Jim drove aimlessly around the city, finally drove home. He was no kid, not one given to dramatics, let alone melodrama. But there was no denying that the effect on him of Rachel Sanders was unlike anything he'd ever known.

Later in his room, trying to read, his mind wandered back to the earlier events of the evening ... to her ... What an extraordinarily beautiful young woman. He got up and went down to the den, poured himself a scotch, sat down and watched the fire's glow. Damn, his life had turned out to be a disaster but until tonight he thought he'd at least come to terms with it. Now he felt that something rather momentous had happened to him. Out of nowhere this young woman had simply entered his life, and he was so startled by the realization that he began to question the compromises that had become so central to his life. ...

Jim Ross had met Kelly Richardson when he was at Harvard and she at Radcliffe. Kelly was the most popular, desirable, sought-after girl at college. Her family was old Boston and his new Pennsylvania. Her father was a Princeton man, as was her grandfather, while Jim's father and grandfather had worked in the steel mills. It wasn't that the Rosses didn't have money, of course. His father and his six brothers had pooled their resources and started a small steel mill of their own, and by the time Jim was old enough to go to Harvard his father had made it possible for him to be accepted into a fine club.

On his wedding day, Jim almost pinched himself, still amazed that someone like Kelly would marry him. But whatever it was she saw in him, he wasn't about to question it.

Shortly after their honeymoon, Mr. James Ross, Sr. opened a subsidiary plant in San Francisco for Jim.

The first years of their marriage had been happy. Kelly was the perfect hostess, the perfect wife and the perfect mother. They adored their daughter Maureen; so far as they were concerned, there had never been a child quite so unique.

Then one evening his whole world came crashing down on him. He'd returned home unexpectedly from a business trip— and found that the devoted Kelly had a lover. In fact, he discovered them making love in the same room, in the same bed, he had shared with Kelly all these years. He stood staring unbelievingly, rooted to the floor. It was not another man ... Kelly was in love with Jennifer Holem, a Radcliffe classmate.

When he finally came out of his paralysis he slammed the door, ran to the bathroom and threw up.

He stayed away from the house for two weeks. But poor Maureen, their daughter, was left alone in that mansion on Pacific Avenue with her mother and her lover.

There was nothing left for it but to go back, try to do what he had to do for his daughter. He laid it on the line to Kelly: "I don't give a damn about your obsessions. The one thing I do care about is Maureen. Unfortunately she adores you, and it would destroy her if the truth about you came out in a divorce. It would be a scandal. So you listen to me carefully. I'll give you a divorce when Maureen is of age and on her own. Then you can fry in hell. But until then you're going to be the kind of mother she deserves to have. It'll be tough to pretend, but that's the way it's going to be. You'll be the devoted mother, and to all outward appearances the Rosses will be a family. I've seen too many children suffer because of a broken home." He bent over her, wishing he could squeeze the life out of her.

Jim took one of the many bedrooms down the hall and stayed as far away from his wife in name only as he could.

When Maureen was fifteen she attended boarding school, which at least made the task of their bizarre situation more simple . . . They only had to play their roles during holidays and summer vacations. . . .

Now Maureen was going on eighteen and was a happy, well-adjusted girl. Didn't he owe himself something now? He got up, poured himself another scotch and looked out to the murky night.

He'd known from the very beginning, when he'd picked Rachel up off that sidewalk, that he had every intention in the world of seeing her again. Think . . . she'd been waiting for a streetcar at about five-thirty on the corner of Montgomery and Market, which meant she must work in that general area, and she also took a six o'clock ferry to Oakland. Finding her again shouldn't be all that difficult. . . .

The next evening Jim parked his car a little after five and waited. When he saw Rachel crossing from Montgomery to Third and Market, his pulse raced like a schoolboy's.

Rachel was startled when she heard her name being called.

"How are you, Rachel?"

"Fine . . . Mr. Ross, and you?"

"Fine. I hope you recovered from yesterday."

"Yes, thank you—"

"Rachel, this may seem a little presumptuous, but I wonder if I might take you to dinner tonight."

She thought for a moment. She'd already let a stranger pick her up last night and what could happen to her in a restaurant? It didn't seem quite so bold after all. Maybe it

226

was the fact that he was older that reassured her. "I don't know that I'm dressed for it, Mr. Ross . . ."

"You look lovely."

"You should have your eyes examined."

"I just did and they're twenty-twenty. Now, may I take you to dinner?"

Again, Rachel considered, then said, "All right."

"Where would you like to go?"

"I don't know San Francisco restaurants, why don't you decide?" . . .

Rachel, of course, had heard of Solari's. It was one of San Francisco's most famous restaurants, but she'd never been there.

The room was all she imagined it would be. Walnut paneling, dimly lit crystal chandeliers, snowy white linen, waiters in tuxedos, roses, candles, paintings, Persian rugs—it took her breath away.

"Good evening, Mr. Ross," the *maître d'*, Émile, said as he ushered them to their table.

When they were seated, Rachel said, "If you'll excuse me, I want to call home."

She hated having to check in with mama, but if she didn't it would just cause another war . . . "Mama?"

"Yes?"

"This is Rachel . . ."

"I know who it is."

Rachel bit her lip. "I missed the ferry so I'll be late."

"What are you going to do about dinner?"

"I'll have something. There's a sandwich shop in the building. I'll wait here for the next ferry."

"Fine . . . papa came home."

Was that supposed to please her? Dear papa, who never gave her a nickel, much less a smile or any indication of interest in her life . . . ?

When she went back to the table, the waiter handed them a large menu. The prices were astounding.

"What would you like?" Jim asked.

"Why don't you order . . ." God knew, she wouldn't dare.

"Do you like sweetbreads? They're very good here."

"That sounds . . . fine." She'd never had them.

First came the fresh green salad with bay shrimp, bouillon and a small portion of vermicelli. The sautéed sweetbreads were accompanied by asparagus topped with hollandaise. Dessert was French pastry and coffee.

227

Jim set down his coffee cup and said, "Someone who looks like you must have a difficult time fending off young men—"

"I don't happen to like young men, so I'm not too bothered with that problem."

He smiled at her candor. Which also gave him more hope. "I'm pleased that you've allowed me to take you to dinner."

"Well, since we ran into each other by—coincidence," she answered, realizing that this was no coincidence.

He laughed, knowing how transparent their "accidental" meeting had been tonight. It hadn't been at all subtle. "What do you do?"

"You mean where do I work? At the telephone company."

This exquisite girl. "You?"

"Why not? There are millions of girls like me, Mr. Ross, but I'm luckier than they. I still have a job."

He sat staring at her.

"What did you think I was last night, Mr. Ross? A society girl out slumming?"

He lit a cigarette and blew out the match. "I don't really know what I thought except, if you'll forgive me, I think you're the most beautiful woman I've ever seen."

She peered over the rim of her coffee cup. Her deep blue eyes and thick brown lashes were a startling contrast to her blonde hair.

"Are you a . . . telephone operator?"

"Would it matter?"

"Of course not, just curious. I don't know *why* I asked."

"I work in the bookkeeping department, comptometers—terribly exciting work, Mr. Ross. Now you know all about my fascinating life, tell me about you."

"About me? Well, I have a daughter going on eighteen." He paused, and for the first time Rachel noticed a bitterness in his voice. "I'm married."

"Happily?"

He looked at her. Not only beautiful, but observant. So it showed that much, did it? "No, Rachel. I haven't been happy about my marriage for a very long time." Strange, he thought, he'd never spoken to anyone about his marriage. In spite of the angelic face, she seemed strikingly mature. Not worldly, quite the opposite, and for some reason he had the odd feeling that her life had been less than all roses too . . . "We're sitting here talking like old friends," he said.

She allowed herself a smile, then, "Why do you stay married, Mr. Ross?"

228

"That's a question an old friend would ask, thank you." He pulled the lobe of his ear, then took a sip of coffee. "I suppose we stayed together for reasons that don't really make sense, although I thought they did at the time . . . I don't know, Rachel, maybe a feeling of failure, a feeling of responsibility. It's a long story, and you have to catch a boat. Better still, would you trust me to take you home?"

"Yes, but I live in Oakland."

"I know, you told me. I'll drive you home."

There was an odd sort of excitement Rachel felt as they drove off the ferry and onto the pier in the blue convertible. They rode in silence until they were within a block of her house.

"If you don't mind," she said, "I'd like to get out here."

"Why?"

"Well, that's a long story too. If your car was seen in front of my house, I think I'd have a lot of explaining to do."

He nodded. After all, he'd undoubtedly react the same way if he saw Maureen getting out of a stranger's car.

Coming around to Rachel's side, he opened the door and took her hand as he helped her out. "This has been a very curious evening, hasn't it, Rachel?"

"Very . . ."

"I won't forget tonight."

"Nor will I. Thank you for dinner."

"Thank you. You're an incredible young woman."

"That's debatable. Good night, Mr. Ross."

"Good night, Rachel." . . .

The next evening when Rachel stepped out of the revolving doors of the telephone building she wasn't really surprised to see Jim Ross waiting for her.

"Any plans for this evening?"

Smiling, "No."

"Dinner?"

"Lovely . . ."

He smiled suddenly, and so did Rachel. Starting up the engine, he drove without asking her for a preference. He'd long ago made up his mind.

Julius's Castle sat high on a hill overlooking the city. The view was breathtaking.

When they were seated Jim watched as Rachel looked out to the bay. She was enchanted with the view, and even more so with her companion. The rain that she had been cursing only seconds before she first met Jim Ross now seemed like a

229

blessing. How had she been so lucky? It was certainly something new. Well, don't look a gift horse in the mouth . . . Suddenly her expression changed. "I almost forgot, I have to make a phone call."

When she returned Jim noticed a peculiar look in her eyes.

"What's wrong, Rachel?"

She tried to hold back the tears. Biting the corner of her lip, she sat for a moment, trying to gain her composure. Finally she answered, "What's wrong is my mother . . ."

"Would you like to talk about it?"

"Not especially, but I will. My mother can't quite cope with the fact that I'm a big girl."

"I suppose mothers are like that, Rachel . . . a little protective. And in your case, I can certainly understand it."

"Can you really, Mr. Ross? Well, my mother's not exactly protective. Domineering is more like it. She's not your everyday run-of-the-mill mother . . ."

"Aren't you judging her a little too harshly?"

Mother Teresa had asked the same question. "I don't think so. It would take a year to explain her, so I'm not going to try. Besides, I don't want to spoil our evening."

"It's a deal . . . Now, what's your pleasure?"

"Just being here."

As Jim ordered their meal, she watched him closely and wondered how it could be that she hadn't noticed before what an extraordinarily handsome man he was. Maybe she'd just not given him too much thought . . . because of his age? Last night she was, frankly, mostly aware of the blue Cadillac, the feel of the fine leather upholstery, Solari's, the ride home, his kindness . . . But as they ate in the dim candlelight, she couldn't help noticing his soft brown eyes and the thick chestnut hair, the healthy glow of a tan and his deep, gentle voice.

Over coffee he said, "I didn't sleep last night, Rachel."

She knew why but asked, "Do you have a difficult time sleeping?"

"Not usually . . ."

"Then what kept you awake?" Oh, God, how coy, she scolded herself.

"You."

"I'm sorry . . ."

"I'm not. You're the loveliest reason to stay awake."

She smiled. "That's probably the nicest thing anyone ever said about me."

230

"I can't imagine anyone not saying the nicest things about you."

"Really, Mr. Ross? Well, I guess, like they say, it's all in the eyes of the beholder."

"Certainly in the eyes of this one . . . I'm going to tell you something very strange, Rachel. When I got home I began to think about my life. I took a long hard look and after weighing all the pros and cons, I came to the conclusion that I owe myself something."

"What's that, Mr. Ross?"

"Some happiness, damn it. I'm forty-two, Rachel, and I'd say I've got some catching up to do." He took a long sip of coffee, and, as though he'd thought about it quite carefully, said, "Rachel, I'd like to ask you to marry me."

Good God, this quickly . . . ? And yet it was exactly what she wanted to hear.

"Does that shock you?"

"Yes, especially since you told me you wouldn't get a divorce until your daughter was of age."

"I said it and meant it, but meeting you changed that. Besides, Maureen's almost eighteen now. Next year she'll be going to Paris to study at the Sorbonne."

How different from her father, who felt that college was a waste of money for girls . . .

"Rachel, I love you. But if you need time to think about it . . ."

She didn't really, and yet she was overwhelmed with how quickly they had come to this point. "Do people fall in love like this?"

"People fall in love in all sorts of ways, but you didn't answer me."

"The answer is—*yes.*"

He took her hand in his, feeling its softness and warmth. "I don't ask the same from you, Rachel. Love is something that I know might take a little longer for you."

"I'm not so sure, Mr.—"

"Jim, for God's sake. I'm not quite that ancient."

They laughed.

Rachel hesitated, then, "I'm Jewish, you know."

"I stopped thinking about religion a long time ago. I don't know what I am."

"Well, so far as my religion is concerned, I do. In fact, I'd never thought of marrying anyone who wasn't Jewish."

"Does that really make a difference? I'll convert if it will make you happy."

"No . . . I wouldn't think of it, it wouldn't be right—"

"But I would, if you wanted me to—"

"No, you can't become Jewish because someone wants you to. But . . . well, my children would have to be raised as Jews . . ."

"Rachel, my dearest Rachel, whatever makes you happy is fine with me."

She shook her head. "Imagine, just because it rained . . . I think I'm always going to love the rain."

"No question, it's our element . . . Rachel, I'd like to meet your parents—"

"Not yet . . ."

"Why? Will you have a problem with them?"

"I'm sure. But first, what about your divorce?"

"I'm going to tell Maureen and her mother immediately."

"How do you think your daughter will react to all this?"

"I'm going to tell her as gently as I know how that people fall out of—and in—love all the time. She's old enough to understand."

"And if she does . . . but doesn't in your case?"

"She will, I know Maureen. I'm going to move out and take a suite at the Fairmont. This has changed everything for me—"

"And for *me*—"

They looked at each other. "It's incredible," he said. "I'd forgotten all about feeling like this."

"And I never knew it was possible." She looked almost fierce as she added, "Jim, I'm going to make you a very happy man."

"You already have, my darling."

When he stopped the car in the same place as the night before, he turned off the ignition, took Rachel in his arms and kissed her. The kiss didn't really arouse her passion—only Sandy had done that—but this was tender, almost reverent and quite wonderful in its special way. Better, in fact, than all the frustrations of the heated passion she'd felt for Sandy and been denied. She was convinced this was the best kind of love—uncomplicated. Anyway, in time she might grow to love him as much as he loved her. Until then, affection would be enough, and she would be a good and devoted wife. She'd promised him, she meant it . . .

After helping her out of the car, he held her close to him,

and she clung to him the way she had never been able to cling to her father.

"I love you, Rachel."

She answered him with a kiss.

"Goodnight, darling."

Rachel smiled. "Goodnight."

As she began to walk away he called out, "I forgot something."

Opening the trunk of his car, he handed her a large box from I. Magnin.

"Oh, Jim, thank you, but you didn't have to, you know—"

"I don't know anything except I love you."

For the first time in years, Jim spoke to Kelly alone. "You'll be pleased to know I want a divorce."

Kelly tilted her head sideways and raised her eyebrows. She knew it would have been impossible for someone as virile and attractive as Jim Ross not to have slept with women, but he was too discreet to ever be openly involved with anyone. They had maintained their image as the ideal couple, and he wouldn't want Maureen to hear about dear daddy sharing another lady's bed. Or, more to the point, mummy sharing another lady's bed . . . too shameful. Why else had he put up with her? But darling James must have finally met the woman of his dreams. Well, it certainly was a long time coming, but better late than never. What a penance this had been . . . Finally she said, "Well, my goodness, will wonders never cease. So you got tired of celibacy?"

He ignored her. "I want you to get the divorce."

Wasn't that noble. Thanks to Maureen, he was doing it all so proper . . . so *decently*. "All right, Jim. Do you have a preference of attorneys?"

Without looking at her he answered, "Go to whomever you want."

"What about Maureen? Have you talked to her yet?"

"If I had, wouldn't she have told you? Don't play games with me."

"How do you think she's going to take it, after having such a devoted mommy and daddy?"

"Don't you worry about her. She had the kind of stability I wanted for her."

"I know, Jim. It took a great deal of sacrifice on your part."

"Get ready to go to Reno."

Well, Mr. James Ross, Jr. was in one considerable hurry. But he was going to pay for the years he'd made her suffer. "I'm not going to Reno."

The muscles in his jaw knotted like twisted rope. "You don't have much choice."

"I think you're wrong. If I were to tell Maureen what caused the breach between us, she'd be quite shocked, I imagine. I wonder how her *stability* would hold up then." She'd never do that to her daughter, but it was like honey from the comb to see the look on his face.

"You perverted bitch. You'd destroy her, wouldn't you. You're just that ruthless."

"Well, it would surely turn her against me, and wouldn't that give you a lot of satisfaction?"

"I didn't know quite how rotten you really are."

She laughed to herself. All he had to do was call her bluff and she would have taken the night train to Reno. "Well, at least now you know all about me. A year's not too bad, James. It passes faster than you can imagine. Seems like yesterday you moved down the hall."

He slammed the door and went to pack his things. . . .

Jim held Rachel's hand as he told her they'd have to wait a year, but he couldn't bring himself to tell her the reasons. He felt miserable that his hands were tied, but he couldn't allow Maureen to find out what Kelly really was.

Rachel was more disappointed than she wanted to show. She could hardly wait to leave home and she honestly wanted Jim Ross and a life with him. But she knew he wasn't having an easy time either. "I know how difficult this will be, but if there's nothing you can do we'll simply have to make the best of it."

He held her close. "Oh, Rachel, I swear to you I had no idea this would happen—"

"Darling, we'll manage it. A year isn't that long."

It was for him . . . forty-two and he wanted a child, Rachel's child . . . A new beginning had been handed him and he couldn't take it; that bitch had the ace. "Rachel darling, I'm going down to Santa Barbara to see Maureen, but of course I'll call—"

"No, please. I still don't want them to know about us."

"Why?"

"Because my family are very complicated people and I know there's going to be a real battle eventually. Please, Jim . . . let's wait a bit longer."

234

She missed Jim more than she had imagined possible. She tried not thinking about him, but that was impossible. If only she could have gone with him. And Jim's thoughts ran parallel with hers. Leaving her had been difficult, but the chore that lay in front of him would be even more so. . . .

When he saw Maureen running toward him, her lovely chestnut hair blowing in the breeze, he thought there had to be a better way than this. But now she was here, hugging him. He looked at her face—those large amber eyes, trusting . . . like Rachel's, innocent yet wise. He loved them both so very much . . .

"Gosh, dad, I'm so glad to see you."

He swallowed, smiled. "Me too, sweetheart."

"I got so excited when they told me you were here . . ."

"Where would you like to go?"

"You devil, you've fixed it so I could get the day off. How about the beach?"

"I'd like that."

"Knew you would. There's a peachy little bistro where they have the best seafood. Sound good?"

"Sounds wonderful."

"Lay on, Macduff."

As they drove along the waterfront Maureen said, "Dad, how would you like to take a very close relative to Argentina on your business trip?"

Jim felt the perspiration on his forehead. "I'd love to, Maureen, but I don't think you should take time away from school."

"It's okay, dad. I'm way ahead—"

"Let's talk about this at lunch."

"Wait . . . slow down, dad. It's that place over there with the green and white awning."

Jim had a reprieve until they'd finished their meal. When the coffee came Maureen asked, "Now, how about . . ."

Jim's face became somber.

"What's the matter, dad? Fess up . . . you can tell this one anything."

"Some things aren't that easy."

"Give it a whirl."

". . . This is something I'd hoped I'd never have to tell you, darling, but I suppose there's no easy way. Your mother and I have agreed to a divorce."

Maureen sighed. "Well, I guess it was overdue."

He looked at her, astonished. "You knew?"

235

"For a long time. I just kept hoping you and mom would make it up somehow. You're both so great. Why can't two wonderful people fit?"

"I don't know, Maureen, but it seems best this way."

"How's mom taking it?"

"As sensibly as you would expect . . ."

"I'm really sorry, dad."

"So am I, darling."

"Dad, I think I should go with you on your trip to Argentina." She thought her mother would weather the storm of divorce better than he would and that he might need some company on this trip. She waited. When there was no answer she said, "Dad, you're a million miles away."

"Not really, Maureen . . . I just don't know how to say this right."

"What, dad? You can tell me anything . . ."

He looked at her. "All right. Honey . . . I've met a lovely woman . . . I'm going to marry her."

Maureen sat like a statue. That was the reason for the divorce, after all these years? Finding her voice she asked, "What's she like?"

"She's beautiful."

"I mean *who* is she?"

"Her name is Rachel—Rachel Sanders."

"How did you meet her, how long have you known her?"

"For several months," he lied, "and I met her quite by accident—"

"By accident? Where?"

"She was waiting for a streetcar in the rain and I happened to be coming around the corner—"

"You met her on the street? How romantic."

"I can't really explain it, honey, I know it sounds pretty strange, but these things do happen, you know . . ."

"How *old* is she?"

He ran his tongue around his dry lips. "Nineteen."

"Nineteen! That's practically child-molesting . . ." She felt sick to her stomach. "Dad, I really think you should see a psychiatrist."

He winced and looked out to the blue ocean washing up against the sand. Rachel was not just nineteen. She was a woman, a lovely woman that he adored . . . "Maureen, I know this is very difficult to understand, but ages aren't always that important between—"

"People in love?"

"Yes—"

"And you think she loves you?"

"Yes. Do you think that would be so difficult?"

"No, I can see where you would be very attractive to a . . . but she's a child, dad."

"Only chronologically."

"I'm going to be as frank as you've been. You're an older man trying to prove you've still got what it takes, and I think she's taking you for everything you've got."

"That's unfair, Maureen, and, frankly, something I didn't believe you'd ever say to me."

"I'm sorry, but, dad, use your head. Why would a girl marry a man old enough to be her father?"

He looked at his daughter. Shaking his head, he thought how wrong he'd been. Maureen took the news of the divorce without flinching, but the fact that he could be in love with someone and she with him was being needlessly distorted. Was she jealous because Kelly was being replaced by someone almost the same age as Maureen? If he'd fallen in love with an older woman would she more easily have accepted that? Or was it that she wanted *nobody* to have her place in his life . . . ?

Maureen was transformed. He'd be taking this . . . this childish nobody to Argentina with him instead of her. She'd always adored him so . . . To her mind he was the ideal man, the kind of man *she* would wait for. Now *this* . . .

"Wait till you meet her, Maureen."

"I don't want to hurt you, dad, but I'll never do that . . . never."

"And you say you don't want to hurt me?"

"I'm sorry. Sorry—" And she ran out of the restaurant to the car.

She was sobbing when he got into the car. He took her to him, put her head on his shoulder. "I wish it could be different . . ."

"Oh, daddy, so do I. I've always loved you so, I still do . . . but I think you're making a terrible mistake leaving mom for her—"

"That's not the reason you're angry, sweetheart, and you know it."

"I know, but why *her?* Why?"

"Meet her, darling, and you'll see. Will you?"

"I'll have to think about it."

"Thank you, darling, for that . . ." And he meant it.

CHAPTER THIRTY-FIVE

JIM MET Rachel every night after work. At first Sara raised a ruckus about her comings and goings, but Rachel didn't really care. She simply said she was going to night classes and would be home when she got there.

The girls Rachel worked with noticed her being picked up each night in a fine automobile, and, of course, there were all sorts of speculations around the office that she was being kept, that she was having an affair with an older man . . . Rachel knew what was being said behind her back and it bothered her no more than Sara's silent treatment. A new stratagem for something new and wonderful in her young life . . .

Rachel was very quiet when she and Jim walked into Sheves Jewelers on the corner of Post and Grant. She had often lingered at the windows of that prestigious establishment, looking at the jewels and gems. But now she was inside, being shown tray after tray of the finest gems.

When the salesman showed her the five-carat solitaire, she marveled at the facets shimmering in the overhead lighting. Was she the same Rachel who had worked for the five-and-dime, who had been an usherette at the Tivoli Theater, Rachel who never had a decent dress until she earned enough to buy one herself? This couldn't be the girl who just a short time ago had stood on a street corner on a rainy evening, thinking that nothing of any consequence would ever happen in her life. It seemed unreal, unbelievable, as Jim slipped the ring on her finger. She trembled inside . . . it was only a dream . . .

"Darling, do you like it?"

She looked up at him. It was no dream. Did she like it? It was difficult to keep her breathing even . . . "Oh, I *love* it."

"Then, my love, this means we're officially engaged."

They laughed and Jim took her in his arms and kissed her as the salesman smiled. "Congratulations, Mr. Ross. And you, Miss Sanders."

They walked up Post Street and went into Gump's. Rachel followed like a sleepwalker. Again the feeling of unreality overwhelmed her. The beauty of the magnificent antiques, the china and silver, the Baccarat crystal—it was simply incredible.

Finally Jim led her to the credit department. "What are we doing here?"

"I want to open up an account, so you can charge."

Rachel barely nodded. Incredible.

They had been engaged for two months when Jim received a letter from Maureen saying that since he appeared to be serious about getting married the least she could do was to meet the lucky lady. He immediately called her and told her how pleased he was and how much he wanted her and Rachel to be friends. . . .

The meeting got off to an awkward beginning. Maureen directed most of her conversation to her father. "What have you decided, dad, about taking your only daughter to Argentina? We never got that settled in Santa Barbara."

Rachel looked stunned. "Are you going to Argentina, Jim?"

He took her hand. "I'll have to, darling, but just for a few weeks. Business . . ."

Maureen was delighted to see that Rachel was upset and in the dark about the trip. She glanced at the sparkling ring on Rachel's slender finger. Rachel might be marrying daddy, but not for love. She'd bet her last biscuit on *that* . . . "Rachel, didn't daddy tell you? I'm shocked at you, daddy. That's no way to start a new life with a new wife. Secrets can be very destructive to a healthy relationship, you know . . ."

Jim knew, and he was also seeing Maureen in a new light. She was the quintessence of charm, but she also, he was sorry to see, had more than a little of Kelly's nature. Now he very much wished he'd never pressed the issue, it would have been better to have had them meet after the wedding. But he had no idea Maureen would behave like this . . . "I haven't kept any secret from Rachel . . . The fact is, I'd hoped I wouldn't have to go."

"But apparently you do."

"Yes."

"Well, then, how about me hitching a ride?"

"Not this trip, Maureen."

"How about you, Rachel? Are you going to let our handsome brute go all alone? You know what they say happens when the cat's away." And she proceeded to smile like one.

"Well, Maureen," Rachel said, "I'm afraid I'm not too up on cats. I think I know Jim, though, and that's assurance enough for me." Jim's attachment to his daughter was going to change, if she had any influence. And she did.

Smug bitch, Maureen thought, and said, "How marvelous to be so sure. I think I'd worry just a *little*."

Jim had had enough, called the waiter and paid the check.

After they had driven Maureen home they sat in silence. It was Rachel who interrupted their thoughts.

"It went pretty badly, didn't it? Maureen, to put it mildly, didn't take this too well."

Jim half smiled. "It wasn't exactly what I'd hoped for, but I still believe in time she'll come around. She's hurt. I suppose that's natural—"

"Maybe . . . Why didn't you say you were planning to go away?"

"Because, darling, I honestly hoped I could get out of it."

"Why Argentina?"

"We're building a steel plant there and it seems I have to do the negotiating personally."

"How long will you be away?"

"Ten days to two weeks at the most. Oh God, Rachel, I know how difficult this is."

"When are you leaving?"

"Thursday . . ."

She bit her lip. Suddenly she felt as if the lifeline had been cut. Especially when she thought of her nights at home with her mother . . . "I already miss you."

He pulled her against him, kissed her. "Darling, when we're married I guarantee you'll never be away from me. You'll probably get sick of me but it won't do you any good. You're stuck, for better or worse, with this old party named Jim Ross . . ."

Nonetheless, it was a sad Rachel who walked upstairs to her room that night.

No sooner had she started to undress than Sara opened the door. "I want to talk to you."

Rachel badly wanted to be left alone.

"I don't know what you're doing, so you tell me, coming home any time you want—?"

"I don't have to tell you anything."

Sara was about to answer when she spotted the ring on Rachel's finger. "Where did you get *that?*"

Rachel was furious with herself for forgetting to take the ring off.

"I *asked* where you got that."

"From a man—"

"You tramp, you rotten little ... I knew you'd come to no good, even with the convent."

Rachel was trembling as she began to get dressed again. She would not remain in this house and take this abuse one more minute.

Sara pulled her around so that they were facing each other. "Where do you think you're going?"

"I'm *engaged,* damn you. You and your mind. I'm going to get *married,* can you understand that?"

"Why, are you pregnant?"

Rachel's eyes were full of tears. "You're crazy, you really are ..."

"Well, if I am it's because of you. And if you're engaged why didn't you come to your parents like a decent girl and *tell* us?"

"Because I don't *have* the kind of parents—"

"And this lover of yours ..."

Rachel grabbed her coat and purse, her blinding tears almost making her stumble down the stairs.

She ran until she found a phone.

Jim was frightened by her voice. "What's wrong, darling?"

"I need you, Jim. Please come and pick me up ... *please.*"

"Can you tell me what happened?"

"My mother found out about us, there was a terrible scene."

"Darling, there won't be a ferry until two this morning. Let me think." Damn, he was in San Francisco and Rachel needed him now. "Darling, I'm going to call the Oakland Hotel and make a reservation for you. Take a taxi and I'll be there as soon as possible."

It was almost three-thirty when Jim knocked on her door. When she opened it her eyes were red from crying. He embraced her and then led her to the settee, where Rachel sat clinging to him. Stroking her hair, he said, "Now tell me what happened."

"It was terrible ... my own stupidity ... I forgot to take my ring off for the first time. When I got home *she* rushed

241

into my room and started her usual tirade. I honestly think there's something a little crazy about her. She said things I'm ashamed to tell you . . ."

"It doesn't matter. I'm going to speak to them. I should have done it before."

"I didn't want you to be hurt. I can't explain them."

"Look, I've faced a few difficult people in my life."

"But not like them—!"

"You're not to worry, let me do that. Now, please get some sleep, Rachel. I'll take a room and later this morning we'll go see your parents."

"Can't you stay with me?"

"No, darling, let me do this my way, will you?"

He kissed her and left. . . .

Sara was in her room when she heard the car stop in front of the house. When she peered through the curtains and saw the blue Cadillac, she gasped. She was undeniably jealous as she watched Jim help Rachel out of the car.

Rachel unlocked the door and for a moment, as she stood in the hall, she thought she'd pass out, but she knew there simply was no way to avoid this. Taking Jim by the hand she said, "Darling, you wait in the livingroom. I'll have to tell them I'm home."

But Sara had already come down the stairs and now stood waiting to be introduced. Rachel almost gasped when she saw that Sara was wearing the dress she had worn to temple. Sara hadn't worn the dress since; she'd had no reason to. For a moment, in spite of herself, Rachel could feel sorry for her . . .

"This is my fiancé, Jim Ross."

"Mr. Ross." Sara forced herself to respond graciously.

"Mrs. Sanders, I'm very happy to meet Rachel's mother."

I'm sure, Sara thought. She could imagine what Rachel must have told him about her. She could hardly stand the sight of them, feeling they must have spent the night together . . . after all, where else would Rachel have disappeared to except . . . "Thank you, Mr. Ross. Now if you'll excuse me I'll call Rachel's father."

Rachel began to tremble. She had reason to. Sara had kept Jacob awake for most of the night with her tales about Rachel, and by morning he could hardly wait to see Rachel and this *man*. He was primed for battle.

When he walked into the room his face was set, his jaw tight as his cold blue eyes looked from one to the other.

"Papa, this is my—"

"I'm Jim Ross, Mr. Sanders," Jim said, extending his hand.

Jacob didn't acknowledge the gesture. "Sit down. All right, now please tell me about this."

Jim remained standing. "Rachel and I are going to be married."

"How old are you, Mr. Ross?"

"Forty-two . . ."

"And do you know how old Rachel is?"

"Yes."

"And you think she loves you?"

"Yes, Mr. Sanders, I do."

"And how long do you think that will last?"

"For the rest of our lives, I hope."

"Don't bet on it. Think about this. When you're sixty-five, she'll be forty-two. You really think a marriage like that can last?"

"It depends on the people—"

"You think so, do you?"

"I know so. There are people the same ages whose lives are hell together."

He ignored that, but didn't overlook it. "I'm sure you know we're Jewish."

"Yes."

"I don't want my daughter to marry outside her religion."

Sara sat back, listening, and watched Rachel twist her handkerchief in trembling hands.

"Well, Mr. Sanders, I'd be happy to accommodate you, but one doesn't have much choice about the religion one's born into."

"That's very clever, but the fact remains I forbid Rachel to marry you."

"Mr. Sanders, I'm afraid you're not in a position to forbid Rachel anything. She's of age. But let me tell *you* something. I have a daughter, so I'm going to give you a little advice. If you want to lose Rachel forever, then continue on as you are and I give you my word that Rachel will *never* want to see you."

Jacob looked at his daughter. "Why didn't you come to me, Rachel?"

"You know why, papa. I was afraid."

"But you weren't afraid that maybe you owed us something, your mother and me? We worked to bring you up as a decent girl, and this is our thanks, sneaking behind our backs—?"

"If you and mama were parents I could confide in, I would have come to you—"

"And we're not?"

"No, papa, you're not," she answered without looking at him.

"All right, Rachel, you can go upstairs and pack and get married by a priest . . ."

"I'm getting a divorce, Mr. Sanders."

Jacob stood shaking his head. "I see. And how long will it be before you're divorced?"

"About eight months."

"What kind of a man are you to take a young girl and—"

"Mr. Sanders, you've said a great many things I wouldn't have taken from anyone else, but because of what Rachel means to me, I have. Let me warn you, Mr. Sanders, don't make a statement you'll regret. Rachel is going to be my wife. As a man, I'm sure you understand what I mean."

It was obvious from the size of Rachel's ring and the way Jim Ross was dressed that Jacob couldn't ask how he was going to provide for his daughter. Still, how had Rachel met him? Well, he'd find out later . . . "Rachel, you have eight months to change your mind. And you'd better be damned sure, because once you get married, young lady, you will *never* come into this house—and I'm sure you understand what I mean by *that*, Mr. Ross."

Jim took Rachel's arm. Looking Jacob in the eye, he said, "I wouldn't worry too much about that, Mr. Sanders. Now if you'll excuse us . . . Come on, darling."

On the way out Jim turned once more to Sara and Jacob. "Mr. and Mrs. Sanders, it's been a pleasure meeting you." . . .

Rachel sat very quietly at dinner, as did Jim . . . The pain was as much his as hers. How, he wondered, could people like that have a daughter like Rachel? Perhaps he ought to ask himself the same question . . . He had sacrificed a huge part of his life for Maureen, and she had badly disappointed him when he needed her most . . . "Darling, I'm not going to Argentina."

Rachel looked up. "But you said it was very important."

"It is, but some things are more important. I'll have someone else take over the project. I'm not that indispensable . . . It's clear you're in for a very bad time and I don't want you to be alone."

"I seem to be coming between you, your daughter *and* your business . . ."

"Nothing's as important as you are, Rachel, nothing."

"I love you, Jim Ross. I really do. I was afraid to at first . . . but I do now. Can you stand it?"

His answer was to take her in his arms.

The following months were filled with the kind of joy and excitement Rachel had never believed could happen to her.

This evening they attended the opening of the opera. Earlier they had dined with some of Jim's friends, and from the looks on their faces he knew that later there would be whispers that he had robbed the cradle. But it didn't bother him at all as he looked at the most beautiful woman in the world, dressed just as Rachel *should* be—in the Schiaparelli that he had bought her.

They shopped together for her trousseau, but most exciting for Rachel was furnishing their home. They selected Royal Crown Derby china, gold Minton serving plates, Baccarat crystal, sterling silver. Rachel found herself adjusting to her new role as though she was born to it. She would not feel guilty, no matter what mama said . . .

When the boxes began to arrive from Gump's at the house in West Oakland, Sara opened them, caught between frustration and jealousy. Imagine Rachel coming into all this. She had fought for years with Jacob to furnish the house, and he still refused. Didn't *she* matter? Her antagonism grew, not only toward Rachel but Jacob. Her depression deepened too as the boxes continued to arrive, day after day.

Rachel was annoyed that the boxes had been opened, but said nothing. Sara's attitude toward her was near intolerable, and Jacob was mostly cold, indifferent. Sara, of course, had never confided in him the things she had said to Rachel that night; she had told him only that Rachel was undoubtedly carrying on an affair. His anger had grown to the point of deep hostility, helped not a little by the fact that Jim Ross made him feel damned uncomfortable. He took no joy in the fact that Rachel was moving up in the world. Thanks to Mr. Wonderful James Ross . . . King of the *goyim* . . .

Three months before Jim's final decree he insisted that Rachel stop working and concentrate on furnishing the apartment at the Brocklebank, and they engaged Arnold Delacourt as their decorator.

The evening they were to be married they wandered from room to room admiring the home they would soon share, looking out to the blue bay and the distant shoreline of Oakland.

Suddenly Rachel was just plain overcome. It couldn't be happening to her ... it would all disappear, she'd wake up and be home again—

"You're trembling, Rachel—"

"I know."

"Why, darling?"

"Because I'm so wonderfully happy, and still not sure it's for real."

"It's real, Rachel. And prenuptial jitters are something most people go through—"

"No, it's not *that*. I can't wait to marry you. I've wanted you so badly, I don't suppose it's been a secret." She smiled.

"It wasn't easy for either of us, darling. I'm not made of wood."

"I know." Her eyes misted with tears. "I only hope I'm up to all this happiness ... I'm not exactly an old hand at it, you know ..."

Two days later Jim and Rachel stood before the judge and were married. In spite of everything Rachel had asked her father and mother to be present, and they had refused.

That night they spent their honeymoon in the suite Jim occupied at the Fairmont. He'd received a bottle of rare champagne from a friend and together they toasted their future.

"To the beginning." They clicked glasses and embraced. Jim held her for a long moment, then released her. Rachel changed her clothes and soon Jim was beside her. She thrilled to his touch. Gently, he took her to him. She had been worth waiting for ...

And she felt the same about him.

The next night, immediately after dinner, Sara said to Jacob, "We're going to furnish the house, once and for all. This time, Jacob, I will not be put off."

He knew from the look in Sara's eyes that it was, finally, time to give in.

Sara was not to be outdone by her daughter ... "She's starting out with more than I've had in twenty-one years. I'm not going to live like this anymore."

"It's a shame you didn't wait and marry a rich man. Rachel didn't meet Mr. Ross at her mother's sink, you know."

"You're not a poor man anymore. I not only want to furnish the house, I want a car."

Before he had a chance to reply, Sara was out of the room and running upstairs. She sat on the bed and looked at her reflection in the mirror. She was fat and close to forty. What did she have to show for all the years? Well, enough of that.

The next day she walked into W & J Sloane and bought with a vengeance. When Jacob received the bills, he was furious.

"We don't need such fancy bedrooms. Who needs to spend money on something no one sees? Doris and Lillian can't sleep unless they have four-poster beds?" But he could have saved his breath.

Rachel's fine marriage revived Sara's determination in another direction as well. Almost daily she received postcards and snapshots from such exotic honeymoon spots as Hong Kong and Tokyo, showing her daughter exquisitely turned out in a Japanese kimono, complete with the ceremonial obi about the waist. But what especially caught her eye was the Japanese parasol . . . evoking as it did memories of that day so long ago when Jacob had proposed to her on the beach in Coney Island, and she'd had a parasol too . . . when she had been young, and delicate, and *thin* . . .

Sara proceeded promptly to put herself on a rigid diet. In less than three months she lost thirty pounds. She felt reborn . . . well, in the flesh in any case. She admired her new self in the mirror. This was the body, at least, that she'd brought to Jacob's bed. And that body would be appropriately clothed, she told herself, as she went on a buying spree, acquiring fine clothes that she had, unfortunately, no place to wear. Well, Jacob would make up for that too . . .

"What do you have in mind?" he said. "A trip to Japan? The opera every night?" And she answered, "Why not . . . it's about time. It's my turn now. You don't have to go to bed every night at eight o'clock to get up at dawn to make more money that you won't spend. Look at me, Jacob. I'm alive too. Take a *good* look at me . . ."

And then she quickly turned away from him, not wanting him to hear the pleading that had drowned out the anger, that left her more naked and vulnerable than ever . . . for all her new clothes, for all her new self. . . .

CHAPTER THIRTY-SIX

IMPOSSIBLE TO believe—three months had passed since Rachel and Jim had been married, but the memories of their glorious honeymoon were relived in Rachel's mind as she now proceeded with the excitement of settling down into the apartment that was even more beautiful than she remembered.

Rachel had no illusions about there ever being a full understanding between her mother and herself, yet something still kept her from making a total break. Sara was, after all, her mother, and maybe now that she was a married woman she would at least accept her independence, rise above past hurts . . .

She found herself making a call.

"Mama, how are you?"

"Fine, Rachel, and you?"

"I'm very happy, mama."

"Really. I'm glad to hear that."

There was a long awkward pause. "Mama, Jim and I want you and the girls to come to dinner."

"I don't know, Rachel . . . We're really very plain people, you know—"

"Please, mama . . . please. Just once let's not—"

"Not what, Rachel?"

"Be so angry at each other."

"Angry? Why should I be angry? Actually I admire you, Rachel, for being so sure of yourself. It's certainly more than I've ever felt."

"How are the girls, mama?"

"Fine. It's very commendable that you should remember you still have a family."

"I remember, mama."

"That's good, because some people who suddenly become rich . . ."

Rachel took a deep breath. Mama, it seemed, was still mama . . . "Mama, I'd like all of you to come to dinner."

"Well, Rachel, I'll be very frank. I don't know if your father would be receptive to that. He's terribly hurt. Your marrying the way you did was a blow to him, especially as his first daughter."

Except as a first daughter he didn't offer to give me a wedding, and we both know why, Rachel thought . . . he's not so much angry over the marriage . . . it's that Jim threatens him, and you aren't exactly overjoyed by the happiness of my marriage that you lost in yours . . . I'm supposed to feel guilty . . . well, mama, I'm not and I *won't* . . .

Sara took Rachel's silence for contrition, which led her to say, "However, Rachel, I'll see what I can do to talk your father into coming . . . Rachel, are you there?"

Softly, "Yes."

"All right, Rachel, I'll call you in a day or so." The line went silent.

Rachel fell across the bed and in spite of herself cried until there were no more tears.

When Jim came home he took her in his arms and held her for a long time before asking, "What happened, Rachel?"

"I called my mother."

"And?"

"She tried to punish me, as usual, make me feel guilty—and, damn it, in a way she succeeded."

"Why do you let her get inside of you like that?"

"You've opened my eyes to a lot of the ways she's manipulated me, and I thought I was prepared to handle whatever she said. But when it came to it, she evoked the feeling I've lived with all my life. It's not easy getting rid of your childhood . . ."

"But you *can* do it, Rachel . . . Did you tell her you're expecting?"

"No."

"Why?"

"I suppose I was afraid. I know, I know, it doesn't make any sense—"

"My God, Rachel, you can't allow her to do this to you, to us, anymore."

"Jim, I'll try . . . but no matter what, just keep on loving me . . . You're my life, darling . . ."

Sara smiled as she went over the conversation. She had no intention in the world of not going to see Rachel's apartment, but she wouldn't be won over so easily. She had her pride too.

That night in bed she said to Jacob, "Rachel called today."

Jacob was relieved, in spite of his feelings about Jim Ross. "Oh, and what did she have to say?"

"How happy she is and how generous her husband is, how lovely her house is—but then, as I always said, Rachel doesn't take after her mother. She always knew what she wanted, and she got it."

The inference landed where it was aimed—on Jacob's head. "I don't begrudge her, I'm glad for her." And in spite of his anger at Ross, he meant it.

"I am too. How many mothers have a daughter who married a millionaire? Well, anyway, Rachel invited us to dinner."

"So."

"Do you want to go?"

Jacob had not forgotten Jim's threat. If you want to lose Rachel, then . . . "We can hardly refuse. She's married."

"You've gotten over her marrying a *goy?*"

"Why do you ask me a question like that? It's done."

"You think we should buy them a wedding present?"

"I suppose so."

"How much do you want to spend?"

He laughed at himself. When it came to the clothes and furniture she didn't ask, but for a wedding present . . . still, she had at least asked . . . "What do I know about presents? Buy what you think is right."

"Well, then I'll call in the morning and say we're coming."

"Fine." And he turned over and fell asleep.

Rachel's anger over having kowtowed to mama had rankled all day, and she had difficulty sleeping that night. When the phone rang the next morning at eight-thirty, she was tired and startled.

"Hello," Rachel said softly.

"Rachel, this is mama."

She sat up in bed immediately.

"You sound a little sleepy, Rachel. It must be wonderful to sleep late . . ."

"Yes, wonderful . . . how are you?"

"Fine. I spoke to your father last night and told him you wanted us to come to dinner." Sara paused. "At first it wasn't easy, Rachel, but I explained that bygones should be bygones, that one has to be flexible. You know your father's not very easy to convince. Unfortunately, he has a habit of holding grudges, but I pointed out that you're his daughter. Finally he said he'd come."

"I'm very happy. What night could you make it?"

Sara laughed. "With my busy social life, any night you say."

"Then let's make it Friday."

"No, not Friday. I always make *Shabbes*. Have you forgotten?"

Rachel sighed. "All right, then Sunday?"

"That would be fine. What time?"

"Six-thirty."

"Make it about five so the girls can get home early."

250

"All right . . . say hello to everyone."

"I will, and thank you for asking us."

Rachel hung up and leaned back against the pillows. Mama still wants her pound of flesh. Was she strong enough, she wondered, to resist her . . . ?

Jacob came through the front door and called out, "Sara? Come on out. I want to show you something."

She took off her apron and smoothed her short, shingled hair.

Jacob still couldn't get over the transformation. He disliked her short hair, but what the hell, it was the style. And Sara had certainly become stylish of late. She was getting so thin . . . too thin. She'd be thinner than Jean Harlow pretty soon. Still . . .

"What's so urgent?"

"Come on outside. Take a look."

"At what?"

"The new car . . ."

For once she was speechless.

Parked at the curb was a secondhand Pierce Arrow, navy blue and shiny. The upholstery was gray-blue and inside was a walnut panel that contained a sterling silver comb, brush and mirror. On either side of the back doors were glass bud vases. It looked as though it had come straight out of the showroom.

Sara gasped. "You bought this car?"

"I sure did."

Jacob had gone mad. A Pierce Arrow in this neighborhood?

"Well, what do you think of it?" he asked anxiously.

"It's simply beautiful, but don't you think it's a little elegant for West Oakland? My God, what will the Welches and the Heannys say? They might think that the Sanders are acting a bit ostentatious—and Jewish."

"The hell with them, *goyim*. You like it?"

"I said it before, it's beautiful."

"Well, it's yours."

"Mine? I'm going to drive that car? Why didn't you get me a chauffeur?"

"Here, get in." Jacob had to smile as he saw her pleasure in the car.

She started up the engine, which purred like a kitten. She couldn't deny it was the most wonderful car she'd ever seen.

251

As they drove around the block, she felt like a queen. She really did. Jacob was certainly making up for lost time. "What did you pay for it, Jacob?"

"I stole it."

"How much did you steal it for?"

"Twenty-two hundred dollars. What do you think of that for horse trading?"

"I think it's some car, never mind the horses."

Some sense of humor all of a sudden, his Sara . . . "Well?"

"Well what?"

"So now you've got your own car."

"It's beautiful, I don't know what to say."

"Well, you could say thank you."

"Thank you, Jacob."

"Are the girls home?"

"Not yet."

"We'll take them for a ride after dinner . . . Wait till your fancy daughter and her dandy get a look at *this* car—"

"Is that the reason you bought it, Jacob?"

"Of course not, who do I have to impress? Admit it, though, not many people have a car like this."

"You're right, Jacob, only millionaires."

A few months before Rachel's marriage she had asked Sara, in the spirit of new beginnings, to come and see the apartment while she was in the process of furnishing, but Sara had begged off, playing as she was then the role of the non-interferring mother. "Rachel, you don't need my advice on this. You have the finest decorator in San Francisco helping you." . . .

Still, without Rachel knowing it, the Brocklebank Apartments were not to be an unknown quantity to mama. One day she crossed the bay to San Francisco, took the cable car up California Street to Mason, then walked to Sacramento Street and stood on the corner viewing the magnificent structure. It looked like many of the buildings she recalled in Brussels. And she remembered taking Rachel and Doris, then little more than infants, uptown to Park Avenue in New York, where she'd stood outside the mansions, just as she was doing now, and dreamed of all the things she had missed because of other people . . . Harry, Louie, Molly . . . She'd led a decent, respectable life, with too little to show for it . . . especially love. And now her fine daughter, who had been seeing a married man old enough to be her father, was

252

rewarded with all this . . . Not, of course, that she begrudged her luxuries. It was just that life, just once, ought to take time out for her . . .

After all, she was equipped to be the lady of such a manor. She had the schooling, she spoke several languages, could pour tea with the best of them, could recite *Hamlet* chapter and verse when she was eleven . . . The tricks life played . . .

She crossed the street and regally walked across the wide cobblestone courtyard.

The doorman, dressed in a handsome uniform, inquired if he could announce her.

"No, I've come to inquire if there is a vacancy in the building."

"Of course, madam," he answered, opening the imposing doors and ushering Sara into the magnificent lobby. Red plush carpet lay beneath her feet. A huge tapestry covered one wall and taupe velvet sofas and matching chairs completed the elegant décor—

"Yes, madam, I'm the manager. My name is Mr. Lawson. I understand you're interested in seeing an apartment."

"Yes, if I may."

"We have four apartments available. If you'd like to wait I'll just get the keys."

Sara waited nervously. What if Rachel should walk in?

As they stepped into the elevator Mr. Lawson said, "Now, we have one on the third floor with a panoramic view of the bay."

"How large is it?"

"This one has three master bedrooms, a butler's pantry, two maid's quarters . . . ah, here we are." The doors slid back and Sara followed Mr. Lawson down the hall, watched as he selected the key, slid it into the lock, and when he opened the door Sara thought she would faint as she saw the lovely foyer and enormous livingroom beyond. At one end was the most extraordinary view she had ever seen—looking out to the shimmering, blue bay. Alcatraz stood like a citadel. Then her gaze wandered to the hills of Marin and back across to the East Bay. The house in West Oakland was there. Slowly, she took in the French mantel, the wood moldings and the high ceilings. Her mind darted back to the hotel in Brussels, where Molly and Louie had once lived in this kind of splendor. Next she walked across to the diningroom. The former tenants had left traces of how they must have lived. The walls were covered in rose damask. She barely heard Mr. Lawson saying,

"Of course you understand, Mrs. Sanders, the apartment will be refurbished to your taste."

"Naturally . . ." and she had followed him down the hall to the bedrooms—beautiful, large, sunlit. A breakfast tray brought in by a maid dressed in a black uniform and a starched white apron—

Her fantasy was interrupted by Mr. Lawson. "Now, Mrs. Sanders, would you like to see the others?"

"What? Oh, yes, of course . . ."

Each was more beautiful than the last.

When the tour was over Sara asked, "How much are they renting for?"

"Well, let's see." He scanned his clipboard. "Now, the one on the second floor is two hundred and fifty a month."

"How much is the one on the fifth floor?"

"The fifth floor . . . ah, here we are. That one is four hundred and seventy-five. Is that your preference?"

Indeed it was. "It's very charming, Mr. Lawson. However, I'd like to have my husband see it before I decide." . . .

Sara stood at the rail on the upper deck of the ferry, but the cool sea breeze could not dissipate what she felt . . . "I'd like to have my husband see it before I decide . . ."

Some joke. Some joke, indeed.

When Sunday came and the Pierce Arrow parked in front of the Brocklebank, it was that other secret day that came rushing back to Sara. When the doorman helped her out of the car, he didn't, of course, recognize her. That brief meeting was of complete indifference to him; she was only one of the many people who had inquired about the apartments. And she looked so different with the loss of weight and the short hair that she hardly recognized herself.

That day she had worn her brown dress and feathered hat, and she knew she had looked matronly. Now she wore a size-eight gray silk frock, a pink hat, gunmetal-gray bag and shoes and sheer silk stockings. Her makeup was flattering, and artfully applied.

Doris was wearing her plaid dress, and Lillian wore the simple little yellow silk, made by Sara's loving hands at home.

Jacob was impressed by the building, and was happier than ever that he'd bought the car.

Sara said to the doorman, "Will you call Mrs. Ross and announce that her family is waiting."

"Your name?"

"Mr. and Mrs. Sanders."

He picked up the house phone. "Your family is here, Mrs. Ross." He pushed the elevator button and the Sanders got in. It stopped at the fifth floor. . . .

Rachel stood nervously with her husband in the foyer. When the bell rang, Jim looked at her reassuringly. "Rachel, you're my wife. Keep remembering that."

"I'll try," she said as she opened the door.

She could not believe this was mama.

Finding her voice, she said, "We're so happy you're here—"

"We are too, Rachel," Sara said, handing her the wedding gift.

Doris kissed Rachel, shook hands with Jim.

Lillian said, "You look gorgeous, Rachel."

"Thank you, Lillian. Oh, mama, what did you do to yourself? I can't believe it's you."

"Is that good or bad?" Sara asked.

"You look so lovely, mama. When did you lose all that weight?"

"While you were exploring the world."

Rachel looked at Jacob. "Thank you for coming, papa."

"It was nice of you to ask us, Rachel."

Jim quickly extended his hand. "Mr. Sanders, welcome."

Jacob's response was a nod of the head and a light handshake.

"What are we all standing in the hall for? Let's go into the livingroom," Rachel said brightly.

Sara looked around at the magnificent furnishings. Nothing escaped her . . . the pastel Persian rugs, the celery-green damask walls, a pair of petit-point chairs and a collection of jade and ivory in a vitrine that could have belonged to the dowager empress of China. Velvet love seats flanked the fireplace, and a Directoire sofa stood against the large wall. But the most staggering of all was the Steinway grand piano. Sara had never seen anything quite like it.

Everyone seated themselves. Silence took over.

Finally Rachel said, "I'm . . . I'm so excited that I didn't even open the gift." She rushed out to the foyer and returned with the box. Sara watched as Rachel took off the wrappings and took out the silver-plated chafing dish. "It's *beautiful*, mama, papa. Thank you so much."

"Well, it was very hard to buy you anything. I went to Gump's, but it seemed you'd already bought most of the store out." Sara laughed.

255

Rachel smiled. "I love it."

"I'm sure it doesn't compare with what you have, but then as you know, we're not exactly rich people."

Jacob wished she'd keep her mouth shut. She was embarrassing him in front of Jim Ross. How dare she say the Sanderses weren't rich? That ridiculous present cost one hundred and fifty dollars.

There were few people Jim disliked, but, never mind how much he might have understood her, he was afraid his wife's mother was pretty close to the top of the list. "One doesn't need to be rich to have good taste, Mrs. Sanders, and *yours* is impeccable. Now, how about some brandy, or sherry? What's it to be Mr. Sanders?"

Before Jacob could answer Sara had said, " 'Mr. Sanders'? My goodness, that makes Jacob seem so old . . ."

The inference was too clear . . . "You'll have to forgive me. Now, what would you like . . . mother? Sherry or brandy?"

Sara's eyes narrowed, but she responded graciously. "Sherry, if you don't mind."

"And you . . . Jack?"

"I'll have a brandy."

"And you, darling?" he asked Rachel.

"Nothing, dear. Doris, Lillian, I'll get you some soda."

Rachel went off to the kitchen and came back with a tray of hors d'oeuvre and two glasses of soda pop, then nervously passed the tray. Sara looked, then declined, feeling very virtuous.

"Papa?" Rachel asked, handing him the tray.

"What's in them?"

"Seafood, crab, shrimp—"

"No thanks. I don't eat seafood. You should know that."

My God, Rachel thought, the family hadn't been kosher in a hundred and four years.

"I'd like one," Doris said.

"You don't need any," Sara told her quickly. "No matter how hard I try, Rachel, I can't seem to get her to diet."

Doris, of course, was on the edge of tears, and Lillian now wouldn't dare accept anything from the tray. Mama and her diet food—it seemed that dieting had become the hub of their whole existence . . . For lack of anything better to say, Lillian tried, "This is the most beautiful house I ever saw, Rachel."

"Thank you, Lillian. I haven't asked if you'd like to see the rest. Mama?"

"Later." She knew what the apartment was like. "I don't

256

think I had the chance to tell you that your uncle is getting married."

Rachel dropped the tray.

Jim was quickly at her side. "Sit down, darling. I'll take care of this."

She looked at him vaguely.

"Are you all right, darling? Would you like a little sherry?"

"Yes . . . I think I would . . ."

"Haven't you been feeling well, Rachel?" Sara asked. Jim might be forty-two but he looked virile enough. She couldn't help wondering what their love-making had been like on that romantic three-month honeymoon. Had Rachel *enjoyed* it? Probably . . . She was brought back as she heard Jim say, "No, Rachel hasn't been feeling too well." He smiled at Sara and added, "You're going to be a grandmother."

Sara almost choked on her brandy. A grandmother? She was only thirty-seven. She was beginning to feel young again, and now she was . . .

Thank God, Rachel thought, when the maid came in to announce dinner.

Dinner was solemn, with little conversation.

Jacob ate without relish. Sara glared at Doris who had heaped her plate with the fine food, and Lillian stared at mama, who hardly ate a thing. Rachel had a dreadful headache, and Jim couldn't wait for the whole affair to be over.

When they were once again in the livingroom and Rachel was pouring coffee into the demitasse cups, Doris asked, "Can we see the rest of the house?"

This time Sara could hardly refuse. And besides, she was very curious now.

The apartment was perfection. One bedroom was done in rose toile. The second had become a study for Jim, all leather and oak with hunting scenes. There were golfing trophies on the Georgian mantel, and an entire wall was covered with photographs of Jim fishing in Mexico and Guatemala, and hunting in Canada. There were enlarged prints of the honeymoon couple in Tokyo, Hong Kong, Bangkok and Saigon. Sara had seen enough of Jim's retreat.

When Rachel led the way into the master suite, Sara had to suppress a gasp. The bed had been custom-made and could easily have accommodated four people. Yellow silk draperies hung in the windows and thick pearl-gray carpet stretched from baseboard to baseboard. The large marquetry dresser, the chaise longue, the writing table with blue monogrammed stationery embossed with "Rachel Ross," the dressingroom and the bath with their profusion of French perfume and bath salts—it was all more than Sara could bear. "It's lovely. Really lovely, Rachel."

"Thank you, mama. I'd hoped you'd like it."

"Mama furnished our house," Doris said.

"That's enough, we won't talk about our great mansion this evening. Rachel will see it when she comes to visit."

When they'd finally left, Rachel fell—collapsed—into Jim's arms, her head against his chest. When she looked up there were tears in her eyes. He took her face between his hands, wiped away the tears.

"It was a disaster, wasn't it?"

"Like the Johnstown Flood." He laughed.

"I've got to lie down."

"I'm not surprised."

Rachel undressed and got under the covers, and Jim sat on the edge of her bed, holding her hand.

"What does she *want* from me?"

"Your mother wants to be you, Rachel."

"I think you're wrong, darling. She doesn't want me at all."

"That's not exactly what I said ... Look, you don't have to be Sigmund Freud to see that the only outlet she has for her frustrations is her children."

"I know. Poor Doris, wasn't that awful? Mama just doesn't have any idea what she's doing to her. She's fifteen, Jim, this should be the happiest time in her life. But she's already lost some of the spirit and fun she used to have. Both of them sat there afraid to say anything. What did you and papa talk about while I was showing the apartment?"

"His favorite subject—the meat business."

"What do you really think of him, Jim?"

"I think he's a little overbearing but—"

"He wasn't always that way, not when we were little. He's not really the strong one, he only thinks he is. It's mama who can influence him without him even knowing it."

"Let's not talk about them anymore ... you, lady, were plain magnificent tonight. And dinner was out of this world."

"I didn't cook it."

"The food was the least of it. It's the *way* you do things, Rachel. God, you really held up well in a very difficult
258

situation. But I'm going to get you away from that situation for a while. I'm taking you to Argentina."

"We just got home."

"I know, but I have to go on business again."

"Is that the only reason?"

"Part of it. I think the time has come when you're going to cut the umbilical cord, once and for all. You're a lovely woman, it's time you took full possession of yourself . . . free and clear of mama . . ."

She looked at him. "James Ross, father-to-be . . . I do believe I love you. Now please shut up and make love to me."

Sara called the next day. "Rachel, I want to thank you for a lovely evening. You were so nice to have invited us."

"You're welcome. I'm delighted you could come."

That sounded more like the old Rachel, Sara thought. "However, next time it doesn't have to be so elegant. The way you catered to us, papa and I felt as if we were strangers."

You are strangers. "Well, I wanted to treat you as nicely as I would invited guests." Rachel applauded herself; she wasn't quite so nervous this time.

"The thought was very nice, but unnecessary. However, I don't think your husband was terribly receptive. Oh, he was polite enough, but sometimes I get the impression he thinks he's just a little bit too good for the likes of us."

"I'm sorry you got that impression. That's really not so at all—"

"Don't be defensive, Rachel, I was merely saying that he didn't really make us feel too at home—"

"That has a lot to do with the attitudes brought to the situation . . . I'd like to thank you for the lovely gift, mama."

"I hope you enjoy it. Now, tell me, Rachel, when are you expecting?"

"I'm about six weeks pregnant."

"Oh. Well, not that it's any of my business, but maybe you should have waited. Children are a great responsibility . . ."

You're absolutely right, this is *none* of your business, Rachel thought. She answered, "Well, we decided to have a family as soon as—"

"On second thought, I can understand that, at Jim's age . . . He'll be rather an old man by the time—"

"Mama, I don't *want* to be rude, but this really is between Jim and me—"

"I wasn't trying to interfere, just making an observation."

"I know, thank you, mama . . . Mama, I'd like to talk to you about Doris."

"Doris? What's there to talk about? She's very difficult to control. I've had her to a doctor and he tells me she's what they call a compulsive eater."

Rachel badly wanted to say that maybe if mama gave her more love and understanding she wouldn't need substitutes, but there was no point in pursuing that subject . . . "How do you like your new furniture?"

"It's all right. You know your father's great generosity. Remember, he wouldn't give you the money to go to college."

And I remember you didn't urge him. "Well, as it turned out, I guess it wasn't necessary. Incidentally, I'm going to South America."

Sara gasped. "You just came back from a long trip."

"Jim has to go again on business."

"So every time he goes, you're going with him? What are you going to do when you have a baby?"

"I'll worry about that when the time comes."

"You have your life very well ordered, Rachel."

"It's not really me. My husband is the planner."

"That's fine, but let me give you just a little advice, Rachel. Don't ever let a man—even your husband—get total control of you."

Rachel didn't know whether to laugh or cry . . . "I'll watch that carefully, mama."

"How long will you be away?"

"About a month, maybe less."

"I hope you're back for your uncle's wedding. From what I understand, he's marrying a very lovely girl. She's Jewish and from a very nice family. They had money before the crash. Incidentally, Rachel, how are you going to bring your children up?"

Rachel was still recovering from the memory of Shlomo, the surprising effect the news of his marriage had had on her. She'd thought she was well over *that* . . . "What did you say, mama? Oh, the children's religion? We haven't decided." But she knew her child wasn't going to find out about being Jewish from a Catholic nun. If she had a son, he was going to have a *bar mitzvah*.

"Well, that always happens in mixed marriages. That's why they usually don't work."

"Don't worry too much, mama. They'll be raised just as religiously as we were."

260

"I certainly hope so. I wouldn't want you to have any problems on that score."

"I won't—"

"Tell me, how do you get along with your husband's daughter? Her being almost your age? It's difficult to think of you being old enough to be a stepmother."

"We get along beautifully," Rachel lied. They hadn't heard from Maureen since their marriage.

"Well, it seems everything in your life is just beautiful. You're a fortunate girl, Rachel."

"Thank you, mama. I know I am."

"All it takes is a little *mazel* and that you've got."

"Thank you, but I've got a lot of *mazel*. It's been wonderful speaking to you, mama. So happy you called . . ."

When Rachel replaced the receiver, she sat looking at the silent phone and thought, finally I've really grown up a little.

CHAPTER THIRTY-SEVEN

SHLOMO HAD had his share of romances during his years in the service, but he had never seriously thought of settling down. The marine corps had exposed him to a world he might never have known existed, and he enjoyed the freedom to explore it.

Of all the places he'd been, Manila was the most exotic. Life was good, he lived like a king. He had risen to the rank of top sergeant, a position as high as any enlisted man could attain. The rank and job afforded him a small house, a Filipino aide named Juan, a car of his own *and* a Eurasian mistress.

Monica was an admixture of English, Portuguese and Filipino. She was not only educated, but beautiful. Her skin was smooth as ivory, and her black hair fell like heavy strands of silk to her waist. Her mouth was tender, her eyes deep, and the feel of her was at once exquisite and sensual.

They met at a New Year's Eve party, where Monica soon found herself dancing every dance in the arms of Sergeant Sandy Sanders. At midnight the whistles blew, balloons floated in the air, champagne bubbled, and amidst shouts of "Happy New Year" Monica was being kissed by a rather inebriated Sandy Sanders.

261

At three o'clock in the morning, Monica found her hand in Sandy's as he led her out of the ballroom to the terrace.

"Where have you been hiding?" he asked with, he realized, something less than originality.

"Where have you been looking?"

"Obviously in the wrong places. Did anyone ever tell you you were the most ... the most gorgeous woman in the—"

She laughed. "On occasion."

He held her very close. "I want to make love to you."

"And what happens on the second of January?"

"That's not until tomorrow." He kissed her soft smooth shoulder, then ventured down to the cleavage between her breasts. "Please, now, I've got to have you ..."

Monica was certain he must have said that more than a few times, but there also was something about Sandy Sanders for her that she neither could nor wanted to resist. She followed him to his car.

He drove silently, one hand on the wheel, the other around Monica's slim waist. When he opened the door to his house he picked her up and carried her to his bedroom. He undressed her and caressed each part of her magnificent body as he exposed it to his touch. She was like no one he'd ever known before. The taste and smell of her ... she was pure pleasure.

Lying side by side in the still, dark night, he said, "You asked me about the second of January. How about the Fourth of July?"

"Or the fifth?"

"Yes, or the fifth."

"Give me a minute—no, two—to think it over."

"I'll give you *one*."

"You're a hard man"—said with a straight face. "All right, in that case the answer is yes."

"You're not only the most beautiful but the most sensible woman I've ever met. I'd never have given up. If you hadn't said yes, think of all the time we'd have lost." ...

Literally from that moment on, there was no other woman Sandy wanted, and it wasn't necessary for Monica to tell him that he'd be the only one for her.

Until Sandy had entered her life she was a woman groping. Her position in the government as an interpreter had been rewarding because it was all-consuming, but her husband, an English pilot, had been killed in the war, and at twenty-two she was left a widow. The world had fragmented into pieces she could not put together. And the few men she had permitted into her life were far removed from what she was searching for, whatever . . . whoever . . . that was. But now her life was complete. Sandy truly had become the center of her world. Her search was over. . . .

Two weeks later the rattan furniture Sandy had lived with in the small stucco house on the base was carted away and replaced with Monica's French, English and Chinese antiques. On one wall stood the tall, ten-paneled, black-lacquered screen, adorned with jade and rose quartz—a treasure that was a family heirloom. A gold Chinese rug covered the terra-cotta livingroom floor and English wing chairs were on either side of the fireplace.

For a moment she stood contemplating where the sofa should be placed, then she called Juan, the houseboy, who left his kitchen chores and came into the livingroom.

"Juan, please help me move the couch. I think it would be lovely facing the sea, don't you?"

He smiled. "And very romantic."

"I thought so too, especially watching the sunset."

When the last picture was hung she stepped back and observed the whole of it. In her mind she saw Sandy sitting in one of the wing chairs during the evening, reading while she worked on her tapestry. She would take the book from his hand, sit on his lap and kiss him, and then put her head on his shoulder . . . God, how dear he was to her . . . she'd die if anything went wrong between them. Her thoughts were cut short when the clock chimed. It was four, he'd be home soon.

She had just finished slipping into a silk dress when she heard his footsteps coming up the garden path. She ran to greet him. This was truly the beginning of their lives together. She took him by the hand and led him into the house, eager to see his reaction.

"Monica, I don't believe it's the same place. My God, this is beautiful. You're incredible. It's like Buckingham Palace." Taking her in his arms, he told her the truth. "Monica, I love you." She led him to the large wing chair, sat in his lap. The fantasy had become real. "You know, darling," he told her, "this is the first time in my life I've ever had a real home of my own. It means everything to me . . . I don't think you realize how much—"

"It's enough for me to hear it."

"It goes beyond what I've said. I don't have the words to describe it, or you, my beautiful Monica."

If she had looked at Sandy's face at that moment she would have seen the start of tears in his eyes.

From that time on, Monica devoted herself to her man's needs and desires. She relieved Juan of the cooking chores to make certain that their dinners were just as she wanted, complete with candlelight and wine. She had opened up a whole new world for Sandy, and he for her. She was the perfect hostess at the small dinner parties they gave. Sundays were spent in quiet contentment, breakfasting on the terrace and then going to the beach. They fished and sailed and danced until dawn. When Sandy was relieved of duty for a few days they would drive up to Baguio and stay at a special inn. Their love only seemed to grow.

The only times Monica was unsure was when Sandy received letters from his family, especially from his brother Jacob. The letters always seemed to upset him, and they were always the same: when was he ever going to get over this craziness and come back where he belonged among his own people. Jacob still found it impossible to understand how a Jew could be content being in the marines. It was for *goyim*. And his mother Esther was concerned, too. She hadn't raised him to be a marine. The snapshots of the children also upset him. "My God, Monica, they've all grown so and I wasn't around . . . it's a wonder they still remember me."

Yes, she had to face it, it was in those moments that she knew in a way he longed to go back. But those moments of confusion and longing were usually short-lived. Monica's fears were always put to rest and replaced with the quiet pleasure they shared.

They were still very much together a year later and once again they stood embracing, wishing each other a happy New Year.

"You brought the world to me, darling," she told him, and meant it.

"Thank you, but if you're the smart woman I know you are you'd look around for someone better—"

Comments like that rather frightened her, but only for a moment.

When he held her in his arms that night, she had no doubts, no shadows came between them. She could banish them with her love, and her fear. . . .

In August, Monica knew she was pregnant, and she was delighted. Sandy would want this child, she was sure of it. A
264

woman knew when a man adored her. His words last night, when he sat on the couch holding her in his arms, were a proof of his feelings. "Darling, how do you think you'd like living in Hawaii?" he'd asked.

She bolted up. "Hawaii?"

"Yes, I'm being transferred."

"When?"

"In January."

"That seems to be the best month of the year for us."

"Every month is the best with you—"

"Oh, God, how much I love you . . ."

As she went over last night's scene in her mind, she wondered if this was the time to tell him. She wasn't sure why she was reluctant, but something down deep told her that this was not the time. . . .

In the following months, she felt the child inside. Although she didn't show yet, she knew she would soon have to tell Sandy.

Finally one night, as she lay close in his arms, she said, "Sandy, we've never talked about this . . . but I want to be your wife."

"You are, as far as I'm concerned—"

"I know, but it's not quite the same . . ."

He got out of bed and sat on the edge, lit two cigarettes and handed one to her. How could he tell her he adored her but couldn't marry her? Eventually he would have to go home to the States, to a world that wouldn't accept them. Could he really bring her home to his mother, to Jacob? Here they fitted, they were right . . . God, why hadn't he considered that a woman couldn't go on indefinitely in a relationship like this without wanting marriage. It was selfish, stupid. It was so fundamental. Even a woman in love wanted, needed, the security that only marriage brought. But he couldn't marry her—*not* only for his sake but for hers. She couldn't realize what life would be like for her in the States. People in love deluded themselves . . . maybe that's what was meant by love being blind. Well, his vision was unclouded, unfortunately, and he despised himself because he had to hurt the dearest person in his life. But not yet . . . so he avoided it by saying, "Monica darling, let's wait."

For how long? "Sandy, tell me now. Do you want to marry me?"

"Of course, I *want* to . . ."

"Then?"

"Monica, we haven't talked about it but one day I'm going

home. The United States isn't the Orient. It's hard enough being a Jew, but interracial marriage would make us outcasts. You'd begin to blame me, to hate me. In the end it would destroy us." He took her cold hand and held it gently. "Try to understand this . . . no one belongs just to himself, not in this world, and it tells us that if we want to survive we have to live according to some of its rules, and if we had children they'd be terribly hurt . . . through no fault of their own. But because of us . . ." He looked at her, and her eyes said more than words. Suddenly he put his face in his hands, knowing how he'd hurt her, unable to see what else he could have done . . .

She took him and put his head on her shoulder. "Shh . . . it doesn't matter. You've given me more than you know—"

"It matters. It *matters* because I love you, Monica, but damn it, I can't change the world. Not even for you . . ."

"Come lie down, darling. We're together now. It's what really matters. It will be enough."

She said it like a judgment. . . .

He woke up at four in the morning. Getting out of bed carefully so as not to disturb her, he went into the livingroom, poured himself a glass of bourbon and settled himself into the large wing chair. He sat in the darkened room and relived the years he and Monica had shared. Who had given him the contentment and joy she had? In his desire to protect her he had felt he had to be totally honest about what would happen to their lives if they married. And what he had said *was* the reality; they would *not* be accepted. But the truth was double-edged. Had he been honest for her sake alone, or had his own fears played a part in it? His mother? Jacob? No, he'd never have been able to bring Monica to them and have her accepted as part of the family, never. But how important was all that? What did living in the United States really mean to him? How much of his life had actually been spent there? And how good had life been for him there? Was it all *that* important to him if he never went back? The Orient had been his world and now he realized that he felt more a part of it than any other world. "Going back" had been a myth, that's what it really amounted to. It was merely an assumption based on his childhood longings to have the family together. Yes, he still loved them and always would, but they had been apart for so long now that they lived in different worlds—and it was more than just the miles that separated them. He had no hope that Esther or Jacob would understand or approve
266

his marrying Monica and he understood what their reasons would be. But they had lived their lives as they had to, and he was entitled to do the same... they would be hurt and he regretted that, but he would regret Monica even more. He would *not* leave her, he couldn't. She was just too much a part of him...

Suddenly he felt a sense of peace and new purpose. He got up and quietly went into the bathroom to shave and get dressed. It was six in the morning when he stood at the side of the bed and looked down at her. *She* was his world, and *nothing* could compare to having her. He checked his impulse to wake her. Tonight he would tell her. He kissed her cheek, then turned and left....

Monica spent the morning thinking about the alternatives. If she had an abortion, what would that solve? Yes, they could go to Hawaii and be lovers as before, but one day he would leave her, go home. *She* was not *home;* she was only a stop-off place. Oh, she knew he'd marry her if she told him about the child, but he would end up hating her, feeling she had tricked him. There was only one way out... she'd really known it from the very beginning. The small fears, the reluctance to tell him—they'd been pushed aside for a long time, as though by not facing them they would go away, disappear...

She sat for a long time reliving the moments they had shared. There would, she knew, be nothing for her when he left, and somehow she also knew that it would be soon. No one could ever come into her life again as he had. But the greatest gift of all was the child he had given her. It would be over soon, but the child would be hers forever.

She sat down at the writing table, calmly took out a piece of stationery and began to write.

My dearest darling,
   I have loved you as I could never love again. There are so many memories I hold dear, and those no one can take away from me. Not even you. If I had my life to live over, I would do the same, just to have known what it was like to be held in your arms.
   Please forgive me, my darling. There is no other choice. With all the love I possess, I give you back to yourself. Be happy, dearest ... please, for your darling ...

She folded the note, put it inside the envelope and placed it against the lamp. She paused for a moment and looked at the bed they had shared, then she slowly walked through the French doors and down the garden path to the sea.

Sandy picked up the phone as he was going through a file of papers on his desk. "Yes?"

"This is Captain Rodriguez of the Manila police. I'd like you to come down here, please."

A peculiar chill went through him. "Why? What's wrong?"

"It would be better for you to come in, sergeant."

"All right, I'll be there." . . .

Now he sat apprehensively in a chair across from Captain Rodriguez. "Sergeant, did you know a Mrs. Monica Hill?"

He frowned. "*Did* I know? I know Mrs. Monica Hill."

A pause. "Sergeant, Mrs. Hill . . . her body was washed up on the beach early this afternoon—"

The shock and the pain were too much. He went into a rage of grief, pounding his hands against the walls until his knuckles bled. He wanted to scream, to break the world to pieces. And then the tears came, and the life seemed to ebb from his body. He sat down.

Captain Rodriguez offered him a brandy. "Here, take this—"

He pushed the glass away, it shattered on the tile floor. He wiped his face, sat staring out the window. He did not see the lovely garden in bloom, nor the palms that swayed in the gentle breeze. All he was aware of was Monica's face, the pain in her eyes, her voice whispering to him, "Shh, it doesn't matter. You've given me more than you know." Oh, he knew. He knew *now* . . .

"We need you to identify the body, sergeant . . ."

The body? Monica was a body? He closed his eyes. How many men had he killed? Except that was in war. Now they wanted him to see Monica laid out on a slab, lifeless. Last night *she* had consoled him . . . Dear God, he had done this to her . . .

"Sergeant, we need you to—"

But he had already gotten up and was walking to the door. They led him down the hall to the sterile white room. A sheet covered the outline of what remained of her. Rodriguez waited for a moment, then uncovered the face.

Somehow he'd known it when he'd picked up the phone . . .

"Is this Mrs. Hill?"

He couldn't speak.

"Sergeant, is this—"

"Yes."

The sheet was put over her face and he was led away.

"We'll be in touch, sergeant. There'll be an autopsy."

He shook his head and walked out into the terrible sunlight. . . .

For three days he stayed home, trying to drink away the truth. Juan came in from time to time, but he threw an empty whiskey bottle at him or roared at him to go away. Finally Juan came again and found him sprawled out on the bed. Juan undressed him and got him under the covers, and for the first time he slept. . . .

The ringing of the phone finally got through to him. Fumbling, hand shaking, he picked it up. Twice he tried to speak, no sound would come. Swallowing hard, he heard his own raspy voice. "Yes?"

"Sergeant Sanders? This is Captain—"

"I know, what body do you want me to identify today?"

"Would you be kind enough to come—"

"No, I wouldn't be kind enough to come down. Whatever you have to say you can say now."

"I would suggest, sir, that you come in."

"Damn it! How much more do you want?"

"Please, sir, we need you to sign some documents."

He mumbled all right and hung up.

Hardly able to get out of bed, he called for Juan, who had been sleeping outside his room for the last four days. "Juan, I need a bath, you'll have to shave me. My hands are so damned shaky I might cut my throat." Which for a moment he thought might not be a bad idea.

He sat in the same chair, looking haggard but presentable. Just like a good marine should. A credit to the corps. Sharpshooter Sandy Sanders. He had a medal to prove it . . . Stick it up your ass, Uncle Sam. He almost laughed at the coincidence. In English that's what his name was . . . the citizenship papers read Sam Sanders . . . The hell it was. His name was Shlomo Sandsonitsky, but that wasn't American enough. Monica wasn't American enough to live in the land of the brave and the home of the free. "What do you want me to sign?"

"Sergeant Sanders, Mrs. Hill and you were—"

"Lovers. In love . . ."

"Yes. Well, could you tell us what religion she was?"

Jewish, he wanted to scream. "I don't know, we never discussed it. Why . . . ?"

"Well, I imagine she was a Christian."

269

"I imagine that's going to make a big difference in heaven. All right, I'm sorry, I guess she was—"

"I assume you will want to take care of the arrangements..." Captain Rodriguez cleared his throat. "I received the coroner's report."

Sandy closed his eyes. Suicide...

"Mrs. Hill was expecting a child."

His shoulders slumped. Oh, my God, she was pregnant and he'd been busy moralizing about... how the hell could he... should he?... live with the knowledge that she had killed herself with their child inside her? Thanks to him...

Captain Rodriguez handed him a brandy and this time he took it, swallowing it down in a gulp. "Thanks," he said, handing back the glass as he stood up to leave. "You've taken more from me than you had to."

He walked out of the room and shut the door behind him. ...

He stood watching the coffin being lowered into the ground. Just himself and the minister. He wanted it to be private, and it was. Two wreaths had been ordered. One for her. One for the child.

"Shall we go now, sergeant?" the minister said.

"No, I'd like to stay for a little while. Thank you, thank you for everything."

The minister nodded, then walked down the path among the graves.

Sergeant Sanders asked to be transferred to Mare Island as quickly as possible. It was time to go home.

CHAPTER THIRTY-EIGHT

SIX MONTHS later his reenlistment term was up, and this time he was going to stay a civilian. He'd had enough of the marines, the travel and seeing the world. Jacob was right; it wasn't such a beautiful world.

Still, if one were to survive in it, one had to find an antidote to the pain of intolerable loss. Shlomo, gradually, opted for survival. And Nadine Blum of Oakland, California, a lovely Jewish girl, was the antidote.

Nadine was not what would be considered a great beauty—he could not, of course, have tolerated that. But her hair was the color of autumn leaves turning gold. She had a sweet face, with soft amber eyes and a nose that had been pleasantly sculpted by Dr. Friedman. Her figure was slim and sufficiently rounded at the hips. Indeed, she was rather voluptuous. Nadine's greatest asset, however, was her ability to accept a situation that had been thrust upon her. As such, she was a healthy object lesson to Shlomo. . . .

At the time of her birth the family had inherited a chain of twenty-seven shoe stores. It looked as if Nadine and her brother Neal would never be in want if they lived to be ninety, but in 1929 Charles Blum not only lost the stores but the mansion in Seacliff, which the Blums had enjoyed ever since the day Charles had carried Mildred over the threshold twenty-nine years earlier. Still, if they had lost a fortune, Charles and Mildred Blum were determined not to be bitter about it.

They took an apartment on Geary Street and Mildred fixed it up with the few pieces of furniture that had not been auctioned off. She also took a job at Gump's in the china department, a place where she had frequently been a customer. Through a long, friendly association with the Leibes family Charles managed to land a job selling shoes, and Nadine through the same set of circumstances worked as a saleslady for Ranshoff's.

Just before the Depression had hit, their son Neal had married his childhood sweetheart, Jean Morris, and they were now the parents of an eight-pound baby boy. As Charles and Mildred held their first grandchild after the *bris,* losing the stores suddenly seemed rather unimportant. They were very, very proud that little Freddy was a fifth-generation American.

As for Neal, he felt the joys of fatherhood so deeply that they almost made him forget the denial of what might have been. In fact, he was grateful that he could bring home a paycheck every week from his earnings at the Florsheim shoe store on Market Street. It kept them in a flat in the Richmond district and it fortified the dream that one day he and his father would somehow start again. After all, nothing lasted forever, the Depression would pass.

Meanwhile, democracy had at last come to America. The Depression was a great equalizer. There was no disgrace in being poor.

Not for Nadine's family, and not for Shlomo, who ended up going to work for his brother, and not in the capacity he might have assumed he was coming home to. Before he had reenlisted Jacob had pleaded with him to be a partner. But now that Jacob was the sole owner of the meat packing company he no longer wanted to give up his title or power. Shlomo was only momentarily disappointed. He couldn't really blame his brother. Jacob had established the business on his own and he had never shown any real interest in it. So Sandy Sanders, ex-marine top kick, became a truck driver for thirty-five dollars a week, which was still more than most people made at the time. He even rented a room, though against Jacob's protest.

"Why spend the money when we have a room, now that Rachel's married?"

"I don't feel it would be right, it would only disrupt your household—"

"What do you mean by that?"

"Well, I'm not exactly a homebody. I tend to stay out late; you know how it is ... I'm grateful, but believe me, it's better this way."

Jacob shrugged his shoulders. Shlomo always was stubborn.

Sandy was often lonely now, but he did his best to keep occupied. Women were no longer the panacea—that had been buried in a small cemetery in Manila. So he joined a gym in San Francisco and he worked out four nights a week. He welcomed the routine of getting cleaned up, having an early dinner, crossing the bay. And the physical effort invigorated him, helped dull the painful thoughts. He would work out on the bars, do a hundred push-ups, then wait his turn at the handball court.

Which was how he met Neal Blum. They were a good match. Neal never returned the volley with the same intensity of Shlomo's serve, but he was very fast and very agile.

After their first game the two men sat on a wooden bench to rest.

Mopping the sweat from his forehead, Neal said, "Boy, you're a real gung-ho character."

"Thanks, and you're no pushover yourself."

"Maybe, but how come you beat the hell out of me?"

Sandy laughed. "I got a scholarship in handball. That's how I worked my way through the marines."

"You were in the marines?"

"Yeah. I enlisted during the war and when Uncle Sam said, 'I want you,' I took it seriously and reenlisted. I just reverted to civilian a little while ago."

"What do you do now, Sanders?"

"Work for my brother, driving a truck. He has a meat packing plant."

"Oh? Well, I guess that's a pretty good business even in a depression. Better than the business we used to be in—"

"What was that?"

"Shoes. People can do with one pair, put paper into the soles if there's a hole or have them repaired for a buck, but you got to eat."

Neal already knew he liked this Sandy Sanders. There was a quality to him . . . not that Neal was a snob, but he sure as hell didn't think Sanders seemed like a truck driver, even if he did have the build for it. "Where do you live?"

"In Oakland."

"Married?"

He took his time answering. "No . . . and you?"

"I sure am. I'd better be." He smiled. "I have a little boy."

Would his child have been a boy . . . ? "That's great, congratulations. Well, hey, I'd better be going. Have to catch the ferry. See you Thursday."

Watching Sandy walk off, Neal wondered whether Nadine would like him. Not that she needed anyone to fix her up, but something had happened to Nadine. The guys she used to date no longer seemed interested in her. . . .

On Thursday night after the game the two sat talking as usual. "Sanders? What nationality is that?"

"How about Swedish."

"Is that what you are?"

Sandy laughed. "Me? My friend, I'm Jewish. My mother inherited that all-American name when she arrived on Ellis Island. It used to be Sandsonitsky, but the processing agent couldn't pronounce it so she became Esther Sanders. She walked around with the name tag pinned to her coat for a week before she knew she'd been rechristened by the U.S.A."

Being a fourth-generation American, Neal had no personal knowledge of such experiences, but he'd heard these immigrant stories. "That's fascinating—"

"You think so? Well, I suppose our family is pretty colorful. Can you imagine joining the marines with a name like Shlomo Sandsonitsky? Fall in, men. This is your new sergeant, Sergeant Shlomo Sandsonitsky. And my brother, a regular Jewish cowboy," Sandy went on. "Yankel or Jacob Sandsonitsky doing business with the Wyoming cattlemen.

273

My brother-in-law from Cleveland became a Harold. Pretty fancy from Hershel, right? Well, it's still a good country, but it will be a better one when we get rid of the illusion that everybody melts into the melting pot. The Negroes haven't and neither have the Chinese or the Jews. The only difference is that Jews are white and names can be changed, but colors don't change and eyes don't lose their slant . . ."

Neal sensed the underlying bitterness. "Have you had any problems? I mean, being Jewish?"

"Of course, haven't you?"

"To be honest, no."

"Well, you're lucky. When I was in the service I had to fight two wars—one with the Germans and the other with my *buddies* in the trenches. When they weren't shooting the enemy, I was a handy-dandy target for letting off a little steam."

"I guess I sound naïve but I never found any of that. Hell, I've gone to school and worked with all kinds of people and I never felt different—"

"Well, you're lucky, my friend . . . I guess I'm looking for a too perfect world that respects people, not labels." Shlomo looked at his watch. "I've got to get going if I'm going to catch that boat."

Waiting at the same corner for their streetcars, Neal said, "If you're not busy this Saturday night I'd like you to meet my wife. How about dinner?"

"Thanks, I'd like that."

Neal scribbled the address on a matchbook. "Is seven all right?"

"Terrific. See you Saturday."

Shlomo's ring was answered by an attractive young woman he would guess to be in her early twenties. Her eyes were the same deep blue as the dress she wore, the hair surrounding her oval face was chestnut brown. There was a warmth about her that put him immediately at ease. "Mrs. Blum, I'm Sandy Sanders."

"I know. Neal told me you beat him unmercifully. Come in. I'm Jean. Neal got home a little late, he's washing up. If you'll excuse me, I have something that needs attending to, but please feel at home. I'll let Neal know you're here."

Sandy looked around the apartment. For all its modesty, there were indications his new friends had once lived more lavishly. Many of the furnishings looked valuable. The

French rug had been salvaged as had a few rare pieces of Dresden. Above the shabby mauve silk Louis XIV sofa hung a large portrait of Jean's mother. A rose marble-topped coffee table with French bronze ormulu was placed in front of the sofa. On either side of the coffee table were the remains of two tapestry chairs ... heirlooms, Sandy was sure, and on the opposite wall, a tall armoire almost dwarfed the room. It seemed incongruous that such fine things were occupying a forty-dollars-a-month apartment.

His thoughts were interrupted as Neal came into the room holding his son in his left arm. "Glad you could come, Sandy."

"Me too. Let me see the tiger."

Beaming, Neal held up the child, who looked very much like his mother ... Who would his child have looked like? Monica? He stifled the inevitable questions. Time for that later when the nightmares took over ...

"I'd like to see you take him on at handball," Neal said.

"He'd probably beat the hell out of me." Sandy smiled. "Here, I brought a little gift."

Picking the box off the sofa, Neal laughed. "Not so little, my friend, but thanks."

Jean came into the room, took the wrappings off. Inside the box was a toy bunny as large as the baby. "It's wonderful. Thank you so much, Sandy." She turned to Neal. "Now, may I please have that child? If he cries until ten tonight you know who we'll have to thank." She smiled when she said it. Taking the baby, Jean said to Sandy, "Don't let him talk your ear off about the glories of fatherhood or you'll be here for the duration."

Sandy kept watching as Jean took the child back to his room, then was brought back as Neal said, "I wish to God Congress would forget this damn Prohibition. What the country really needs now is a little booze. Luckily, I just happen to have a few jugs of brandy stashed away from the good old days."

It was as Neal handed the glass to Sandy that the front door opened, and Nadine walked in. She kissed Neal. "Sorry I'm late, but it's so difficult getting good streetcars these days."

"You're telling me. We have the same problem with butlers. Meet Sandy Sanders. Sandy, this is my sister Nadine."

It was falling into place. Neal's machinations weren't subtle, but Shlomo didn't feel uncomfortable or offended.

What should Neal have said? Have I got a nice Jewish girl for you, who just happens to be my sister ... "Nice to meet you, Nadine."

"Thank you. Neal told me how you beat the pants off him."

"She's exaggerating. I don't think you're that good, just lucky."

Jean came in then with a plate of hot canapés, bent over and kissed Nadine on the cheek. "Hi, darling. You're a little late."

"I know ... Can I see my favorite fellow?"

"If you take just a peek. Your brother keeps changing schedules ..." She turned to Shlomo. "Have one of these while they're still hot, Sandy."

God, how long since he'd been in a home like this? These people weren't poor, they just didn't have any money.

"How about a drink for me?" Nadine said. "It might soothe my aching feet. Jean, you have no idea how difficult women can be. I had one today who spent two hours trying on everything in stock and then said she wanted to look around a little more. Did you ever have a deep-down desire to clout someone with a hanger?"

"Did you hit her?" Jean asked.

"No. The customer is always right, so I went into the back room and hit myself."

"Hey, Sandy, how about another brandy?" Neal cut in.

"Thanks, this is really great ... no wonder it was Napoleon's favorite."

"I'll have another drop or two—or maybe three. Got to keep the working class happy," Nadine said.

As Neal filled her glass, Shlomo noticed how really attractive she was. Or was it the brandy? ...

After a delicious dinner they were once again seated in the livingroom.

"Neal tells me you've been in the marines, Sandy. That must have been fascinating," Jean said. "Do you miss it?"

"Well, it's been a little tough getting back into civilian life. At first I used to lie awake in the morning waiting for reveille."

"How about you, Neal?" Nadine asked.

"No problems, shoes are shoes. Jean's the only pampered one in the family."

"Only in between nursings. Speaking of which, I think I hear the call." She got up and went to the bedroom.

"I'll join you," Nadine said.

276

Picking up the child, Jean unbuttoned the front of her dress and sat on the bed. She smiled at Nadine as she reached out to touch the child's little head. "Isn't he incredible?" Nadine said.

"Oh, I'd say so." Jean kissed her son's chubby hand. "How do you like him?"

"I just said he was incredible."

"Oh, you know who I mean."

Nadine half-smiled, shrugged. "He's nice, interesting. How did you like him?"

"I think he's gorgeous."

"But do you like him?"

"For the first time out of the barn, I'd say so. What about you?"

"How can you tell? As you said, the first time out of the barn . . ."

"Look at this, our Freddy already fast asleep. Here, let me put him down." . . .

When the two women went back into the livingroom, Nadine said, "I hate to eat and run, but I'm really beat. Thank God tomorrow is Sunday, the most special day of the week. I'm going to be wicked and sleep till noon. So you see, Jean? Careers do have their compensations."

"You think so," she answered, looking at Neal.

Nadine looked at them. "Well, in some cases. Now I've really got to go." Slipping into her coat, she said, "Jeanie, it was marvelous, thanks so much for inviting me. Sandy, it's been nice meeting you. And Neal, you'd better be at dad's tomorrow or you'll stand a good chance of losing your inheritance. He grumbled all last week because you stood him up on the court."

Sandy stood up. "May I take you home?"

"No, thank you . . . I wouldn't think of breaking up the evening—"

"It's getting late and I have to catch a ferry to Oakland."

"Thank you, Sandy, but I'm sure it would take you out of your way—"

"No, it wouldn't . . . Jean, Neal, this has been the best evening I've had in a long time, but I don't want to wear out my welcome—"

"Our pleasure, Sandy. Please come again," Jean quickly told him.

"I'll see you Tuesday night, Neal, and everything you said about your wife is absolutely true." . . .

On the streetcar, they chatted easily about inconsequential things until they found themselves in front of Nadine's building and Nadine was saying goodnight, that it was nice to have met him. The compliment was returned but with no mention that he would call.

Later, as Shlomo stood at the rail on the ferry and looked out at the dark blue bay, he reviewed the evening. It had been so wonderfully *pleasant*. They were lovely people and they had a fine little boy . . . he'd wanted very badly to hold him. And Nadine? Nice girl, very. Plenty of character and a good sense of humor. About twenty-two? She wasn't coy or anxious. In fact, she showed no special interest in him. Maybe he'd been wrong in thinking that the dinner invitation had been a ploy to have them meet. When they stood there saying goodnight it was altogether casual. Come to think of it, he had real *chutzpah* to think that someone with her background and education would be interested in him. Who the hell was he? An ex-marine, a truck driver. Okay . . . fine . . . he wasn't really interested in her either . . .

Over the next few weeks he saw Neal several times and no mention of Nadine was made. But each time the two met she crossed his mind along with small details of the evening of warmth and domesticity.

One night he found himself unusually depressed. He could no longer ignore the facts of his life. He lived in a rooming house, for God's sake, and he had no anchors, no roots, no love . . . Where the hell was he going? How long could he continue to come "home" to an empty and lonely room at night? When the hell was he going to settle into a normal life? If he went on as he was he'd wind up an old bachelor, eventually kicking the bucket and leaving no trace that he'd ever been around. Neal had said, "That's some little guy I got. Makes living worthwhile—something to work for."

And suddenly Nadine began to figure more largely in his thoughts. But what the hell would she want him for? The thirty-five bucks a week? She probably had the most eligible guys around to pick and choose from. She was San Francisco born and bred, had been brought up with the best of them. Still, it was worth the try. Yes, the more he thought of Nadine, the more he thought she might be the answer . . . He couldn't go on living with a ghost. Monica would always be there in that special place he reserved for her, but he knew that kind of love would never come his way again. So turn the page, or give up . . . get on with the business of living or drop dead . . .

Waiting now for her phone to ring, he thought it was a hell of a time to call a girl. They'd met only once and for almost a month he hadn't even made an attempt to get in touch. Would she even remember him—?

"Hello."

"Hello . . . this is Sandy Sanders."

"Hi, how are you?"

She remembered. "Fine, and how are you?"

"Great—"

"What are you doing Saturday night?" Like a damn school-boy . . .

"Nothing."

"How about dinner?"

"I don't think so, Sandy, but thanks very much."

He felt set back. "But you said you weren't busy?"

There was a smile in her voice now. "I did say that, didn't I?"

"Right, so what about Saturday?"

"I'm sorry, Sandy—"

"Why not?"

"Well, this is Friday night."

"What does that have to do with it?"

"It is rather last minute . . . makes a girl feel she was the last one in the little black book—"

"I'm sorry, I really am. I told you I haven't caught on to being a civilian. Suppose I told you I didn't even own a little black book, and if I did you'd be top of the list?"

"Well, for a new civilian you do pretty well in the flattery department."

"Then how about it? Look, suppose we pretend this is Monday, okay? Now, Miss Blum, may I have the pleasure of taking you out on Saturday night."

She'd never let herself be taken for granted, but he seemed a nice enough guy, maybe she was being too hard on him . . . "I've never done this before, Sandy, but please, if there's a next time—"

"You've got a deal. What time can I come by?"

"Where would you like to go?" These days it was only polite to ask . . . A dollar and a half for a pitcher of punch at the Mark could set a fellow back a week in his rent.

"Do you like dancing?"

"Love it."

"How about the Saint Francis? I think Freddy Martin's band is playing there this week."

Sandy Sanders was clearly one of the last of the big spenders.

"How about seven-thirty?" he was asking.

Seven-thirty . . . that meant dinner. She hadn't done that in a long time. "It sounds fine."

"Great, see you tomorrow. And, Nadine, please forgive me if I sounded a little sure of myself—"

"Well, this is only Monday so there's nothing to forgive."

Early on Saturday morning he bought a secondhand bottle-green Chevrolet on terms he hoped he could afford. Then he fitted himself out with a navy-blue suit for thirty dollars, a white shirt and a striped tie. Okay, he told himself, welcome back to the living . . .

When he saw Nadine opening the door he thought she looked wonderful. She wore a long pink chiffon dress with a shocking-pink cummerbund around her waist, and her trim legs were sheathed in sheer silk stockings.

Closing the door behind him, he handed her a box and watched her eyes light up as she saw the two white orchids inside. "They're beautiful . . . now, come meet my parents."

He followed her into an apartment that was furnished much like Neal's. Mrs. Blum rose to shake his hand as Nadine made the introductions. She was a tall patrician lady with blue eyes and the same oval face as Nadine's. Sandy was sure that the silver streaks in her hair had widened with the hardships of the last few years, but there was no bitterness in her face.

"Sandy, this is my father. Dad, Sandy Sanders . . ."

Charles Blum peered over his wire-rimmed reading glasses and appraised the young man. So it's come to this, he thought. Really hard times . . . Nadine going out with an ex-marine. Damn that idiot Hoover for getting us into this, and I *voted* for the fool . . . "Yes . . . well, nice meeting you," he said, picking up the newspaper once again.

What Mr. Blum thought of him was no secret, but Shlomo couldn't really begrudge his feeling that his daughter was special. Besides, if it hadn't been for the times, he knew he'd never have gotten into this home. Not that he felt inferior, but Blum was an impressive man who still gave one the feeling he was sitting behind a desk in a plush office.

Nadine kissed her parents goodnight and led the way out of the apartment. In the elevator she struggled with the corsage. "Here, let me help you with that . . ." She handed him the pin and soon the flowers sat properly on her shoulder. . . .

The orchestra was playing a romantic tune in the dimly lit ballroom when Shlomo asked her what she would like for dinner.

A few years earlier she would never have looked at the prices, but now . . . The steak dinner was six-fifty, chicken was five . . . "You order, Sandy."

"Steak?"

"Fine." She hadn't allowed herself a steak since the crash.

As they waited for their entrée they danced to the music not of Freddy Martin but Ted Fio Rito, and to the voice of a long-legged blonde named Betty Grable. Sandy danced very well . . . she could feel the hard muscles in his back under his flannel jacket. Jean was right . . . This one was a considerable man . . .

Sandy noticed the waiter putting the steak on the table. "I think we'd better sit down or our food will get cold."

"Anything you say, sergeant."

Seated once again across from each other, Sandy said, "This is perfect. The only thing missing is a bottle of good wine. It's crazy, a country that doesn't allow wine."

"I know . . ."

They didn't seem to need more small talk. Looking at each other, they feasted on more than the dinner . . . When the music began again Nadine found herself in his arms, being twirled around the dance floor. She liked the way she felt, she liked the feel of him . . .

They danced until the ballroom closed. When he brought her to the front door of her apartment, this time they looked at each other for a lingering moment, he wondering if he should kiss her, she hoping he would. She handed him the key. He put it in the lock, turned it and the door opened. Now he stood outside and she inside. "It's been a lovely evening, Sandy. Thank you . . ."

"For me too. And since this is Saturday, how about next Saturday?"

She laughed. "I think I can just make it."

"Great. What time?"

"Same time, same place. Goodnight, Sandy."

He started to turn when she said, "Sandy, may I have my key?"

He looked down at his hand, then burst out laughing as he handed it back to her. "I don't know if it's according to

Hoyle in the States, but would it be rushing things, Miss Blum, if I kissed you goodnight?"

"I think it's pretty much the same here as most places."

He took hold of her and kissed her gently, but firmly. . . .

After he'd gone she shut the door and leaned against it. I think I like you, Sergeant Sandy Sanders, I think I more than like you. You're not Stanford or Harvard and that's fine with me . . . because I think there's a devil of a lot that goes on inside your head that I'd like to know about. And I think I will . . .

Saturday night came and Nadine waited a little nervously. When the bell rang she felt almost giddy.

"Ready, Miss Blum?"

"Since six." They laughed easily.

Over the next few months they started spending Saturdays and Sundays together, going for long walks in Muir Woods, or lunch in Sausalito, dinner at Fisherman's Wharf.

One night at dinner Nadine asked, "Do you like San Francisco, Sandy?"

"I love it. One of the most beautiful places I've ever seen." ·

"And you've certainly seen a lot of places—"

"If you believe the posters . . . Join the marines and see the world."

"Sandy, I think that's the navy, isn't it?"

"Well, I get them mixed up, but the marines aren't stingy about travel."

"Was it a rough life?"

"No, a good one really. I saw and I did a lot of things I'd never have had the chance to do otherwise, especially when I look back and consider where I came from . . ."

"And where was that? We've never talked seriously about the past."

"Maybe sometimes it's better not to . . . Anyway, I was born in Europe, in Poland. My mother came to America . . ." He wasn't going to tell her about his mother leaving his father when he was born . . . "She opened a restaurant, made a bare living. I've told you about my brother and his family. And I also have a sister, Gittel."

"Gittel? That's one name I've never heard before."

"She was the only one who didn't need to change her name. I can't imagine calling her Greta."

He smiled briefly, an ironic, even bitter smile, she thought.

"Anyway, the war came along and I enlisted in the marines. Thought it was the class of the service, had a spiffy uniform . . ." He thought back to the time he had enlisted and Jacob had beaten the hell out of him. "To make a long story short, when the war ended I couldn't get a job so I decided to make the marines a career." He paused, remembering the headstone he'd ordered . . . "Loving Wife of—"

"What changed your mind, Sandy?"

"Oh, I suppose I just got tired of always being on the move. One day I woke up and decided it was time to go home." He'd made it very short. But wasn't it better this way . . . ?

"Where's home for you?"

He looked at her closely now. "I think *you* are, Nadine."

She looked away and fumbled with the broken fortune cookies. "You've never mentioned love, Sandy."

He reached for her hand across the table. "I love you, Nadine . . ."

"Do you really, Sandy? Somehow I have a feeling there was once someone very important in your life and you haven't forgotten—"

Don't lie, he told himself. "There was, but you have to get over things, move on."

"Does it still hurt?"

"Yes. She died . . ."

"Do you think you can ever love anyone else like that again?"

"Probably not . . . But what I feel for you is love too, believe me . . . I want to be with you. I *need* to be with you . . ."

She didn't answer.

"Of course, being the suave type I am, I haven't even asked if you'd have me. I'm not too much of a bargain, I grant you, but for whatever it's worth, I want to marry you and spend the rest of my life with you. I want to try to make you the happiest lady in the world—"

She started to cry softly. He came around to her side, lifted her face and kissed her. "Please marry me, Nadine . . ."

"Yes, Sandy. Wonderful, sweet, dear Sandy—"

He lifted his cup of tea in salute. "Here's to very lucky Sandy, who's going to wake up in the morning next to Nadine, and wonder why he should be so lucky."

She smiled. "All right, Mr. Lucky. Now please shut up and take your intended home. We've wasted enough time already." . . .

One month later they were married at Temple Emanuel. It was a small wedding—Mr. Blum had to take out a loan from the Morris Plan, but it had all the charm and grace one would expect from Charles and Mildred Blum.

Gittel and her family and Esther came. They couldn't afford the trip because the Depression had all but wiped them out, but Jacob had sent the money. The memory of the way Hershel had treated them when they were in Cleveland hadn't faded, but Jacob saw to it that his mother would see her Shlomo married.

Shlomo watched as Nadine walked down the aisle on her father's arm, stood by his side in a white organdy dress and a tulle hat with satin streamers down the back. It was not a time for lavish gowns. He held her very close to him, and when they were pronounced man and wife, Shlomo knew he had indeed come home.

Doris cried that her beloved Uncle Shlomo had abandoned her. And Rachel could barely look at him when she remembered that awful moment in the back bedroom, that one frenzied night . . . She clung to Jim's arm, feeling embarrassed and wishing she hadn't come . . .

For sentimental reasons the wedding luncheon was served at the Saint Francis, where their romance had really begun.

During the meal Sara kept looking across the table at the Blums. In spite of Sara's elegant clothes she felt oddly out of place. She knew she would never be like Nadine's family—Jean Morris was from one of the so-called best families in San Francisco. Well, "best" was a sometime thing . . .

Esther cried to think she should live to see this day, and Gittel blessed Jacob for being so good to send for them. Hershel, of course, said not one word of thanks. He didn't seem so talkative these days . . .

The luncheon was over before they knew it, and soon everyone stood on the wide steps of the hotel to watch the newlyweds drive away in their green Chevrolet for three days in Carmel. . . .

After their honeymoon they moved into a furnished apartment on Jones Street. Nadine put away her lovely organdy dress in moth balls.

At nine o'clock the next morning she was at work at Ranshoff's and Shlomo was crossing the bay to Hayward, but they felt they were the richest people in the entire world.

CHAPTER THIRTY-NINE

AT SIX o'clock in the morning Sara hurried down the stairs to answer the phone in the front hall.

"Sara, this is Jim."

Her heart pounded. "It's about Rachel?"

"Yes, you have a grandson."

Sara's hand trembled. "I don't understand. Rachel wasn't due for another two months—"

Jim was very tired, he didn't want to explain all the details. Still, it was Rachel's mother . . . "She went into labor yesterday afternoon and the doctor decided to do a Caesarean at three o'clock in the morning."

"A Caesarean? And you didn't let me know Rachel was in the hospital since yesterday? Jim, I'm her mother . . ."

Yes, Jim thought, how well I know it . . . "I really felt the ordeal might be too much for you and I didn't see any point in having you wait around—"

"Oh, I *see.*" She fought to control her irritation . . . "How is Rachel?"

"Fine, thank God."

"And the baby?"

"A little small, but healthy."

"Would it be all right if Jacob and I came to the hospital?" she asked cautiously.

He was now holding the receiver so tightly that his knuckles showed white. "Please do . . . but not today. Rachel's been through a great deal, you're of course welcome to come tomorrow—"

"Well, thank you, that's very generous."

He hung up without a good-by.

So Rachel had a premature baby? Sara doubted it. She'd suspected Rachel was pregnant when she married Jim Ross. She called Jacob at the plant.

"Hayward Meat Packing Company."

"Let me speak to Mr. Sanders."

"Who's calling?"

"Mrs. Sanders."

"Sorry, Mrs. Sanders. He's out in the yard sorting cattle. It may take a while . . ."

It was eleven o'clock when he called back. "Sara?"

"Who else would it be—"

This was one of those days for Sara. "Yes, what is it, Sara? I'm very busy—"

"When aren't you busy . . . Do you know what *I've* been going through since six-thirty this morning?"

"Okay, Sara, what's the problem?"

"Rachel had a boy."

"A boy!" he shouted. "That's great. How's Rachel?"

"She's fine . . ."

"So what's the problem?"

"The problem? Rachel went to the hospital yesterday afternoon and the doctor did a Caesarean at three o'clock in the morning. I don't remember when I've been so upset—"

"A Caesarean? But she's all right?"

"Fine . . . from what your son-in-law said."

"And the baby?"

"A little small, but fine."

"Well, thank God."

"That's what your son-in-law said—"

He'd be damned if he could understand her. This was their first grandchild and she was upset. "What's the matter, Sara?"

"Don't you know?"

"Know what?"

"The baby was seven months. Don't you know what that means?"

"What does it mean?"

"That she must have been pregnant when she got married. Maybe that's why she didn't call as soon as she went to the hospital, but even so . . . We're the grandparents and he didn't think we should be present when our first grandchild was being born. But what can you expect from an old *goy?*"

Sara was stirring the resentment Jacob already had for Jim, but he tried to suppress it. "Didn't he give a reason for not telling us earlier?"

"Sure. He thought it might be too much of an ordeal for me. Wasn't that considerate?"

"I'll be damned . . ."

"Well, at least now you know why I've been so upset."

"Yes, I do . . ."

"I wanted to go to the hospital today and was told to stay away, can you imagine? Keeping grandparents away? It's the cruelest thing I've ever heard of."

"Well, if that's the way he wants it, then I think that's the way he'll get it. I'm not going."

286

"I agree with you, Jacob. We've been good parents and this is our thanks. Mr. Jim Ross doesn't think we're quite good enough for him."

"He's going to find out differently . . . but Rachel should have insisted we be there—"

"Well, now you know."

He shook his head, so upset that he could hardly work for the rest of the day. He had a grandchild—a grandson—and his daughter and her husband didn't want him to share the pleasure of it. Hard to believe. Terrible . . .

Jim sat by Rachel's bed in a chair waiting for her to wake up. When she opened her eyes, she reached out for his hand.

"Happy, darling?" she asked weakly.

"More than any time in my life," he said, stroking her hair. "We have our beautiful little son and he has a beautiful mother."

"Did you call my mother?"

"Yes . . ."

"And? Was she happy?" Rachel half-smiled.

"Very, very happy, darling . . ."

"She was pleased it was a boy?"

"Beside herself."

"Well, thank God for that . . . And I know my father will be proud. He always wanted us to be boys."

"I'm damned glad he didn't get what he wanted."

Rachel's room was filled with flowers from friends and associates of Jim's, but, strangely, nothing from her family. Not even a phone call. She and her mother had hardly had an easy relationship, but that mama would ignore her now went beyond her comprehension. Was it possible mama was ill and no one wanted to tell her? Three days had passed . . . She asked the nurse to hand her the phone. After six rings Sara finally answered.

"Mama, this is Rachel."

"Well, Rachel . . . how nice of you to call."

Rachel was in tears. "What's *wrong*, mama?"

"You don't know?"

"Know what?"

"That your husband told us not to come to the hospital?"

Rachel blinked back the tears. "I can't believe that . . ."

"Oh, so you're saying I'm not telling the truth?"

"I can't imagine Jim saying—"

"Parents have feelings like anyone else, you know. As you'll find out . . ."

Rachel was trembling. "There must be some misunderstanding . . ."

"I don't think so. When I asked to see you, your husband told me not to come. Furthermore, I always thought it was common courtesy for parents to be called when one of their children is taken to the hospital—"

"Mama, it all happened so suddenly. We didn't have time for anything . . ."

"Well, no matter, Rachel. It's obvious, we're just not important in your life anymore."

In spite of herself, Rachel felt guilty. "I want to apologize for not letting you know. I suppose it was wrong . . ."

Silence.

"Please, mama. Please come and see the baby."

"I'll have to talk to your father. His feelings have to be considered too. Now, how are you, Rachel?"

"Fine, mama, fine . . ."

"Well, that's good to know. And the baby?"

"He's beautiful."

"We'll come over tonight."

When Rachel hung up, she was crying near-hysterically and could only be calmed with a sedative. . . .

When Jacob saw the baby through the nursery window he could barely resist picking the child up. His grandson . . . It seemed like only yesterday that Rachel had waited for him at the subway station . . . My God, where had all the years gone? Looking at Jim, he thought, Lucky old buck has a son and a lovely young wife like Rachel. But what the hell, this was a different situation, a different time . . . They never knew the hunger and the wants of mere survival. Nobody had left him a steel mill. He'd had to fight his way out of the sewer and he'd done it with his own two hands and his own mind . . . . Still, was it really so bad that his grandson wouldn't have to struggle as he had?

The next day Doris came to see Rachel. She kissed her and seated herself in the yellow leather chair. "You look so beautiful, Rachel, in that blue bed jacket."

"Thank you, Doris. Why did you wait so long to come see me?"

"Don't you know mama and papa by now, Rachel? If they get mad, then we all have to be mad."

"I know . . ."

Doris sighed. "Since you got married she simply doesn't leave me alone. You're lucky you escaped . . ."

"I'm lucky on all counts, but some day you're going to meet the right person too and—"

"Me! Who's going to marry fat Doris? I'm seventeen and I've never even had a date. Next week I'm graduating from high school and everyone's been invited to the prom except big little old Doris."

"You won't feel bad if I say this, will you, Doris?"

"I know what you're going to say. Why don't you get thin, Doris? Am I right?"

"Well, yes . . . Why don't you try—?"

"I really have, Rachel, so help me God. But every time mama starts at me about my diet I go out and buy a dozen candy bars."

"Don't do it for her, Doris. Do it for *yourself*."

"Do it for myself . . . sure. And what about you, Rachel? How come now that you're married and don't need them for anything, she still gets to you? You had to beg them to come and see their own grandson. And I really have to laugh. Papa's supposed to be the strong one, but the heck he is . . . She's got him wound around her little finger. She can twist anything to suit her purpose and he doesn't even know it. I don't understand them at all."

"I know—"

"Then how come you still put up with it?"

"Jim asks me that too, but I can't explain it, Doris. I should never have called mama. I'm angry at myself for always giving in to her, for always letting myself be made to feel guilty . . . but it won't happen again. I've made up my mind . . ."

"Well, you have more nerve than I ever did. I thought the only way I could survive was to keep my mouth shut. I'm still doing that, for all the good it does . . ."

"Oh, forget them, Doris. What are you going to do when you graduate?"

"Golly, I don't know. Remember, I was going to be a big movie star?" Doris laughed. "Well, the blimp's going to look for a job. Funny, I've no ambition to do much of anything. Funnier still is I made it through high school. In fact, I'm the youngest one in the class because mama lied about my age when I started school. Can you believe it, dumb Doris managed to get through."

"Doris, why don't you go to secretarial school?"

"Yes, and who's going to pick up the tab for that? Papa? I'm so sick and tired of asking for nickels and dimes. I asked for an allowance of five dollars a week—"

"And?"

"And papa said, 'What do you need an allowance for, don't you have enough food?' It went on and on with the same old things we've heard all our lives. He still doesn't understand. Finally I said, 'You're absolutely right, papa.' Who wants to argue?"

"Why don't you go to night school and take a course? I did."

"You had more ambition. The heck with it, I'll get a job doing something. Well, enough about the hard life and times of Doris Sanders... You're really happy, aren't you, Rachel?"

"More than I can tell you ..."

"And you're really in love with Jim. I can tell that much."

"Didn't you think I was?"

"Not at first ..."

"Well, for anyone's information, I adore him."

"Did you always?"

"Not in the very, very beginning, but soon enough. He's the best thing that ever happened to me. Or ever will ..."

"I'm glad, it must be wonderful."

"It is. And it will happen to you—"

Doris burst out laughing. "You want to make a bet?"

"Yes."

"Okay, six candy bars."

"You're on."

Chapter Forty

THE NIGHT of the senior prom, Doris lay in bed and thought about the other girls getting into their long white dresses, then waiting for their dates to arrive.

"Holy cow, Gladys, you look terrific... Here's your corsage."

"Oh, Howie, it's beautiful! Tie it around my wrist... Goodnight, mom, dad."

"Have a good time, Gladys, and drive carefully, Howie." The front door shuts.

"Didn't she look beautiful, Willie?"

"Imagine our little girl . . . just like her mother."

"Oh, you told me that when you picked me up for our prom." . . .

"Wow, you got your pop's car!"

"Yeah, pop's terrific . . . Gosh, Gladys, you look so beautiful."

"Oh, Howie . . ."

"Gladys, let's go to lover's lane and park. I got a flask filled with my pop's favorite booze." . . .

"You're dripping it on my dress . . . Howie! Take your hands off my—"

"Don't talk now, Gladys . . ."

Doris started to cry. Her life was hopeless. She had no direction, and although she had lots of desire there was no Howie on the horizon. . . .

Doris got a job at Goldman's Dress Shop from nine to five. She stood on her feet six days a week, and the only thing that made life bearable was her lunch hour and the movies on Sunday. On Saturday nights she came home, ate, took a bath, went to bed to read movie magazines; it was better than being seen without a date on the traditional big date night.

By the time her birthday came in January she knew more about Hollywood than Louella Parsons. But then, she wasn't Louella Parsons, she was still fat Doris and it was yet another lonely Saturday night. Already eighteen and no closer to any romance than she'd been in June. At forty she'd probably still be living at home. God, what would happen to her if mama and papa died? She was afraid to think about it. She'd be all alone. Rachel had Jim and little Larry. Lillian would be married, probably a grandmother by then. And fat Aunt Doris would float from one to the other for Sunday night supper because everyone would feel so sorry for her . . . Thank God she finally went home, they'd say, old maids were a pain . . .

She went downstairs and poured herself a large glass of milk, took the chocolate Oreo cookies she kept stashed away and wolfed them down. At least she had no fear of reprisals tonight. Mama and papa were at some kind of nightclub with Nadine and Sandy to celebrate Mr. and Mrs. Blum's anniversary. Mama was really dressed to the teeth tonight. God, if she got any thinner she'd be able to take a shower without getting wet . . . And Lillian was at a meeting of the Girl Scouts.

Finishing the last Oreo cookie, she felt as though her life was one long, dateless prom night. To hell with it . . .

Doris sat having her lunch of macaroni and cheese at her usual spot in Clinton's Cafeteria. Sitting across from her at the long communal table, she saw a girl about her own age but at least thirty pounds lighter. She was eating a hot fudge sundae, heavy with whipped cream. God wasn't fair. How come some people could eat themselves into oblivion and never gain a pound? It had to be glandular, it had to be. Rachel was raised on the same diet of starches and fats that mama used to make when food was the center of their existence, and she never put on a pound. Doris was convinced that fat was a disease the medical profession had never researched.

"Boy, I bet you never had a problem with your weight," she said to the girl.

"Actually it's the other way around. I have to eat to keep the skin on my bones. I'm so thin I hate myself."

God sure got mixed up when He was handing out the bodies. She had to eat? What a curse . . . "Yeah, I'll bet it's tough . . ."

"It is . . . really. I hate to get into a bathing suit. I feel like Popeye's girlfriend, Olive Oyl."

"And I hate to get into a bathing suit because I look like a zeppelin."

"There's just no in-between, is there?"

"Never a more astute statement was made—"

"Yeah. Golly, I have to get back to work—"

"Well, so long. Nice meeting you."

The thin girl nodded and Doris sighed as she watched the size-six disappear. . . .

From then on, the girls ran into each other frequently at lunch and got to know each other quite well. Amazingly, they discovered they had the same birthdates. But the similarities stopped there. Murial was born in Oakland and her family well well-known in the Jewish community. The Silvermans were prominent members of Temple Sinai and, in fact, Murial's grandfather had been there the day the cornerstone was laid.

. But the differences in the girls' backgrounds made very little difference in their friendship. Doris had at last found a friend, and her devotion to Murial had no bounds.

Soon Doris was invited to the Silvermans', and in a short

292

time their home became her refuge ... she adored the whole family.

Mr. Silverman was a soft-spoken, slender gentleman. Mrs. Silverman was a gentle woman whose understanding nature made all four of her daughters feel the value of their individuality.

Sylvia, the oldest, was like her father in manner. She was twenty-three and not especially attractive, but her parents' love had given her an inner and outer composure that more than compensated. She had been going with Henry Levin, a doctor, for three years on an on-and-off basis, but the family kept assuring her that one day he would pop the question. All he needed was to establish himself in private practice. After all, he was only thirty-three and doctors were the first to be called and the last to be paid. Sylvia was advised to be patient, and Doris thought it was wise advice. Doris had never really talked to the doctor, but she thought he seemed nice. He always said hello to her when they met at the Silvermans', and he seemed to like her jokes.

Janice, eighteen months younger, had any number of dates, but no proposals. In spite of the fact that she was the beauty of the four sisters.

Auburn-haired Alice was seeing Martin Gold, the furrier's son. There were no intentions on his part, but then this was the Depression and fellows generally didn't or couldn't think of marriage.

Murial had lots of friends, gave lots of parties, but that was as far as her social life went. She had her heart set on Sidney Stein, although there was little hope that anything would materialize there. Still, she was going to keep trying ....

Doris loved the nights she could spend with Murial. They would lie on Murial's bed and fantasize about the boys ... about the bliss of being Mrs. ...

Now Doris had a friend she could share her dreams with, and a whole family who actually liked her and laughed at her jokes. Her life had decidedly taken on new meaning. She really dieted, and, miracle of miracles, took off twenty pounds. It was torture, but she did it.

Mama said another thirty and she'd look human. ...

Murial worked for her father in his haberdashery shop and she had Saturdays off, but this was a problem for Doris. She worked six days a week, and as a result she couldn't go tea dancing at the Saint Francis Hotel on Saturday afternoons.

After hearing Murial and Eva Kahn's tales about those

fabulous guys who twirled you around the floor, Doris was desperate to go to the tea dances. Finally she called in sick one Saturday—the hell with being docked three dollars—and joined Murial and Eva. . . .

Dressed in a brown and chartreuse print and a small pillbox hat with veil, she sat excitedly at the table and watched the fellows asking the girls if they would like to dance. Today she ignored the plate of small sandwiches on the table. She was waiting for someone to walk into her life.

Skinny Murial was whisked away to the dance floor, where Eva, the Clara Bow of Doris' new circle of friends, was already dipping and twirling in the arms of some tall boy with the remains of adolescent acne.

Doris suddenly felt that she was only a spectator. She wasn't jealous of either of her friends . . . not really jealous, only very aggravated. What the hell had she taken off the twenty pounds for! Was this her reward for all the hunger pangs and near-sleepless nights when her stomach had rumbled so? She had gone down two whole dress sizes, and at a hundred and thirty, although she was only five-feet-two and large-boned like papa, she thought she looked reasonably svelte. Everyone had praised her accomplishment—except mama, of course. But in this case, maybe mama was right.

Holding back the tears of anger, she grabbed for the dainty cucumber and mayonnaise sandwiches. Murial was so busy dancing she wouldn't have time to eat hers anyway . . . She washed them down with the sugared tea. What was wrong with her? She'd even had her hair cut short and marcelled into small waves and had carefully learned to apply the dark lipstick Joan Crawford used. Well, Doris, she muttered to herself, make up your mind, this is it. She sat leadenly in her unnoticed spot and watched all the pelvic bones, thin arms and thin legs gliding past the table . . . .

"Wow," Eva said as they sat on the ferry going back to Oakland. "I was asked out by some guy who gave me his card."

"Did you accept?" Murial asked.

"Are you crazy? Here, take a look at the name . . ."

Murial held the card, while Doris peeked. Timothy McCarthy, Esq., Attorney at Law.

Murial laughed. "How did he get into that profession? I thought it was restricted."

"Just my luck, he's in the right profession but the wrong pew." Eva tore up the card into small pieces and let them blow into the salty breeze. "Well, there goes my last chance at motherhood."

Doris smiled in spite of her depression, "With your luck and figure, I wouldn't worry." . . .

That night she decided not to stay over at Murial's. If ever she owed herself a treat, it was now.

She went to the Pig and Whistle, where she had a banana split and a piece of German chocolate cake with coffee. She expected the binge to be heaven after the months of dieting, but somehow it just wasn't. She took the streetcar home, went to her room and cried most of the rest of the evening. Tomorrow she'd diet. Tonight she gorged.

In February, Murial announced that they were having a surprise birthday party for Sylvia. "But how are we going to decorate the house with balloons and streamers and not have her guess? Holy cow . . ."

Doris thought carefully. "If I could get my mother to say yes, would it be all right if it was at my place?"

"Say, what an idea! We could bring the food in the morning, work all day and you can tell Sylvia you're having a party. Oh, Doris, you're a genius."

"Let me ask my mother first . . ."

"Do you think she'll say yes?"

"Well, I'll ask her—"

"Thanks, and tell her she doesn't have to do a thing. Everything will be spick-and-span before we leave."

"Sure, well, I'll ask." . . .

Sara had begun a strict regimen of exercise. Doris sat on the edge of her mother's bed and watched, and in between the bends and kicks tried explaining to her about the party.

"Don't be ridiculous, Doris. Do you really think I'm going to have a bunch of kids jumping all over my furniture—?"

"Mama, these aren't kids. Sylvia's going to be twenty-*four*. Besides, Murial and her family have been so good to me, I think it's the least I could do."

Sara wiped the perspiration from her face and looked at Doris as she went on.

"Besides, mama, I never had a party."

"Well, that's not exactly my fault. You never had any friends—"

"Well, I do now. Can I tell Murial it's all right?"

Sara hesitated. Should she cover up the furniture? Doris really asked for very little . . . "If I say yes, can you guarantee me that no one smokes or gets wild?"

"Yes, I give my word."

"All right. On one condition—don't let anyone put their feet on the furniture."

"I promise. Thank you a lot, mama, I really appreciate it." And she did.

The girls had come to Doris' to help with the preparations for the party, and at the end of a frantic day everyone had rushed home to shower and dress.

Doris was ready a half hour early and was dressed in a long beige chiffon dress with a pink taffeta sash around her waist that ended in a large bow at the back. Some fashion expert said big bows covered a multitude of sins ...

The bell began to ring promptly at seven, and Doris ran down the stairs and nervously greeted her guests for the first party she'd ever given.

The bell kept ringing, and Sara stood at the top of the stairs wondering how long this was going to last ...

Finally Murial came in with Sid, and it was just in time. Going into the livingroom, she gathered everyone around. "Okay, now when the bell rings and Sylvia and Henry arrive, wait till Doris takes their coats and when they come into the livingroom everyone sings 'Happy Birthday.' "

From then on, everything went as planned. Sylvia and Henry arrived at seven-thirty, and Sylvia was genuinely surprised and pleased that the party was for her. She was aware as never before that she was still unmarried, especially after she excitedly opened the small box Henry gave her and found only a small rhinestone pin. But this was her birthday, and she was determined to have a good time with the family and friends who had thrown this party for her.

Her surprise and good spirits set the party rolling. The Victrola started to play the latest dance tunes. Someone brought the records of that wonderful new singer, Bing Crosby, and before Doris could protest, the punch was spiked. She prayed mama wouldn't ask for some if she came down. But on second thought, that was unlikely. Mama go off her diet? Not if she was entertaining the Prince of Wales.

The sandwiches were quickly eaten, and the girls went into the kitchen to fix another batch while Doris stood sentry, making sure no one was smoking. The lights were dimmed, and since the livingroom wasn't large enough for twenty people to dance at one time, a little heavy necking was going on in the corners.

Pearl Grossman sat on the sofa with one dainty leg tucked

under her, while Ben Schwartz groped for her lips. When he finally made contact, his breathing rasped as though he were having a sinus attack. As diplomatically as possible Doris asked if Pearl would be kind enough to keep her feet on the floor—a request that did not endear her to Ben Schwartz, who was just getting ready to thrust a sweaty palm inside Pearl's bodice.

The evening was far from enjoyable for Doris. She was so anxious for it to be a success, but her concern over mama's instructions had made her a policeman rather than a hostess. Exhausted, she stood ladling out the punch... The hell with it, she thought, she was going to have a piece of cake—

"Would you like to dance?" Henry asked.

Doris looked around to see whom Henry was addressing, but it could only be her. Sylvia was dancing with Mel Harris, who was the only extra fellow. And Mel, like herself, was not exactly beating off the competition. He wore thick glasses and was much too thin for his height. He and she had become known as the fill-ins.

"Would you like to dance, Doris?"

She looked at him. He was five-feet-eight, one hundred and twenty-five pounds. She hadn't weighed that since she was four. He had curly black hair and a neatly-trimmed mustache *and* a nice face with a sweet smile. Somehow he didn't seem quite thirty-three tonight in the navy-blue suit and white shirt. Nor did he seem to feel particularly out of place although the other fellows were only about twenty-two. Maybe it was just the punch she'd had, but she felt that things were beginning to look up for her.

"I'd be very happy to," she told him. Damn right, she would . . .

She found Henry's arm around her waist, and they were, miracle of miracles, dancing. "You look lovely tonight, Doris."

It must be the dim lights, or maybe he was too vain to wear glasses and was stumbling through life. If he was, she sure as hell wouldn't want him to take out her tonsils.

"Thank you, Henry. It's very nice of you to say so . . ."

"Well, it's true, and I've always thought so."

Maybe it was Henry who'd had too much punch. Or maybe men of thirty-three began to get senile. Now she was terribly embarrassed, and she repeated the same scintillating words. "Thank you, Henry—"

"What are you doing tommorrow?"

She stepped on his toe and immediately hoped she hadn't

broken it. He'd never be able to stand up in surgery on Monday. "I'm *sorry*, Henry—"

"It didn't hurt."

"I'm glad . . ."

"Now about tomorrow. I'd like to take you out."

There must be a touch of insanity in his family. She glanced over at Sylvia, who was doing the rumba to a Paul Whiteman record. The Silvermans had been filling Sylvia's hope chest for three years now so that she'd be ready at a moment's notice if Henry should forget himself in a weak moment and ask her to marry him.

"I don't think so, Henry, really."

"Why?"

"Because you're engaged to Sylvia . . ."

"Who said I was?"

"Well, you've been serious for a long time."

"Serious? Who told you that?"

"Well, haven't you?"

"Not to my knowledge . . ."

Was it possible Sylvia had been keeping it a secret from him?

"You've been going steady with Sylvia for three years, Henry," she said indignantly.

"Steady? I just take her out sometimes."

"Well, anyway, Henry, I just couldn't."

"Because of Sylvia?"

"Yes . . . Besides, Murial is my best friend and it wouldn't be right."

"If I had had any intention of being serious with Sylvia, it wouldn't have taken three years."

If Doris was ever grateful to her mother, it was at this moment, as she whispered in Doris' ear, "It's time to break up the party. Your father's complaining about the noise."

"All right, mama . . . Excuse me, Henry."

Sara left and Doris went to find Murial. "Listen, my folks want us to call it a night. I'm sorry."

"Oh, no problem, everyone wants to go to Checker's for waffles anyway."

Murial got on mama's chair, which almost made Doris faint, and announced, "All right, gang, the party's over."

Doris was pleased with how well the party had gone. Mama and papa had been so decent. But now she was exhausted, and really happy to be free of Henry.

"You're coming, aren't you, Doris?" Murial asked.

"No, I don't think so, Murial."

"Come on . . ."

"No, really."

"Well, you've been swell. I can't thank you enough . . . and Sylvia was so thrilled . . ."

On the way out, everyone said the party was great, Doris had been great, the punch was great . . .

Sylvia kissed her, then said, "I'll never forget what a wonderful party it was. You're a doll, Doris. We'll see you tomorrow."

"Yes . . . goodnight, Henry."

"Goodnight. Sure you don't want to come?"

"Real sure, Henry, but thank you."

When the door closed she leaned against it, trying to remember what waffles tasted like with real butter and maple syrup. She dismissed the thought as she turned on all the lights and worked until four in the morning getting the house in order.

She finally plopped into bed at four-thirty, thinking what a louse Dr. Henry Levin was. And *he* had to be the first man who had ever asked her out . . .

It was ten o'clock in the morning when Lillian came into Doris' room to announce: "Doris, get up. There's a *man* on the phone who wants to speak with you."

She bolted up in bed. "And what's his name?"

"Dr. Levin."

She hesitated, then, "Okay, tell him I'll be there in a minute—"

She went to the bathroom to wash the sleep from her eyes and then walked wearily down the stairs and picked up the receiver. "I'm sorry but we already have a family doctor."

"Now that's not very nice, Doris. I called to ask if I could take you out."

"The answer is still *no*, doctor."

"Listen, Doris, if I thought I was doing anything dishonorable I wouldn't be calling. But I'm *not* going steady with Sylvia or anyone else."

"But you *have* been taking her out for three years—"

"And several other girls as well. Sylvia knows that."

Doris paused, really wanting to accept the date but feeling very guilty about it.

Lillian had been standing close enough to understand what was being talked about. She whispered, "Go, go . . ."

Doris hushed her. She had to have time to think. "Call me back in half an hour. I just got up."

"Okay, in half an hour . . ."

Doris padded into the kitchen, where mama was eating her grapefruit. She sat down, slumping forward with both elbows on the table, and wondered how mama could eat that without sugar.

"I want to compliment you, Doris. The house was immaculate this morning. I was worried but I must say you handled it better than I ever would have thought."

Maybe mama was mellowing in her *thin* age. It was the first real compliment she could remember in a long time. "I appreciate your saying that, mama."

"Well, it's true and I think the girls were wonderful to stay and help you, just as they promised."

"Oh, yes, they were terrific . . ."

Taking a bite of grapefruit, Sara asked, "What's wrong?"

When Doris remained silent, Lillian answered for her. "This doctor wants to take Doris out and she doesn't want to go—"

"A doctor wants to take you out and you don't want to go?"

Doris glared at Lillian. "You've got a big mouth, Lillian. That's one of your most unredeeming qualities."

Sara repeated, "Did I hear right? You don't want to go out with a doctor?"

"Well, yes . . ."

"Why, do you have a date with Cary Grant?"

"You don't understand. Big Mouth here didn't tell you he's practically engaged to Sylvia Silverman."

"Practically! Instead of taking you to a doctor for your weight, I should take you to a doctor to have your head examined. What, you're so popular you can turn down a date, and with a doctor?"

"Mama, I just got through telling you—"

"I know what you told me. But if he was so crazy about Sylvia he wouldn't be calling you. How long have they been going together?"

"Three years . . ."

"Three years! My God, how could I have a daughter with so few brains? When a man wants to marry a girl, he doesn't *shlep* around with her for three years."

"But Murial is my best friend and it wouldn't be right . . ."

"To hell with what would be right. Murial isn't going to be your husband."

300

Doris was shocked. Husband? She hadn't even been out with him . . . "Well, I'm not going."

"Yes, you are, Doris. You certainly are." . . .

When the phone rang, Doris told Lillian to tell Henry she was sick.

"You go to that phone, Doris, and tell him you'd be happy to go out with him."

Doris sat looking at mama. God, hadn't she ever heard of loyalty to one's friends?

"Well," mama urged, "by the time you get to the phone, he's liable to change his mind and ask Sylvia."

Let me make up my own mind, Doris thought, but she knew her mother wouldn't give her a moment's peace unless she went out with Henry. Impatiently, she picked up the receiver.

"Hello, who is this?" As if she didn't know . . .

"Henry. Henry Levin."

"Oh. Yes, Dr. Levin?"

"You told me to call back about today—"

"What about it?"

"As I said, I'd like to take you out. And I'm not going to say it again . . ."

"Okay, Henry . . ."

"What? Oh, good . . . What would you like to do?"

"Anything . . ." What do you do with a man on a Sunday afternoon? Big Mouth Lillian. Mama always pushing. Poor Sylvia . . . "I don't know, Henry, I suggest you suggest something."

"Well, I thought it might be nice to take a ride down the coast to Santa Cruz and have lunch."

Everything seemed to revolve around food. What would she do, sit there and watch? She was sure that after last night she must have put on easily nine pounds, which would bring her to one hundred and fifty-nine. God . . . but she had to give him an answer. "That sounds fine—"

"What time can I pick you up?"

In about twenty years. "Twelve will be all right?"

"Great."

"Yes, great. Well, I'll see you then."

"I'm looking forward to that, Doris . . ."

The man was absolutely not well. "Thank you. At twelve then."

Doris turned around and saw her mother and sister standing behind her. Her mother was all smiles. The dialog must have gone exactly according to her script.

"Oh, Doris," she said, "I'm so thrilled. Now, let's go upstairs and see what you can get into."

What a nice way to put it. Let's see, out of my large wardrobe I think I'll wear my simple little size-sixteen silk, the demure and adorable little dress that all the fellows at the Saint Francis so admired as they waited their turn to dance with me.

CHAPTER FORTY-ONE

AT TWELVE noon on Sunday, Dr. Henry Levin was invited into the livingroom to meet mama and papa and Lillian.

"It's a pleasure, doctor," Sara said in her most gracious manner. He was good-looking, she noted with surprise, quite dapper in the white flannels and the double-breasted blue jacket. Imagine *him* asking Doris out . . .

"And this is my father," Doris said. "Papa, this is Dr. Levin."

Jacob shook hands, thinking that at least this one he could be proud of—not only Jewish but a doctor too. Doris should grab him. "Nice to meet you, doctor."

"Henry. It's a pleasure, Mr. Sanders."

"The pleasure is mine . . ."

I'll bet, Doris thought. Hadn't papa noticed he was a little bit old? Well, any port in the storm for little Doris. Papa had complained that Jim was too old for Rachel, but the eminent doctor was only ten years younger. Mama, on the other hand, never let the girls forget that she was only seventeen years older than Rachel. Well, at least the doctor had outdone mama; he was a mere child, only fifteen years Doris' senior. "Henry, this is my favorite sister, Lillian."

Lillian ignored Doris' sarcasm; after all, she had performed a *mitzvah*. "How do you do, doctor."

"Nice meeting you, Lillian. Please call me Henry."

Mama was right for once, Lillian thought. Doris should have her head examined. The doctor was handsome. He looked like Clark Gable. Well, sort of . . .

Now that all the introductions had been made, Sara asked, like any normal Jewish mother, "When will you be back, Doris, dear?"

"I don't know. Does it matter—?"

"No, only that I thought if the doctor—"

"Henry."

"Yes, Henry. If you'd like, we'd be pleased to have you join us for dinner."

Well, mama didn't waste any time initiating the doctor—Henry—into the intimacy of the Sanders' close-knit family circle.

"That's really very nice of you, Mrs. Sanders."

"Sara . . ."

"Sara. I'd like that, that is if Doris would."

Anything to bring a little sunshine into everybody's life.

"Sure, what time do you want us to be back, mama?"

"Oh, would seven give you enough time?"

"Oh, that's more than enough time. Let's make it six, mama."

"Then six . . . Have a lovely day, Doris . . . Henry."

"It's been a pleasure meeting all of you," Henry said.

"The pleasure is ours." Sara smiled, devoutly meaning it.

When the door closed Sara took a deep breath. "If Doris could get a date, we'll live to see a bridge built across the Bay. How do you think she looked, Jacob?"

"Nice."

"Nice?" Lillian echoed. "She looked beautiful."

"Who could tell," Sara said. "The dress looked like it was made at the American Tent and Awning Company."

Lillian wanted to say that this was unfair, but she held her tongue.

"All right, Lillian, go change your clothes. I want you to help." Let's see, Sara thought, soup or salad? Soup. Every good Jewish boy likes soup. They'd have chicken, her noodle *kugel*, fresh peas . . . And for dessert? Strawberry shortcake. Wait! Was he kosher? Well, in case he was she'd bake an extra sponge cake.

"Lillian, take out the good dishes . . . Jacob, pick the roses."

"What am I, a gardener?"

"Forget it. Lillian, go pick the roses."

"I can't do everything, mama. What do you want me to do first?"

"Set the table—and don't get fresh. Then pick the roses."

Lillian was already taking the china out of the diningroom cupboard.

Henry helped Doris into his new De Soto, and she sat rigidly as he shut the door. When he started the engine up Doris asked, "Please don't go down Webster Street."

"Why?"

"Because I'd die if any of the Silvermans saw us."

"Doris, please, I'm going to ask you not to be worried. I have no understanding with Sylvia."

But I do . . . she's Murial's sister and Murial is my best friend. Damn mama for putting her in this position. If Murial ever found out it would be the end of their friendship.

Her unease grew with each mile. She didn't notice the sky or the lovely waves that lapped against the jutting rocks. All she could think of was her betrayal, forced or not . . .

She answered his questions woodenly and asked none in return.

Finally they arived in Santa Cruz and strolled silently along the boardwalk. By now Henry was disturbed that she was being so quiet. He'd observed her at the Silvermans', where she had been open and lighthearted. Well, maybe it just took her a while to warm up to people. He intended to give her every chance.

"Doris, are you ready for lunch? It's almost two."

"If you like . . ."

"I could eat if you could."

Her one hope was that God would let her go to heaven on a full stomach . . . "Yes, Henry, I could."

"There's a great place at the end of the pier. Let's try that." . . .

Seated at a table near the window, they found the view spectacular.

"It's lovely, isn't it, Doris?"

"Just lovely—"

"Are you having a nice time?"

"Very nice."

"I've very glad you said yes, Doris."

The man had to be desperate. What was wrong with him?

"What would you like?" Henry asked after the menus were brought. "The French dipped prawns are a specialty."

Well, that would add a week's torture. "Is that what you're going to have?"

"I think so."

"All right—"

"Make that two," Henry said to the waitress.

"French fries or coleslaw?" she asked.

"Doris?"

Both. "Coleslaw."

When the waitress walked away Henry generously buttered the French bread while Doris watched intently.

"Tell me about you, Doris."

"Where would you like me to begin, with my life on the stage?"

"Were you on the stage?"

"No, I was just being funny, or trying ..."

"What do you do?"

"Work in a dress shop."

"Oh. Do you like it?"

"It's a job ..."

"I get the feeling you're qualified for something better—"

"For what? And besides, how can you tell? This is the first time we've ever had more than a nodding acquaintance."

"I noticed you, whenever I was at the Silvermans'."

God, he had to go and spoil it by bringing up their names, but the waitress arrived with their plates and saved Doris from having to answer.

"Too bad we can't have a little cold beer with this," Henry said.

"I never had a beer in my life."

"I keep forgetting you're eighteen. You seem so mature for your age. Why, Prohibition has been around for almost that long."

Was that supposed to be a compliment? Mature? I suppose being fat makes one look wise, jolly *and* mature. "Thank you for the compliment—about being mature, I mean ... Now what about you?"

"Well, my mother and father came from Russia, but my three brothers, my sister and I were all born on the East Side of New York."

Where papa and mama lived ... "And?"

"My father got into the fish business. In fact, until I was eleven I didn't know there was anything else. Eventually my father got us out of the East Side and we moved to Syracuse."

Henry went on with his memories of New York, and Doris found herself interested in spite of herself. Finally Henry noticed the time and said they'd better be getting back.

On the way back to Oakland, he continued with the saga of the Levin family's rise from poverty, and all in one generation. "As I said, we moved to Syracuse and then to Denver because my father had relatives there. My brother Al—he's the oldest—got into business. Would you believe it? By the time he was twenty-six, he'd made over half a million dollars."

Henry wasn't bragging, Doris knew, because he spoke with such admiration. "What did he do, rob banks?"

They both laughed, and Henry was pleased to see her more at ease now.

"Pretty much. He made a bundle in the market, sold at the right time and went into the lending business. He wound up with a vault full of jewelry plus some property at a time when no one could pay back their loans. He even bought the mayor's house for us—a great big brick house on Spear Boulevard. What a character. He was the best-hearted guy in the world. He bought a Persian rug for my mother. When she asked how much it cost he said three hundred, although it really cost three thousand. She said we didn't have to walk on such an expensive rug, so she sold it."

"I'm afraid to ask for how much."

"Four hundred dollars—and thought that she'd made a profit. Then there was the dog he bought her . . ."

"What kind?"

"A pedigreed spaniel."

"Would she have fainted if he'd told her the price?"

"She would have if he'd told her. Anyway, the dog never understood anything but Yiddish. Can you imagine calling a dog Yankel? Unless you talked Yiddish to that dog he wouldn't lie down, do his tricks. Nothing. My mother's been in America forty-five years and she still can't speak a word of English, God bless her."

Doris was fascinated. She loved stories, and one day, she'd told herself secretly, she'd write about things like this . . . "Then what happened?"

"Well, it was the twenties and my brother was one of the few people in Denver who had any money at the time. He got himself involved in politics, and before you knew it he was getting the mayor, chief of police and the governor elected. He had more influence than the Pope. Spent money like confetti."

"What happened then?"

"Well, he got the bright idea that what Denver needed was a nightclub. So he became an entrepreneur and opened up the first nightclub Denver ever had. It was called the Marigold Gardens. He went to Chicago and booked the most expensive acts he could get. Al Jolson, believe it or not, and Ted Lewis, Belle Baker—a lot of people you probably never heard of."

"I've heard of all of them. I spent the best part of my life going to the Orpheum. In fact, I wanted to become the new Fanny Brice or Sophie Tucker." At least I had the figure for it.

"Really? I knew you were special—"

"Thanks. Then what happened?"

"Well, he made all kinds of money, but with his wine, women and song he spent it faster than he made it. And bookkeeping was out of Al's line. Everyone stole from him. The place folded and he wound up broke..." Henry's voice had trailed off.

"Gee, I guess you must have felt terrible after that..."

"In the beginning, yes, but Al's a happy-go-lucky sort of person. The only problem is that you get just one break like that in a lifetime, and somehow he lost that golden touch, just couldn't do anything right after that. Anyway, he lost everything and the Levins were right back where they started when they arrived in Denver."

"How did you get through college?"

"Worked at burlesque shows selling popcorn, peanuts and chewing gum, waited on tables... But I belonged to a good fraternity—"

"You had enough money to belong to a frat?"

"I worked hard enough for it. Anyway, I'd gone to high school with most of the guys so no one looked down their noses at me. Those were great times for me. In fact, the happiest time of my life was at college. The worst was when my father died two months before I graduated. That was tough..."

Yes, it would be. She'd never forget the face of death... "How did you happen to come to California?"

"When I applied for my internship I chose Fresno, California, because they had a course in urology I wanted. We got ten dollars a month."

"How come you didn't go into practice in Fresno?"

"I spent two dollars on a bus ticket, and I guess you could say it changed my life. I took a Greyhound bus to San Francisco one day, and when I saw the hills, Chinatown, the Bay, I just said, 'San Francisco, I love you.' This is where I want to be."

"Then?"

"So I came to San Francisco after my internship with twelve dollars in my pocket, took a room in a little hotel. Next day I went to the Flood Building and rented two rooms, then went down and bought some secondhand furniture for the treatment room, some instruments that I took on credit— and I was in business."

"You sound very enterprising."

"Well, I don't know if I was so enterprising... It was a tough struggle but believe it or not, after five months I brought my family out. I rented a flat on Thirty-eighth Avenue in the Richmond District."

"What do your brothers do?"

"Sell haberdashery, and my sister works at the Emporium."

"You all sound like quite a ... devoted family ..." She thought of her own "devoted" family, and decided not to explore that subject. "How long have you been in practice?"

"Five years now ..."

He must be making a fortune, with a new De Soto and—

"My God, I don't believe it, Doris, do you realize we're already back in Oakland?"

Oakland ... The Silvermans ... "It's none of my business, but how come you never married Sylvia?"

"Because I don't love her."

"She's awfully nice and the Silvermans are such lovely people—"

"I know they are—"

"Well, then, how come you've been going together for three years?"

"Doris, this is where we began. I told you I just take her out from time to time ... Well, here we are at your place."

Yeah, here we are.

Sara was graciousness itself as she welcomed them at the front door.

"How was he?" she asked when she finally cornered Doris in the kitchen.

"Very nice ..."

"Here, take this into the diningroom, Lillian. What did you do, Doris?"

"We took a ride to Santa Cruz and then went to lunch."

"Doris, I hope you watched your diet."

"Yes, I was very careful." Well, at least not one piece of bread and butter.

Doris followed as Sara imperiously announced dinner.

Thanks to Dr. Henry Levin it was like old times tonight— no rabbit food. But mama was still keeping an eye on Doris' plate.

"May I help you to more *kugel*, Henry?"

"No thanks, but it was really wonderful. I haven't eaten like this in years."

"Oh, Henry, how can you say that with a Jewish mother?" Sara asked.

"I love my mother, but she can't cook like you, Mrs. Sanders."

When a young man said someone cooked better than his mother, it was tantamount to a proposal. She brought in the two cakes. "Strawberry shortcake or plain?"

"The strawberry, thanks ... Did you really bake these?" Henry asked in honest admiration.

"Yes, of course."

"Well, it's the best I've ever had."

"Oh, thank you, Henry. Doris is a very good cook too, you know."

Oh my God, and I can't even boil water without burning it, Doris thought.

Jacob ate as usual, without compliments or comments. But he liked this young man, and after he was through he suggested they all go to the livingroom.

"How long have you been in practice?"

"Five years ..."

The story was fascinating, but once in one day was enough. Doris wished mama would get out of the kitchen so she could go in and sneak a piece of strawberry shortcake, which she'd been denied at dinner.

Seeing Sara finally come back into the livingroom after her chores, Doris excused herself, went through the hall and proceeded to the kitchen. When she got there and rummaged through the refrigerator she found that mama had outsmarted her ... She'd thrown out the strawberry shortcake.

Frustrated, she walked back and settled herself into a chair as far away from Henry as possible. Everyone was still listening to his saga.

Jacob was definitely pleased ... he'd met a *landsman*. "You were born on Chrystie Street?"

"That's right."

"Well, it's a small world. I used to box at a gym—"

"*What?* You never told me you boxed," Sara said, astonished.

He looked at her, then turned back to Henry ... "Now doctor—"

"Henry."

"Yes, Henry, well anyway, I think it's wonderful that you brought you whole family out here and supported them."

"Well, I don't exactly support them, I've just made it possible for us all to live together."

"I still give you a lot of credit for doing that and for working your way through college. You see, Sara? If a person wants something enough he'll find a way. And you once told me it was all luck."

This time Sara ignored him. "What decided you to become a doctor, Henry?"

"I always wanted to be a doctor, but especially when I saw the way my father and brothers struggled without a profession."

"That's admirable, Henry." Sara smiled.

Well, this could go on far into the night, Doris thought. Her mother was being just too obvious . . . you'd think *she* was being courted by Henry. Before she could catch herself, she yawned. Sara's eyes opened wide at her in an expression not uncommon to Jewish mothers. It meant any number of things, such as: stop yawning, act interested or I'll speak to you later—and that's exactly what mama did. . . .

When Doris finally said goodnight and stood against the door, Sara said, "When is he calling you?"

"He didn't say, and besides, I can't go out with him again—"

"You what?" Jacob said. "Let me see if I heard you right . . ."

"I said I can't go out with him again, papa."

Jacob's foot began to tap rapidly, a sure sign he was about to blow up. "For the first time you meet a fine gentleman—not only nice but a Jewish doctor—and you're not going to see him again? All I've heard from you is that you're going to wind up being an old maid. And you know something? You will. What's wrong with you, Doris? Your mother's right, you should have your head examined. Damn it, in the old country children listened to parents. Here in America children do what they want, ruin their lives and to hell with the parents."

"But you're not going out with him, I am."

"I thought you just said you weren't."

She started to cry. "I don't know what I said. You're both mixing me up."

As she ran up the stairs to her room, Jacob called out, "If you weren't mixed-up, you wouldn't say—"

She slammed the door and Jacob looked at Sara in exasperation. "First we have one who marries a *goy* old enough to be her father, and now we've got one who's total *meshugge*. I don't understand any of this." Walking up the stairs, he continued to mumble, "It could only happen in America . . ."

Trailing behind him, Sara said, "Now you see what a

parent goes through. You only want the best for them but they fight you every step of the way."

He nodded. On this, at least, they were together.

Now Doris knew what Jennie Harrison had meant that Easter Sunday so long ago when she'd told Doris about purgatory. But Doris' soul wasn't burning in hell; it was burning in Oakland, California.

On Monday she sat across from Murial at Clinton's Cafeteria and for once the cottage cheese stuck in her throat.

"Where did you go yesterday, Doris? We tried to call and thank you for the party, and say how sorry we were we didn't stay and help after."

Doris finally managed to swallow the lump of cottage cheese. "That's okay, I didn't mind cleaning up. It was no big thing." She hoped that would divert Murial from the first part of her question, but no such luck.

"What did you do yesterday?"

It was like the Spanish Inquisition. "Oh, stayed home and cleaned closets . . ."

Murial frowned. "That's funny. Your mother said you were out on a date."

Doris took a long drink of water. "My mother said that?"

"Yeah . . ."

"She didn't say you called."

"I did, about one. What did you do?"

Oh, how she wished she could disappear. "Went for a ride."

"Really? Who with?"

Oh, boy, think fast, Doris. "With a cousin of my aunt's."

"What aunt?"

"My Aunt Nadine."

"You never told me about your aunt's cousin."

"Didn't I?" Doris answered a little too brightly.

"No. A guy or a—"

"Girl."

"Your mother made it sound like a guy. She said, 'Doris isn't home, she has a date.' Gee, and here I was really so glad."

"Sure, well, it was a bore and besides, my mother has a habit of making things sound like what they're not."

"Oh, I think she's really very sweet, Doris."

Doris swallowed. "She's darling. Anyway, what time did you get home after the party?"

311

"About three. We all went to Checker's, except Sylvia and Henry. He said he was tired and wanted to make the one-thirty boat. Poor Sylvia, when the heck is she going to wake up? Well, anyway, everyone went to Eva's and danced for a while. Her folks are away in Los Angeles and, boy, did we have fun. Sid got fresh . . ." Murial giggled. "And Pearl got into a little heavy necking with Marty—I mean, heavy. Ben got high and started a fight so the fellows made him lie down in his car."

"Boy, that sure sounds like—God, Murial, I've got to run."

"Talk to you tonight, Doris."

"Yes, sure, call." . . .

After closing time at Goldman's Doris was summoned to the office.

"Yes, Mr. Goldman?"

He looked over the rim of his glasses and Doris knew beyond a doubt that he was furious.

"Take a look at these sales tags—"

Doris looked them over, then at Mr. Goldman. "What seems to be the matter, Mr. Goldman?"

"Can't you add, Doris? We're not a charity organization. Add up this tag."

Doris looked down at the charges. They totaled seventy-three dollars when she added them up, but the tag she'd written up said fifty-one dollars. God, how could she have made such a terrible mistake? She'd been upset all afternoon after meeting Murial. And this morning hadn't been much better. Mama had really started her day off by ignoring her at breakfast. Not just ignoring her, but *hostilely* ignoring her. The only small comfort of the day was that papa had gone to work at four in the morning, so at least she hadn't had to face him too.

"Gee, Mr. Goldman, I don't know what to say. I never made a mistake like that . . ."

"Well, I know what to say. You're going to make up the difference."

"I don't blame you, Mr. Goldman . . ."

"Okay, we'll take it out of this week's paycheck—and don't let it happen again."

"I sure won't, Mr. Goldman." . . .

But where papa was concerned, she was not let off so easily. Dinner that night was eaten in silence, but if looks could kill she'd have been dead.

And Lillian didn't exactly help. She just sat and ate, not even daring to look at anyone.

Finally Jacob broke the silence. "Shlomo wants to buy a house."

"So? Why don't they buy one?" Sara said.

"He needs the money for a down payment."

"Oh, I see, and he wants you to give it to him."

"Not give, loan."

"Why doesn't Nadine go to her father?"

"They don't have any money, Sara, you know that."

"So who are you? Mr. Rockefeller? If anyone needs a new house, it's us. Did you ever consider how I feel living in this mausoleum?"

"This is no mausoleum, it's a beautiful house—"

"Beautiful? Then why don't you sell it to Shlomo. For God's sake, we have our daughters to think of. This neighborhood is so bad, no wonder Dr. Levin didn't say he'd call Doris."

Well, they did remember she had a name, although they didn't seem to notice she was sitting with them in the same room . . .

"It wasn't because of the house, Sara, and you know it. I didn't marry you because you had such a beautiful house."

"Let's not get started on that, all right? Look, Jacob, it isn't even proper for a man in your position to live like this. My God, you're a well-to-do man."

"I'm not that well-to-do. Besides, we weren't talking about us. I asked about loaning the money to Shlomo."

He was still a frightened man when it came to money . . . The more he acquired the more he was apprehensive about losing it. Of course he wanted to help his brother, but at the same time . . .

"What do you think, Sara?"

"Why do you ask me? You'll do what you want anyway. You care more about Nadine having a baby than you do about your own children. If you were that considerate of your own family and would realize that Doris needs a decent place to bring a fellow to, maybe she'd stand a chance of getting married. Maybe if we'd had a decent home, Rachel wouldn't have married a *goy*. For God's sake, Jacob, when we bought this place we were lucky to have a roof over our heads, but things are different now . . ."

Doris got up and walked out unnoticed. Did her whole life depend on a house? Didn't they think that maybe someone

313

might like her just because she was Doris? No, she was just a bargaining point for mama to use to her own advantage.

On Thursday night the phone rang and Sara ran to answer it.

"How are you, Mrs. Sanders. This is Henry."

She stammered, "Wonderful, Henry. How nice of you to call."

"I should have called sooner to thank you for dinner but I've really been busy and haven't had a moment—"

"I can imagine what a doctor's life is like . . ."

The truth was, he had hoped that not calling would give Doris a chance to miss him. "Is Doris in?"

"Well . . . I'm not sure. She has a date tonight, but maybe she's still home."

"Thanks, I'll wait."

She ran upstairs and burst into Doris' room. "The doctor's on the phone."

Imagine, mama, he called in spite of the mausoleum . . . "Tell him I'm at the library."

"You go downstairs this very minute."

This was the first time she'd heard a voiced directed to her in nearly a week . . . She got out of bed and went down the stairs, with Sara close behind. When she picked up the receiver, mama's look said, "If he asks, you say *yes.*"

"Henry?"

"Hi, Doris. I'm glad you're still home."

Still home? "Oh, yeah, that was a lucky break."

"How are you?"

"Fine, Henry, and you?"

"Are you busy Saturday?"

One look at mama and she said, "No, the fellow I had a date with broke his leg."

"Oh, that's a shame . . . Then I can see you?"

Doris could hear mama's breathing. "Sure, that would be fine, Henry."

"Where would you like to go? Is the Mark Hopkins all right?"

What about Buckingham Palace? My last date was there. "I love the Mark Hopkins."

"So do I. Seven-thirty?"

"Swell." Doris hung up and was about to go upstairs when Sara cornered her. "I want to talk to you, Doris."

My goodness, mama remembered she had a name. "Yes,

314

mama, what would you like to talk about?" As if she didn't know.

"Let's go into the livingroom."

Wow, this had to be special. The livingroom was reserved for royalty.

"So tell me, what did he say?" Sara asked, abruptly all smiles and solicitude.

"It seems Dr. Levin wants to take me to the Mark Hopkins Saturday night."

"Oh, Doris, I'm so pleased . . . You see? There's a difference between the boys Murial and the others go out with—those law students who spend a whole dollar to take a girl to the Clairmont Hotel for dancing and a pitcher of punch."

It should only happen to me, thought Doris. "Well, I don't suppose it matters so much if you're having fun and you like the fellow."

"Now, you listen to me, Doris. Henry likes you. That's *obvious*."

"Why is it obvious?"

"That's stupid, Doris." For once there was no bite in her words, just motherly concern. Even weariness.

"Why is it stupid?"

"Because if he didn't why would he call?"

"I think it's maybe because he's desperate, mama." Mama was really pushing. Still, she seemed really to care . . . "I'm sorry, I didn't mean to sound sarcastic. I suppose he thinks I'm . . . oh, I don't know what he thinks . . ."

"Look, Doris, please be smart for once, use your head. When you want to you can be very bright, you know."

"Thank you very much, mama. So tell me how to be bright now."

"He's not a boy with a crush, and you're not the most popular girl in Oakland, Doris. I don't mean to say you're not nice or attractive, especially when you get dressed up. But Henry called because he likes *you*. Do you think he doesn't have every Jewish girl in town after him? Ugly, he's not. In fact, Lillian said she thought he looked like Clark Gable."

"But the truth is, mama, I'm not looking for someone who looks like Clark Gable."

"What are you looking for?"

"For someone I like."

"And you don't like him?" Sara asked with total, genuine dismay.

"I like him . . . But first of all as undesirable as I may be, I

315

do have some standards. I'm *grateful* he asked me out, but I also feel like he's an uncle and I owe some loyalty to—"

"Doris, please be smart. I'm begging you. Rachel married a man your father's age and she claims she's divinely happy."

"But I'm not Rachel, mama. I'm trying to be Doris."

"Then be Doris, and be smart. How many eligible men are around these days who can make a living for a girl? How many?"

"I believe at the last census it was four-point-two, on the Jewish community scale."

"Doris, I'm trying to be patient. I'm your mother and I want the best for you. Don't you know that?"

Looking at her mother's pleading eyes, Doris nodded.

"Well, then, why don't you listen to me? If you gave yourself a chance and really put your mind on it, you'd find out what a catch Henry is. Sylvia's been praying for three years that he'd marry her, and you say the Silvermans are one of the best Jewish families in Oakland."

"All of that's true. But even if I liked him, I wouldn't get serious . . ."

"Why?"

"Because, as I started to say, of my friendship with Murial, who happens to care about her sister. It just isn't right, mama. I'd never be able to hold my head up. I'd feel so ashamed."

By now Sara was beginning to run out of patience. "Listen to me, Doris, and listen carefully. If you had a fellow Sylvia liked, do you think for one moment she'd hesitate to take him away from you? If you think so, you're living in a dream world. As far as I'm concerned the Silvermans, including Murial and Sylvia, can go to hell. You miss this chance and you'll regret it. Both papa and I think he's perfect for you."

"It's very nice, mama, when parents approve. But you and papa seem to have overlooked one small item . . ."

"What's that?"

"He hasn't asked me to marry him."

"That's up to a woman. If she knows how, she can get any man she wants. If a woman's smart, she knows how to please a man. Flattery is important—men are egotists. Don't boast or show off how smart you are. Agree when he says something."

Oh, that was rich, coming from mama. "Is that how you got papa? Being shy and coy?"

"That's exactly how. Papa thought I was the most naïve, submissive girl in the world."

316

"Then suppose a woman wants to assert herself later. It must come as a shock to the poor unsuspecting husband . . ."

"Worry about that later. Now, Doris, you listen to me, I'm counseling you, the way any good mother should."

Doris suddenly felt frightened to see her mother like this, so calculating, never mind the reasons. She had always wanted to love her mother, had *needed* to, which was at least partly why she put on the smart-aleck front, to cover up the hurt she felt . . . But sometimes mama just went too far for her, and that was when it hurt the most . . .

"I see you're thinking this over carefully, Doris."

"Oh, you bet I am, mama. There's a lot in what you say."

"Thank you, Doris. It's nice when children occasionally listen to parents. Now, tomorrow I want you to buy a new dress. Get a long black one—it's slenderizing. And a very tight girdle . . . No, I think you'd better get an all-in-one, it'll help the bulge around your waist. I have a black beaded bag so there's no use spending the money on that. And you'll get the things at Goldman's so you can get your ten-percent discount."

"Yes, that's quite a saving . . ."

"At least you're not extravagant like Rachel."

Mama should only know what her paycheck was going to be with the deficit she had to make up. But maybe they'd let her charge it.

"Doris, it's really wonderful when a mother and daughter can have a heart-to-heart like this . . . It's the way it should be. Now go upstairs and take a bath. You look tired."

She felt dead.

That Saturday, when Doris came home from work she was met at the door by Lillian. "You got orchids!"

"How do you know?"

"Because I couldn't resist looking inside the box."

For the first time, Doris wanted to slap Lillian right in the mouth. "How dare you? Did it ever occur to you that I might like the pleasure of taking off the ribbons and opening my own present?"

"I'm sorry, I didn't mean anything."

"Nobody ever means anything. If, God forbid, I should get a present or a letter, mama always opens it. Goddamn it, I'm sick and tired of it."

"You better not let mama and papa hear you swear."

317

"I learned it from them." And then she smiled quickly at Lillian. It was difficult to stay angry at her. She was the wrong target, and Doris knew it . . .

CHAPTER FORTY-TWO

THE BELL rang at seven-fifteen. Of course, it was the divine Henry. Well, she'd take her time. Papa was crazy about him. They could discuss Chrystie Street and the gym papa used to work out at.

At seven twenty-five she walked into the livingroom feeling like she was in a straitjacket. The all-in-one was killing her—if she inhaled too deeply the dress seam might bust wide open. She stood in the livingroom in her black chiffon. The full skirt would hide the hips, the saleslady had advised, but Doris really loved it. The lace running around the neck and cuffs was flattering, the rhinestone buttons down the bodice were dazzling and even the cummerbund around her middle looked pretty good. Mama was right—to be svelte you had to suffer. And the all-in-one sure made her suffer, but at best her waist looked a size smaller. Her hair had been cut and marcelled, and her lips and nails were painted ruby red.

She knew she looked all right when she saw the look on Henry's face. "Doris, you look beautiful . . ."

"Thank you, Henry. Now if you'll excuse me for a minute, I'll be right back. Please, just go on visiting with papa." She walked out to the kitchen where she knew her mother would be waiting to examine her.

She was right. "Let me look at you, Doris."

Doris stood under her scrutiny, feeling like a lump of clay.

"You look like a different person."

Different from what or whom? "You approve?"

"Yes, the dress is perfect. Just a little less lipstick."

Mama was the Jewish Elizabeth Arden. Doris ran her pinkie finger over her lips. "Better?"

"Perfect."

Doris reached into the refrigerator to take out her flowers.

"Doris! You're not going to eat anything?"

"Just my corsage."

She opened the box and saw two of the most beautiful white orchids she'd ever seen.

318

Sara smiled. "See? That's what I call a man with class."

Doris didn't hear mama, she was genuinely touched. The first corsage she'd ever received . . . orchids. As she began to pin them on, Sara said, "Why don't you let Henry do that? Men like to feel they're doing you a favor, makes them feel manly."

Doris was more than willing to let Henry feel manly. Carrying them in her hand, she went back to the livingroom, with her mother and Lillian not far behind.

"Thank you for the orchids, Henry. They're really lovely."

"I'm happy you like them . . ."

Doris attempted to pin them on, but as mama predicted, Henry said, "May I help?"

"Thank you, Henry. How nice . . ."

Mama smiled . . . Doris smiled back. Papa was beaming and Lillian was thinking how romantic it was. She was secretly in love with Henry. Just like Clark Gable . . .

They sat in the Room of the Dons at the Mark Hopkins. No one would guess there was a Depression on; everyone was dressed to the nines and dancing to the rhythm of bandleader Al Kavelin, with Carmen Cavallaro at the piano.

The dinner was salad, filet mignon, duchesse potatoes and green peas, and for dessert there was vanilla ice cream with chocolate sauce. Doris had no trouble being careful about what she ate; the girdle was a constant reminder.

Henry, she had to admit, was a great dancer for a man his age—in fact, for any age. He was decent and nice and kept telling her how beautiful she was. Maybe if he kept at it, she might even believe him. . . .

When they left the Mark Hopkins, Henry asked her if she had ever been to a speakeasy.

To a speakeasy? This was the first time she'd ever had a date. Who did he think she was, Carole Lombard? "No, Henry, never."

"Would you like to go?"

"I'd like to, but I don't think I should."

"Why?"

"Because I understand they're always getting raided . . ."

He laughed. "That's in the movies. I know a place that, believe me, no one's going to raid. How about it?"

"Are you sure? I mean about getting raided?"

"You can trust me."

They were greeted by a man behind a peephole at the top of the stairs in a building on Howe Place and Ellis Street.

"I'm Dr. Levin," Henry announced, as though he owned the first mortgage.

The door opened and Doris found herself inside a room filled with lots of smoke, lots of people and lots of illegal booze. The dancing girls were dressed in pink sequins with ostrich feathers around their behinds, and they were tapping vigorously to the tune of "Mississippi Mud."

Next a buxom lady, endowed with the reddest hair Doris had ever seen, came out in purple spangles and belted out: "Some of these days you're gonna miss me, honey . . . some of these days you're gonna feel so lonely . . ."

Doris felt Henry's hand on her arm, leading her to an alcove table with parted curtains.

Henry noticed that she sat as far away from him as possible, and when she crossed her leg it seemed to twitch nervously beneath the long black dress. He was about to reassure her when the waiter came for their order.

"Doris?"

"Oh, I'll have a straight ginger ale and three cherries."

Henry ordered a bourbon, and soon the waiter was back with their drinks.

She was really beautiful tonight, Henry thought. He'd never known anyone as amusing as she was, and if he sometimes detected a slight sadness in her it only made her seem more vulnerable. He touched his glass to hers. "To you, Doris, for a wonderful evening."

She smiled, somehow knowing he really meant it. But she was still uncomfortable here. She knew they were going to be raided any minute, and papa would have to come down and bail her out of the police station. She couldn't wait to get out of here. . . .

God heard her. Even speakeasies closed and once again they were on safe territory in Henry's De Soto.

When they arrived in front of her house, Henry said, "Doris, I don't know how to say this, but . . . I think I'm in love with you . . ."

He waited. She said nothing. He ventured further. "Do you know what I did last Sunday night?"

She shook her head.

"When I got home I said to my mother, 'Mama, I met the girl I'm going to marry,' and she said, 'Henry, if you love her, I'll love her.' "

Doris didn't know whether to laugh or cry. He'd told his mother he'd met a girl? Did it ever occur to him that maybe Doris would say no? It was obvious he hadn't, as he put his arm around her and started to . . . my God, kiss her.

She pulled away from him. "I used to laugh when the girls in the movies always said, 'This is so sudden,' but I'm not laughing now, Henry. But really, you don't even know me."

"I know all I have to . . ."

"What do you know?"

"That you're beautiful, sweet, intelligent, wonderful—"

"And fat and—"

"You don't fall in love with fat or thin, Doris. You fall in love with a person."

She couldn't believe her ears. To Henry she was a person? A real honest-to-God person? Beautiful, sweet, intelligent and he loved her. And somehow it stirred all the old insecurities. "Well, you really could have fooled me, Henry. I sure had no hint I was any of those things until tonight—"

"That's hard to understand, but I'm not sorry to be the first to tell you. I come from a long line of brothers who don't believe in getting married. I never really believed in it either, but when I met you I changed my mind." He took her in his arms and kissed her, and this time she didn't resist.

It didn't stir any of the frantic desires she had imagined, but it was tender and pleasant, and Henry was such a gentle man, as well as a gentleman. He made her feel like a woman, and maybe she'd learn to believe that all the nice things he said about her were true. Yes, by God, Henry was going to be the answer to her prayers, and she hadn't even given him a thought. Mama was right—she was stupid. To hell with romance and bells ringing. At least with Henry she wouldn't hear shouting and cursing. At last she'd be Mrs. Somebody and not merely Sara and Jack Sanders' daughter . . . She'd be Doris Levin. Or rather, as mama would quickly point out, the esteemed wife of Dr. Henry Levin . . . Dr. and Mrs. Henry Levin . . .

"Will you marry me, Doris?"

It would take a little time to get used to the idea that someone could love her, but . . . "Yes . . . whenever you say, Henry."

He kissed her more ardently than before. There were still no bells, but she could wait . . .

When he took her to the front door he said, "I can't wait to see you again. I'd like to tell your folks tomorrow."

"They'll approve, I assure you."

"So will my family. My mother can't wait for me to bring home a wonderful Jewish girl. Wait till she sees *you*."

She kissed him so she wouldn't have to say she loved him. Still, what she felt for Henry Levin was more affection than she'd ever felt for anyone in her life, except for Lillian and that was different . . .

Doris slept until eleven o'clock on Sunday morning, and by the time she came downstairs Sara was a nervous wreck. "Well?"

"Well what?"

"How did it go last night? Did you do everything I told you?"

"Didn't miss a thing, mama."

"Really? So tell me."

She looked at her mother coolly, then, "I'm engaged."

"Engaged!"

"I believe that's the way it works when a fellow asks you to marry him."

"My God, I can't believe this. Jacob," she called out, "come in quick."

He came into the kitchen, looking concerned. "What's wrong?"

"Wrong? For the first time, everything is right. Doris—our Doris—is engaged."

Jacob was dumbfounded. "I can't believe it. The doctor asked you to marry him?"

"Yes, papa, the *doctor*. Can you believe it? He thinks I'm beautiful, sweet, intelligent and wonderful. So what if he's blind?"

"Well, *mazel tov*. You're a good girl, it pays to listen to a father."

"How true that is, papa. Without your love and advice I could never have done it."

They beamed, and Sara stood with tears in her eyes. "Our Cinderella . . ."

"Cinderella? Oh, mama, she wasn't really so much—and she couldn't have been Jewish. What Jewish girl would have lost her glass slipper?"

They all laughed—Doris not quite for the same reasons, but let them be happy, she told herself. It wouldn't kill her.

"Doris, with your sense of humor you could have been a comedian."

322

"I am, mama. Incidently, Henry's coming this afternoon to ask for my hand. Please be sure it's the left one you give him, papa."

Sara just sat and shook her head. "I can't believe it, our Doris . . . Go answer the phone, Doris, that's probably him."

The following Saturday night Sara and Jacob took them to the Palace Hotel to celebrate the engagement.

During dinner, Jacob continued to reminisce about the lower East Side of New York. Henry told Jacob how his wonderful Jewish mother had bathed them all in a pickle barrel, how all the kids had slept in the same room and about his father's unique bookkeeping system when he owned a fish store on Hester Street and had allowed his customers to charge on Thursday nights. Mr. Levin, it seemed, wrote his accounts on the wall, and everybody in the neighborhood knew that Mrs. Rubinowitz owed forty-five cents, that Mrs. Cohen hadn't paid for five weeks . . . there were accounts in the dozens. Then the catastrophe happened. One day, when Mr. Levin was at home with a very bad cold, Henry's mother decided that the store should be painted. And there went Mr. Levin's bookkeeping system, covered over with white wash. When everyone denied what they owed, Mr. Levin refused to give any more credit, so the ladies took their business to Farber. He trusted them.

Jacob laughed so hard he had tears in his eyes. And thank God, Sara was so engrossed with Henry that she didn't notice Doris cautiously sneaking tiny bites of strawberry tart . . . .

After dinner Henry asked if his future in-laws would like to see his office, and it was obvious this was the moment they'd both been waiting for.

When Sara walked into his reception room, she was clearly impressed. It was all done in Chinese. Against one wall was a tall black wooden settee with arms carved with a dragon motif. An altar table covered with a satin runner sat against the opposite wall, and was flanked by a pair of teakwood chairs with carved bases that were so beautiful Sara wished she had them. But the *pièce de résistance* was the cream-colored Chinese rug with the deep blue border. Sara didn't notice that Henry's consultation room doubled as a treatment room or that there was no office for a nurse. She was simply too taken with the impressive *décor*. "Oh, Henry, really, we're so proud of you."

Which made Henry's evening complete.

Doris asked that no wedding notice be placed in the Sunday society section, but Sara placed it anyway—without telling her.

On Monday morning, Murial came rushing into Goldman's and in front of everyone announced that Doris was the most disgusting, deceitful human being she'd ever had the displeasure of knowing. Doris knew that Henry hadn't loved Sylvia, but Murial's denunciation had really hurt. Murial had been her one and only friend. It was what she had been so afraid of . . .

As for Henry, he reassured her again, and bestowed on her a three-carat blue-white gem that he bought for seven hundred dollars from Jerry, a friend who was in the wholesale jewelry business.

Not to be outdone, Sara got Jacob to buy her one, just a little larger, almost the size of Rachel's. . . .

Now the engagement was in full swing. Henry's mother had the Sanderses to dinner, then the Sanderses had the Levins to dinner. Rachel entertained them but excluded Nadine and Sandy. And Nadine, Sandy, Jean and Neal had a family dinner at a restaurant, excluding Rachel and Jim.

And Sara was commencing to plan in earnest. She selected the china—a service for six since a new bride didn't have to entertain in large groups. Sterling silver could come later; for now, Oneida would do. Two changes of sheets and pillow slips, a comforter, a set of towels and the minimum amount of kitchenware. The furniture was selected by Sara and Jacob at Redlick's—more for its price than its beauty. That's where the best buys were.

It was the wedding itself that was the important thing, and Sara took charge of the wedding plans. The date was the seventh of June. They would be married at Temple Sinai, with Dr. Coffee officiating and the family would come from Cleveland.

Doris was outfitted from Goldman's bridal salon, with the help of her ten-percent discount. She could hardly believe it when she saw herself in the white satin gown with the little seed pearls around the neck, and the long veil with the Juliet cap covering her hair. My God, this was exactly what she used to talk about to Lillian at night when she dreamed about floating down the aisle. She was beginning to fall in love with love, and Henry couldn't have been more adoring . . .

Sara bought a gown of oyster-white taffeta in the newest Paris style. She'd been some bride with the fifteen-dollar dress

324

Jacob had bought her and the reception in Esther's restaurant . . . What difference would it make if both she and Doris wore white?

Lillian was ecstatic. For the first time in her life she had a store-bought dress—a long peach organdy with a velvet sash, and her shoes were low-heeled silver slippers.

And Jacob was fitted for a rented tuxedo. The only thing that annoyed him was that he had to buy pearl studs and black patent-leather shoes. Jacob took Henry's De Soto and traded it in for a brand-new blue Reo. He paid the difference of seven hundred dollars, which was their wedding gift. The flowers were ordered, the photographer hired, the invitations sent and at long last Sara could relax and wait for the glorious event.

CHAPTER FORTY-THREE

ONE EVENING Doris met Henry at his office before they were scheduled to go out to dinner. They were waiting in the garage where Henry parked every day when Henry's sister happened to be passing on her way home from work.

Rosalie was a dear person, Doris thought, and she knew she approved of her baby brother's fiancée.

While the attendant was bringing up Henry's car, Rosalie said to Doris, "I don't think Henry looks well."

To Doris, Henry had never looked better. "Why, Rosalie?"

"I think his late hours are showing."

"What hours?" Henry asked.

"I mean that all that commuting back and forth to Oakland is giving you dark circles around your eyes."

"I hadn't noticed," Doris said.

"Well, I think you should. Doris, if I make a suggestion, you won't think I'm interfering?"

"Never. I promise."

"Well, I think big weddings are stupid, a waste of money. And I can't see why when two people are in love they should wait. Especially with you living in Oakland and Henry having to commute every night. Why not elope?"

Rosalie meant well, but she was definitely interfering, Doris thought. All her life she'd dreamed of being a bride. That was almost the most important thing about getting married—being queen for a day, having a unique moment of glory . . .

"You're an absolute genius, sis. Why didn't we think of that instead of wasting all this time?" Henry sounded as if he'd just discovered oil in his backyard.

"We've only been engaged three weeks, Henry . . ."

"I know, darling, but just think. By June the seventh, we can have been married more than a month. What do you say?"

She looked from Rosalie's smiling face to Henry's pleading one. "Let me have a dime so I can call and see what my mother thinks of this . . ."

When her mother answered, her knees nearly buckled. "Mama?"

"Yes, Doris."

Silence . . .

"Doris, are you there?"

"I think so . . . Mama, please sit down."

My God, there'd been an accident, the new car was ruined. Or maybe Henry was calling off the wedding . . . "Yes, I'm sitting."

"All right, mama. We happened to run into Rosalie, and she thinks Henry's health is suffering because he's commuting—Oh, it's all so mixed-up . . ."

"For heaven's sake, tell me already."

"Well, she suggested we elope and Henry's so excited I don't have the courage to disappoint him . . ."

Sara was quiet for a moment. The wedding gown and veil—that could be canceled. Her own dress? Well, she'd think about that. Jack's suit was only rented, Lillian's dress could be returned, so no problem there. And for what the wedding would cost they could pay for the furniture and have money left over. Jack wouldn't have to spend the money to bring his whole family from Cleveland. And what was it all for anyway? Only a show. All that money for one evening . . . "Doris, how much does this mean to Henry?"

What about me, mama . . . ? "Well, he'd like to get married now. He thinks it's foolish to wait and Rosalie obviously thinks it's foolish to spend all the money—"

"Let me talk to your father."

"All right. Should I call back?"

"Yes, in about an hour. I want him to eat and rest . . . make it an hour and a half." . . .

When Jacob heard the news, he hit the ceiling. "Damn it, why does every father but me get a little pleasure from their kids? Gittel's kids got married at a wedding and Shlomo had

326

a wedding. But Rachel went to a judge, and Doris—I don't know what kind of kids I have."

"Calm down, Jacob. It's not the end of the world. They're in love, they want to get married. Remember when you said at Coney Island—"

"I know what I said, but that was a different time."

"Jacob, be reasonable, they want to get married. Is that so terrible?"

"I didn't say it was terrible. I just wanted the *naches* of walking down the aisle with my daughter."

"Well, you still have Lillian," she added quietly. "Look, we have to face it. Doris is getting someone we never in a million years thought she'd marry. In fact, we should go down on our knees and thank God she got such a man. Of all girls, Doris marrying a doctor . . . You should be happy, Jacob. How would you feel if he backed away and broke the engagement? I don't think I could stand it. Could you . . . ?"

"But what about all the arrangements? The invitations have been sent and my family are probably out buying clothes right now. What are we going to do about that?"

"I can send out notes saying they've eloped. And people can always return clothes . . ."

"I just hope no one thinks they had to get married. Who runs away?"

"I know how you feel. I'd like to see my child married just as much as you, but we have to learn to accept certain things—"

"All right, all right, fine, so it's *settled*." . . .

When Doris called, Sara said, "It was a great disappointment to papa and me. We always dreamed of seeing you stand under the *chuppah*—but this is America where parents have to learn to understand. Besides, Rosalie is right. It's difficult for Henry to keep commuting from San Francisco every night, staying up late. Look, he's a doctor and he needs his rest. Although it's not our wish, you have our blessings. However, it's really up to you and Henry to decide."

You and Henry decide . . . Some joke. Why didn't she have enough guts to say, "Look, Henry, all my life I've dreamed of walking down an aisle, wearing white satin and a long veil, holding a bouquet of lilies of the valley, having my wedding pictures taken and everyone toasting us with champagne, then changing into my going-away suit and rushing to the car while everyone was showering us with rice. And wearing something borrowed, something blue . . . ."

She walked back to their table and Henry held out the chair as she slid into it. When he reached for her hand across the table he saw the tears in her eyes and knew she must be relieved. "I know you're happy, darling. Elopements are more exciting and romantic. I know just how you feel . . . What did your folks say?"

"Well, they were disappointed, naturally."

"Of course, but this is really more sensible, Doris. And to tell the truth, I'm not really so crazy about big weddings." He squeezed her hand. "Just think. By tomorrow, we'll be married. Well, as long as we're this side of the Bay we'll go out to my place and I'll pack a few things, then we'll go get yours."

This couldn't be happening to her. "You mean leave tonight?"

"Of course."

"Where are we eloping to?"

"Reno."

Reno? And here she'd been stupid enough to think she'd be married in the rabbi's temple study, with mama and papa and Henry's mother there, and *then* they'd elope.

Stupid Doris . . .

While Henry packed, Doris looked sourly at the virginal Rosalie. Already forty and never been kissed, and she would surely live the rest of her life with her mama and brothers. She didn't need a husband; she already had four. What a Jewish family—kosher and celibate. At least Henry was breaking the Levin tradition . . .

In Yiddish, which Doris could hardly understand, Henry's darling little mother was saying, *"Oy,* to see my Hershela married."

Doris managed to smile as Rosalie interpreted.

Since Roosevelt had declared a bank moratorium the day before, Henry had very little cash on him and asked his brother Al to loan him whatever he could manage.

There were shy congratulations from brothers Irving and Meyer—no wonder they never got married. And Al, the Diamond Jim Brady of the family, actually shook her hand.

There were some tears from mama as she clung to her baby boy of thirty-three, and a kiss for her very own Doris, who was going to be like a daughter. *Oy,* such *naches.*

With Henry's bag in the car, they were now on their way to Oakland . . . .

It was a rather different scene at the Sanders'. Jacob was

328

sullen and would barely look at Doris and Henry. But when Doris and Sara went upstairs, he did look at Henry sitting there in the livingroom and thought, Well, maybe the doctor was right. He wasn't exactly twenty-one. Still, he was disappointed.

Sara had already packed Doris' enormous trousseau of two silk dresses, a bridal nightgown and some underwear. Mama, Doris thought, surely seemed to have taken care of everything rather quickly . . . With her overnight case in her hand, she went to join Henry. But when she looked at him and realized the finality of this moment she wanted to cry. Difficult as it had been growing up in this house, still it had been home— and would be so no more. She was going off with a stranger she hadn't known until a few short months ago, and suddenly there was an unreality about the whole business . . . She went to her father and held him tightly.

It was difficult for him to return the gesture, but he did. "Couldn't you have waited, Doris?"

She wanted to say, I didn't have the guts, I'm not strong like you and mama, but instead she started to cry.

Brides always cry, Henry thought knowingly.

Sara took her daughter and kissed her. "Doris, we're so happy for you."

When Doris took a look at her father she knew he was disappointed. At least mama still had her oyster-white taffeta dress and her ruby-red shoes and the cape with the fox collar. Have a wonderful wedding, mama.

Then Lillian started to cry too. After all, without Doris at home she'd be the only one left for mama to vent her frustrations on. Besides, she'd miss her favorite sister . . .

When Henry helped Doris into her coat she saw that it had a big grease spot right in front. Some bride.

The final good-bys were said and Doris and Henry set off for Sacramento, the halfway point between Reno and San Francisco . . . .

Henry registered at the Capitol Hotel, took Doris to her room, kissed her goodnight, then walked down to his own room. He wanted to get a good night's sleep. They had to be on the road by seven in the morning and Henry wanted to be bright-eyed and bushy-tailed. Tomorrow was his wedding.

Doris spent the night wondering what in the world she was doing here.

It was eleven o'clock when Doris read the highway sign. Welcome to Reno, the Biggest Little City in the West . . .

Henry parked on the other side of the bridge—where divorcees usually threw their wedding rings into the creek. As they walked to the courthouse Doris realized there was still one missing ingredient. "Henry, we don't have a ring."

"Oh my God, I've been so excited, it never entered my mind."

"Well, what do we do?"

He didn't have enough money with him for a ring. Besides, when they got home he could get it wholesale from Jerry.

Just then Doris spotted the five-and-dime. Realizing Henry's temporary financial dilemma, she suggested, "We could buy a ring in Woolworth's. What difference does it make?"

He hugged her. "God, you're so understanding, Doris."

"That's one of my great virtues . . ."

Doris selected a thin gold band that looked like it might turn green before the wedding was over. They stood in line waiting for a license, which was issued with all the pomp and circumstance of getting a subscription to the Oakland *Tribune*. Doris eyed it as she signed her name, then the date—May 10, 1933. This was certainly the no-nonsense way, as Henry said, to get married—

"Next," a voice interrupted.

They found themselves standing in front of a one-armed justice of the peace, who quickly said, "Do you, Henry . . ."

Doris was looking up at the pictures of George Washington and Abraham Lincoln hanging on the wall. Not bad. It wasn't every girl who could boast that two Presidents had attended her wedding.

"And do you, Doris, take this man to be your wedded husband, in sickness and in . . ."

Her stomach began to churn but her knees were trembling too badly for her to run out now. Almost inaudibly she answered, "Yes . . ."

"I now pronounce you man and wife. Congratulations. Pay two dollars to the clerk on the way out. Next . . ."

Henry held her in his arms in the hall. "Well, you're now Mrs. Henry Levin."

She didn't know what to say, because there was no more Doris. She'd finally become extinct. What would mama have said? "It's wonderful, Henry, and thanks." Yes, that's what mama would have said. He kissed her . . .

As they sat having their wedding luncheon at the Riverside Hotel Doris looked from the beige coat with the grease stain to Henry. She didn't feel married, she didn't feel too much of anything. The lunch was plain everyday food. There was no

330

cake with a bride and groom, no rice, no shoes—just Henry who sat across from her, now her husband because a one-armed justice of the peace had said he was.

After lunch Henry suggested they leave if they were going to make the drive back in one day.

"Wouldn't it be kind of fun to walk around and see the gambling casinos?"

"Darling, I don't believe in gambling, and I'm sure you don't. And besides, I really think we should get started. We have a long drive ahead of us."

Henry signed the register at the William Taylor, one of San Francisco's better second-class hotels, and led her to their room on the eighth floor. After he unlocked the door, Doris found herself standing awkwardly in the middle of the room, waiting for Henry to tip the bellboy.

When the door shut Henry came to her, held out his arms and said, "Well, darling, can you believe it? We're *married* ..."

"It's ... thrilling, Henry."

"You are ..."

She shuddered. That was the wrong choice of words; she'd have to remember never to say "thrilling" again.

"Doris, darling ... would you like ... to go to the bathroom?" ...

She lay in the tub soaking for what seemed like an hour, and finally Henry knocked on the door. "Are you all right, darling?"

"Fine."

"Well ... I'd like to use the bathroom."

"I'm getting out." She lifted the plug and wished she could flow down the drain along with the water. Unfortunately science hadn't made that giant stride yet.

When she came out in her negligee, Henry said, "I've never seen anything so lovely."

She was anything now, not someone or even anyone.

He kissed her, then walked to the bathroom and closed the door. She sat listening to the water running in the tub. She was not only nervous but on the verge of tears. She picked up the phone and asked the operator to call Ashbury 3–4842. Her pulse was racing.

Sara answered.

"Mama," Doris said, holding back the tears.

"Doris? Where are you?"

"In San Francisco, at the William Taylor Hotel."

"I'm so happy to hear from you. How was the wedding?"

"Beautiful . . ."

"Oh, I wish I'd had the *naches* of seeing it."

"I would have liked that too, mama . . ."

"How's Henry?"

"Wonderful."

"I suppose he's walking on clouds."

"Actually, he taking a bath."

Sara laughed. "Oh, Doris, you're happy, I can tell from the sound of your voice. The way a bride should sound on her wedding night."

"How's papa?"

"How's papa? Like papa, he's still upset."

Doris bit her lip. The guilt and the fear were almost too much for her at this moment. "Can I speak to him?"

"Wait, darling, I'll see if he'll speak to you. Be happy, Doris. And let me know where you're going on your honeymoon.'

"I will, except to tell the truth, I don't know where we're going. Henry and I never got around to discussing it."

"Well, dear, have a wonderful honeymoon."

"I will, mama. Let me talk to papa."

Henry was out of the bathroom and getting under the covers. "Who are you talking to, darling?"

"My folks . . . papa?"

Her father's voice did not conceal what he was feeling. "Yes, Doris?"

"Papa, I want you to know how much I love you."

"That's very nice to hear, Doris."

"Don't be angry, papa, please—"

"So if you ask me I shouldn't feel—"

"I'm sorry if I hurt you, papa, from the bottom of my heart."

"All right, fine. So now you're married, have a good life."

"Thank you, papa, I hope so. May I speak to Lillian?"

Doris heard papa calling.

Henry shut his eyes and Doris prayed he'd fallen asleep.

"Doris," Lillian cried. "Congratulations, it's so wonderful. I miss you, though."

"I miss you, Lillian . . ."

"Are you going away for as long a time as Rachel did?"

"I don't think so. Keep well and I'll talk to you tomorrow."

"Aren't you going on your honeymoon?"

332

"Well, not at eight in the morning, I don't suppose."

"Have a good time, Doris."

There was a long pause, then, "I'm sure I will, Lillian. Goodnight."

Henry opened his eyes. "Honey, I think you should get some rest. It's been a . . . tiring day."

The Levins must take resting seriously. That's how she happened to be here tonight, because Rosalie had said Henry looked so tired. "I will in a minute, Henry. I just want to say hello to Rachel. I didn't call and tell her we were eloping."

"I'm sure your mother must have told her by now."

"I know, but I'd like to call . . ."

"Darling, you can call tomorrow. Remember, Doris, this is your wedding night," her husband said, holding out his arms to her.

She switched off the desk lamp, then the bedside lamp, took off her robe and cautiously slipped into bed. Henry was soon beside her. He held her close to him, kissed her, then whispered, "Darling, get in the center of the bed."

Obediently she moved over and lay very still. Henry's breathing was speeding up and something strange was touching her . . . Henry gently pulled up her gown. "Darling, spread your legs apart."

As gently as he could, he tried putting himself inside her, but she let out a whimper. The pain . . . Oh, my God, why had she ever thought of getting married? Now he was working himself in little by little. "I know this is slightly painful, but only the first time. There, there, darling. Now lie still."

One or two more slides, in and out, and it was all over. Just as quickly as their wedding . . .

So *this* was what everyone whispered about? This was how Ruby Fox had a baby?

Henry kissed her, mumbled, "I love you, Doris," and before she could figure out what to say back, he had rolled over and was fast asleep.

She got out of bed and went to the bathroom. The sight of her nightgown reminded her of that day long ago when she'd run home to Rachel. I got blood on my bloomers . . . She soaked the gown in the wash basin and let the water run in the tub. As she lay back in the soothing warm water she wondered if any of the people who wrote those romantic love songs had ever . . .

CHAPTER FORTY-FOUR

IN THE morning Doris was awakened from her restless sleep by a brush of tender lips touching hers. Slowly she opened her eyes and saw Henry's mustached face. For a brief moment she wondered what he was doing in her bed and why she was in this strange room ... oh, yes, she'd been married yesterday and Henry was asserting his right—for which he had paid two dollars.

In between kisses he said, "Good morning, darling ... did you sleep well?" Sleeping was going to become a very big subject in their repertoire.

"Like a rock, Henry, and you?"

"Never better ..."

And soon Henry's breathing was beginning to crescendo and what had happened the night before was starting all over again. As Henry pumped away Doris glanced at his wristwatch on the nightstand. It was seven in the morning. Exercise in the evening *and* the morning? Well, at least it didn't hurt so much this morning and, fortunately, Henry didn't take long to be satisfied.

"Doris, you don't know how wonderful it is to make love to you."

"Oh, you're wrong, Henry ..."

"What a difference to make love to your wife."

"What's different about it, dear?"

"There's a big difference between just going to bed with someone and making love to a person you're in love with."

"Did you go to bed with a lot of women?"

"I'm thirty-three, Doris, and man does not live by bread alone." He laughed.

"Well, I'm beginning to find out a lot about you, Henry. You must have been quite a lover."

"I wouldn't say that. I had my share of girls, but I never really loved anyone before you."

"When was the first time?"

"She was a lady I used to deliver fish to, a buxom blonde who liked to play with little boys, I think."

"Did you enjoy it?"

"No, not really ... She invited me into her bedroom and pulled down my pants, and I didn't know what to do. In fact,

334

I was scared to death. She took my penis in her hand and began playing with it and naturally I had an erection. Before I knew it, she had me in bed and was telling me about the facts of life—or should I say showing me . . ."

"Weren't you embarrassed?"

"Sure. Also scared that her husband might come home unexpectedly, but she said he worked until six."

"How long did your basic training take?"

"About three days. Then I told my father I didn't want to deliver fish to her house."

"Then?"

"Then what?"

"I mean, how did your love life progress?"

"Well, at college there were always enough coeds . . ."

"You mean college girls did that kind of thing?"

"Oh, my darling innocent Doris . . . sex has been around for a long time—"

"I heard . . . but how come you weren't afraid of getting a girl pregnant?"

"Honey, your sex education has really been badly neglected. You don't know anything about the facts of life, do you?"

"Well, it wasn't one of the topics at the dinner table, but I'm honestly not that dumb. I knew a girl who had a baby out of wedlock, as the neighbors so subtly put it. I wasn't sure how it all happened until last night . . . As the novels say, do you think I could be with child?"

"No."

"Why?"

"Because . . . look at this."

She observed Henry's shriveled organ. Only a few minutes ago it had been extended like a small sausage but now it looked like something in the casing of a hot dog, and at the tip there was a fluid . . . This was the first time she'd seen a penis, shriveled or otherwise, and she found it embarrassing. She had to remind herself that Henry was her husband and she had a right to look and ask questions.

"What's that?"

"It's called a condom."

"Oh? And that's how you know I'm not with child?"

He laughed again. "That's how I know. When we come home from our honeymoon, you'll go to a friend of mine and be fitted for a diaphragm."

"What's that?"

"A rubber disc that's inserted in the vagina to cover the cervix—"

The *cervix?* Well, she wasn't going to go into anatomy this morning. Presumably they had a whole lifetime to make this a topic of conversation . . . "Henry, we've never talked about our honeymoon . . ."

"I thought it would be nice to drive down the coast to Los Angeles. I have a lot of school friends there who moved from Denver to go into practice. I know they'd love to meet you and you'll be crazy about them."

Henry knew so many things.

The drive along the coast was long and bumpy, and to make it worse the car was acting up. By nightfall the car chugged into San Luis Obispo, where Henry immediately found a garage. He was shocked when the mechanic told him he had forgotten to put oil into the crankcase and that the transmission was shot. Henry was fuming, the car was fuming and Doris knew papa would be fuming if the new Reo couldn't be repaired. Well, a man in love forgot a lot of things, like buying his bride-to-be a bunch of daisies or a wedding ring, or taking her to a lovely restaurant for a wedding-night dinner.

"What the hell is this going to cost?" She hadn't heard that tone in his voice before.

"It could cost eighty or ninety dollars," the mechanic said, wiping his hands on his overalls.

Well, Henry thought, if he ran out of money he could always get a loan from one of the Phi Sigma Delta brothers in Los Angeles. "Okay," Henry said, none too happily, "get started on it first thing in the morning. We're on our way to Los Angeles."

"Do my best . . . Now give me your name."

"Mr. Levin."

Mr. Levin! Of course, Doris would later find out that Henry never used his title when dealing with tradesmen. It always drove up the price. Doctors were millionaires . . . .

When John Steinbeck . . . or was it Bobby Burns? . . . had so profoundly written, "The best laid schemes of mice and men . . ." Doris was sure he must have had the Levin newlyweds in mind.

The three days in San Luis Obispo were hardly Doris' idea of a honeymoon. They stayed at the Mission Hotel, an adobe building that looked like it dated back to the Spanish Empire, and its monastery atmosphere made Doris feel that perhaps some of the monks were still stomping on the grapes in the cellar.

336

The weather was a scorching hundred and ten in the shade, and the only shade was at the Mission Hotel. The two dresses she had were not only inappropriate but impossible to wear in the heat because of their long sleeves and weight, so she stayed in her room and read movie magazines or wrote notes home.

After Henry's anger over the car had simmered down, he was very attentive and catered to her every whim. Well, almost. They ordered room service for breakfast, but lunch and dinner were a bit steep so Henry returned with sandwiches at noon and delicatessen at dinner. The sardine cans were carefully put into a paper sack along with the empty carton of potato salad and carted down the back stairs, where Henry had found a garbage can. . . .

When they finally rolled into Los Angeles, Doris took one look at the Biltmore Hotel and knew that at last she was to have the kind of honeymoon she'd always dreamed about. The room was truly beautiful, and every night the maid turned down the bed and left one light softly burning on the nightstand. It looked romantic, just the way it should. . . .

Henry spent most of the first day calling his "frat" brothers . . . "Benjie, guess who's in town?"

"Cookie! What the hell are you doing here?"

"You better sit down . . . I got married." Henry beamed.

"You son of a gun, and you didn't let me know? We went through school and college together . . ."

"I can't wait for my wife to meet you. Let's get together tonight, Benjie."

"Sure. I've got news for you too. I'm engaged. Where do you want to meet?"

"Here at the hotel. I'm at the Biltmore. I'll get some booze—bellhops know everything if you slip them a few dollars."

"By God, Henry, I can't wait to see you. By the way, have you called Jerry?"

"No, you were the first. Do you have his number?"

"Yeah, wait. I'll look it up . . . Here it is." Benjie gave Henry the number. "Wait till you see Jerry. Remember how shy he used to be? Well, he lost his shyness when he married Pamela Rose—of the movie houses by the same name, no less. Thanks to her dad's connections, Jerry's got some practice on Wilshire Boulevard. And a house in the Valley to boot."

"But he was already a rich kid."

"I know, but nothing like he fell into. Anyway, we got a lot to catch up on. Congratulations, and I can't wait to meet the little bride. See you at seven." . . .

Ben Schwartz and his fiancée, Elaine Halpern, arrived promptly at seven. Talk about Betty Boop, Doris thought. Elaine was five-feet-two with eyes of blue and was a perfect size-six. She was dressed in yellow strapless taffeta, with shoes to match.

Then Jerry came in with his rich new wife, but any resemblance between Pamela Rose and her name was purely coincidental. She was unattractive in a way that made it impossible not to notice her. Her hair was a dull pitch-black, and her small eyes were outlined exotically. Her figure was another matter, however, and the black satin dress accented her curves and made one forget her lack of good looks. With her money, she didn't have to worry about winning any popularity contests, which was a good thing. She wasn't the most lovable person Doris had ever met. Condescending was the kindest thing she could think of to describe her.

Pamela extended a diamond-bangled hand to Doris. "Congratulations," she said through clenched teeth, enunciating the word in a way that branded her Vassar, or at least Wellesley.

Davy Marks knocked on the door just then, calling out, "House detective, open up and get the broads out." A real funster.

Henry opened the door and planted an arm around Davy's shoulder, they shook hands in the secret shake of the Phi Sig—with the pinkie finger and the index interlocked.

"Davy, this is my wife, Doris. Did I say she was gorgeous?"

"You sure did. Doris, you're a doll . . . Congratulations. This is my wife, Ethel." . . .

Suddenly the room became crowded with an assortment of "brothers" and their spouses, and it all began to look like a Phi Sigma Delta reunion. They also all seemed stamped out of the same mold, and Doris couldn't remember half the names. Henry was busy filling the glasses. There was a lot of laughing, and Henry received any number of pokes in the ribs . . . "Well, kiddo, how does it feel to be married?" A wink, another elbow in the rib . . .

Doris went unnoticed into the bathroom and locked the door. This wasn't a honeymoon, and just when she'd begun to think she might want Henry to herself she couldn't have him.

338

Henry knocked. "Honey?"

She swallowed back the tears. "Yes?"

"You okay?"

"Terrific."

"Come on out, honey, everyone wants to go to dinner."

"I'll be out . . ." She washed her face with a damp cloth, put some makeup on, refreshed her lipstick and took Henry's arm as everyone walked down the hall to the elevator.

They went off to the Cotton Club, a very posh place, they said. Doris sat at the long table, looking at everyone dancing in their beautiful gowns and felt like a reject from the Salvation Army. The girls had all but ignored her and their self-confidence intimidated her. Henry was so involved with Benjie, Davy, Jerry and whoever the rest were that she wondered if he remembered she was a bride of only four— no, five—days. . . .

That night, as Henry took her in his arms, he said, "Well, didn't I tell you they were real people? I knew you'd love them, Doris . . . and everybody raved about you, honey."

When they'd arrived in Los Angeles last night, Doris had almost looked forward to their love-making and the tenderness of lying in his arms. Not so tonight. Tonight she was weary and disappointed and she added a new ploy to her growing sexual knowledge. "Henry, I really have a terrible headache tonight."

"Oh, do you, darling? I'm sorry, and I don't even have an aspirin. Some doctor . . . well, just lay your head on my shoulder and rest, honey." . . .

The next day they took a tour bus to see where all the stars lived, and when they returned at five to freshen up Henry suggested having dinner at the Brown Derby.

It was eight-thirty when they left the restaurant, the shank of the evening . . . "How about a walk down Wilshire Boulevard. The stores are beautiful, Doris."

"How about a movie, Henry?"

"On a night like this? It's so warm and balmy."

"You're right, we'll save the movies for cold winter nights—"

He held her hand as they walked and walked and walked and . . . finally Doris saw a sign that must have been sent from heaven. Van Camp's Confections and Bakery.

"Henry, let's have an ice cream soda?"

"Sure, honey."

Once they were seated she changed her mind. She decided

339

to order a pineapple milkshake. "Make that extra thick and don't spare the whipped cream," she said, looking up into the face of the guardian angel who had just saved her honeymoon.

"Darling, do you think you should?"

She looked at him. "You don't fall in love with fat or thin, you fall in love with a person, Doris . . ." he'd once said. "Why not, Henry? Let's live it up. This is going to be the only honeymoon I ever have, and I want to remember this night." Sweetly.

He took her hand across the table. "You're right, sweetheart."

When she had almost finished her milkshake she finally had the courage to ask, "Henry, how would you like to go home tomorrow?" When she saw his face brighten she almost sighed with relief.

"You know, I didn't want to say anything because I wanted this to be your moment. But I would like to go back. The office has been closed for a week, and it's about time we started our new life together."

"Oh, for heaven's sake, Henry, why didn't you talk up?"

"I don't know. As I said . . ."

"You didn't want to spoil it for me. That's so sweet," she said, and she meant it.

They took the Wilshire bus back to the hotel.

That night as Henry made love to her she was gratified that it was beginning to hurt less each time, but what especially helped was thinking of that delicious milkshake . . .

CHAPTER FORTY-FIVE

THEY ARRIVED in Oakland at nine the next evening.

"My children have come home," Sara greeted them at the door. The first thing she suggested was that they have something to eat. Mama was getting thinner, while Doris was getting fatter. But mama didn't seem so concerned about that now that she was married.

"Mama, dear, we ate on the way home."

"Are you sure you don't want something after that long drive?"

"No, really . . ."

"Let me look at the two of you." She sighed with *naches*.

"You look like lovebirds. All right, go to your room, you must be tired. I'll see you in the morning."

Going up the stairs with Sara at her side, Doris asked, "Is papa still mad?"

"No, he got over it. Now, darling, I'll see you in the morning."

Doris went into her room with Henry and closed the door. As Henry began to undress, she suddenly felt embarrassed. They couldn't do anything in her virginal bed, not with mama and papa down the hall and Lillian across the way. They'd simply have to find an apartment, and the sooner the better. . . .

Henry didn't have office hours on Saturdays, so right after breakfast they crossed the Bay to San Francisco with Sara. Henry had a friend whose father owned an apartment house on Pacific Avenue and, fortunately, there was a one-bedroom apartment on the second floor. It had a livingroom, dinette and kitchen combination, a bedroom and bath. The rent was forty-two fifty a month, plus utilities.

For the first time since meeting Henry, Sara was a little annoyed with him. "Don't they have a two-bedroom, Henry?"

"What do we need a two-bedroom for?"

"Well, where would I sleep if I came to stay for a night?"

Doris looked at him and became nervous.

"I'm afraid I can't afford more than this—"

He, the doctor, couldn't afford better? "Henry, I don't like bringing this up, but we were under the impression you could support Doris a little better than this—"

"I'm sorry if I gave you any false impressions, but I will support Doris in the best way I can. I've only been in practice five years and it takes time. There's a depression going on, and I'm not exactly Dr. Mayo—"

"That wasn't necessary, Henry. I was merely saying that Jacob and I thought you were doing very well."

"I'm sorry, but I'm struggling to pay off what I owe now." Henry turned to Doris. "Do you like it, honey?"

"Yes, Henry, I love it. I'm sorry, mama, that you don't—really."

"Why should you be sorry? You're the one who has to live in it. So I won't come and stay." Funny, Sara thought, two married daughters, and she couldn't spent the night with either one. In Rachel's case she knew she wasn't welcome, but

341

at least in Doris' house she would have been. She had hoped to have a place to spend a few days when Jacob was away; it would have been a wonderful change and it would have eased the loneliness she often felt. Oh, well, it was just give, give, give. She'd bought the furniture for this place so the doctor could enjoy, but the second bedroom set would have to be returned . . .

Doris did like the apartment. It was cheerful and the neighborhood was one of the best in Pacific Heights. She felt guilty mama was so unhappy with the apartment, but she was more than happy to settle for it. Poor Henry, it must be hard to establish a practice. There had been a glimmer in the back of her mind that Henry was making a good living, but her thoughts hadn't gone much beyond that. Her great concern had been to escape home, and she'd done that . . .

There was complete silence on the drive back to Oakland. When Henry parked the car in front of the house Sara got out of the back seat and walked sullenly to the front door, with Doris and Henry behind her.

Maybe they should stay at a hotel tonight, Doris thought. When mama got through with papa there'd be all kinds of arguments. And to make matters worse, he was coming home from the country today.

Sara was hanging her coat in the closet when Doris asked, "Mama, maybe it might be better if Henry and I stayed in a hotel until the furniture is delivered."

"Do you think Henry can afford it?"

Doris bit her lip, and when she looked at Henry she saw the hurt in his eyes.

"Look, Mrs. Sanders, I won't accept that from anybody."

"Really? And what about the furniture and the car? You didn't mind accepting those—"

"The car? Well, I'd like to remind you that more than half of the car was paid for from what you got out of my car. Also, please remember I never asked for it or even wanted it—Doris, I'll wait for you in the car."

Doris felt ill. No one spoke to mama like that except papa. Henry had no idea how much wrath he'd brought down on them. God, poor unsuspecting Henry. If only she had explained that mama's personality was a country mile from what it had appeared during their courtship . . .

"You heard the way he spoke to me?"

"He didn't mean it, mama . . ."

"Take his part. Who am I? Only your mother. You'd better go to your wonderful husband."

342

Doris tried to kiss her mother but she turned her cheek.

Doris was hysterical by the time she sat next to Henry in the car. He put his arms around her and held her close. "I'm sorry, Doris . . . sorry if your family thought you were marrying someone like Jim Ross, whom they don't seem too fond of either. Anyway, I'm known as a struggling doctor. That's all I am, but I'm not going to allow anyone to talk to me the way she did. I can't get over it. You'd think she almost had a split personality . . ."

"She's just really a very high-strung person, she doesn't mean half of what she says—"

"Maybe, but how could anyone have been so sweet before our marriage and then say the things she did today?"

"Believe me, Henry, she didn't mean it—"

"I think she did, Doris. And while we're at it, let me say I can't get over the way your father was so upset about our eloping. I never saw such anger."

"Can't you understand how disappointed he was?"

"Of course, but such hostility? You've got a very strange family, Doris."

As miserable and frightened as she was, somehow Henry had gained her respect. He wasn't quite the pussycat she thought he'd be with mama. He hadn't given an inch and she liked him for it . . . "What are we going to do about the apartment?"

"What about it?"

"Suppose my mother cancels the furniture?"

"Then we'll just have to take a furnished apartment for a while. In fact, I'd much rather not accept anything from them."

"Where are we going to stay tonight?"

"At my mother's. She may not be able to speak very good English, but she's not in the business of hurting people."

When Doris called the next day, papa came right to the point. "I heard about what happened, Doris."

I don't think so, papa. Mama didn't tell you how she insulted Henry, only what Henry said to her . . . "I'm terribly sorry, papa, but there was a misunderstanding."

"That's what you think insulting your mother is? A misunderstanding?"

"Things just started to happen and before you knew it—"

"Your husband walked out of the house."

"That's not exactly what—"

"Here, talk to your mother."

343

"Yes, Doris?"

"Mama, I want to apologize for yesterday," Doris said. Peace at any price . . .

"Well, I'm not so sure I'm going to accept that."

"Henry's sorry, too, and would like to speak to you."

Henry was sitting beside her on the bed, and he put his hand over the phone. "I'm not sorry, and don't apologize for me."

"Please, Henry. *Please* . . ."

If he didn't love Doris so much he'd tell her mother and father to go to hell, but seeing her so upset was hurting him. Finally he took the phone. "I . . . I'm sorry about the unfortunate incident yesterday, Mrs. Sanders."

Sara was silent a moment, then answered, "Yes, a good many things have been rather unfortunate, Henry."

Looking at Doris' pleading eyes he said, "That's true . . . Since this is Sunday, Doris and I would like to come over and spend the day with you."

Doris kissed him, while Sara clamped her hand over the mouthpiece. "They want to come over this afternoon. What do you say, Jacob?"

"Do what you want to."

"Well . . . all right, Henry, if you'd like."

Henry thought, anything to stop Doris from feeling so miserable. "Yes, we'd like that. Fine. We'll see you then." . . .

When they arrived about two Sara and Jacob were cool, but as the day wore on Sara began to warm up now that she had a sympathetic audience for other grievances. As she prepared dinner she and Doris talked about Rachel—or rather, Doris sat listening to Sara's recital. There was nothing new . . . she complained about Rachel's extravagance, and that she'd given a party but hadn't invited them. In fact, Sara reported, she hadn't spoken to her snobby daughter in over a week, and she had no intention of giving Rachel the satisfaction of calling. On it went, with Doris nodding her head in sympathy. In fact, she did sympathize. Mama was hurt and angry, and although she'd brought it on herself, Doris still felt badly for her . . . .

At the end of a very tense day Doris and Henry finally went back to his mother's. When they were in bed Doris said, "Mama told me the furniture will be delivered on Tuesday."

"I'm glad for your sake, but I'm going to ask you to do me a favor."

"Anything, dear . . ."

344

"Please don't apologize for me again. And don't ask me to spend Sundays with your folks."

"Henry, try to understand. They don't have anyone else—"

"What about Nadine and Sandy?"

"Mama doesn't like Nadine. Besides, they're used to having their children around."

"Well, children grow up, and have a life of their own—"

"I know. We won't go every Sunday, but we do have to see them, Henry."

"As little as possible, I hope . . ."

First thing the next morning, Doris checked in with mama. She told her what a wonderful day they'd had, thanked mama for being so nice to Henry. And would she please ask papa not to be so cold to her and Henry?

Mama said she was happy Doris had called and, yes, she would speak to papa . . .

When she hung up Doris sat on the edge of the bed wishing she could run off to an unknown island . . . unknown to all of them . . . and then she called Rachel.

"I'm sorry I haven't called since I came home, Rachel, but things have been so hectic—"

"There's nothing to forgive. You're making a new life and it's a tremendous adjustment."

"Thanks for your understanding, Rachel."

"Don't be silly. What are you doing today?"

"Nothing—"

"Why don't you come over?"

"You mean it?"

'What a question! Come for lunch."

"I really should skip it . . ."

"I'll have cottage cheese and fruit. You'll be safe from temptation, I guarantee it."

"I can't wait to see you and the baby." . . .

Doris sat in Rachel's fine diningroom, eating her cottage cheese and pineapple off of Minton china. It was like being in another world, especially after yesterday. "It's so lovely and peaceful here."

Rachel saw the look in Doris' eyes. "What's wrong, Doris?"

"Oh, God, I don't know where to begin . . ."

"Well, since that goes back to the cradle, tell me what's new?"

"It's not new, Rachel, just a continuation of the same very old story. It's mama. She and Henry had their first confrontation and the poor guy was really unprepared for her." It was

345

a painful memory, but Doris told her the story of the apartment and the storm that had followed with papa. "She still scares the hell out of me, Rachel, and so does papa . . ."

"Well, let me tell you, Doris, the time to start is now. You're married and you're going to have to learn to break the cord."

"Funny, you saying that, Rachel. A little over a year ago when Larry was born I said that to you and remember what you told me?"

"I know, Doris, but that was then and Jim helped me . . . made me grow up. I'm not going to allow them to dominate my life any longer. In fact, I've gotten to the point where I see less and less of them. And one of these days it's going to be just a Christmas card from Spain."

"It's easy for you to say that, but I really feel so damned insecure, or is it unsure . . . ? Oh, I don't know what I feel . . ."

"You love Henry, don't you?"

"I don't honestly know about that either . . . Yes, I do, I love him but I don't feel very secure about his making a living for us . . . Look, I can say this to you because you're my sister. The truth is, I didn't really want to marry Henry. They kept up a steady barrage about how fat and hopeless I was until I began to believe it. And then Henry said something that made me like him so much, and he was nice and decent . . . and I guess I saw him as my best chance to escape . . . you understand? It hasn't exactly been a marriage made in heaven, but there's a compensation . . . Henry loves me, I have no doubt about that." She smiled. "He certainly didn't marry me for my dowry—so it's hardly the worst marriage in the world either. He's really very kind and loving . . . sweet. Crazy as this may sound, he even thinks I'm beautiful—"

"You are, Doris."

"I'm not and you know it. Why kid me?"

"You know what you have, Doris? And it would be a miracle if you didn't."

"What?"

"A raging inferiority complex. When you've had it drummed into you how fat you are, how awful you are, from the first day you were old enough to understand a word they said, how could you not believe them?"

"I guess you're right, but how do you suggest I get over it?"

346

"By telling yourself you're *not* any of those things. My husband helped me to believe it."

"Henry tries. Funny, isn't it? We have to grow up through our husbands. You know what he said about mama? That . . . she isn't really too well . . ."

"He's right, I think . . . You can also tell him she's crazy jealous and one of the great neurotics of all time. And papa doesn't have time to wonder if there are two sides to a story."

"You're right, she tells it her way and he seems to believe it . . . But what hurts so badly, Rachel, is that they pushed me into this marriage and now they're angry because Henry's not rich like they expected him to be . . . does that make any sense?"

"Nothing they do makes too much sense. I haven't spoken to them in a week, did you know that?"

"She told me yesterday."

"That's par for the course. What did she say?"

"That you had a party and didn't invite them."

"That's not true. I did, but mama wanted to come in the afternoon and start taking over. I thanked her for offering but said I had a catering company and wanted her to be as much a guest as anyone else. Well, that did it. She told me she was a mother, not a guest, and if she wasn't welcome in my house as such I could go to hell. Does that sound like mama turning things around?"

"Sure does . . ."

"Well, I'm not putting up with it any longer. I can't help begging her for forgiveness—and love."

"Mama says you wouldn't even let her see Larry."

"Oh, Doris, don't you know mama and her fears about growing old? She doesn't even want to be called 'grandmother.' Larry's supposed to call her 'sissy.' Isn't that adorable? Can you even imagine mama taking Larry to the park? She told me once that she'd never baby-sit. She raised her family by herself and no one sat for her children." Rachel was working herself up now. "That's some joke about being denied her grandson. When we do talk she forgets to ask how he is. You know what we talk about? Her problems with you and Lillian, her health and how stingy papa is, how good I've got it—My God, it makes me angry that I'm getting so upset even now, but at least I don't need her the way I used to—and neither do you really, not now that you have Henry."

347

"But I'm not you, Rachel . . . she has such a hold on me I can't even make a stupid, simple decision without consulting her. I talk big but I'm still dependent on her—"

"You'll learn."

"I hope so. Can I see the baby?"

Doris picked him up out of the crib. He was going on fifteen months, a gorgeous, golden little boy, with blond hair and blue eyes like Rachel and papa. He laughed and said the most incredible inarticulate things. "He's beautiful. I love him. Jim must be wild about him."

"You can imagine."

"What does his daughter think of the baby?"

"She's never seen him. In fact, she and Jim have almost no relationship at all. She still can't forgive him for marrying me, but luckily she's going to the Sorbonne. But even if she weren't I would have put my foot down. I'm not going to be darling and adorable to *anyone* who doesn't approve of me, Jim's daughter or not. I've had enough of that all my life."

"Boy, we're sure the ones when it comes to families . . ."

"Well, I won't let anyone interfere with my happiness. No one, and that includes his daughter and our mother."

"I wish I could be strong like you."

"Teach yourself."

"Yeah, well, I'll work on it . . . I'd better be going. It's been a wonderful day—and thanks for the advice. I don't think it should take more than a hundred years to remake myself."

"With your sense of humor, you'll make it. I'm betting on you . . ."

She went to Henry's office and waited in the reception room. It was the end of the day and there was only one patient in the room.

Soon the door opened, and Henry stood framed in the entrance. He smiled at Doris, then asked the patient to come in.

Sitting alone now, she was free to admire the reception room Henry had so painstakingly decorated.

After the patient left, Henry said, "God, I'm glad to see you, honey."

She kissed him and went into his office. She wondered how many patients he'd seen today. There were only three charts on his desk, but she didn't want to pry.

After he wrote up his case histories, he smiled at her and said, "What brought you downtown, darling?"

348

"I had lunch with Rachel. It was so nice to talk with her again, just the way it used to be."

"How is she?"

"Fine, sends her best. And Jim and the baby are great. I really had a lovely day."

"Good. How'd you like to cap it off by staying downtown to have dinner? Besides, we have to make the move into our own apartment tomorrow."

"Really, Henry? I'd love to."

It would be a relief to be free of *all* families. They'd really be starting their marriage. It would be wonderful, she told herself . . . wanting desperately to believe it . . .

CHAPTER FORTY-SIX

AT NINE the next morning Henry packed their suitcases in the car. They kidded Henry's mother, and Doris thanked her for all she had done. Mrs. Levin shyly said it had been a joy to have them.

When they stepped into the apartment, Henry took her in his arms and hugged her. "Well, here we are. This is the real beginning . . . I wish I didn't have to go to the office today, but I'll help you out tonight. If you need anything, call . . . I love you very much, Doris."

"And I love you, Henry." It was getting easier to say now, and she truly meant it. Except the moment he shut the door behind him she didn't *feel* like a new bride in her first love nest. What in God's name was wrong with her? She was supposed to be all trembly with excitement, but something down deep was weeping.

She went into the small kitchen and began to line the shelves with paper, then she unpacked the carton of dishes they'd brought back from mama's on Sunday. She washed them and put them inside the cupboard but her hand was trembling so that she dropped a cup, and it fell to the floor and shattered.

She sat on the floor and just looked at the pieces. Doris, what's wrong with you? Get used to the idea that this is it. Just because Henry placed a ring on your finger you thought you were going to turn into a fairy princess? Yes, dummy, you did . . . you thought getting married would bring instant magic into your life, that it would change you into a whole new different person . . . Wake up, Doris. *Grow* up . . .

At eleven o'clock the doorbell rang. It was Redlick's. One of the two husky men asked, "Where do you want this?"

Doris looked at the couch. "Well, bring it in and we'll see."

They tried getting it through the door, twisting and turning, but it didn't fit.

"We'll have to take the door off the hinges, lady."

Off came the door and in went the sofa.

Mama and papa had selected the sofa while she was at work, so she had never seen it before. It was kidney-shaped, persimmon-colored, oversized . . . The nine-by-twelve rug was no better. Next came the large matching chair and two smaller chairs in a *green* green. All three occasional tables were red mahogany. The gray-painted dinette set with the four matching chairs was at least the right size. She then directed the movers to the bedroom . . .

When the movers left she walked from room to room, shaking her head in disbelief. Her fantasies had run toward chintz, Currier and Ives prints, brass, copper and—the doorbell was ringing.

She opened it. It was mama, laden with food.

"Here, Doris, take this."

She took the pot of soup to the kitchen and went back to help with the rest.

"How are you, mama?"

"Exhausted. This stuff was heavy and I had to carry it for two blocks. Couldn't find a place to park."

Doris kissed her mother. "You shouldn't have done all this." She *shouldn't*.

"Well, you had to have something to eat, didn't you? Let me take a look at the furniture."

Sara stood in the livingroom, then looked at Doris. "Is this lovely?"

"Beautiful, mama . . ."

"You like it? Papa and I knew you would. Here, let me arrange it."

"Aren't you too tired?"

"I always work hard, so what's new?"

They pushed and tugged at the furniture and finally Sara stood back to examine her handiwork. "Perfect. See what a difference arrangements make? What do you think?" She beamed. "Now let's see the bedroom."

Doris followed her down the short hallway. Sara stood in the doorway, taking it all in. "Beautiful. Is this a beautiful set?"

"Beautiful, mama. In my wildest dreams I never thought I'd ever own anything like it."

"If you waited for Henry—well, let me help you make the bed." That accomplished she said, "Well, Doris, you got your home."

"Yes, mama, thanks to you and papa."

Stop it, she lectured herself . . . so it isn't what your little heart wanted. It's mama being kind to you, at least trying to please . . . in her fashion. Don't be a snot . . . You'll *learn* to like it, to love it—just like with Henry . . .

And all unaccountably Doris started to cry, and she heard herself saying, "I love you, mama. Thank you . . . thank you for everything."

"Well, Doris, if I didn't do it, who would?"

"No one, mama, no one . . ."

"I know you're crying from happiness. I remember my first apartment. In fact, I'll never forget it. It was a lot prettier than I have now, if you can believe it, and your father was a lot poorer, but I guess a bride's first home is something she never forgets."

They were on two separate tracks—mama going on about her life, Doris trying to believe mama really was here with her, caring about her the way she wanted her to . . . so much so that at this moment, at least, she really did believe . . . "I love you, mama . . . And I need you very much—"

"Well, I'm here."

Suddenly the furniture didn't seem quite so ugly, nor—more important—did it really matter . . . .

It was getting on toward five when Sara put the food on the stove to heat. Doris sat in the breakfast room and watched. Mama seemed very happy.

"Papa should be here any minute, Doris."

Doris prayed he'd be nice to Henry. It would mean so much to her after the good day she'd had with mama. They hadn't had *one* word of disagreement. Of course, she'd been careful to stay away from things that might have started an argument—like when mama had asked if she had spoken to Rachel and she had lied and said no.

Henry came home soon after papa arrived, and was, understandably, surprised to see Sara and Jacob. He would have preferred to spend the first night in their home alone. He kissed Sara on the cheek, said he was glad to see her and shook hands with Jacob.

When Doris hugged him, he knew she was happy and he

351

wasn't about to spoil it. She took him by the hand and led him to the livingroom. "Isn't it beautiful, Henry?"

She squeezed his hand hard, and he got the message. "Thank you, Sara...Jacob. You've made Doris very happy."

It made Doris very happy? And you, doctor, are you going to enjoy it with her...But tonight, Sara used restraint. "We've always tried to make Doris happy. Jacob, are you proud? A little different than when we got married, wouldn't you say?"

Sure, my mother-in-law gave such a lot..."That's what good parents do for their kids."

"Thank you, papa. Now come and see the bedroom, and you too, Henry."

"Hurry up. Dinner is ready," Sara called out, holding to her priorities.

When Doris and Henry finally lay next to each other in their very own bed—their very first—Doris said, "It's *pretty*, isn't it, Henry?"

"We've gone through this, honey. I'm very happy."

"The folks were too. Didn't you think so?"

"I'm sure they were—"

There was an edge to his voice. "What's wrong, Henry?"

He paused, not wanting to hurt her but knowing it had to be said. "Well, it's not the most unusual thing for parents to furnish an apartment when a daughter gets married, but your parents would have us think it's never been done before."

"You sound a little strange, Henry, almost like you resent them—"

"I don't resent them, I just don't think it's all that unusual a thing for parents to do. They can afford it, you know..."

It's more than you could have done...Oh, God, she was beginning to think like mama. "I suppose you're right, honey ...I just wish you'd said *you* appreciated it—"

"I do, but I'm not going to kiss their toes, and I'm sorry, but that's what they want me to do."

And Doris started to cry, not because of what he said but because she knew he was right, and it still upset her...

"For God's sake, please, stop crying..." Sara and Jacob really weren't going to be satisfied until he kissed their feet. What a lucky guy Jim Ross was. He had enough money to tell Jacob to go to hell, and Rachel had been so fortified by his strength that she could just walk out of their lives. But

352

Doris was an insecure little girl, and he was afraid he was going to have to bow and scrape to them for the rest of his life just to make her less frightened of them, to keep her from falling apart . . . maybe even leaving him . . .

The next evening Doris met Henry at the door after work, all hugs and kisses. She was very proud of herself . . . she'd cleaned the apartment, cooked, washed his underwear and some towels . . . today she honestly felt like a housewife. She fairly beamed as she served him a bowl of Campbell's tomato soup.

"Honey, now don't feel badly about this, but I don't much like canned soup, especially tomato."

God, she didn't even know what he liked to eat. "We have tuna casserole . . ."

"I never had that in my life . . . how about some scrambled eggs?"

"You won't even give it a whirl?"

"Honey, I don't really like tuna, in or out of a casserole."

So, he didn't like tuna. Well, she'd learned all about sex . . . now it was foodtime . . . Come to think of it, she did remember that he liked steak, which cost a fortune, and chicken, which she had had up to her eyeballs all these years at home . . . "How do you like your eggs, Henry?"

"Scrambled, please, well-done with no whites showing."

She put some butter in the frying pan, beat the eggs until they were thick and foaming, then poured them into the melted butter and stirred . . . "Here, how are these?"

"Great, may I have some toast?"

She popped the bread into the toaster.

Doris watched him eat as she played with the tuna casserole on her plate. "I'm sorry about the dinner, dear. Tell me what else you like."

"Just plain food, no sauces and nothing highly seasoned."

"What about desserts?"

"Apple pie, custard . . . We'll work it out, honey, don't worry. Now, how did your day go?"

"I cleaned and washed, then I cooked this sumptuous meal." She laughed.

"Listen, it's not your fault if you have a crazy husband who doesn't like every food there is."

"I have the best husband in the world, and the kindest."

"That's a big thing with you, isn't it, Doris?"

"Without kindness, what have you got?"

Henry smiled and took her hand in his. "I called your mother this afternoon, thanked her . . ."

"You did? That was sweet . . ."

"And so was she. I suppose she has a problem with insecurity too. She wants to be told she's important."

"Don't most people?"

"Of course they do. I told you in the beginning you were mature—"

"For my age, you said."

"For any age. And you're also beautiful. I hope you realize *that* by now."

"No. Henry, you're the first person who ever told me that and meant it. And do you know something else? You're the first person who ever called me by an affectionate name. When you called me 'honey' for the first time I couldn't get over it for days."

"I'm going to keep on doing it for the rest of my life."

"Henry, you're the most . . . comfortable person I've ever been with. Also, doctor, I love you, I really do."

Keep thinking it, Doris . . .

That night as she lay close to him she realized how truly important he was to her. No . . . she wasn't in love with him, and the truth was that she never would be. But she loved him with all her heart, the way you did a best and beloved friend. There was a gentleness she had needed all her life, and that above all was what he had brought to her. She might never have more with him, but what she had was more than most people ever achieved in a marriage, for all their claims and pretending about how much they were in love.

"Doris . . ."

"Yes?"

"Doris, I've thought carefully about this. I think we should have a child . . ."

Oh God . . . let's wait and get a little more used to each other. Let me adjust more to being your wife and learn how to be a . . . person. I need at least a year, how can I be a mother when I don't even know who I am? . . . But then a residue of the old fears surfaced; if she didn't please him, maybe he wouldn't love her . . . and she needed so badly to be loved . . .

"I'm thirty-three, Doris, and it's getting sort of late for me," she heard him say.

But Jim Ross had a baby at forty-three and it didn't seem to worry him. Except, she reminded herself, that wasn't a fair

354

comparison. Jim had been married before, had already had a child. Of course it didn't worry him, but this was Henry's first marriage, first child . . .

"Darling, I want to be young enough to grow up with my child. I'll be thirty-four this October."

And if I get pregnant tonight, in nine months I'll be nineteen . . . But I owe Henry a lot. He rescued me, and when things get rough with mama and papa he'll always be there . . .

"I'd love a baby," he whispered. "Wouldn't you, darling?"

The tenderness in his voice touched her, and maybe it would be the best thing that ever happened to her . . . a child to devote herself to, something of her *own*, someone to love and to be loved by . . . "Yes, Henry, I would."

Henry was jubilant when Doris told him, "Don't start handing out cigars yet, dear, but the rabbit died."

"Oh, Doris, I'm the happiest man in the world—"

"That seems to be the standard phrase." She laughed, happy that she could do this for him, especially when she looked at his face.

But when she called mama it was a different story. "You couldn't wait? Henry can barely make a living now and you're going to have a baby?"

"We talked it over, mama, and decided we wanted a family right away."

"Did you also talk over how you're going to support it? Children cost money."

"Mama, I don't want to argue with you, but children are a treasure. You had us, didn't you? And for all the hardships we managed to grow up . . . okay."

Sara sighed. Another grandchild, no less. Well, if it was a boy, at least Doris would allow Jacob to enjoy it—not like Rachel. Or even like me, Sara thought guiltily as she recalled the abortion. "Well, be that as it may, I hope you know what you're letting yourself in for."

"Mama, I know you mean well, but don't be upset. This is the most wonderful thing that could happen to us."

What was the use of talking. "Look, Doris, this is your life and you're the one who's going to live it. If that's what you *want*, then good luck to you."

Chapter Forty-Seven

WHEN DORIS began her fifth month of pregnancy she and Henry realized they really must move into a larger place. But money, as usual, was the problem. Whatever they found seemed above their means.

At five o'clock one evening she was driving down Geary Street to pick Henry up at the office. This had now become a daily ritual so they could save the twenty-five-dollar-a-month parking charge.

Suddenly it began to rain. Doris thought, isn't it lovely, the first rain of the fall. It hadn't been forecast, but then, the weather was no more predictable than the events of a person's life. How long ago was it that she hadn't even had her first date, and now . . .

Crossing the intersection at Hyde and Geary, she was suddenly jolted and found her car spinning around, then skidding to a halt. She was dazed and in shock.

A man came rushing over and opened the door. "Are you all right?"

She was shaking so badly that she couldn't answer.

He asked once again, "Are you all right?"

"I don't know . . ."

"God, I'm so sorry. With the rain and all, I didn't see your car until I hit it."

She had heard the crash, but didn't know it was hers. "You hit my car? I thought I'd just skidded on the . . ."

"No. I bumped into you. I'm so sorry—"

She just nodded.

When the police arrived she was helped out of the car. And when they saw that she was pregnant, their concern deepened.

"Lady, maybe you should sit down. Better take it easy," said the officer. She obeyed automatically, too numb to think as he helped her ease her way out from behind the steering wheel.

"Now, can you tell me what happened?" the officer asked, taking out a pad and pencil.

She shook her head.

"It was my fault, officer," the other driver put in.

356

"The lady was actually across the street when you bumped into the back of her car?"

"Yes. My windshield was so frosted up I didn't see her."

The officer turned again to Doris. "Do you have a driver's license?"

Doris fumbled in her purse and handed him her license. Suddenly, she became hysterical. "I'm going to lose my baby . . .".

"We'd better call an ambulance."

"No, call my husband." She gave him the number by rote and he went off to place the call.

"Dr. Levin speaking."

"Dr. Levin, this is Officer Johnson . . . Your wife has been in an accident—"

"An accident? Is she hurt? You know she's expecting a baby?"

"Yes, doctor, I know, and she's asking for you."

"How is she?"

"Very frightened. I think you'd better come right down."

Henry was given the name of the intersection, grabbed his hat and ran out of the office. By the time he reached Geary and Hyde his anxiety was as great as Doris'. "Are you all right, sweetheart?"

She shook her head. "I don't know, Henry. I'm so frightened I can't stop trembling."

"I know, darling. Try and relax . . ."

When Henry spoke to the man who had hit the car he could hardly contain his anger. "You realize how serious this is? My wife is pregnant."

The man was a head taller than Henry but he almost cowered. "I sure do, doctor, and I can't tell you how sorry I am—"

"If anything happens to my wife, you're going to be a lot more than sorry—"

"Listen, I didn't see the car and—"

The officer intervened. "I have all the information and I think you should take your wife home, doctor."

When he turned to her she was weeping hysterically. "I want to go home . . ."

"Do you have any pains, honey?"

"I don't know. I just want to go *home*."

He helped Doris into bed, wiped her face with a damp cloth, and sat by the bed and held her until she relaxed. She

357

seemed okay, he thought, but he wasn't going to take any chances. He went to call his friend Gary, who was her obstetrician.

When Gary arrived, Henry stood nervously beside the bed while Doris was examined. With the examination complete, Gary snapped his bag shut and asked, "You have no pain now?"

"No, Gary."

"I think you're more in shock than anything else. I don't find anything wrong, thank God, but I want you to stay in bed for a few days. If you need me, don't hesitate."

Standing at the door with Gary, Henry asked, "She won't lose the baby?"

"I don't think there's much to worry about, but we'll watch her."

"Thanks, Gary, I really appreciate it."

"It's okay, now, keep her in bed and I'll be in touch in the morning."

Henry went back to Doris, who was a bit more composed now.

"Henry, please call my mother . . ."

"Tomorrow."

"No, dear, please . . . now."

He sighed, God knew he didn't want Sara here, but . . . "Sara, this is Henry."

"Yes?"

"Sara, please don't be alarmed but Doris was in a slight accident."

"An accident! My God, what happened?"

He told her.

"I'm coming right over."

"You're more than welcome, but it really isn't necessary tonight. The doctor just left and assured me she was all right. She's just shaken up—"

"Wouldn't you be?" she said, but this time there was more concern than anger in her voice.'

"Of course. What I'm saying is that she's fine and just needs a little rest. Why not come tomorrow?"

"All right, I'll be there first thing in the morning." . . .

Sara rang the bell at seven-thirty the next morning, greeted Henry with a quick hello, then hurried back to the bedroom, where Doris was still sleeping.

Henry was shaving, when Sara abruptly appeared in the doorway. "Why didn't you take her to the hospital?"

The razor slipped and cut his chin. "Her doctor didn't think it was necessary." He felt almost guilty as he answered, then realized that Sara was working her way on him too.

"Well, I think she should be watched carefully."

What the hell did she *think* he was doing? "Well, you're here and I'll be home at five."

"But I have to leave because there's no place here for me to sleep."

"You can sleep with Doris if you like and I'll sleep on the couch."

"You should sleep on the couch even if I'm not here. Doris shouldn't be disturbed."

"I guess that's a good idea . . ."

"Have you gotten in touch with the insurance people yet?"

"It only happened last night. Besides, there's a full police report. Everything will be taken care of—"

Sara went into the kitchen and put the coffee pot on the stove. Henry soon joined her. "Doris is so tired that she's still asleep, but she'll be happy you're here."

"Where else should I be? What do you want for breakfast?"

"Coffee and toast will be fine."

She joined him at the table. "Now tell me again what happened."

He repeated what he had told her the night before.

"You realize, Henry, that this could mean a very large settlement, in Doris's condition?"

"To be honest, Sara, I've been so upset I haven't given it any thought."

"Well, I suggest you hire an attorney."

"Fine, I'll talk to an attorney."

He got up from the table and walked to the bedroom to see Doris before leaving. She was awake, and smiling.

"How are you, Henry?"

"How are *you*?"

"I feel fine, just a little tired."

"I can imagine. Now rest, honey. I'll call later. Oh, your mother's here."

"I'm glad. Please have her come in."

Kissing her again, he said good-by, and on the way out told Sara that Doris wanted to see her. . . .

Sitting in a chair near Doris, Sara said, "Now don't be upset, but sometimes I wonder how bright Henry is. His wife has an accident and he doesn't think to hire an attorney? If I hadn't suggested it I doubt he would even have thought of it."

"He was very upset yesterday, mama."

"And I wasn't?"

"Of course you were. Now, mama, everything will be fine. Please don't get yourself all worked up."

"All right . . . What would you like for lunch?"

"I don't feel hungry."

"You should have something."

"Later, thank you."

"A cup of tea maybe?"

"Nothing, thanks—"

"All right. Now, Doris, I brought enough food for at least three days and I wrote out all the instructions for Henry. I don't want you to get out of bed. Let Henry do it when he comes home. It seems he doesn't work so hard."

"He'll manage, I'm sure. You won't be here then tomorrow?"

"Well, since you're feeling well and you're in no danger. . . . I do have other responsibilities. Your father comes home early from the plant now. Suddenly he doesn't eat lunch anymore and wants dinner at four in the afternoon. Did you ever hear of anything so insane? How can I make a social life? Suppose I was in the middle of a bridge game? I'd have to say sorry, I must go home and feed my husband. I think I'm the only woman in the world who has such a crazy kind of life . . ."

Poor mama, she wouldn't face it that the reason she had no social life was not because papa came home so early but because she couldn't accommodate herself to anyone, put them off with her manner even when she was trying not to . . . It was easier to pretend that everybody else stood in her way, was at fault. Still . . .

"I know, mama, it's not easy for you."

"Well, that's the way it is, Doris. Believe me, I've had my share of trouble."

"I know, mama." . . .

When Sara left, Doris sighed in relief. It was so quiet and serene now, and she was glad mama wasn't coming back tomorrow. The tension of always trying to keep the peace and always trying to make mama feel better was terribly wearing.

She was especially happy when Henry came home. He was very easy on the nerves.

360

"How are you, honey?" he asked, kissing her. "When I see you like this, I realize how grateful I am. I could hardly work today. All I thought about was you."

Doris smiled at him. "Honey, do you think you can manage dinner tonight? Mama left everything out. It just has to be heated. You can bring it in here and we'll eat together."

Together . . . it was taking on some real meaning.

The next day Henry was sitting at his desk in the office when the phone rang.

"Doctor Levin? My name is Mr. Robinson. I'm from the insurance company that represents Mr. Milman, the gentleman who accidentally hit your wife's car. I wonder if I might come over and speak with your wife?"

"She's in bed under doctor's orders. I don't think she should be disturbed for a while."

"When might I be able to see her?"

"Let's say Thursday, about seven-thirty in the evening."

"Thank you, doctor, I'll see you then." . . .

Doris sat in the big chair, her stomach bulging under the flannel robe.

When Mr. Robinson saw Mrs. Levin's condition, he knew it would be hands down as to what she would be awarded in court. A pregnant woman? If they got a sharp attorney, they'd collect a bundle.

"Doctor, I have an offer here that we think is very fair. In your wife's condition, I'm sure you wouldn't want her to go through any lengthy court proceedings. Would you mind going over this?"

Henry did not read the fine print. All he saw was *twenty-five hundred dollars* . . . That was half a year's earnings. Could he get more if he hired an attorney? Maybe, but it could drag on for a long time and they needed the money now so that they could move. Besides, attorneys got one third of the settlement.

"Mr. Robinson, I'd like to talk to my wife for a moment." He helped Doris up and led her into the bedroom. "Doris, do you know how much they want to pay? Twenty-five hundred dollars."

"Do you think we should take it?"

"Well, it's a lot of—the point is . . . I don't know how to say this—"

"Say it, Henry."

"If you hadn't been pregnant, they'd never have made such an offer and so fast."

"Do you think we should get a lawyer?"

"Maybe so. But on the other hand, these cases can drag on a long time. The rent is up on the fifth, which is Saturday, and that means staying another month. You'll be in your sixth month and—"

"Take it, Henry."

"I'm sorry the money had to come because of an accident . . ."

"God's looking out for us, honey. It's a lot of money for us and we need it now. Sign the papers." . . .

Doris and Henry had moved two blocks away, to an apartment on Broadway. It wasn't as bright as their other apartment, but it had the extra bedroom and a full dining-room.

Now it was November. The days grew shorter, the weather more overcast. The constant drone of fog horns was somewhat eerie.

Doris had become so large it was impossible to drive Henry to and from the office. Now she rarely left the apartment. There was nowhere to go anyway. Her days were lonely and the only moment of excitement was when she sat at the window about five o'clock and saw Henry's car turn into the driveway. . . .

One morning a crib and dresser set arrived from mama and papa, and she spent most of the day sitting in the baby's room on a dinette chair and looking at the set and waiting for Henry to get home before calling the folks.

"Mama, the set arrived. We're thrilled with it."

"Well, enjoy it. Papa and I are happy to do things to make your life a little easier." She, and papa especially, had exercised monumental restraint in not letting her or Henry know how foolish they thought he'd been to settle the insurance claim so fast. Well, everybody knew doctors were lousy businessmen . . . and that parents had to protect and do for their children regardless of the mistakes they made . . . "Yes, Sara, we love it. Thank you." . . .

After dinner Henry settled down to the evening paper, but Doris was restless. She hadn't left the apartment for several days. Not that anything held her back, but she needed someone to share an hour or so with. Rachel was away and she had no friends, so the days were very long.

"Henry, could we go to the movies?"

"When?"

"Tonight."

362

"It's already eight o'clock, honey."

"So?"

"It's such a miserable night out. Let's go right after dinner tomorrow so we can be home early. Is that okay?"

Henry was so damned sweet, how could it not be okay . . .

She went to bed early that night and fell asleep in minutes. She could only guess what time Henry climbed into bed, but it must have been around ten. It was becoming the nightly routine.

On a cold December morning Doris went down to the mailbox and found two envelopes, hurried back to the apartment and sat on the couch to open them. One was an announcement—Nadine and Sandy Sanders wish to announce the birth of their son Mark, nine pounds. A son! That was going to fry papa's bananas; everyone seemed to have sons except him. If only she had been a son, what a difference that might have made . . .

The other envelope contained an invitation to Larry's birthday on January fourteenth. Imagine, he was already two. Should she call Rachel? She had begun to feel a little awkward with Rachel. Was it that ol' debbil inferiority complex? Probably. She was never invited to Rachel's house socially, but that was understandable. Rachel's life was so totally different. Still, Rachel was her sister.

She picked up the phone and dialed.

"Ross residence."

For a moment she wanted to hang up. "May I speak to Mrs. Ross? This is her sister Doris."

Rachel was quickly on the phone. "Hi, Doris. How are you?"

"Getting a little too big for my belly. I got your adorable invitation to Larry's birthday."

"You're coming, I hope?"

"Sure, you picked the right month. Did you ask the folks?"

"Yes. I take it you haven't spoken to mama."

"Since when?"

"Since yesterday. Believe it or not, she was *most happy* to do me the honor of coming. Will wonders never cease?"

"Well, anyway . . . just wanted to thank you. Hope I see you when you get back from your holiday."

"Of course. Incidently, since I won't see you at Chanukah, I've sent something. Hope you like it."

"It's not a tent, is it? That's what I'm wearing these days."

Rachel laughed. "No, it's a layette for the baby."

"Oh, Rachel. Thank you, darling."

"You're welcome. Just have a healthy, happy baby. Hey, wait a minute. Why don't you come to dinner tomorrow night?"

Doris hesitated, then thought, why not. "All right . . . we'd love to."

When Doris hung up she sat and stared around the room a moment, then once again picked up the announcement from Nadine. She'd have to send them a gift too. Everyone's life seemed to be turning out pretty well. Sandy and Nadine had bought a lovely bungalow in the Sunset district and had furnished it beautifully. Sandy still drove a truck, but papa was paying him a really good salary now. Well, be glad for them, Doris . . . don't be like mama. And be glad for yourself too, damn it . . .

At five o'clock she was at her usual post at the window, eager to share the day's news with Henry. At five-thirty she was still at the window when the phone rang.

"Mrs. Levin? This is Mount Zion Hospital calling. Your husband wants to talk to you . . ."

From the pain in Henry's voice, she knew he wasn't seeing a patient. "Henry, what's wrong?"

"Don't get upset, but——"

"For God's sake, please tell me what happened?"

"Well, it's pretty stupid . . . I got a crate of oranges for Christmas from a patient and as I lifted it into the trunk rack it fell out of my hands and I landed on my back. I broke four vertebrae. I couldn't get up. Someone called an ambulance and I was taken to emergency. The doctor's putting me into a bodycast."

A bodycast . . . There had to be a mistake . . . she was dreaming all this. A nightmare . . . "I'm coming right over——"

"Please don't, honey, please . . ."

What do you mean? My husband is in the hospital and I shouldn't come? "I'll take a cab. I'll be there in a few minutes." . . . .

She wobbled into the emergency room and saw Henry lying on the hard table. She held his hand in hers and kissed it. "Oh God, darling, why did this have to happen to you——"

"It's rotten luck, but I'm more worried about you."

"Don't, I'm only going to have a baby. There's one born every three minutes."

364

The nurse was standing next to him. "Doctor, has the pain lessened any?"

"Holy cow, how dumb. I didn't even ask if you were in pain."

"I was, but it's better now."

"Are you sure? Oh, Henry, I just want to die." She put her head down on his chest.

"It's not that bad. Honey, I want you to go to my mother's and stay there. Call and tell them."

She nodded, then watched as they wheeled him out of the room.

She was in tears when she called her mother to tell her what had happened. Sara was genuinely shocked. "You'll come and stay with us."

"Thanks, mama, but I think it's best to stay at Henry's mother's, since I want to be in the city, I mean."

Sara agreed rather quickly, and that was that.

Irving answered when she called Henry's mother and repeated the whole story. He said the family would come over immediately. While she waited she called Rachel. "It's really been a nightmare. Sometimes I don't think the gods like me too much. Well, anyway, I won't be seeing you tomorrow."

"Oh, Doris, I'm so sorry . . . is there anything I can do?"

"Thanks, you're an angel, but Henry's family will be here soon. Besides, you have things to do getting ready for your trip and all . . ."

"Well, all right, and don't worry, Doris, I know Henry will be fine."

"I know he will." Doris hung up, knowing nothing of the sort. She had no idea how long he'd be in the cast or what the long-term effects would be. She shuddered. Was it possible he'd be an invalid? The thought was too much for her to hold . . .

The Levins arrived en masse. Fortunately Henry's mother was not a woman to go into hysterics and run to *shul* to pray for her baby son. In fact, she was very comforting to Doris.

In Yiddish she said, "You'll see, Doris, Hershel will be all right. God will take care of everything."

Doris wasn't so sure God would have the money to pay Henry's office rent and take the time out to care for his sparse practice, but those fears had to be put aside. Her husband's future was in God's hands, and she prayed that Mrs. Levin was right. What else could she do?

Meyer picked up Henry's car downtown and drove it

365

home. Irving shyly ushered her down the hall and Al consoled her. "It'll be all right, kid." Rosalie held her hand and said not to worry. Doris had never been more grateful than at this moment . . . she felt a security in their numbers. . . .

The next morning she took the streetcar to visit Henry. The bodycast extended from his groin to under his arms. He was still groggy from the anesthesia of the night before, so their conversation often lapsed as he nodded off. Still, she sat in his room all day.

When the doctor came in at five, Doris asked, "How long will he be in the cast, doctor?"

"About six weeks and then I'm afraid he'll have to remain in bed for a month or so."

A month or so . . This was December tenth, and she was expecting in February. "When can he leave the hospital?"

"Maybe by the end of this week."

That was something to be grateful for . . . She sat near the bed, looking at Henry encased like a mummy. "Are you very uncomfortable, darling?"

"I guess you could say that."

"And the pain?"

"Not too bad . . . How are you, darling?"

She tried to smile. "Great, Henry . . . but I've been thinking . . . I think we'd better give up the apartment—"

He winced, not from pain but from the stupidity of the accident and what it would do to their lives.

Doris went on. "We'll store the furniture and I'll stay with your mother. She's a dear, I really love her."

"She loves you too, honey . . ."

"Well, I guess Dr. and Mrs. Levin need all the love they can get. Thank goodness we have a little money in the bank. At least we can afford to pay the rent on the office. Irving put a sign on the door saying the office will be closed for two months. I'm getting so efficient, Henry, I surprise myself—" She stopped abruptly when she saw the tears begin in his eyes. "Oh, please, darling, don't do that. It could always be worse."

Actually there was nothing she could think of that would be worse.

"Well, I'll promise you one thing, Doris. If I have to saw this damn cast off, I'm going to be out of it when you have to go to the hospital."

"Of course you will, but let's not worry about that now. By February, I just know you'll be well."

She knew nothing of the sort.

Henry's brothers helped pack and get eveything ready for the movers.

Sara came over to help out. She smiled sourly when she saw the layette Rachel had sent. Rachel, the good sister, showing off how much more she had than Doris. And what bothered Sara most was Doris' lack of pride in accepting Rachel's charity.

But again, she held her tongue, monumental effort that it was.

As Doris looked out of the window and saw the last of the furniture being loaded into the van, she turned quickly away. Going from room to room in the now empty apartment she thought, Well, it was nice while it lasted. They had moved in about this time last month. She waddled to the front door and closed it behind her.

Her mother tried to console her as they waited for the elevator. "You found this place, you'll get a better one. In fact, to tell you the truth, I never liked it. It's so gloomy and dark . . ."

Doris tuned her out. . . .

Three days later Henry was carried up the stairs on a stretcher to his mother's flat, then put down carefully in the bed by the two ambulance attendants.

Every few days Sara dutifully called to inquire about Henry. The conversation could really have been recorded . . .

"How's Henry?"

"Feeling better."

"And you, Doris?"

"Fine, mama."

"And how is Henry's family treating you?"

"Wonderful."

"Don't work too hard, Doris. After all, it's Henry's family."

"That's right, mama. After all, it's Henry's family . . ."

Today the conversation had a slight variation.

"It's a shame that you can't be here tomorrow, Doris. Christmas will be so lonely with just papa and me and Lillian."

"I know it's sad for you being alone."

"Well, that's what happens when your children grow up."

"That's why it's so important to enjoy them while they're young, mama."

"I suppose so, my daughter the philosopher, but it's also painful, let me tell you."

Sara took Doris' silence to mean she too was recalling fond childhood memories, while actually she was thinking about the Levins. They celebrated Chanukah instead of Christmas, and they'd always be together in spirit even if they were separated.

"Yes, Doris, it's painful when your children grow up and find a life of their own. Parents don't seem to matter so much. I don't mean you, of course, but look at Rachel—" Well, she could hold her tongue just so long . . . what was she, a martyr? "We got a case of pineapples from the Royal Hawaiian Hotel with a note . . . 'Have a lovely holiday.' It hurts, Doris."

"I know, but try to have a Merry Christmas, mama. I'll call and talk to you and papa tomorrow."

Rachel called when she returned from her holiday. "How are you?"

She hadn't written to ask while she was away . . . "Well, under the circumstances I guess it could be better." Careful . . . don't be like mama . . .

"I know. How's Henry?"

"Improving. Some of the cast has been cut away and he's a little more comfortable. At the end of the month it will be removed and he'll wear a body brace. I keep praying."

"I do too, Doris."

"Thank you . . ."

"And thank you for the darling gift you sent Larry."

"I wish it could have been more—"

"It wasn't necessary, Doris, but he adores it."

Good God, was she jealous of Rachel? Yes, to be honest. Life had been good to Rachel, but—Doris, you are getting to be like mama. Nobody escapes, everyone has problems . . . "How was your trip?"

"Lovely." Rachel was beginning to feel uncomfortable. "Well, Doris, if there's anything I can do, please don't you dare hesitate."

Again the thanks, you're very kind, I appreciate it . . . and, unspoken, I wish I could jump off a cliff.

On New Year's Eve Doris and Henry sat listening to the radio.

"This is Guy Lombardo, coming to you from the Starlite Roof at the top of the Astor Hotel . . ."

Doris shut her eyes, visualized the sequins and spangles, the black satin, the emeralds, the bubbling champagne . . .

The announcer was now shouting above the din of voices, "The crowds in Times Square have gone mad and—"

Doris switched off the radio, bent over and kissed Henry. "Happy New Year, dear."

"Happy New Year, honey. Let's hope nineteen thirty-four will be better."

Or at least let's hope it's not worse, she thought, and said, "Henry, I love you."

CHAPTER FORTY-EIGHT

AT THE end of January Henry's cast, to Doris' relief, was removed. He was fitted for a steel brace and could now at least walk about the house. At first he tired quickly but soon he was able to be up for longer periods of time. Doris decided God was getting to like her a little better when she and Henry took their first short walk . . . .

February came, and now her pregnancy was almost to term. She marked the calendar every day, certain that this had to be the longest nine months in history. . . .

On February 28 at seven o'clock in the morning her water broke. Niagara couldn't have looked so beautiful. Her little overnight case had been packed for weeks.

A stiff and uncomfortable Henry managed to rush her to Children's Hospital, as he'd promised. After she had been taken to her room, she asked him to call her mother.

"Let's wait a little while, it's only nine—"

"Henry, please. Please call . . ." How well she remembered what went on when Rachel had Larry. The thought was almost worse than the few sharp contractions she was beginning to have. She wanted no repetition. . .

Henry placed the call with great reluctance, only too well aware that the Sanderses had neither visited him nor given Doris the kind of moral support he felt they should have during these last months of high anxiety. . . .

When Sara and Jacob came to the hospital, they found Henry pacing the hallway. They shook hands and went quickly to Doris, who smiled when she saw her mother come into her room. "I'm so glad you came, mama."

"Glad, what do you mean? I'm your mother. How are you, Doris?"

"A little scared. I suppose having your first baby is always—" Doris broke off as a contraction came on.

Sara winced and held her hand. "Is it bad?"

Doris let out her breath as the pain ebbed. "It's okay . . . Is papa here?"

"Naturally. Did you think he wouldn't be?"

"No, I knew—" Doris shut her eyes tightly and clenched her hand, then relaxed. Boy, having a baby was a lot harder than getting pregnant. "I'd like to see him."

As Jacob walked into Doris' room he felt himself being carried back in time . . . Hold on, Gittel, squeeze my hand . . . The thought of his own child going through that agony pained him in a way he could not express in words. "Doris?" he said almost inaudibly.

"Thank you for coming, papa . . ." Doris felt all the past hurts dissolve in that moment. If papa was here, nothing could happen to her.

"I'm glad to see you, Doris."

"Me too, papa—" She broke out in beads of perspiration, and her father grasped her hand and told her to hold tight as yet another contraction came on.

The nurse came in then and asked Jacob to leave. He leaned over his daughter and kissed her forehead, then turned to leave with tears in his eyes . . .

Miss Williams examined Doris. For contractions coming so close, she had barely dilated. Now she was getting another.

"Bear down and breathe out," Miss Williams said.

Letting out a cry, she lay back, exhausted. "Boy, that was a good one."

"And you're a good patient, Mrs. Levin."

At six o'clock Gary came in to examine Doris. Although her water had broken at seven in the morning the difficult labor hadn't begun until four that afternoon. Two hours of labor wasn't that bad for a first baby.

Henry rushed over to Gary as he came out of the room. "Well?"

"Doris is having a little difficulty, but I don't think there's anything to be alarmed about."

"You don't?"

"No, Henry, keep calm and I'll be back later."

Jacob had heard the conversation and was concerned. "Listen, Henry, I'm not going to let this go on. I don't think your friend the doctor knows his ass from his elbow. I want a specialist brought in. Damn it, I want a consultation."

Henry shook his head. He was worried too, but Gary Goldman was one of the best, he explained.

Nevertheless, when Gary came down the hall later that

evening Jacob confronted him with his decision. "I don't give a damn if this hurts your feelings or not, doctor, but I want to call in a specialist."

Gary looked at Jacob and narrowed his eyes. "That's what I happen to be. However, if you don't think I'm doing a good job, I'd suggest you do that. Who do you want me to call?"

"Who's the best?" Jacob asked Henry.

"Dr. Philip Barnes."

"Why didn't you have Doris go to him in the first place? Call him."

There was no point in upsetting Jacob further, so Henry gave in. "Gary, will you call Dr. Barnes?"

"More than happy, Henry."

At eleven-thirty, Dr. Barnes arrived, and he and Gary went in to see Doris.

By the time they came out, Jacob and Sara stood like statues, as if they expected only the worst.

"How's my daughter?" Jacob asked Barnes.

"She's ready to be taken up to delivery. I concur with Dr. Goldman. It was a difficult labor, but he was right to have waited."

"Thank you, doctor," Jacob said, wiping his forehead with his handkerchief.

The baby was born at one minute to twelve. It was a breech birth, but there were no other complications.

When Gary came out of surgery he said to Henry, "Well, dad, you have a little girl, eight pounds and two ounces. Congratulations."

Henry put his arm around Gary's shoulder.

"Thanks, Gary—for everything."

"Nature should get a little of the credit." He walked away without a word to the Sanderses.

"Well, Jacob," Sara said, "we have another grandchild."

A girl . . . He and Henry were some combination, but at least Doris and the baby were okay. "So, how does it feel to have a daughter?"

"That's what I prayed Doris would have." He wiped away his tears unashamedly . . . .

The next morning, Henry came into Doris' room with a bouquet of flowers. "Well, darling, we have our little girl."

"I can hardly wait for the nurse to bring her."

"She will, I stopped by the nursery and they were just feeding the babies. A nurse held her up for a minute."

"What's the color of her hair?"

"Dark."

"I can hardly wait." She sighed happily. "How did your mother take the news?"

"She can't get over it. All morning she kept saying, 'I'm a *bubbe,* I'm a *bubbe,*' like it was the world's first grandchild."

"Henry, she's really so good, I'll never forget what your family has done for me... How are my folks? You know what I mean."

When Henry recalled the events of last night he wondered how he had taken all that bullying from Jacob without blowing up. "They were great, Doris."

"Was my father disappointed because we had a girl?"

"No, really... Well, I'd better get to the office. My family will be here later. I'll call."

"Darling, please call Rachel."

"Your mother already did."...

At ten that morning, the nurse finally brought Doris her child. She could hardly believe that the small bundle wrapped in white blankets had been inside her the day before.

"Well, here we are," the nurse said, handing the child into Doris' waiting arms.

Her first look at her child made her face pale. It was... wizened... all black and blue. The eyes were tightly shut and it had a thin little patch of black hair. Henry said she was *beautiful?*

Doris brooded for the rest of the day. She had never seen a newborn baby, and actually thought they were born all pink and healthy and cuddly.

When Henry arrived that evening he saw her distress at once and asked her what was wrong.

"Henry, I know I shouldn't say this, but are you sure you saw the right baby?"

"Why?"

"The one that they brought me... I don't think it's ours."

"How can you say that?"

"Because she's just—all black and blue."

"That's from the instruments, but it'll go away."

"No, she's just—"

"Honey, the poor little thing had a very tough time."

Henry was right... but he was also making her feel guilty. She wondered if she would ever get over that first shock...

Over the following week, the forceps marks had completely disappeared, much to Doris' relief. In fact, the baby was

372

getting as pretty as her original fantasy ... her eyes were violet, her hair straight like mama's. The most beautiful thing about mama was her hair, and Doris could tell even now that the baby's was going to be the same color and texture. Indeed, the more she saw her child the more she prayed that God would forgive her for having such awful first thoughts. She had already fallen totally in love with this adorable little child and suddenly the name began to fit the child. Michele ... Doris had always loved that name. If she said it fast it sounded really lovely ... Michelelevin, Michelelevin ...

CHAPTER FORTY-NINE

SARA SAT at the kitchen table, having her usual breakfast of grapefruit and coffee, but this morning the grapefruit soured her stomach. Why was she dieting so much? What was she trying to prove? She had asked herself that question several times recently, but this morning she knew the answer. Quite simply, she didn't much like herself and never had. Nor had anyone else, she added. She had thought that getting thin would give her a sense of accomplishment, and somehow change her. At first it did bolster her morale, but deep down she knew she was still the same person, the same little girl who had lived her life in longing and loneliness. She had spent her childhood drifting from one place to another because her mother had preferred Louie to her. When she looked back and unraveled the years, her mind stopped at the first year of her marriage. That was the one and only time she had felt a true sense of happiness, an intimation of hope, when she and Jacob were in love in that little place on Washington Heights. But much too soon the world had come crashing in on her ... on them. When they moved back to the lower East Side, she had been cast into long years of poverty and denial. Of course she wasn't poor now, but life had deprived her of more than material things and she could never go back and reclaim them. She had never known what it was like to be at peace; she had never been given the time. She had become a mother before she'd become a woman, and the responsibilities of motherhood hadn't allowed her to do anything with her life. That wouldn't have hurt so much if her children ... ah, the children ... and the promise of Jacob's strength and ambition had not brought what she had

373

hoped for. She had struggled by his side for well over twenty years, but he was more frugal with his love and his money now than when he had been poor.

Her life was more lonely now than at almost any other time. And now she was a grandmother, whether she liked it or not. She was going to be forty-one in December and she'd never been young herself. Life had gone by her ... run over her ... so quickly she hadn't had the space or time to establish herself in life ... Or was it possible, she was frank enough to ask herself, that she had been hiding from life, using her children as an excuse? Maybe, but she doubted it ... It seemed more the other way around. They had so consumed her that there was little or no time left for her to develop a social life, and Jacob ... when he had first started in business he was away so much that she was left with all the responsibilities of the home. Besides, a woman couldn't establish a circle of friends without a husband as host and escort, and the circumstances of their lives had only brought her in touch with people who were his roughneck associates or simply miserable downtrodden people. She was as poor as they were, but at least she had had some education, she was smart, but who was there to talk to, to be really friendly with ...? Soon Lillian would be grown up, and then what ...?

She got up from the table, threw out the uneaten grapefruit and went upstairs to dress. Sitting at the dressing table, combing her thick black hair, the house seemed strangely silent and she felt frightened. Was this what her life ...

A sudden thought made her pause as she walked to the closet. Why not have Doris come home and live? Having Henry around would be no particular joy ... he was a constant reminder of how mistaken she had been ... but then again, he'd be at the office all day and it was Doris who was the important one. So happy-go-lucky, such good company ... The baby should be a bonus. Babies took up one's time and she was such a sweet little thing. Henry could baby-sit in the evenings so she and Doris could go to a movie.

The feeling of loneliness was beginning to lift as she now hurried to dress.

It was with a rare sense of exhilaration that she got into the Pierce Arrow and drove down the driveway, and before going to catch the ferry she bought a nightgown for Doris and a silver comb and brush set for the baby.

Sarah felt in command of life once again ...

She opened the door to Doris' room and smiled at her daughter . . . her redemption. Kissing Doris with more than her usual affection, she handed the gifts to her and watched as Doris unwrapped them.

"They're beautiful, mama. Thank you."

"It's nothing compared to what I'd like to do for you, darling, but you know papa's not the most open-handed man in the world. Well, do I have to tell you? To get a dollar out of him . . ."

Mama seemed so pitiful today, Doris thought, and what she said was true. Papa was a difficult man. She was sure papa did love mama, but he was just not able to show it. Strange man . . . At times Doris thought he was deliberately trying to punish mama for some unfathomable reason, and at other times it was as though he wanted to reach out but couldn't.

"How's the baby, Doris?"

"That little doll is so adorable I could eat her up. I have to admit that I didn't feel that way at first, though. The first time I saw her I thought she looked like a shriveled little old woman."

Sara laughed. "And now you think you'll keep her?"

"Oh, mama, I adore her."

"Why not, she's your child . . . Have you thought about where you're going to live?"

That was a question she wished she didn't have to answer. "I think for the time being, we'll stay with Henry's mother."

"Why Henry's mother? I'm a mother too."

Doris was surprised that her mother wanted to bother with them, especially with the baby. Her nerves weren't the best, and now that she was going through the change of life her emotions were even more on the surface and more conflicting.

"I think it might be difficult for Henry," Doris said, hoping it would discourage mama.

"What would be difficult for Henry?"

"Commuting back and forth, and he still has problems with his back."

"As a good mother and a good friend, Doris, I'm going to tell you something. You cater to Henry a little too much."

"Please, mama. Let's not talk about Henry and—"

"I'm not talking about him. Please let me finish. I was starting to say that a woman can spoil a husband when she thinks *only* of his welfare. Women have something coming to

375

them too, you know. If you don't, ask me. You and I, darling, have a tendency to allow a husband to walk all over us."

"Henry doesn't do that, and I *do* have to consider him . . . He's my husband."

"That's true, he's your husband. But he's also not the most . . . ambitious man in the world, Doris, so you're going to have to look out for yourself too."

"He does the best he can, mama."

"So the best he can do, a man with a family, is to live with his mother?"

"Look, mama, the little money we had is almost gone. What with his illness and my pregnancy it's—"

"Well, since you have so little left, why don't you just come and stay with me? We can give you more space and more privacy. Isn't it nicer for a daughter to be living with her parents? While you were pregnant I could understand the necessity of staying in the city while Henry was sick, but now it's different. You don't have a nurse to help take care of the baby, like Rachel did. Her *mazel* you didn't have, much as papa and I hoped . . . well anyway, it's still your home and while you're with us Henry can save. In fact, it would give him a chance to get on his feet financially. Look at the money you'd be saving. No food bills, no rent . . . It could really be a blessing for you, Doris."

What mama said made a lot of sense, Doris had to admit, and she seemed so eager to help. It was as though she were trying to make up for having neglected them during Henry's illness, and it really touched her. But still . . . "You're sure it wouldn't be too much for you?"

"Doris, what are parents for? You know how much papa loves babies. I don't want to influence you, but a daughter goes to *her* family."

"I can't tell you how grateful I am, but you do understand, mama, I'll have to talk with Henry."

"Of course."

"You're really a very good woman, mama. I'm—"

"Don't talk foolish."

Sara left, confident that Doris would be coming home. And if Henry continued to be as successful as he was, she would be home for a very long time.

That evening Doris talked to Henry about the advantages of living with her family for a little while.

At first he wouldn't hear of it. He hated the idea of living off the Sanders' charity. But the accident had taken care of the little nest egg he'd so carefully guarded, hoping it would be a down payment on a house. And although his mother would gladly have them live with her, her small home was already overcrowded. He was touched by Doris' happiness over reconciliation with her mother, but also knew it would be short-lived. Well, so be it. By the time Sara was on the warpath again, he was determined to have saved enough money to get their own place. So with many misgivings, he acquiesced . . . .

After Doris' ten days of confinement, she was sitting next to Henry, looking down at their lovely baby, as they crossed the Bay on their way to Oakland.

Henry parked their Reo in front of the Sanders' and helped Doris out of the car as Sara came out to greet them.

"Welcome home, Doris . . . and Henry."

Doris felt she was really coming home, where she could love and be loved as never before. After all, this time she had her beautiful Michele and her adoring Henry . . . .

For a while, Sara coped well enough with all the clutter and fuss of having a new baby in the house. But day by day, month by month, things began to change. Little things that build to large troubles . . .

Henry complained that he spent so few evenings with his wife. Doris tried to explain that mama had so few friends and so little to occupy her that she enjoyed getting out once in a while and going to the movies.

Sara began to complain about the bathroom always being so messy, that she cooked and cleaned all day long. Her nerves became so frayed that she took to locking herself in the bedroom nearly every time the baby cried.

Doris felt terribly guilty that this was all so hard on her mother. When Sara would come out of hiding, in contrition, Doris would say, "Mama, I'm really so sorry, but I just don't know what to do . . ."

And at such moments Sara would look at Doris, remember her former loneliness and consider that perhaps she wasn't trying hard enough. Michele was just a baby, after all, and the two o'clock morning feedings would eventually have to stop. Sara would compose herself and life would go on peacefully for a day or two, but then revert to the tensions of before . . . Nothing Doris did was right. The sterilizer was in the way. Couldn't Doris do the washing later? Couldn't she bathe the baby earlier?

"It was a mistake from the beginning," Sara blurted out

377

one day. Doris looked at her mother's face and realized she should have known better. Doris knew she had meant well, that she had really tried . . . but mama was mama . . .

The breaking point had come. That night, when Doris and Henry had gone to their room, Doris said, "This has been a bad mistake. I'm sorry, it's my fault for talking you into it, but please, Henry, can't we get a place of our own? You're a doctor, you ought to be able to make enough at least for that—"

Henry lay looking at his wife, feeling as though he'd been slapped in the face. "I'm sorry. I guess your mistake was in not marrying someone like Jim Ross."

Doris closed her eyes and shook her head. Oh, God, she was turning into a shrew like mama. Poor Henry, how damned unkind of her . . . how *unfair*. Sitting calmly on the bed she took hold of his hand. "Please forgive me, Henry. That was cruel. I'm making excuses for myself, but I've been under a lot of pressure. I'm tired and my nerves are shot. I know you're doing the best you can. Please forgive me, dear. I love you. You're the only one . . . who really loves me."

"Your mother's enough to make anyone crazy. I'm going to look for a flat first thing tomorrow morning."

"Oh, Henry, thank you, I don't care what it is or where, just as long as it's *ours*."

Henry called at eleven the next morning and was grateful that Doris answered the phone. He couldn't have spoken a word to Sara this morning.

"Honey, I found a two-bedroom flat in the Marina."

"How much is the rent?"

"Seventy dollars a month—"

"Can we afford it?"

"We'll manage. Can you meet me? I'd like you to see it before I sign the lease."

"Take it, darling."

"Suppose you don't like it?"

"I'll love it. When can we move in?"

"Anytime, tomorrow."

"Sign the lease. And Henry, I love you." . . .

At lunch, Doris sat silently at the table, watching mama eat her tomato and drink her tea. She didn't feel up to the challenge of breaking the news to her mother, but it had to be done.

She said quietly, "Mama, that was Henry on the phone."

"So?"

"He found a flat."

Sara stopped chewing. "He found a flat? Where, in the Mission? How's he going to get the money to pay the rent?"

"We have it," Doris said, fidgeting with her napkin.

"You have the money?"

"Enough . . ."

"And you told me that day in the hospital you had to go live with Henry's mother because you were so destitute?"

"Mama, you twist things . . . I said most of what we had was used up by the accident and my pregnancy. Look, mama, I don't want to get into a fight over this. *Please.* It's been too much for you with us living here. You cook and clean, and nothing I do suits you . . . I know you meant well, but it just hasn't worked out. Besides, *I want a home of my own.*" Doris' voice had risen and she was shocked to hear her vehemence. This was the first time she'd ever spoken to mama like this.

"Well, that's the kind of gratitude I should have expected from you and your so-called husband. I took you in when you didn't have a nickel to pay for the streetcar, fed you, clothed you . . . it was all for—"

"What do you *want* from me? Never mind, I'll pay you back for all your goodness—"

Sara got up and slapped Doris across the mouth. "Listen to me, young lady, just who do you think you are? I gave birth to you and don't your forget it. I had labor pains just like you. Now I want you out of my house today, do you hear? And we won't impose our terrible hospitality on you anymore . . . you won't get a quarter from us—"

Doris ran out of the room, up the stairs and locked herself in her room. She threw herself across the bed, and cried. Mama could be so damned cruel . . . Henry was right, she was mad, but not in the way he thought. She saw her mother for what she had become, and that's what counted. No more making excuses for her . . . I've got to get away, got to get away, she kept repeating to herself.

When Henry returned that evening Doris was packed and waiting for him. He took the things and put them in the car and then waited for Doris. He couldn't go back into that house and look at Sara.

With the baby in her arms, Doris knocked on her mother's door.

"Come in . . ."

"I'm going now, mama. I know you tried, really I do. I also know you meant well, and—"

"Please spare me the farewell speech."

"I'll call—"

"Don't bother, you don't need me. You have a husband who can take care of you."

Doris turned and shut the door.

Lillian was downstairs, waiting in the hall. "Doris, I'll miss you . . ."

"I know, Lillian—"

"Do you? I'm the only one left—"

They both started to cry then, because there was nothing else to say. Lillian had said it all.

"When we get settled, you'll come and see us, Lillian."

"If she lets me . . ."

Another kiss and Doris closed the front door behind her . . . .

That night they stayed with Henry's mother, and the next day the furniture came out of storage and was delivered to the flat on Scott Street in the Marina. Doris felt she was home at last. Not free, but home.

When Jacob came back from his trip Sara filled him in on his daughter's sudden departure.

"Do I understand that they had money?"

"Well, I guess he must have. When Doris decided she didn't need as much help with the baby she told me Henry had rented a flat. And he didn't even say good-by or go to hell. Imagine, after all I . . . we . . . did. Slaved, never left the house . . . I'm sorry to say it, but they used us, Jacob, our own flesh and blood . . ."

Lillian sat unnoticed during all this, wishing she had the nerve to speak out. But she kept still. All mama had to do was give her one of those special looks . . .

"Well, you'll see if I give them a penny from now on," Jacob said. "We sure got ourselves a couple of wonderful sons-in-law. And as for our daughters—well, the less said . . ."

Oh, how Lillian would have loved to tell papa everything. And there was a lot she could tell, not only about what mama had told him about Doris, but about the times mama took her to the Century Theater on Telegraph Avenue and left her there for a few hours. A few hours? She sat through the same movie twice. The first time she had become so worried that something had happened to mama that she walked out into the lobby and looked out through the glass doors. Suddenly she wished she hadn't. Mama was standing on the street with a man. She knew who he was; she recognized him from the bank. Lillian felt sick when she saw him kiss and hold mama for a minute before he turned and left. Lillian had run back to her seat as fast as she could, and soon mama was tapping her on the shoulder.

They went to the Pig and Whistle and mama had seemed happy as she said, "Lillian darling, I don't want you to tell papa I left you alone in the movies this evening. Will you remember that?"

"Yes, mama," she answered, but she couldn't look at her mother. She had loved her better than anyone in the world, even Doris, until that night. And then there were the phone calls that used to come almost every night when papa was away. Mama would say, "Lillian, go to your room and study." She went to her room, but she didn't study. She listened to mama laughing and whispering. Lillian caught a word here and there. All during that time mama was . . . was nice, sweet. It had all happened a little while after Doris got married. Then one night she heard mama crying when she was on the phone. She'd stood at the top of the stairs in the shadows and listened to mama say, "I can't go on like this anymore. You're becoming more important than I intended. I just wanted a friend . . . No, I can't do what you want. It's all over. The guilt is too much. I hate sneaking around like this and if your wife or Jacob found out—No, I can't."

Lillian had shut the door then and cried for a very long time.

And so she could not have told papa that mama had also cried . . .

Sara had not been unfaithful to Jacob physically, but her guilt was no less than if she had. She'd been so awfully lonely, and with Doris getting married a door seemed to have slammed in her life. Oh yes, she'd wanted someone to look at her too and see that there was still a woman . . . only thirty-nine, after all . . . but it had terrified her all the time it had buoyed her, made her feel for a little while like a woman again . . . But that was all she'd wanted, all she'd dared, and he had not understood . . . No matter what she did, it just didn't seem to turn out right. . . .

And now with Doris gone, the awful depression and loneliness came over her again. She'd said some harsh and unfair things to Doris, she knew. Doris had really been the only child who seemed to try to understand her. But Doris had also deserted her in the end, which made her anger, and her depression, all the greater . . .

381

CHAPTER FIFTY

AFTER DORIS moved into her flat it took a great deal to try and forgive what had happened, but she *had* gotten out. Don't be vindictive, she told herself. She called mama.

At first Sara all but hung up, but Doris persisted and Sara, who'd been dying for the call, finally relented.

Doris had mama and Lillian to dinner. She wished papa had been home. But he was in Wyoming . . .

Sara said nothing about the flat, which was to be expected, but her daughter's happiness in her home had started the wheels in motion. That evening when Sara left to go home, she knew a change was going to take place in her life. Oh, yes, without question, tonight she had come to a great decision.

Monday morning the house in Oakland went on the market, without Jacob's knowledge. Within a month she had a buyer. It made no difference how little she'd gotten; she was ready to move to San Francisco and she now had the money to do it. Jacob had had his way long enough. Turn the page, end the chapter, start a fresh new one . . .

After dinner she said quietly, almost casually, "I've sold the house, Jacob. Eleven thousand dollars—"

He stood up abruptly, the chair toppled to its side.

Lillian was afraid he was going to hit mama.

"What? You're crazy . . . Who the hell do you think you are that you can twist me around your little finger? And how *dare* you sell this property at such a price?"

"Such a price! You payed twenty-five hundred dollars and I sold it for eleven thousand and you're complaining?"

"Property has gone up. This house is worth at least fifteen—"

"Stop hollering. You got your money's worth out of it. Besides, if I'd asked, would you have sold? No. Now, Jacob, you listen to me carefully. I'm moving to San Francisco. I will not go on living like the poor relations. Your brother lives better than we do—"

"And since you made all the decisions, what are you going to do? Buy a mansion?"

"No, I'm going into an apartment."

"An apartment? That's like living in a jail—"

"Rachel's apartment is like a jail? A jail like that I should only have."

"Well, I'm not going to live in an—"

"And I'm not living in a two-story house. I'm through climbing stairs and being a slave to the house ... In case you're having a difficult time making up your mind, let me remind you why Doris and Rachel married who they did. It was because we lived in this lovely anti-Semitic neighborhood, in this *place* ... Who could they have brought home? Who did they come in contact with? Father Gallagher? If you think I'm going to allow you to make the same mistake with Lillian, you're mistaken."

In spite of himself Jacob had to admit there was some truth in what she was saying. Lillian was sixteen and soon she'd be grown. What chances did she have here? He didn't want her to wind up the way Rachel and Doris had, one with a *goyisher* old man and the other with a weak failure ... Suddenly he began to see other reasons for the move. He had been so hell-bent on providing his family the security that he'd never had that the source of that security—the plant—had been all that mattered. But he was rich now and there was only Lillian left. Didn't he owe himself something too ... ?

"All right, sell the damn place, but I want to buy a house!"

"Oh, no. I want a doorman to park my Pierce Arrow, carry up the groceries, and announce the guests. Why not? What's good enough for my daughter is good enough for me ... This time it's going to be a little my way ... and as long as we're talking, you're going to give me an allowance every month too."

He swallowed hard, face reddening. "How much do you—?"

Sara knew she for once had the upper hand about money. Obviously he wouldn't have agreed to move if he didn't want to ... and he wasn't going to do it alone ... "Five hundred dollars a month."

Jack was staggered. "Five hundred a—"

"Yes."

"What in God's name do you need that much for? I pay all the bills—"

"Is that so? Well, I'll pay my own personal bills from now on. You're not going to continue to interrogate me about

383

everything I buy . . . no more doling out nickels and dimes, not after twenty-three years of marriage, thank you very much."

Jacob hated the idea of the confinement of an apartment, but Sara plunged ahead and somehow ended up selecting one on the corner opposite Rachel's building. It was really a coincidence, she told herself, but she wanted to live on Nob Hill and especially at the Park Lane. The building, she was pleased to see, was just as prestigious as the Brocklebank, and the rooms and floor plans were much the same. The apartment could accommodate three live-in maids, but for the time being she settled for one.

She was a changed woman, but the fact that Jacob had given in to her demands was not exactly the victory she thought it was. Once the realization he was a wealthy man had caught up with him, he too wanted to live according to his means.

He walked along the aisles of Gains Walrath's Fine Furniture Company on Post Street feeling as if he owned the world. Suddenly he found that nothing was quite good enough for him. As in the case of most born agains, he went to the opposite extreme.

The Italian diningroom furniture would take four months to be carved and shipped from Florence, but Jacob had fallen in love with the massive high-backed chairs, the enormous buffet, the exquisitely carved china cabinet. As he sat in the host's seat and looked down the long refectory table, he felt like a conquering hero returned from the wars, victorious over poverty. Poland seemed very far away, as did Ludlow and Rivington Streets. His *bubbe* and *zayde's* house was now only a vague childhood memory. Mostly they would be something to boast about when he reminisced about his rise to wealth and how he had overcome all obstacles. Yes, indeed, he was beginning to like the feel of luxury very much, especially when he walked on the thick Persian rugs and looked at the fine painting that would hang on his wall.

Sara stood to one side, amazed at the transformation in him. But what amazed her most was his innate good taste. It was impeccable. So Sara let him select what he wanted. And what he wanted was more than she would have ever dreamed of asking for. He insisted they buy the best and most expensive sterling silver tea set, as well as the candelabra and crystal.

Sara remembered her feelings when Rachel's wedding boxes began arriving from Gump's—how she'd admired and

384

frankly envied the contents, never even daring to dream that she would not only be living across the street from her daughter but that her possessions would be comparable.

It had been a long way from that time to this, she thought. Things could change. People could change. Jacob was a living example.

They had been living in the apartment for four months now. Sara spoke to Rachel on occasion, but never did she suggest a visit. She would show Rachel that she too could be independent.

Except Rachel didn't feel neglected—to the contrary. She had established an extensive social life—which mama just wasn't a part of—and she could do as she pleased without having to explain or make excuses. Mama's "punishment," in fact, had been a blessing, helping as it had to set her free. Thanks to mama, she was able to separate herself from the family without feeling the kind of guilt that, for example, Doris did.

Sara herself was preoccupied with her decorator and her trips to Elizabeth Arden's Salon, and then there was her regimen of body massage and facial treatments. She managed to phone Doris, of course, but she had become a very busy woman. Lillian was also included in Sara's concerns. She bought her a beaver coat and carefully selected her clothes and her diet. She was sent to Hamlin's School for Girls, where she would make the kind of friends Sara felt were essential to her future. Lillian was her last hope, and she was going to make sure that her daughter's destiny was turned in the right direction. She was going to mold one of her three daughters to suit. Lillian, at least, was going to love her.

Jacob was traveling more and more, but Sara's life was so full that she found herself not resenting or even missing him.

She attended concerts, theater, opera and the ballet with Lillian. San Francisco, it turned out, was where she belonged. Oh, the wasted years—but she refused to look back. This was a time to savor; she had been redeemed . . . .

With the apartment finally complete, Sara was now ready to invite the family. She sat at her marquetry desk, making out a guest list. It was rather foolish since she really had no outside friends and knew exactly whom she would invite, but the idea of a guest list intrigued her. It included Nadine and her family, although she certainly had no special love for them. Doris, of course. But before she finished the list and made up a menu befitting a state dinner, she wanted to make sure that Rachel could come. Otherwise she'd call it off and set a different date. She was going, by God, to show the Rosses the way the Sanderses lived. Of course, she'd have to be careful not to mention that Nadine and Sandy were coming. Rachel felt awkward with them, she knew, although she'd never understood the reason for it.

Sara now dialed the number and greeted Rachel as if they'd just spoken yesterday, although it was actually some weeks since their last conversation. "Good morning, Rachel. I hope I'm not calling too early?"

"Well . . . we were out rather late last night so I was sort of indulging myself . . . but it's nice hearing from you, mama. How've you been?"

"Never better. Thank God the apartment is finally done. Waiting for that damned set drove me mad. But your father had to have that set, and no other."

"I'm sure it was worth waiting for."

"Well, yes, it's nice. As long as your father likes it . . . Rachel, I'm having just the immediate family to dinner for the first time and I want to know if you'll be free on October twelfth."

Rachel hesitated, knowing mama was bursting at the seams to show off the wonders she had achieved. "As a matter of fact, mama, we are free."

"I'm delighted, make it seven."

"Thank you for inviting us. Send my best to papa . . ."

"I will."

After hanging up, Rachel called Gump's and sent mama and papa a silver-plated chafing dish for one hundred and fifty dollars. Now they were, in a way, even. She smiled, knowing mama would get the message . . . .

Sara next proceeded to issue the rest of the invitations. When she called Doris she told her that everyone was wearing long dresses.

"Why, mama?"

"Because it's a very special night—our housewarming. And you know Rachel would never go out to dinner in a short dress—"

"Well, I think that's lovely, except I'd really like to wear a short one."

"No, I want it to be formal. And besides, you look best in long."

What the hell was she going to wear, Doris wondered. Well, it would have to be her heirloom, the one she wore the

386

night of Sylvia Silverman's surprise party. Which had really turned out to be her own party. That was the night, after all, that Henry had asked her to dance, and in a way she was still recovering from the surprise of it . . . "Okay, mama, anything you say."

The night Sara had fantasized so long was about to begin. She dressed in her new flowered chiffon and considered which of her new jewels to wear. Jacob had stumbled into a great deal of jewelry for nineteen hundred dollars, which he had insisted on having remounted. She didn't quite understand why and it had irked her at the time, but the new settings were every bit as beautiful as the originals. Among the cache were a diamond bracelet, a large ruby and diamond pin, a wide gold bracelet and earrings, a dinner ring, and a five-carat diamond ring for himself.

Jacob was handsomely outfitted in a velvet maroon smoking jacket with satin lapels, patent leather shoes, a white shirt and black trousers. A regular Beau Brummell, yet.

Sara went to Lillian's room and looked approvingly at the hyacinth-blue taffeta dress. Lillian's startling black hair and her makeup were done just right.

The doorbell rang at seven. Doris and Henry—who stood speechless. This couldn't be mama! She hadn't seen her mother in the four months since the move, but they talked on the phone frequently and not once had mama mentioned she'd become a *blonde*. She looked stunning, no question.

"Come in, don't stand there like you saw a ghost." Sara was smiling at Doris, but she was thinking how heavy she still was and wondering why had she worn *that* dress?

When Doris saw papa and Lillian her astonishment was complete. The three of them looked like they'd just stepped out of a Noel Coward play.

"I can't get over you, mama."

"Is that good or bad?"

"Good, great. You're gorgeous, but you should have prepared me for the shock. I could drop ten pounds."

Sara laughed. "Well, thank you. Now let me show you around."

But the doorbell rang and this time it was Shlomo and all his in-laws.

Sara couldn't have been more gracious . . . "Nadine, you look so lovely."

"So do you, Sara, I can't get over your hair, you look ten years younger."

"How nice of you to say so. And I'm so happy you and

387

Charles could come," Sara said as she turned to Mildred Blum.

"Thank you for asking us," Mildred said, remembering acutely how catty Sara had always been toward them.

Sara then gave a formal, if cordial welcome to Jean and Neal, followed by, "Now, let's go into the livingroom and have a *long* chat."

Jacob was soon serving drinks from the built-in bar, as if he'd done it all his life, which caused more than a few looks to be exchanged among the guests, although neither Sara nor Jacob noticed.

Doris sat observing the performance, as practiced, she thought, as if there had been a dress rehearsal, and feeling as ill at ease as Henry did. If there was a depression, everyone certainly seemed to be keeping it a secret . . . Nadine was wearing a black velvet dress with pearls left over from better days, and Jean wore a green silk dress that showed off her lovely slender arms. Mildred Blum was poised and distinctive in a gray lace dress.

The only cloud over Sara's moment of glory was that Rachel still had not arrived. She was beginning to wonder if Rachel was doing this deliberately, but before the thought could develop into anything more explosive Rachel and Jim had arrived in the foyer.

"Well," Sara said, "since you just live across the street I was beginning to get worried. My goodness, you're a half-hour late."

Rachel couldn't find her voice, Sara's transformation was so startling. "My God, what did you do to your hair?"

"Obviously, I had it tinted. Do you like it?"

Mama had always loved her blonde hair and now, thanks to Elizabeth Arden, she had what nature had denied her. "Well, it's certainly becoming, but I also thought you were striking as a brunette."

"Did you? Well, you'll get used to it . . . now come and join the others."

When Sara opened the double doors to the livingroom, a flush of embarrassment rose to Rachel's cheeks. Shlomo was standing in front of the fireplace with a drink in his hand. The memory of the night she had all but seduced him . . . and he had rejected her . . . still, in spite of herself, was very much with her. He must have had more than one good laugh over that dreadful moment, she thought, and the humiliation was somehow no easier to bear now than it had been originally.

388

He kissed Rachel on the cheek and shook hands with Jim.

"I haven't seen you for such a long time, Rachel, but you're as beautiful as ever. It seems motherhood has made you even more so."

Rachel cringed inwardly, wondering if he had ever discussed that episode with Nadine ... "And being in love," she answered, looking at him coolly.

Shlomo understood her feelings and pretended to ignore her abruptness. She needn't have worried. He saw the episode as a matter of adolescent confusion, and as he looked at her now, standing there with her husband, he was relieved that what must have seemed to her a rejection had apparently left no lasting scar. Had it been anyone other than Rachel he would not have worried, but he knew she was not a person to take things light-heartedly, no matter what her pretense. She was a bit like Jacob in that way. He answered, "You're quite right, Rachel. Love makes all people beautiful."

She smiled mechanically, then quickly left him with Jim and sat down next to Doris.

"I'll never forgive mama for this, Doris," she said under her breath.

Bewildered, Doris asked, "For what?"

"For pretending this was going to be a simple little family get-together."

"Oh? Well, you're dressed perfectly. So she didn't give the guest list."

"That's just the point. She doesn't feel that these people are family any more than I do. In fact, she probably can't stand most of the people in this room. She just wants to show off."

"Oh, Rachel, don't take it all so seriously. They *are* family.., It's only for one night ... after all, it's mama's housewarming and she's worked and waited a long time to have such a home. Why shouldn't she show off, and who else has she got to show off to?"

"Look, Doris, I'm a little tired of your being so noble, always playing the part of the arbitrator .... I'm going to get a drink."

Doris was more bewildered than ever. She and Rachel had become almost strangers. Rachel seemed so intolerant, self-centered. Maybe her husband over-indulged her, what with her rich gown and jewels ... And Doris suddenly felt very much that she didn't belong here.

Dinner was announced, and the food and service were lavish beyond belief. Doris looked at mama sitting so regally

389

at one end of the table and papa at the other. And Lillian in between, looking like a mannequin. Oh, the memories she had of them all sitting in the kitchen in West Oakland. Those hadn't always been happy occasions, but at least it hadn't all been so artificial.

Rachel had been seated across from Shlomo, and her discomfort grew with each course that was served. When dessert finally came, she had stood as much as she felt she could. She nodded her intention to Jim, got up and went to Sara. "You'll have to excuse me, but I thought this was going to be a very early evening, just for the family, I think you said. Anyway, we're leaving tomorrow and I still have a million things to do ... Don't bother to get up, please ... it's really been delightful. Thank you for including us." She turned then and left, Jim following her with a brief nod of thanks.

Sara and Jacob were seething but they carried off the rest of the evening with as much composure as they could manage. Conversation was forced and the party broke up early, but at least the other guests seemed duly impressed.

Sara would deal with Rachel and Jim Ross later. For this evening, she'd sworn to be a lady even if it killed her.

What a night of revelations this had been. For the first time, Doris understood why mama and Rachel had fought so through the years—they were both so alike. She hadn't really seen the similarities until now. She had always believed Rachel was defending herself against mama, but in truth they were both self-centered people who demanded satisfaction regardless of the effect on others. . . .

Doris went home with a headache for more than one reason. Yesterday Henry had told her they could no longer live in the flat ... he just couldn't afford the seventy dollars a month. She lay in bed that night wondering why Henry hadn't been able to develop a better practice. She didn't have Rachel's or mama's desire for wealth; she only wanted him to make a living for them. She thought, sadly, that papa really hadn't been so wrong. Henry was a decent man, but he just seemed to have no ... ambition. It was a painful truth, but she had better face it ...

When they were married she had no idea how doctors improved their practices, but now she did, and Henry really wasn't even giving it a chance. His personality seemed better-suited to a nine-to-five job. He loved his *routine* ... shower

390

and shave at nine in the morning, have a leisurely breakfast of corn flakes and scrambled eggs, take the baby out in the go-cart . . . He was not at the hospital with his peers, who at seven A.M. were conducting a clinic. He did not go to conventions to improve his skills and keep up with the latest methods, and isolated as he was, he received few referrals from other doctors. The practice of medicine had changed from the good old family doctor who treated everything from tonsillitis to phlebitis. Specialization was demanded and that required a five-year residency plus taking boards. But Henry had been so eager to hang his shingle that he had never thought about his future, and the result was his practice was stagnant. His office hours were from eleven in the morning to twelve-thirty. Then lunch, followed by a leisurely walk, and the office again from two to four-thirty. In between the few patients he saw, he would peruse his medical journals, some of them not very up-to-date.

Well, she would just have to accept the fact that Henry was Henry and would not change. She had to fight down her annoyance, and fear, and come back to the sustaining consolation . . . Henry was kind. He was a loving husband and he adored her and Michele with a devotion that she could hardly take for granted—not after the loveless childhood she had had. All reasons enough for her never to let him know about her unhappiness. She never wanted to make him feel less than a man; it would only have resulted in breaking his spirit, and who knew better than she what a broken spirit felt like . . . ?

When they moved from the flat to the one-bedroom apartment, Michele was given the bedroom and they slept in the hideaway wall-bed. The only time Doris gave in to her tears was their first morning in the new apartment, but she was careful to save them until Henry had left for the office. She owed him that much . . . and much more . . .

CHAPTER FIFTY-ONE

THE NEXT year moved slowly for Doris. There was little time to acquire friends, or even the means to do so, but as her inevitable resentment grew, she still remained silent. It seemed, God help her, that her life was running parallel to her mother's early married life. The biggest difference was that she never allowed herself to complain and mama had never stopped. But like mama she desperately wanted at least a small home and as the years went on enough to educate their child . . . .

Almost a year after the housewarming party at her parents, her prospects didn't seem any brighter and she knew things would only get more difficult as Michele grew up. Out of desperation she finally went to her parents.

She sat nervously in their livingroom and finally she couldn't hold it back any longer. "Papa, I'm desperate. I have to get out of that apartment. It's choking me—"

"If you weren't married to such a lazy s.o.b. you wouldn't be so desperate."

"Please, papa, I beg you. Don't make things worse by running Henry down. He's my husband and I live with him. All I ask of you now is, will you help me?"

Jacob looked at Sarah . . . She nodded.

"All right, Doris, I'll give you the money to move, and then what? How will your husband be able to pay the rent?"

"Things are improving some . . . his practice is getting a little better. He'll take the streetcar so we can save twenty-five dollars a month on garage fees. I just know somehow we'll make it . . ."

"If you can't manage now, how will you manage in a more expensive place?"

"We will, somehow . . . I'll be more careful, but I need help to get settled . . ."

Jacob hesitated, then nodded. "So find a place and I'll pay the first month's rent—"

"But we need money for the movers and we don't have any diningroom furniture—"

"How much will it all cost?"

"I don't know. I found a flat on Beach Street for sixty-five dollars a month. The movers will cost about forty—"

"And the furniture?"

"I found a set at Redlick's for two hundred—"

"So you need about four hundred and fifty dollars, right?"

"Yes," Doris whispered.

"Fine, so I'll give you money. But listen to me, Doris, I am not going to continue to make things so all-fired easy for your husband, so he begins to expect his father-in-law to support him. . . . That's really why he doesn't try, that's why he hasn't taken out any life insurance. He thinks one day his wife is going to be an heiress—"

"Oh, please, papa. Can't you remember how it felt to be

poor? We don't want you to support us, just to help now when we need it so badly . . ."

"I told you I would, didn't I? But I want you to know I never had any help. I didn't have a rich father to go to. I got where I am . . ."

But you also wanted to get rid of me so badly that you practically threw me at Henry, she thought. To have to ask, and take, from them was choking her.

Jacob wrote out the check and handed it to her. She looked from her mother to her father, unable for the moment to show the gratitude that she knew was expected of her for what to them was a pittance.

She blinked back the tears. "I don't know how I can thank you for all this—"

"Don't be silly, Doris." Sara spoke for the first time. "We'd do a lot more for you, believe me, if Henry showed just a little initiative. But as papa said, we don't feel his attitude toward you is right. You're his responsibility . . . ."

When she gave Henry the check, she prayed she could forget what her parents had said about him. Her prayers were not answered. Hard as she tried to shut it out, the echo of papa's words rang in her ears. She had no illusions about Henry, and in a way she did feel trapped, but complaining would only add to Henry's sense of his own inadequacy in the rat race. The look on his face when she handed him the check told her how badly he already felt, and she had no desire to add to his pain.

She was not, as Rachel had said, being noble. At least she hoped she wasn't. She had no desire to play the long-suffering wife. But she also hated fights . . . Thank God, they never fought . . . she'd had enough and seen enough at home to last a lifetime.

And besides, as mama would say, she'd made her bed, she'd lie in it. Never mind that she'd had more than a gentle push in getting there . . .

It was four o'clock in the afternoon when Doris walked into Foster's Cafeteria on Powell Street. Holding Michele's hand, she picked up a tray and slid it along the metal counter. On the other side of the glass partition she saw the steam table— chicken and gravy, spaghetti, salads . . . But today she wasn't hungry. She looked down and smiled at her three-year-old daughter. If there was a true joy in her life, Michele was it.

"Would you like some Jell-O, sweetheart?"

"Could I have the red?"

"Of course, darling. Let's sit over near the window where you can see the cable cars."

Doris watched as Michele ate, but her thoughts wandered back to earlier in the day . . . "You're pregnant, Doris," Gary had said.

She had missed her period this month and although she'd hoped against hope, she wasn't really surprised. Upset, yes . . . Not because she wouldn't have loved another child, but it was difficult enough trying to raise Michele. She was rapidly outgrowing her clothes and the expenses were mounting. What was Henry going to say? She felt, ironically, empty inside. But she wasn't empty and that tiny fetus deserved more consideration. It hadn't asked to be conceived.

She had been grateful to Henry for having talked her into getting pregnant so soon after they'd married. Funny, how reluctant she had been at the time. Now, as she looked across at the child three years later, the miracle of it overwhelmed her and she almost felt guilty for having been saddened by today's revelation. Besides, she told herself, it was wrong to raise an only child. They were struggling now, so another mouth to feed wouldn't be all that bad . . .

After Michele finished, Doris asked if she would like to go and see daddy.

"Could we, mama?"

Michele loved riding the elevator up to her father's office. It was an old open-grilled cage, vintage 1910, installed the same year the Flood Building had been erected. She watched as the iron grill slid back.

They walked down the marble-floored hall until they came to the door of Dr. Henry Levin and rang the buzzer. Soon Henry was opening the door.

"Doris, I'm so glad you came down. And look at my beautiful little sweetheart," he said, picking Michele up and kissing her.

"Can I be a nurse?"

Henry laughed. "Okay, I'll make you a cap." He took a paper towel out of the dispenser and folded it, then slipped it on her head. "There you are, Nurse Michele."

"Daddy, can I have the squeezer, the one you use to clean out my ears?"

He laughed as he lifted her onto the chair near the corner sink. Michele was quickly engrossed in squeezing the rubber bulb and watching the water rise in the glass cylinder of the syringe.

Doris sat looking out to the courtyard, her mind a million miles away, and when Henry kissed her she was startled.

"How'd you like to stay downtown for a bite to eat?"

"I'd like that, Henry."

She looked strange—tired, down . . . "Did you have a fight with your beloved mother today?"

"No, why?"

"You seem so quiet. Is anything wrong?"

"Well, not exactly wrong, Henry . . . I went to see Gary this afternoon."

He frowned. "Are you feeling all right?"

"I'm feeling fine, just slightly pregnant . . ."

"How can you be pregnant?"

"Because diaphragms are only ninety-nine percent safe, as you know."

The next moments were strained. As she looked across the desk at him she suddenly felt that she had placed him in a very difficult position. But she hadn't done this as a conspiracy. Things were as rough for her as for him. For God's sake, it just happened. Still, seeing his worried face softened her anger. "I'm sorry Henry, I really am."

He took a deep breath and smiled. "Why should you be sorry, darling? It's just one of those things . . . Did Gary say how far along you are?"

"About six weeks—"

"Do you know something, Doris? I'm really happy—"

"Are you, Henry? Honestly?"

He got up and took her in his arms. "Yes, sweetheart, I am—"

She knew he wasn't, and the clearness of his attempt to cheer her touched her so that she clung to him gratefully. "Thank you, darling. You're really so understanding—"

"Understanding? Doris, I love you. We should be happy about this . . ."

"I feel better now. But please don't ever tell anyone that this was an accident. I wouldn't want our child to ever feel it was an accident and unwanted."

As she knew she had been . . .

The next morning Doris called her mother. "Good morning, mama, how are you?"

"Fine, Doris, and you?"

It's not how I am, but what. "Could I come over and see you?"

"When?"

"Now. That is, this morning—"

"All right . . . Are you bringing Michele?"

No, I'm leaving her with the governess . . . "Of course."

Sara was always so apprehensive when Michele visited. She touched everything, opened doors, closets, drawers, almost broke a piece of Dresden last week.

Doris' pulse seemed to beat a little too rapidly as she stood ringing her mother's bell.

"Michele, don't touch any of sissy's things. Okay?"

The little girl remembered being reprimanded. "I won't mommy."

Doris smiled down at her. "I know, you're a good girl."

The door was opened by Mary. "How are you, Mrs. Levin?" she asked in her soft Southern accent. "And how's my precious little sugar plum?" she said to Michele, who was clinging to her mother. "Here, let me unbutton your coat, honey . . . There we are. Your mother is in her bedroom, Mrs. Levin."

Doris found Sara sitting at her dressing table. "I'm glad to see you, mama."

"Me too, Doris." Sara kissed Michele and sent her off to the kitchen to get a glass of milk and a cookie.

"Could I have it in here, sissy?"

"No, dear. Go in with Mary like a good girl," Sara answered quickly.

"I am a good girl, mommy said so—"

Doris told her, "Of course you are, darling, but go and have something with Mary."

"Couldn't I bring it back, mommy?"

"No, honey." . . . We mustn't eat in sissy's boudoir, no crumbs on the carpet, God forbid . . .

When Sara saw Michele leave she visibly relaxed.

"Don't let me keep you from what you're doing, mama."

Sara went back to her makeup.

Why did she feel so damned uncomfortable, so unsure of herself sitting in her own mother's house? "I have some wonderful news for you, mama." Doris swallowed hard.

"Really? That would be nice for a change—"

"I'm pregnant."

Silence. Sara observed Doris's reflection in the mirror. *"How* could you allow yourself to get pregnant? Don't you take precautions?"

"Of course I do . . ."

"Well then?"

"I wanted to have another baby . . ."

Sara shook her head. "Doris, I don't understand you at all.

396

How could you think of having another child in your financial position?"

"Because I decided it was time."

"Why, are you so old? You're only twenty-two."

"Yes, but Michele is three and I didn't want to wait any longer." She listened to her own lie, and felt it was in a good cause. She was not going to admit the accident to mama, risk having the child know from her at some point and suffer for the "sin" of being unwanted as she had, even if mama didn't realize it . . . "I think it's important for children to be close in age . . ."

Close in age, Sara thought. Oh, that foolish girl . . . Rachel, for all her snootiness, was the smart one . . . she'd had her child, a son yet, and now she and her husband were off in the Bahamas sipping rum and Coca Cola . . . My God, Sara thought, if there had been precautions when she was first married . . . Well, she couldn't put her head on Doris' shoulders. If Doris wanted to struggle needlessly all the rest of her life, well, that was her decision . . . "Well, *mazel tov*. How far along are you?"

"About six weeks. Henry is so thrilled and Michele keeps asking if she's going to have a little sister or brother—"

"That's wonderful," Sara said, her tone belying her words.

Michele came back into the bedroom and climbed on to the chaise longue.

"Doris, please take her off the furniture . . ."

Doris felt the old nervous feeling with mama . . . Damn it, why did it still seem to matter to her so much if mama approved, why did it hurt so badly when she didn't . . .

"Doris, I asked you to take her off the furniture."

"Come sit on my lap, sweetheart," Doris said, lifting Michele down.

But Michele didn't want to sit on Doris' lap. "Can I play the piano, mommy?"

"Mama?"

Sara nodded.

Doris took her by the hand and they went to the living-room, where she sat Michele down on the piano bench. "Just play softly, honey."

Michele was already engrossed in the black and white keys as Doris went back to her mother's room.

"How's papa?" That was usually a good diversion.

"Fine, works terribly hard . . . Not a lazy bone in his body, even at his age. That's why he's such a success."

No question who *that* was about . . . They were almost like

397

strangers, Doris thought. What did they talk about now? Ah, Lillian . . . "Imagine, Lillian graduating this year . . ."

"Yes, it's hard to believe, but children grow up and parents are left alone."

Michele's discords on the piano were giving Sara a terrible headache. "Doris, you'll have to forgive me, but I must get dressed. Please take Michele home, she's getting a little restless."

"All right. Well, it's been nice seeing you, mama. Have a lovely afternoon—"

Sara got up and looked at Doris. "I'm happy for you, Doris . . . if this is what you want. I just hope for everybody's sake that Henry makes a better living—"

"I'm sure he will . . . but I'd be very happy if you meant it."

"Meant what, Doris? About Henry?"

"No. I wish you were happy about me having a baby. Children can be a blessing to . . ."

And a heartache and a headache, and can also make you feel guilty as hell . . .

Sara took out a five-dollar bill from her wallet and gave it to Doris. "Here, dear, take Michele to lunch. It'll be nice for you . . . And God bless you, Doris. I'd help you more if I could, but you know how little I get. Papa isn't the most generous man. I still have to fight for everything. Life isn't ever all roses."

Doris almost smiled. Mama really believed it. She had said it for so long now that in her mind it was the truth . . .

"I know, mama dear. I know."

CHAPTER FIFTY-TWO

SARA WAS preparing for Lillian's graduation as though she were making her debut into society. She did ask Lillian what she wanted, but she called Doris a dozen times a day to consult with her. *Consult* was hardly the right word; she was calling to tell Doris about her fabulous ideas. She was going to make this the extravaganza of the year.

Doris listened with one ear while her thoughts strayed back to her own graduation. She remembered coming out of her bedroom on prom night and going to the kitchen to gorge on Oreo cookies and a large glass of milk . . .

"We've hired an orchestra," Sara was saying, "and I want you to come with me to pick out the flower arrangements."

"I'd love to, mama, but in all honesty, don't you think you're going a little overboard? It's only a graduation party—"

"Do you resent Lillian, Doris? I seem to get the impression . . . Remember, I couldn't give you a party like that. I wasn't in that position at the time."

"I'm sorry, that's not what I meant—"

"Then what did you mean?"

"That I thought it might be nice to have a party at home instead of a formal dinner dance at the Palace Hotel. Unless times have changed a lot, it seems rather . . . adult."

"You forget, Doris, Lillian is going on nineteen."

"No, I remember. All right, mama, I'll go with you."

"Could you get a sitter for Michele?"

"I don't have the money. And besides, she's awfully good—"

"I'll give it to you. Please get a sitter."

Lillian was crying when she called Doris. "I've got to see you—"

"Sure, honey, come on over . . ."

Lillian started talking as soon as she walked in the door. "Oh, Doris, I don't know what I'd do without you. Mama's gone absolutely off her rocker. Do you know about the party?"

"Do I! If I had what this shindig is costing I'd be independently wealthy."

"But that's not all . . . she invited girls I hardly know. Doris, it's plain hell, I can't stand it—"

"I know, honey . . ."

"She's so possessive and she's completely taken over my life. It's as though I were some kind of a puppet. She never asks my opinion. She just goes merrily on her way. I don't understand it—"

"I do, darling. She's living her own long lost youth through you." And God help you . . . .

"But it's my life. Why doesn't she make friends of her own, get out and make a life like other women do?"

"Because it's easier for her this way. Besides, who could she be friends with? She can't even stand her own daughters, except you."

"How lucky can I get? And papa's just as bad. He interrogates me about every guy I have a date with, but all he seems interested in is who the boy's father is. I know they want the best for me, but they never let me go out with anybody I like."

"Don't let them do that to you." Doris shook her head ... "God, what a family. Rachel's disappeared and mama punishes me for reasons I don't even understand—maybe because I was unwanted, as if it were my fault ..."

Lillian looked shocked. "What do you mean by that?"

"I mean one day she let it slip in a fit of anger that she hadn't wanted me, that I was a mistake ... Isn't it great to know you weren't wanted?"

"God, what a thing to tell someone—"

"Well, mama would never get the prize for diplomacy. And papa never forgave any of us for not being boys. How many times has he said, 'You should have been a boy'?"

"She's got a new wrinkle now. You know how religious mama is? Well, she just joined Temple Emanuel and guess why?"

" 'Cause she just discovered God?"

Lillian laughed. "So that I can attend every crummy social function and meet a nice rich Jewish boy. And she has a new obsession—Steward Gold. He's going to be my escort to the party. I don't like him, but mama and papa do."

"Well, honey, you're their last chance—"

"Yes, but the point is I'd like to have a chance to make up my own mind. Is that asking too much?"

"Let me give you a little advice, darling. If you *don't* make up your own mind, you'll wind up marrying someone they choose and you'll have the rest of your life to deal with that ... *your* life, not theirs ..."

When Jacob received the bills for Lillian's party Sara and he had a true battle royal.

"You've gone crazy, absolutely crazy. How the hell do you think I earn my money? I know what's going on in that mind of yours."

"What?"

"You're trying to outdo Rachel, but this is one bill you're going to pay. I'm not giving you a dime. I'm not working this hard just so you can play your games."

"What do you mean you're not giving? Half of what you have is mine and don't forget it. Besides, what do you give me? Affection, companionship? What do I have from you? Tell me ..."

400

"You have this place, which is all you've ever wanted. But you brought up a good point. What have *you* given me? Since we've been married have I had a moment's peace? You're not a wife to me anymore, Sara, and no matter what I gave you it wouldn't be enough . . . I'm the money machine—"

"You're a machine, period."

"And you? The whole world revolves around you. This apartment isn't a home, it's somewhere I sleep—and alone at that—"

"You don't need me, Jacob . . . You're in love with your plant, your money. You have a mistress, Jacob."

Tonight's argument was more upsetting than most to Jacob. Although fights had become a way of life, this was the first time he had to face it that there were feelings he could no longer push aside. Look at your life, Jacob . . . For years his only concern had been getting ahead, becoming rich, but what had started out of concern for his family had become an obsession, a substitute for the love and feeling of belonging he had searched for all his life. Sara, of course, figured largely in his immersion in his work.

After she'd had the abortion she had become obsessed with not getting pregnant again, and the result was complete abstinence. The abortion itself was a blow to him, but he had still needed her. In fact, he had needed her more than ever, but he was compelled to face the realization that she was a woman who thought almost exclusively of herself. She had pushed him out of her life, and Jacob was not a man to beg or plead. But his resentment was too great to resist punishing her when he had a chance, and that had been one reason he had fought her so hard about money. In a sense, it was a sexual outlet for him. For a long time he had never considered sleeping with another woman. He may have grown away from Judaism, but he still believed it was a sin to commit adultery.

He had married too young. What boy of eighteen considered anything more than having met a pretty girl who brought out feelings of burning desire? It had seemed only fitting to marry. He certainly hadn't considered that she would eventually become a manipulative and, in the vernacular of the times, a neurotic woman. He laughed at how some thought she'd manipulated him into selling the house and moving. Nobody forced him to do anything he didn't want to do.

For a time the change had sustained him, but gradually he had realized that the only thing he had changed was his address. His sexual desire and loneliness had only been temporarily put to rest. He could have gone to a brothel, but the memory of that long ago scene, when he had awakened in a dirty room to find he had not only slept with a prostitute but had almost killed her, had left an impression. In fact, he still woke up from time to time with the nightmare fresh in his mind. God, how many times had he been invited to join the boys . . . But a brothel? Never.

Damn Sara for bringing up a word that had been haunting him for six months now. Mistress . . .

It had started the day Gloria Allen came to work for the meat packing company as a telephone operator. She was a beautiful young auburn-haired woman with lovely eyes, a supple body and a lilting voice that made him uncomfortably aware of her. That's why he'd reacted so when Sara had said he had a mistress. Tonight's argument brought Gloria sharply into focus. He suddenly realized he wanted to go to bed with her, and the revelation not only startled him, but made him feel terribly guilty . . .

The next day Jacob simply couldn't face going home and sitting across from Sara at that long dinner table. Not tonight . . .

He walked into the Frenchman's, the only decent restaurant in Hayward.

While waiting for his dinner to be served he looked across the room and was startled to see Gloria Allen. For a moment he was tempted to ask her to join him, then immediately dismissed the thought. With last night's revelation still fresh in his mind, that would be tempting the gods. In fact, he almost wondered if he should fire her . . .

After dinner he slid out of the booth and walked toward the cashier. When he had paid his check he turned around— only to find Gloria Allen standing behind him.

"Good evening, Mr. Sanders . . ."

He answered formally, "Good evening." He paused, then said abruptly, "Here, let me pay for that." He took the check from her hand.

"Thank you, Mr. Sanders . . ."

He held the wide door open as she stepped into the soft twilight.

"Well, goodnight, Mr. Sanders. And thank you for dinner."

"Where do you live?"

"Oh, not too far. I take the streetcar and get off one block from my place."

"Here, let me take you home——"

"You're sure it's not putting you out?"

He looked at her . . . What the hell was wrong with him? Maybe he should let her take the streetcar, but impulse overcame logic. "No, it's not putting me out. My car's across the street."

There was something sensuous about the sound of Gloria's high heels tapping against the concrete . . . He slid into the seat behind the steering wheel, and she let herself into the passenger seat and sat silently as he started the car. Except for the directions to her place, not a word was exchanged.

Soon they reached the three-story building in which she lived, and she let herself out of the car. "Well, thanks a lot, Mr. Sanders——"

Before he could respond she had shut the car door and was walking up the stairs.

Once inside she leaned against the door, feeling very embarrassed. The meeting must have been so transparent. How was she going to greet him at work tomorrow? . . .

She greeted him as usual the next morning, and his cold reply made her feel even more ridiculous.

CHAPTER FIFTY-THREE

AFTER CLOSING time Jacob sat behind the steering wheel for a long contemplative moment, then turned the key and started the ignition. Although he sat a moment longer, he knew what he was going to do.

Gloria was standing on the corner, waiting for the streetcar, when he pulled up at the curb beside her and leaned over to open the opposite door.

"Get in, Gloria, I'll drive you home . . ."

"Thank you, Mr. Sanders," she said as she got in.

"For what?"

"Driving me home——"

"Listen, do you feel like going out to dinner?"

Now her pulse raced. A few weeks ago she would have encouraged him, but tonight her instincts urged her to be sensible. Besides, he had hardly said a word to her since that meeting in the restaurant, and although she still found him attractive she was ill at ease with him.

"I'd like to, but my kids are expecting me for dinner."

"Who's with them now?"

"My mother. She has a little house in Livermore, that's where I'm going—"

"So why can't you call and tell her you're going out?"

"Because my kids live with her and I haven't seen them all week."

"Another day won't make that much difference, will it? I'd like very much to have dinner with you."

"Well . . . I suppose they'll be a little disappointed . . ."

"They'll get over it. Here's some change. Why don't you call?"

She hesitated, then took the change. . . .

The restaurant Gloria had recommended was small. There was only one other couple in the place—for which Jacob was grateful. He was beset with an assortment of feelings as he looked at Gloria across the round, candlelit table. Guilt was at the head of the list. But still, he was happy to be with Gloria. She was . . . soft, and there was a tenderness in her lovely eyes . . . although a sadness too.

After their orders had been given, Jacob said, "How old are your children?"

"My youngest, Barbara, is six and Julie is eight."

"It must be difficult raising them alone."

"Well, it hasn't been easy, but thank God for my mother—"

"Are you divorced?"

"No . . ."

"Separated?"

"Deserted—"

Deserted . . . He knew what that felt like. No one ever forgot, no matter how long one lived. From his childhood in Poland through his marriage with Sara, it seemed he'd been deserted time and time again. At this moment he felt a special bond with this young woman sitting across from him. "How long have you been alone?"

"Since Barbara was born . . . And you don't know how grateful I was for the job, Mr. Sanders."

He understood that too. The sign in Mr. Mendlebaum's window . . . he had been alone until they took him in and gave him a job . . . and their love . . .

"Why haven't you gotten a divorce? You can, you know."

"I suppose, but I don't need a divorce. I don't want to get married again, ever—"

"How do you know? You're a young woman."

"I just know, Mr. Sanders."

404

When the food was brought to the table he asked, "Do you come here often?"

"No, only once before . . ."

Did she have a lover, he wondered? "That night I saw you at the Frenchman's, I thought you were meeting someone . . ."

"I was just feeling very down and thought I'd give myself a treat."

She immediately regretted the lie. She knew now that he was interested in her. Why couldn't people simply say what they felt instead of playing games? "Did you ever do anything you regretted, Mr. Sanders?"

"More than once. What do you regret?"

"I deliberately went to dinner that night, knowing you were going to be there."

He looked puzzled. "How did you know that?"

"When you told me to call your house, I just figured you were going to have dinner alone. That's how I happened to be in the restaurant that night. I even know why you weren't going home . . . When you work as an operator you find out an awful lot of things and I just gave way to an impulse . . ."

Jacob was shocked that she'd thought about him at all. And in those terms? He didn't think of himself as a romantic figure but she seemed to be telling him that he was.

"Gloria, I have a very . . . warm feeling for you. In fact, I have for quite some time now—"

She looked bewildered. He had all but ignored her in the office.

"We're two rather lonely people, Gloria, and I think we need each other."

"I need you, but I want to make it clear right now that it has nothing to do with your wealth or your position. There's just something good in you that I sense, and I want to know that part of you better and to share things with you. I hope that doesn't sound too forward . . . it's the plain truth . . ."

He reached over and took her hand. Nobody had ever said such things to him. In the beginning Sara had said she loved him, but he learned she didn't love him as much as the security of being with a man who would protect her. Lotte had said she loved him, but he suspected her feelings might have been like Sara's. Who had ever liked him for himself . . . ?

"I can't promise you anything, Gloria. It's only right that I tell you I can never get a divorce—"

405

"I don't expect that. You have children and you must love them a great deal."

"That's not the reason."

"I hope this won't hurt your feelings, but I feel very sorry for your wife—"

"For my wife?"

"Yes. She has a good man and for reasons I couldn't guess she doesn't know it. I think all you ever wanted was . . . to be loved, and appreciated?"

This *stranger* seemed to know so much more about him, and he had already told her things he'd never told anyone. . . .

They drove to Gloria's small studio apartment, and there Jacob discovered something he had never experienced—the kind of lovemaking that was uniquely shared by two people. Even early in his marriage Sara had been passive, as if she were somewhere else and it wasn't happening to her . . .

Later as they lay together he said, "Gloria, I don't know what to do for you. You've made me feel so good . . . and I'd like us to continue seeing each other, but will you be satisfied with that?"

"I never thought I'd have you on any terms—"

"Maybe you should stop working? I'll take care of you and your children—"

"No. If I did, look what I'd be giving up. I'll see you more than your family."

"All right, all right, anything you want—"

"I want you, Jack, just the way it is now and just the way you are now."

He heard what she said, but it was hard to believe it. He'd make the effort . . .

The longer the liaison with Gloria lasted, the more secure he became. He didn't have to worry about Sara seeing a change in him. His routine was the same, and he was no more or less demonstrative with her than he'd ever been. He also knew it would never occur to her to think that he might be . . . unfaithful. She thought she had him securely under her thumb and that he was so busy that the last thing in the world he'd have time for was another woman . . . An ill-chosen word . . . "mistress" . . . He almost thanked her for it. It had been the catalyst to something, the deep need in him that had been building longer than even he knew . . . . He'd found a woman who gave of herself, who wanted him for himself, and wanted nothing more . . .

406

In the beginning it was difficult to convince himself she wouldn't turn away from him one day—and that kept him from trusting her completely. Even during their most intimate moments, he had thoughts of . . . his mother abandoning him, Lotte betraying him, Sara's self-centeredness that pushed him out of her life—he'd never forgotten the abortion, he always lived with the haunting feeling that the child she destroyed might have been that boy . . .

As his relationship with Gloria went on he learned to accept that she was what she seemed . . . a woman of understanding, of compassion. He thanked God for her . . . she gave him so much and demanded nothing in return. And because she did, Jacob wanted to do more and more for her, give her as much as she would accept. It was difficult not to make comparisons between this girl who took his gifts only reluctantly and his family, who always seemed to want more . . .

Nights after the passion was spent he would lie there with his arms around her and allow himself to talk about his childhood. She helped him to do it, seeming to feel the pain he felt. Only to her could he confess his boyish heartbreak over Lotte that never left the man, his maddening frustrations with Sara. Gloria was, as he told her, the only person he'd actually felt loved by, and it was a continuing mystery to him how or why she had fallen in love with him.

"I think," she said, "it was because I sensed from the start how much you needed to be loved, how open you were to it, even if you didn't know it. And your need was also mine . . . I needed to give . . ." She laughed lightly. "At the *very* first I didn't really know why I felt drawn to you . . . and then I did. I realized you were afraid of me . . . yes, you were . . . and you tried to hide it. You're a man who never showed his true feelings. Call it instinct, anything you want. Maybe that's where love begins, I don't know." She kissed him and smiled. "But you underestimate yourself, Mr. Jack Sanders. It wasn't just instinct on my part. You also happen to be just about the most handsome man I've ever met. In or out of bed."

She knew he wouldn't respond to the compliment, nor did she expect him to. Compliments embarrassed him. Still, she knew he not only liked hearing it, but *needed* to hear it said. She also knew he could never use the word *love* or return a compliment, but the way he made love left no doubt about his feelings.

CHAPTER FIFTY-FOUR

DORIS SAT in the park watching as Michele played in the sandbox. It was her ninth month now, and her belly bulged so that she could make a bet it was going to be triplets. Nothing would surprise her.

The thoughts that crept into Doris' head were surely not new, but somehow, today they were more acute. You're feeling more than a little sorry for yourself, she told herself. You're damned right, but why now? Well, I suppose it has to do with what's inside my belly and that adorable little girl going down the slide. I'm trying to sort out the pieces, to figure out what brought me to here, to now . . . but to answer that would take me back to my parents' childhoods, even further back than that. Still, I suppose it's all one and the same, the way one generation affects the next. . . . All right, then, so let's talk about mama and papa. Papa first . . . he came out of a different set of circumstances than mama, but both were unloved, unwanted—at least papa *thought* he was unwanted, which is what counts. Their similarities might have been what had attracted them to each other from the start, but the similarities had eventually led to driving them apart— and their children had been paying for it ever since . . . Two people meet, their children's destinies as well as their own seem set. In our case, our parents are people who probably shouldn't have been parents in the first place. Just because people can give birth doesn't qualify them to take on the responsibility of molding other human beings. Children need understanding, not just a roof over their heads and food in their stomachs. They need *love* to grow on too . . .

Of course, I'd love to give my children all the things I didn't have, but if I can't do that, my children are *still* going to get all the love and understanding I possess. I just can't remember a kiss from papa or a kind loving word from mama—but they didn't understand each other, so how could they understand us, give to us . . . ? The only one of us who fought back was Rachel, and she escaped. Hooray for her. Me? I'm like a frightened bunny, scared to death of everyone, afraid of rejection, of insecurity . . . I'm afraid to let go for fear I'll end up living my old age on charity. And what did they give us spiritually? Nothing much, I'm sorry to say.

Well, the time has come for you, Doris, to take the clue from all their mistakes and *reverse* them, figure out how you're going to raise your children and what you owe them. Okay, Doris ... you've thought it all out and you're still sitting on the bench. Only remember one thing before you go home—love your kids, not till it hurts, but till it makes you feel good. They're all you have or maybe ever will. But they don't belong to you. They're only on loan, so love and enjoy them while you can, then let go when the time comes. Don't hold the strings, and never make them feel beholden to you. They don't owe you anything ... I'm going to be the best damned mother because I'm going to listen. No sermons. And I'm going to give them spiritual values so they'll have something to lean on ...

The day suddenly became cold. Doris got up quickly and tried to button her coat, but she couldn't quite close it over her belly. She walked to Michele and hugged her. "You've been such a good girl, Michele." Oh, God, I love you, she said silently.

Michele heard the sound of the ice cream man. "Could I have an ice cream, mommy?"

Doris blinked back the tears. "You know you beat me to it, I was just going to ask you." ...

It was seven in the morning. Doris woke Henry up, pushing him urgently. "Darling, I think I'm in labor—"

"My God, when did it start?"

"About five—"

"And you tell me now?"

"Don't get excited, I have a feeling it won't be for quite a while. No, please get dressed and I'll get Michele. What do you feel like having for breakfast?"

"Breakfast? How can you think of that? Just get ready. I'll take care of breakfast later."

As they were about to leave, Doris said, "Henry, take Michele and I'll be right down, okay?"

"What do you want to do, the kitchen floor?"

"I did that yesterday. Go ahead, dear—"

"This is ridiculous," he said, taking Michele's hand.

Doris went from room to room. It wasn't much to look at, but it was home. Please God, let me come back with a healthy child ...

When they arrived at Henry's mother's house Doris felt a lump in her throat at the thought of being parted from Michele. "Let me look at my little girl."

"Mommy, do you have to go?"

"Would I leave you if I didn't have to? We talked about this, remember?"

"I'll miss you—"

"And I'll miss you too, but it's only for a little while. I'll call you every day and you can call me too, honey."

Michele nodded reluctantly, took her father's hand and went up the stairs to her grandmother's. . . .

At eleven that morning, the contractions were coming closer together. She pressed the button to summon the nurse and asked her to call Henry.

Soon he was standing at the edge of the bed, taking her hand in his. "Are you all right, darling?"

"Couldn't be better. I just spoke to Michele—"

"You called?"

"Yes, I didn't want her to feel . . . alone . . . Darling, please call my mother."

He needed Sara like a hole in the head, but he picked up the phone and called. "Sara, Doris is in the hospital."

In spite of her feelings about Doris' pregnancy, she became anxious when she remembered her last delivery. "How is she?"

"Well, nothing much has happened yet."

"When did you take her?"

"About nine."

"Nine, and you just called? Why do you do this to me, Henry?"

"Sara, *please*, let's not start that today."

There was a long silence. "I'll be there." . . . She hung up and called the plant to tell Jacocb.

"Doris is in the hospital, Jacob—"

"You go and I'll meet you there."

"I'm very nervous . . ."

"With the help of God she'll be all right." But he was as nervous as she was. For some reason, when Doris was sick or in any trouble it came crashing down on him like a hammer. He always remembered when Sara had given birth to Lillian how he'd taken care of Doris, hovered over her. He had felt so responsible . . . protective . . . needed. Today he felt the same way . . . .

Jacob found Sara and Henry waiting.

"How are things, Henry?"

"Thank God, not like the last time. You can go in to see her for a minute, if you want."

He walked down the hall eagerly but when he saw his child

410

he couldn't understand why he felt so uncomfortable inside himself. Had he, after all, been a bad father? God, he'd tried so hard when they were growing up to give them a good life—

"Papa, I'm glad you're here."

"I am too, Doris. Is it very bad?"

"Pretty bad, but it'll soon be over. Hold my hand."

With tears in his eyes, he took her outstretched hand and held it. There was another contraction coming on, and Doris let out a scream that cut through him too. Why couldn't he help this child now? A peculiar thought, but this it was . . .

Before he could say anything more the door opened and Gary Goldman walked in. "I think you'd better leave. I want to examine Doris."

"I'll be outside with your mother, Doris." He blew his nose. Why was he feeling this way? He proceeded to pace the halls, along with Henry. . . .

At five that afternoon the door to Doris' room was opened and she was wheeled down the hall. The next forty minutes seemed an eternity.

At long last the doctor came out. "Well, Henry, you have a boy . . . nine pounds, two and a half ounces."

Henry hugged him joyfully. "A boy! My God, I have a son—"

Jacob and Sara looked at each other, one with envy, and one with guilt.

"Thank God it's over," Jacob said, "and congratulations, Henry. I guess you're a better man than I was."

Sara's anxiety abruptly turned to anger . . . he was saying that to remind her . . .

Henry answered, "Not 'better.' You had Doris." . . . The next morning a happy Doris greeted her husband. "Well, one thing we can do is make beautiful children together. Henry, I'm so happy I could scream. I saw that beautiful little darling with ten fingers and ten toes . . . my father must have been thrilled."

"For the first time since I've known him. I think he was actually humble."

"Because you did something he couldn't. You surely did . . . Would you mind if we called the baby Gary? I think he should be immortalized."

"That's beautiful, and it will please him."

After Henry left, Doris lay thinking what a glorious feeling motherhood gave her. Thank God, she thought, some destinies are taken out of our hands. Otherwise, she wouldn't be

411

here now, reveling in the gift that had just been given her. Thank you, God, for giving me a healthy baby. I'm going to try to earn the right to be called mother. Love and devotion and understanding are a child's birthright. And I'm going to see to it that they have some spiritual belief, something to sustain them. I guess in a way I should thank mama and papa for making me so aware of what parents owe the lives they're responsible for ... She picked up the phone and called Michele.

"Darling, you have a baby brother."

"I wish it was a sister—"

"Yes, but this way you're still my one and only very special little girl."

Michele considered this, and decided she liked it.

Chapter Fifty-Five

LILLIAN HAD graduated from high school in June, and there were feelings inside her that cried out for her to do something constructive with her life. But she also felt she never would. Mama wanted her to become a social butterfly, and that's pretty much what she had become. She went along ...

On Saturday afternoons she and her friends met at the Sir Francis Drake Hotel. It wasn't a revival of the tea dancing. Rum and Coca Cola had replaced tea and tiny sandwiches, ladies' hems were slightly lower, trousers had zippers, and couples rumbaed instead of dancing cheek-to-cheek. But the girls still sat at round tables and eagerly waited to be asked to dance. And now they smoked. It was not only acceptable for women to smoke in public, but almost a must in the new sophistication. To be caught without a cigarette was to be labeled a "square." Although Lillian didn't like cigarettes and would never have dared smoke in front of mama or papa, that was her one bit of rebellion.

This afternoon she sat watching her best friend, Amy Harris, dancing to "Begin the Beguine."

When was her beguine going to begin? She was so tired of her life, and mama, and all the guilt she generated that she felt melancholy even now, right in the midst of all the excitement that was going on around her. Lillian knew she would never live up to mama's expectations; she wasn't the beautiful, winsome creature mama had tried so hard to make her.

What mama would have liked was to see herself reflected in Lillian. Pretty, gregarious, cultured—the kind of personality her mother saw in herself. Lillian found it all but impossible to find her own identity because mama practically lived inside her skin. She didn't own a single dress she liked—if she liked it, mama didn't. Mama screened the fellows she went out with. And papa never asked if the boy was nice, only who the boy's father was and what he did.

Now they were trying to cram Stewart Gold down her throat. The Golds were an old established family of attorneys, and that pleased papa very much. He had even made it a point to look up their Dunn and Bradstreet rating. Lillian had as much strength as a jellyfish when it came to defying them, but she knew she would eventually have to take a stand on Stewart Gold. Marriage was something she was going to have to decide for herself. She shuddered at the prospect of telling them, knowing papa felt it was her responsibility to make up for the experiences they'd had with Rachel and Doris . . .

Lillian stopped twirling the straw in her coke and looked up when she realized that someone was standing by her chair.

"Hi. Feel like dancing?"

What she saw was a young man about six feet tall, with a handsome face, square chin, black eyes and thick dark hair to match. "Sure, why not?"

"You're a good dancer," he said after they'd been on the dance floor a few minutes.

At least the dancing lessons weren't a total loss. Maybe mama was finally getting her money's worth. "Thanks, so are you—"

When the music stopped, he took her back to her table and walked away without a word.

Amy had been watching. "My God, who was that?"

"I don't know. Except for Clark Gable, everybody's face looks the same here."

"I always find out," Amy said, applying a little extra lipstick.

"Really? Did you ever think of joining the FBI?"

"Oh, Lillian, you're so backward in some things."

"That's an understatement. In everything—"

"I just meant you weren't aggressive enough."

"What did you want me to do? Seduce him on the floor?"

"I'll ignore that. But holy cow, he's really gorgeous."

"So why don't *you* go over and talk to him? He's standing at the bar."

"I thought you didn't notice."

"I noticed. So?"

"So why don't *you* go over and talk to him."

"And would I gain your respect plus a medal for aggressiveness?"

"You sure would." Amy smiled. "Dare you . . ."

Lillian looked toward the bar. She began to stand up, but suddenly felt that it would be too brazen to approach him. She sat down again.

"For God's sake, Lillian, do just one thing that's a little unconventional, will you? Stop being so inhibited. Mama's not going to spank you. Get out of your playpen. You're a big girl now."

Lillian got up quickly and walked across to the bar just as the music began. "What's your name and would you like to dance?" She could hardly believe those words had come from her virginal mouth.

"My name is Jerry Gould and I'd love to . . ."

When they danced past the table where Amy sat, Lillian glanced at her and winked.

When the music stopped, Jerry Gould said, "Thanks for asking me to dance, and what's your name?"

"Lillian Sanders, and it's been my pleasure."

"You're a terrific girl, Lillian Sanders."

"You must be new in town, because everyone knows that." She was getting a smart mouth on her, like Doris . . . and for the same reason . . . ? To cover her fear . . . ?

"As a matter of fact, I am new in town. That's probably why I just found out. Would you like to join my friends and me for dinner?"

"Who are your friends?"

"The two fellows standing over there at the bar."

"Where are you going?"

"To Chinatown."

"I don't know. I'm with a friend . . ."

"Ask her to come along. Incidently, this is going to have to be Dutch treat. I don't have very much money."

"That's okay. Let's talk to Amy." She introduced them, then said, "Jerry wants us to join him and his friends for dinner."

"What about Arlene's party tonight?"

"I just came down with a very bad cold."

I've created a monster, Amy thought. "Well, thanks a lot, Lillian, but I'm going to the party."

"Have a good time . . ."

"I will. Listen, I have to powder my nose. Want to come?"

"Sure. Be right back, Jerry . . ."

On their way to the ladies room Amy said, "You sure grew up in a hurry. I didn't want you to make a lifetime hobby of picking fellows up, I just wanted you to see how much fun it is to flirt."

"Well, you're right. It was fun."

"But fun is fun, Lillian. You can't go out with three guys you don't know anything about."

"You just said the wrong thing. You sounded like my mother. As you suggested, I'm getting out of my playpen."

"Lillian, this is crazy, believe me—"

"I believe you, but I want to be crazy."

"How will you explain it to your mother?"

"Did you ever hear of less than the truth?"

"But suppose she finds out?"

"She won't unless you tell. Besides, I think it's about time to break the tradition. In my case, honesty doesn't pay."

"You know the way she checks on you. Remember the night I slept over and your mother called me the next day to ask what you had for breakfast?"

"Do I remember? She asked me the same thing. Only she had to call you to verify that I had toast and coffee. She's paranoid about being thin. When I left today she said, 'Watch your diet.' That was her good-by."

"How are you going to manage?"

"I'll call and say I'm going home with you."

"But she knows about Arlene's party. And what about Stewart? Besides, you have to change your dress for the party."

Lillian was stumped. Here she was, nineteen years old, and still having to check in with mama on every detail of her life. She'd never break out at this rate, and had no idea how to go about it. "Okay, Amy, you're so worldly, how do you think I should handle this? I really want to go out with this Jerry Gould, just for the hell of it."

"I'm against it . . . But let's think. Call Stewart and tell him you don't feel like going to Arlene's and to meet you for dinner instead."

"What will that solve? I want to go out with Jerry."

"Yes, but if he joins you, it would give you a sort of cover. Then you could have a headache, ditch him and meet Jerry later."

"How am I going to explain three guys? Tell you what I'm

going to do, I'll call Stewart and say a cousin of mine just came in from Cleveland unexpectedly, then I'll call mama and say I don't have time to come home to change my dress for Arlene's party because it's informal."

"I think you're nuts, Lillian, but maybe you can get away with it."

"I'm sure it's nuts, but maybe once God will be on my side. Since she doesn't believe me when I tell the truth, she just might believe me when I tell a lie. I don't know, Amy, I feel pretty jittery about it, but I want to do it . . ."

"Well, if you don't get back, Romeo will be gone. Talk to you tomorrow. Keep your fingers crossed."

"As well as a few other things. I'd better make my phone calls." . . .

Lillian's heart pounded as she told her mother that she was going to wear the same dress to the party.

"A sheer wool, Lillian? I don't know, it just doesn't sound like a party dress to me."

"Don't worry about it. Really. I'll get some beads from Amy and it'll jazz up the outfit."

"What time will you be home?"

"Around twelve."

"Tell Stewart to drive carefully."

No, he's going to speed right down Market Street. "I'll tell him."

Now for Stewart . . . "Sorry about breaking the news at the last minute, but it was so unexpected—"

"Why don't you bring her along?"

"She wouldn't feel comfortable, but you have a good time. And incidentally, I won't be home tomorrow . . ."

"Where are you going?" he said with an irritability that Lillian resented. She wasn't beholden to him. They weren't engaged or going steady, although he thought so—and so did mama and papa. "My mother and I are taking my cousin to Carmel for a few days." At least that would keep him from calling the house. If only he'd back off, but no such luck.

"Well . . ." Stewart said, "I can't say I'm not disappointed about tonight."

"Me too, but it's just one of those things."

"Yes, well, have a good time. When you come back I'd like to meet your cousin and take you both to dinner."

She doubted that Stewart was going for any of this, but she told herself she didn't care. What bothered her was her trembling when she hung up. My God, it was hard climbing

416

out of that playpen . . . She composed herself and walked back to join Jerry and his two friends, Nat Fried and Mike Robinson . . .

As they left the hotel Jerry said, "Do you mind walking?"

"Not at all, but I have my car parked in the garage." . . .

It wasn't until after the waiter took their order and had brought them their drinks that Lillian began to relax. This was the first time she'd had anything stronger than a Pink Lady, but whatever this concoction was it certainly helped to soothe the nerves. The lights were dim and Jerry looked like Cary Grant. Funny, she thought, Henry had looked like Clark Gable when she first saw him . . . It sure took a lot of *chutzpah* to do what she had done tonight. In fact, her boldness still frightened her. Amy was right, this was crazy. But still, it was more fun than she had ever had in her life.

"I'm going to have another one," she announced.

"Those drinks aren't as innocent as they look. They creep up on you," Jerry warned.

"Really? Did you ever see a drunken coconut?" Lillian said, thinking it must have been pretty witty because they all laughed.

"Never. You're absolutely right. I'll have another one too."

"Make it three," Mike said.

"Four. The coconuts have got to make a living," Nat wittily added.

Halfway through the second drink Lillian thought, Now this is a party, a real party. She felt like quite the *femme fatale*, out with three good-looking guys. If she only had the nerve to invite them home for a nightcap. Wouldn't *that* be something? But that brave she wasn't . . .

Now the food was being passed back and forth and Lillian was sampling a little of each dish. "This is really delicious, Jerry."

"I told you, best and cheapest dinner in town. Here, how about a little more almond duck?"

"Would you like some more rice?" Nat asked.

She'd never felt so at ease and happy in her whole life. She turned to Jerry. "How did you all meet?"

"We grew up in the Bronx together and decided to come west and make our fortune." He laughed. Lucky if he had ten bucks on him . . .

"Do you like it here?"

"I love it. What about you?"

"Native Californian."

"You mean people are really born in this state? I don't believe it."

"Swear . . . I was born in Oakland, California, that great metropolis across the bay." . . .

When she finally looked at her wristwatch it was eleven-thirty, and that could mean trouble. "I really hate to break this up, but I've got to go. It's been great. What do I owe?"

She settled her share and then got up to leave, but Jerry stopped her. "You're not going home alone at this hour. I'll go with you."

"And how would you get to where you live from my place?"

"Where do you live?"

"On Mason and Sacramento."

"Near the Fairmont Hotel?"

"The same."

"In that case I can walk it. I live on Golden Gate and Hyde."

"You don't have to, Jerry, really—"

"I don't have to do anything, but I want to." . . .

Lillian parked the car a block away from her building—she didn't want the doorman to see her. They talked for a few more minutes, then she said, "I really have to go. It was the best time I've had in a long time . . ."

"Me too. You know, Mike had to drag me there this afternoon. I almost didn't go."

"Well, I did something tonight I've never done before."

"What?"

"Pick a fellow up—"

"Is that what you did?"

She laughed. "You know I did."

"So what? It was harmless enough."

"But now that I think about it, it could have been the other way around."

"Sure could have, but I have a feeling you wouldn't go out with anybody you didn't trust."

"How do you know so much about me?"

"Just instinct. I think you're a very classy girl, Lillian."

"Thanks. Is that the way you tell if someone is, or isn't, a pushover?"

"Sure, if you'd come on too strong I would have treated you differently."

"I'm going to take that as a compliment."

"That's the way it was intended—"

"Thank you. Again, it was one of the best times I've ever had."

Jerry laughed. "It doesn't take much to make you happy, does it?"

"I wouldn't say that. It takes a lot, and that's why I had such a good time."

Jerry got out of the car and came around to her side. "Well, goodnight. Hope I see you around."

"I go to the Drake every Saturday—"

Jerry smiled, nodded and walked down the Jones Street hill.

When Jerry opened the door to his room, Mike was reading the Sunday paper in the twin bed next to his. Looking up, he asked, "Well, how did it go?"

"How did what go?"

"The price of bananas in Guatemala . . . Lillian, stupid."

"Why is that your business?"

"I know you didn't screw her but—"

"But *nothing*, I didn't even kiss her goodnight."

"You didn't like her, huh?"

"I liked her very much."

"You're a *putz*, you know that?"

"Thanks," Jerry said, getting out of his trousers.

"You're not only a *putz* but a *schmuck*," Mike went on. "The first classy girl you met since you've been here and—

"Will you leave me the hell alone?"

"Why? Someone has to take care of you."

"For God's sake, Mike, you should see where she lives. What the hell would she want to go out with me for?"

"She did tonight . . ."

"Tonight was for kicks. She wanted to go slumming, see how the other half from the Bronx lives."

"She went out with you because she likes you, dummy, and if you had a brain in your head you'd rush her. The way to get ahead in this world is either to have a rich father or marry a rich girl."

"If anyone needs their head examined it's you, buddy. Even if I was crazy about her, what would she want with a guy who sells ties at Roos Brothers?"

"Because, as you said earlier tonight, you're fascinating."

"Very fascinating. I couldn't even pay for her dinner. I felt rotten taking four dollars from her."

"She didn't seem to mind—"

"No, because she was out for kicks tonight."

"Well, let me tell you. If I had such *mazel* I wouldn't let it slip through my hands. You can fall in love with a rich girl—in fact, it wouldn't be too hard. She's a good-looking broad—"

"She's not a broad. Rich, yes, and good-looking—but *not* a broad."

When Jerry walked into the bathroom and shut the door behind him, Mike shook his head, as though the loss were his own.

Lillian sat looking at the entrance door of the Drake for two Saturdays.

"Well," she said to Amy, "I guess I just don't have what it takes. I really thought he'd call."

"You didn't give him your number."

"He's a big boy. He could have looked it up in the phone book."

"Well, so what did you lose?"

"A lot. I liked him—"

"Lillian, don't tempt the fates. You got away with it once, but even if he called, would you bring him home?"

"I've thought about it a lot, Amy. If I have to repent for my sins against my parents for the rest of my life, I'm going to marry who *I* want."

"He hasn't even called!"

"I wasn't talking about him in particular. I meant anyone who loves me and I feel the same about. I'm not going to let them do to me what they did to Doris, and Rachel too in a way."

"Lillian, don't look now, but guess who just came through the door."

Lillian didn't dare look toward the door. She took out a Camel and lit it. God, she was nervous. Suddenly she felt him standing at her side.

"Hi, Lillian. Want to dance?"

She smiled and got up without a word. They danced silently and she couldn't bring herself to meet his eyes, but when the dance ended he asked if he could buy her a drink.

As she perched herself on the stool next to him, she said, "Mike must have been very persuasive . . ."

"He had nothing to do with it this time. I just wanted to see if you were for real."

420

"What do you think?"

"You're for real ... Can I take you out to dinner? I got paid today."

"Could we go to the same place?"

"Why, are you that crazy about coconuts?"

"No, about you—" She heard herself say it, and couldn't believe it ...

"Really? After one meeting—?"

"After one meeting. I've been seeing someone for several years ... zero."

Jerry laughed. "Funny about chemistry."

"I don't know much about chemistry. It wasn't my best subject."

"What was?"

"I guess I did postgraduate work in feelings."

"Good subject ... feel like dancing?"

Lillian passed Amy's table without even seeing her. All she was aware of was Jerry touching the tips of her fingers. She wasn't dancing, she was floating—five feet off the ground. ...

She sat at ease in the dim light of the restaurant and listened to Jerry's voice as he answered her questions ...

"I didn't see any reason to stay in New York after my mother died. She was all I had."

"Tell me about her."

"Tell you about her? She was just a great person. When I was thirteen—incidently, do you know anything about *bar mitzvahs?*"

"Of course, I'm Jewish. Couldn't you tell?"

"No, why should I? Your name is Sanders."

"Yes, but my nose isn't—"

He looked carefully. "Your nose? I think it's beautiful. Where did you get that idea?"

"From my mother, I guess ... she's a little unhappy because she thinks it looks like hers. That's the only flaw I have in her eyes. Otherwise, I'm perfect."

"Forgive me, but I don't think she ever took a good look at your profile."

Lillian smiled. "There's a lot of things she never looked at ... well, you were telling me about your mother and your *bar mitzvah.*"

"Right. My father had a stroke two days before, and obviously I thought she was going to cancel the *bar mitzvah.*" Jerry paused as though he were reliving the moment ... "She was broken-hearted, of course, but she insisted on going

421

ahead with it. That's just the kind of person she was. She took care of my father until the day he died. She was a wonderful mother, and wife . . ."

"You're a very lucky fellow, Jerry. It must be marvelous to have all those memories."

"You sound sort of strange, as though in some way you're almost jealous of me . . ."

"Well, it doesn't take you long to catch on—"

"With all you've got?"

"Well, I just couldn't talk about my family in the glowing terms you use for yours."

He was hesitant about pressing her on what was obviously a painful subject, and so he grasped at the first thought that came to mind. "What do you do?"

"That's one of the problems. I don't really do anything, and from the looks of things, I doubt I'll ever win the Florence Nightingale prize."

"What about the men in your life?"

"Men in my life? I date, but no one I could think of getting serious with. What about you?"

"Oh, pretty much the same. But I couldn't think of getting serious even if I did meet the right girl."

"Why?"

"It's a little tough to support someone on the salary I get. Selling ties at Roos Brothers isn't the best paying job in the world."

"Don't people ever get married just *because* or *in spite of* anymore? It seems people no longer go by their hearts, only their heads—"

"It's obvious you've never been poor, Lillian."

"That's how much you know. You think the Sanderses were born with silver spoons? We lived in a crummy house in Oakland until about five years ago. That's when my mother decided that we should move to San Francisco."

"Yeah, but it takes a lot of dough to live the way you're living. How did you get from rags to riches in so short a time? Did your father win the sweepstakes?"

"Hardly. And besides, it wasn't so short a time. My father's been a wealthy man for a long time . . . he just had to get used to the idea."

"What's he like?"

"Strong, handsome. He's also really tough . . . difficult. Everyone who works for him is so . . . subservient that you'd think he was running for God in the next election."

"You sound bitter. I'd have never believed it."

"Well, it just goes to show you can never tell too much about anyone when they've had too many coconuts to drink . . . Yes, as a matter of fact, I guess I am a little bit bitter. For instance, I'd love to take you home and say, 'Mama, papa, I want you to meet Jerry Gould—' "

"And you can't do that?"

"The understatement of the year."

He was beginning to get the picture. "Do they know you're out with me?"

"Are you kidding? Do you have a Dunn and Bradstreet, Jerry?"

"I have exactly twenty-two dollars and fifty-two cents. Do you think that would qualify me? . . . By the way, why *did* you go out with me tonight?"

"Did you ever hear of liking someone? I just happen to like you a whole lot, Jerry."

"Well, I take that as a very great compliment . . . but it doesn't make things any easier. Much as I'd like to go on seeing you, what you've just told me seems to make that impossible."

"Not as far as I'm concerned."

"You're not only beautiful, you're also smart. You're the reason I came today. In fact, I spent a week debating the issue. But maybe I came to the wrong decision. Now that I know about your situation, there just doesn't seem to be any place for us to go from here."

"I wouldn't say that. I've spent my whole life being obedient, and it's meant that I've never had anything I really wanted. But this one time, Jerry, if I have any guts at all, I'm going to do something I want—and that's to keep on seeing you."

"What's that going to prove?"

"If you feel the same way I do, let's keep meeting and then worry about it."

Jerry sat back for a moment and looked at her. "There's a very fine line between liking and loving, Lillian. What then?"

"Let's wait until we cross that line, if we do . . ."

Amy's loyalty and Lillian's growing skill in deceiving her mother allowed Lillian and Jerry to see each other frequently during the next few months. The initial chemistry between them had only grown stronger; as Jerry had predicted, the liking had grown to love.

One Saturday evening Lillian sat in their favorite Chinese restaurant, waiting forty-five minutes for Jerry. Finally she began to worry that something had happened to him, and she went to the phone and called his hotel—only to be told that Mr. Gould had picked up his key and was in his room. She looked at her watch. It was nine-thirty. Suddenly she knew why he hadn't come.

She left the restaurant and drove to his hotel. She didn't care if it was brazen or not, nor was she going to worry about the consequences.

It was ten o'clock when she knocked on his door. As she stood in front of it, her anger began to turn to anxiety. When the door opened, the shock on his face was undisguised.

"Would you like to come in?" he finally asked.

"I thought you'd never ask." She walked in and looked vaguely about the small room while Jerry closed the door.

"You're angry at me for not meeting you tonight, and I can't say I blame you."

"No, I'm not angry, just a little shocked that you're such a coward."

"I guess you're right . . . except that when you're confused about things you can do the wrong thing—"

"And why are you so confused?"

"Oh, come on, Lillian. It's no big fat secret I've fallen in love with you. And for your sake I just thought the best thing to do was to get out of your life—"

"Why, what makes you think that would be the best thing for *my* life?"

"Well, what are you going to do, keep me in a closet forever?"

"No, as a matter of fact I'm taking you out of the closet right now. Get dressed. You're going to meet my parents."

"Now wait a minute, Lillian, this isn't right. I'm not going to walk in like some sort of damn charity case. What I did tonight was not impulsive—it was inconsiderate, but it wasn't impulsive. Unfortunately for me, I had to meet you, the right girl from the wrong neighborhood. I deliberately did this to get out of your life. And believe me, lady, that's not so easy."

"If that's really the truth, then get dressed."

He stood there shaking his head. "What do you think is going to happen when you bring me home? What are you going to say? Meet Jerry Gould, I'm in love with him, I want to get married?"

"The bombs are going to fly, anyway, Jerry. Are you ready for that?"

"Yes, I'm ready. But this is the first time in your life you've

424

decided to do something you want and I think you're doing it the wrong way."

"So what do you suggest?"

"That you go home and tell your family about me before you bring me there. You'll make it easier on everybody, especially yourself."

She smiled. "Okay, but be prepared."

"And you'd better be prepared, Lillian, because I only make a hundred and twenty-five dollars a month. That probably covers your stocking bill. Are you ready for that?"

"You bet I am. As a matter of fact, I'm going to get a job."

"Well, you can't say I didn't give you a chance, Lillian. Except, damn it, I do love you and today was hell. Ever since I've known you it's been hell, because I know damned well I'm wrong for you—"

"You're getting to sound a little bit like my parents, Jerry. Remember I told you I took a postgraduate course in feelings? You're right for me, Jerry. I *love* you . . . thank God, Mike made you go to the Drake that day."

They both smiled, embraced tenderly, then more warmly . . .

Sara was so shocked that she felt suddenly faint, disoriented. Lillian had been her last hope . . . She sat down and started to cry hopelessly. "How could you have deceived me like this, Lillian? How? I've done everything possible so that you would marry the right man . . ."

"I have met the right man, for me."

"*No!*" Jacob weighed in. "Stewart Gold is the right man for you. How do you pick up with a nobody at a bar? You've been seeing him and haven't said a word. If he was anything so special, why did you keep him a secret?"

"Because of what's happening now. But to begin with, Jerry Gould doesn't happen to be a nobody. He's a man I'm in love with, and I'm not in love with Stewart Gold. Papa, for the first time in my life I'm going to say what I feel, whether you like it or not. Doris married Henry because you picked him out . . . and whether you're aware or not, she's suffering because of it. At least if I'm going to be poor, I'm going to be poor on my terms. I love Jerry Gould. Doing without things won't be painful at all—"

"You think so, do you? Money, as you'll discover, is a very important thing—especially when you don't have it . . . Just ask your mother. If you marry this man I'm not going to do a single damn thing for you. You could have had anything, but

425

now I'm *through* . . . I wouldn't give you a red cent. The only reason Doris is suffering, as you put it, is because she has a husband who can't support her, just like you will."

"And the reason you're not helping her is because you thought Henry was the rich doctor, and you can't admit your own mistake. In my case, at least you know the truth, so you won't have any illusions. But this should make you happy . . . Jerry's religious . . . he had a *bar mitzvah* and he comes from a very loving family, unlike some I could name. So, that's his complete dossier. And please, papa, don't keep reminding me about how important money is. For all your wealth, it doesn't seem that you and mama have had the greatest life together."

He looked at Sara, who was still crying. "Okay. You want this fellow, you can have him. But I repeat, I'm not going to give you anything, Lillian."

"I don't *want* anything. The only thing I ask is that you meet Jerry and accept him. He's going to be my husband." . . .

The next evening Jerry Gould found himself standing in the grand livingroom, being introduced to his sullen future in-laws. However, Lillian had prepared him for their attitude and she was glad to see that at least he wasn't going through the inquisition Jim Ross had. Dinner was a nearly silent affair, but at least there were no fireworks.

After Jerry had left, Jacob said, "You can forget about any big wedding, Lillian. If you think I'm impressed, you're mistaken, and if he thinks he's marrying an heiress, he's got another guess coming—"

"You know what, papa? Jerry didn't want to marry me. In fact, I proposed to him. And as for a big wedding, we don't want one. We'd rather go away to get married."

Jacob walked out of the room without another word.

After he'd left, Sara shook her head sadly. "Lillian, Lillian, you've hurt us so. May God forgive you for what you've done—"

"I'm terribly sorry I've disappointed you, mama, truly. I've always done what you wanted me to. I've tried to be a good obedient daughter, but this is one thing that's too important for me to allow anybody else to decide. I'm going to go to Reno tomorrow, mama . . ."

"No, no, don't do that. My God, at least let us have the *naches* of seeing you married . . . Tomorrow I'll call Temple Emanuel and you'll be married in the rabbi's study . . ."

Lillian went over and kissed her mother. "Thank you,

426

mama," she said, tears in her eyes. "What about papa? He said he didn't want me to have a wedding."

"I'll talk to him, I'm sure he'll feel as I do . . ."

Jerry and Lillian were married the following Saturday after sundown. Doris cried, Mike Robinson smiled to Nat Fried, Sara wept, Jacob stood rigid and tight-lipped.

After champagne and cake at Sara's and Jacob's apartment, the happy bride and groom spent the night at Jerry's hotel. Lillian was neither frightened nor shy. She undressed quickly and waited longingly for him to finish in the bathroom.

From the first moment he lay beside her, he aroused a passion she had never believed existed. Their lingering kisses before their marriage had strongly aroused her, but this . . . oh, God. Jerry's lips brushed hers, lightly at first and then with more intensity as he held her gently in his arms. As her breathing became uneven the kiss ventured to her distended nipples . . . Suddenly nothing existed in the world except this place, except Jerry and herself . . . Now. Then his body was on hers, she instinctively spread her legs as he entered her gently, carefully. For a brief moment there was a slight pain—and then ecstasy. It was the only word. She responded to his every movement as though they were of one body. Nothing was equal to this. The passion built with every thrust, and she arched her back to receive him. The moment of climax came with such intensity that she cried out.

As she lay back in his arms, she told herself that Mr. Jerry Gould was everything she'd ever dreamed a lover should be. And then she told him. . . .

On Sunday they drove in Lillian's convertible to Marin, where they had lunch at a wharf-side café. Lillian was entranced; she couldn't have been happier if they'd gone to Venice. She fought for Jerry, and, by God, she had won . . .

On Monday morning Jerry went back to work at Roos Brothers and Lillian found a job at the City of Paris in the glove department. At this point, neither was at all concerned about finding an apartment or planning for the future. Nothing mattered, except that they had each other. . . .

After Lillian had been married a month, Sara had a long talk with Jacob.

"Look, Jacob, I know the disappointment we often feel our children have been, but we just can't go on letting Lillian work as she is. And whether we like him or not, Jerry is our

427

son-in-law and Lillian's husband. I think you ought to take him into the plant. At least he can make a living there. Try not to be so bitter. After all, she's still our daughter."

The strangest thing was that of his three children, the one he had the greatest feeling for was Lillian. Perhaps it was because she was the youngest and had been with them the longest—he didn't analyze the reasons. He wasn't eager to take Jerry into the plant, but on a hundred and twenty-five dollars a month, how could he decently support Lillian?

So Jerry went to work as a truck driver at a salary of two hundred and fifty dollars a month. It was the only job Jacob could offer him, since he didn't know the first thing about the meat business. Besides, Jacob didn't want to make life too easy for him.

Sara shopped at W & J Sloane and furnished a three-room apartment that rented at seventy-five dollars a month. The linens, dishes, silver and china were *almost* comparable to her own. Jacob was indignant over the expense and the gesture itself, but Sara was determined to give Lillian this surprise, to set her up in life as she should be.

With the job completed, she called Lillian at work. "Lillian darling, we have a great surprise for you."

"What is it, mama?"

"Come to dinner tonight and I'll let you know . . ."

Sara's surprise was unveiled after dinner, when she took them to see the apartment. Lillian was almost as indignant as Jacob—she should have been the one to select the furniture. But then, of course, that would have deprived mama of keeping her beholden.

They picked up their belongings at the hotel that same night and moved into their new home, but neither felt comfortable surrounded by all the luxury.

As they lay side by side, tucked between the linen sheets and the satin comforter, Lillian could hold in her frustration no longer . . . "You know, I'm really damned mad, Jerry."

"About what?"

"For being so taken for granted. What they've done is certainly more than I expected under the circumstances, but why couldn't we at least have selected our own furniture and our own home?"

"You're right. But the thing that makes it so cockeyed is how they can expect us to pay seventy-five dollars a month rent, buy food, pay the expenses on the car and insurance when I only make two hundred and fifty dollars a month?"

"I know. By the time we get through with all the expenses

428

we'll be lucky if we have enough money left to go to a movie . . ."

"Well, honey," he said, turning toward her and taking her in his arms, "at this particular moment, I don't feel like talking about furniture and expenses."

Moving closer to him, she whispered, "And neither do I."

At the end of the month they found themselves owing the grocer and they knew things would get no better unless they moved.

One night after dinner Lillian told Jerry she'd found an apartment that rented for forty-seven dollars, all utilities included. There would, of course, be hell to pay with mama, but it seemed the only answer at the moment . . .

Lillian's prediction was right. Sara hit the ceiling. "After all I went through to find that apartment and decorate it, you're going to take all the beautiful furniture into some dump—?"

"The apartment doesn't happen to be a dump. It's in the same area, just two blocks up from where we live. But twenty-eight dollars a month is a lot to us."

"Why can't you sacrifice a little bit to live in a beautiful place like that? Everything is so perfect there—"

"It's beautiful, but it's not perfect—not when I have to owe even the grocer."

"Let me tell you something, Lillian. I'm putting up with a great deal from you and I'm getting very sick and tired of it. Do you know what I think you are?"

"What?"

"An ingrate. Do you know what I had to go through to get your father to do this for you? He was right . . . As far as I'm concerned, I'm all through helping and giving. Believe me . . ."

When she'd left, Lillian sat down, took out a Camel and puffed furiously, trying to hold back her tears. Mama simply can't stand the idea that maybe I've got a few guts, she thought. She still wants me to be subservient, as if I were fourteen years old. But knowing the truth didn't make it easier to accept, or to cope with . . .

So they moved into the new apartment, and were very content with it. At least they had selected this one themselves . . . it wasn't to show off to the world, it was for them.

Peace was wonderful, but it was also short-lived. Mama called Lillian every day, demanding that she accompany her downtown for lunch. Lillian went along, but she resented missing the bridge club with Amy and her other friends, who now were also new brides. Even worse was that Jerry came home every night to find Sarah *and* Jacob at dinner. He had enough of Jacob at work. It seemed nothing he did was quite good enough for his father-in-law, and Jacob didn't hesitate to call him out in front of other employees—but Jerry knew his independence wasn't just for himself anymore... he had a wife he loved, this was the Depression still, and the job came first for their sakes, in spite of *where* it came from ...

The real blow-up came when Lillian told Sara she was pregnant.

"My God ... just like Doris. You move into an apartment to save twenty-eight dollars a month and now you're going to have a baby? Do you have any idea what it takes to raise a child?"

"When Jerry and I decided, we didn't compute the cost. We just wanted to have a baby, mama."

"Well, *mazel tov* to you ..."

Thank you very much mama, even though I know you don't mean it, or can't let yourself mean it ...

CHAPTER FIFTY-SIX

JACOB HAD never liked the apartment. Although it was quite large he felt confined in it. And it certainly hadn't served its alleged purpose; Lillian hadn't exactly married into society ... a tie-salesman, for God's sake ... Well, the girls were all gone now, it was time he thought of himself a little more ...

One morning he called Sara from the office. "I'm going to pick you up at eleven-thirty."

"Why?"

"Because I've got a surprise for you."

"What's the surprise?"

"When I pick you up, you'll find out ..."

At eleven-thirty, Sara found herself being driven down the highway toward the Peninsula. When they stopped at their destination it was in front of an enormous two-story Tudor mansion in Woodside.

Sara looked at him. "What's this all about?"

"It's about the surprise."

"What do you mean?"

"That's your new home. I just bought it."

430

"You did what?"

"I just told you, I bought it."

"And why didn't you tell me?"

"Why didn't you tell me when you sold the house in Oakland?"

"So now you're punishing me?"

"Every Jewish woman should be so punished to live in a fifteen-room house—"

"Fifteen rooms? If anybody's gone crazy, it's you."

"No, I don't think so. This is the way Jack Sanders should live."

"And what about Sara Sanders? I've just adjusted to my life in San Francisco. That's where my children are—"

"And I adjusted to San Francisco for your sake. You'll get over it. . . . Now come and see the house."

It was large and sprawling. On the first floor was a forty-foot livingroom, a wood-paneled library, a diningroom with English murals and a wing with three guest rooms, each with its own bathroom. The flagstone terrace overlooked a lush green golf course. From the central foyer, a winding staircase led to the four master bedrooms and baths. The dressingrooms and built-in closets were mirrored, and the bathrooms had sunken tubs, marble basins and solid gold hardware. The left wing could accommodate four servants, and the kitchen was probably the size of the one in the Saint Francis. In fact, most of the appliances were restaurant-size.

As though the house were not startling enough, the grounds of the three cultivated acres were like a park, with enormous oaks and a nursery and rose garden. The outdoor dining area and swimming pool seemed like a resort. It was so spectacular that the change it would mean in Sara's life didn't really penetrate at the time.

"Well, Sara, this is a little different than Washington Heights, huh? And you were so afraid I wouldn't make it off Rivington Street. So now you think you made a mistake when we lay there in the sand at Coney Island?" There was no anger in his voice, only pride.

"What did this Buckingham Palace cost?" she asked quietly.

"Plenty, but isn't this what your mother brought you up to expect?"

That finally brought tears to her eyes. "She would have approved," Sara conceded softly, wishing her mother could have seen it . . . "What did it cost?"

"Seventy-five thousand dollars. They wanted more but you know me when it comes to horse-trading. I've had a little experience along those lines. So what do you think?"

"It's really beautiful, Jacob—but so far away from the children."

"So they'll come down. There's enough room. Maybe even Rachel will condescend to visit. If so, at least Mr. Jim Ross will find out he didn't marry beneath him." . . .

He was right about the children coming down. Every weekend, rain or shine, Doris and Henry brought their children, and Lillian—her tummy bulging now—and Jerry also made the trip. At the end of the weekends, though, everyone went home with frayed nerves. Jacob maintained only a minimum staff and Sara once again found herself doing housework and trying to shut out the sound of Doris' crying children. The housework wasn't that heavy but she found it an ordeal to entertain—and let everyone know it.

Every Monday she stayed in bed to recuperate and every Monday morning both Henry and Jerry said, "Are we going to be on call for the rest of our lives because your folks bought a Taj Mahal in Woodside?" . . .

When the high holy days came Doris said, "Mama, I'm awfully sorry, but we're not going to be able to come down for dinner. It's going to be too difficult to get back and forth in time to make the services. Why don't you and papa come in and go with us to temple? Lillian and Jerry will be here too."

Sara was surprised to hear that her daughters were observing the holy days and thought briefly of insisting that they come anyway. But as much as she would like to have had the children at her table, she realized that Doris was right. Under the circumstances, the trip was simply too far. So who said she was so unreasonable? . . . Jerry called Sara to tell her that Lillian was in labor and wanted her parents to be with her at the hospital. They left immediately to make the long drive into the city, Jacob driving their Pierce Arrow a bit faster than usual and Sara fidgeting anxiously beside him.

When they walked into Lillian's room, Doris was already there and the two girls were talking quietly, Lillian taking an occasional puff on her cigarette.

"What is this?" Sara said. "Are you in labor or was it a false alarm?"

"No, it was no false alarm."

"How come you're so calm? I can't believe you're having a baby."

432

"According to the doctor, you'll see differently in about eight hours. They gave me a spinal block, so why should I enjoy? The only one having labor pains is Jerry. Please go calm him, mama—no, Doris—please go out and hold his hand." ...

Candice Gould was born at six in the morning—blonde, blue-eyed, like her grandfather. "I would have accused you of having an affair if it weren't that blondes run in the Sanders family," Jerry said happily.

The day before Lillian was to be discharged from the hospital, Jerry laid a long-stemmed rose across her flat abdomen and kissed her when he came to visit. "Honey, I'm glad you're lying down, 'cause I think you're going to have delayed birth pains—"

"What are you talking about, Jerry?"

"Well, I didn't want to talk about it until you were feeling better, but—your mother decided that the apartment was too small for a family of three. We had quite a long discussion about it ... but the outcome was that she offered to store the furniture so we can move to Woodside and live in the guest suite."

Lillian gasped. "I don't believe you, Jerry!"

"Believe it, honey, believe it. In fact, she hired a nurse and has decorated a nursery. We may be nonpaying guests for quite a while until your mother at least sets us free..."

My God, it was Doris all over again. Mama's loneliness in that magnificent mansion must have sparked it off. It was crazy... Lillian didn't know whether to cry or to take the baby, Jerry and herself to Siberia.

"Jerry, how could you allow her to do that? I want to take care of my baby and I was happy in our apartment—"

"How did I *allow* it? Lillian, you're really not well. Would you like me to read you chapter and verse on how persuasive your mother can be?" Besides, he thought, with the expenses of a new baby, what alternative did he have on his salary? And even at that, he was doing better working for his father-in-law—tight as he was—than he could do on his own, with things as they were.

"Well, too bad we didn't have triplets, *that* might have been a deterrent."

"Not even quintuplets would have helped. Your mother needs company. And, honey, we need a break."

In more ways than one, she thought. ...

At the end of the four months, Lillian had her doubts that she'd make it through the next twenty-four hours. What had

433

happened with Doris was happening with her. Sara wanted her cake, but she couldn't quite swallow it. When she wasn't complaining, she was in her bedroom in near-hysterics. Poor mama just didn't seem to understand that she couldn't keep picking at Jerry and expect him to just stand there like a pussycat. The baby's crying and her irregular hours, the clutter in the bathroom—mama's reactions created a scene Lillian well remembered from Doris' short stay after Michele was born.

The final break came when Lillian announced that she and Jerry were going to get a place of their own. She didn't know quite how they would manage it, but that was something she kept to herself.

Tears flowed from Sara. *"Why* was I cursed with the most ungrateful children? Other people have children who love and are appreciative of their parents . . . no matter what I do, it's not enough . . . I cook and I clean and your father, the grand seignior, he keeps a gardener and two maids for a fifteen-room house—so he can show the world how Jacob Sanders lives."

"I understand what you're saying, mama, but Jerry and I still want to get a little place of our own. We have to . . ."

"Then move . . . move. This mansion isn't good enough for you? Move—"

"Mama, it's not our mansion, it's yours."

"What did you think I bought it for if not to have my children with me?"

"Well, I'm sorry if that's the reason you bought it, but we should really be on our own. Jerry and I found a little bungalow in Redwood City . . ."

The day Lillian moved out, Sara lay sequestered with a hot water bottle at her feet and an ice pack on her head. Oh Lord, what was she going to do alone in a fifteen-room house . . . ?

For the first time since Candy had been born, Lillian was able really to enjoy motherhood . . . and what a joy it was. She bathed the baby in the morning, holding the chubby infant in her arms and watching her swish and kick and coo. She put her on top of the bassinet, dried and powdered her, brushed her sparse blonde hair—and thanked God it was now just the three of them.

The afternoons were a different matter, however. Sara was there almost every afternoon, and she either had dinner with Lillian or brought her back to the mansion for dinner. When

Lillian came back home in the evening she would look around her tiny livingroom with the chintz slipcovers and thank God again for the little two-bedroom bungalow. It wasn't that she didn't ever want more, but she was so in love with Jerry and the baby that she would have settled for a hut in the Mojave Desert.

Of course, Sara would never allow that, and as far as she was concerned the bungalow was indeed no better than a hut. At four o'clock one afternoon, she walked into Lillian's house and announced: "Lillian, get the baby ready. I want to show you something."

There was that command tone in mama's voice that told her changes were about to take place. Lillian could only guess what the price would be this time—and there was always a price. She took Candy out of the playpen, put the bottle of orange juice in with the diaper bag and followed mama out to her new Cadillac.

As they drove along El Camino Lillian said, "Mama, you look like the cat that swallowed the canary."

"Well, you will too when you see what I have to show you."

Suddenly Sara veered to the inside lane, swung left on Atherton Avenue and drove into the Flood Estate area. She drove slowly through a magnificent wooded area and stopped in front of a rambling one-story ranch house that was shaded by the tall oaks. The "For Sale" sign had a "Sold" sign tacked across it.

Before getting out of the car, Lillian looked closely at her mother. "This is the surprise?"

"Yes." Sara beamed.

"Mama, I think it's lovely—"

"Wait, you haven't even *seen* it. When you do, you'll go absolutely wild about it—"

"I'm sure I will, mama, and thank you, but did it occur to you that the reason we had to move out of the first apartment was because of Jerry's salary? Mama, we have to be practical—"

"Don't worry about Jerry's salary. Obviously you can't live in this house on what he makes now. You think I'm that stupid?"

"I never thought that, mama, but it's a fact you're not very good at mathematics. What can Jerry earn as a truck driver? Nadine and Sandy can't own a house like this and he makes a better salary than Jerry."

"There's a big difference between you and Nadine. Your

future is set. *You* have a mother and father who are going to provide for you."

"That's very reassuring, but what I'm worried about is right now. How are we going to afford this?"

"Lillian, you're either very stupid or you're not listening to me. I told you that Jerry's salary was going to be . . . commensurate."

"Jerry isn't going to be too happy about that. He wants to *earn* his money, mama."

"Believe me, he'll earn it. In fact, he's going to be a salesman."

Lillian sighed. "Look, mama. I don't want to bring up anything unpleasant and I beg you not to get upset about this . . . but Doris is really having a struggle. Don't you think it will be a slap in the face to her if you buy this for us? You've already done so much more for us—"

"Henry's a lazy *doctor*, and I'm not going to make life easy for him. At least Jerry's not lazy."

"Even if that were true, *Doris* is the one having a rough time. I'm not."

"Well, that's too bad. She should never have married him . . . well, she's his responsibility now. If she had any brains in her head she'd leave him."

Lillian shut her eyes. Poor Doris . . . mama was punishing her for what was really mama's and papa's mistake . . .

"Okay, enough about them, let's take a look at the house," Sara said.

The double doors opened onto a flagstone foyer, and beyond was a twenty-five-foot livingroom and a lovely field-stone fireplace. The diningroom was light and airy, and a short hallway led to the kitchen, and a longer one to the three lovely bedrooms and two baths. It should have been the dream of Lillian's life, but it was not—not when she thought of the demands that were going to be laid on Jerry to produce. . . . There just ain't no Santa Claus, and Lillian knew all too well she was going to pay for this house in more than money.

"*Well,* Lillian," Sara said, "what do you think, is it gorgeous?"

"Gorgeous . . . What did it cost?"

"Seventeen thousand dollars. Papa and I are giving you the down payment and the rest you'll pay out like rent."

"And how much will the payments be?"

"I don't know. You'll talk to papa about that. The important thing is you'll be living like I always wanted for you."

436

But what about me? And why do you want me to live this way? To show off to the world how good you've been to your children? Or is it because you and papa can't stand living together and you need us to fill up the void in your life? . . .

On the first Sunday in June, Sara's help, Otto and Helga, were at Lillian's house for the housewarming, and several waitresss had also been hired. Sara planned the whole affair. All of Lillian's friends from the city had been invited. And, of course, Nadine, Jean and the Blums—Sara especially wanted them to see the house. The only disappointment for Sara was that Rachel had been invited down to Pebble Beach, she said, and couldn't make it.

When Doris arrived with her two children, Sara was rather irritated. "Doris, don't you think you could have gotten a baby sitter—?"

"No, mama, I couldn't afford it . . . I'll be sure they don't step on anybody's furniture." There were no words to describe her feelings as she looked through the house, and no one was more aware of her pain than Lillian—nor felt more guilt . . .

Shortly after Doris had arrived, she said she wasn't feeling well, and mama had felt badly about that and said she'd call in the morning . . . Doris was silent all the way home. It was true . . . mama hadn't wanted her and was still busy proving it. And Lillian? What price would she pay for allowing mama to run her life? The way she'd tried to run hers . . .

CHAPTER FIFTY-SEVEN

WHEN CANDICE was a year old, Lillian had another little girl. Cindy was just as beautiful as Candy, but she looked exactly like Jerry, which greatly pleased Lillian. Lillian and Jerry were as happy a couple as ever, but the Sanderses were a continuing presence in their lives—a presence that was less and less bearable.

Jerry had become a salesman, and the promotion had made Jacob more demanding than ever before. Finally Jerry just couldn't take it any longer . . .

"Lillian, I don't know if I can go on with your father. All he does is complain, no matter what I do. The only peace I have is when he's away. And I'm getting damned tired of never having a moment to ourselves. They're either here for dinner or we're over there almost every night of the week.

And your mother's always letting us know how much she does for us and how they bought the house for us and how little we appreciate it, and so forth . . . I'm very sick and tired of the whole damned thing, if you want to know the truth."

Lillian sighed. "Honey, I know, I agree with everything you say. But you tell me—what *choices* do we have?"

"Look, we don't need this house. I don't even feel like it's ours anyway. Your father makes me feel like he's supporting me. If I want to take my family to Tahoe for a week he makes me feel like it's *his* money I'm spending."

"Jerry, you just got a little off the subject. What can we *do* about it?"

"What we can do is sell this damn place and move somewhere further away from them, back to the city. At least they won't be able to drop in so often—"

"Jerry, you know what this means, don't you?"

"You bet I do. It means your father's going to fire me and your mother's going to go off like a rocket because I'm taking away not her daughter but her *companion* . . . You once said I was a coward, right? Let's see how brave you are . . . . Are you ready?"

"I don't know how my ulcer will take it, but I do know you're right, absolutely right . . ."

"Okay, shape up the kids. We're going over and have it out with your dad tonight."

"But what are you going to do for a living?"

"Look, I can always go back to Roos Brothers. In the meantime, property values are better and we'll make a little profit on the house. I'll give back the down payment to your father and with the rest . . . well, I thought I'd look around for a little store, maybe open up a haberdashery shop. Maybe Nat and Mike will go in as partners." . . .

They found Sara and Jacob sitting in the library. Jacob beamed when he saw his grandchildren. Candy climbed into his lap, just the way his daughters had done when they were young. Candy even reminded him of Rachel at the same age . . .

"Oh, I'm so glad you brought the children over," Sara said—as though she hadn't just seen them this afternoon.

Lillian and Jerry looked at each other. Who would go first?

Jerry sat down in one of the leather chairs, cleared his throat nervously. "Jacob, Lillian and I have talked this over very carefully and the truth of the matter is . . . we feel we're living above our means."

438

Jacob set Candy down from his lap and stood up. "What are you saying, you want me to give you a raise?"

Trying to keep calm, Jerry answered, "No, as a matter of fact, I think you give me far too much money for the amount of work I do . . . Lillian and I have decided we're going to sell the house—"

Sara dropped four stitches and Jacob found full voice. "You're absolutely right. You don't earn half of what I pay you. And as far as you're concerned, Lillian, you don't deserve parents like us. What do you do for us? The only pleasure we have is in seeing our grandchildren, and now you want to deprive us of that? As far as I'm concerned, Jerry, you just gave me your notice." With that, he stormed from the room and went upstairs.

Sara went on where Jacob had left off, and she was shaking visibly. "Everything your father said is *absolutely right*. You're unbelievably unfair to take our grandchildren away. And as far as I'm concerned I don't want to have anything to do with either one of you—"

"I'm sorry you feel that way, mama . . ."

"You were never sorry about a thing in your whole life. See how it's going to feel, being on your own. We've just made life too good for you . . ."

Without another word, Lillian got up and put the children's coats on, and the four of them left. . . .

After putting the children to bed, they sat in the living-room, silent for a moment.

Then: "Jerry, I think we really burned our bridges." Lillian was trying to hold back her tears, but she was very frightened.

"Maybe, but I'm not going to let them control my life. I'm sorry it's so hard on you, but it had to be done."

"What are we going to do in the meantime, until the house is sold?"

"I've still got this month's salary coming, and we've got a few dollars in the bank. I'll start looking for a job tomorrow." . . .

The house was sold a month later. Jerry sent Jacob a check for the original down payment, paid off the mortgage and netted out twelve thousand dollars in equity and profit. Lillian thought it would be far better for the children if they remained on the Peninsula, so instead of moving to San Francisco they bought a lovely two-story Spanish house on Row Hampton Road in Hillsborough, with the minimum of ten percent down and a four-and-a-half-percent thirty-year loan.

Jerry commuted to the city by train and was working at Roos Brothers while he looked for a small store. His salary was three hundred dollars a month, which barely paid expenses—but they lived very frugally. . . .

Finally Jerry took what little money they had and invested it in a tie shop on Powell Street. He was happy to be finally working for himself and at first he had been certain he could make a good living—until the daily receipts showed differently. If he took home twenty-five dollars at the end of the day he was lucky. The unit sales showed that the average customer bought three ties at the most, so he knew that he'd have to expand stock to include men's shirts. But he didn't have enough capital, and as a result had to ask his best friend Nat Fried, whom he'd grown up with in the Bronx, to come into partnership with him. At first Nat resisted. He had a fairly good job and two thousand dollars saved, and to invest in a business that was barely making it didn't quite make sense. But Jerry hammered away. "So, okay, Nat, you saved two thousand dollars. Tell me, how long did that take you? Five years? What kind of future do you have working as a salesman?"

"What the hell future do you have in a tie shop you can hardly make a living in?"

"A big one if I had the money to stock up better. Sure, I can't make it just on ties. But if we expand I know we can make it."

Nat thought carefully. The location was very good, he couldn't argue about that. And if Jerry knew anything it was how to buy, and he had good taste. Maybe this *was* his opportunity.

"Okay, Jerry . . . I'm a little nervous about taking the plunge, but you just got yourself a partner, partner . . ."

It wasn't too long afterwards that Jerry was to regret taking Nat in. . . . As soon as the business was beginning to show a small profit, Jerry's best—and most trusted—friend commenced to tap the till. When Jerry found out, he hit the ceiling and the fight they had ended in Jerry saying, "You and I are through. I should have listened to you when you said you didn't want to come into the business. Now I want you out."

"Really? Okay, buy me out."

"Fine. I'll raise the two thousand dollars you put in and that's finished."

440

"How are you going to raise the money?"

"I'll take out a personal loan."

"You better take it out for five thousand, because that's what I want."

"You bastard. I have ninety-five hundred dollars invested. *I* started the business. The lease is in *my* name. I took you in for two thousand and you want five?"

"You asked me, remember?"

Jerry slowly shook his head. "I would never have believed in a million years that you'd do this to me . . ."

"Friendship is one thing, business is another. I want to survive, same as you. You forgot I left a good job."

"You left a good job? You were president of Macy's, right? Well, I'll tell you what. I'll get a loan of three thousand dollars and you can go to hell."

The partnership had largely been dissolved when the lease on the store came due and the landlord raised the rent. Jerry sat in his small office with his head in his hands and knew it was over. He couldn't make it, no matter what. The competition was too great. The merchandise he sold could be bought in every department store in the city, where people could charge and pay their bills off later. He couldn't compete with that.

The next day, "Going Out of Business" signs were plastered across the windows. Lillian came down to help, and there was tension between them for the first time since their marriage . . . but it remained unspoken. Lillian just couldn't help feeling angry that Jerry had been so impulsive in leaving his job with papa. At least he'd made a good and dependable salary, and if need be she could always have gone to papa for help. But where did they go from here? . . .

Jerry's thoughts were no different. Damn it, he guessed he should have overlooked Jacob's tirades for the sake of his family . . . When the last day of the sale was over, he came out with a whopping four thousand dollars. What now? What, indeed?

After Lillian moved away Sara and Jacob refused to have anything to do with her. At first Sara turned back to Doris, but Michele was now in nursery school, which made it impossible for Doris to go along with Sara's requests that she come to stay for long periods of time. After a while Sara was reduced to calling Rachel more often, but there too she found only frustration. Rachel and Jim had bought a house in Palm Springs, where they spent the winters, and Sara knew it was a deliberate attempt on Rachel's part to divorce herself from the family. So Sara had lonely hours to spare in the huge empty house . . . thinking about the people who had passed through her life, and left her . . . Mollie, Louie, Jacob, and now every one of her children . . .

It was through Doris that she heard about Jerry's failure, and after a week thinking about it she finally was ready to call Lillian. Maybe *now* she would realize how important her parents were . . .

Lillian could not hold back her tears over having to admit Jerry's failure.

"Look, Lillian," Sara said, "don't feel it's the end of the world. After all, I'm not going to allow you and the children to starve. I'll talk to your father about having Jerry come back to the plant . . ."

Except the task that lay before Sara was not quite as simple as she'd thought; Jacob's anger toward Jerry was far from appeased. Still, with Sara's pleading, he finally relented and allowed Jerry to come back to work—but not as a salesman. His salary would remain the same, of course, but Jerry had to realize that Jacob was in command.

Once again, the husband of the heiress was back at work as a truck driver.

CHAPTER FIFTY-EIGHT

DECEMBER 7, 1941: The bombing of Pearl Harbor. It not only changed the course of world history, it even changed the course of Doris and Henry Levin's life.

Doctors were being inducted into the armed forces and Henry went down for his physical, but to his great surprise he was rejected. When he was given the eye test, it was discovered that he was color blind—which immediately put him into the category of 4-F. With the shortage of doctors in civilian life, Henry now hit a bonanza. Almost overnight he was deluged with patients. He not only expanded his office space and acquired a nurse, but also a house in Seacliff.

It was love at first sight when Doris saw the fifty-year-old Georgian two-story house. The moment she walked into the octagonal foyer and looked at the spiral staircase, she knew this was the house she had dreamed of all her life. She moved on to the sunken livingroom, spacious and filled with sunlight.

The oval diningroom with wood molding and the large old-fashioned kitchen charmed her, as did the paneled library. She walked slowly, softly, up the stairs, went from one bedroom to the next. Michele would have the canopy bed she'd wanted so, and Gary would have all the room he could use for his pennants and books . . . and the drum set would stand in the corner. The master suite had bay windows and seemed as large as some of the apartments she had lived in. The fourth bedroom would be a guest room. The only thing she found superfluous were the maids' quarters, but she would use those rooms for storage, shut them off, or maybe use one for an office . . . She walked back to the living room and began to visualize how she would furnish it. What a job it was going to be to shop—and she was not going to have a decorator. She wanted *her* house to be invitingly elegant—not like mama's where one felt as though there was an invisible rope saying, "Do Not Enter," nor like Rachel's, where you felt you really ought to remove your shoes. Her house would be filled with spring blossoms and big informal vases of flowers. And this time everything was going to be her choice, reflect her personality. . . .

They furnished the house, paying it out on terms, and for once Doris didn't worry whether Henry was able to afford it, and Henry, for the first time, was a man who felt a sense of accomplishment.

Doris' life seemed complete. In more ways than one the best part of her time was spent with the children. She took them to and from school . . . her days were filled with the PTA, the Brownies, Sunday School, piano lessons, the orthodontist. Henry bought her a Chevrolet coupé, which gave her life a new horizon—she was able to acquire friends and keep up with them socially. . . .

Her mother was not so happy. Jacob traveled more and more as his business expanded to enormous proportions, and she was left for even longer periods of time in the isolated mansion. Otto and Helga, the live-in help, were the only human beings she had any contact with, and she clung to them as though they were not only her family but her redeemers. She carefully furnished their apartment above the garage. If she thought something would please Helga, she bought it for her. In fact, Sara meticulously went through her closets and gave armloads of clothes to Helga to send back to her sister in Germany by way of Switzerland.

When Doris heard about it she was horrified. Millions of

443

Jews had been annihilated or were struggling to put their lives back together, and mama was helping Helga's sister fill out her wardrobe?

"Mama, don't you realize what a bad thing you're doing?"

"What Helga does with the things I gave her I don't know."

"But of course you do, mama."

"The only thing I know is that I could live and die here alone if it weren't for them. They love me better than my own children."

"I'm sorry you feel that way, but the point is—"

"I don't want to discuss it anymore. What I do with what's mine is my business. Now I want you to go home. I'm very tired and want to rest."

For mama, the big war was still inside. And she had no planes or tanks to fight it with . . .

Yes, Sara thanked God for Helga and Otto, but they hardly filled the void in her life. The more time she spent alone, the more the old fears and angers haunted her . . . "What can I do with my life, my days and nights? Please . . . help me." She had finally broken down and called Doris.

Doris all but begged her to become involved in the community. There was so much that needed to be done, especially with the war effort. Sara thought maybe that could be a solution to her problem, so she joined the Red Cross. But she really hated it. She made brief attempts to get involved with other activities, but nothing seemed to satisfy her for long.

Her unhappiness grew so unbearable that finally she decided anything would be better than the way she was living . . . She confronted Jacob when he returned from one of his trips. "I can't go on this way, Jacob. I want you to sell the house. There's simply got to be more to my life than this . . ."

She begged him to understand her reasons but one word led to another and the argument left her in such a state that she issued an ultimatum to end all ultimatums. Unless he sold the house and moved back to the city, she was going to get a divorce.

Jacob was stunned into silence, then said that was craziness, that she couldn't just walk out. Would she . . . ? But he didn't say he would sell the house—and he didn't say how much he needed her. In the end, she packed her luggage and left. . . .

Doris opened the door to find mama standing surrounded by her suitcases . . . . Sara simply moved in.

That night they sat in the den and talked about her problems. "Sara, I can't say that I totally blame you," Henry said. "Loneliness drives people to do some very desperate things. But I can't believe there's no other way for you and Jacob to work out your differences. I think you've made a very, very serious error. Jacob isn't a man who forgives easily, as you know, and before you do anything drastic I think you should try to—"

"I know you mean well, Henry, but I'm not exactly a child. I'm a fifty-year-old woman and this wasn't an impulsive act. I just can't go on living the way I've been. Tomorrow I have an appointment with an attorney. Once and for all, I'm going to find some kind of life for myself."

"Well, divorce is a drastic step. If you have any doubts, think is over carefully. Jacob may never forgive you, take my advice, let things cool down for a while—"

"No, this is one time in my life I've made up my mind and I'm going to stick to it . . ."

The next day Sara went downtown, bought herself a new mink coat, an entire wardrobe at Elizabeth Arden, then went to the travel agency to get a flight to Palm Springs. Then she went to a rental agency and inquired about a house. Sight unseen, she leased an estate . . . Yes, indeed, she had made her decision. She was going to make friends, join clubs, entertain. Life was going to be everything she'd expected it to be, and about time too . . .

That evening when she came back and told Doris and Henry what she had done, they knew she had no idea of what she was doing. "Mama, in your present state of mind you just don't realize what you're doing. Please, for your own sake, don't do this . . . It's wrong. Try to fix up your differences with papa, somehow, some way. If you can live alone in Palm Springs why—"

"Doris, I've been married over thirty years and please don't tell me that I don't know what I'm doing. For the first time in my life I know what I'm doing."

"But this shopping spree will only aggravate matters. When papa gets the bills he's going to know why you've done this—"

"I'm not returning anything. I have it coming to me—and that's not all he's going to pay for. He's going to pay for every lonely minute without any love or affection . . . He only gets the message through his pocketbook."

There was nothing either one of them could say to reach her. But maybe Lillian could get through to her? Doris called her late one night.

"Lillian, mama's gone absolutely around the bend . . . she's spending money right and left, and nothing Henry or I say can stop her."

"I hate to tell you this, Doris, but papa's just as angry at you as he is at mama. He thinks you've taken sides with her."

"What would you have done, Lillian, if mama came to your house with her bags all packed? What would you have said . . . No, you're not welcome? Would you have turned her away?"

"Yes, as a matter of fact I think I would, and that's what you should have done."

"I haven't sided with mama at all, Lillian. I pleaded and begged with her to go back to papa. But I can hardly throw her out, can I? I tried to get in touch with him but he refuses to talk with me."

"I just told you why."

"Well, when it gets down to taking sides, Lillian, haven't you taken sides with him against mama?"

"No, not really. He's rambling around the big house in Woodside and the only time we see him is when I invite him to dinner. Obviously, he's very lonely. Not only lonely, but embarrassed and frightened about what this is going to mean to his finances. And the thing that hurts him most of all is having been served with divorce papers. You do know, Doris, that mama's attorney subpoenaed his books? They want a settlement of half of what he has, plus five thousand dollars a month in temporary alimony. Look, nobody has to tell me what a difficult man he is, and I hardly blame her for everything, but the truth is she isn't the only woman in the world who has a husband who makes his living traveling. It's just that she has no . . . resilience, no desire or maybe ability to accept compromises of any kind . . . Other women do it, why couldn't she? Instead of depending on all of us . . . Anyway, I think you've made a big mistake, Doris, by letting her stay with you . . ."

When they hung up Doris felt caught . . . Mama had not only disrupted her entire household, but had put her in the middle of something she wasn't responsible for and had no idea what to do about . . .

After a month of separation much of the frenzied excitement of Sara's previous determination began to subside. Now she began to miss her home, badly, and the thought of starting a new life at her age began to seem more and more frightening. In spite of herself, she also began to miss Jacob.

446

Even though he was rarely home, at least there was a feeling of . . . permanency with him . . .

As the days wore on, her regrets and insecurities deepened. Now she privately hoped she could resolve things with Jacob, but how in the world could she put things right?

Henry and Doris noticed her worsening depression, and one afternoon Henry knocked on Sara's door to talk to her about it. "Sara, we all make mistakes in our lives and some are irrevocable. But I honestly believe that you should try to make up with Jacob. You're not happy without him . . . marriage becomes a habit. Believe me, Sara, I know what you're feeling. Now if I suggest something, will you at least listen carefully?"

She nodded slowly.

"I know Jacob's sentiments about our having taken sides with you—which doesn't happen to be the case, as you know—but I'm more than willing to drive you home this evening and try to get the two of you back together again."

Sara, in spite of herself, began to cry. Because, of course, that was really what she wanted, to go home to her husband. However, Henry would never be the person to bring about a reconciliation. Only one person could do that . . . Shlomo.

She called him immediately.

"Do you want me to come to Doris', Sara?" She could hear the anxiety in Shlomo's voice, and knew he was anxious to help.

"Thank you, but would it be all right if I came to your house? I want us to be alone."

"Of course, Sara, come anytime—"

"What about eight o'clock?"

"Why don't you come now? Nadine will hold dinner."

Nadine was the last person she wanted to talk to, not under these circumstances . . . "Thank you very much, but we're about to sit down. I'll be there at eight. And you won't mind if we speak alone? I'm sure you understand." . . .

At eight o'clock Sara was sitting with Shlomo in his den. "You know that my life with Jacob was no bed of roses, Shlomo, and feeling desperate can push a person to do a lot of foolish things . . . but, well, emotions and feelings don't stay the same. I've been separated a month, and I've taken a little different look at my life. Jacob and I were mere children when we met. I suppose the fact I've been married to him for so long makes me feel lost now . . . that's how I feel, lost . . . Oh, God, I want to go back to him, tell me what I should do—"

"Well, Sara, to be honest, I don't think Jacob's going to be too receptive. He's been badly hurt and the articles in the paper haven't helped. I don't know whether you know this, but his credit has been affected, too ... banks get a little jumpy when they hear about divorces. All in all, it's been tough on him, believe me ..."

"You're saying you don't think there's a chance ..." Sara was chilled by the thought, and blamed herself for being so damned impetuous ... well, what else was new ...

"Nothing is impossible. Let's go see Jacob tonight. He's home, and I'll try anything to get the two of you back together—"

"Do you think there's a chance?"

"We'll try." ...

When they arrived at the mansion in Woodside Jacob was sitting in the library. Shlomo suggested that Sara go up to her bedroom and wait while he'd had a chance to speak to his brother.

"Jacob," he began, "look, brother, I know the kind of hell you've been through, and I also know that Sara isn't exactly the easiest or calmest person in the world ... But still, you've been together for a long time. This is no kind of life for you ..."

Jacob got up agitatedly from his chair, but Shlomo persisted. "Now keep calm and listen. Sara realizes she's made a very bad mistake, but you've got to realize her life with you *has* been difficult. There are two sides to every story, you know. She was lonely the first day she met you and she still is. But more now than ever. She'd like to come back ..."

Jacob was pacing the floor. "Oh, would she? She'd really like me back? Do you know what this damned mess has cost me? Attorney's fee, twenty-five thousand dollars, to start with. You want me to take her back? If I did, how long do you think if would last?"

"Look, Jacob, shocks can change a person. I think Sara has begun to realize her life wasn't as bad as she thought it was. Being separated has given her a chance to take stock ... She misses her home ... Let's be realistic about this. Sara's not going to become a saint and neither are *you*. But if you go through with this divorce, it's going to cost you one hell of a lot more than twenty-five thousand dollars. And forgetting money ... what are you going to do? Live alone for the rest of your life? Get a new wife? You've got five grandchildren. My God, you're both middle-aged people. You've lived

448

through so much in your lives together and shared so much . . . What are you going to do, break up this beautiful home?"

"All right, everything you say is *right*, but how in hell could a woman have gone to such lengths, airing all our differences in public? How do you forgive a woman who does a thing like that?"

"The first thing I'd suggest is sitting down and talking together. Sara's upstairs—"

Jacob stopped in his tracks. He thought of the years . . . he thought too of having to give her half of what he'd worked so desperately hard for . . . weighed the losses, the gains . . . And Gloria? He felt great affection for her and gratitude for her love, but he knew he wouldn't marry her even if he did divorce Sara. He wouldn't marry anyone. Still, how did he go back to a wife who'd stopped being a wife so long ago and try to start fresh? Who knew? What were the wonderful alternatives . . . ?

"All right, have her come down."

While Shlomo went to get Sara, Jacob opened the double doors to the bar and poured himself a full tumbler of bourbon, took a long swallow and sat down in his leather chair. When she came into the room, red-eyed and contrite, he felt more anger than sympathy, but still . . .

Finally Sara said quietly, "Jacob, I know you'll never believe how much I regret having done what I did, but I wasn't entirely to blame. The pressures put on me were greater than you can imagine . . ."

Jacob took another swallow of whiskey. "What pressures, Sara? I can't be in two places at one time. If I was home you'd be complaining you were living like Gittel—you'd be living in the back of a store. You have this mansion and money means as much to you as it does to me. So when you talk about pressures, what do you think you've been deprived of? And *how* could you have gone so far as to serve me with papers for a divorce? How am I supposed to forget that?" He was working himself up now . . . "And how the hell did you get hold of an attorney like Brandon?"

"I was advised . . . what do I know about divorces or attorneys?"

"You were advised? Who advised you to go to Brandon?"

"Jacob, I'd rather not tell you."

"Damn it, Sara, I want to know the whole story."

A long pause, then Sara began quietly. "You must understand that I was in a very emotional state when I left. I'm not

449

blaming anybody, but things began to build up . . . I had spoken to Doris at one point when I was really upset and she suggested that perhaps the best thing that could happen to us was a brief separation . . . If you could only understand the emotional strain I was under at the time. I thought perhaps she was right. When I said I was going to divorce you, it was only a stupid threat. I had absolutely no intention of going through with anything like that. But after staying with Doris and Henry—particularly Henry . . . He made me begin to realize that I was a young woman, and that if I wasn't happy with you I could still make a life of my own. You're a very rich man, and I could have a wonderful new life, travel . . . Well, people can be persuasive, and it hurts me to admit that in my state of mind I wasn't thinking for myself. I was listening to him—"

Jacob sat silently until he recovered from the full impact of what Sara had said. He realized that, of course, Henry probably thought that if she came into a great deal of money, he could feather his nest. He wasn't excusing Sara, not for one moment, but that son of a bitch Henry had tried to coerce her. That's how she'd found out about Brandon, the biggest damn bloodsucker in the world . . . "You mean to tell me that Henry was the one who persuaded you to go ahead with this divorce?"

"I hate to admit that I was weak enough not to have seen through it to Henry's reasons . . . But yes, Jacob, as a matter of fact he did."

Sara began to realize what she had done, and she could only pray that Jacob would believe she had indeed been a victim. If she lost this gamble, she would pay a double price. And if she won? She lost Doris . . . God, she *must* be desperate. She was almost at the point of recanting when Jacob got up and filled the glass once again. "Well, Sara, as of this moment your daughter Doris and her so-called husband are out of my life. Betrayal like this is something I'll never forget. I disinherit them, you're my witness . . . and as for you, if you ever do anything like this again, as there's a God above me, I'll never take you back—not if it means giving you everything. How we're going to resolve our lives I have no idea, but we'll try to go on . . . nothing is going to change . . . I intend to do exactly as I have, and what you do with your life is strictly for you to decide."

Sara could almost hear the sound of thirty pieces of silver being paid to Judas. That's what it amounted to—she had

450

crucified Doris . . . The daughter she'd never wanted . . . For this, she was sure, there could be no forgiveness . . . .

It was midnight when she called Doris. "Doris, papa and I have gone back together."

"Oh, mama, I've been waiting on pins and needles, hoping and praying that you'd make up."

"Yes, Doris, we did . . . But I did something that I regret very much, Doris . . . I put you in a very awkward position—"

"I don't care, mama, as long as you're back together."

Sara swallowed hard. "Well, I do care, Doris. Unfortunately, papa doesn't want to have anything to do with you as long as he lives—"

Doris was stunned. "Why?"

"He feels that you took sides against him. I tried to explain to him that that wasn't the case, but papa has to have a reason for taking me back. The only way he seems to be able to save face is by believing that you and Henry influenced me . . . I mean, by allowing me to stay with you. We know the truth, Doris, but he feels that you were very disloyal to him. No matter how I try to explain it to him, he refuses to speak to you—"

Doris' outcry was like a knife in Sara—she was paying the piper already for getting Jacob back . . .

"Well, mama," Doris said, trying to compose herself, "I guess what really matters is that you and papa are together again . . . I just hope and pray you'll be happy . . ."

CHAPTER FIFTY-NINE

BECAUSE OF the breach between Doris and her father, the relationship between Lillian and Doris also changed. Lillian's and Jerry's livelihood depended on Jerry's job, and Jacob made it clear that their loyalties had better lie with him. As painful as it was for Lillian, she couldn't endanger her family's security.

But it was Doris for whom the next few years were the greatest trial, requiring the greatest emotional adjustment. It was particularly wrenching when the holidays came, when the family normally gathered together to celebrate. As dearly as she loved her husband and children, spending the holidays with just the four of them left her with an incompleteness she could not seem to overcome. She was bewildered that papa could hold her responsible for the separation from mama.

One day she got up enough courage to drive to the plant, but her father all but threw her out, called her and Henry ungrateful *gonifs* and said he would never see them again as long as he lived.

She came home in a state of total despair and called Lillian. Lillian knew that Doris was unaware of mama's treachery, but she was too frightened to reveal the true story. To take Doris into her confidence would jeopardize her own position—and only add to Doris' heartbreak. . . .

The adjustments Doris had to make were more than just emotional ones. She even had to change temples. The family had always gone to Temple Emanuel and she saw them there once, but they had made a point of avoiding her.

She joined another temple. As she sat in the strange pew during the high holy day of Yom Kippur, she wondered what papa was thinking during the part of the service that said not until we learn to forgive one another can God forgive us. How could papa read that in the *Union Prayerbook* and not realize that he was giving lip-service to his religion, which in itself was a sin against God? And what had her terrible sin been, to offend her father so? My God, hadn't mama explained that she'd come to Doris and that they had begged her to go back? Well, it really did no good, all the thinking, the wondering . . . The reality was that she was going to have to accept the fact that she was no longer wanted, that the lifeline had been cut and she was left adrift.

Sara had resumed her marriage but things were as they were before. Jacob was away much of the time, and she still made no attempt to create a life of her own. More and more she clung to Lillian.

Not a day went by that Jerry didn't come home to find Sara present at dinner, and Jacob was frequently there too.

And now Lillian and Jerry began to have their troubles. He complained that he couldn't put up with seeing Jacob all day and come home to him at dinner too. Other changes too . . . Lillian had become quite heavy—which Jerry noticed—and she was under such pressure that the house was often neglected.

Jerry's resentments became more vocal as time went on. Jacob had even begun to pick up the little girls on Saturday mornings to take them to spend the weekend with him. But if

Jerry complained that he wanted the pleasure of spending the only free time he had with his own daughters, Lillian said that, after all, papa did enjoy the children so much . . . Jerry well understood that Jacob was using the children as an excuse for not being left alone with Sara . . .

At this point, Lillian was fighting a battle on both sides, but what distressed her most was the change in Jerry. He didn't sleep nights, and if she asked him to tell her why he seemed so upset, he shook his head and told her she was reading things into his attitudes.

Then one day she no longer had to worry, or wonder. Her life came crashing down on her.

Jerry was stopped by the police and his truck was searched. A bag of money was found. Almost simultaneously, Shlomo and Smitty were picked up. All three had been under surveillance for some time for collecting black-market money, and all three were booked and held.

Jacob was frantic when the case broke. He'd made the deal with various meat markets that had approached him, telling him that rationing restrictions were actually hurting the homefront and for no good reason . . . there was plenty of meat for the war effort but bureaucratic redtape was making hardship totally unnecessary for the people of America who sustained the war effort from home . . . It was a persuasive presentation, and so was the money promised. Jacob knew it was technically wrong, but it made sense . . . he knew all about the bureaucrats who had never met a payroll in their lives, didn't understand the profit and loss that made America great . . . . So he made a deal, and to protect his brother and son-in-law and friend he had kept them in the dark as much as possible . . . or hoped he had. Of course, they were grown men and if something happened . . . well, they'd all lived off of him anyway, and life was full of risks, as he well knew, nobody put a spoon in his mouth . . . And now, well, in a private conference with his attorneys it was clear somebody had to take the fall. To implicate him would only destroy all of them—he was the meal ticket, after all, as his attorneys pointed out again and again. And what would the disgrace do to Sara . . . ? It would kill her, as they well knew, and would any of them like that on their conscience? The burden of guilt fell on the three men who had collected the money—although they'd had no share in it—and a deal was made. Jacob would not be implicated, but he would use his influence to shorten the sentence and he promised that when they were released

453

they would be well compensated for the time they'd done. In the meantime, he would provide for their wives and children.

Lillian and Nadine went to visit their husbands as often as they could. Both women were, of course, devastated. It all seemed like a nightmare they couldn't wake up from.

After six months the men were finally released, and now they sat in Jacob's private office as he wrote out a check for each man—five thousand dollars for six months in jail and three shattered lives.

When Shlomo was given his check he just shook his head in wonder, then looked up at his brother. "I'm having a little difficulty remembering the little boy who walked into mama's one winter morning, looking for a home and family. What happened to you, Jacob? How did you turn out to be a man who would allow his brother, son-in-law and friend to spend six months in jail to protect himself? You wound up with thousands and thousands of dollars and you think that writing out a check will wash away your guilt. I never thought the day would ever come when I'd say this to you, Jacob, but I hope your soul burns in hell . . . Take your damn check. I don't want your blood money." And he tore the check into pieces and threw them on Jacob's desk.

Jerry very much wished he could do the same thing, but he wasn't as strong, wasn't ready yet. Not yet . . . Also, he didn't have any money put away, as Shlomo did.

Smitty had no such inhibition and gave it to Jacob with both guns, calling him, among other things, a cold-blooded son of a bitch.

As far as Nadine was concerned, there was no money in the world to compensate for the disgrace and injustice that her husband had been through. But at least he had endured it. When Sandy finished telling her what had happened in Jacob's office, she sat quietly, then said to him, "For six months now, I haven't been able to put this whole picture together. But now . . . Jacob sat in his ivory tower making the deals with the buyers, and you weren't even aware that you were collecting blackmarket money when the receipts were handed to you. Why did you feel your brother should be protected? Why did you feel that his life was so much more important than yours? He was the one to blame for all of this, and he's gotten away scot-free!"

"As much as I hate what he's done, I couldn't bring myself to throw my brother to the wolves. Look, Nadine, it does no

454

good to go over this again and again. It's over. As far as I'm concerned, Jacob is no longer my brother."

"What are we going to do now?"

"Well, I'm going to talk to Neal and I think we can make some money in the salvage business. There's a place we can buy in Los Angeles. That will mean selling the house and moving, but thank God we've saved a few thousand dollars ... The truth is, no amount of money he could have given me would make up for this ... he can rationalize it for himself, maybe ... I can't, won't. Never. Something terrible has happened to Jacob. I don't know how, or when, it happened, but it did." ...

The next day, Nadine called Doris and asked if she was free for lunch. Doris was happy to hear from her. Nadine and Sandy were the only ones in the family who kept in touch with her, but they hadn't seen much of each other since Sandy had been in jail.

As they sat at lunch, Doris was saddened by the lines of bitterness around Nadine's lovely eyes. There was an awkwardness between them, and making small talk was difficult. Finally Nadine looked searchingly at Doris. It was about time Doris knew the truth about her family ... about time she shared the burden of the knowledge ...

"You know, Doris, your uncle and I have the very deepest affection for you. That's why I wanted to see you today. We're moving to Los Angeles to make a new start. This has been a nightmare, the boys have suffered so ... Perhaps I'm being vindictive, but I'll live with that ... Doris, if you're under the impression your father isn't speaking to you because you took your mother's part during their separation, that isn't quite the truth. She used you ..." And Nadine proceeded to tell Doris everything.

By the time she was through, Doris was so shaken that Nadine had to take her home. She almost regretted having told Doris the truth, but maybe it was better that Doris at last be freed of her illusions ...

Leaving a city where they had spent their whole lives wasn't easy for the Blums. But in time of trouble, one put one's own feelings aside, and Charles and Mildred knew they needed their children and grandchildren more than the comfort of a familiar place. Neal was going into business with Sandy and the family would be separated for the first time. The prospect of that was too painful, so Charles and Mildred picked up and moved to Los Angeles as well.

Sandy and Nadine found a large old Spanish house with five bedrooms, with a minimum down payment and a twenty-five-year FHA loan. During the twenties the neighborhood had changed to lower income families, but they ignored the surroundings and concentrated on the realities. They had all agreed to pool their resources and live together; it would be cheaper than paying for three separate homes.

Nadine and Jean found jobs in a dress shop. Mr. Blum went to work for Florsheim's. Mildred assumed the responsibility of homemaking, and it was probably the most exciting and gratifying chore she'd ever done. She was already home when her grandsons returned after school, waiting for them with milk and freshly baked cookies.

Sandy and Neal found a salvage business to buy—it could hardly have been called a gold mine but the books showed it made a meager profit and Sandy felt that with hard work it could be developed. They bought the business for five thousand dollars, to be paid out over a period of a year. Neal took over the bookkeeping, Sandy the buying and selling. He worked almost beyond his endurance, and with the help of Jason, a strong young black man who had walked into the lot one day asking for a job, he sorted the scrap into piles so that they knew every nut and bolt in the yard. Sandy began to realize that one of the biggest demands was for old auto parts. Hot-rodding had become a national hobby. So he bought old mufflers, pistons, fenders, hubcaps, vintage wire wheels—anything and everything that a kid needed to build a jalopy. By underselling the competition the business grew rapidly and soon the lot became a hunting ground for enthusiastic collectors of these indispensable items.

The business of Sanders and Blum was not only making ends meet but also made it unnecessary for Nadine and Jean to work. They joined the temple, Nadine became involved with the sisterhood and even became president. The boys were thriving too. Neal's and Jean's son Freddy became captain of the Little League baseball team, and Sandy's son Mark showed the makings of a rabbi—he had decided he wanted to be one almost from the first day he attended Sunday School. The scholar of the family, after school he attended Hebrew classes and, in fact, was most helpful when it came time for Freddy to be *bar-mitzvahed*.

Sandy never spoke of Jacob, but he did think of him occasionally ... had Jacob shown more remorse—*any* remorse, in fact—the chances were he'd have forgiven him, never mind what he'd said at the time. In a perverse sense he

456

had Jacob to thank for his new life. He could face the world and hold up his head without shame. His sleep was never disturbed with guilt or nightmares. He wondered if Jacob, for all his money, was so fortunate, and knew the answer . . .

Life did not resolve itself quite so satisfactorily for Jerry. He was not only angry over Jacob's betrayal but he felt he had considerably more coming to him. Jacob had slept peacefully in his mansion while he had been unjustly suffering in jail. Five thousand dollars hardly made up for that. He demanded that Jacob establish him in a butcher shop, Jacob told him that he didn't feel he was qualified and that he wasn't going to allow him to intimidate him, to blackmail him . . . The antagonism between them grew to such a proportion that Jerry left his job with Jacob and went to work as a butcher.

Lillian found the arguments and pressures almost more than she could bear. Her parents went so far as to say that Jerry gambled and they even questioned his fidelity as a husband (Jerry, after all, had committed the cardinal sin— had declared his independence). At first, Lillian refused to believe any of it. She had no reason to question Jerry's faithfulness to her, but Sara and Jacob especially kept up a barrage about Jerry's inadequacies as a man, saying that he would never provide for her, that she could expect nothing in her life with him, that he was a failure, and in spite of herself she did finally have some doubts . . . She found herself questioning Jerry about why he stayed out late. Because, he said, there were nights he just couldn't go home and face seeing Sara and Jacob, so he sometimes met with his friends to have a few drinks and a little dinner . . . And then one night he came home drunk. A dreadful scene built and Lillian actually accused him of being unfaithful. Jerry accused her of finally having become her parents' daughter in every way, told her he had no intention of listening to Jacob talk through his daughter . . . she snapped back that he was protesting too much . . . The next thing Lillian knew Jerry had packed his suitcase and left the household . . . .

The following night, Jacob and Sara were once again at Lillian's house.

"I've been trying to warn you," Jacob said. "Your husband is no good, he'll never amount to anything. He thinks I should hand over the whole business to him . . . let me tell you, Lillian, the best thing that could happen to you is to get rid of him. He's not a good father or a good husband . . ."

Each time Lillian tried to defend Jerry the condemnations became more overpowering, more convincing ... the awful doubts kept creeping back into her mind. Eventually the tension and pressure unraveled the marriage. Unbelievably ... inevitably ... they were getting a divorce, something that they had never thought possible took on an internal momentum that overwhelmed them. Jerry was miserable, Lillian was stricken. ...

After the final decree, Jerry took himself to the house one evening. Lillian was alone. He was shocked at how thin and withdrawn she'd become, and his heart went out to her as they sat quietly in the livingroom.

"Jerry, I still can't believe this has happened to us."

"Neither can I. The whole thing is a nightmare. I do know one thing ... we made a terrible mistake, you and I. We should have gotten away from them, the way Sandy did. You and I shouldn't be divorced, but there was just too much against us. You can't battle people like them, we were never left alone ... that's really why we're divorced. I was never unfaithful to you, Lillian. I've always loved you, I think I still do ..."

"Jerry, do you think there's a possibility we could go back, even now?"

He had asked himself the same question ... and regretfully answered it ... "Eventually the same thing would happen ... they'd never leave us alone. They've lost Rachel, driven Doris away. You're all they've got left. They can't live with—or without—each other, you're going to become their answer, their target, their bail-out ... I love you, Lillian, and I feel very sorry as hell for you because you'll never be able to leave them behind you. We might have had a chance if you'd been able to keep them from having so much power over you. I don't blame you ... I just hope you find a little happiness."

She tried to hold back the tears ... "What's going to happen to you, Jerry?"

"I don't know, I haven't thought that far ahead. The Sanderses aren't easy to get over ..."

Jacob sold the house in Row Hampton for twenty-five thousand dollars and took over all of Lillian's affairs. She felt it was only right that Jerry should get half of the money, but Jerry refused it since he wasn't in a position to pay alimony. When the furniture was moved out, she realized that Jerry was—really—out of her life now. It was a reality that she'd still not been convinced of—or willing to accept—until that very moment.

That first night she slept at her parents' house she asked herself, as she had before, how she could have allowed them to so dominate her life, how she could have sacrificed even her marriage for them. Of course she'd known what was going on, but it was as though it was happening to someone else . . . not to her. Life wasn't perfect with Jerry, but compared to *before* Jerry . . . and now that's where she was right back to . . . feeling powerless to reach out for the one thing she wanted—just as she always had. . . .

The next long three years brought no changes for Lillian. She and her mother warred as before. Her father kept promising that he would send her to Europe, where she'd meet a man who was worthy of her, but somehow he never got around to it. She knew that she was too necessary as a focus for her parents. Her presence was the only thing that made their marriage tolerable to them, except the specter of the absence of it . . . .

Each Sunday Jerry came to pick up the children, and from time to time he would ask if she'd like to join them, and their day would be spent so pleasurably that it was difficult for her to believe he was no longer her husband. In fact, she was just beginning to hope that she'd have the courage to leave her parents for him again when he said uneasily to her one day . . . "Lillian . . . I've met somebody . . . I'm going to be married . . . I'll never feel about anybody the way I felt about you, Lillian. In fact, I want you to know that I still love you—"

"Jerry, please, don't you think it might be possible for us to start again? We did have so much that was good between us. More good memories than bad . . ."

"How many times do you think I've thought about that? And what do you imagine it's been like for me these last three years? But it still gets back to the same old story. You just can't fight them . . . I'll never completely understand why, but then I'm not a psychiatrist. I just hope something good happens for you in your life. God knows, you deserve it . . ."

CHAPTER SIXTY

LILLIAN MADE up her mind she at least had to do *something* with her life. All right . . . it wasn't exactly the route to social eminence, but never mind that . . . she'd take a secretarial course. . . .

One day after class she was walking to her car when she happened to see a fetching coat in a store window. The one thing she didn't need was a coat, but maybe it would at least help bolster her morale . . .

Lillian went in and tried it on. It didn't really achieve what she'd hoped, hadn't brought the lift she'd anticipated. But still, it was pretty, jaunty—red with brass buttons.

When she got out her checkbook, she found that the balance in her account was rather low. Since she wasn't going to make a deposit till Thursday, she said, "Why don't I open an account?"

"We'd be delighted. Here, let me take you into the credit office and introduce you."

After filling out the application she handed it to the credit manager. Woodside, Hayward Meat Packing Company, Mrs. Gerald Gould . . . When he finished reading it and took a look at the way Lillian was dressed, he decided there would be no need to check on her credit. "If you'd like to take the coat today, Mrs. Gould, you're more than welcome—"

"Thank you, how nice of you."

"Not at all. I hope we'll be seeing you more often." . . .

Two days later she was sitting at the counter of Liggett's drugstore having a cup of coffee after her class.

"Mrs. Gould, how nice to see you."

She turned around and smiled. It was the credit manager from the store. "Thank you . . ."

"Do you mind if I join you?"

"Not at all, if I can charge it."

He laughed. "Your credit is very good with us, Mrs. Gould. Incidentally, my name is Dan Fuller."

The conversation was light and impersonal, and Lillian didn't give it a second thought. Over the next few months, however, they seemed to keep running into each other whenever Lillian walked into Liggett's for coffee.

One day he took it further ... "I confess, I'm a little curious about you."

"Why?" A divorced woman and still coy, Lillian?

"Well, judging by your application and credit sources you haven't remarried. How does a beautiful woman like you happen to be single?"

Lillian looked down and stirred her coffee. "It wasn't exactly my choice ..."

"Do you have children?"

"Yes, two little girls, Cindy and Candy."

"How long have you been divorced?"

"Three years."

"How did you get away with that?"

She smiled. "Just unlucky, I guess."

"I hope you won't feel offended at this, but I'd very much like to take you to dinner. We've become coffee buddies after all these months and—"

"I'd really like that—"

"Great ... when?"

"Well, with my busy social schedule, just about any time."

"How about tonight?"

"Why not?" Why not, indeed. How long had it been ... ?

"I don't have a car."

"Oh, don't worry about that, Dan. I'll pick you up. What time?"

"About five-thirty? At the store?"

For the first time in three years she felt alive, actually excited. She'd wear the lucky red coat ...

When she went home and started to dress Sara said, "What are you doing?"

"I'm getting dressed, obviously. I have a date."

"You have a what?"

"A date." Mama, leave me *alone* ...

"With whom?"

"With a man."

"What man, who is he?"

"I think his father owns the Chase Manhattan Bank."

"That wasn't necessary. Who is he?"

"He's the credit manager for Carolyn's Dress Shop. Mama, I'm not fourteen years old ... I'm an old divorced lady—"

"Well, I'd certainly think you'd be more discriminating—"

"Do you, mama? Where are all those marvelous eligible young men that you and papa said would find me so irresistible. It happens to be the best offer I've had in three years.

461

Don't get excited, he's only taking me to dinner. It should help my credit rating . . ."

She arrived at five-thirty on the dot, just as Dan was closing up.

"You look beautiful, Lillian."

"Thank you very much, sir . . . that's the nicest thing anybody's said to me in a long time."

"That's hard to believe . . . where would you like to go for dinner?"

"How about Tahiti?"

"I'm game . . . except it'd be a little difficult opening up the store in the morning. Would you settle for Monterey?"

A little more than an hour later Lillian found herself sitting across the table from Dan Fuller in a restaurant called Cannery Row, and the restaurant's atmosphere was certainly conducive to making a very lonely lady feel a little romantic.

During the months that they had met in the drugstore, she had found him to be charming and witty, and she felt enormously comfortable with him. He certainly wasn't Jerry, but it was a little late to start making comparisons. Over dinner, he told her amusing anecdotes about a day in the life of a manager of a dress shop. By the time dinner was over and they found themselves once again in Palo Alto, Lillian was sure she would see him again, even though he didn't so much as kiss her goodnight or, for that matter, mention another date. There was just something in the air, and they both knew it was only a matter of time . . .

Two days later, he called her at seven in the evening and asked her to go to a movie.

"I'd like that."

"Great, I'll pick you up in a cab."

"Don't be silly. Where do you want to meet me?"

"How about in front of John's Pub?"

"I'll be right down . . ."

Again there was a confrontation with mama, but Lillian managed to ignore it. Progress . . . ?

Instead of going to the movies they spent the evening at John's Pub. It was the first time they'd talked about him . . . Without embarrassment he told her that he'd been born in Kansas and that his mother was a lady who took her drinking very seriously and her husband for granted. When she found that her husband had taken up with someone else, she wasn't too upset; there were any number of men she could call, and

462

she often did. The result was that at a very early age Dan refused to live with his mother any longer. When he was twelve years old he went to live with his grandmother, whom he adored. He had almost gotten married once, but it hadn't worked out and he'd never met anyone else he could seriously think of marrying. After his grandfather died his grandmother had decided that she wanted to move to California, where her sister lived, and that's how they'd happened to wind up in Palo Alto.

"I don't think it would make much of a movie," he said, "and I know they'd never make a musical out of it . . . Anyway, now that I've revealed the shattering saga of my life, how about you and yours?"

"Well, my story would make a great movie, but I'm not sure if it would be comedy or tragedy. Or maybe farce. I married, no kidding, for love . . . one of the most terrific people I've ever known in my life. We've been divorced for three years now and he's remarried."

"Are you still carrying the torch?"

"After lots of sleepless nights and tears and frustration, you finally come to the conclusion that over is over—or at least that there's nothing you can do about it."

"So you're really still in love with him?"

"You don't get over someone just because you're not together. And ours is a rather special situation. Even though he's married, we're still friends. Real civilized, wouldn't you say?"

"Why did you get a divorce?"

"Oh, my mother and father thought it might be a good idea . . . Anyway, here I am, Dan Fuller, sitting in John's Pub with you, and liking it."

His own childhood had taught him a lot about what parents could do to their children, and he understood it better than she would ever have imagined . . . "Did you ever think of getting married again?"

"Sure, except you know that corny expression . . . it takes two to tango."

"I tango."

"To do it with me could be dangerous to your health. Especially your nerves."

"You need strong nerves to be a credit manager . . . Enough badinage, Lillian Sanders Gould . . . what I think I'm trying to do is propose to you . . ."

She nodded, unsmiling. In fact, deadly serious. "That's something I'm going to have to think about—"

"You take all the time you want, as long as you say yes in twenty-four hours."

She looked at him. "You don't know what you're letting yourself in for, Dan."

"What are you so frightened about?"

"Just about everything . . ."

"You're frightened about getting married again?"

"That's part of it."

"Don't you think you could love more than once in your life?"

"I would hope so, but the point is, I have a problem—"

"What's your problem?"

"I happen to have a mother and father who not only want someone around in their old age, but who've picked me to keep them from having to live alone with each other."

"And you're going to settle for that? That's giving up, being a coward . . ."

"I once said that to someone . . . you're right, though. I am a coward—"

"What are you afraid of?"

"Oh, my God, Dan, it would take me years to explain it, and I'm not sure you'd understand it even then. I'm not sure that I do, for that matter."

"Well, I'm not afraid of too many people, so let me tell you now—I happen to be in love with you. And if you feel the same, I'd like us to get married. That's fairly clear, isn't it?"

"I'll take those twenty-four hours." . . .

That night as Lillian lay in the dark staring up at the ceiling, she knew that what she felt for Dan was at least a kind of love. Not the kind she'd felt for Jerry, of course, but there was something about Dan that she couldn't walk away from—and it wasn't because she hadn't been out in three years and was on the rebound. More than that . . . much more. But she also wasn't going to rush into this without giving it some real thought . . . To begin with, she had two children. How could Dan provide for them all on his salary? Papa was carefully guarding every cent she had so that no fortune hunter could bilk her out of the enormous sum. Dear trusting papa wanted to make sure that no one would take advantage of her. Well, she'd fought for Jerry once—for all the good it had come to in the end—and although she was afraid that the same pattern would be repeated if she married Dan, she also knew she had to take the chance. It might damn well be her last . . . Lillian met Dan the next day after

464

work. As they sat in John's Pub, each sipping a martini, Lillian said, "I've thought it over, Dan, but there are some questions I have to get out of the way before I can give you an answer . . . I know you haven't met my little girls yet, but how do you feel about taking on the responsibility of them?"

"If they're anything like their mother, I don't think we're going to have any problems there."

"I'm Jewish . . ."

"And I'm not, what does that have to do with anything?"

"I just want you to know that my children are being raised as Jews."

"Listen, I really don't care how you raise them, as long as they have religious training of some kind."

"I'm glad to hear that . . . now, for the good stuff—my parents . . . I don't know how to prepare you for this, but introducing you to my parents will be like throwing you to the lions."

"Then the sooner the better. Tonight's as good as any."

When they stood to leave, Dan took her in his arms and kissed her. "Lillian, let *me* do the worrying."

"That, I assure you, will be a pleasure, Dan." . . .

When they arrived in Woodside, Dan Fuller looked at the moonlit house in amazement. "Is this where you live or where you work?"

Laughing, she said, "No, this is where I'm incarcerated." She took him by the hand and they walked down the flagstone path that led to the front door. She paused at the door and kissed him. "Man the battle stations, you're in for a rough time."

She opened the door and led him across the forty-foot livingroom and into the library. When they entered, Jacob and Sara both looked up with questioning expressions.

Lillian decided to plunge right in. "Mama and papa, I'd like you to meet my fiancé, Dan Fuller."

Sara sat speechless. Jacob quickly sized up the situation and decided it would be the wrong approach to go into a rage. He had seen Lillian's growing discontent in these last years, to spar with her now would only push her further away . . . Besides, he had tried that tactic with Jerry and she had married him anyway. This time he would try a different tactic.

"Sit down, Lillian and uh . . . you, Mr. Fuller. Now tell me, Lillian, how long have you two been going together?"

"About three months," she said, looking him directly in the eye.

"And Mr. Fuller knows all about the children?"

"Yes, papa, obviously."

"And you think Mr. Fuller is prepared to take on the responsibility of two growing girls?"

"Mr. Sanders, since you're talking about me, I'll answer. Yes."

"What do you do for a living, Mr. Fuller?"

"I'm the credit manager for a large dress concern."

"And your salary will support Lillian and her children in their current manner of living?"

"Papa, if you don't mind. I haven't always been so accustomed to luxuries. There have been periods when I didn't have money for groceries . . . besides, I think that's a subject Dan and I should discuss—"

"You do that, but I want you to know, Lillian, that I don't intend to do anything for you—absolutely nothing."

"You've done enough for me already, papa. All I want is the money you've taken care of for me. We're going to be married as quickly as we can arrange things."

Jacob turned white, but he fought to control his anger. "You're taking on a very great responsibility for a young man," he said to Dan.

"I'm accustomed to responsibility . . . and I happen to love Lillian very much. I'd say that's a good combination for the future. Mr. Sanders, I don't expect you to give us any help, nor do we need it."

Jacob felt the words like a blow to his stomach . . . His favorite daughter—his only daughter, in some ways—was leaving him too. Well, she'd regret it . . . "You've made your decision, Lillian. Now I want you out of this house as quickly as possible."

"That's what I'd planned on, papa."

Everything had been said.

Sara just sat there, without a word.

Lillian had a long talk with the children, and she and the girls spent Sunday with Dan. It was obvious there were going to be no problems there. Dan adored them, and they quickly took to him.

On Monday they had their blood tests and got their marriage license. But when they tried to find a rabbi, from San Francisco to San José, there was no rabbi who would marry them. They finally were reduced to arranging with a justice of the peace to be married on Wednesday, at seven-thirty in the evening.

466

On Wednesday afternoon, as she put on her beige wool suit, Lillian certainly didn't feel like a bride. The tension created by her parents' hostility had been unbearable and she couldn't wait to get away.

At six o'clock she went to the diningroom, where Cynthia and Candy were having dinner. They ran to her and she hugged them tightly. "We'll all be together very soon, darlings. Tomorrow night I'll come for you and we'll have dinner together."

"I wish we could come and live with you now, mommy," Cindy said.

"I do too, darling. But as you know, the apartment that Dan has is too small. We're going to get a bigger place very soon though, and then we'll all be together."

As she was about to leave, Jacob said, "I'm taking the car back."

She stared at him expressionlessly. "Papa, I would have thought that you, of all people, would be happy for me—especially after what you did to my last marriage."

"Don't worry about how I feel. You go ahead and do what you want—and see how happy it makes *you.*"

Sara walked out of the room and up the stairs. . . .

Lillian took a taxi to Carolyn's Dress Shop, where Dan was anxiously waiting for her with a bouquet of lilies of the valley. She promptly broke into tears when she saw them.

"Honey, I hope you're crying for the right reasons. You don't have regrets already?"

"God no, Dan, I'm just sorry that it couldn't have been different."

"It'll be okay, I'll make sure of that. Listen, we'd better get going or you may not be a bride at all."

They hailed a taxi, and when they got in the taxi driver smiled and said, "Hi, lady."

She looked at him. "Hi."

"We're not even married and you're cheating on me?" Dan said.

"Well, as a matter of fact, I am. No, actually, he picked me up in Woodside to bring me down."

When they arrived at the justice of the peace, the door was opened by a diminutive gray-haired lady. "Come in, my husband and I have been expecting you."

When they entered, the J.P. smiled solemnly and his wife went to the organ and began pumping out "Drink to Me Only with Thine Eyes."

Suddenly Lillian turned to Dan and he saw the distress in

467

her face. "What's the matter, honey? Having second thoughts?"

"No, but you'll never believe this. We haven't got the license . . . I left it in the glove compartment of my car that I don't have anymore."

Dan groaned and shrugged helplessly at the justice of the peace. "Your honor, we'll have to hold this up for just a little while, if we won't be putting you out. We seem to be without the license . . ."

Lillian called a taxi and when it arrived they were greeted by the same charioteer with the same friendly "Hi."

"Would you drive us up to Chapin off of Woodside Drive?"

"I know, I know the way."

"Wait a minute," Lillian said. "I don't have the keys to the car or the garage. You wait here, and I'll call home and ask whoever answers to open the garage doors . . ."

Sara answered and when she heard Lillian's voice she broke down and cried. "Are you married?"

"I would be but—"

"Did you change your mind?"

"Not a chance, mama, but I left the license in the glove compartment of the car. Mama, do me a favor. Open the garage door and leave the car keys in the door."

Jacob was in the room and was asking what Lillian wanted.

"Lillian wants you to open the garage door and leave the keys in the door . . . she has her license in the glove compartment."

"I said she couldn't come in the house and I meant it. Tell her she can pick up the license in the mail box."

"Jacob, enough is enough already. She's the only one we've got left—"

"And she's left us—"

Quietly, Sara said, "Lillian, papa says to pick it up in the mail box . . ."

They drove to the house, Lillian picked up the license, and soon they were on their way back to the justice of the peace. When they arrived the driver said, "Do you think you're going to need me any more this evening?"

Dan laughed. "I'd bet on that. If you want to hang around, we won't be long."

"Why not . . . you people have been through a lot tonight, I think you need a break . . ."

At eight forty-five, wilted bouquet and all, Lillian Sanders

Gould became Mrs. Dan Fuller. The only prayer she made was that God would be good to her and help her finally to grow up.

The justice of the peace congratulated them, gave Dan a fatherly handshake and Lillian a peck on the cheek, and once again they were back in the taxi, where Dan took her in his arms. "Lillian Fuller, you're the most beautiful bride that ever was."

The taxi driver looked at them in the mirror. "Congratulations. God, I feel like I've spent the honeymoon with you two . . ."

When they got to Dan's apartment, he had champagne, caviar and a small two-tiered wedding cake waiting for them.

"You did this?" Lillian said. "You're more romantic than I am—"

"But you're better looking . . . now, let's see how good I am at popping the cork." As he struggled with it, Lillian said, "Honey, *this* you're not going to believe, but I left my overnight case in the taxi."

"Well, you can always wear my pajamas . . ."

As it turned out, Lillian didn't need her overnight case, nor Dan's pajamas.

After they had made love Dan said, "You know, darling, if I'd known how it was going to be, I'm damned if I'd ever have given you even those twenty-four hours."

She snuggled closer to him. "I'll do my best to make it up to you for lost time."

"How about now?"

Her eager kiss was his answer.

CHAPTER SIXTY-ONE

THE NEXT morning Lillian was in the kitchen, wearing Dan's robe and slippers, measuring the coffee into the Silex. "Honey, what do you want for breakfast?"

Dan was shaving in the bathroom. "Who can think about breakfast after last night?"

"Well, I hoped you'd worked up a big appetite."

"I have, and don't tempt me . . ."

Twenty minutes later, they were sitting across from each other at the table, eating their wedding breakfast of waffles

469

and very crisp—according to Dan's prescription—bacon. She looked at her tall, sandy-haired, hazel-eyed new husband and smiled to herself. Isn't this remarkable, she thought. When my life ended with Jerry I would have laid odds that a morning like this was something I'd never see again. It's too incredible for words. Which she didn't try to find.

"You know," Dan said, "the day you walked in Carolyn's I had a feeling you probably made the best waffles in the world."

"So that was it. And all the time I thought you were after me because of that seventy-nine-dollar coat I bought."

"That too . . . I'm greedy," and he proved it by taking her off to the bedroom for the best part of their wedding breakfast.

Afterward, in between kisses, they polished off the rest of the champagne, and he announced it was now time to consider the honeymoon.

"Terrific . . . where are we going?"

"I thought we'd splurge and hire a car, take a little ride, stop for lunch on the coast, and maybe drop in to see my grandmother. She got back from Kansas yesterday—"

"How come you didn't tell me, Dan?"

"Because you would have insisted she be at the wedding. I told her how adorable your family is, and that since they weren't going to be there I thought it should be just the two of us. And Mabel agreed." . . .

Everything Dan had said about his grandmother was true. She was what everybody wished a grandmother to be, and she was genuinely pleased that Dan had at long last found the person he wanted to share his life with.

As they sat with her in her small cozy apartment she said to Lillian, "I was beginning to worry about your husband."

"Why?"

"Well, at twenty-six he had all the makings of a confirmed bachelor. Thank God you came along and saved him from *that*."

"Well, it works both ways, Mabel. He rescued this blushing bride of thirty-one . . ."

When the time came for them to go, Mabel said, "Lillian, I just want you to know how pleased I am that Dan found you. Somehow I know the two of you are so right. Just be happy, my dear. I think you both hugely deserve it."

The next day, after Lillian had straightened up the apartment, she called her mother to see how the children were doing. To her surprise, Sara urged her to come out to the house.

As she sat in her mother's bedroom the conversation was stilted, but this morning Sara seemed more hurt than angry.

"So, now you're married again—"

"Yes, thank God, mama. When Jerry and I broke up, the world just fell apart for me. I never thought I'd ever be able to put it together again—but it *happened.*"

"Well, I hope it continues, for your sake, but I think you've made a terrible mistake, Lillian. Your husband is a handsome young man and women age a lot quicker than men. What's going to happen ten years from now?"

"Mama, it seems to me I've heard this same thing before—though in a slightly different form. Jim was too old for Rachel, but they seem to be perfectly happy together. Marriage has nothing to do with people's ages. It's understanding and being able to communicate with each other that makes a marriage."

"That's all very philosophical, Lillian, and on the surface it sounds very good. But reality is something else. When a woman is married to a younger man, as time goes on she has to work hard to keep up with him and that can be a very great strain . . ."

If anybody was unqualified to give advice on marriage, it was certainly mama. She and papa had no greater understanding of each other now than they had when they first married.

"What happens, Lillian," Sara went on, "when you're not quite as lovely as you are now? Men do stray, you know. It's in their nature."

"That depends on the woman, the marriage and especially the two people involved. Besides, it's not true—not all men stray," she said, thinking of Jerry. "So, if you've any worries about my marriage, don't add that one to your repertoire. Well, I didn't come to talk about that . . . I'd be grateful if papa would arrange to give me my money. And I want to take the girls as quickly as possible."

Sara paled at the thought of losing the girls. She really needed them, though she'd never stopped to analyze the reasons. Lillian's remarriage had left her feeling lost—just as lost as when she'd been a little girl in Belgium, unwanted by her mother and Louie but always hoping that some day . . .

There was a pleading note now in Sara's voice that she was not aware of . . . "Lillian, you've just been married. Why don't you give yourself a chance to adjust. Anyway, your present living situation is hardly suitable to having the children live with you—"

"Obviously, I'm going to take a larger place."

"Lillian, don't be selfish. Please think of the children too. They're accustomed to this being their home, and they have every advantage here. Leave them for a little while..."

"I think the sooner they adjust to their new lives, the better it will be for all of us, mama."

Sara began to cry. Sometimes, Lillian thought, crying seemed to come as naturally to mama as breathing...

"Please don't take them yet, Lillian. Leave papa and me with something..."

Lillian couldn't help it... all the hostility and anger that had dominated their relationship was washed out from her for the moment. She needed time to find an apartment and get settled anyway, and it would do no harm to have the girls here for a little while...

"All right, mama, but the girls are going to come live with us as soon as we're settled. Papa's not traveling as much and he'll be around to keep you company... But if that isn't enough, remember that there's still a big world out there, mama... If only you'd make an *effort* you could find a life for yourself. Other women do. Mama, you can be a very charming woman when you want to be. There is no reason you can't make friends. There are a million charities..."

"Lillian, you're just talking foolishness. Your father still goes to bed at eight o'clock at night and gets up at four in the morning and I have to be home to get his dinner in the early afternoon. I don't have a normal life, like other women do."

Well, there was just no use pursuing it. Mama, it seemed, just wasn't going to try. She would live—and die—feeling victimized... "Well, be that as it may, mama, I think there's a great deal you could do to help your situation. Now, I'm going to pick the girls up after school every day. And I want them to spend a little time in the evening with Dan, so they'll come to dinner too."

"You mean every night?"

"Well, maybe not every night, but often. They're going to have to get to know Dan, although I expect them to go on seeing and loving Jerry too. For the first time in our lives, let's try to be sensible and mature people. Okay, mama?"

Sara nodded....

Jacob was as upset about Lillian's intention of taking the

children as about her request for her twenty-five thousand dollars. "You call her on the phone," he told Sara. "I want to see her—and tell her to come alone."

But when Lillian arrived, Dan was with her. If papa was going to be a tough adversary, so was she. When they walked into the library, Jacob was fuming.

"I told you to come alone."

"Since I no longer *am alone,* I don't intend to start out my life with secrets. Anything you have to tell me can be said in front of my husband."

Jacob's face was rigid. "What, if I may ask, do you intend to do with twenty-five thousand dollars?"

"Since it's mine, I don't really think I need to answer that. But I suppose you'll find out sooner or later . . . I'm going to put part of it down on a house and then Dan and I are going to open a dress shop—"

"You know what's going to happen, don't you, Lillian? You're going to take that money and it's going to be like sand going down a rat hole."

"As I said, it happens to be my money, money that Jerry *earned*—and a damn sight less than you owe for the things he did for you. I have the right to take it and throw it in the ocean if I want."

"Damn it, do you think I don't know why this . . . this person married you?"

"Now just a minute, Mr. Sanders," Dan shouted, "I won't take that from you. I haven't seen any great dowry that you've bestowed on Lillian. I got along okay without you and I intend to keep it that way."

"But you'd never be able to get into business without my daughter's money, would you—?"

"I'll answer that if you don't mind, Dan," Lillian interrupted. "I happen to be the one who suggested going into business, not Dan. And for your information, I resent your talking to my husband that way. I want my money, it's as simple as *that*."

"Why you ungrateful girl, after all I've done for you."

"You broke up my first marriage and you dare call me ungrateful?"

Jacob stood up, about to strike Lillian for the first time in his life. But he caught himself and merely glared at her before he finally walked from the room.

For a moment, Dan and Lillian sat quietly, each with their separate thoughts. When she looked up at him, she said, "There are feelings that are very, very hard to explain. What

473

I said to my father was true about my marriage, but I'm sorry for having said it. This may be difficult for you to understand, but no matter how hard you try, you never stop being a child, someone's daughter or son. I can't apologize for my father, but I hope you can forgive the way he talked to you tonight . . ."

Two days later Lillian received a registered letter. She knew what was in it without opening it, but when she took the check out and looked at it she couldn't help feeling that it should really have been made out to Jerry. . . .

The next week she found a charming one-story ranch house in a good section of Menlo Park. It was in some disrepair, but Lillian saw great possibilities in it, and the price of eighteen thousand dollars attracted her even more. She showed it to Dan, who approved, and they promptly bought it.

"Lillian, I want this to be in your name."

"Oh, no. We're not starting out that way. What I've got is yours, and vice versa."

"Well, I'm afraid vice versa ain't going to buy you much more than a bus ticket."

"We're not going to have to worry about bus tickets. Tomorrow we're going to sign the lease on the store on University Avenue."

He pulled her to him and held her tightly. "How the hell did I ever get so lucky?"

"Well, you said you did a mean tango. And damn it, Dan, we're going to tango on our own."

"You mean on *your* own."

"Dan Fuller, let's get this out of the way once and for all. There isn't going to be one towel that says *his* and one that says *hers*. They're going to say *ours*."

He looked at her once and shook his head. "I still say I don't know how I lucked out."

"Tell me that twenty-five years from now."

"I intend to."

The next months were filled with scarcely any leisure moments for either of them. Between the house and the store, Lillian was finding out how to use a hammer and a saw, how to wallpaper, install linoleum and lay ceramic tile. Their first priority was getting the store ready so they could open.

Dan was extraordinarily artistic, and very handy with carpentry work. They remodeled and decorated the store at a minimum expense, and the result was far above their expectations.

Having been connected in one way or another with the dress business for twelve years, Dan's expertise amazed Lillian. He chose his stock judiciously, and the use of mirrors and lighting not only made the store appear larger but the stock more plentiful.

Announcements were sent to all the customers from Carolyn's—which didn't exactly endear Dan Fuller to Carolyn Hodge. Still she smiled graciously when she attended the opening, although it was already apparent to her that he was going to present some tough competition.

Once the store was in operation Lillian turned her attention to finishing and restoring the house. Within two months her furniture was being arranged and all was ready for the girl to move in.

Lillian went up to the house to collect the children in her secondhand Oldsmobile. As usual, she found Jacob and Sara sitting in the library.

"Mama, papa, in spite of all that's happened, I want you to know that you're both welcome in our home."

Jacob didn't answer, Sara couldn't. When Sara saw the two little girls standing before her in their coats, she . . . inevitably . . . began to cry.

Cindy said, "Don't cry, sissy, we don't live very far from here. You're going to be seeing us all the time—"

"I know, I know. You'll call . . . you won't forget." Oh God, she thought, what was she going to do tomorrow? She could already hear the empty echo of that enormous house. . . .

The children's adjustment to Dan was everything Lillian had hoped for. They loved Jerry, but their affection for Dan was undeniable—as was his for them. On weekends they all worked in the garden. Dan bought three rose bushes, dug the holes for them and made a great ceremony out of planting them. Each had its own name plate. He said they were for his three American beauties.

CHAPTER SIXTY-TWO

JACOB WAS reading in the library when the phone rang.

"Jacob?" The tremulous voice on the other end was familiar, but he was startled by the sound of it. "Gittel?"

There was a long pause, then: "Yes, Jacob."

His hand shook. Why was Gittel calling, especially at this time of night? It would be eleven o'clock in Cleveland. "How are you, Gittel?"

"Oh Jacob . . . Jacob, how can I tell you this?"

"Tell me what?" His face tightened.

"It's Shlomo . . ."

Jacob shut his eyes, began to shake. "What about Shlomo?"

"Oh God, Jacob, Shlomo is dying."

Silence, except for Gittel's sobbing. Finally Jacob found his voice. "Why . . . what . . .?"

She could hardly get the words out. "He has cancer, Jacob . . . I don't know what happened between you, but please, whatever it was you should make it up."

Tears started to his eyes. *I knew one day you would come . . . mama always said you'd come . . .* He could see Shlomo's large soulful eyes as he'd said that . . . "Gittel?"

"Yes, Jacob . . ."

"I'll send money for you and mama to go and I'll meet you in Los Angeles."

"We're already here."

He was stunned. "How long have you been there?"

"For three days. We left as soon as Nadine called."

"And you didn't try to contact me?"

"They . . . I mean Shlomo's sons made me promise I wouldn't, but I know God will forgive me for not keeping my word. They didn't understand as I do. Yes, Jacob, you should come."

"I'll leave right away . . . What hospital?"

"Cedars of Lebanon."

"All right, Gittel, I'll be there as soon as I can get a plane."

"God bless you, Jacob."

No, God damn me, Jacob thought as he hung up. He went to Sara's room. "I just spoke to Gittel." His voice broke. "Shlomo is very sick and I'm going to Los Angeles. I know you haven't been feeling too well yourself, but I think it's only right that you should go too."

"I would, Jacob, but you must believe me, I don't think I feel strong enough to make it. I'm sorry about Shlomo but I feel too sick to even get out of bed." She *was* ill, of that he had no doubt. He would rather not go alone but he had no choice. "All right, Sara, I'm leaving tonight . . . I don't know how long I'll be there but I'll call." . . .

476

Jacob was shocked when he saw Gittel. Her once beautiful, soft face was creased and pale, but worst of all was the sight of his mother. Esther looked shrunken. She looked at him vaguely. "Jacob?"

"Yes, mama..." He held her frail body close to him as a flood of memories came back... You're a fine man, Jacob ... Gittel's first child had been born that night. Here's your father's *tallis*. Wear it with the dignity he did... You hate me, say it...

He didn't hate her tonight. He needed her more than anyone in the world at this moment. From her he found the strength to go to Shlomo's room.

When he opened the door a handsome young man got up from the chair and approached him. With an abrupt gesture he summoned Jacob out of the room and in the hall said without preamble, "I'm sorry Aunt Gittel asked you to come. My father's wish is for you not to be permitted to see him or to attend his funeral."

Jacob stood remembering how he had hit Shlomo, then had held him close in his arms like a child. Oh please, God... don't let Shlomo die... "I don't care," he said to Shlomo's son, "I don't care what happened between your father and me. I'm going to see my brother."

"No, you are not. You almost ruined his life once, but I won't allow you to make his death any harder than it is." Without another word he turned and went back to his father's room, closing the door softly behind him. Jacob sat down on the wooden bench, alone.

Shlomo died near dawn on Friday, but he did not die alone. His wife and two sons were with him, and the last words he uttered were to Nadine... "You've been my resting place, my love..."

According to tradition the funeral had to be held on Friday before sundown.

Jacob waited alone in his hotel room during the funeral, but he could see it all. A still body lay on a slab, waxen and yellow, and coins covered his eyes... *Yis-ga-dal, v'yis-ka-dash....* Sleep well, Shlomo. No matter what I did, or you said... I loved you. I'd give everything I have to make it up to you. Too long... too late...

After the funeral Gittel and Esther stayed with Nadine and her family for a brief time, but the house was full of friends who had come to pay their condolences and Esther was tiring. Gittel took Nadine aside. "Forgive us for leaving so

477

soon, but mama must go to the hotel and lie down. And Nadine, may God be good to you and see you through this. I must take mama home tomorrow . . . and there's poor Hershel. He needs me so since he had the stroke."

"Yes, Gittel, darling . . . you have your burdens to bear. Shlomo loved you very much."

When they found Jacob sitting in his room, he hadn't shaved and what he was feeling was clearly written in his eyes. The scars of too much to remember . . .

"Jacob," Gittel said, "I have to take mama home. Do you think it would be possible for you to get us a flight tonight?"

"I'll go with you. I'll get the tickets." He called home. "Shlomo's gone, Sara." He could hardly go on. "I thought I would come home, but I feel I should take Gittel and mama to Cleveland, not let them go alone . . . My mother hasn't even spoken since . . ."

"I'm sorry, Jacob, of course."

"You understand, Sara."

"Yes. You do what you feel is right."

"Are you feeling better?"

"I'll survive, Jacob." I've managed for a long time, she thought. When they hung up Sara thought about her survival. It was a survival without much love . . . yet she could not forget Shlomo as he was when she'd first come to live with Esther. What would have happened if Esther had refused to take her in? What would her life have turned out to be? What foolish questions . . . The past was history. Did she have a future . . . ?

Jacob's mother was living in the Hebrew Home for the Aged. Was this what happened in the end? He had condemned Esther for what she had once done to him, what kind of a son had he been? He hadn't seen her in years, hadn't even bothered to inquire how she was living, had barely provided for her. He had known she was in an old people's home, but this, he couldn't have imagined. Doddering old men and women sat aimlessly in the hall, staring out into space, forgotten . . . It was as though they were nonexistent, as though they were simply waiting, hoping for death to rescue them.

Gittel had gone home to Hershel and Jacob sat now by his mother's bed, watching as she lay motionless. The effort of talking was too difficult for her. He stayed this way by her

478

side for two days, and had a cot brought into the room although he hardly slept. Listening to his mother's shallow breathing, he could almost hear her thoughts ... no mother should outlive her child ...

The next morning, Ester Dubin Sandsonitsky was gone. It was as though she had willed herself into death. The only words spoken before the end were, "I'll be with you, my Shlomo ... my baby ..."

Jacob threw himself across her, holding her close. Even at the end, mama, you died for Shlomo. Oh God, and even at the end I was jealous ...

The next day, as he saw his mother being put into the ground, the memory of his father's funeral came bark to him. God, there was so much to remember. He looked at Gittel's children, three tall and handsome sons and a lovely daughter. In spite of Gittel's financial problems, somehow she'd managed to educate her children. Two were pharmacists, one a lawyer, and Bertha, Gittel's daughter, had become a schoolteacher. Rachel's words rang loudly in Jacob's ears ... "I want to go to college, papa" ... But he'd turned away her request. He hadn't really been the good father he'd thought he was. No ... he hadn't helped Doris when she needed him. At the time he had justified it to himself, but the truth was he'd denied himself the joy of giving, and he'd done to her what he'd blamed his mother for doing ... yes, he had abandoned her, as surely as he'd thought Esther had abandoned him. And Lillian? He had deliberately broken up her first marriage because Jerry had become a constant reminder to Jacob of his own guilt ... and so Jerry had to be eliminated ... But it had done no good. The nightmares persisted. Shlomo's words would not go away. When Jacob had called him after he'd stormed out of his office, he'd said, "You're not my brother. You're dead as far as I'm concerned ..." As the last shovel of dirt was thrown over Esther's gravesite, Jacob wept. He had too much to be forgiven for ...

After the funeral was over they went back to Gittel's house, and when he saw Hershel, a sick, crippled old man, all the hostility toward him was gone as well ... replaced by the chilling knowledge that he could never undo, or make up for, the past.

When Jacob returned home he was not alone in his bereavement. After the little girls had moved, Sara became very ill. For two weeks, she had hardly been able to eat, and

479

had excruciating pains in her abdomen. The night Jacob came home, she rang the intercom to his room at midnight. Barely able to speak, she said, "Jacob, please come."

Within moments he was standing before her bed. "What's wrong—?"

"I don't know, Jacob, I just have these terrible pains in my stomach."

"I think we'd better call the doctor."

He sat with her while they waited for Dr. Forster to arrive. When Jacob met the doctor at the front door he had no need to tell him where Sara's room was. In the last two weeks he'd been there nearly every day.

After examining her, Dr. Forster walked out into the hall, where Jacob was waiting. "Mr. Sanders, I think we're going to have to take your wife to the hospital. For surgery . . ."

Genuinely shaken, Jacob asked, "What is it, what's wrong—?"

"Mrs. Sanders has a gastro-intestinal problem, and I'm afraid it may be quite serious. She's in a very weakened condition . . . she hasn't eaten in weeks, which I warned her about. But I'm going to be perfectly frank with you, I think there's a good deal more to this. For some reason, your wife seems to have given up . . . Well, we'll talk about that later. Let me call the hospital."

When the ambulance arrived and Sara was taken out, Jacob was trembling inside, and as he got dressed he knew he couldn't face this alone.

He called Lillian.

It was two o'clock in the morning. Lillian answered groggily.

"Lillian . . ." His voice broke.

She sat up in bed immediately. "What's wrong, papa?"

There was no anger in his voice tonight. "Mama's just been taken to the hospital at Stanford."

Her heart was pounding. "What do you mean, papa, what happened?"

"Well, for the last few weeks mama's been pretty sick . . . I admit I didn't take it too seriously at first, but . . . the doctor was here and she's going to be operated on . . ."

"Oh, my God. Look, papa, you want me to come and get you?"

"No, I'll pick you up."

"All right, I'll be waiting."

Dan was awake now. "What's wrong, darling?"

480

"It's my mother, she's going to be operated on—"

"I'll go with you."

"No, darling, we can't leave the children alone and I have no idea when I'll be home. Please get the girls ready for school in the morning. Mama's at Stanford. I'll be in touch with you later."

Suddenly she began to cry, and Dan took her in his arms.

"It's strange, I can't remember any of the bad times at all . . . I just hope that . . ." She couldn't finish the sentence.

Lillian and Jacob waited in the hall as Sara was being prepared for surgery. Her nurse summoned Lillian. "Your mother's asking for you."

Swallowing hard, running her hand over her dry lips, she walked into the room. Taking Sara's hand in hers, she bent over her mother. "Yes, mama?"

"Lillian, if anything happens to me, take care of papa. He's not as strong a man as you think he is—or as he thinks he is."

"Nothing's going to happen to you, mama."

"Promise me, Lillian."

"I promise, mama—"

Lillian stayed until the injection took effect, then went out in the hall and waited with her father. It was nine hours before Sara was wheeled back to her room.

Both Lillian and her father were exhausted when he dropped her off at her home. The house was terribly quiet. The girls were at school and Dan was at the store. Lillian took two aspirin, walked into the kitchen and prepared a cup of coffee. As she sat drinking it, the yellow phone on the wall kept staring back at her. Finally she got up and dialed.

When she heard Doris say hello, she almost wanted to hang up. Her guilt for neglecting Doris came flooding back over her. "Doris . . . it's good hearing your voice."

"Thank you . . . It's been a long time, Lillian. How are you?"

"How am I . . . well, a great deal has happened since we last saw each other."

Doris really hadn't needed to be reminded. "How are things with you, Lillian?"

"They could be better . . . I'm sorry I didn't call when I had really good news to tell you. I've remarried . . ."

"Congratulations—"

"Thank you, I wish that was the only reason I was calling . . . Mama's had an operation. It's serious and I felt it only right to tell you . . ."

A long pause. "I'm sure you mean well, but I honestly wish you hadn't called. I think it's a little cruel. Now that you've told me, what do you propose I should do?"

"I guess I'm just not thinking right, but somehow I thought you should know, would want to—"

"I'm sorry mama's sick and I hope with the help of God she'll recover. Much more than that, I can't say." Yes, Doris wished she were a saint, had no feelings . . . but being human, it just seemed impossible to set aside her feelings . . . she'd been so *used*—and by her own mother . . . She wondered if Rachel would be contacted and would come rushing to mama's side . . .

After she'd hung up Lillian realized it had indeed been cruel to involve Doris in their lives after what they'd done to her. She just wasn't thinking. Even if Doris had come to the hospital, the residue of papa's feelings would have surfaced, and chances were that there would have been a confrontation. His feelings for Doris were never going to change.

But damn it, Rachel's feelings shouldn't be so sacred. Lillian picked up the phone and called Rachel's apartment, only to be told that she was in La Paz, Mexico. "This is an emergency and I have to get in touch with my sister. Would you be kind enough to tell me where they are?"

After Lillian was told, she placed the call to La Paz. Rachel was not available at the moment, but when she returned the message would be given to her. How nice . . .

She called Dan, took a bath, changed clothes and was almost out the front door to pick up Jacob when the phone rang. Her heart pounded—it was either Rachel, or the hospital. She yanked the receiver off the hook. "Yes?"

"Lillian?"

"I'm sorry, Rachel, but I'm calling to tell you that mama is seriously ill."

"I'm very sorry to hear that Lillian. How seriously?"

"Well, how serious is serious? I just got through telling you. She had surgery and she's not out of the woods yet. As a member of the family, I thought you might like to know."

The strain in Lillian's voice was apparent, as was the edge. "I'll be there as soon as I can get a plane."

"I think that's very decent of you. I'll see you when you get here." . . .

As Lillian sat in the hall with her father she said, "Papa, I called Rachel and she'll be here as soon as possible. She's flying from Mexico."

He reached for the handkerchief in his back pocket and wiped his eyes. But the images, and sounds, of the past persisted . . . pushcarts being rolled over cobblestone, vendors hawking their wares on Hester Street, a kosher restaurant on Rivington, a little boy by the name of Shlomo, a sister Gittel . . . "push harder, Gittel, hold on, Gittel . . ." A six-year-old blonde, blue-eyed little girl holding his hand on a hot summer night . . . charlotte russe, ten cents . . . The pain he was feeling was so acute, so personal, that he got up and walked to the end of the corridor and stood looking out to the lawns beyond.

And suddenly, breaking through, was his relationship with Gloria . . . another selfish indulgence he'd neatly rationalized. He'd help her, provide for her any way he could, but he was through. He'd been using her, as he'd used so many others . . .

Jacob was a frightened man. He had never been able to reveal his weaknesses to others, or to himself. Sara had seen it, and now her illness brought to the surface things that no longer could be pushed aside. He missed Shlomo terribly, and the pain of his death, of being told that his brother didn't want to see him, was still acute. And Gittel? Gittel was an old lady who cared for Hershel, and Jacob sent her a check each month to compensate for his neglect of them. When Shlomo died Esther could no longer face life and willed herself to death. The Hebrew Home for the Aged—it was a sight never to be forgotten. To end one's days in such a place . . . And now with Sara's illness, his greatest fear was that he would end *his* life alone, shut away without a soul to mourn him. He had lived too much of his life without love. Would it end that way . . . ?

At four o'clock the next afternoon Rachel walked down the corridor toward her father and sister. She caught her breath when she looked at papa . . . My God, he'd aged so. She threw her arms around him. "Papa . . . why does it take tragedies for people to come together?"

"I don't know, Rachel. I don't seem to know the answer to too many things today."

And then she embraced Lillian. "Thank you for calling . . ."

Lillian could only nod and force a smile . . . .

That night Rachel stayed with Jacob, and Lillian went over

483

to join them after spending a little time with Dan and the children. There was a chill that seemed to permeate the very walls.

After Jacob excused himself and went to bed, Lillian and Rachel talked. "Why didn't you let me know that you got married, Lillian?"

"Would you have cared?"

"Lillian, I know you're angry, so I'm going to ignore that remark. Of course, I would have cared."

"Well, I'd never have guessed it from your actions. There's no debate that you were right not to let mama dominate your life. I don't think anybody can blame you for that. But for God's sake, Rachel, you've removed yourself so totally from all of us that we're strangers. I know you live in a different world from any of us, that we can't have a kaffee klatsch, but you might at least have tried to keep in touch. You never seemed to want anything to do with us even when we were growing up. You haven't really changed, Rachel, not really . . ."

"But you have, Lillian."

"Well, I think the things that have happened to me would have changed anybody . . . Anyway, I suppose when all is said and done, you've got your life and you're entitled. The one who really breaks my heart is Doris. Boy, if you think you had it bad—well, the Lord made it all up to you, Rachel. But poor Doris didn't even have to try to get rid of the family, the family got rid of her. And she's left paying for everybody else's sins . . ."

"You make me feel like a heel—"

"The truth may hurt. So you don't like mama and papa, but Doris and I are your sisters. How come you never thought it important to be in touch with us?"

"I'm not sure . . . I guess my life just changed without my realizing it. It's not a great excuse, but it's the only one I can come up with . . ."

"Well, at least that's honest . . . you should call Doris."

"I will . . ."

"Well, it's been a long day and I think we ought to get a little sleep. I'm going home, I'll see you in the morning." Lillian paused at the door and looked at Rachel. "I have to say one thing for you, age certainly hasn't been too unkind to you. You're as beautiful as ever, Rachel."

"And you are *more* beautiful than ever." . . .

Gradually, Sara began a slow recuperation. If there had been an unkind word between her and Jacob in the past, now no one would ever imagine that he was anything less than the most loving and adoring of husbands. His only concern now was that Sara should survive.

For three months Sara was indulged and pampered. The cost of the private nurses was the least of Jacob's concerns. He saw to it that special food was brought to her, as well as her own linen and towels. By the time the doctor began to talk of discharging her, she dreaded leaving the hospital. She had never felt so loved and protected as she had during these last three months. And for the first time ever, Jacob really seemed to need her.

It was enough to make her believe in miracles . . .

CHAPTER SIXTY-THREE

DURING THE most critical time in history, when the civilized world was being threatened with Fascism, Doris' life seemed to be the most secure. Henry's practice was at its best, allowing him to support his family in a most comfortable lifestyle. They lived in a lovely home, entertained graciously. Doris' life appeared to have a sense of permanence and security. Still, when it came to buying things for herself, she thought twice before indulging herself . . . even old habits died hard. She continued to look for bargains, watched the sales. To others, though, she was more than generous. One of the joys of her life was indulging her children. Although she was not able to give them great luxuries, she was inclined to look the other way when the price of a cashmere sweater, or a Schwinn bicycle for Chanukah, was more than she knew she should have spent.

Her life centered around her children, but she was careful not to believe she possessed them. True to her promise that long ago day in the park, she maintained the attitude that they were gifts, to be cherished and enjoyed. She did not expect perfection from them and was grateful that they had developed as two well-adjusted and delightful teen-agers. She was a mother who tried to understand the needs of her children and the importance of allowing them to express themselves. She trusted them, and, not surprisingly, they adored her.

She had made it a point not to confuse her childhood with Michele's, but there, was, nonetheless, a tremendous gratification that Michele was the kind of normal adolescent who dated and talked on the phone for hours about all the things girls talked about. Gary was a popular boy. Doris was terribly proud and happy for her children.

And then, just as Doris was beginning to feel her life was moving forward, the bombs of Nagasaki and Hiroshima not only ended a war, but also Henry's success. The patients he had acquired gradually began going back to their former doctors. His practice had somehow never developed on its own, and his earnings began to diminish. Once again Doris had the old fears, could see her lifestyle being taken away ... what to do? She would supplement Henry's income, she would try out her Godgiven talent, such as it was ... She would get off her duff and pick up her pen and start to write ...

She hardly met with any national acclaim, but if she was anything, she was prolific and hard-working. Her financial needs spurred her on to keep submitting her work in spite of numerous rejections, and gradually she began to sell to some small magazines. The turning point came when she received a letter from a national women's magazine saying that a serial she had submitted had been accepted. Her joy was far greater than the revenue, but it did help to pay the taxes on the house. She felt wonderful.

Henry had suggested that they sell the house, but this time Doris refused. She knew what would happen. The money they'd get from the sale of the house would gradually disappear and soon she'd find herself moving from one place to another. At any cost, she was going to stay in the house in Seacliff. She continued with her chores during the day, wrote in every free moment and far into the night. If she couldn't have anything else, she was going to live with dignity in her life.

There were other ways Doris changed during this period. In order to salvage her self-esteem, she dieted until she found herself with a slender, attractive figure. Her exceptionally green eyes had become more expressive with time, and she'd had her hair straightened. In fact, a complete metamorphosis had taken place. She began to believe in the beauty Henry had always seen in her, and she had acquired a natural elegance and ease. Her hair had turned prematurely gray with light streaks of silver, and instead of making her look older it only added to her beauty. Now she had the ability to wear an inexpensive dress with such flair that her friends were under

486

the impression that she dressed rather extravagantly. But if she was more aware of herself now, it was not a matter of conceit or vanity. Fat Doris had simply begun to take charge of her life instead of eating it away . . .

The years after the war were an uphill battle for the Levins, but with Doris' contribution to their income they managed to get by without changing the way they lived in any substantial way.

It was 1952 now, and Michele had grown into a beautiful young woman who everyone said was even prettier than Elizabeth Taylor. In truth, the resemblance was very strong. At eighteen, she was seriously dating a young attorney whose law firm had been established long ago by his grandfather, and now they were planning to get married. Joshua Wolf was everything Doris could want in a son-in-law.

It was all wonderful, except that Doris found herself caught up in the deceptive facade she had created by a lifestyle they could barely afford. Michele wanted a large wedding, and if anybody knew the importance of that it was Doris. Had she been a woman who thought with her head instead of her heart she would have been honest with Michele, would have told her, "Darling daddy and I would love to give you a big wedding but the truth is, we really can't afford it. You can be married in temple and have a lovely open house reception here at home . . ." But thinking back to the disappointment of her own wedding, Doris couldn't bring herself to do that.

The day they shopped for Michele's wedding gown at I. Magnin, Michele fell in love with one that was far more expensive than Doris could afford. But when she looked at her daughter's violet eyes and saw the bright excitement in them, she knew she would take it on time and pay it off. The trousseau was expensive, especially since Michele needed two wardrobes—one for a Mediterranean cruise and one for San Francisco when she returned to take her place as a young matron.

The financial burden was heavy, as Henry told Doris, adding that in his present situation the extravagances just weren't justified. He was a man of moderate means, Doris was making up for her own lost youth and living it through Michele . . . Doris refused to accept that last explanation and in fact felt that Henry was pretty insensitive to make such a remark. Besides, he had no idea how important it was for a girl to be able to look back on her wedding day. "Somehow, Henry, we'll be able to do it. Let's give this to Michele, we'll do without other things—"

"Why should we do without? Does she need anything so lavish?"

When Doris thought on it, she had to admit he was more honest than she was. Their so-called affluence was a sham, and she knew it. She secretly resented that Henry hadn't done more to make it a reality, but she tried to rise above the anger—as she had for so many years. She was determined that Michele would have this most important day, no matter *what* the cost.

She bought a blue chiffon dress for the wedding in a small specialty shop for thirty-nine ninety-nine, and with her own hands she beaded the entire skirt. Henry's white tie and tails were rented, as were Gary's.

When the bills began to arrive for the ten bridesmaids' dresses, Henry hit the ceiling. "Why does she need ten bridesmaids? This is turning into an MGM extravaganza."

"Henry, these are Michele's dearest friends, girls she's gone all through school with. And those dresses are the least expensive I could get, believe me."

"Twenty dollars times ten is two hundred dollars, Doris. Frankly, I think this whole thing is ridiculous."

"Please, Henry, we've been through this. Remember, we're not going to have to furnish a home for them . . . she's marrying a very wealthy young man and somehow we'll weather these expenses."

Over Henry's protest, Doris sold her engagement ring for five thousand dollars. Michele was going to have the wedding of her dreams. . . .

During the three months of their engagement, the couple were fêted extensively, with any number of Jewish mothers in the community looking on from the sidelines and envying Doris Levin for having her daughter Michele pluck the most eligible plum—indeed, Michele and Joshua became known as the most beautiful couple in San Francisco.

Josh Wolf and his family loved Michele, with good reason. She was warm and sweet, and the fact that she was not the least bit impressed with her beauty endeared her to almost everyone who knew her. Doris had explained through the years that being beautiful was like having a talent. It was merely a fact of life one was privileged to enjoy, and not too much credit should be taken since it wasn't something one earned. What counted most was what went on behind the facade. Doris should know . . .

They were married at Temple Emanuel. The *chuppah* was magnificently adorned with a crown of roses, lilies of the valley, carnations and white satin streamers. The gold candelabra glowed, and two giant, flower-filled urns adorned the altar.

Doris was escorted down the aisle by Gary, then she sat next to Henry's mother in the first row alongside his family. When the wedding march began, she turned to see Michele in her magnificent gown and veil, holding onto Henry's arm. Whatever the cost, the sight of this was well worth it . . .

When they were pronounced man and wife, Josh lifted Michele's veil and kissed her for so long that there were stifled laughs . . . which he was unaware of. Then the smiling bride and groom walked hand in hand back up the aisle and waited in the stone foyer to greet the two hundred and fifty guests. Pictures were taken of the bride and groom, smiling adoringly at each other, then of the ensemble of ten bridesmaids and ushers with the bride and groom standing in front of them. And finally pictures of the families. But Josh only had eyes for his Michele. Amid a flurry of excitement, she was being escorted now out of the temple to a rented limousine and found herself being kissed in the back seat as the chauffeur drove them to the Fairmont Hotel.

The superb wedding dinner was in the Gold Ballroom. Just before dessert was served, the waiters came out with the traditional parade of colored ices carved in the forms of hearts, flowers, a bride and a groom. Doris sat at the main table, along with Irene and Monroe Wolf, Irene's sister, Monroe's brothers, Henry's family, the rabbi and his wife.

The music began as the bride and groom cut the first slice of the six-tiered wedding cake. Speeches were made, telegrams read, and the dancing began. When Michele and Josh danced alone a hush fell over the room. Few had seen a more beautiful couple nor one that seemed to have such a bright future.

After their solo performance, the bride and bridegroom were joined on the dance floor by their family and friends, and the next few hours passed in a flurry of dancing with ever-changing partners.

Suddenly it was midnight, and Doris and Michele went upstairs to the room they'd reserved for the bride to change

489

in. Michele threw her arms around Doris. "Oh, mama, this is the happiest night of my life. Thank you . . ."

Doris well recalled the conversation she'd had with Sara on her wedding night at the William Taylor Hotel. How she would have liked to have been able to say the same thing to her mama, but seeing Michele's happiness now made up for all those memories.

When Michele emerged dressed in her pink raw silk going-away suit, everyone standing at the foot of the staircase gasped. Soon she was on Josh's arm as he came down in his gray flannel suit, and amid waves and showers of rice they drove off in Josh's Jaguar . . . .

Michele lay awake long into the night in the bridal suite of the Saint Francis Hotel, feeling the exaltation of giving herself to her husband. This was the second time they'd been together like this, and when she thought about it she was grateful to Josh for having convinced her that they should make love before their marriage. The first time for a woman was not always the most pleasurable experience, and he'd wanted to have that behind them so that their wedding night would be as wonderful for her as for him. Making love to Josh this night had brought out the deepest passion she'd ever known, or imagined . . . yes, she had been right to let him convince her.

That same night Doris had great difficulty trying to sleep. In spite of her happiness, there were thoughts that would not go away. Life, it seemed, was never meant to be enjoyed without some pain . . . not one member of her family had attended the wedding. Rachel sent regrets, along with a check for five hundred dollars; they were taking Larry to Europe for the summer as a belated twenty-first birthday gift, and so forth.

How vividly she recalled the morning when she had sat at her desk addressing invitations, and wondering whether the years might have mellowed her parents. Was *she* strong enough to forgive and forget? Suddenly their differences seemed so unimportant compared to the joy Sara and Jacob might have in seeing their first grandchild married—and maybe it was the catalyst that would reunite them. So she wrote a personal note to them and placed it inside the invitation. The days passed with no word from them, then the answer came with the return of the unopened letter. Doris felt the rejection keenly, but she was also beginning to feel

490

pity for them for depriving themselves because of their foolish pride.

At least Lillian had the courage to call Doris and wish Michele all the happiness in the world, but under the circumstances she couldn't possibly attend, inevitably papa would find out and she just couldn't risk that now... At first the conversation was stilted, but it seemed Lillian had a great need to confide in someone... It had built up for a long time. Although the dress shop was doing well, Dan had to expand in order to compete with the big stores, and for that he needed added capital. It was papa, of course, who was co-signing their bank notes. But papa was papa—it simply wasn't in his nature to do things without extracting his pound, more or less, of flesh. He was after Dan constantly about making certain the notes were paid on time... "The strangest thing is, Doris, we've never missed a payment. My God, you'd think he was *giving* us the money. And as for mama, in a way these years of her illness have been the best. She's catered to, indulged, and we've all become her lackeys, at her beck and call day and night. She spends her time in and out of the hospital. I know you won't believe it, but... well, she's enjoying being sick. The doctor told me in confidence that she brought it on herself, that her illness is self-imposed."

"How can an operation be self-imposed?"

"It was because of her extreme dieting. Most of her stomach has been removed by now. Let me assure you, Doris, whatever I get from them I earn the hard way... they make me feel guilty because they buy the girls so much, so how can I say no to anything? You remember when Rachel wanted to go to college? Well, they're sending Cindy and Candy to Stanford in shiny bright new cars. They insist on indulging them, and you know why... It makes yours truly just a little more beholden, tightens the noose, so to speak. But the one I feel really sorry for is my husband. Like Jerry, he really got himself a bargain. I feel terrible, there isn't enough money in the world for things he has to put up with."... And yet, she realized, it was she who let him do it...

When they hung up, Doris had similar thoughts. If Lillian found it all so distasteful, she *could* have refused. She wasn't forced to own the most lavish dress salon on the Peninsula. No, Doris didn't feel sorry for her baby sister... not anymore... And as for papa, money still seemed to be his god—and mama had apparently found her fulfillment in her illness. Lord, what a family...

491

And what of her own family? She had taken on enormous financial obligations and was afraid she wouldn't be able to meet them. What happened if she couldn't write, if she lost what skill she had, if she ran dry? But she refused to think on that. God, for some reason, loves you, Doris. When the chips were down, He was always there. You're a Capricorn, a mountain climber, for God's sake. Don't be frightened, Doris, you've gotten through worse storms ... And with that thought, she finally fell asleep ....

The next morning she woke up with a distinctly renewed spirit. The anxieties of the night before seemed to have been washed away. She got out of bed, showered and dressed. Just before leaving she looked at herself in the mirror. "Doris Levin, I think I like you this morning. I've decided you're a lady who's been tested and I think you're going to be equal to the challenge. So there. And besides, I think you look rather smashing today. Hell, with your silver mane and the tan, you look at least two and a half minutes younger."

As she got into the car alongside Henry he didn't seem nearly as happy as she. It was easy to guess why ... he had probably been going over the bills mentally last night too.

At noon they boarded the ship and went to visit Mr. and Mrs. Josh Wolf in stateroom thirty-four on the promenade deck.

The scene in the stateroom was a continuation of the previous night. Almost everyone in the family was at the cocktail party. The first one Doris saw was Irene Wolf, who made her way through the crowd and embraced her. "Doris, I didn't have time to call this morning but the wedding was absolutely marvelous. I don't know about you, but Monroe and I talked about it until the early hours of the morning. In fact, I was so excited I don't think I slept at all."

Doris smiled. She looked at Joshua's mother, thinking, Kiddo, you had company, but your reasons for not sleeping were a little different from mine. However, she said, "I just hope we have more occasions like that to stay awake for." Then she heard Michele call out to her.

"I'm so happy to see you, mama. You look gorgeous."

"Well, I'm no competition for you, darling."

"Oh, mama, thank you again for last night. Where's daddy?"

Doris looked around. "I know I brought him aboard. You go look while I say hello to my handsome new son."

When Michele came face to face with her father she had

tears in her eyes, "Daddy, *thank* you so much . . . for everything. You're the most wonderful father a girl could ever have. And you're still my favorite man, even though now I have two special fellows in my life."

"Darling, just be happy. That's all your mother and I want."

The boat whistle blew and there was a last call for visitors going ashore.

Once again, Michele hugged her mother. "God, it's a terrible thing for a bride to say, but I'm really going to miss you, mama."

"I'm sure that won't last long, darling. By the time you get out into the middle of the ocean it will all wear off. It better . . ."

Everyone stood on the wharf and looked up at the newlyweds standing at the rail. Handkerchiefs were waving, confetti was flying, balloons were floating—and once again, Doris knew that it had *all* been worth it.

CHAPTER SIXTY-FOUR

THE NEXT year brought both enormous joy, and sadness, to the Levins. Henry's mother passed away in her sleep, as gently as she had lived. In the very beginning, Henry grieved terribly. There had never been a day through all the years that he hadn't called her. But much as he missed her, as the months wore on the sorrow lightened and he felt that his memories of her were a gift to be cherished.

One of the things that most helped him recover his spirits was that Michele was expecting. It seemed to Doris that the events of life rather balanced out. There were beginnings and endings. Michele said that if she had a little girl she would name her Rebecca, after Henry's mother . . .

And this was an especially good time for Doris. She wrote more and better, magazines were beginning to approach her and ask to see her work. She needed little prompting, since the financial rewards were becoming increasingly greater.

On Friday nights, she observed the Sabbath with her children around her table. The first Passover the children were married was not only a large affair but an exciting one, celebrated with the Wolfs, Irene's sister and brother-in-law and Henry's family. At last Doris had a family. The joy of sitting in temple with her children and son-in-law was the fulfillment of a lifetime. She had almost forgotten the dreadful pain of having been exiled by her parents.

Thanksgiving came, and again it was at the house in Seacliff. Christmas—which they all considered merely a secular holiday—was at the Wolfs' . . . .

In Michele's sixth month a series of baby showers were given, and she seemed to blossom with her impending motherhood. Josh would lie in bed at night, put his hand on her tummy and feel his child gently kicking and moving about. "You know, honey, I have a feeling you're going to be a little disappointed. I think you're going to have to save the name Rebecca for another time. This one's a little too active to be a girl."

"So what do you suggest we call him—Dempsey?"

"Dempsey Wolf?"

"Well, it would certainly be different and we might even get a pair of autographed boxing gloves." . . .

In Michele's eighth month, she woke up one morning to find she had a few sharp pains and was spotting. Josh called Dr. Stevenson, who advised him to bring her to the hospital immediately.

"I'm scared, Josh," Michele said quietly.

Trying to keep his voice even, he said, "Dr. Stevenson assured me there was nothing to worry about. Darling, please, don't let this upset you . . ."

Apprehensively, she slipped into her coat and picked up her overnight case, and Josh drove her to the hospital.

While Michele was taken to a room, Josh called Doris. "Mom, I think you and dad should come to the hospital. What's wrong with me? I haven't prepared you for this, I'm so upset. I'm sorry. Michele had pains this morning and she's spotting a little . . . I think you and dad ought to come over. I'd feel a lot better about it . . ."

Doris was about to walk out the door when it occurred to her that she hadn't called Henry, and she hurried to the phone. "Michele's in the hospital. Henry, tell me the truth, is it serious when a woman spots in the eighth month?"

"Well, it's not such a good sign, but please stay calm. Everything's going to be all right, I'll meet you at the hospital . . ."

When Henry arrived he found an apparently calm Doris, and a very upset Joshua. Nothing he could say seemed to dispel Josh's fears.

494

Finally Doris said, "Josh, if you don't mind, I think your mother should be here."

"You're right, I hadn't even thought about it."

"Would you like me to call?"

"Would you? I'd like to go in to Michele."

The Wolfs arrived within the hour, and all that day they sat together, trying to reassure each other, in spite of their worries.

Dr. Stevenson arrived at five, and after examining Michele came out into the hall and told them that everything was going to be all right. However, he added, Michele should stay in the hospital for a few days.

Everyone relaxed. When Dr. Stevenson left they all went into Michele's room to say goodnight and that they'd see her first thing in the morning. Then they left Josh and Michele alone together.

At nine o'clock Josh was asked to leave. He kissed Michele goodnight and went back to their apartment, where he poured himself a double scotch, sat in the livingroom and turned on the record player. Nothing, though, seemed to shut out the sound of Michele's voice or the loneliness he felt without her.

At eleven o'clock he decided to turn in, but as he lay alone in the dark his thoughts kept him restless and wakeful.

He was still awake when the phone rang at three o'clock. "Mr. Wolf, I think you'd better come to the hospital."

His heart thumped. What good would it do to ask a lot of questions? "I'll be there immediately . . ."

When he got to the hospital and walked into Michele's room, she was nowhere to be seen. He ran out into the hall and called over the first nurse he could find. "Where's my wife—Mrs. Wolf? I just came from her room—"

From the look on her face, he knew something dreadful had happened. "I'll have Dr. Harrison, our chief resident, talk to you."

"Damn it, tell me what happened to my wife . . ."

Before she could answer, Dr. Harrison was standing in front of him. "Mr. Wolf, please sit down."

"Tell me what happened to my wife . . . where is she?"

"She was taken to surgery—"

"Why, what happened?"

"Mr. Wolf, your wife was delivered of a stillborn child."

The shock was so great that for a moment he merely stood speechless, unable to comprehend. When he recovered, he asked without looking at the resident, "And my wife?"

"She's fine."

"Thank God, when can I see her?"

"Well, it'll be a little while, an hour or so . . ."

Although Michele was unaware of it, he held her hand as she was being wheeled down the hall on the gurney. He looked at her beautiful face, still unable to understand—or accept—how this had happened, but his chief feeling was that she had survived. He sat in her room, waiting for her sedation to wear off.

At seven o'clock that morning he called Doris, whose reaction was much the same as his. At first she was too stunned to say anything, then she said quietly, "I'll be there right away, Josh."

It wasn't until after she'd hung up that she gave way to tears. Henry, for all his tenderness, could not begin to console her.

The two of them drove to the hospital, arriving at about the same time as Irene and Monroe Wolf. They didn't know what to say to one another, but, indeed, what was there to say at such a moment.

Doris kept remembering how she'd given birth to Michele twenty years ago in the same hospital. How silly she'd been those first few days, thinking how ugly her baby was . . . Oh God, the things life does to people. How could she ever have guessed she'd be sitting here this morning with a greater pain than she'd ever known in childbirth . . . ?

Josh came out of Michele's room unshaven and disheveled, his tear-stained face showing clearly what he had been through in the past few hours.

Irene went to her son. "Darling, how is Michele?"

He had to clear his throat before the words would come. "Fine, thank God, thank God . . ." And then he began to cry. "It was a little boy . . ." Irene held him very close, the way she'd done when *he* was a little boy.

"Darling, why don't you go home and get some rest? We'll all stay—"

"No, I'm not leaving until Michele wakes up . . ."

They all sat and waited in silence.

At nine o'clock the nurse came out and said to Josh, "Mr. Wolf, your wife would like to see you."

He followed her like a child. Opening the door quietly, he walked to the edge of the bed and looked down at Michele. When their eyes met, she said quietly, "We've lost our child." And then she cried, "I lost your child . . ."

496

"Darling, the important thing is that you're fine and well. Let's not think beyond that."

"Oh, Josh, I'm so sorry, I'm so terribly sorry."

He couldn't say a word, just held her tightly to him.

A week later Josh was able to take her home, and while he was at work either Doris or Irene would come to stay with her.

For two weeks, Michele refused to get out of bed. Her depression was so intense that she spoke to no one. No matter how reassuring Josh tried to be, her guilt was so great she couldn't even look at him. And nothing he could say could bring her out of it.

A month had passed and by now Michele should have begun to accept the loss, but it was clear that she had not. She felt that she had let Josh down, that it was somehow all her fault.

Doris kept trying to jog her out of her depression ... "Michele, darling, losing a child is a terrible thing for a woman, but you're young and you can have other children. The time has come to start picking up your life. It's been a tragedy, but it isn't the end of the world ..."

But nothing she said seemed to do any good.

Over the next few weeks Josh would come home from work and find that Michele had been drinking. She had also begun to take two Seconals to fall asleep at night, and when she woke up during the night and found herself unable to go back to sleep she'd take two more.

A pattern began to form and Josh was increasingly concerned. Finally one night he said to her, "Michele, when we lost the baby I think my grief was almost as great as yours, but I've learned to accept it. It's happened to other people and there's no reason we can't have other children ..."

Without looking at him she said with chilling calm, "I'm not going to have any more children."

"But there isn't any *reason* why you can't. Dr. Stevenson assured me that physically you're well and healthy—"

"Then why did I lose the baby? Eight months I carried that child ... why did I lose him?"

"Darling, Dr. Stevenson explained that to you. And he also said that the best thing in the world for you would be to go ahead and have another."

"No. I don't want to take the risk. I'm afraid ..."

Nothing he could say would convince her.

The next day he called Dorris and told her about the barbiturates, the drinking, the depressions and that he frankly didn't know how he was going to reach her... she just seemed inconsolable.

Doris went to see Michele that afternoon. When she entered she found her daughter lying on the livingroom sofa, drinking vodka. Doris took the chair opposite her.

"Michele, I'm not going to stand by and see you destroy yourself and your marriage—and that's what's happening. Just how much do you love Josh?"

"So much that I want to die ... I feel I've failed him—"

"You haven't failed him, and if you love him enough to die for him then you should love him enough to live for him. Michele, I've done something I wouldn't ordinarily do, but I'm not going to let you feel this sorry for yourself any longer. You don't seem to realize what's happening between you and Josh, so I've taken the liberty of making an appointment for you to see Dr. Goldstein. He's a psychiatrist and—"

"I'm not going to see any psychiatrist."

"Why? Are you afraid you might find out something about yourself? Maybe I don't know you as well as I thought I did, Michele. You've had a terrible disappointment. All right. But that tragedy isn't nearly as great as what's happening to you now. If you love Josh and want to keep your marriage together, I suggest you get dressed and keep that appointment." ...

After three months of seeing Dr. Goldstein four times a week, Michele showed a remarkable recovery. Gradually she became the Michele of old. She no longer needed to be fortified with vodka, and the barbiturates were flushed down the toilet. Once again, thank God, she was able to make love the way they had in the beginning.

Josh now could consider when would be the best time to bring up the subject of having a child. Should they sit down over a cocktail before dinner in a dimly lit restaurant? Or during lovemaking? If he did the latter, though, she might feel he'd tricked her.

One night he kissed her gently and ventured, "Michele darling, I think tonight might be a good time to start a family."

She tensed and drew away from him. But she couldn't go on denying Josh forever. Besides, she wanted a child too and she wanted to make up to Josh for what she felt she'd

498

deprived him of ... so, in spite of her fears, which had never left her, she said, "Yes, darling, I think the time has come ..."

Michele called Josh early in the afternoon at his office. "Darling, since tomorrow is your birthday, would you mind terribly if the two of us spent it alone together?"

"I can't think of a better way to spend my birthday—in fact, every day."

"Your mother won't feel hurt, will she?"

"You know her better than that. But are you sure you wouldn't rather go out?"

"No, I want to spend it with you alone, just the two of us."

Josh wasn't aware of it, but Dr. Stevenson had told her that morning that she was pregnant. Tomorrow would be the perfect day to tell Josh. ...

When he came home the next evening, the house was filled with the aromas of the dinner she was preparing. Michele was exuberant. She embraced her husband with a vigor that he'd been pleased to know many times in their marriage, but somehow he knew that tonight was very special.

When they sat down together for a drink, there was a fire glowing in the grate and Michele had put some melodic music on the record player. They discussed his day, which he said had not been easy ... he had one particularly difficult client who kept changing her will every time a member of her family fell from grace. Her grace, that is. Michele was bursting to tell him her news, but she was waiting for the perfect moment. Excusing herself, she went to the kitchen and put the roast duck *à l'orange* stuffed with wild rice on a platter, surrounded it with an array of vegetables, placed it on the brass serving cart and wheeled it into the diningroom. The silver champagne bucket was next to Josh's chair. The candles were lit. It was perfect. She went into the livingroom, kissed him and led him by the hand into the diningroom. Her eyes reflected the flickering candles.

She waited excitedly as he poured the champagne into the hollow-stemmed glasses. Then she held up her glass to him. "Happy birthday, darling. I have a present for you ... but I won't be able to give it to you for another eight months."

He got up and took her in his arms, then almost reverently held her face in his hands. "Thank you, darling. That's the greatest gift any woman can give a man." ...

From that day on, Michele did everything very cautiously. She decided not to drive. Her morning exercises were suspended, she held on to banisters, avoided crowds, braced herself while riding in the car. Each month that passed made her feel a little more secure—

Then, six months into her pregnancy, she had a miscarriage.

This time nothing could console her. Her visits to Dr. Goldstein did no good. The depressions became so acute that Josh began hating to come home at night. The drinking and the sleeping pills began again, and now Doris was not only concerned for Michele's sake but for her marriage, which was gradually beginning to disintegrate. And then another change took place. Michele became enormously restless, wanted to go day and night. She gave one cocktail party after another, never refused an invitation, turned away Josh's lovemaking and, in fact, took to sleeping on the couch in the den. . . .

One night after coming home from a cocktail party she was so drunk that Josh had to carry her to bed. After softly closing the door to their room, he went down to the den and stayed up for the rest of the night, wondering how he was going to go on this way. He thought briefly of adopting a baby, but he wasn't sure if that was the answer. At this point, he didn't know what the answer was.

In the morning Michele was humiliated by what she had done. Sitting down across from him, she said, "Joshua, I'm so sorry about last night."

"So am I, darling, but we have some serious things to talk about. We can't go on like this much longer. I know you've been through a great deal, but, frankly, so have I. I've talked about the drinking and the sleeping pills, but it hasn't done any good. We can't ignore what this is doing to our marriage. I sat up all night wondering what to do, but I found only one answer. Since you can't have children and we both want one, why don't we adopt a child—"

"*No*, Josh, it would only make me feel more . . . I don't know . . . inadequate than I already do, raising another woman's child . . . a child that some woman gave birth to, then gave away . . . No, Josh—"

"All right, what do you suggest? We have to do something, there has to be some change that will put an end to your depression."

"I don't *know*. I'm just too confused about so many things—"

500

"Michele, I'm trying to tell you something . . . I can't go on living this way."

She fought back tears. "I'm not doing this on *purpose*, Joshua, I just feel as though I've been such a total miserable failure in my life. I don't want to hurt you, but I don't know what to do . . ."

"It hurts me to say this to you, honey, but really . . . there's a time for sorrow but there's also a time for acceptance and getting on with life and you don't seem to be able to face the reality of that."

She went over to him and put her arms around him. "Josh, please, let's try. God, I can't even begin to imagine what life would be without you—"

"Same for me, but unless things change, Michele, I'm really afraid for our marriage."

"I'll *try*, Josh, I promise I'll try." And she meant it, and she honestly tried very hard to reconcile herself to the fact that they would be childless, but somehow she never could, never could overcome her sense of failure. Finally she could only pretend that she had changed, and when the pretense became too much of a strain she started the drinking again. When Josh returned at night, she was radiant and lovely, if slightly incoherent. She burned the vegetables and dropped the dishes, she walked unsteadily as she brought things to the table . . .

Finally one night Joshua said, "I know you've tried, Michele . . . but it's just not going to work—"

"But I love you, Josh—"

"I know, and I love you. But that doesn't seem enough. Maybe I've failed you too. I don't know, but I do know this . . . it's over . . ."

When Josh moved out she wanted to die. Through her own weakness she had driven away the most important person in her life, and she despised herself for it. God, why hadn't she inherited her mother's ability to face reality? But she hadn't, she was Michele—whoever *that* was . . .

She packed a bag and went to her mother's house. It was in the den that she told her mother and father everything. Doris had no answers. All she could do was to try to help her child through this ordeal.

Since the apartment was Joshua's he moved back in, and Michele went to live with her parents.

501

There was no community property to settle, so Michele was awarded five hundred dollars a month in alimony, which she didn't for a minute feel she deserved.

After living with her parents for three months she told her mother that she simply had to get away from San Francisco, that it was no good for her . . . "Everywhere I go, I seem to see Joshua. I can't stand being in the same city with him. It's destroying me. I don't want to see anybody, meet anyone, I don't want to go anywhere . . . I've simply got to go away."

Doris swallowed back her fear for her child. "Michele, if ever you need your family it's now, people who love and care for you. I know how terribly painful things are for you, but running away isn't the answer. Believe me, Michele, you can't run away from your problems. They follow you wherever you go. Your only chance is to stay and try to face them . . ."

"You know how much I love you, mama and papa, but I've thought this over and I've decided that I *can't* be this close to Josh."

Doris saw that she meant it. "Have you thought about where you'll go?"

"Yes, I think Los Angeles might be a good change."

"But you don't have anybody there—"

"I *know*, and maybe that's one of the reasons I think it might be good for me. I won't keep running into people who feel sorry for me—or the ones who gloat that our marriage broke up. In case you hadn't noticed, nobody's all that sympathetic. Those dear friends I used to have haven't even called . . . oh, the hell with them . . ."

"Well, that may be, but please, think it over carefully, darling. And whatever you decide, remember I'm always here. I'm your mother and I love you, and so does your father."

Michele sat down alongside her mother, put her head in her lap, and cried like a child . . .

CHAPTER SIXTY-FIVE

MICHELE WAS able to find a lovely little apartment in Beverly Hills on Crestview Drive off Wilshire Boulevard. She furnished the apartment on time payments, then took a job at I. Magnin. This was a kind of loneliness she'd never known, cut adrift from her family and living among unfamiliar faces. In the evenings she couldn't even concentrate well enough to read. Weekends were the most difficult time. On Sundays she felt she had to get out of the apartment, and she spent hours just riding around in the bus. By Sunday evening, she couldn't wait for Monday morning to come so that she could go back to work. She and her mother called each other frequently, but it was hardly the same as seeing her. . . .

It was three months before she made a friend.

One of the ladies who worked at I. Magnin was an enormously wealthy widow who found that her life had fallen apart after her husband's death. She traveled for a while, but then ran out of places to visit. She had no children and found that playing canasta with the girls bored her to tears. In desperation, she walked into I. Magnin one day, went to the manager, who knew her well, and announced, "Herb, I want a job."

"Sandra Heller, what do *you* need a job for?"

"Did you ever hear of sanity? Is that a good enough reason?"

"It is . . . okay, where do you want to work?"

"Well, the only thing I'm qualified for, I guess, is fine jewelry."

"You're telling me. Between what you're wearing and what you've got in the vault, you have more stock than we do."

"In that case, if you're running low I can sell my own stuff."

"Okay, okay . . . when do you want to start?"

"Is tomorrow pushing things?"

"No, that could be arranged. Now, let's talk about salary."

"Screw it." . . .

One day Michele was browsing in the jewelry department during her lunch hour and Sandra Heller asked if there was anything she could help her with.

Laughing, Michele said, "You could help me with a lot of things. I wouldn't mind the emerald, the aquamarine, and that beautiful little bauble over there with the star ruby in the center."

Sandra laughed. "Do you want me to put them in a paper bag for you?"

"I wouldn't mind a bit. Incidently, I work here too. My name is Michele Wolf."

"How is it I haven't noticed a beauty like you before?"

"Well, they keep this beauty sort of stashed away."

"The ought to keep you right out front. What department are you in?"

"Junior sportswear, you should forgive the expression."

"Oh, that's the reason I haven't seen you. I'm a little beyond that age."

"But not the size."

"With that compliment, you've just earned my undying loyalty. My name is Sandra Heller and as you can see I hold forth here."

"Well, *I* wouldn't mind switching if you're interested."

"Truthfully, Michele, they could have put me in the wrapping department."

"Oh, you'd have been wasted there, you're far too glamorous for wrapping."

"I'm getting to like you better by the moment, you certainly know how to jazz up an old gal's morale . . ."

In the next few weeks, Michele often stopped in at the jewelry department and said hello to Sandra, and the more Sandra saw Michele the more she grew to like her.

One day, when Michele happened to be passing by, Sandra called her over. "What are you doing Saturday night?"

"The same thing I've done for the past six months—nothing."

"You are now, if you want to. I'm having a party and I'd love you to come."

"I wouldn't miss it for the world. What time and what do I wear?"

"Oh, something long and sexy, and say about seven-thirtyish?"

"How long does it take to get to your place? I don't have a car so I'll be taking a taxi."

"Don't be silly, I'll have you picked up. Where do you live?"

"On Crestview, off Wilshire."

"Okay, write down your address and phone number and I'll have a very nice guy pick you up. His name is Richard Stein. He's an architect. Don't worry about him, I've had him screened since he was about four years old."

"In that case, I won't have to call the FBI. Thanks a million, Sandra. Two million. I really am looking forward to Saturday." . . .

Michele found her hands trembling as she began to get dressed. She'd had no idea when she accepted Sandra's invitation how traumatic this would be. She had been so lonely that she had accepted eagerly, quickly, but now the idea of meeting new people once again frightened her. Richard Stein was surely not a particular concern of hers, nor did she think of him as a date—but he'd be the first man she'd met since her divorce, and the idea suddenly terrified her. She felt so damn unsure of herself that she changed into four different dresses. Nothing seemed right. In frustration, she picked the first thing off the bed. She started to slip into the black long-sleeved gown but then suddenly remembered that it was one of Josh's favorites and quickly yanked it off.

She went into the small livingroom and reached for the only consolation she seemed to have. As she sat there, sipping vodka, she thought of calling Sandra and saying she simply wasn't up to it, but she realized that that was no answer to what she was feeling tonight. *You can't go on living like this,* she told herself, *spending all your time alone. You've got to break with the past and tonight's the night. Now get yourself up and get dressed . . .*

Drinking down the last of the vodka in her glass, she walked back to the bedroom and dressed in the red chiffon, the dress Joshua had liked the least . . . She combed her hair carelessly, applied a little more lipstick and without a second glance at her reflection went to sit in the livingroom, where she waited nervously for the bell to ring. When it did, she took a deep breath and called through the intercom, "Who is it?" She was only prolonging the agony. She knew damned well who it was.

"Richard Stein."

"I'll be right down."

If Richard Stein was a little surprised that she hadn't asked him to come upstairs for her, he was even more surprised when he saw her. There was no shortage of beauty in Hollywood, Burbank or Beverly Hills, but the girl who was standing in front of him now had no competition. Damn that Sandra Heller. When he'd asked her what this new girl looked like her only reply had been, "She's very pretty, you won't be embarrassed."

Well, that was the understatement of the century. He was a divorced man who'd had his share of romances, but Michele's beauty left him tongue-tied. He opened the door and awkwardly helped her into his Thunderbird.

As they drove to Sandra's he could elicit very little conversation from Michele. She answered his questions in as few words as possible and sat looking out the window as they drove along the fine boulevards and streets.

By the end of the ride he had decided that she might be beautiful but that she was also dull and going on dumb. Still, with a face and figure like that . . . .

Sandra Heller lived in a beautiful apartment house in Bel Air. The door was opened by a positively glowing fifty-five-year-old Sandra, dressed in Pucci lounging pajamas and decked out in a profusion of jewels. She embraced Michele as an old and dear friend.

"You look absolutely divine, Michele. Let me take your wrap and show you off a little."

She followed Sandra like an obedient child. It seemed that half of Los Angeles was on hand. She was introduced to John, Nancy, Paul, Judy, Alan, Nicky, Tony, Erica . . . the list went on and on, and after the introductions were made Michele wouldn't have been able to call anybody anything except "darling" or "dear" if her life had depended on it. Soon she was being asked what she'd like to drink . . . Vodka on the rocks, thank you. She turned down the hors d'oeuvre, then stood uncomfortably in the corner, smiling as though she had already heard the punchline to the funny story being told by Michael Somebody-or-other. She wandered off to another corner and caught fragments of conversation about who said what in *Variety*, and she wandered a little further on and heard bits of gossip about somebody who'd just run off with somebody else's wife. Then she found herself being escorted to the buffet table by Richard. She had hardly given him a second thought all evening, and by now she was so ill at ease that she merely said, "Thank you very much."

At about eleven o'clock she walked out to the terrace and stood at the rail, looking out to the magnificent vista beyond —but all she saw was Joshua's face. She kept asking herself what she was doing there without him, wondering what he was doing tonight and who he was with. Was he reaching out to her as she was to him? I'm really lost . . . No matter how much she wanted it to be otherwise, she simply hadn't been ready for tonight. It was too soon . . .

Suddenly she felt the presence of someone beside her. She turned and saw Richard.

"Penny for your thoughts . . ."

"You'd get short-changed, I'm afraid."

The answer changed his mind about her. Not dull or dumb, as he'd thought. Sad, lonely maybe . . . and he knew what the feeling could be like in a crowded room.

"Would you like to go home, Michele?"

"Not unless you're ready—"

"I'm ready."

"You're sure? I wouldn't want to take you away—"

"Look, when you go to four thousand parties a year, one more or less isn't going to make a big dent in your social life."

She smiled for the first time, and although the smile was a little wan, it made her even more beautiful. Taking her by the arm, he said, "Let's say *au revoir* to the Perle Mesta of Bel Air."

Catching up with their hostess as she circulated among her guests, Richard said, "Sandra, the party was terrific as usual. Hate to cut out early, but I'm going to drive Michele home."

She looked at Michele. "If you have a headache, I've got aspirin. Why don't you stay?"

"Thanks, Sandra. I don't have a headache, but I've had an awfully good time and thanks very much for inviting me. I mean that . . . it's been a beautiful party."

Kissing her on the cheek, Sandra told her, "Well, it won't be the last one. I warn you . . ."

As they walked to the car Richard said, "How about a nightcap?"

"I don't want to seem like a wet blanket, but if you'll forgive me I'm really a little tired. Saturday's always a big day in Junior sportswear."

Driving off, he said, "I. Magnin ought to have their heads examined. They should have you modeling."

"How did you know I worked at I. Magnin?"

"Sandra told me."

"Oh, of course, I'm not thinking . . ."

When they got to Michele's place Richard parked the car, opened the door and helped her out. Without asking, he took her by the arm and led her into the lobby, then into the elevator and up to the fifth floor. At her door he hesitated a moment then asked, "What night are you free next week?"

She was tempted to say she had all kinds of social engagements and wasn't free, but she knew she had to stop that . . . "Wednesday, I think."

"Damn, that's the one night I'm busy. Tuesday? Thursday?"

"Thursday . . ."

"Great. Any special place you'd like to go to?"

"No, you decide."

"Is eight all right?"

"Fine."

He wanted to kiss her, but sensed tonight was probably not the night.

"Thank you very much for everything, Richard. I'll see you Thursday."

When she'd shut the door behind her, she stood for a long time in the darkened hall. Suddenly she wanted to talk to her mother, but it was twelve-thirty. God, she'd have given anything to have heard mama's reassuring voice... She walked to her bedroom without turning out the light and went to the bathroom to undress, letting the red gown fall to the tile and kicking it away.

She took a long hot shower but it didn't stop the shivering, and when she stepped out she knew that tonight she was going to have to take two Nembutals. . . .

The next morning she sat with a coffee cup in one hand and the phone in the other. As so often in the last three months, when she heard her mother her first impulse was to say, Mama, I want to come home. But what she said was, "God, you sound so good."

Better than I feel, Doris thought. "So do you, darling. How are you?"

"You want to know the truth? Kind of lousy this morning."

"Why, darling?"

"Well, Sunday's the most lonely day in the week, never mind what they say about Saturday... I miss you terribly, really... And I went to a party last night that wasn't exactly my cup of tea. It was a beautiful party but it was just kind of rough... going out for the first time..."

"Did anything interesting happen?" She hoped, she hoped...

"Not especially... but I have a date with a man I met there, Richard Stein, for Thursday night."

"I'm happy to hear you're finally beginning to get out. That's very important." And a relief to hear.

"Hmm, I suppose you're right, mama. How're dad and Gary?"

"Dad's fine. And Gary made halfback on the football team."

"That's terrific. Is he still seeing Barbara Levy?"

Doris hesitated. Trying to be off-handed, she answered, "No, as a matter of fact, Gary and I have been having quite a dialog. Suddenly he has a thing about taking Jewish girls out. Or rather not taking them out. I can't say it doesn't bother me

508

because it does. But unlike dad, who's been puttting pressure on him, I feel the best way is to just let it run its course."

"It seems there's never a dull moment lately."

"Well, it's not all that critical. He and dad had a little argument because he's been taking out a gentile girl, but he's only eighteen so I wouldn't take it too seriously."

"That makes sense . . . Mom, do you think you could come down for a few days? Maybe next week?"

"Of course, darling. I'll call and we'll make arrangements.

"Look, I could spend the day on the phone with you, but the phone bills are staggering as it is. I'll speak to you soon, though."

Thursday came and this time Richard came into the apartment. As he entered her livingroom he looked around appreciatively. "God, you have great taste."

"Thank you . . . what would you like to drink?"

"Scotch, please."

"How do you like it?"

"Rocks, with a twist."

"The rocks I have, but the lemon I don't." She smiled.

"Well, if you keep smiling like that I won't miss the lemon. Incidentally, I have a reservation for Chasen's at eight-thirty."

"In that case, we'd better drink up."

Michele studied him closely as she raised her glass to her lips. On Saturday night she'd been so disconnected that she hadn't noticed how good-looking he was. He was about medium height, with thick brown hair that was just slightly graying at the temples and deep blue eyes. He dressed impeccably, expensively, but it was his beautifully modulated voice that caught one's attention, without a touch of stuffiness.

When they got to the restaurant, Michele was surprised to find herself feeling very much at ease as she sipped another vodka.

"Michele, I've ordered something sort of special. Chasen's is famous for its hobo steak. I hope you like it."

Before she could answer, the waiter was standing by their table, carving the steak, and it was every bit as good as Richard said it would be. . . .

By the time they finished dinner it was a quarter to eleven . . . and this time when they stood in front of her door he took her in his arms to kiss her goodnight. She backed away from him. "I'm sorry, Richard, but ... thank you, it's been a lovely evening ..."

For a moment her pulling away bothered him but he was certain she wasn't just being coy. There was more to her than that. He said goodnight as she opened the door, then closed it and proceeded into the safety of her apartment. ....

Afterward, back in his apartment, the lights out and trying to sleep, Richard couldn't get Michele off his mind. He was intrigued by the reasons for her defenses, and in a way he admired her for holding him off tonight ... clearly it wouldn't have been honest, it would only have been done to please him. ....

At his drawing board the next afternoon, he found his mind drifting away from the electrical outlets on the blueprints to the Junior sportswear department at I. Magnin. Finally he couldn't resist the impulse, went to his desk, picked up the phone and called Michele at I. Magnin.

"Yes, this is Mrs. Wolf."

"Mrs. Wolf, this is Richard Stein. I'd like to find out if you have a size thirty-six waist in Bermuda shorts."

Michele laughed. "We just happen to be out of that size. Maybe you should take a bit off ..."

"I'd rather take you out—to Scandia tonight?"

She hesitated. "All right, I'd like that. By the way, thank you for dinner last night. It was really lovely."

And so are you, he thought, but instinctively knew better than to say it. If anybody came on too strong with her, he knew what the answer would be—thanks, but no thanks. "I'm glad you enjoyed it. What time can I pick you up?"

"Seven-thirty?"

"See you then. And cancel the order for the shorts." ...

Over the next week they saw each other three times ...

After dinner on Saturday night Richard said, "I think the least you can do is invite a friend in for a nightcap."

Michele wasn't foolish enough to think she could keep putting him off. He'd been damned sweet, and damned patient, as it was.

He settled himself on the white sofa and once again looked about the room. It was almost as beautiful as Michele, and it seemed right that she should live in such surroundings. He put his drink on the table beside him and shook his head

510

admiringly. "I have to say once again, this is one of the most charming apartments I've ever been in."

"Thank you. Not too many men would notice."

"I notice more than furnishings. During the past week, for example . . . you."

He reached over and drew her toward him, but when he started to kiss her she gently released herself. "Richard, you're going to have to forgive me, but it seems I'm still not ready for this."

"Ready for what, Michele?"

"To have even a casual relationship with a man."

"Why?"

"I . . . I don't think I'm ready to talk about it either."

"Michele, I don't believe in preaching. But if you'll forgive a little amateur Freud and a lot of practical experience, I'd like to suggest to you that the more we repress things, the deeper we bury them—and then it becomes difficult as hell even to *try* to peel off the layers. If you feel like it, it might help to talk about whatever's bothering you to somebody who's a comparatively new . . . friend."

She got up and walked over to the bar cart. When she sat down again she took a long swallow of her drink before looking up at him. "I'm getting a divorce and apparently I'm doing a lousy job of facing the reality of it. I just keep hoping that phone is going to ring and it's going to be Joshua saying, 'Honey, I just can't live without you.'"

"And if that doesn't happen, what are you going to do. Sit for the rest of your life by the phone? Michele, maybe this will make it a little easier to talk about. I graduated from M.I.T., picked up my diploma and invited myself into the navy during the war. I was crazy in love with a girl, had been for a long time, and we were married two days before I shipped out. Now, after four years of going with somebody, you think you know them pretty well. But when I came back I found that Linda and I were not only total strangers, but that being faithful wasn't one of her long suits. It knocked the props right out from under me. I did all the things that your average well-rounded all-American male does when he finds out he's come home to an unfaithful wife. I sort of went a little off my rocker, did pretty good in the booze department and made up my mind then and there that I was never going to take a woman seriously again. A few years later I met a lovely girl by the name of Bonnie and we lived together. One day she said it was either-or, but much as I

511

liked her I had to say that marriage was out of the question. It's not so easy to live with someone for a couple of years and suddenly lose her. There were nights I'd lay awake and wonder if I hadn't made a mistake. But by that time Bonnie had found someone else and gotten married. Well, I'm thirty-seven now, and I feel there has to be somebody special in my life, and that the word *we* instead of *me* is very important ....probably the only parallel in our stories is that we both loved somebody very much. Believe me, I know how rough this is. But don't let it make you bitter or frightened. We all have to go on living, and unless you leave that door open, you're going to wake up one day and find you're one very, very lonely lady. Sandra Heller's going that route."

"There's a difference between death and divorce. At least in Sandra's case, she knows that phone's never going to ring."

"True, but you know it too, don't you?"

"Yes, I guess I do. I just keep hoping ... but there's also a slight difference between your story and mine. I lost two children and I feel guilty as sin ... as if I've criminally failed ..."

"I don't think you're as much a failure as you imagine you are—"

"It doesn't matter what you think, it's what I feel ..."

"Michele, don't beat on yourself. Give yourself a *chance*. And while you're at it, give me a chance. I'd like us to be friends. Good friends. How about it?"

She looked intently at him. "I'd like that."

During the next few months she dated other men, but they distinctly weren't Richard. He had a sensitivity that she needed, and the more she saw of him, the more she liked him. More important, much as she knew he wanted her he never pushed her, and there was a kindness and understanding in that attitude that she appreciated more than she knew how to say. . . .

One evening at dinner she was unusually withdrawn.

"Trouble, Michele?"

Reaching into her purse, she took out a large, legal-size envelope and handed it over to him.

He looked at the size and at the name in the lefthand corner. "I've had one of these before, I don't have to look."

"It hurts a lot, though, doesn't it? Knowing it's really over ..."

512

"It does, but the best answer to that is try again."

She had known it would come to this eventually. It had become as inevitable as receiving the divorce papers that had come today. But it seemed too early and she was still so preoccupied with the past. "I'll have to think about it, Richard. Today's really been pretty rough. Would you mind if we left? I'd like to go home." . . .

When they got back to her apartment she realized how grateful she was that he was here. To go through this alone . . . it would have been nearly as bad as the night Joshua left her.

Sensing her need to have him with her, to feel wanted, he gently put his arms around her and kissed her. The kiss became urgent, and Michele found herself responding to his intensity. She needed to obliterate the past and to feel that she too could go forward. Tonight she wanted Richard, and he sensed her unspoken thoughts. When he carried her into the bedroom she made up her mind that Josh would not become a part of this moment. She was here with Richard. She needed him and he made love to her with a passion she had thought she would never know again . . .

Later, when they lay in each other's arms, the release she'd found with Richard made her feel more clear-headed and more alive than she'd felt in a long time. Richard was very good for her and she refused to make comparisons. Joshua was out of her life, Richard was *now*.

"Michele . . . marry me . . ."

She wanted to wait, but she knew that eventually it would be Richard anyway. Why delay what she'd needed for so long? "Yes . . . but I want to fly home and have you meet my family. In fact, let's call my parents now. I want to tell them."

"Don't you think it's a little late?"

"For this, my mother won't mind." . . .

The next few days in the Levin household were spent in preparation for Michele's homecoming. Doris had the cleaning lady come in, the house was scoured from stem to stern. She cooked and baked for the meals they would share together as if she were preparing for a three-day banquet. As she took a few minutes to sit down and catch her breath, she thought, thank God, if we can just ride out the storm, not give up, we can *survive* . . .

When she finally saw Michele standing in her foyer with

513

Richard Stein, somehow she knew it was going to be all right.

Later that night, Michele crept into Doris' bedroom, knowing her mother would still be awake. Listening to Henry's snoring, Doris slipped out of bed and the two of them went down to the kitchen. Doris fixed a fresh pot of coffee and took out a tin of home-baked cookies. When they sat down at the table they simply looked at each other, remembering all the wonderful secrets and memories they'd shared and all the heartbreak they'd lived through. And somehow, like childbirth, it now seemed to have become merely a part of the past.

"Michele, darling, I have no words."

Michele laughed. "Gee, mama, for a lady who makes her living with words, that's one big confession. Don't let it get around, it could ruin your career."

"Well, there are some feelings I don't think anybody can put on paper. You're really happy, Michele, and your happiness is so important to me."

"Yes, I really am, mama, and in a very *nice* kind of way. Maybe it takes a lot of growing up, but I think Richard's helped me. There isn't the same excitement I had with Josh, but I don't really want that anymore. I feel so good with him, at ease . . ."

"Well, these are certainly aspects of love, and who's to say which parts of love are more important . . . ? Not this lady, I guarantee you."

"You're a very smart lady, mama. I'm never going to bring his name up again, but I guess it can't be avoided. Joshua was my first love but I just couldn't handle it. I guess if I could, we'd still be married in spite of the lost babies. But in all the months I've been seeing Richard, I've learned that liking someone very much is almost better than loving someone so much you want to kill yourself over failing him . . ."

For the first time, Doris was a little uneasy with that rationalization. That's the way she had felt about Henry, but although her marriage had turned out to be so workable, she wanted so much more for her daughter. She could only hope that Michele's reasons for remarrying were the right ones, that she wasn't marrying on the rebound or trying to prove anything . . .

"Michele, dear, I don't know what you've planned, but I'd love to have you married in the rabbi's study, and then perhaps have a few friends over for a reception at home . . ."

514

Michele looked at her mother, then said, "Thank you, darling, but getting married in San Francisco . . . Richard and I think it's best to go to Las Vegas."

"I suppose it was a stupid suggestion, if I stop to think about it."

"It wasn't stupid at all. It was exactly what I would have expected from you and I would have loved to have you and papa and Gary. But I know you understand. . . ."

The next morning after breakfast Michele went upstairs to knock on Gary's door.

"Yeah, who's there?"

"Your one and only favorite sister."

"Come right on in, favorite sister."

Michele smiled broadly at the blond, blue-eyed six-footer. He was going to make some gal mighty happy from the looks of him.

"Boy, I'm glad you came, Michele. Sure have missed you this year."

"Same here. Gary, I came to talk to you about something very important."

"Okay, shoot."

"Mama tells me you're not going with Barbara Levy anymore. How come?"

"I was never *really* going with her. Just took her out—"

"It seems to me you had quiet a crush on her, and for a long time."

"Yeah, well, sixteen isn't exactly eighteen. My ideas on women have changed."

"I know, to little *shiksas*."

"Oh, come on, Michele. You're not going to start on that, are you? I get enough of it from dad. Besides, just because I'm taking out a non-Jewish girl doesn't mean anything—"

"True. But on the other hand, what happened to all the Jewish girls you always went with? What's wrong with them?"

"Look, Michele, you and I have always been close. We could level with each other. So here it is . . . I've come to the conclusion that most Jewish girls are spoiled rotten and want things their own way."

"And gentile girls don't? Besides, what about me . . . ?"

"Come on, Michele, you know it's *generally* true . . . I mean about Jewish girls."

"No, I don't, Gary. As you say, you're making a generalization and it just doesn't hold up. As a matter of fact, I think Jewish girls make damned good wives."

"Now I *know* you've been talking to dad. He thinks every Jewish girl is like mom. But let me tell you, sister, dear, they're not. Anyway, why are we talking about this? I'm not serious with anybody."

"In other words, this Robin Baker you're seeing is just a date?"

"Just a date, Michele, believe me. When I get married, which isn't going to be for a long time, she'll be Jewish, honest Injun."

"I hope so, Gary. God knows, it would be a blow to the folks if you didn't. They've had one disappointment with me already . . ."

"They were pretty cut up about it, but they don't think you were a disappointment. Anyway, Michele, you've got to marry the person you love, don't you?"

"I can't argue with that, Gary, and I won't."

"Good . . . Now I just have to get dad off my back about my so-called future profession . . ."

"Why?"

"He thinks if you're not a doctor, you're nothing. But I don't want to be a doctor."

"You still want to be an engineer?"

"You know I've always wanted to be. But it's a battle royal with dad. He's just hell-bent on having Doctors Levin and Levin on that door, and I'll be damned if I understand it. He's never qualified for any Nobel prizes, and if it wasn't for mom the living wouldn't be so easy—"

"I'm in your corner there . . . I think you should be what you want."

"Yeah, but when dad goes off on one of his tangents and begins arguing the merits of the medical profession, he's tough to convince. He's got an obsession about this."

"Well, Gary, you just stand tough . . . not that I'm one to give advice . . ."

"Never mind . . . that's exactly what I intend to do. And, Michele . . . congratulations, I think you've got one great guy."

CHAPTER SIXTY-SIX

THE FOLLOWING weekend Michele and Richard were married by a rabbi in Las Vegas. Michele wore a lime-green silk shift, and as she stood in front of the rabbi she found herself

516

recalling the white satin gown, the magnificent long veil with the Juliet cap, the pink going-away suit . . . But the recollections was wiped from her mind when Richard took her in his arms and held her. "We're going to have a long life together, Michele. And I want to spend it making you happy . . ."

Josh, God help her, had said the same thing . . .

When they returned to Los Angeles they moved into Richard's house in Encino. Every nook and cranny had been designed by Richard. There were four bedrooms and a den, and a combination livingroom-diningroom that looked out to the pool site. It seemed there wasn't an electrical invention known to man that Richard had missed. If you pressed a button the record player started, press another and the bed revolved for a full view of the pool, another button and the TV went on . . .

She thought it was one of the most incredible houses she'd ever seen—but she didn't like it. It just seemed to go on for miles, and the brown suede walls, the leather and corduroy furniture made it so masculine that she wondered what she was going to do with her little French pieces, for example. But Richard always had a solution. He converted one of the bedrooms into a sittingroom and put her furniture in it so that she could feel more at ease among her own things.

For months it seemed that their life was one continuous round of parties. She'd never known people quite like Richard's so-called friends, but maybe she was just having trouble geeting accustomed to the Encino scene? There were barbecues and the swimming parties every weekend. And no one ever had to ask, "Tennis anyone?" That was a Sunday morning must.

Michele knew that it should have been exciting to her, but truthfully it wasn't. Somehow it all seemed too . . . superficial, and everybody seemed stamped out of pretty much the same mold. The girls took their shopping seriously, and conversations were mostly about who wore what to whose party. Still, she reminded herself, as a successful architect he needed the contacts, and as his wife she had to play the social game.

Richard's newest project meant frequent trips to Scottsdale, Arizona, and between all the parties and the travel it seemed their life was in a constant uproar. The only times that seemed to bring a semblance of stability and sanity into her life were those occasional weeks when her mother would come down, but since she was writing more furiously than ever now it wasn't as often as Michele would have liked. . . .

Six months ... half a year of whirlwind living. Finally, not wanting to carp but ... Michele said to Richard, "Darling, I feel as if I'm spending my life as window-dressing. Would you mind if I took a job?"

"I guess I would, Michele. I'm sort of old-fashioned about some things—"

"Well, is there anything I could do around the office to help you out?"

"Sweetheart, please ... just be the lady in my life."

"The lady? What about the woman ... ?"

Over the next three months Michele became so weary of her shallow women friends and the exotic parties that she found herself retreating from the forced gaiety and standing in corners with a glass of vodka in her hand. And more and more often, Richard would say to her, "Darling, I really think you've had enough." Which echoed menacingly to her of another time, another place ...

As time went on she found herself almost avoiding Richard at the functions they went to, and lately she had begun to develop migraine headaches. She also had periods of deep depression but she fought them as best she could so Richard would not suspect her unhappiness. And for a time he hadn't noticed, because she always made it a point to be buoyant, radiant, fortified with vodka and an occasional upper by the time he came home. But then she couldn't sleep, and so she took a Seconal ...

One night, though, Richard came home to find her sprawled across the bed too drunk to reply when he said her name. When she woke up later that evening, she could no longer deny the thought that this was a continuation of the pattern she'd had with Josh. But at least then she'd had some reason ... she'd lost two children. What was happening to her now? Why couldn't she adjust to *this* new life? She had everything a woman could possibly want, yet she was, face it, desperately unhappy.

Late that evening she went in to the library and found an equally unhappy Richard.

"What's wrong with us, Richard?"

"I don't think anything is wrong with me. But, baby, I think you've got a lot of problems. Just exactly what do you want, Michele? What did you think your life was going to be like with me?"

"All I wanted was someone I had a deep affection for and wanted to be with, hopefully all my life. I really didn't know it was going to turn into a circus—"

518

"Well, we went to enough parties before we were married."

"Yes, but I didn't know that was going to be the centerpiece of our life. Do you realize, Richard, we've been married over a year and I don't think we've had an evening alone?"

"That's not the problem, Michele."

"Well, maybe not entirely, but it's a big part of it."

"What's the rest?"

"I feel like a parasite, so *unnecessary*. I'm just not doing anything constructive. I asked you to let me take a job, and I'd still like to go to work——"

"And you think that would solve the problem? Let me tell you what I think the problem is, Michele. I knew it before we got married, but I foolishly hoped it would change."

"What's that, Richard?"

"You're still in love with your ex-husband, *plus* you're still playing the part of the bereaved mother."

She was stunned. "That's cruel . . . I haven't heard you say that *you* wanted a family. That might mean settling down for you, wouldn't it, Richard?"

"To be quite honest, no, I don't want a family, but that's not the point. The point is that you're still living in the past and you can't put up with realities or make the compromises we all have to make. I wouldn't have married you if I hadn't thought it was going to succeed. But then, I'm not a soothsayer, so I couldn't predict you weren't going to be happy living my kind of life, even now that you've had two years to adjust to it . . . You'll never be happy with me because you want something I can't give you. You want me to be somebody I'm not—namely, Joshua. So I think before we really sour on each other we had better call it quits——"

"But I love you, Richard——"

"No, you don't, and you never did. I loved you and I thought that would be enough. Wrong, it's not."

Michele was reeling. "Richard, I know part of what you've said is true. Yes, I have lived with a ghost. But your life is so fast and furious I just don't feel I can keep up with it. I feel like I'm running to stay in place all the time . . . Richard, we've both made mistakes in our lives . . . maybe I can learn to adjust to all of this. Please just give me the time, believe me . . . I'll *try*——"

"Michele, please, I've known more than a few women in my life, but when I met you I was overwhelmed. You were and are the most beautiful woman I've ever known, but that's not enough. You don't love me or need me because you're

519

still clinging to the past. But the past can never give you any satisfaction. You'd better get rid of those ghosts. Until you do, believe me, you're not going to live with any man and be happy."

"And you're willing to give up, just like that?"

"Just like *that?* My God, this has been coming almost since we first got married. It *isn't* that I don't love you anymore, it's just that I'm facing the facts. Someone has to . . ."

A long silence. Michele got up and poured herself a drink. She turned around. "Would you like one?"

"No, I don't have to get bombed to face the facts of my life."

She looked at him, suddenly knowing that he was right and that she had to accept it. "I don't think I can ever tell you how I feel about this . . . I'm so terribly sorry, Richard."

"So am I. Nobody wanted this to work more than I did."

"What do you want to do?"

"You can go to Las Vegas or Reno. A year is a hell of a long time to wait for a divorce, and you've been through enough."

"I'll do anything you say . . ."

The next morning Michele was on a plane to Reno. Las Vegas, like San Francisco, had too many memories . . .

Richard sat in his den for three days. Much of the time he was drunk—despite his rather stuffy words to Michele earlier about not needing booze to face reality—and all of the time he wondered if his decision had been the right one. Damn, he loved her. In fact, he knew full well that no woman in his future would ever measure up to her. But she wasn't in love with him, and never would be, not five years from now, not ten years from now. There'd still be Joshua. God damn him . . .

Doris not only felt Michele's failure, but her own.

That day, so long ago, sitting in the park watching Michele come down that slide, sitting there with her belly bulging . . . that day she had thought she had the answer to what children needed. How wise she was then. Now she found herself feeling she didn't know much of anything. She had tried to direct her children, give them her moral strength, always hoping she was directing their destinies in the right channel, that eventually they would become happy, fulfilled people with spiritual values to sustain them. But she had failed with both her children, though in different ways.

Last night Gary had come home and sat in the den with

herself and Henry, trying to explain. "You've got to understand, mom and dad, I hadn't meant to fall in love with
Robin Baker, I just did. And the fact that she isn't Jewish is
something that neither one of us can help. I don't want to
hurt you and I wish to God for *your* sakes it could have been
Barbara Levy, but it's not . . . it's Robin."

Doris was shaken. "The thing that hurts more than anything, Gary, is that you weren't honest with us. I kept asking
you how serious you were with this girl and you kept evading
me. Why couldn't you just have told me that you loved her?
At least we might have been prepared."

Henry took it even harder. "I will never accept this girl as
my daughter-in-law. In fact, if you marry her, she can't come
into my house." Oh God, Doris thought, where had she and
her sisters heard *that* before . . .

"Gary, leave your father and me alone for a little while,
will you?"

When he did, Doris sat quietly with Henry. "Henry, I do
know how you feel. We've tried to be aware of our children's
needs, but let's be sensible and good parents. Whether *we* like
this girl isn't really all that important. What is important is
that Gary is our son. If you threaten him, you'll only end up
losing him. Believe me . . . he'll still choose her over us. I
haven't spoken to my parents or my family in nearly *twenty*
years, and who do you think gains? Nobody. Parents have
disappointments, but Gary loves this girl. She comes from a
decent family, and whether I like her or not I'm going to
accept her. I believe you should do the same . . . our children
are all we've got."

Henry stood up, shaking his head. "How could that boy
have done this to us—?"

"Henry, to *us* . . . ? Look, it isn't in the scheme of things
for parents to choose mates for their children. Gary's in love
with this girl. Make up your mind to accept her, Henry.
Pretend if you have to, but don't lose your son because of
your own disappointment."

Henry didn't have to answer. Doris knew he was hurt,
deeply disappointed, but she was sure he would see the
wisdom of accepting what she said. She got up and called
Gary back in. He sat down nervously.

"Gary, your father and I, as you know, don't approve of
the marriage, but if this is the girl you want to marry, we give
you our blessing."

Gary now had tears in his eyes. "I'm just sorry you're both
hurt and that she couldn't be the girl you'd like to see me

marry. But I'm very much in love with her . . . and if this will give you any comfort, she's converting."

"If you're doing that for our sake, don't. It's a very great mistake to force—"

"No, mom. As a matter of fact, when Robin and I decided to get married I told her that my children were going to be raised as Jews. She insisted on becoming Jewish. As a matter of fact, she's been going through the training now for six months."

"How does her family feel about this?"

"Well, Mrs. Baker was quite upset, but Mr. Baker less so. It seems a shame that religion gets in the way like this . . ."

"If two people love each other, it needn't."

Gary knew his mother's heartbreak, but he loved her for having said it.

"When are you going to be married, Gary?"

"In two weeks, at Sherith Israel. That's where Robin's been studying."

"And how are you going to manage your financial affairs? You still have a few months of college to complete."

"Robin's going to work and I'll take a part-time job. In fact, I already have one, pumping gas at Shell Oil. Her family's going to help us a little."

"Well, dad and I will help you out with a check every month. At least you have the prospect of going into a good firm as soon as you graduate." She got up, put her arms around him. "No matter what, you're still our son, and we love you. Never forget that."

Two weeks later the Bakers and their younger daughter sat on the right side in the temple and Henry and Doris sat together on the left and witnessed their children's marriage.

After the ceremony the seven of them went to dinner at the Fairmont Hotel. The disappointment the newlyweds' parents felt was in the back of their minds, but for the sake of their children they pushed it aside. The occasion was amiable, if subdued. When dinner was over, Mr. Baker shook hands with Henry. Doris pecked Mrs. Baker on the cheek, smiled and said, "I hope the children will be very happy. I'm sure they will . . ."

Then they all left, Doris and Henry driving silently to the house in Seacliff, the Bakers to the house in Precita Terrace, and the newlyweds to their Spartanly furnished studio apartment.

And so life began for the Gary Levins . . .

522

When Doris went to bed that night, she lay awake thinking of the year Michele had first married, when Henry's mother had died and Michele had become pregnant. At the time she had thought that life balanced out, with beginnings and endings. But the events since then had made her wonder, especially now, with her pain over Gary's marriage and Michele's divorce. She could only pray that God would help her children find their way, where she had failed.

CHAPTER SIXTY-SEVEN

AFTER THE six weeks of legal residence were up in Reno, Michele was once again free to come and go as she pleased. No obligations, no husband, no children... only herself. Wonderful. She was awarded seven hundred and fifty dollars a month in alimony.

She came home to spend some time with her mother. They avoided talking about the past and the future, but the time finally came when Michele knew she'd have to pick up her life once again.

She couldn't stay in San Francisco, particularly now that Josh had remarried and had a baby girl. She couldn't go back to Los Angeles, because that too was a reminder of failure, with Richard. The six weeks in Reno had been lonely, but somehow that seemed to be a place that offered a little hope, a little excitement... a place where there could be a new beginning...

Doris was opposed to Michele's living in Reno, it just didn't seem the proper environment. But if Michele felt more at ease there, she'd simply have to accept it. Still, she ventured to say, "Darling, before you make the decision, there isn't any need for you to leave San Francisco. I'd be less than honest if I said my feelings are completely unselfish... of course I want to have you with me. But San Francisco is a big city and a lot of time has passed. Why don't you think about staying?"

"Mama, I have, but I don't think it would be good for me ... really."

"Well, you do what your heart tells you." And let's just hope it isn't a foolish one ...

Michele's adjustment to her divorce from Richard was not quite as traumatic as it had been with Josh. The sense of failure was there, but the feeling of loss was not the same. Her affection for Richard had been genuine, but it had never been the love she'd had for Josh. Forgetting was simpler.

Her greatest regret was having hurt Richard so badly, but she knew he had done the right thing. Their marriage could never have worked, no matter how hard they tried.

She found a small apartment, and Richard was very kind and concerned when she called to ask that her furniture be shipped. In fact, he had been so sweet she had spent a few days in an emotional turmoil, caught between her regret over the past and her fear of the future. But in those moments she found her mother's strength helping to sustain her ... "Darling, the only answer to most problems is work. It doesn't give us time to feel sorry for ourselves."

Also, somehow Reno was not quite as lonely for her as Los Angeles had been. That had been the first time she'd ever been cut off from the people she loved, and because she had led such a sheltered and protected life she hadn't been prepared to cope on her own. But her mother was right. Time was the greatest healer ...

Michele found a job in a dress shop owned by a delightful middle-aged couple, and almost from the very beginning Paul and Fran Kaufman took a great liking to her. They began to include her as a member of the family, and Fran's affection was returned a thousandfold. Michele needed the stability of a mother surrogate, which Fran was pleased to be.

Michele even went to temple with them on the high holy days. It wasn't quite like home, she wrote her mother, but she had an anchor. It was what she needed.

And Doris thanked God that at long last her Michele actually seemed at peace.

During the Christmas season the Kaufmans gave a party. This had been a yearly event for the past twenty years, and since the Kaufmans had lived in Reno most of their lives there were few people they did not know.

The party was noisy and cheerful, and Michele was enjoying herself. As she stood thinking about the contrast between this party and the ones she had attended with Richard, Fran came bustling through the crowd to find her. "Michele, darling, I want you to come and meet a very, very dear friend ..."

The friend turned out to be one Eliot Burns.

Michele wasn't sure if it was the Christmas punch or Eliot Burns, but he was surely the most attractive man she'd met in a very long time. The fact that there was no resemblance at all to Joshua or Richard helped. And what pleased her even more was that he wasn't Jewish, which meant, of course, no involvements, no reminders.

Eliot was a lanky six-footer, with sandy hair and eyes that seemed to change from gray to green. Her father would immediately have labeled him a typical *shaygets*, but Michele liked his easy manner. In spite of the well-tailored suit, somehow she could visualize him tall in the saddle. Except there was no Western twang in his voice. He was Nevada-born and Purdue-educated.

"How come you waited till tonight to introduce me to this beauty?" he said to Fran.

"Why, I thought the only thing you were interested in was that little spread of yours."

"Well, I have other interests from time to time—like right now."

Without asking permission, he took Michele in his arms and the two were dancing.

"Well, I have to say one thing about you. You're not shy . . . and you don't waste any time," Michele said, smiling as she did.

"Don't believe in either. Especially wasting time. How do you feel about leaving this party and—"

"I don't believe in it. I'm enjoying myself and I haven't done that in a long time."

"Oh? Then how about breakfast tomorrow."

"I'll think about it."

"What about lunch and dinner? You might as well say yes now, because when I get set on something I'm not too easily put off. Just stubborn, you might say."

Michele was sure he wasn't being a bit serious, but she was intrigued nonetheless. "And if I said no?"

"Wouldn't do a bit of good. I'll be keeping you up day and night answering the phone."

"You're crazy, you know that?"

"I've been trying to tell you that for the last ten minutes. Now that you know, where do you want to eat?"

"Surprise me."

"Okay."

Michele was indeed surprised. He picked her up after work in his jeep, looking exactly like the image she'd had of him the night before. He was dressed like Gary Cooper in *High Noon*, except for the six-shooters. Since she couldn't quite

525

manage the height of the step into the jeep, he hoisted her into the seat, got in on the other side and took off like a rocket down the middle of the busiest street in downtown Reno.

As they were heading out of the city limits, Michele asked, "Where is this restaurant?"

"Can't hear you. Knew I should have had this damned bucket turned."

"I asked where we're going."

"With a little patience, you're going to have the best damn dinner you ever had."

"How far is this place?"

"Oh, could be a day or a week."

"Will you be serious, please?"

"That's exactly what I'm being. However, the part of it we're going to is another half hour, give or take."

Michele sighed and sat back, trying to relax in the bumpy jeep. Eliot didn't seem to want to miss a single chuckhole.

When Eliot at last brought the jeep to a grinding halt, it was in front of an enormous two-story house that looked like something out of *Gone With the Wind* ... and highly incongruous in the rustic landscape.

He lifted her down and escorted her to the front door. This couldn't be real, she thought as she stood in the front hall. It did indeed look like Tara. The furnishings were French and English antiques, the draperies satin, and the upholstering silk, velvet and damask. What was this doing in the wilds outside Reno, Nevada?

He helped her out of her coat and led her into the giant livingroom. Before she had a chance to catch her breath he was asking, "What do you drink?"

"Oh ... Vodka over ice."

"How about a martini instead?"

"Sure ... fine."

"It makes it more like a party. Besides, I make a damn good martini. You just relax and I'll be right back with all the fixings."

Michele wanted to laugh. This was the little spread that Fran had mentioned? Eliot was back carrying a silver bucket of ice. With his free hand he took hers and said, "This is not my favorite drinking room."

He led her to what she supposed would be considered the den. One wall was taken up with a glass-encased gun collection, and mounted above the stone fireplace were the antlers of a long-deceased antelope. The draperies were wool tartan

526

plaid, the furnishings a caramel-colored leather. In front of the large sofa lay a bear rug—head, claws, and all. Michele's gaze turned toward Eliot. He was standing behind a barrel-shaped bar, complete with brass rail, making quite a production out of mixing the martinis.

Glasses in hand, he handed her one, looked at her and said, "Here's to you, lady. You've got to be the prettiest damn thing I ever saw in my whole life. You might as well drink up, 'cause I got a real special announcement to make. You don't have to give me your answer right this minute, of course. But I made up my mind last night that we're going to get married."

Michele started to laugh. "Well, you were right about not wasting any time. The only thing you didn't consider was that maybe I'm not about to try that again."

"Why? What have you got against marriage?"

"I'm a two-time loser and I just have a feeling that marriage isn't one of my greatest talents."

"You can't be totally against it if you tried it twice."

"True, but I don't want to be a three-time loser."

"Oh, that's nonsense. Your problem is you should have met me first."

Suddenly it didn't seem quite so funny, especially when she thought of the unhappiness she'd already had. "Where's that best damn dinner in the world you promised me?"

"That's a pretty good strategy for evasion. But maybe after dinner you'll change your mind."

Eliot sat at the head of the table in the large diningroom, and she to the left of him. Dinner was served by Chang Lee, who'd been with the family for more years than anyone could remember. He served them Chateaubriand *bleu*, potatoes *au gratin* and fresh garden peas, all of it prepared to perfection.

Stirring his coffee, Eliot said, "Well, didn't I tell you that was the best damn dinner you were ever going to have?"

"You did and you were absolutely right."

"Well, isn't that enough to make a lady say yes?"

Michele took a sip of her coffee. "I don't know if you're serious or not, I really don't. But in case you are, the answer has to be no."

"Nobody jokes about asking a girl to marry him. You could get a little buckshot in your butt—and that's painful, let me tell you. Daddies don't like a man who doesn't go through with a proposal."

"Eliot, I'm beginning to think you really are serious."

"Damn right. I told you last night I don't waste any time when I see something I want. And I really want you, lady."

"Maybe you won't when you find out about me."

"I know enough for me."

"Eliot, let's be serious. We just met last night. We don't even know each other."

"By the time you get to know me, you're going to find out I'm just about what I am now. I don't want to rush you or anything, but why don't you just say yes? Then if you change your mind you can always send me a telegram. A deal?"

She ran her fork around the now empty dessert plate. "I'd like to go back and sit in front of that lovely fire."

"Anything for the new lady in my life."

When they were back in the den and seated in front of the fire, Michele said, "Eliot, I've never met anybody quite like you, and I'd like us to be friends. But before even that happens I should tell you a little about myself . . . a lot about myself, everything." And she proceeded to tell him about falling in love with Joshua and the happiness they'd had, her stillbirth and miscarriage, the subsequent breakdown and inability to accept reality, and how she'd turned to Richard, a truly loving and understanding man, but that too had been a failure . . . "If it hadn't been for my mother, I doubt I would have survived at all."

Eliot sat staring into the fire before he spoke. "During this whole conversation, I've heard you mention your mother quite a lot. I hope this won't hurt your feelings . . . I think it's great and all to love your mother and I'm sure no shrink, but what strikes me is that you seem dependent as hell on her to bail you out. Apparently you don't think you have her strength, so you always go chasing after it when you're down. Hell, your mother's not to blame for the lousy things in your life, but maybe she just protected you too much, didn't toughen you up enough, let you think the world was snug and safe like the old homestead. Frankly, lady, you need a man around the house. Me."

Well, he was right about not being able to cope like her mother. Crises just made her go to pieces and then she ran to her mother . . . She said quietly, "Facing the truth hurts like hell, Eliot, but what do you do with the nature you're born with? I'm just not very resilient, to put it mildly."

"Like I said, the answer to that is a strong man, with a lot of patience."

528

She got up and paced back and forth. This was crazy. He wasn't at all the kind of man she'd ever thought she would seriously consider. And worldly as she thought she was, the fact that he wasn't Jewish suddenly became a problem of consideration. True, her mother had never made a fetish out of religion, but there was no doubt how important it was to her and how hard she had tried to imbue her children with the faith that apparently had so often sustained her.

"This is going to take a little longer than you're going to like," Michele said.

"It's against my nature, but in this instance I'll make an exception. Now come over here and sit down."

"I've told you about me, what about you?"

"Well, there's not really a hell of a lot to tell. My ancestry, as they say, is Scotch, Irish and English. My grandfather built this house for his Southern bride, who wanted to bring Atlanta to Nevada ... Don't particularly like parties, although I like my share of excitement and going into Reno to kick up my heels some. Maybe one of the reasons I don't like parties so much is that my mother's so crazy about them. She lives in New York, Madrid—and I wouldn't be at all surprised if you met up with her in Istanbul. My father's not crazy about Istanbul so he lives here. He's got a house on the ranch. I've seen my share of the world, but something hauls me back here, I guess it's in my blood. I was born and raised in this house and intend to die here with my boots on in the same bed I was born in. And there you have it, all the skeletons in the closet."

"Why didn't you ever marry?"

"Well just after I got out of Purdue, they started a little thing in Korea, so it didn't give me much time to think about matrimony. That just had to be the damnedest place in the world to find a bride. Honey carts, yes; brides, no. Anyway I have a feeling I've been waiting around for you. And besides, I don't think at thirty I should be considered an old bachelor. Sure as hell don't feel like one."

"Well, you don't look like one either."

"And how old are you?"

"Twenty-three, and Jewish."

"Really, I don't remember asking you that question. But in case you're interested, they've got a dandy little temple right down there in the heart of Reno. And any Saturday matinee you might be interested, I'd be more than happy to drive you there in the jeep."

She laughed in spite of herself. She couldn't even begin to

529

analyze what it was she so liked in him. All she knew was that he kept sneaking through the defenses she'd built up.

"Okay, enough for the family histories and the past. The hell with it all. Now that we both know all about each other, how about the answer to my first question. Did you make up your mind?"

"Eliot, let's get to know each other better—"

"Okay, I'm going to make a different kind of proposal to you. The only way two people can get to know each other better is to spend a lot of time together. How would you like to move out here with me? See if you like the life?"

This time Michele was totally taken aback. "Eliot, I couldn't do that—"

"Why not?"

"To begin with, I'm not even sure how I feel about you . . . And it's something that I just couldn't do."

"As far as how you feel is concerned, I don't think you're going to give yourself much of a chance to find out since this Joshua fellow's still sleeping in your bed."

My God, that sounded like Richard . . . but she didn't think it was really true any longer, that she'd overcome . . . "Eliot, please, let's go slow on this. Let's at least get to know each other better . . ."

He took her in his arms and kissed her. "That's exactly what I'd like to do, get to know you better. A whole lot better." They lay back in front of the fire. Her response to him was far greater than she would have imagined. He aroused feelings in her that no man had ever done, not even Josh . . .

Their responses grew more and more eager, and finally he lifted her in his arms and carried her upstairs.

Kissing her, he unzipped the back of her dress and unfastened the lace bra. What overcame them both was undeniable. All thoughts of the past, present or future were driven from her mind. She only knew that there had never been anyone who filled her with more excitement than Eliot Burns. He loved her as a woman should be loved . . .

When they lay quietly together he said, "Now, lady, when do you want to be married? Tomorrow?"

"Although I'll be considered a fallen woman, I think I'm going to accept your second proposition first, Eliot. Yes, I'd love to live here with you. And crazy as this may sound, I think maybe I am in love with you . . ."

"Happy to hear you say that, but I knew it was just a question of time till you got that first guy out of the way. But

530

I won't settle for the second proposition for too long. When do you figure you'll accept the first one?"

"Give me a little more time, Eliot. June, maybe . . . I'm going to have to get used to this . . . and I'm also going to have to prepare my parents for *both* propositions."

"You do that. And incidentally, any time they want to come out to the ranch they're more than welcome."

Michele laughed. "You don't know my father. If he knew where I was right now he'd probably faint."

"Well, we wouldn't want him to do that."

"But how am I going to explain all this? Not only to them, but to the Kaufmans?"

"As far as I'm concerned you don't owe anybody any explanation. You're a big girl, Michele, trying to make your own way on your own . . . I think Fran will understand. And as for your folks, if it would make you feel better don't give up the apartment. Just have all the mail forwarded here."

"That isn't going to work . . . the phone calls, but I'll tell you what I think I'll do . . . I'd like to go home this weekend and see my folks."

"That's a hell of a thing to do to me. I already feel like a jilted groom . . . Seriously, Michele, if that's what you want, do it. Much as I'll miss you, you should handle this the way you think is best."

"Eliot, I think I do love you. Of all the crazy things that have happened in my life, I think you . . . us . . . may be the one sane thing. God, I'll never get over the way this has happened—"

"Nor me, lady. I guess it's something called life, and fate, who cares . . . ?" With that he took her in his arms, and they made love with a passion greater even than before . . .

Doris stood looking through the window at the San Francisco airport. When she saw Michele walk down the ramp and then run across the field, she was sure something wonderful had happened. When they found themselves in each other's arms, each renewed the special feeling she had for the other . . . and for Michele coming home was always a special event. What was it the man said, "My country right or wrong"? She felt that way about her family, especially her remarkable mother . . .

That night at dinner, Henry kept looking at her and thinking how much he had missed her . . . if only he could turn the clock back and make her a little girl again . . .

After Henry had gone to bed, Doris and Michele sat in the

531

den. "I don't know how I've been able to hold myself back from telling you about it till now," Michele said, "but I've met somebody incredible . . . everything about him and me is incredible to . . . including that we're in love . . . truly in love." She began with how they'd met and even told her mother that they'd made love. How Eliot had asked her to marry him but she'd felt that after the disasters of her previous marriages she had to be sure this time. Not that she'd exactly rushed into either of her other marriages, but she still felt that she needed more time. "I hope you won't be too upset or think less of me for it, mama, but I'm going to live on the ranch with Eliot. I know it's kind of shocking to you, but I also want to be sure that I'm going to be able to adjust to his life. This time it's *got* to be right. I just don't want to fail again. This seems to be the best way to make certain I don't."

Strangely enough, the thought of Michele living with this man didn't really bother Doris. She didn't advocate it, of course, but in Michele's case there seemed to be a wisdom in it. If it were merely an affair she would have been strongly opposed. But under the circumstances, she felt Michele was being very wise, and mature.

"There's only one thing, Michele. Your father must never find out about this, so from time to time you're going to have to come home, just as you always have. I don't want to deceive him, I never have, but this is one deception I think is necessary—"

"Mama, you're really a remarkable lady."

"Okay, I'll buy that," and she said it with a straight face as they embraced. "But, darling, I would like you to spend a weekend here at home with Eliot." Smiling, she added, "In separate bedrooms. Your father and I will want to meet him, and I think the sooner the better."

"No wonder I love you so much . . . how did I get so lucky?"

"I've no idea . . . Now the next chore that I have is trying to prepare your father for another member of the Levin family who isn't Jewish."

"You can do anything."

"Hardly, but I'll work on it." . . .

While the plane was making its descent to the Reno airport Eliot ran onto the field and waited for the motorized stairway to be rolled up to the plane, then brushed by the passengers coming down as he went up and swooped Michele into his

532

arms. "Welcome home, lady, forty-eight hours is a hell of a long time to take out of my life."

"Next time," she said when she'd regained her breath, "you'll go home with me. Besides, I'll try to make it up to you somehow—"

"Damned right you will—and tonight's the night," he said as he carried her all the way down the ramp and across the field and put her in the jeep.

Doris' talk with Henry wasn't exactly as jubilant as Eliot's reunion with Michele. She was sitting with him after dinner, trying to appease.

"Henry, the important thing is that Michele seems to have found someone she really loves. Yes, I agree with you, too bad he's not Jewish—but he's not."

Henry said angrily, "What are you, an apostle of mixed marriages?"

"That's unkind, Henry, but the truth is the truth, whether you or I like it or not. Robin has turned out to be a wonderful wife for Gary. She worked and helped him through college, and look how devoted she is to the baby. Imagine calling him Mordechai. How Jewish can you get, Henry? Would we have named a baby Mordechai? We went all-American with Gary ... Since they've been married, I haven't seen one thing that I could find fault with. In fact, she's become so Jewish that she puts me to shame. She goes through the whole thing, with the candles and the *Shabbes* and the recipes I gave her for *matzo* balls ... to tell you the truth, she's maybe going a little overboard. She even gets upset when people say she doesn't look Jewish—"

"*Oy vay*, you keep talking so I can't even interrupt. That's always your best way of winning arguments—"

"I'm not arguing, Henry, merely trying to suggest—"

"Your suggestions are longer than the Bible. Thank God my mother didn't live to see her grandchildren marry *goy-im* . . . ."

"I think that's unfair."

"What's unfair? You think she would have been proud and happy?"

"I think she would have been very proud of Robin, yes. Your mother was a very fair-minded woman, never mind she came from the old country and could barely speak English."

"All right, on Friday night I'll go to temple and thank God because Michele's marrying a *goy*."

"I think you should go both Friday night and Saturday morning and thank God that Michele is marrying someone she *loves*, someone who's going to be good to her, take care of her and protect her—"

"You sure you didn't leave anything out? Sounds like a commercial to me."

"No, I think I've just about covered everything, except . . . to let you know that Michele and her fiancé are coming home this weekend so we can meet him."

"*Mazel tov*, I can hardly wait. *Naches* like this I'd never thought I'd have. Now I'm going to bed . . . and I think that *you* should write a story about how to be a Jewish mother."

"I can't do that, Henry, it's already been done."

"So sue me, I'm not up on my literature." After kissing her on the cheek, he smiled and said goodnight before he went up to their room.

Doris went to her desk, rolled a sheet of paper into the typewriter and began an article:

ON BECOMING THE PERFECT JEWISH MOTHER-IN-LAW

1. Keep your ladle out of your daughter-in-law's chicken soup.
2. Ask for *her* delicious chicken liver recipe but eliminate the mayonnaise and use the traditional chicken *schmaltz*. If you keep your Jewish mouth shut, she'll never know the difference . . .

High literature, she said to herself, and settled in for the night . . .

Chapter Sixty-Eight

Doris had rarely been in better voice or form than this day. While Maria, the cleaning lady, went about her chores, Doris was busy in the kitchen, working amid a clutter of mixing bowls and pots. She sang happily as she poured the noodle *kugel* into the casserole. To strains of "On the Sunny Side of the Street," she took the sponge cake out of the oven and sliced it for the base of a strawberry shortcake.

When the table was set, she stood back and observed and was taken back to a long-ago afternoon . . . she'd just left Rachel's, and she recalled now the longing she'd felt wandering through the china department at Gump's, never daring to hope she'd have anything. But God had been generous to her, the talent she'd been given had helped make today's luxury possible . . . The service plates and crystal goblets, the silver bread-and-butter dishes, the Minton china, the candelabra, the epergne filled with roses . . . all had been bought with the money she had earned, and the feeling was good. But the greatest luxury of all was that her children were going to be together with Henry and herself tonight. This was a very special *Shabbes* indeed.

At four that afternoon she went upstairs to shower. As she looked at her reflection in the mirror she also thought how far she'd come from that fat, frustrated, curly-haired girl of eighteen that Henry had married. She'd come to terms with life since then. The hope of being reunited with her family had been put in its proper place; she knew after all these years that there would never be a great reconciliation. She had shed tears but she had also built a life from them. It wasn't a question of resignation, but of facing the realities of her life. She accepted Henry as he was. If, after all this time, he had not developed intellectually or grown financially, it would be foolish to think things would change now. Dreaming was self-defeating. No, the compromises, the adjustments to reality were better.

Tonight Henry would sit at the head of his table as the father and man of the house. Although she and Henry had little in common, he was still a kind man who loved and adored her as always, and it was a very good and treasured feeling. His obstinancy about Gary was something she just couldn't seem to help him to overcome, but there too she met Henry on his terms, as she did herself. For all the struggles, she had managed to hold onto the house and to help send Gary to college—and now, with the help of God, Michele would at long last find a happy life for herself. Today she felt a sense of peace. Her stories were more in demand than ever and her contribution to the family income had increased accordingly. She was hardly the female counterpart of Shakespeare, but she accepted herself and recognized her own limitations. When a story was good she knew it, and when it wasn't she tore it up. The standards she set for herself were hers, no better, no worse. . . .

A little after five o'clock Henry found her with an apron on over her chiffon hostess gown, arranging the *gefilte fish* with a sprig of parsley and a piece of carrot on top. She looked radiant and excited. Kissing her, he said, "Why don't you let Maria do it?"

"Oh, darling, she's filling the water glasses and thank God she's here to serve. Now, Henry, please be a darling, go upstairs and get washed, then set up the bar . . . Oh God, Henry, I'm so nervous I can't stand it. What time is it, dear?"

"About five-fifteen. You know something, Doris? I have to give myself a little credit . . . I always knew you were beautiful, but you're even improving with age."

"With the steel-gray hair I still look young and beautiful? I was thinking of changing it to red."

"Do that and you've just lost the most wonderful husband in the world."

She kissed him once again. "In that case, I'll keep this color. Now, please hurry up. Michele should be here soon."

She put the fish back into the refrigerator, turned down the temperature of the oven, basted the chickens, and stood thinking for a moment, wondering if there was anything she'd forgotten. Then she took off her apron, washed her hands and walked into the den.

"Henry, you want me to get you the ice?"

"Honey, calm down. I'll take care of everything."

"I'm calm, Henry, I'm really very calm."

"I could tell the minute I came home."

She walked from room to room, fluffed up the pillows, arranged one daffodil that seemed to be a little out of place, then went back to the den. "You think everything looks all right, Henry?"

"What are you making such a big thing out of this for? When did anything not look all right?"

Before she could answer, the doorbell rang.

"Oh, my God, they're here." She ran to the front door and there was Michele, dressed in a Kelly-green suede pants suit with a black mink coat hanging over her arm. Doris was about to say, "You look gorgeous . . ." But then she saw Eliot, dressed in his best cowboy finery, including high-heeled tooled boots and a Stetson that sat on his head at the perfect angle.

The two of them looked so incongruous that it took every bit of Doris' self-discipline not to break into laughter. For a moment her thoughts went back to the little girl who had sat in the Golden State Theater, watching William S. Hart and knowing how much she loved him.

Michele was kissing her mother and saying, "Mama, I want you to meet Eliot."

536

Who immediately planted a big juicy kiss on Doris' cheek, then held her at arm's length. "You got to be kidding, this isn't your mother. Why, she's the most beautiful thing I ever saw in my life."

Laughing, Michele said, "That's what you said about me. Can't you make up your mind?"

"I did that the first night I met you . . . but to think there are *two* of you. Boy, this is a shock. I wasn't sure what I was going to call you, but it sure isn't going to be *ma*."

Doris laughed delightedly.

"I knew I was going to like you a whole lot," he went on.

"Same here. Now let's go into the den. I want you to meet Henry."

Henry was just preparing the bar glasses when he looked up at Eliot. Oh, my God, he thought, we've got Gene Autry in the family. He looks like he just came from the rodeo.

Michele embraced her father. "Oh, dad, I'm so glad to see you."

"Yes . . . me too," still staring at Eliot.

"Let me introduce you to Eliot."

Any further thoughts of likes or dislikes were banished when Eliot shook his hand warmly and said, "Michele talks about you a lot. I'm very glad to finally meet you, doctor."

"Thank you . . . likewise. What would you like to drink?"

"Just anything, bourbon, gin, vodka . . . anything."

"Daddy, can you make martinis?"

Doris was already into the kitchen to bring back a jar of olives.

As Henry began mixing the drinks, Michele said, "Dad, Eliot makes great martinis. Would you mind?"

"Not at all, but I'll have bourbon and Seven-Up."

"Doris, how about you?" Eliot asked.

"I'll have one of your specials."

When the drinks were served, Doris raised her glass in a toast. "Congratulations to both of you. I can't tell you how happy Henry and I are that you're with us this evening."

"Well, Michele didn't have to urge me too much. I couldn't wait to meet her family."

"Thank you," Doris said, her face suddenly very serious.

As she went into the kitchen to get the chopped liver, Michele followed her.

"What do you think of him, mama?"

"He's everything you said and more."

"I'm so happy you like him."

537

While Doris and Michele were in the kitchen Eliot went to work on thawing Henry out. What every man liked best was to discuss his business, so . . .

Before Henry had realized Eliot's strategy he had launched into the saga of how he had arrived in San Francisco with twelve dollars in his pocket, started the office and . . . Henry had succumbed to Eliot's charm. In fact he had almost forgotten he was a *goy*.

A little after six-thirty Michele said, "Where are Gary and Robin?"

Doris laughed. "They'll be here soon. Robin had to wait until sundown before leaving, so that she could light her candles. She's turned into a regular *rebbitsin*, but they should be here any minute."

As predicted, the doorbell rang minutes later and Doris hurried to the door. She kissed Robin and Gary then led them to the den, carrying little Mordechai in her arms.

After all the introductions were made, Robin said, "Here, mom, let me take the baby and put him to bed upstairs. He's already had his *Shabbes* dinner." . . .

When they were seated, the *gefilte fish* was already on the table.

Eliot took a bite and said, "Boy, these are the best damn fish cakes I ever tasted."

Henry paused momentarily, then continued to eat without looking up.

"It's *gefilte fish*, dear," Michele whispered.

"Is that so? Well, best damn *gefilte fish* I ever tasted . . ."

Maria removed the fish plates while Doris carried in the silver tureen of chicken soup and *matzo* balls and ladled it out.

"You've got to get the recipe for this, Michele," Eliot said when he tasted the soup. "These are the best dumplings I ever had."

Again, Henry swallowed hard.

"They're called *matzo* balls, dear," Michele told him.

Henry was the only one who was disturbed by Eliot's gaffes. For Doris, this occasion was deeply satisfying. The hardships she had survived had brought her to this moment. She not only had a family gathered around her but a family that promised to grow. Imagine, she even had a grandchild sleeping upstairs—it was as though the family denied her in her life was now richly compensated for . . .

As they sat having coffee, Gary said, "We have an announcement to make."

538

Doris and Henry looked at him expectantly—Henry thinking, My God, maybe he's changed his mind and is going to become a doctor ... and Doris hoping that this one would be a girl.

"Yes, Gary? What's the announcement?" Doris prompted.

"Well, this is going to be a bit of a shock to you but ... we're moving to Israel."

Doris and Henry could only stare for a moment. Then, finding her voice, Doris asked, "Why?"

"For one thing, because there's a great need for engineers there."

Before he could go on, Henry said, "What's the matter, in America they don't use engineers anymore? What kind of nonsense is this? You're Americans. How can you go to live in Israel?"

Robin answered, "Dad, the only place you can really be a Jew is in Israel."

"Why, there's not enough Jews for you here in the United States?"

"But it's not the same. We've thought this over very carefully, dad. Gary and I want to go live on a kibbutz in the Negev. That's why we named the baby Mordechai ... we knew it even then. There's a quality of life there that we just don't have in the United States."

"I think this whole thing is crazy," Henry said. "Where would Israel be without the contributions of money from American Jews?"

Gary interjected, "It would have been a lot harder for them, but we weren't doing anything so noble, dad ... If there had been the State of Israel during Hitler's time, six million Jews wouldn't have been annihilated ... You might as well know the whole truth. We've also become Zionists."

"Zionists!" Henry rasped.

"Yes, dad. I'm not saying that every Jew should be a Zionist, but it happens to be right for us. I'm sorry if you don't approve, but we have to do what's best for us, follow through on our own beliefs."

Doris sat thinking back on all the years and all the worries she'd had over her children. Somehow the Book of Ruth came to mind ... "for whither thou goest, I will go ... Thy people shall be my people, and thy God my God." How ashamed she was this evening that she had questioned Gary's judgment the night he told them about marrying Robin. Well, Israel wasn't really so far away. Woodside, California, was a lot closer and she hadn't seen her parents in over twenty years. "I think we should raise our glasses to Robin and Gary for the part they want to play in maintaining our heritage. I love and admire you both very much."

Gary came around and kissed his mother. She looked very special to him tonight; he knew the conflicts and the pride she was feeling. Then he went to his father, put his arms around him and said, "Dad, thanks for everything. I'm very proud to have a father like you."

"And I'm proud to be your father," he said, and he genuinely meant it. He wasn't really angry with their decision. It was more that he knew how much he would miss them. How much he and Doris both would miss them. My God, what's wrong... If Gary had married Barbara Levy he'd probably never have moved, would have settled down here. So he marries a *goyisheh maidel* who converts and becomes more Jewish than any of them. She even wants her *country* to be Jewish...

Doris looked on, also thinking of the ironies of life. Her mother and father had come to America from the old country, but papa had divorced himself from the beliefs he had once held so dear. And yet here were Gary and Robin, who had the faith papa had lost and were going to fight to perpetuate it... "Have you decided when you're leaving?"

"In about two months, I think.... Incidentally, you'll have to address your Chanukah cards to Mordechai Ben Lev."

Doris laughed. "And what are you going to be, Mr. and Mrs. Gary Ben Lev?"

"No, I'm changing my name to Ari, and Robin's will be Rahel."

Eliot picked up his glass and said, "I think we should all drink to Rahel and Ari, keepers of the faith. In the words of my dear friends the Kaufmans, *Mazel tov* and *L'chayim.*"

Michele looked at him lovingly. This extraordinary man seemed to understand it all.

Six months had passed. Doris had waved good-by to two of her children, going off to a new world, and today she and Henry had just arrived at Eliot's ranch for their daughter's wedding.

Chang Lee's wife had prepared a room for the Levins and for the sake of propriety Michele had been moved from Eliot's room to a room down the hall. If Henry had guessed that this wasn't the first time Michele was sleeping in Eliot's home, he gave no indication.

That night they gave a dinner party for Doris and Henry. The Kaufmans were present, along with a number of Eliot's close friends. At seven-thirty, Eliot's father arrived. Ben Burns was a tall husky man who lived in a sprawling ranch house at the east end of the property with Juanita, his housekeeper-mistress of twenty years.

Two days later the house was prepared for the wedding. Michele hadn't told her parents that she was to be married by a rabbi, but when he arrived to perform the ceremony she could see the pleasure and gratitude in their faces. When the rabbi pronounced them man and wife and Eliot embraced his Jewish bride, dressed in violet Chantilly lace, Doris and Henry looked on with tears in their eyes. God was in his heaven, all indeed was right with the world.

That night the newlyweds spent their honeymoon in Eliot's room, while Doris and Henry were sequestered in their room at the other end of the long hall. As Doris lay awake she thought, Good Lord, how the world had moved on. It seemed only yesterday that Rachel, Lillian and herself were sitting in a Dodge truck on the Fourth of July, going to Alum Rock. She thought about the letter she'd received last week from Rachel, who was living part of the year in New York to be near her son Larry, who had married the daughter of an illustrious banker . . . Imagine what mama and papa had missed. They not only had grandchildren whom they had never seen, but even a little great-grandson by the name of Mordechai Ben Lev. What a pity to be deprived of such satisfactions because of anger and pride. These joys could have enriched their lives. That's what families were really all about, growing together and sharing the blessings and sorrows and love. . . .

The wedding breakfast was real Western style, with pancakes, oatmeal, hash browns, eggs, slabs of ham, country-churned butter, biscuits and honey.

Doris, smiling broadly at Eliot, said, "This has got to be the best damn ham I ever tasted."

"Sorry, Doris, that's kosher corned beef," he said.

"Best damn corned beef I ever tasted." . . .

As soon as the plane back to San Francisco was airborne, Doris turned to Henry as she put her hand over his. "I think our Michele's got herself quite a man this time, don't you, honey?"

"I always said you were smart, Doris, and even if you do

541

outtalk me, you always have the right answers. He sure is quite a man. How they got the rabbi to marry them I'll never know."

"Oh, I have a feeling that Eliot can accomplish most anything he puts his mind to."

"Well, let's just hope and pray that they have a good life."

CHAPTER SIXTY-NINE

HENRY'S HOPES and prayers during the next year were more than realized. Michele found life with Eliot as close to heaven as anything on earth could be.

Often she would recall the first week of their marriage, which Eliot considered "the best damn honeymoon" in the world. They had spent the week touring the ranch, but it was impossible to cover the entire seven thousand acres in that little time.

He took her first to the corral, where she sat on the fence and watched him show off his equestrian ability. He called attention to his special tooled saddle, which he used only on very special occasions—like honeymoons. Then he showed her the bunkhouses and introduced her to the cowhands.

The first night of the tour he drove the jeep up to the timberline and came to a halt. "Honey, this is where we're going to bed down for the night. It's not going to be *matzo* balls, *gefilte fish* and your mother's noodle *kugel,* but I make the best damn baked beans and venison you ever tasted..." When they turned in for the night, she was shivering in the cold Nevada air and climbed into her sleeping bag to undress. "Don't bother with that flannel nightgown," Eliot said. He got in alongside her, zipped up the bag, and before she knew it she was very warm and cozy. Very.

The first real bath she had on their honeymoon was the night they spent at Ben's. Juanita was a beautiful woman, of Mexican, Indian and Irish ancestry, and Ben clearly adored her. How could he not? Michele thought. Dinner that night was thick bean soup, roast leg of venison and peach cobbler.

When they got back to the house after the honeymoon it seemed that Eliot thought she still had a few things to learn about the life she'd live with him.

For example—how to ride. "It'll toughen up your butt," he said.

But when she sat in the dust after her first spill, she said, "I'm not getting back on that thing—"

"Of course you are, that mare's damned sensitive."

"Really, what about my butt?"

"After a few more falls, it won't be quite so tender. Now, up you go."

"Eliot, I'd do anything in the world for you, but I'm not going to get up on that—"

Before she could finish the sentence, she was back in the saddle again. By the time autumn came she was an accomplished enough rider to accompany Eliot to the round-up in the northwestern part of the ranch.

If their life took on a pattern, it was one that Michele never found boring. From time to time they spent a weekend in Reno, where Eliot thought he had a little catching up to do at the gaming tables. One night his winnings were so great that he bought drinks for everybody and ended up going to bed drunk as a hoot-owl. The next morning, without any apologies, he said, "I sure had one hell of a time. How about you, lady?"

"Well, I was okay after you simmered down and I was able to get your boots off, but I must admit I was thinking of taking another room."

"Why?" he asked, nibbling on her ear.

" 'Cause you snored."

"I always do that when I get drunk as a skunk. But drunk or sober, I expect to wake up and find you right alongside of me . . ."

Once a week she drove into Reno and shopped, had lunch with Fran Kaufman, then was at the ranch in time for dinner. She always bought Eliot some crazy little thing she knew would make him laugh. And he always did.

In December, Michele and Eliot trudged through the snow until they found the perfect Christmas tree. As they took a rest from their efforts to chop it down, Eliot said, "I know it's a little against your principles, the Christmas tree thing, but I'll help you light your Chanukah candles and you help me trim the tree. That way we'll work out the whole damned thing . . ."

Doris and Henry came to spend Christmas with them, and the uproarious Christmas Eve party included the Kaufmans, Ben and Juanita, and an assortment of Eliot's relatives. Eliot was especially fond of Aunt Effie, who was a little hard of

543

hearing except when it came to being offered what she'd like to drink.

Eliot also decided that this year there was going to be a Mr. and Mrs. Santa Claus giving out the presents, so after dinner he and Michele went upstairs and changed into their costumes. She put on a gray bouffant wig that came to a topknot, granny glasses, shoes laced to the ankle and a long red skirt with a white ruffled blouse. When she stuck the pillows into her blouse, Eliot came over and took a good handful. "You know something, lady? I wouldn't mind a bit if I could nosh on those."

She laughed and danced away from him. "Eliot, you're crazy."

"Is that any way to talk to Santa Claus?" Flinging the sack over his back and handing her an enormous basket, the two of them walked back into the livingroom with the record player blasting "Jingle Bells."

Eliot dusted the fake snow off his shoulders, and suddenly Mrs. Claus was calling out the names . . . .

After everybody had gone to bed, Eliot whispered, "Lady, this was the best damn Christmas I ever had in my whole life."

She said quietly, "I got a secret to tell you. You're going to be the best damn father—"

He let out a whoop. "You mean you been holding out on me?"

She answered hesitantly, "Yes, darling, I guess I have."

Catching the apprehension in her voice, he turned on the lamp and said, "For how long?"

"As long as I could. I'm in my fourth month."

"Why?" he asked. "Michele, I thought we got rid of all those ghosts. I thought riding that mare would strengthen your butt *and* your courage. Now I've got news for you, lady. As of today, and this is an order, you're going to take it easy. And you're going to leave the worrying to me. I can be a tough buzzard. You've got something that belongs to me and I mean to collect."

"Oh, Eliot, I love you so much, and I don't want anything to go wrong for us."

"Well, you just stop worrying about it and keep thinking about what we've got ahead of us. If there's anybody that ever loved a woman, it sure as hell is me."

In the months that followed, Eliot did everything he could to reassure her, and made certain that she was not subjected

544

to stress or strain of any kind. He called Doris and told her that he thought it would be good for Michele to have her mother there toward the end of her pregnancy, and so Doris came out in the beginning of May to spend a few weeks with her daughter and son-in-law.

A week before the baby was due, Eliot took a large suite of rooms at the Riverside so that they would be close to the hospital. His timing had been quite accurate. At the Reno Presbyterian Hospital on May 15, 1959, Michele was delivered of a boy. When Eliot saw Steven Burns for the first time, he threw his hat in the air and twirled Doris in his arms. "By God, you're the best damn looking grandmother in the world."

She laughed, with tears in her eyes. "And, Bill S. Hart, I love you too. You've got to be the best damn son any mother could be privileged to have."

After seeing Michele, who was every bit as joyful as he was, he walked down the hall toward the nursery and waited, looking through the glass. When he saw the nurse bring his child out to be taken to Michele he said, "Here, give me that little fellow."

She protested that it was against the rules. He told her, "To hell with that. I'm going to take him in to see his mother. You better get used to that rule."

"But you don't have a mask and a gown on."

"I don't think this kid's going to mind a bit," and he strode down the hall with the little blanket-wrapped bundle and swung open the door. Laying the child alongside Michele, he said, "Here's your Christmas present . . . best damn present you're ever going to get from me." He bent over, kissed her lingeringly. "Thank you, lady. You're one hell of a woman."

"And you're the best damn man I've ever known in my life."

The whole household revolved around Steven, and no matter where Eliot happened to be Michele always heard the sound of his jeep coming round the bend at feeding time.

He dashed up the stairs to the nursery, kissed her generously, and settled into the big wing chair to watch as Michele held the child to her breast. Eliot loved the look and sound of his son's enjoyment. From time to time, she would glance over and smile at him. When she'd finished nursing he'd say, "Here, give me that kid. Burping's my job."

"Eliot, you'll have to put a diaper over your shoulder."

He obeyed reluctantly. "You know, this kid's going to get a few germs anyway, diaper or no diaper . . . Wow, fellow, that was a good one." Then he'd hold the child in his arms and look down at him. "I'll be damned if you're not the best-looking kid I ever saw. You look just like your mother."

"Eliot, he looks exactly like you and you know it."

"Only his plumbing. The rest of him is you, Michele."

"Have it your way, but he's absolutely a duplicate you. Your father swore he thought he was seeing you for the first time again."

Looking at the child and smiling, he said, "You really think so?"

"Well, it wouldn't be the worst thing that ever happened to him."

"Yeah, come to think of it, he does look like me. And he's a damn good-looking kid in spite of it." . . .

Doris and Henry came out to spend the week for Steven's first birthday, and there wasn't a happier grandfather than Henry. As for Doris, she couldn't understand why Steven wasn't the most incorrigibly spoiled child in the world. Michele doted on him, and Doris doubted if there was a toy left in Reno. The things that Eliot bought were absolute insanity. A panda the size of a six-year-old, a huge red fire truck, an electric train set . . . On the momentous occasion of Steven cutting his first tooth, Eliot insisted it had to be on beef jerky . . . By the time Steven was two, he was riding on Eliot's lap in the jeep, and on Steven's third birthday, Eliot took him into Reno and had him outfitted with boots, a Stetson and chaps . . . "Here, let me take a look at you. Yeah, terrific. Okay, buckaroo, let's go home and show mama . . ."

When Steven was four Eliot kept him out an entire week during round-up, but this was one excursion that backfired. When they came home, Steven was put to bed with a very bad cold, which made Eliot more than a little nervous. Maybe this time he'd gone too far. The humidifier in Steven's room ran day and night for a week, and Eliot wouldn't leave the child for a moment. He slept on a cot in his room and it was only when Steven was up and around, "full of piss and vinegar again," that Eliot began to relax . . . .

At six, Steven looked like a miniature Eliot and could ride a horse almost as well. Eliot gave him his first rifle, which didn't please Michele in the least. But Eliot said that his father Ben had taught him to shoot at that age and Steven was going to do the same. If Michele had any funny ideas

546

that he was going to grow up to be a sissy, she had another guess coming . . . .

When Doris came at Thanksgiving that year, she proudly announced that Michele had a little niece, a *sabra* by the name of Aviva, born at the Hadassah Hospital in Jerusalem.

"Mama, I know you miss them terribly and eight years is such a long time. Why don't you and dad go and visit? Imagine how thrilled they'd be for you to see the new baby. And Mordechai is almost nine now."

Doris sighed. "I'm dying to see them, and dad and I have thought about it, but the trip is so expensive . . . Then again, if we don't do it now . . . You're right, we're going this summer."

"Oh, I'm so happy, mama. What are you smiling at?"

"The differences in my grandchildren's lives—one a cowboy living in Nevada, the other living on a kibbutz in the Negev, and my new *sabra* . . . Isn't that a magnificent name, Aviva?"

"It's beautiful. What does it mean in Hebrew?"

"Robin . . . I mean Rahel said it meant spring, the most beautiful time of the year."

Indeed it was, Michele thought, remembering the spring morning she'd given birth to Steven. That morning had been the final proof to her that her ghosts were a thing of the past.

CHAPTER SEVENTY

BUNDLED IN his hooded Mackinaw coat, Steven sat in the jeep between his mother and father. It was a tradition that Steven was familiar with, the cutting down of the Christmas tree. He had chosen this year's tree almost a year ago, and he knew it would be ready for cutting.

It was cold and crisp, a winter wonderland. The boughs on the towering firs and pines were bending under the weight of the snowfall.

They got out of the jeep, eagerly took the axes and lanterns and trudged through the snow to Steven's tree.

As Eliot swung back his axe to make the first cut, they heard the sound of gunfire. None of them were startled since hunting jackrabbits in the snow was not uncommon, but "some crazy bastard" was poaching on Eliot's land and he didn't like that.

"Wherever the hell you are, get off my land," he called out.

The echo of his voice hadn't even died when another shot rang out and Michele and Steven watched Eliot double over and fall face down into the snow.

It was so sudden, so unexpected, that Michele wasn't quite sure what had happened. When she saw him lying motionless, she cried out, "Get up, Eliot." When he didn't move she bent down, her knees sinking into the snow, and tried pulling him onto his back. But she was trembling now, and she wasn't strong enough. "Steven, help me. Help me roll daddy over!"

They finally got him on his back, but when she saw the blood rushing from Eliot's mouth she became hysterical. "Eliot, get up, get up!" she pleaded. "Don't do this, Eliot, get up." She bent down, took his head in her arms and held him against her. "Oh, my God, Eliot you can't, you can't . . ."

Steven stood wide-eyed, tears streaming down his cheeks. "Mommy, dad's hurt. Let's get a doctor."

She took off her coat and covered Eliot. "Please, Eliot, get up." But all she heard was the sound of his labored breathing. "Darling, we'll be right back," she said frantically. She grabbed Steven by the hand and they drove to Ben's.

When she arrived and opened the door, Juanita saw the blood on Michele's hands and cheek. "My God, what's happened?"

"Eliot's been shot—"

"Oh, my God, no . . ."

"Where's Ben?"

"He's in bed." She ran through the house and came back moments later with Ben. "Let me get my coat, Michele. Juanita, call Dr. Mason to get an ambulance out there. Have Nick and some of the boys meet us . . . where's Eliot?"

"Over at the east acres . . . we were cutting down a tree . . ."

Ben took Michele and Steven out to the jeep and drove them back to where Eliot was, and minutes later four of the hands had arrived. Ben had told her to stay in the jeep while he went to Eliot, but suddenly she couldn't stand to just sit there, to be without Eliot. As she got out and started across to her husband, one of the men stopped her.

"Mrs. Burns, let me take you home. The others will take care of Eliot."

Trying to push him aside, she screamed, "No, I want to see Eliot."

548

"Mrs. Burns, come on, let me take you home."

"Michele, I think you'd better listen to Mac," Ben said. "Go ahead now, and I'll meet you up at the house . . ."

By the time they brought Eliot back, there was no need for the ambulance. The men carried him into the house and up the stairs to his room, with Ben following.

Michele started to go in, but Ben stopped her.

"Don't go in, Michele."

"Get out of my way, Ben."

"Michele, listen to me . . . Eliot's gone."

She looked at his face. "It can't be true. Just an hour ago we were . . . Get *out* of my way, I'm going to see my husband." She opened the door . . . . His face was covered, and he was lying so still. She refused to believe it, he was going to get up any minute. She walked slowly to the bed, took the sheet off his face and spoke to him as though he would answer. "Eliot, darling, please wake up, please . . ." And then she threw herself across him and let the anguished, soundless cries wash over them both . . .

When Ben called Doris she understood what was being said but she couldn't believe it. It wasn't possible . . . "How is Michele?"

"In pretty bad shape."

"Steven?"

"About the same, I'm afraid. I guess it's going to take us to see this thing through."

"Yes, Ben. Henry and I will be there as soon as we can get a plane." . . .

When they went up to Michele's room and saw her sitting in the large wing chair and staring quietly into the fire, Doris wished she could die rather than see her child like this. "Darling, daddy and I got here as soon as we could."

Michele did not respond.

"Michele, darling, come lie down."

She looked at Doris. "You know Eliot's dead."

"Yes, darling, we know. Now please come lie down."

"No, I can't ever sleep in that bed again. I just want to sit here alone, mama."

"Please, Michele."

But Michele wasn't listening. Then, quietly, "I want to die, mama."

"Don't say that . . . Eliot wouldn't want you to say that."

Henry said, "Come on, darling."

She looked up at her father. "Dad, I want to sit here, this is what I have of Eliot."

"You have more than that. You have Steven—"

"No, I can't look at Steven. When I do, I see Eliot."

Taking her hand, he said, "Come, dear . . ."

Like a child, she followed him down the hall to another room. Tucking her under the covers, he said, "I want you to take one of these."

"No, I don't want to go to sleep. I never want to go to sleep, I don't want to do anything."

"Please, Michele, do this for me—"

Doris had a glass of water handy as Henry put the Nembutal to her mouth. They sat in the room until she finally fell asleep, then they went to see Steven.

He was crying and angry. "Somebody killed my dad and I'm going to kill them."

Henry held the little boy very close. "You mustn't say that, Steven. It was an accident."

"No!" he screamed. "I'm going to kill them like they killed my dad."

"Steven, listen to your grandpa. If you love your father you won't say that kind of thing, because you know he wouldn't want you to. Now, I know it's going to be very hard, but you must try to be a brave boy and remember, your mother needs you. Your father would want you to remember that."

He clung to Henry and cried out his broken heart.

The day Eliot was buried, Michele stood like a statue watching the coffin being lowered into the ground. There was nothing real about it. In fact, it wasn't happening to her. She was watching a young woman dressed in black, standing there with a little boy . . . It wasn't happening to her, not to Michele . . . not to Steven . . .

After the services were over they went back to the house, which was full of people who had come to pay their respects. Fran and Paul Kaufman were the last to leave.

After Steven and a sedated Michele had been put to bed, Ben and Henry sat silently as Juanita said to Doris, "Ben and I thought maybe we'd take Michele over to our place but she refuses to go. In fact, she won't leave the house. Doris, I don't want to upset you, but I think we've got a very sick young woman on our hands. She was a little *too* quiet today."

Henry said, "That happens after tremendous shock. But of course she can't be alone, so Doris will stay for a while until we feel that she's ready to make a change of some kind. Then we'll all decide what's best."

"You can count on me for anything. Now, is there anything I can do for you before I leave? I think I should get Ben home," Juanita said.

Ben spoke now for the first time. "No parent should live to bury his own child." He got up and walked out of the house without another word.

Juanita said goodnight and followed him . . . .

Doris stayed for a month, and Ben and Juanita came up to the big house every night. Michele seemed composed and resigned now.

One evening Ben stood in front of the fire in Eliot's favorite room and said, "What do you want to do, Michele?"

She replied almost inaudibly. "I want to stay here."

"But you can't live here alone, Michele, in this big house," Juanita said.

"Yes, I can . . . it's all I have left of Eliot and I can't leave."

"Why don't you come and stay with us for a little while, or go home with your mother and father for a bit. It would do you good to get away—"

She shook her head. "No, I'm going to stay here."

"Michele," Ben said, "your mother can't stay forever and I don't think its good for you to be here alone."

"That's what I've decided to do."

Juanita said, "Well, if you've thought about it, Michele, and that's what you'd like, then Ben and I will be here every day."

Michele just sat, making no reply.

When they were on the plane going home, Doris felt she shouldn't be leaving, that Michele still needed her. When she got home she called two and three times a day. There was a peculiar serenity about Michele, and she wished she felt the same way. If only she could convince herself that Michele had come to terms with her tragedy . . . .

Two weeks after Doris returned home, she received a phone call from Juanita. "Doris, I don't know how to tell you this, but . . . Michele is in the psychiatric ward at the hospital."

Somehow she'd known all along that Michele's reaction had been unnaturally calm. "Tell me what happened, Juanita."

"Well, I wanted to spare you this, but she simply went berserk. A few days ago she left Steven and drove into Reno. Then Chang Lee called and told us that she hadn't been home for a few days—"

Doris let out a gasp. "Tell me exactly what happened."

"Michele was found wandering around in quite a state. She was incoherent ... dazed. She was picked up and taken to the psychiatric ward. Ben's been in Reno for the last several days so that he can be near her."

"Where's Steven now?"

"With us, but I think you'd better come up so we can decide what to do."

She was met at the airport by Ben, who silently drove her to the hospital.

When Doris walked into Michele's room, she was trembling very badly. Michele didn't recognize her. She took hold of Michele's hand. "Michele, I'm here. Darling?"

Michele looked at her vacantly.

"Darling, it's me, mama."

Michele didn't respond.

God, Doris thought, if I have any strength give it to me now, please.

The psychiatrist was frank with her. Michele's breakdown was so complete that it was going to take a very long time for her to recover.

"What do you suggest we do, doctor?"

"Well, as I said, it's not only going to take a long time, but she'll have to be watched carefully. This is difficult, Mrs. Levin, but we really have a suicidal patient on our hands."

"You mean that she tried to—" Doris couldn't finish.

"Yes. We don't know how many barbiturates she took, but the clerk at the hotel said he found two empty bottles of Seconal. It was close for a while, but at least we've got her to this point."

"Obviously she'll have to stay here until Mr. Burns and I decide what to do ..."

Doris stayed the rest of the day with Michele, then drove out to the ranch with Ben. After Steven had gone to bed, she sat with Ben and Juanita in the livingroom.

"Ben and I have talked this over carefully, Doris, and we'll go along with whatever you decide to do. You have our support on this in any way you need it. But let us make a suggestion—which you're free to reject if you think we're wrong. You can't stay here indefinitely, you have other obligations, and obviously you're going to want to be with

Michele. We thought maybe the best thing is to take her to a sanitarium where you'd be able to see her, and that would mean someplace near San Francisco. As for Steven, you know how Ben and I feel about him, but we're not so sure this is the best place for him. The adjustment is tough . . . . In fact he's been going up to the east acres every day. Ben found him sitting in the snow, by himself right near the tree—"

Doris interrupted. "I really think I could stand a drink, Ben."

When he handed her a bourbon and sat down again, he picked up Juanita's thought. "Doris, what Juanita is trying to say is that we think the best thing that could happen to Steven is to get away from here. He's *got* to get away, much as we love him. And it seems the best place would be with you and Henry. I think you have the kind of stability he needs now."

Doris took a long sip of the drink. . . .

The next day she spoke to the psychiatrist and asked when Michele could leave and fly to California, to be in another hospital. She explained what had been discussed the night before.

"As a matter of fact, that strikes me as a wise decision. There's a fine place in Belmont, about thirty miles from where you live. We believe she's going to come out of this eventually, though we don't know to what degree. And when she does, she'll need the security of her family."

"When do you think we could take her?"

"Probably in the next few days. However, I suggest that one of our staff nurses go along with you until she's all settled."

"Do you think we should take Steven at the same time?"

"No, I'd suggest he stay till you get Michele settled, then, as you all decided, have him come to live with you and Dr. Levin." . . .

It was a silent, vague Michele who sat on the plane to San Francisco. From time to time Doris tried speaking to her. No response.

If ever there was a moment of truth in Doris' life it was at Belmont Hospital. Signing the papers to commit Michele was one of the grimmest tasks she had ever faced. After seeing Michele settled into a room she kissed her good-by, then walked down the corridor and out into the sunshine and made the drive home in a daze.

Doris and Henry waited for Steven to come out of his room.

Juanita and Ben had had a dreadful time trying to tell him that he was going to be living with his mother's parents.

"I'm not going," he had screamed. "*You're* my grandparents and I'm going to stay here."

Ben tried to reason with him. "Look, Steven, you know that as much as we love you, your other grandparents do too. We think it would be good for you to have a change for a little while."

"I'm nearly seven years old and I can make up my own mind what I want to do. If you don't want me, I can get along. I can go live in my dad's house."

Juanita said quietly, "Steven, it's not whether we want you, it's a question of what's best for you. And besides, you're going to want to be near your mother—"

"No, I don't. I don't want to see her at all. I hate her."

"Don't let me ever hear you say that, Steven. Now you act like a man," Ben said sternly.

"But she went away and left me—"

"Your mother didn't leave you. She's very sick and I think you're old enough to know about it. Your mother's in the hospital, a sanitarium—"

"That's for crazy people—"

"Well, Steven, you're not quite the man I thought you were. Your father would certainly have been disappointed to hear what you just said."

He didn't answer. Instead he turned his back on them and pulled the covers up, under his chin.

Juanita and Ben were up late that night, talking about the boy.

"If I thought this was the place for him, that's where I'd have him," Juanita said. "But I know in my heart he's never going to get over this if he doesn't get away."

"You're right. Besides, Doris is the only one of us who's really young enough to be able to handle a little boy. What is she . . . going on fifty? Still, it's not going to be easy for them, even if it is the best thing for the boy."

Ben's observations proved all too true. Doris and Henry did feel their inadequacy to handle the situation. Steven had been raised with Ben and Juanita from the cradle. Although he had always been affectionate toward his other grandparents, he resented them for taking him away from the people and the home that he knew best . . .

When Ben drove them all to the airport, Steven sat sullenly in the back of the car, looking out the window. Ben deliberately avoided the road going past the big house.

When the announcement was made for boarding, Steven looked up at Ben. Biting his lip hard so as not to cry, he said "You're not going to forget to call me, are you, gramps?"

Ben looked down at him. Jesus, he looked just like Eliot. "Well, of course I'm going to call."

"And you're going to come and see me this summer?"

"We'll talk about that, Steve."

It seemed no one really wanted him, Steven thought. When he looked at Juanita, he could no longer hold back the tears. "I don't want to leave, grams, I don't want to go."

"Steven, your other grandmother and grandfather are just as important as we are, and they love you just as much. Now, remember what I told you the other night, that this is rough on all of us and that we all have to cooperate. We think it's what your dad would have wanted—"

Without another word, he released himself and walked down the ramp and onto the plane, leaving Doris and Henry behind him.

Doris looked at Juanita. "Thank you for everything. You're a remarkable woman."

"So are you. And unless I miss my guess, you're going to see it through. You're a strong lady, Doris."

The two women embraced, then Doris went to Ben and put her arms around him. They had both lost a child, one in life and one in death.

CHAPTER SEVENTY-ONE

DORIS' LIFE required a complete readjustment. Before Steven had come she would write into the early hours of the morning. Her sleeping habits were so erratic that she had often indulged herself and slept until ten. But that came abruptly to an end.

Now she woke Steven at seven in the morning, fixed breakfast for him, then drove him to school, and at two-thirty she dropped whatever she was writing and picked him up. Once again she became consumed with the PTA, Sunday School, the orthodontist and shopping for clothes.

Because of the time she spent away from the typewriter doing other things, she now wrote at a frantic pace and was lucky if she slept three to four hours a night. Her mind seemed befuddled and when she proofread her work she wondered how any of it made any sense. It seemed she was now relying on a pat formula. Nothing creative . . . just names, places, a few variations on the same themes. For the first time she was ashamed of what she was doing and she submitted her work without pride. But that was really the least of her problems.

After a year and a half, Dr. Weingarten felt Michele should begin to gradually learn how to live once again in the outside world. When patients stayed too long in the security of an institution such as Belmont, very often they were reluctant to leave. So he advised Doris that Michele should go home for short periods of time.

On her first visit home, Michele was very nervous and unsure of herself. When Doris suggested it might be nice to lunch out, Michele refused. She didn't like crowds and noises frightened her. But the greatest of her anxieties was Steven. Although he was a painful reminder of Eliot, she wanted to try to establish some rapport with him. But Steven's resistance left her feeling even more unsure of herself. He was difficult and belligerent toward her, and Doris was beginning to worry that there was no way to reach him. No matter how hard Michele tried, she couldn't break through Steven's rejection. The tension became so great that Michele often begged to go back after being home for just a few hours. She just couldn't be the kind of mother Steven wanted.

When Doris returned from her visits to Michele, Steven glared at her at the dinner table as though the visit to Michele was a disloyalty to him.

Finally, Doris spoke to Henry about sending Steven to see a child psychiatrist, and he agreed it would probably benefit them all.

It did. After six months the tension and overt resentment began to lessen. Steven assumed the attitude of a well-behaved boarder, and while Doris wished he could be happier with them she was grateful that he didn't seem as angry as he had.

At least it was now a period of greater peace. Michele seemed to be making progress, and each time Doris visited her she noticed a decided change in her. When she left for the thirty-mile drive home, now it was with a glimmer of hope.

The years were moving on, and although Doris realized she still knew nothing of what went on in Steven's mind, she was glad their lives had become more compatible.

They were preparing for his *bar mitzvah* now, and Doris wanted it to be a very special occasion for him. She invited

556

Ben and Juanita, who arrived two days before the ceremony. But during their stay, Steven had as little to do with them as possible. It was as though he was punishing them for having rejected him. . . .

Doris and Henry sat in the same pew they'd occupied for Gary's *bar mitzvah*, and in spite of—or perhaps because of—the problems they'd had with Steven, Doris was very proud when she looked at him during the service. He was magnificent. He neither stammered nor stuttered, and he made not a single error. At the end of the service Steven walked to the lectern to deliver his speech.

He looked down at Doris and Henry, and then at Ben and Juanita. Suddenly the speech he had prepared seemed false and somehow he couldn't bring himself to say it. The whole evening seemed unreal. He had had three years of training in Judaism, but he didn't feel anything about it, it all meant nothing to him. He resented his mother for not being there, although he understood the reasons, he *felt* that she was selfish and thought too much about herself. Without thinking, he blurted out, "I wish I could honestly say I did this for my grandparents, but I didn't. They taught me that today I would become a man, so I guess I have to be honest. This was in memory of my father." With that, Steven took off his *tallis* and walked from the pulpit. The rabbi awkwardly continued the service.

Doris and Henry were crushed, and Ben wanted to horse-whip Steven. He maintained his composure only out of respect for Doris and Henry. Somehow they all got through the reception, but Doris had to close her ears to the whispers . . . What an ungrateful little boy, how terribly sad Michele couldn't have been here . . . that Doris and Henry had to assume the responsibility of raising a young child . . . Doris ignored it all. She had too many other problems to worry herself over what other people thought. . . .

After seven long years of being in and out of Belmont, Michele was ready to leave. The day before she was to be released, Dr. Weingarten phoned Doris and asked if they might get together.

His opinion was that what Michele needed most at this moment was to build a life of her own and resume the responsibility for her child. Although she was going to need the love and support of her family, she had to build up her own strengths.

"Dr. Weingarten, I think for the past seven years you've

557

been trying to tell me something, that maybe you feel that a part of Michele's inability to cope is basically my fault."

"How do you feel about that?"

She thought for a long moment. "I don't really know. It's strange, I raised both my children the same way, loved them equally, but Gary has a strength that Michele lacks. Maybe I let Michele think that the world was a safe, warm place like home, maybe I overprotected her."

"Do you think it was because of your childhood?"

"Yes. Strange, isn't it?"

"What?"

"My own childhood was not too happy. I was completely dominated by my mother, and one would think I should have grown up a beaten person. At one point in my life that was true. At one time I had the most tremendous inferiority complex even you could imagine, and it took me a long time to get over it. But with a lot of hard work, on my own, I not only did but I've come to feel secure within myself. Until now, anyway. What have I done to make Michele unable to face her realities?"

"I thought you said you didn't know if you'd done anything."

"Well, I do know I've made mistakes, and I don't want to go on making them."

"But what makes you feel you were responsible for Michele's weaknesses?"

"In one way or another children are the by-product of their parents—"

"True, but parents aren't quite that omnipotent, they're not totally responsible for the way their children turn out. And it isn't just one parent who forms a child either. Michele also has a father, who, I've observed, is a very kind man. But during some of the discussions we've had, I've found that he has some weaknesses. In fact, Mrs. Levin, I believe he leans on you too. But that's getting off the track. The point is that you can't continue to let Michele lean on you. The best thing you can do is to allow—encourage—Michele to take up her life. Never mind who's responsible for what . . . she needs to get on with being a mother. Let's all of us watch her grow."

"What happens if there's an SOS?"

"You'll have to deal with that if and when. You used the word overprotective, and I think it was apt. Now it's time for Michele to have her chance to try to make it on her own. If we find that she can't, we'll both be there. And let me add

558

that I think Michele is very fortunate to have a mother like you. In my line of work, I don't get to say that too often."

Doris brought Michele home the next day. The reunion with Steven was very strained. He was so like Eliot that she could hardly embrace him. Even after seven years of therapy, seeing him brought back all the painful reminders. And his reaction to her was subdued hostility. They greeted each other like civilized strangers, and Doris could only hope that when the two of them were living alone there would eventually be a coming together of mother and child.

During the next week Doris and Michele looked for an apartment and found a two-bedroom one on Leavenworth and Clay streets. Michele cried bitterly the night before she was to move. If only she could go on living here at home, where she felt safe, as if she belonged. . . .

After a sleepless night she and Doris went to the apartment and waited for Steven to come home from school. When he came in he merely acknowledged them, then went to his room and turned up the stereo full blast. Doris wonder whether she should have them home for dinner that night, but then she remembered what Dr. Weingarten had said. At a quarter of five she got up as casually as she could and put on her coat to leave."Well, darling, I think I'd better go home and get something for your father's dinner."

Michele stood there, trembling inside, and calling on what she'd learned from her therapy sessions. The time had come. The umbilical cord had to be cut. She was Steven's mother, and that was the role Dr. Weingarten had been preparing her for, that she'd been trying to prepare herself for.

But after her mother had shut the door, Michele was left with all kinds of conflicting thoughts . . . She and Steven were unknown quantities to each other; she hadn't been a mother in seven years. She remembered the day Eliot had first tried to teach her to ride and had made her get back on the horse every time she'd fallen off. But how did she get back on without him? She heard his voice . . . Lady, you're going to have to do it on your own this time. I'm sorry I'm not around to help, but hang in there, lady. You'll make it . . .

Unsteadily, she went to Steven's door and knocked.

"Yeah."

"Steven, may I speak to you?"

"What about?" he called through the closed door.

"I'd just like to speak to you."

"Okay—"

When she opened the door he was sprawled on the bed, looking much older and taller than a boy going on fourteen.

"Steven, you and I have never really talked together . . . I want you to know how much I love you and have missed you—"

Glaring at her he said, "Yeah, I'll bet . . ."

The trembling started. "Steven, I want us to have a good life together and I hope you'll help me—"

"You didn't help me after my dad died."

"Steven, don't you *still* understand what happened to me?"

"No, the only thing I understand is that you were feeling so sorry for yourself after dad died that you didn't even have time to think about what was going to happen to me."

"Steven, I didn't deliberately leave you. There were many things in my life you know nothing about, and losing your father . . . well, it was just too much for me. I know how you feel, but as time goes on and you grow older I hope you'll understand what happened to me and—"

"What do you think happened to me? I never felt that living with your mother and father was my home. I wanted to stay with gramps. In fact, I'd like to go home to him right now."

"This is your home and I'm your mother."

"This is *not* my home, and as far as I'm concerned you're someone I don't even know."

Tears blinding her eyes, Michele turned and went to her room and called Doris. "Mama, this isn't going to work. I can't reach Steven. I don't know how to handle it. I don't know how to get through to him . . ."

Against her better judgment Doris said, "I'll be right over."

As Doris got into her coat she said, "To hell with Dr. Weingarten. I'm not going to stand by and watch my child disintegrate."

When she arrived at the apartment she found Michele almost incoherent. The first thing she did was get Michele into bed. Then, without knocking, she walked into Steven's room and sat down. "Now you listen to me and listen carefully, Steven. Grandpa and I have given what we could to you. We could have left you with gramps, but he didn't think that was good for you. But we didn't have to take you. We could have said, 'What do we need with the responsibility of raising a child at our age?' We didn't do that, because we

560

agreed with your gramps that you needed a change. And now, whether you like it or not, you're going to live with your mother. And I'm not going to allow you to blame her for something that wasn't her fault. She didn't do anything to you any more than if she'd had had a bad heart or some other serious physical illness. You have a problem? Sure you do. We all do, but you're so angry at the whole world you'd like to use your mother to hit back at it. But I'm not going to allow you to do that, Steven. You treat her the way your father would have wanted you to. Do I make myself clear?"

Steven didn't answer. He heard her, even half understood, but mostly he didn't, wouldn't, and in the anger and confusion he was now feeling he wondered if his father hadn't in some way let him down too. . . .

CHAPTER SEVENTY-TWO

OVER THE next years Michele was truly put to the test. Steven's resentment only seemed to grow. He fought with her over even the smallest differences, he found fault with her and angrily shut himself up in his room after slamming the door. There seemed no way Michele could get through to him.

The year he turned sixteen, Ben managed to have him spend the summer on the ranch. Though it wore Ben out, it was the best and happiest time Steven had known since he was six, but when he returned to Michele he not only returned to his old ways but became more impossible than ever. He stayed out until all hours of the morning and often refused to get up for school. The strain was becoming so great on Michele that the only way she could cope—forget— was by drinking. But when Steven would return and find her in a stupor, it only added to his resentment. The two were bringing out the worst in each other . . . Michele was at the breaking point. Seeing all the signs, Doris once again tried to talk with Steven, with the old results.

Finally one night Michele received a phone call from the police saying that Steven had been picked up for possession of marijuana. By now, Michele knew that Ben was the only one who could handle Steven at all, so she called him, and he promptly took the first available plane to San Francisco.

When he saw Steven walking out of the door of the detention hall, he almost wished he had his whip with him.

No, sir, he wasn't going to put up with Steven's nonsense anymore. None of them had this coming to them, especially not Eliot.

When Steven was seated across from his grandfather, he kept his eyes on the floor as he listened to the angry voice. "Maybe your tantrums and your play-acting are going to work with your other grandparents. But I have news for you, laddie. I think you've gone just about as far as I'm going to take. You're going to shape up or ship out. Now, I've asked you this before, and I'm going to ask you again. What have you decided you want to do—*if* you should ever get out of high school?"

"I want to go home—"

"I thought home was with your mother. That's what every kid wants, but by God, *my* mother would have beaten the hell out of me if I'd done a lot less than you. Now you said you wanted to go home, right? Okay, you're going to go home . . . you'd better believe you are. But you're not going to live in the big house, buddy, and you're not going to live with me, either. You're going to bunk up with the rest of the boys and get paid what they do. And I'm going to see that Mac works your ass off. Now, is that enough home for you?"

Steven smiled for almost the first time in many years, but Ben went on even more forcefully. "When I get through with you, buddy boy, you'll be lucky if you've got a smile left in you. Now let me get you out of this place, and after we get you bathed and shaved the whole family's going to have a pow-wow. And damn it, you're going to beg your mother to forgive you and you'd better mean it. You're also going to tell your grandmother and grandfather how much you appreciate what they've done for you. They've sacrificed a hell of a lot for you, we've all taken as much bull from you as we're going to."

Steven went to Ben and put his arms around him as he unashamedly let the tears pour down.

As Ben predicted, Mac worked the butt off him, and the hard work was beginning to make him take a good look at himself. Ben didn't fool around. Sunday afternoon was the only day in the week Steven had dinner with Ben and Juanita. No, sir, Ben wasn't going to indulge him with a lot of fancy food and all the comforts of home. He was going to eat the same grub that the rest of the guys did. . . .

During the next two years Steven had a good deal of time to think about his life, and what he discovered was that he not only loved his mother, but even *missed* her. He couldn't just turn off the love he had felt for her as a child, and he was beginning to feel guilty for only having made things rougher for her. There wasn't a week that passed that he didn't phone or write to Michele, and he was just as conscientious with Doris and Henry. . . .

Just before his eighteenth birthday he called Michele. "Mom, I'd like you to come up with grandma and grandpa. You think you could make it?"

Michele thought she'd never hear Steven say that to her. It broke her up. "Of course, darling."

"You want to tell grandma and grandpa or do you want me to call?"

"What do you feel is right?"

"I guess I'd better call. Now don't forget, you're going to come up and spend a week with me, right?"

"Damn right."

That week brought the greatest happiness Michele had known in years.

When the plane landed, Juanita, Ben and Steven watched his mother and grandparents come across the field. Steven was shocked. His mother was just as beautiful as ever, but there were silver streaks in her hair that he hadn't noticed two years ago. He knew very well he'd been responsible for putting them there.

His greeting was so affectionate that Michele was immediately at ease. The one worry she had was driving back to the ranch. But once again, Ben deliberately bypassed the big house. . . .

One day Michele took Ben's car and drove up to the house. She sat behind the steering wheel for a long time, reliving the memories that house had stored away in its walls. When she felt up to it she got out of the car, walked slowly up the stone path to the double doors and stood in front of them as she thought of the first time Eliot had brought her here. She knew if she ever was going to recover she would have to walk over that threshold again, and this time she had to do it on her own.

Slowly she turned the heavy brass knob and walked into the enormous foyer.

Chang Lee had heard her footsteps in the hall and appeared immediately. His usual Oriental composure was forgotten in the excitement of seeing Michele . . . "Miss Michele, I'm so happy to see you."

563

"It's been a long time, Chang."

"Yes, a very long time." He smiled and excused himself, sensing that she wanted to be alone.

She retraced her steps, trying to remember every moment. First she went to the enormous drawingroom, sat in the exact spot she had sat that first night . . . This is not my favorite drinking room, he had said. She got up and walked into the den. The first thing she saw was the gun cabinet. She quickly looked away to the stone fireplace, vividly remembered the dancing flames, the dim lights . . . She could almost see him standing at the bar, going through the careful ceremony of mixing the martinis. She felt as though she were being carried up the stairs to Eliot's room . . . I want to marry you, lady . . . But we don't know each other . . . If you knew me a hundred years, I'd be the same . . . She looked at the bed where they'd shared so much love. It was where both Steven and Eliot were conceived, and where Eliot had died . . . She walked down the hall to what had once been the nursery, and saw herself sitting in the rocker with Steven at her breast, Eliot in the wing chair with his arms folded about his legs stretched out in front, watching and smiling . . . She wandered slowly now, from room to room, then went back down the winding staircase and crossed to the front door. Without looking back, she opened it and let herself out.

As she sat behind the wheel of Ben's car she asked herself, Now that you've made that trip into the past, do you think you can make it to the east acres? And she thought that Eliot would be damn proud if she could . . .

She started the car and set off into the countryside. How different it looked on this beautiful spring morning. What was it her mother had said about spring? She recalled now . . . the renewal, the promise . . . the beginning.

She got out of the car and walked up the incline to Steven's tree. It had grown a great deal since she'd last seen it, and was no longer dwarfed by the trees that surrounded it. She lay down on the very spot where Eliot had fallen. As though embracing him, she said, "I've done it, Eliot, I've been able to do it. Thank you, darling, for your strength."

She lay there for a few minutes longer before calmly getting up and brushing the pine needles away, then walked down the hill to the car and went back to Ben's. . . .

The night before she left Steven asked if he could be alone with her for a little while. They sat now in Ben's study.

"Mom," he said, "you know, this is the place I'm going to spend the rest of my life. I was born here. And like my dad,

I'm going to die here. How about us finally becoming a family, you and me? I mean, is there any chance you could come live here?"

She was sure he was psychic: it was what she had been wanting all day. This was the place she'd known the greatest happiness, and she had realized today that part of her problem had been that she'd been so cut off from Eliot. Here she felt his presence in everything—and especially when she looked at Steven. Here, in this place, he was the living proof that Eliot had been real, that she and Eliot had been real and always would be . . . "I'd like that very much. This is where we both belong."

He got up and kissed her. "I know it's sort of late in the day"—he smiled awkwardly—"but I'd like to say how ashamed I am for what I've done. I was rough on everybody, including myself, but I promise you, mom, I'm going to be the best damn son that any mother could ever have."

She laughed. That was exactly the way Eliot would have said it . . .

That night at dinner Steven turned to Ben. "Sorry, gramps, but I think you're going to have to get yourself a new hand. Mom and I are moving up to the big house."

Ben smiled. Juanita looked at Doris, knowing what she must be feeling . . .

Doris hadn't really lost her children, she told herself, but still, she wasn't going to have the pleasure of having them close by either. Gary and his family were in Israel, and now her daughter would live in that house for the rest of her life. And she and Henry might never again know the joys of spending *Shabbes* or the holidays with all their children. Well, if this was Michele's salvation, if she had found herself at last, then Doris would be content. More than content . . .

CHAPTER SEVENTY-THREE

A YEAR passed. Henry was well over seventy now, and at last preparing to retire, which left Doris feeling anxious about their finances. The social security he received, plus the interest he got from his meager savings, was barely adequate. So she now spent more and more time with her writing, which left little energy to devote to any social activities.

She accepted this with good grace, but she began to worry when she noticed Henry's lack of interest in developing hobbies or any interest to take up his new leisure time. He had never been a golfer or a Sunday painter, and was no more eager to spend an afternoon playing gin rummy with a few old cronies now than he'd ever been. He spent his days puttering around in the garden or taking long, aimless walks, and gradually Doris began to notice an undeniable decline in his mental acuity.

The first sign was when he began asking her the names of people he'd known for forty years. Then she noticed that during casual conversations his responses were out of context with the subject. And when he started asking the same questions over and over again she finally was forced to the realization that Henry's vagueness was a sign of approaching senility.

At first, the shock was more than she could accept. She began to urge him to take a part-time job in the medical field, doing anything just so that he would use his mind. But that was one subject on which Henry was perfectly lucid and adamant. "I put my fifty years in and I've had enough of the medical profession. I want to be rid of all that, to take it easy..."

He had never exactly worn himself out to create security and leisure time for his family, but when Doris looked at him she really couldn't be angry or even resentful. She had to deal with him as he was now, and she was dealing with a man who was not entirely responsible.

Still, Henry's condition became an increasing burden. In some ways it was like living with a large child. It was also a little scary. For the first time in all the years of their marriage, the pressures became so great that she even thought of leaving him. They had never had many interests in common, and now they could not even communicate on the most simple matters. He seemed to take everything she said literally and seriously, and the result was that his feelings were often hurt. She had to be very careful... oh, so careful...

In her desperation she turned for the first time to writing a novel. She gave few thoughts to its success—she knew that few novelists ever gained much recognition or financial rewards. The overriding concern for her was the necessity of saving her own mental health. So much besides herself depended on it...

Steven was twenty now, and had just married Pamela Rogers...

566

As Doris and Michele sat in Michele's bedroom the morning after the wedding, Michele realized that her mother was not quite the exuberant, outgoing woman she'd known. "Mama, you've been here now for a week and I've noticed a change in you. Do you think you're overdoing it? Too much work on the novel?"

"No, Michele, thank God I have that to fall back on—"

"Look, mama, something is wrong. I know it and **you** know it. You don't have to be so brave. Talk about it."

Tables turned, Doris thought . . . "All right, Michele, have you noticed any . . . change in your father? This week or the last few times we've been up to see you?"

"Yes, mama, I have—and I wondered if I should mention it . . . he doesn't always seem to understand what's said to him. I've had to repeat the same things over and over again to him, and there's a sort of vagueness about him."

Doris shook her head. "It's that obvious?"

"Very, mama—"

Doris started to cry about it, for the first time. "Michele, I'm afraid it's getting worse. I don't know what to do. I've even thought of a nursing home, but I can't bring myself to do it. It's awful even to think about it . . . But how can I live in the same house and not communicate with somebody? It's almost worse than living alone. Still, no question about it, I have responsibilities to the man who is my husband. God knows I don't blame him, Michele, any more than I would if he had anything else wrong with him. And I hope I don't sound like some damn martyr. But how do I live with this?"

"The one time *you've* asked *me* for help . . . and I just don't have any answers."

"Well, don't feel so bad, neither do I. I may as well tell you, though, that I've started seeing a psychiatrist to help get me through this. It seemed to help you . . ."

"Has it helped?"

"Not especially, I'm afraid . . . I just feel so desperately sorry, for both of us, and I can't find any answer."

"Well, maybe things will resolve themselves, mama," Michele said, knowing her father's condition could only worsen.

Doris smiled briefly. "Well, it's true, they usually do . . . But that's not a subject we should be talking about today. The wedding was beautiful, Michele, and Pamela's a lovely, lovely girl. Looking at you, it's hard to believe that you could soon

567

be a grandmother, and me a *great*-grandmother. If it happens very soon I might not look too bad for a great-grandmother. What the hell, next year I'll only be sixty-five."

Michele smiled. "Mama, I keep telling you, you're more gorgeous and glamorous at sixty-four than you ever were. Not a wrinkle on the horizon—it's scary, really, you're incredible. In fact, you were hands down the most beautiful woman at the wedding yesterday. Everybody talked about you. More people came up to me and said, 'I don't believe that's your mother.' "

Doris laughed. "Did they really? Must have been the candlelight and champagne . . . Getting away from the subject of my great beauty, I didn't want to tell you this before the wedding, but my sister Rachel's husband passed away last week. Not that you knew him, of course, and I'm not too worried about how Rachel will adjust to being a widow. She generally adapts pretty well . . . Still . . ."

"How did you find out, mama?"

"She called from New York. That's my family . . . they usually get in touch, at least about the bad things. Anyway, I guess Rachel will survive. She told me in all her bereavement that she's decided to mourn in the best of two worlds—she'll divide her time between New York and Paris . . . Well, enough of the family hour . . . I'm thinking that with the help of God, when and if I finish the book, I just might take a little hike for myself to Israel. It's about time I saw my kids. The pictures are getting stacked by the dozens and I'm running out of albums."

"It's a shame Gary hasn't been able to come home. I know you miss them so much . . ."

But Michele didn't know the extent of Doris' fears. Gary had moved from the Negev to a kibbutz in the Hula Valley. It sat just below the Golan Heights and not a day passed that their lives were not in peril. Her grandchildren slept each night in a damp bunker. Doris subscribed to the *Jerusalem Post,* and every issue added another strand of silver to her hair. It seemed there was no end to the conflict. Israel had been besieged with one long war, ever since the War of Independence in 1948, and her son was fighting in many of the battles. He had fought in the Sinai campaign and in the war of 1967, to free the Golan Heights above so that in the Hula Valley below his children no longer had to sleep in a damp bunker. But above all, he fought for the survival of a homeland with a courage and determination that Doris found awesome. And most remarkable of all was Robin. She literally stood shoulder to shoulder with her husband, without a complaint. What extraordinary human beings they were and how proud she was that she had the privilege of being their mother. She sighed, "You're right, I do miss them. But I promise you, even if I have to hock the old homestead, I'm going. I have faith. You wait and see, everything will work out."

CHAPTER SEVENTY-FOUR

DORIS DIDN'T know how prophetic her words to Michele would be. Things did indeed work out. It was almost like a Cinderella story.

The first publisher the book was submitted to accepted it, and no one could have been more surprised than Doris. It was an old-fashioned story about Jewish immigrants who worked themselves up from starvation to *poverty* in one generation, and she couldn't imagine what the ingredient was that made it a success. All she knew was that people seemed to like it, and before long she found herself going in a million different directions. It was funny, really . . . in her old age she was becoming a sort of celebrity, and she was making money that came in very handy. She was even going to be introduced to the press in New York and she needed to buy a few outfits that would be appropriate to the occasion. She bought a smashing cocktail dress and a black mink coat, if you please.

When her publisher asked her to come to New York, she had invited Henry to take the trip with her, but he'd said no, he didn't like flying and the memories . . . sensations . . . of New York and the lower East Side were too painful. It was ironic, Doris thought. He couldn't remember the names of some of their oldest friends, but he could remember his early childhood, being bathed in a pickle barrel . . .

She hired a competent housekeeper for Henry, and rather than put him through the task of seeing her off at the airport she took a taxi and set off on her own. On her own . . .

When Doris arrived at Kennedy Airport she still couldn't accept the reality of what had happened to her. The fat, curly-haired kid who used to go to the Orpheum and say,

569

"Someday I'm going to be a star," found the doorman at the Plaza Hotel in New York City opening the door for her. The suite of rooms her publisher had reserved left her speechless. Before taking off her coat, she walked over to an enormous bouquet sitting on the French desk, took out the card and read it. "We're so happy you're here. Welcome." She stared at it. Publishers were real people after all, it seemed. Imagine being thoughtful enough to make such a beautiful gesture. And all of this happened because she'd written some funny little book about a Jewish family that *didn't* make it from rags to riches. Thank you, Ida Cohen, my favorite character. I really have you to thank for all this, because you're what every Yiddish mama wanted to be . . .

In the next twenty-four hours Doris found herself catapulted into an unknown world. A cocktail party was given for her. She was interviewed on television, had her picture taken, met a lot of very important people whose very important names she couldn't remember if her life depended on it . . . However, there was one lady this evening she did remember. Her name was Annette Mayer.

"Any relation to Louis B.?" Doris had asked, trying to sound smarter than she felt.

"That's not my claim to fame, sorry to say."

Annette was taken with Doris, and wanted to arrange a dinner party at her apartment on Central Park West for the following Tuesday, provided Doris was available. Doris was available. . . .

She arrived at seven-thirty, dressed in a Pucci print and her black mink coat and toting two pounds of Lady Godiva chocolates for her hostess. Annette introduced her to all the guests. Considering that they were sophisticated New Yorkers, Doris was more than somewhat surprised by how excited they apparently were to meet her.

"I've read your book and adored it" was what she heard over and over again. Funny, the thought, at home I'm just good old Doris Levin, and here on Central Park West I'm a big star, yet—Her thoughts were interrupted when the doorbell rang and she overheard Annette's greeting to the latecomer.

"Aaron, why do you insist on being a prima donna? You're always late."

"That's very unkind, Annette, and the traffic was horrible as usual. Besides, I didn't come here to argue with you but to meet your author. That's what you invited me for, right?"

570

"You're incorrigible, I don't even know why I put up with you. But come on . . ."

Leading him to Doris, Annette said, "I want you to meet a very dear and constantly late friend, Aaron Brauch . . . Doris Levin."

"This is a pleasure I've been looking forward to, Mrs. Levin."

Doris smiled uneasily. "Next thing you'll tell me you read the book—"

"I'm not only going to tell you I read it, but even reread it."

"Well, Aaron Brauch, I can tell you have extremely good taste in literature."

"Indeed I do. As a matter of fact, if you don't mind comparisons, I think it comes as close to Sholom Aleichem as anything I've read in a long time."

Doris laughed. "Thank God you didn't say Tolstoy."

"Well, Sholom Aleichem wasn't exactly a piker either."

"Thank you, I accept that as a great compliment."

Aaron was seated next to Doris at the dinner table and she found herself enjoying his company, to say nothing of his good looks. In fact, she hadn't met a man this good-looking in a long time, or even seen one. He was of about average height, but was well-built and gave the impression of being taller. He had a thick crop of salt and pepper hair and the loveliest brown eyes. When he reached for his knife and fork, the cuffs on his sleeves rose above his wrists and exposed what promised to be masculine, hairy arms. Doris was surprised to find herself even thinking about such a thing . . .

The evening passed much too quickly, and since Doris had an early interview, she begged to be forgiven for leaving before the party was over.

After a very busy day, when she returned to her suite she found several messages. And one was from Mr. Aaron Brauch. As she sat down and kicked off her shoes to relax for a moment she thought, Oh, go ahead, Doris, what the heck, be brazen, call. She dialed for an outside line and then quickly hung up. Doris, don't be brazen . . . Look, maybe you've never had a huge lot of fun in your life, but then you never got into trouble either. So be a good girl, put yourself together and get on with your appointment tonight.

Her appointment that night was with her publisher and some "media" people . . . Watch it, you could get to like this life . . . but it was also very tiring, especially after the kind of existence she'd led. When she returned to the hotel after dinner she removed her makeup, took a fast shower and hopped into bed, thinking how glad she was that tomorrow was Sunday. A day of rest . . .

But Doris' morning of sleeping in was interrupted at ten o'clock. When the phone rang she wasn't sure if she didn't want to just pull the cord, but then she realized it could be Henry's housekeeper. Sleepily, she took the phone off the cradle and said, "Hello?"

"Did I wake you?"

"Who is this?"

"Aaron Brauch. Did I wake you up?"

She shut her eyes and shook her head. "Well, as a matter of fact, Aaron Brauch, you did."

"I'm very sorry about that—"

"You don't sound a bit sorry."

"I really am. But now that you're up, how would you like to go roller skating?"

This I'm going to put in my next book. "Roller skating? Are you out of your mind? I take my car to mail a letter across the street. Athletics don't happen to be one of my passions."

"Don't knock it if you've never tried it."

"I'm not knocking it, but I'm not going to try it either."

"Okay, if you want to be difficult, how about lunch?"

"Now *that* was a good suggestion. You just made yourself a deal, Mr. Brauch. Food used to be one of my big hobbies, but I've reformed." Sort of . . .

"You haven't given it up entirely, have you?"

"Not likely."

"Where would you like to go to lunch?"

"Tavern on the Green? It's been a long-time fantasy of mine."

"Well, fantasize no more, my dear. Is twelve-thirty all right?"

"Could we make it closer to one?"

"Pick you up at one. . . ."

Sure enough, one o'clock came and Aaron Brauch was standing in the lobby, dressed in a Russian-style beaver hat and a fur-trimmed overcoat. The smile on his face was genuine. He seemed pleased to see her again, and she certainly didn't find that offensive. In fact, there was a distinct excitement about just walking alongside him as they walked out of the lobby and hailed a cab.

572

Seated in the restaurant having Bloody Marys, Doris said, "I don't know whether you know or appreciate it or not, but you live in the most fabulous city—"

"You like Manhattan?"

"I adore it, there's an excitement and energy I can't describe. The other day I stood at Rockefeller Center and looked from the skaters below to the skyscrapers above. An awesome sight."

"You come from a magnificent city too, you know. Probably one of the most beautiful I've ever seen, and I go there quite often."

"I can't argue with that, but there's a magic about this place I'll never forget—"

"And there's a magic about you that nobody could forget—"

"Aaron Brauch, I'll bet you say that to every rubberneck lady author you take to lunch."

"No, as a matter of fact, you're the first author I've ever had lunch with. Not the first lady, true . . . but none as special as you—"

Doris was actually blushing. "You're not going to believe this, but you're embarrassing me."

"Never get embarrassed at the truth—"

"You're right, but I wasn't exactly raised on compliments by—"

"By men?"

"Yes . . . well, sort of." No one would guess she was a middle-aged grandmother with a successful career. She was acting more like a schoolgirl with her first crush. My God, Doris, you've lived in a cloister for too long . . .

Quickly changing the subject, she said, "How about lunch?"

"Would you like another Bloody Mary?"

"Please, but I tend to get sloshed on two drinks, so I really think we should have something to eat."

"Do you have a preference?" Aaron asked. "The eggs Benedict are very good."

She heard the echoes of Santa Cruz in the far, far distance . . her first date with Henry, when he had suggested what she order at that restaurant on the pier. "Sounds marvelous," Doris said, and felt herself beaming like a ridiculous teenager. Good Lord . . .

Lingering over coffee, he asked her how she had started to write.

"I just didn't have anything to do one day, so I got up and I

573

said, 'You know, Doris, I think you should write a book, either that or get into basket weaving.' "

He laughed. "I'm glad you didn't opt for the basket weaving. Otherwise I might never have met you."

"You think you would have missed so much?" Now, for God's sake, she was even fishing. *Doris . . .*

"I do."

"You do? Oh, yes . . . well, what about you?"

"What about me? Am I married? No, divorced, for ten years now."

"How did you get away with that?" And now she was flirting . . . ?

"Never met anybody I was interested in."

"Do you have a family?"

"Yes, two grown daughters. One in Florida and the other in Westchester."

Aaron watched as she stirred the remains of her coffee. "Do you see them often?" she asked, suddenly subdued.

"As much as possible, but they have lives of their own and I have mine. Occasionally I get a terrific desire to visit my grandchildren. I have four of them now."

Without looking up, she said, "Well, you're one up on me, I have three."

"I noticed a change in that beautiful face," he said, watching her intently.

"I'm not much of an actress . . . I have a son and daughter-in-law living in Israel. And would you believe it? I've never even seen my granddaughter, and she's almost fourteen."

"How is that? Israel isn't that far away, you know."

"Oh, you keep promising yourself you're going next summer, and next summer never comes around."

He reached across the table and took her hand. "Well, Israel will be there this summer. Just got to make up your mind to go."

Looking up at him now, trying to be offhanded, she said, "I think maybe I'll take your advice. You're not in the travel business, are you?"

"No, advertising."

"That must be fascinating." Dumb remark, Doris, but it beats thinking about how much you miss your kids.

"Like they say, it's a living. Tell me about you, how did you really get into writing?"

"Oh, it's just something I started when I was about eight. I started doing plays, but the publishers were unreasonable . . .

574

they just didn't line up to buy the inspiration of an eight-year-old."

He smiled. "No, really . . . how did you get started?"

"There was a point in my life when I needed an outlet and more income and it just seemed natural to roll a piece of paper into the typewriter. Like you say, it's a living."

"I think you're being a touch too modest. Your book's a tremendous success."

"And no one was more surprised than me. In fact, I still can't believe the reviews. And imagine getting published with a name like Doris Levin. I thought of changing it to Doris Day, but I was afraid they'd send her my royalties by mistake."

"Tell me about your marriage . . ."

Just like that? Tell me about your marriage? Doris sighed and leaned back in her chair. "Where would you like me to begin?"

"With now."

She hesitated for a moment. "Well, I have an enormously sweet, kind husband. I guess when you've been married since you were eighteen you get sort of . . . I mean I think that marriage becomes a little bit of a habit—"

"Are you in love?"

What is this? An interview for *True Confessions*? "Of course I love him. My God, it seems like I've been married all my life."

"That doesn't mean a damn thing. You didn't really answer the question."

"Yes."

Her tone and abrupt answer told him otherwise. "How come he allows a beautiful woman like you to take off on her own? Is he that sure of you?"

"He doesn't take me for granted, if that's what you mean."

"So how is it he let's you wander off by yourself?"

"He doesn't enjoy flying—and I think I'd like to get out of here and take a good long walk."

Aaron paid the bill and they walked through the crisp, cold streets of Manhattan. Doris was relieved to find that the Big Apple seemed to have a tranquilizing effect on her emotions. Aaron's questions had certainly stirred them, arousing all kinds of feelings, feelings she had tried so hard to divorce herself from on this trip.

When they returned to the Plaza Aaron asked, "What are you doing for dinner tonight?"

"Nothing. But I've really had a very big week and . . . well, I just sort of feel like playing hooky this evening."

"Hotel rooms can get very lonely on Sunday night—"

Any room, anywhere can get lonely on Sunday night, she thought, and on Monday and the Fourth of July and . . .

Sensing her mood, he said, "Look, why don't you do this. It's only four now, so relax and let me pick you up at eight. You'd be surprised what four hours can do to change a lady's mind."

She looked at him as a small warning signal went off in her mind. Break if off, Doris, right now. You're much too attracted to him and you know it. Now be a smart girl and say . . . "Thanks a lot, Aaron, but I'm going to beg off tonight—"

"Tell you what. I'll call you at seven. See how you feel. Maybe you'll change your mind. Now would you call that a compromise?"

"Okay, I guess so . . . and thank you for the delightful day. I mean that . . ."

When anything really bothered Doris she found that soaking in the bathtub was the best place to think. And think she did, about Aaron Brauch. She couldn't get over the way he had affected her. Even in the short time she'd known him, they seemed to have more in common . . . than she and Henry had had in forty-six years. That wasn't a very admirable thought, and in a way it was superficial, but face facts, Doris . . . Aaron was on the same wavelength with her . . . he enjoyed doing all the things she dreamed of, adored the theater, the arts, traveling, exploring . . . He'd had enough guts to walk away from a marriage, in spite of having two daughters, when he knew it wasn't going to work. His wife was remarried, his children seemed to be happy mothers and housewives and his life had apparently turned out to be very satisfactory. No guilt, no recriminations . . . But for all her supposed strength she'd never have the guts to do that . . . What do you think you're doing, Doris? Pipe dreams among the pink bubbles? But you know the answer, you need the same thing you've always needed. It isn't the success that's so important but the need to share it with someone. That's really what it's about . . . What are you going to do, go on talking to pillows for the rest of your life? Why don't you face it, Doris. You're not sure if it's love, but you certainly do want to have an affair with this man. But that's pretty silly, isn't it? Of

576

course, it is ... sixty-four years old with three grandchildren? And then when the affair, if there is an affair, is over, do you just go home to Henry and pretend nothing happened?

Suddenly she realized the water had turned tepid and the bubbles were beginning to disintegrate.

When she got out of the tub and started to dry herself, she glanced at her nude body in the full-length mirror and stood looking, as though she were really seeing herself for the first time. Doris, you've emerged on the scene at sixty-four in better shape than some I've seen at thirty-four. So don't ask yourself if you're desirable. That's just being stupid-coy. So you're a late bloomer ... okay, so now what ...?

Slipping into her robe, she went back into the bedroom and looked at the bedside travel clock. A quarter to six ... Okay, kiddo, get yourself together because Aaron's going to be calling by seven. Besides, you don't have to make any rash decisions tonight. He only asked you out for dinner and that will be just about the most wicked thing you ever did in your whole unwicked life ...

Slipping into the black brief girdle, then fastening the black lace bra, she thought, Boy, those aren't the worst-looking boobs in the world. Then she slipped on the sheer black hose and silk pumps. As she attached the garters to the top of her stockings, once again she looked at her image reflected in the mirror. Putting one foot on the desk chair she sang like Marlene Dietrich, "Falling in love again ..." Okay, Marlene, she said to herself, let's get the show on the road.

Going through her closet, she reached for the cocktail dress. It was black, revealing her hard-won curves. She loved it, completely backless and high at the neck. She looked at her firm arms in the sleeveless dress. Not too bad for a fat little kid who couldn't get on the basketball team. Boy, what would the kids in West Oakland think of her now? She was a star. Thin....

When the phone rang promptly at seven, she wasn't so much startled by its sound as she was by the excitement she felt as she picked up the receiver.

"Hi. Do you feel rested?"

"You have no idea what a little nap will do ..."

"In that case, I'm down in the lobby."

This one surely didn't fool around. Talk about being taken for granted ... "I'm taking the first elevator out of here. I'll be right down."

As she grabbed her mink coat she felt giddy and almost

girlish. Of all the crazy things that should cross her mind now, she was suddenly remembering prom night, when she had lain there on her bed visualizing all that she was missing. Well, it was a little delayed but she was finally having her prom night. And then some . . .

Aaron was standing there as she got off the elevator. He smiled. "You look gorgeous . . . Where to?"

"Surprise me . . ."

And she was surprised. As they sat in the dimly lit Four Seasons restaurant, she watched the skeined draperies that rippled as if they were being gently blown in the wind. Here she was, fat Doris, sitting next to one of the most attractive men she'd ever met. The conversation was easy, comfortable, and there were no pretenses or games. But the feelings that he was bringing out in her made it difficult to remain as calm on the inside as she hoped she appeared on the outside.

When dinner was over, he said, "And now what would you like to do?"

"It's getting to sound like a cliché, but I love surprises . . ."

Again, she was surprised. When the taxi stopped, it was in front of the Martinique.

After Aaron paid the fare, Doris smiled at him uncertainly. "You mean we're going to go in there? When you said dancing, I thought you meant waltzing. Like at the St. Regis, which is a little more suited to grandmothers . . ."

They were ushered into a room where the music was deafeningly loud. There was a group on stage that didn't exactly sound like the Stones, but they were perilously close. There were strobe lights, lots of smoke, lots of alcohol and lots of bodies trying to see how much their sacroiliacs could take.

Suddenly she found Aaron leading her out onto the crowded floor. "Aaron, you've got to be out of your mind, we may never come out of this alive. We could get stomped to death." But he couldn't hear her over the sound of the music.

Before she knew it, she was catching on to the gyrations of the dancers she saw around her. She thought fleetingly of the speak-easy Henry had taken her to on their second date . . .

When the place closed down and the taxi stopped in front of the Plaza, Aaron got out and opened the door for her.

A gentle rain was falling. He took her in his arms and kissed her. "Where are you going tomorrow?"

Subdued, she answered, "I'm going home."

"Why?"

"Because that's what the itinerary reads."

"Itineraries can always be changed."

"True, but I've been away ten days now and I do have a husband who's beginning to miss me."

Holding her close, he said, "Change your reservations. Call and tell him something unexpected came up."

"Oh, Aaron, I can't do that—"

"Why? The days of slavery are over . . . Lincoln, remember him? And then there was a fellow by the name of Freud."

Doris looked up into his eyes and thought, Face it, Doris, you're still chicken. "Aaron, I'd stay if I could, but really, I must go home."

"I have tickets for *A Chorus Line* tomorrow night."

She laughed. "Aaron, I'll take a rain check."

Holding her very tight, he kissed her again. "Then is this going to be it? All of it?"

She almost ached as she said it, but . . . "I'm afraid so, Aaron—"

"Well, if you change your mind, you have my card. And then some . . ."

Before he could say another word she had turned and walked into the lobby.

He stood in the damp night air for a long moment, then dismissed the cab. What he really needed was a good long walk to clear the disappointment from his mind. And then maybe an after-hours bar. . . .

Doris was sitting in bed in the dark, watching the smoke from her cigarette curl in the dim glow from the streetlights outside. She felt the presence of Aaron Brauch just as surely as if he were lying by her side . . . Boy, I've really got it bad and that ain't good. Sixty-four years old, and for the first time in your whole life you've found someone who . . . so why don't you reach out and grab the brass ring? Don't you owe yourself anything? You've paid your dues to Henry and everybody else. You dummy, get rid of that fat kid inside, pick up the phone and call TWA . . .

She turned on the lamp, picked up the phone and canceled the flight with TWA, then spoke to the hotel operator and placed a ten-thirty wake-up call so that she could call Henry and tell him of the change in her plans. . . .

When she called Henry at ten-thirty she was still terribly uncertain of what she was going to say to him.

"Hello?"

"Henry, how are you?"

"Doris, how are you, honey?"

"I'm wonderful, Henry. How are you?"

"I'm lonesome, honey . . . I really miss you."

"It's nice to be missed, Henry, but I hope Mrs. Henderson is keeping you busy." She paused momentarily before she went on. "The reason I called was to tell you that this trip has become much . . . more involved than I thought. There are some things that have come up and I'm going to have to stay on for a bit—"

"Oh . . . How long do you think that'll be?"

"It's hard to say. It may be a week or so, maybe less. I'll let you know, I'll keep calling you every day."

"I'm happy to hear your voice, honey. Come home as quickly as possible."

"I will, take care of yourself, Henry."

She sat with the silent receiver in her hand. Had this been one of his less lucid days, she might feel less badly . . . but then, maybe not. She felt as though she were abandoning a child . . . and a mate . . .

Quickly, she put the phone back on the cradle and went into the bathroom. She poured some perfumed bath oil into the tub while it was filling, and put tons of moisture cream on her face. If at this late date she was going to make her maiden voyage, so to speak, into the sea of . . . what? . . . at least she ought to go smelling like a rose. Suddenly she was very happy. Yes, by God, she was *very* happy, and she wasn't going to do one bit of damage to Henry. Maybe it was the steam, maybe it was the pink bubbles, maybe it was Aaron Brauch and Manhattan . . . She didn't know what it was, but somehow she didn't feel guilty, she didn't feel she owed anybody. She was almost, for the moment, at peace with herself . . .

After breakfast in her room she waited impatiently until noon, a decent hour to call after their late date last night. Although she no longer felt guilty, she felt a peculiar kind of embarrassment when she placed the call, and for a moment she faltered when she heard his voice.

Well, she was too old, or young, for games . . . "Aaron, I thought carefully about what you said yesterday and I decided that seeing *Chorus Line* was too big an opportunity to pass up."

He laughed. "God, I hoped you'd call this morning. In fact, I didn't sleep. I kept wondering if I should call you back to try to persuade you, but now I'm glad I didn't. The decision had to be yours." . . .

580

Sitting in the darkened theater, Doris neither heard the dialog nor listened to the music. All she was aware of was Aaron holding her hand, caressing it gently.

When the theater let out he said, "Where would you like to go?"

"Surprise me..."

Aaron laughed, then looked at her more seriously. "I don't have any etchings but I'd really like you to see my apartment."

She didn't say no.

It was almost exactly what she had imagined. A living-room-diningroom combination. Beyond the sliding doors to the balcony she could see the lights of the Fifty-ninth Street Bridge. The walls were brown suede, as was the three-piece sectional sofa. A glass-and-brass coffeetable sat in the center, a pair of plaid winged chairs on either side of the fireplace and a lush carpet of autumn yellow was a startling contrast. Maybe Aaron didn't have etchings, but he had taste.

Her attention was diverted when Aaron handed her a glass of chilled champagne.

Touching glasses, he said, "Here's to new beginnings, and no excuse for endings."

Doris smiled as she sipped her drink.

Taking her by the hand, he led her up the staircase to the second floor. As she stood beside him in his bedroom, she paid very little attention to its décor. Suddenly she found herself wanting to say, I've changed my mind, I really think this has got to be the craziest thing I've ever done in my life... But before she could give in to the impulse she found herself in his arms, being kissed tenderly as he unzipped the back of her dress and let it fall to the floor. The black lace bra was slipped slowly off her shoulders, and now she was standing nude, her body being held closely to his... What happened from then on seemed so natural that it was as though she'd known him all her life. Carrying her to the bed, he lay down alongside her, kissed her gently on the mouth, the neck... The kiss ventured down to her breasts. He aroused parts of her she'd never known could respond this way... If she had ever thought she was sexually cool, she now knew how wrong she'd been. She just had never known that anything like this could happen to a woman. To *her*... She discovered pleasures she'd never believed possible, and the feelings that had been so long dormant were brought wonderfully to life when he gently entered her. For the first time in her life she knew what being a woman truly was...

581

Later, as they lay side by side, Doris said, "Aaron, I don't know why I feel I should tell you, but this is the first time I've ever had an affair."

"If most any other woman told me that, I don't think I'd believe it. But I do believe you."

"Why?"

"I have a feeling about you. You play it straight down the middle."

"Aaron, this may sound strange, but I want to thank you for knowing me so well in so short a time."

"Time has nothing to do with it, and I think maybe I know you a lot better than you know yourself."

She kissed him. "Would you think I was terribly wicked if I asked that we . . ."

She didn't have to finish the question, and this time was every bit as intense as the first. Maybe more so, though it hardly seemed possible.

As she lay in his arms afterward she suddenly began to feel awkward. What did she do now? Was she supposed to stay or just say goodnight and leave?

When she got up and began to dress, he asked, "Where do you think you're going?"

"I'm not trying to be coy, but unaccustomed as I am to . . . well, sir, I'm afraid I really don't know what's customary . . . What I'm trying to say to you, Aaron, is that I don't want to wear out my welcome."

Getting out of bed, he swooped her up in his arms and put her gently back in bed. "There aren't any rules, it's not like bridge. With some women it's once over lightly. And since this is confession time, there are damned few women who spend the night in my bed."

Indulging herself, she said, "Am I an exception?"

"You're *the* exception. As a matter of fact, madam authoress, you just might spend the rest of your life sleeping alongside of me."

This was something Doris certainly hadn't considered, and his statement sobered her up in a hurry. She spoke hesitantly. "Aaron, I think you recall I said I had a husband?"

"I know you did and I also recall the look in your eyes when I asked you if you were in love with him. I knew you weren't at the time, and now I'm sure of it. You wouldn't have loved me the way you did tonight—Doris, your mouth is open. You're a very bright lady, but just in case you didn't get the gist of it, I just proposed."

"Proposed what?"

"Proposed that you get a divorce. Proposed that you marry me . . ."

My God . . . people married forty-six years don't get a divorce. She had grandchildren . . . and what about Henry? My God, he'd been like a father to her. And why was she even asking those questions . . . ?

"Doris?" he prompted.

"I heard you, Aaron, but how do you imagine I could just walk out on my husband after all these years, a husband who's been good and kind, believe me . . . My God, I've been married to him since I was eighteen . . . How could I do that, Aaron? Could I . . . we . . . build a life on the destruction of somebody else?"

"It isn't easy to walk away from any marriage. My marriage was lousy and it still wasn't easy to walk out. But the thing is, my wife survived, my kids survived and I've had ten good years, as they have. But now I've met you, I realize there's something else I want and need, and that's to share my life again with somebody. With *you*."

. . . You've got to have someone to share it with . . . she'd been thinking the night before about her success . . . "Aaron, this is an impossible decision. I'm absolutely confused, I don't know what to say—"

"Well, in that case I'll say it for you. After hearing you talk about your children, and very guardedly about certain areas of your life you didn't want to get into, I'd say you've played the role of the sacrificing wife and mother long enough. You owe yourself, Doris, and if you feel at all about me the way I feel about you, then your answer ought to be *yes*."

"But Henry's a sick man—"

"I'm very sorry about that, but what do you think is going to happen in the next few years, Doris? You told me tonight that he's already slipping. It's only going to get worse and eventually you're not going to be able to cope with that. If you face the reality, Henry should probably be in a good convalescent home right now. I know I sound hard, but I've got my life at stake here too. And you have yours. If Henry had a disease that could be arrested or reversed, it would be one thing, but from what I gather his is the sort of thing that involves blood supply to the brain . . . I've had a little experience with this myself in my own family . . . It's a damn shame, but eventually—"

"Yes, I know, but . . . Aaron . . . I need *time* . . . time to think . . ."

"Do you love me, Doris?"

"Yes ... even though it doesn't seem quite real to me. Imagine, to fall in love at my age ..."

"Look, I'm sixty-five, which isn't spring chicken to me, but I *feel* young and so do you ... we've got a lot of living ahead of us."

"Will you give me time, Aaron?"

"Some, but time is important to us. We've lost too much already."

"I just don't know what to do—"

"Get Henry settled and proceed with a divorce—which should be done as quickly as possible. Les Vegas, Reno, whatever ... Meanwhile, New York is only five hours away. In fact, I have to be in Los Angeles in about ten days, we can meet there ..."

How much she wanted to say yes. But it had just happened too quickly. She hadn't really thought it would go beyond a lovely, unexpected romance ... "Aaron, I simply must have time to get used to this whole—"

"Maybe spending the next week together will help. Just remember, *you're not hurting anybody.*"

If she could just believe *that* ... Without giving her any more time to think, he took her in his arms and once again ...

During the next ten days Doris desperately tried not to think of Henry. Instead, she played a game, living each day as if it were going to last forever.

But the days defied her. The night before she left, as she lay in Aaron's arms, he said, "Well ... what have you decided?"

"To spend the rest of my life with you."

Holding her very close, he said, "Doris, remember, I'm no further away than the telephone."

"Twenty-five hundred miles away."

"I'm practically a commuter. I've forgotten how many times I was in San Francisco this year."

As she sat in the plane on the flight back to San Francisco, she couldn't tear her thoughts away from Aaron. He seemed to fill every part of her being, and how she had managed to wrench herself away from him in those last few minutes before the departure she would never know ...

She tried to divert her mind by looking at the in-flight movie, but what she saw on the screen was herself in his arms. They belonged ... they really belonged together.

584

SHE REALIZED her need for Aaron even more when the taxi stopped in front of the house in Seacliff. But when she stood in the hall and looked at Henry's sweet face . . . he seemed so pathetic, almost childlike, that she could hardly hold back the tears. How was she going to do this? He was so overjoyed at seeing her. She knew what Aaron had said was logical and realistic, but how could you take your happiness at somebody else's expense?

The moment Henry went for a walk with Mrs. Henderson, Doris called Aaron. "Darling, I just got home a little while ago and I haven't been able to get you out of my mind. I miss you so—"

"Same here . . . How was it when you got home?"

"Difficult, but I'll keep working on it, Aaron."

"It'll get easier, darling . . . now, don't forget next Thursday. I'll meet you at the airport. Get the twelve o'clock PSA and I think we'll just about have it timed right. Oh yes, please remember that this not-so-old party is crazy about you . . ."

The day before she was to meet Aaron, Doris went with Henry for his walk. As they sat in Union Square, she watched as he threw bread crumbs to the pigeons. Again, it struck her how much he was like a sweet child . . .

"Henry, come on, darling. Let's have a cup of coffee."

"Oh, no. I couldn't drink coffee, Doris."

"Well, then I'll have a coffee and you can have sherbet."

"I'd like orange, I'd like that . . ."

As they sat in a small coffee shop on Geary Street, she said, "Henry, I have to go to Los Angeles to do a promotion spot, and to see my agent."

"That means you have to go on a plane?"

"Yes, I have to take a plane."

"I don't like flying, Doris . . ."

"I know, Henry, but that's a part of my life now."

Thankfully, his protests were mild, and the fact that he liked Mrs. Henderson so much made it easier for her to leave him.

The next morning when she waited for the taxi, he said, "Have a good time, honey. Are you going back to New York?"

"No, dear. I told you I was going to Los Angeles, but I'll call this evening."

That night at dinner at the Beverly Hills Hotel she said, "I never knew falling in love at any age could be so painful, and wonderful . . ."

"I haven't exactly been Mr. Tranquillity since you left. I've missed you, Doris . . ."

"How, with my compulsive calling? I've just discovered something about myself that I didn't know existed. I can be very possessive . . . I know I'm already jealous of every moment we're not together. So you'd just better be aware of what you're getting into . . ."

He smiled. "Madam, after all these years of not having anybody care that much . . . that's music to my ears . . . and while we're on the subject of dark revelations, I should tell you that being patient isn't one of my strong suits . . . Have you made any plans yet?"

"Well . . . I've looked into some good places . . . now it's a question of getting up the courage to talk to him—"

"How long do you think that will be?"

"First I want to discuss this with a psychologist and find out what the best approach is—which I realize I should have done before . . . Once I have him settled, I'll go to . . . Las Vegas. And if it's possible during the time I'm there, maybe you'll be able to spend a little time with me. Otherwise, I'm liable to run off with a croupier."

"Be assured that I'm not going to go through six weeks without seeing the lady in my life."

"Aaron, how did I ever get so lucky? And so late? I just keep saying it's happening to someone else."

"You know, darling, we ought to send your publisher a special invitation to the wedding."

"Why?"

"Because if he hadn't been smart enough to publish your book, I'd never have met you. I don't like to think about it."

"Me either. I'll bless him forever."

The next days went by all too quickly. The love between them had been so good, so complete . . . Aaron saw Doris off at the airport—then waited around to catch his flight to New York. . . .

The moment Doris arrived home Mrs. Henderson told her, "Mrs. Levin, your sister, Mrs. Fuller, has been calling."

Doris felt a sinking feeling, as though she were being towed under. As she dialed the number and sat listening to the ringing, she thought, God, I've never even met Lillian's husband. Wasn't that unthinkable . . . ?

Finally, Lillian answered.

Awkwardly, Doris said, "How are you, Lillian?"

There was a long pause. "Terrible, Doris. Mama's in the hospital. She's dying and has asked to see you."

Doris started to cry as Lillian told her that mama was dying of leukemia—The betrayal, the years of rejection—it was still very real but it seemed so insignificant in the face of this news. Strange, all this time mama hadn't called once. But now, at the very end, Doris was being forgiven for *her* sins . . . "Will you come, Doris?"

"Yes, of course."

Doris' hands were trembling so that she could hardly hang up the phone. All the old fears and uncertainties from the past seemed to come over her . . . Mama was throwing her out after she'd had a new baby . . . Please, Henry, I can't go on this way, I beg you, find a place for us, anything . . . Papa, help me, I need some money to get settled, don't you remember what it was like to be poor? She needed Aaron, and started to dial his number, then realized he wouldn't have arrived in New York yet. Try to control yourself, Doris. But she had to speak to him, feel his strength before she could go to the hospital. Thank God, Henry was out with Mrs. Henderson. She couldn't have faced seeing him, not now. Today she wasn't up to any more dissembling . . .

She backed her car out of the garage and drove up to Coit Tower and sat on the parapet, feeling the misty breezes of the Bay, looking out at the green hills of Marin and the enormous span of the Golden Gate Bridge. It somehow made her feel very small and very lonely, but there was also a comfort in the serenity of the scene. Finally she glanced at her watch and got up to leave. Aaron would be home by now . . . Quickly she walked back to the car and drove down the winding hill to Lombard Street and then home.

When she opened the door she heard the sound of the television. Henry was watching the news. She went up to the privacy of her room and placed the call to Aaron.

"Hello."

That simple word spoken by him was what she most needed at this moment. He was there, and God, how she needed him.

"Aaron . . ."

"You're psychic . . . I just came through the door."

"I know. Aaron—" Her voice broke.

"What's wrong?"

"My mother's . . . dying. I just wanted to hear your voice before going to the hospital."

"Oh, God, Doris . . . I wish there was a way I could help—"

"You have . . . I don't know what's going to happen. I may not be able to call for a few days but at least you'll understand why."

"Of course. I love you, Doris. If you need me, I'm here."

When Doris walked into her mother's room and saw her frail, withered body, it seemed impossible that life could be quite so cruel. Her mother, who had once been so beautiful, was all but unrecognizable.

Sara feebly put out her hand. "Thank you for coming, Doris . . . I should have called you long ago, I really meant to, but . . . guilt is a terrible thing, it's a killer . . . I just hope you'll forgive me . . . and forgive papa too. We make terrible mistakes in our lives, Doris . . . just forgive us if you can . . ."

"I did that a long time ago, mama. Now you have to forgive yourself . . ."

There was really nothing more to say, for either one of them. The feeble old lady cried with the few tears she had left. Doris bent over and kissed the wrinkled face. Swallowing back the tears, she walked down the hall to where Lillian and Rachel stood with Jacob.

The change in him was almost as shocking as in her mother. His hair had gone entirely white, and his once magnificent body seemed bent and wasted. At first he didn't even recognize her because he could barely see, and he didn't hear her footsteps because his hearing was impaired. Oh my God, the toll that time had taken, how handsome papa had been. She couldn't help remembering . . . looking out of the window that long ago Fourth of July and watching him hose down the truck. How vivid the memory was, even after all these years of separation . . .

Doris walked to her father and put her arms around him, crying openly . . . some for her loss, more for his. He'd been such a stubborn, proud man. How painful for him to be dependent on someone to be his eyes and his ears. Papa . . . mama . . . their lives hadn't even really gotten off to a very good beginning, but maybe they weren't responsible. Maybe they had just done the best they knew how . . .

588

"Doris," she heard her father say.

Holding back the tears, she nodded her head. "Yes, papa. I'm here."

They felt no recriminations, no anger, no bitterness even . . . just lost years that could never be recaptured. They both felt it in that moment of closeness, and sensed that each accepted it. . . .

The three sisters waited in the corridor through the long night. Doris kept her own counsel . . . Rachel, a grandmother four times. Still blonde, but a little brassy now. Still beautiful, but age and indulgence had left their mark on her face. Lillian too had aged. She was matronly now, gray, and seemed faintly weary. Doris was surprised that she herself seemed to have emerged looking the least scarred, being the least scarred, in spite of everything. Like she'd once said to herself, she guessed she was a late bloomer . . .

Rachel sensed the transformation in her sister. "You certainly have changed, Doris. In fact of all of us, you the most," Rachel said.

Doris noticed she didn't say "for the better" . . . It was almost as though Rachel were jealous of *her* . . . the funny little kid, fat Doris. Except fat Doris was, thank God, no more.

"Well, Rachel, I guess I just had to try the hardest, I needed the most remodeling."

"Well, it seems to have turned out fine for you . . . I understand you wrote a book?"

"So they say, Rachel. No big deal."

Rachel smiled coolly . . . "Well, maybe the next one will do better for you."

Lillian was getting annoyed with Rachel. Yes, her husband had died and she'd not been the same since, but this was no time for a show of bitterness, and especially at Doris, who hardly deserved it after the trouble the family had already given her. Unlike Rachel, Lillian took some pleasure in Doris' success and had followed her career carefully, if secretly. It helped assuage some of the guilt . . .

They talked about their mother, Lillian telling them about the last few years of her life. She had spent her time in and out of hospitals, but although her illness only became more serious it seemed that she had at last found peace. She had Jacob's full love and attention, which was perhaps all she had ever really wanted . . .

Sara died at three that morning, and though they left together, the mourners—sisters and father—were very much alone, each in their separate thoughts. . . .

After the funeral, they all went back to Jacob's. Doris sat and surveyed the people who were gathered in the room. A family reunion. Rachel's son Larry and his wife and children were present. Doris was seeing Cindy and Candy for the first time since they were little girls, and here they were with children of their own. Dan Fuller seemed to be a man she would like to have known better, and his devotion to Lillian was obvious. Michele had flown from Reno with Steven and Pamela. Strange, Doris thought, mama had perhaps never even realized they existed . . . The only grandchildren and great-grandchildren missing were Gary and his family. But other members were missing too, Jim Ross was gone, Shlomo . . . Jerry Gould gone too . . .

Dear God, the lives that had been spent, Doris thought. But she was also beginning to realize that what counted wasn't so much that lives had been spent as *how* they had been spent. Looking at her father, sitting broken and inconsolable, she thought back to the life he had led with her mother. It was the past that had brought them all to this moment, and the memories would not be stilled . . . She was a child once again, listening to the name-calling, the violent arguments, the front door slamming, the screech of tires as the car wheeled sharply out of the driveway, followed by mama's bitter weeping, and her own fear that mama and papa were going to get a divorce . . . It was a way of life for her parents. But after sixty or more years of battle, at the end papa loved mama and showed a protectiveness and affection he wasn't able to give her in health. How complicated human beings were, Doris thought. She didn't entirely understand her father but one thing she knew for sure—papa would not survive long without mama. He was lost without her. Whatever the quality of their life together, she had become the core of his existence. They had shared so much for so long . . . this Jacob Sandsonitsky and Sara Edelstein. And now their story was over.

After everyone had left and Jacob had gone to bed, the three sisters discussed what should be done about papa.

"Well," Lillian said, "he certainly can't go on living in this house. What do you think we should do?"

"Obviously there's only one solution to this," Rachel said. "We're just going to have to put him in a home. I mean, even if we had help here to take care of him, he'd die of loneliness. Their marriage wasn't always a bed of roses, but in his own way he did love her. After living with her for nearly seventy years I don't think he's going to be able to deal with the loneliness."

Doris spoke up now, "Well, I think there's maybe another alternative."

Both sisters looked at her.

Rachel said, "And what's that, Doris?"

"Papa's going to come home and live with me."

Both sisters were shocked, though for different reasons.

"Doris, do you know what you're saying? You're taking on the responsibility of an old man who's almost sightless and deaf," Lillian said in exasperation. "I think you've gone a little crazy."

"Well, maybe... But one of the reasons papa bought this house was because it gave him the space he needed. I don't know why, but he always seemed terribly afraid of being shut away. There's just no way he can be happy in a convalescent home."

"You can't be serious," Rachel said. "Why are you doing this? To prove how noble you are and how terrible we are—?"

"No, I'm doing it because papa has the right to live out his life in dignity and not be shut away like an animal. And don't tell me about my nobility. It's what I *want* to do."

Rachel put her hands on her hips and looked at Doris. "After the way you've been treated, you'd take the responsibility of papa?"

Doris lost her patience. "You know something, Rachel? I think you've inherited a lot of the worst in mama, no matter how much you wanted to get away from her. Maybe that's why you two had so much trouble... Where were you all these years? I needed the family, I had no one else to turn to. And now that I don't need your help you're worried about me!"

"Doris, what happened wasn't our fault," Lillian said. "It was papa and mama who—" Lillian broke off when she saw the look on Doris' face.

"Lillian, I'm surprised at you. You made your choice with mama and papa. I don't know all the reasons and I don't care... it doesn't matter anymore... But I do know you never had enough guts to say, Look, Doris never did anything to me... But as for what we're really here to talk about, the other reason I want to take papa is because I have to live with myself, too... Anyway, it's my decision, and if it makes you feel guilty, that's your problem. And as for what mama and

591

papa did to me, it doesn't seem very important when you think of where mama's sleeping tonight."

Lillian began to cry. "I don't blame you for feeling that way about me, Doris . . . But I mean very, very sincerely for your sake, you're taking on an enormous responsibility—"

"Well, I guess mother's day is never going to be over for me. Who knows, maybe that's what I was put on this earth for . . . Well, if it's okay with everybody, I'm going upstairs and get some rest. It's been a hard day for all of us."

When she'd gone, Rachel lit a cigarette and said, "Lillian, do you honestly think she's doing this from the goodness of her heart?"

Lillian looked at Rachel as she thought back to that Christmas when Doris had taken her to Capewell's Department Store and all the other times they had shared. How great their love and devotion had been then. How had they come to lose that feeling? Her own weakness and fear were to blame, and she knew it. "I don't quite get what you mean, Rachel."

"Don't you really? Well, consider that papa's a very, very rich man and—"

"Rachel, Doris implied it and she was right . . . I paid the price for what I got from mama and papa. And the price was high, take it from me, Rachel. But you . . . you've all the money you could ever need, and you're worried about papa's money? Well, to answer your question, yes, I think Doris is doing this out of the goodness of her heart. As a matter of fact, I wonder how she ever got into this family."

CHAPTER SEVENTY-SIX

OTTO AND Helga had been with Sara and Jacob for so long there was little problem persuading them to move into the city and continue on as members of the family. Otto had lowered his eyes in gratitude when Doris told him how much he was needed. With Sara's death they had felt their services would no longer be required, and they had wondered how they could ever find another position, especially at their ages.

Otto would take over Jacob's care, Helga would maintain her status as housekeeper, and Mrs. Henderson would continue in her roll as Henry's companion. But Doris would provide the love, making sure that their days would be spent as human beings, not outcasts.

All the pieces would fall into place, Doris thought. Lillian, her children and grandchildren, would be frequent visitors. The holidays would be spent as a family at Doris' home, and if Rachel happened to be in town the door wouldn't be slammed in her face. It was late in the day for slamming doors . . . better to open them . . . Michele, Steven and Pamela would come from time to time—and by God, she was going to send for Gary and her grandchildren, once and for all.

When she brought Jacob home, he was settled in Michele's old room with his own familiar furnishings around him. After a week or so he seemed somehow more at peace and the adjustment was really not as difficult as Doris had anticipated it would be.

It was nine o'clock of an evening when she looked in to see if he were still awake. The radio was playing softly, although he had fallen asleep. She removed the tiny ear phone, turned the knob off and pulled the covers under his chin. Then she looked in on Henry. He too was sleeping peacefully.

She walked down the stairs to the den, poured herself a large scotch and drank it down before she leaned her head back against the sofa pillow. As she looked up at the ceiling she wondered how she was going to handle the next, and most difficult, chore. For a moment her courage wavered. A letter to Aaron would be the simplest way, but it would also be the most cruel and cowardly. God, this wasn't going to be easy, but when the hell had anything ever been easy? Now pick up that phone and call.

"Doris, I've been going crazy. I know you said you'd call when you could. But for God's sake, one call last week for three minutes?"

"I know, Aaron, but a lot of . . . changes have taken place—"

"Changes? Such as?"

Calmly, quietly, she told him all of it. "It seemed the only thing to do, Aaron. Human beings shouldn't be discarded like old shoes. I couldn't do that to my father."

A long, long silence hung between them before he responded. "Well, that's quite a project you've taken on for yourself. Where does that leave us?"

Swallowing hard, trying to delay it, she answered, "I'm not sure . . ."

"What does that mean?" he said, with more anger in his voice than he intended.

"I guess it means that I just can't bring myself to abandon Henry . . . Aaron, please try and understand. Let Henry live out his days decently. As for my father, he's an old man . . . I want him to know that at the end he was wanted and loved and—"

"And what about me?"

She could no longer hold back the tears. "Aaron, I love you. But nobody owns themselves . . . we're born with obligations. More and more I believe the choices were really made for me a long time ago . . . Giving you up is the most difficult thing I've ever had to do. Don't you know that?"

Of course he knew, and it was just as difficult for him to give her up. But he also felt she wasn't thinking realistically. The day would soon come when Henry would no longer be able to even feed the pigeons and her father's days were numbered. And what would happen to her after that? He had to do some thinking for both of them now. Yes, he had pushed her into a decision, not only because it seemed sensible in terms of her life but because he wanted his happiness too. Now he felt ashamed in the face of her strength and conscience. Still, he wasn't going to allow her to make this kind of a sacrifice alone . . . At this moment he saw only one alternative. Compromise. They were both healthy, vital, productive people with years ahead of them. She was more than worth waiting for, and the odds were in his favor . . . "Forgive you? I love you more, if possible. But, Doris, you *do* have a choice."

"What, Aaron?"

"Well, it's less than I would have liked . . . but as they say, half is better than nothing. Do you think you could be satisfied with a part-time, sort of unofficial husband? I'm going to be in San Francisco at the Fairmont on Thursday."

Doris could scarcely believe what she was hearing. Finally she answered, "I hadn't thought in terms of choices . . . I felt there was only this one road to take—"

"Well, you're wrong, you know. There *are* alternatives. What do you think?"

"You mean about the sort of unofficial husband? You say you'll be here Thursday?"

"Yes."

After a long pause she answered, "We'll talk about it then . . ." Dear God, Aaron, how much I love you . . .

594

After she hung up she looked across the room to her type-writer sitting on her desk. Rags to riches . . . And she had the greatest wealth of all. With tears of gratitude, she took out a sheet of paper, put it into the roller and began with the title:

PORTRAITS

CHAPTER ONE

Jacob was born in a village which is no longer on the map. History and war have changed that . . .

ABOUT THE AUTHOR

CYNTHIA FREEMAN was born in New York City and moved with her family to California. She has lived most of her life in San Francisco with her husband, a prominent physician. They have a son, a daughter and three grandchildren. A believer in self-education, Cynthia Freeman has been determined since childhood to pursue knowledge for its own sake and not for the credentials. Her interest in formal education ceased in sixth grade, but, at fifteen, feeling scholastically ready, she attended classes at the University of California as an auditor only, not receiving credit. Her litarary career began at the age of fifty-five, after twenty-five years as a successful interior designer. "People seem quite shocked," she remarks. "It doesn't seem strange to me. You do one thing in life and then another. I'd been writing all my life—little things for Hadassah, plays for the Sisterhood. I never thought of myself as a writer, but the simplest thing seemed to be to put a piece of paper in the roller and start typing." That typing has led to her very successful novels. *A World Full of Strangers*, *Fairytales*, *The Days of Winter*, *Portraits*, *Come Pour the Wine*, *No Time for Tears*, *Catch the Gentle Dawn*, and *Always and Forever*.

Now there are two great ways to catch up with your favorite thrillers

Audio:

☐ 45116-2   **Final Flight** by *Stephen Coonts*
Performance by George Kennedy
180 mins. Double Cassette
    $14.95

☐ 45170-7   **The Negotiator** by *Frederick Forsyth*
Performance by Anthony Zerbe
180 mins. Double Cassette
    $15.95

☐ 45207-X   **Black Sand** by *William J. Caunitz*
Performance by Tony Roberts
180 mins. Double Cassette
    $14.95

☐ 45156-1   **The Butcher's Theater** by *Jonathan Kellerman*
Performance by Ben Kingsley
180 mins. Double Cassette
    $14.95

☐ 45211-8   **The Day Before Midnight** by *Stephen Hunter*
Performance by Philip Bosco
180 mins. Double Cassette
    $14.95

☐ 45202-9   **The Minotaur** by *Stephen Coonts*
Performance by Joseph Campanella
180 mins. Double Cassette
    $14.95

Paperbacks:

☐ 26705-1   **Suspects** by *William J. Caunitz* $5.99
☐ 27430-9   **Secrets of Harry Bright** by *Joseph Wambaugh* $5.99
☐ 27510-0   **Butcher's Theater** by *Jonathan Kellerman* $5.99
☐ 28063-5   **The Rhineman Exchange** by *Robert Ludlum* $5.95
☐ 26757-4   **The Little Drummer Girl** by *John le Carre* $5.95
☐ 28359-6   **Black Sand** by *William J. Caunitz* $5.95
☐ 27523-2   **One Police Plaza** by *William J. Caunitz* $4.95

— — — Buy them at your local bookstore or use this page to order: — — —

Bantam Books, Dept. FBB, 414 East Golf Road, Des Plaines, IL 60016

Please send me the items I have checked above. I am enclosing $_____
(please add $2.50 to cover postage and handling). Send check or money
order, no cash or C.O.D.s please. (Tape offer good in USA only.)

Mr/Ms _____

Address _____

City/State _____ Zip _____

                                                  FBB–6/91

Please allow four to six weeks for delivery.
Prices and availability subject to change without notice.

THE LATEST IN BOOKS
AND AUDIO CASSETTES

DON'T MISS
THESE CURRENT
Bantam Bestsellers